D1450877

Thatcher

The unauthorized biography of
Blackbeard the pirate

Published by

PAMLICO & ALBEMARLE
PUBLISHING
P. O. BOX 234•NAGS HEAD NC 27959

ISBN-10: 0988571501
ISBN-13: 978-0-9885715-0-1

Acknowledgments

The authors wish to express their thanks to the many family and friends who suffered through the two decades it took to bring this work to fruition. You know who you are, and we pay tribute to you throughout the body of this work

Three such people require overt recognition, and this work would not have been possible without the advice and support of Anne Skinner McMullan, Elizabeth Porcher Jones and Julie Glasgow Best. The completion of such massive works would not have been possible without the loving support of good people willing to endure endless prattle, speculation and discussion of characters and their motivations. It is only because they love your characters as much as you do that you trust your instincts enough to present them to the world.

Finally, we dedicate this book to our beautiful daughters, Abigail Adams Carroll and Eleanor Roosevelt Carroll. We hope it inspires you to dream over the horizon and then chart your course.

A FORETHOUGHT ...

A work of historical fiction is never complete. At some point, you have to arrive at a conclusion to your research and commit yourself to the writing, and that's what we did in the summer of 2006. After fourteen years of mining every page of source material that could be found pertaining to the central character of our story, we took a year off from our traditional lives on the coast of North Carolina and relocated the family to a small village in the volcanic highlands of southern Mexico to piece this story together.

In 2007, we returned to the Tarheel State fully intent on publishing our work. Coincidentally, our protagonist was receiving a whole new historical examination as remnants of his flagship were being unearthed just a few hundred yards off the North Carolina coast. As underwater archeology both confirmed previously conceived notions and also revealed new facts pertaining to this larger than life character known as Blackbeard the Pirate, whole new reams of source material previously inaccessible to struggling writers became available as vast troves of early 18th century imperial and colonial records were making their way online. And so, with the pressures of daily American life again at hand, work to insert some of these new treasures into the narrative made for slow going. But at some point that figurative line is drawn in the sand of time, and it becomes necessary to "go with what ya got," knowing fully well that, at least from our perspective, this will have to be revisited as new insights are given into lives and times three hundred years past.

Probably the biggest surprise we encountered in our research was the discovery that, as far as we have been able to ascertain, there is no comprehensive history of the period surrounding Queen Anne's War, the time central to the action in this work. Hollywood has done much to shape the misperception of pirates, but alas these caricatures do little to convey an understanding of the lives of common men and women of that period. What drove them to pursue their lives of crime? How were they different, or indeed the same, as others who found themselves in similar situations throughout the history of the world? We have tried to educate a little – in fact ended up purging a good bit of interesting material for want of space – and have worked diligently to dovetail the fiction seamlessly into the fact. For those interested in finding out where one ends and the other begins, we will publish a comprehensive list of historical references at the conclusion of Chronicle Three.

While getting the history correct was essential, this is, indeed, a work of fiction. While many characters are real people and great pains were taken to accurately portray them as historical record suggests, great liberties were taken to put words into their mouths, words likely never spoken. We are unapologetic in our affection and defense of our protagonist, and if a little mud was tossed in the direction of his detractors, we hope their descendents will be understanding and be reminded that, again, this is a work – mostly - of fantasy.

November 22, 2012
Nags Head, NC

The unauthorized biography of
Blackbeard the pirate

CHRONICLE ONE
The Prince of
Preobrazhenskoe

by David W. Carroll
& Penelope W. Carroll

Prologue

The Princess and the Giant

I

As the bedraggled and breathless one-time pirate clawed his way through the final stand of myrtle trees, their branches permanently reaching westward from the omnipresent ocean winds, it was immediately obvious that his desperate flight had been for naught. He drew next to the oversized dog that sat at the water's edge, bending at the waist and placing his hands on his knees, and tilted his head to mimic the Mastiff's stare as both took in the ferocious battle before them. On the deck of the ship just a few yards off shore, the legendary pirate captain he'd come to warn was locked in mortal combat with a dozen men whose collectively engaged pistols and sabers could not seem to fell the black maned giant. The look on the battling brigand's face was not one of desperation or anguish, despite the many slashes and bleeding stab wounds evident on his body. Rather, it was an expression of exuberance as if, through this inhuman demonstration of ferocity, he were indeed confirming the myth that he was a demon, impermeable, inviolable, incapable of dying. The contest on the quarterdeck was certainly more intense than the low grade slaughter on the bow. One by one, the crew succumbed to their foes, freeing up one very stout fighter to take up his axe and charge toward the stern to join his comrades in their quest to fell this bearded dragon. One more man should not have made a difference, but the messenger who had come so far so quickly in an attempt to avert this engagement struggled fruitlessly to muster the breath to warn his former commodore. The woodcutter's tool rose high, flashing brilliantly against the morning sun, then crushed down on the great pirate's shoulder, bringing the melee to a standstill. The axe buried deeply into the skeletal frame of the legendary buccaneer, a voluminous plume of crimson gushed from this latest of two dozen wounds as the pirate slowly whirled, at last collapsing to the deck from this near decapitation. His expression had now changed, betraying his own surprise that, perhaps, the rumors of his immortality been exaggerated.

In his dying moments, his eyes turned to his dutiful first mate who had been an uneasy sentinel aboard the deck of their own ship. The large African took this sudden turn of events as the sign to execute their Doomsday Plan requiring him to shimmy his immense frame into the narrow confines of the hold, offering him no time for pity, grieving or remorse as he prepared to ignite the stores of black powder beneath him. This most notorious of sea raiders had hard earned his reputation for giving no quarter and never taking any in return, and he was pleased that his most loyal companion would at least, if not give them the victory, snatch it from the jaws of the mercenary pirate hunters. His duties completed, the heralded King of Pirates dismissed all further thought of his foes and their fate, averting his attention to the beach, noting his dog faithfully manning his post where he had left him and, beside him, his old Quartermaster. He smiled at the notion of Spotty having acquired a new and equally surly companion. As his view shifted, his expression changed once again as his eyes were drawn to three men now standing near the failed messenger. He smiled more warmly as he took in the aged cleric whose face was etched into the deepest cores of his memory, standing in the strange company of a frail-looking fellow with pale skin and an unmistakably regal nose. Next to him was a tall African radiating a dignity reserved for only the most tested of warriors. Their presence brought a countenance of long sought and hard won peace. But then his eyes softened, his smile broadened as a delicate young woman, with a tiny frame and luxurious blonde hair, emerged from behind the masculine retinue. She walked slowly toward the water's edge, her gentle smile confirming for him that, indeed, all was well, encouraging him to yield to the easy peace that had eluded him for four decades. It was a peace that could only come as the pirate hunter who had bested his much sought after quarry used the last of his waning strength to deliver the final blow. The gentle countenance of bliss was eternally fixed upon the pirate captain's face as his head was violently slashed from his body, a necessary final act to seal in blood the legend of the most infamous pirate of the Caribbean Sea.

Abigail woke with a start from the decapitating blow. She sat silently, letting her breath catch and taking in the still unfamiliar surroundings, feeling the yawing of the ship around her as hemp lines and pitched wood responded to the motions of the sea. She listened for movement, hearing only the footfalls of sailors pass cadence-like on the deck above her. Nightmarish visions were all too often dark residents in Abigail's somnolescent imaginings and one of the many reasons why her mother abhorred her daughter's fascination with the macabre and lowly. Such terrible and wonderful stories were all the rage in the salons throughout Europe in the waning years of the 17th century, and Abigail Edwards considered it her duty to keep abreast of the latest topics of idle conversation. Before drifting off to sleep, she had curled up in her tiny stateroom aboard the Dutch merchant vessel that cruised east through the Mediterranean, passing the time reading *The History of the Bouccaneers of America,* which detailed the nefarious deeds of high seas colonial brigands. This first hand account of life among the pirates who had settled into the Caribbean Sea in the 1660s under the leadership of Captain Henry Morgan may have been beneath the dignity of the more quality works preferred in her mother's house, but to her good stepfather it was a page turner and a recurrent topic of parlor conversation among the frequent male callers. And, as had been the case these last ten years or so, whatever intrigued Yvgeny would eventually pique Abigail's interest as well.

Thinking of her stepfather, Abigail could not help but reflect on the good fortune that had brought him to her mother's opulent home in the Redcliffe district of Bristol. She realized, too, that a bastard's life could most certainly be far worse than hers. For the auspicious, the best one could hope for was boarding schools far afield. For the less fortunate, there was the very real threat of death. Though boarding schools had not been part of her childhood, she had been raised with the benefit of the best tutors that tainted money could buy. As the product of Beatrice Parker's illicit relationship with a lesser royal, Abigail was spared adversity by virtue of the abiding affection the young, gullible noble felt for her mother, a one-time indentured servant at his estate. Knowing that exposure could very easily ruin his life, he offered her compensation for her silence, and Beatrice was pleased to accept the gift with which she built a large home on a sizeable tract of land on the south side of Bristol. In November of 1663, an enchanting blonde haired, fair skinned little girl was born, and despite her agreement of discretion, Beatrice couldn't resist putting the noble family on edge by giving her daughter the last name of Edwards. While she never publicly revealed the actual identity of the father, astute royal-watchers were quick to catch the implication of the name.

Almost as quickly as her body would allow, Beatrice put her whorish reputation to work in her lavish new Parker House. As no respectable nanny would take the job of caring for the daughter of a prostitute, Beatrice recruited wayward girls from the streets of Bristol to take on the overflow of her business as well as share in the duties of caring for Abigail. The young madam's talents and charms, along with those of her ladies, became all the rage among the wealthy men of Bristol. The English town was rapidly becoming the principal port-of-call in southwest England, a reputation that brought a steady flow of merchantmen and mariners who, naturally, sought the company of women who understood their particular needs and desires. Bristol was a market municipality, administered by the town corporation, who, publicly, took a dim view of the woman and her very successful business practices. Being good Christians, they were required to extend an open condemnation of her activities. Privately, however, the men of the corporation knew all too well the valuable and enjoyable commodity they had in Beatrice Parker.

With so many men coming in and out of the house, the brothel was a virtual breeding ground for disease. Doctor Fenton was the one doctor who would provide Beatrice and her girls with a modicum of health care to help check the spread of syphilis, a disease commonly believed to have been brought back from the New World by the sailors who made up the most generous clientele of Parker House. Having survived Doctor Fenton's peculiar and painful mercury fumigation box treatment once, Beatrice took Doctor Fenton's spore theory quite seriously and dedicated hours each day to cleaning every nook and cranny of the house and its highly social residents. While Beatrice and her staff did all they could to keep the house meticulously clean, the random unchecked spore proved to be too elusive even for the ever-tidy Beatrice. Abigail developed a horrible cough that seemed beyond the mercurially centered treatments of Doctor Fenton. Beatrice grew frantic with concern for her daughter as her maternal instincts grew even more dominant than her business ones. As the cough lingered, Beatrice was less than amiable one afternoon when a representative of the town corporation brought word of their need of her services for a visiting dignitary. A very generous offer of money beyond the standard bedding fee convinced her that she should make time for the guest, and she conceded to the request. Beatrice was at her daughter's side when Allison Simms, one of her young "ladies," brought word of the guests' arrival. Beatrice asked Allison to attend to Abigail while she went to meet the gentlemen.

As she came down the stairs, she was greeted by Stanley Greene, a member of the town corporation, who escorted her to the drawing room. The gentlemen seated there stood respectfully as the grand lady of the house entered. She was quite familiar in many ways with most of them: Stanley Greene, who had purchased a rather heavy hair brush in Paris with which he insisted on being punished; Andrew Anson, a prominent merchant with a taste for incestuous role playing; David Huelin, the town harbormaster and the quintessential 60-second customer; Bartholomew Rollins, the town counselor and a man who had confided the true reason for his bachelorhood as his secret yet insatiable preference for visiting Mediterranean sailors. These men she knew and acknowledged with professional civility. But what caught her eye immediately was the giant, black haired and heavily bearded man who, upon introduction, graciously kissed her hand. He was an imposing figure with flashing, brilliant eyes that conveyed incredible intelligence and perceptiveness.

England was in the throes of imperial and commercial expansionism, and goods from her colonies helped Britain gain a competitive respectability in the ever-expanding world market. While the Dutch still controlled shipping via their highly efficient merchant vessels, England was quickly establishing itself as a not-too-distant second commercial power. Since 1555, England had enjoyed a close trade association with the burgeoning Russian Empire, which was still woefully behind the times in its quest to compete at sea. For over a century, trade had been exclusively controlled by the Muscovy Company based in London. But the Great Fire of London which leveled most of the nation's capital just two years earlier had created an opening for the Bristol Society of Merchant Venturers in their efforts to break London's monopoly. As the great city on the Thames would be busy for years rebuilding its commercial center and waterfront, Bristol jumped at the chance to begin the process of wooing Russian business to their bustling port, and these members of the Bristol Corporation knew Beatrice Parker's could be instrumental in helping them make their case. Among her many talents, Beatrice Parker was one of the most reputed hostesses in Bristol despite her running its most notorious house of irrepute. And if anybody could intrigue their esteemed Russian guest, it would be Beatrice Parker. Despite her personal concerns, she welcomed with open arms Yvgeny Thatcherev, an exceedingly westernized Muscovite who had been dispatched as special trade emissary to Bristol on behalf of Alexi Romanov, Tsar of Russia. As well as being a gifted politician and scholar, Yvgeny held a unique esteem as a modernizing priest in the Orthodox faith. Unlike Catholics, Orthodox priests were not bound by vows of chastity, and this made the services of Beatrice Parker invaluable in charming the pants off of a man like Yvgeny Thatcherev.

"Miss Parker, I so deeply appreciate the invitation to your grand home," Thatcherev intoned in heavily accented yet flawless English. Beatrice could feel her heart racing as the big man gently held her hand, his eyes drawing hers like magnets. An expert on men, Beatrice could sense the depth of this one's passion, a trait she had heard was common among Russians.

The group lingered for a few moments and then, in the most tactful of means, excused themselves so Yvgeny and Beatrice could converse more intimately. As the town council made their leave, Allison appeared at the door, beckoning for a conference with Beatrice. Her sudden and dramatic change of expression did not go unnoticed by Yvgeny. Beatrice excused herself, and while Yvgeny could not hear their conversation, he sensed that they discussed a matter of some gravity. As Allison went back upstairs, Beatrice returned to her guest and attempted to resume conversation. Yvgeny could tell that her thoughts were elsewhere.

"Mistress Parker," Yvgeny gently offered. "Please do not consider me too obtrusive, but I sense that your pleasant attention to an uninvited guest has caught you at a bad time." Yvgeny was about to stand and bid the woman good night.

Beatrice, the consummate professional, chided herself for her rare absence of composure, a hallmark of her hospitality. She smiled breezily as she placed her hand on the rising knees of her guest. "It's a minor domestic issue, Minister Thatcherev," she replied. "Please pardon my distraction."

Yvgeny could tell that this was not a woman prone to distraction but, rather, being a distraction. He placed his hand on hers and smiled kindly. Beatrice was strangely moved and, for the first time she could remember since yielding to her former master, she felt strangely compelled to tell the truth.

"You must forgive me, Minister Thatcherev. My daughter has been ill these last few days and it appears her cough has worsened. But, really, I need not trouble you with…"

Yvgeny's face took on a look of concern. "Mistress Parker, it is I who should apologize," Yvgeny rebutted as he stood. "Your place is with your child."

"Really, Minister Thatcherev. She's well attended and I have greater responsibilities to the house and to your … associates."

"Your duty, Mistress Parker, is to your child." He bowed and allowed her to escort him to the door. Beatrice watched from the window as the tall, muscular Russian, quickly bounded down the front steps and strode purposefully away. While part of her believed she may have offended him with her domestic concerns, the other side of her frankly didn't care. When he had disappeared among the growing shadows of dusk, she returned to join Allison at her daughter's bedside.

Abigail was just a few days short of five years and was growing to be a devastatingly beautiful little girl. That fact was in less evidence at this moment as Beatrice sat helplessly beside her, the spasms of cough racking her small body. The perspiration on her face and flushed cheeks were signs of a quickly manifesting fever. The painful bout of coughing brought tears of frustration to both mother and daughter.

"Mummy, when will this cough go away? It hurts so," Abigail pleaded through coughs.

Beatrice held her daughter close and rocked her gently, brushing the fever-dampened locks from her face. "Soon, my love. Soon."

Bernice Waters, a buxom, young brunette, quietly stole into the room, her face bearing a mixture of concern and surprise.

"Mistress Beatrice, a gentleman is downstairs. He says he has something to help Abigail."

Beatrice looked at her, reading the confusion. "Is it Doctor Fenton?"

"No, ma'am, it is the gentleman who was here earlier."

"Which gentleman, Bernice?"

"The tall, bearded one."

Taken aback, Beatrice told Allison and Bernice to stay with Abigail. She hurried down the long hall to the head of the stairs. Pacing in the foyer was Yvgeny, and in one hand he held a small leather satchel. Beatrice studied him for a moment, than made her way down the stairs. The brush of satin and lace signaled a feminine approach and caused Yvgeny to look up and see the beautiful woman coming slowly down the staircase, her face a picture of wariness and motherly concern.

"Emissary Thatcherev, I am surprised to see you again so soon."

"Dear lady, I apologize for the intrusion. However, when you told me of your daughter's illness, I grew quite concerned. We people of Russia live in a cold climate, and our children quite frequently suffer its ravages. I have something," he said, indicating the leather bag he held, "which may help relieve some of her suffering. I would like to administer it, with your permission."

Beatrice studied his face for a moment and sensed sincerity, a concern that touched her. While she had gone to great lengths to keep her daughter separated from the clientele, something told her that this would be one of those times when she should make an exception.

"Your kindness and consideration are appreciated, Emissary. Indeed, I'm a bit surprised. I did not realize that you are a doctor as well."

"No, mistress, I shall not pretend I am a doctor. However a dear friend back home is one, and I have learned a great deal from him. I, too, sometimes suffer from a cough, and I have found that this potion helps alleviate the suffering."

"Please, then, follow me."

She led him up the expansive staircase and down the long hallway where she opened the last door on the right, leading to yet another hallway that was reserved for the family of Parker House. As soon as the door opened, they could hear the little girl's persistent coughing coming from the far end of the hall. Beatrice entered through the last doorway on the left, Yvgeny a few paces behind her.

Beatrice rushed to Abigail and cradled her as she lay helpless on her bed, a mass of pillows behind her to help her sit up. The girl's labored breathing, a series of gasps and wheezes between coughs, was even worse now than when she had departed moments ago. Most heartbreaking of all were the pitiful whimpers and sobs that emitted as she struggled to find breath. Yvgeny watched with a compassionate eye, listening to her futile attempts at normal breathing and the loving care being administered by her mother.

"Abigail, darling, Mother has brought someone who may be able to help," Beatrice stated confidently, trying to hold back tears.

Abigail looked weakly toward the door and caught her first sight of the massive figure standing just inside the frame. His long dark hair and beard would have been frightening were it not for the very reassuring and gentle smile on his lips.

"Hello, Abigail," Yvgeny declared, much more jovially than one would expect from such an imposing figure. He veritably floated across the floor and stood beside the bed. Realizing what a sight he must be, so far above the bed, he knelt beside her and took her hand in his.

"You are a very hairy man," Abigail stated weakly.

"And you are a very pretty girl," he responded, smiling even more warmly.

Beatrice observed this with interest. It was hard to believe that such an august man could be so sensitive to a child. Most interesting was Abigail's immediate response to him. Having spent the first five years of her life primarily in the company of women, she tended to be very withdrawn around men, particularly strangers. Beatrice was astonished as the normally reserved little girl reached out with her free hand to stroke the long, flowing beard of the big Russian.

"It is very soft."

"That is because I do not like for it to feel rough, particularly when such a lovely lady as yourself is so kind to express an interest in it."

In a moment she removed her hand and Yvgeny lifted the bag he had brought with him onto the bed, removing from it an ornate flask and a silver spoon. He popped the cork and filled the spoon with an odd smelling elixir.

"This is a medicine we use where I come from when we have a cough," he informed the child. Abigail leaned forward, taking a whiff of the noxious concoction and wrinkling her nose in revulsion.

Yvgeny smiled. "It is not as bad tasting as it smells. Here, let me show you." He lifted the spoon to his lips and tipped the fluid into his open mouth and swallowed. He demonstrated no notable disdain for the flavor.

"See. What did I tell you?"

Abigail looked first at him, then the spoon. Suddenly, she was grasped by a seizure of coughing. Yvgeny sat patiently and waited for the bout to pass, never taking his eyes off the little girl.

Beatrice, on the other hand, let her gaze pass repeatedly between her daughter and Yvgeny. As the seizure slowly subsided, Beatrice intoned, "Abigail, maybe you should try the elixir. Perhaps it will help you feel better."

Abigail considered for a moment. "Well, if you promise that it does not taste bad, maybe I will."

"On my honor and word as a gentleman," Yvgeny swore seriously. He took the cue and slowly brought the spoon to the little girl's feverish lips, allowing her to sip the contents from it.

She looked at him with surprise. "It tastes sweet!"

"That is because of the honey. The medicine will make you sleepy in a few moments." Yvgeny put the bottle and spoon on the table beside the bed. He felt her head gently with the back of his hand and noted the temperature. "Perhaps you would like to hear a story to help you sleep and to dream pleasant things," he offered.

"I like stories," Abigail responded weakly. Beatrice noted that her breathing had relaxed and that she was not coughing.

Yvgeny smiled. "Well, this tale is in the language of my people, but the story is simple. It is about a little princess who stole the heart of a giant from the snowy country of the north. I think you will like it."

Yvgeny cleared his throat. To everyone's surprise, he began singing in a beautiful, rich bass tone. The Russian song was sad and melancholy, but Abigail took to it immediately. Beatrice could feel the little body she held relax. Before Yvgeny was finished, Abigail was fast asleep.

Seeing her slumber, Yvgeny checked her temperature once again. Obviously pleased with his finding, he gently stroked the little girl's cheek, whispering a few words in Russian. As he stood to leave, Beatrice signaled for Allison to sit with Abigail, and she followed Yvgeny out of the room and down the hall. She stopped him at the door that emptied out onto the main hall.

"You are very good with children, Yvgeny Thatcherev."

He smiled, slightly pained. "At one time, I had a wife and children of my own. Unfortunately, they, too, developed coughs. Had I possessed such an elixir as this then ..." His voice trailed off.

Beatrice felt suddenly lost for words. She diverted her eyes from the obviously pained man and felt a pang of ... something. Compassion, perhaps? Perhaps something else. She thought of the elixir.

"Well, the potion you used. You mentioned that coughs are common in your country. Necessity, as they say, is the mother of invention. Your doctors are now able to do great things because of the need."

Yvgeny smiled again. "No, our doctors cannot take credit for this. The inventor is a countryman of yours who came to Russia long ago and brought many new ideas. It is his thinking, and many others from the West, who are making vital contributions to the progress of my country. Unfortunately, not everyone embraces these changes as readily as Tsar Alexi or me."

"I would like to thank you, Emissary Thatcherev. For the medicine. For the song. Perhaps," she virtually purred as her gaze began to soften, "we can pick up where we left off earlier."

Yvgeny studied the attractive face, which stared intently up at him. The need was there, but it was not as overpowering as the other emotion he was feeling that he still had not identified.

"Mistress Parker, I thank you for your kind offer. But instead, I will ask you: would you care to dine with me some other time, when that little girl is not in such great need of you?"

Beatrice smiled. "Yes, Emissary, I would be honored to dine with you. But only on the condition that you call me Beatrice."

"Very well, Beatrice. And please address me as Yvgeny. I would like to call on your little girl as well to check on the progress of her health, with your permission."

Smiling contentedly, Beatrice responded, "I think she would like that. Both of us would."

"Then until tomorrow... Beatrice."

He gave a gallant, crisp bow, taking her hand and gently kissing it. Beaming through his dark beard, he hastily departed down the hall. Beatrice followed until she reached the head of the stairs and watched as Yvgeny collected his hat and coat. He gave one final glance toward the top of the stairs, smiled at the lovely Beatrice and departed.

"Until tomorrow, Yvgeny," Beatrice whispered to herself.

II

Over the next dozen years Yvgeny became an almost permanent fixture at Parker House. For the first few, he pursued the lovely Beatrice like a teen-aged suitor. While romance was a very prevalent part of their relationship, most important to both was the deeply abiding friendship and esteem they held for one another – that and the paternal love that existed between Abigail and Yvgeny. To the casual observer, one could easily mistake the three as a loving family unit, which, in all but name, they were.

Yvgeny happily took to his role as a surrogate father. He assumed the duty of Abigail's education, at least for the half of the year that he was in Bristol. Every fall, Yvgeny would return to Moscow to bring news of the progress they were making in expanding trade with Europe. Bristol was evolving into a major port, and a continuously growing number of the ships that departed its expanding harbor were en route to Kiev or the far north White Sea port of Arkhangel'sk. Despite his love for his mother country, he was always anxious to return to Bristol where his very non-traditional family awaited.

Abigail was quickly blossoming into a gorgeous young woman who was versed in several languages including Russian, Latin, Greek and Polish. Her insatiable appetite for reading prompted Yvgeny to return from Russia each year with trunks full of books, which Abigail greedily consumed. During his absences, Beatrice would return to the active practice of her avocation as, during his stays, she reserved the use of her body exclusively for Yvgeny. But as the years passed, she found herself slowly tapering off her professional duties. One reason was the dimming of her beauty, but the other was her growing commitment to Yvgeny. Yvgeny was well aware of her practices while he was gone, but never did he realize that in the last half of the twelve year span Beatrice had ceased to practice her art. In truth, she didn't need to. The brothel, which now boasted twelve ladies in permanent residence, did more than enough business to allow her to concentrate solely on its administration and other enterprises. Beatrice had an uncanny nose for business. Through Yvgeny and her talkative customers, she learned of the many lucrative trading deals available and, with her influence over them, she was able to persuade the members of the town corporation to let her invest – discreetly, of course.

In the fall of 1678, Beatrice's world took a sad but significant turn. Yvgeny returned from Moscow, and she could immediately sense that something was on his mind. Since the death of Tsar Alexis, Yvgeny had taken on a much expanded role as a chief trade advisor for the new leader of Russia, Tsar Fedor, who had succeeded his father at the tender age of fifteen two years earlier. Yvgeny was a confidant of Simeon Polotsky, a reformist priest who had long held the ear of Alexis and molded the minds of the Tsar's children as court teacher.

Polotsky enjoyed the support of an ever growing body of Orthodox priests who eschewed the Dark Ages mindset of the Old Believers and embraced the west and the opportunity to modernize Russia. Polotsky's opinion of Yvgeny contributed greatly to his being in Bristol as trade minister. And now, he was greatly influencing a decision weighing on Yvgeny's mind. For the first few days of their reunion, she let his thoughtfulness pass without comment. Finally, one evening, while lounging in the private study, she could not let his contemplative nature go without explanation.

"You have looked so very troubled since your return, Yvgeny. What has happened in Moscow that has made you so?"

"Oh, my dearest Beatrice. I do so apologize for my mood. I assure you it is nothing tragic."

The Russian's beard was showing streaks of grey, and his eyes possessed a tiredness that Beatrice had not noticed before. "Tell me, how are the people taking to Tsar Fedor?"

"Fedor is well received by the modernists, though I fear that many of the boyars ..."

"Boyars?" Beatrice inquired.

Yvgeny smiled. "I'm sorry, my dear, I know you find all these class distinctions quite ridiculous. They are the nobles - actually lesser royals, hangers on, but politically very powerful. They feel threatened by his continuing reforms. There is anxiety that his weakened health will make for a short rule, and there is growing concern that there may be no successor. There is pressure for him to marry, and, well, then there is Sofia, Fedor's sister, who has her own ambitions for the throne."

He paused for a moment and then took the hand of his beloved Beatrice and looked deeply in to her eyes. "But Russian politics – it's all very complicated. This is not what troubles me greatest, Beatrice. I bring news that is both good and, very possibly, bad. This is to be my last year in Bristol. I have brought a young successor with me, and in the fall I am to return to Moscow permanently. Vasily Golitsyn, Fedor's most trusted aid and a very westernized boyar, is pleased with my progress here in Bristol and wishes for me to return to Russia to take an administrative post, coordinating all of our trade emissaries throughout the world."

Beatrice felt her heart drop at this revelation. While she and Yvgeny had never spoken of a lifetime together, she had always felt that an eternal bond existed. The thought of his leaving forever had never crossed her mind.

"I understand, Yvgeny. And I know you must take the post. It is a great honor," Beatrice replied earnestly, doing her best to choke back the tears and the sadness that was permeating her heart. "Abigail and I will miss you very much, of course, but I respect that you have a duty to your country."

She stood quickly and turned her back to him, no longer able to control the tears. He followed and gently placed his hands on her shoulders, gingerly turning her to face him.

"This does not have to mean a parting of the ways for us, sweet Beatrice. I asked you many years ago to marry me. And I ask you again. Do me the honor of becoming my wife, and together the three of us can return as a holy consecrated family to Moscow."

Beatrice smiled as Yvgeny wiped a tear from her eye. She attempted to gather her strength and responded as rationally and sincerely as she could.

"Yvgeny Thatcherev, I love you as I have never loved any man. That is a truth that I am not afraid to admit. But as I told you so many years ago, I will never marry. Not even you, my dearest Yvgeny." She sighed heavily. "Besides, I could not leave Bristol. I have too many responsibilities here. And, let us be honest, wedding a prostitute from England would not be to your political advantage."

"No one ever need know, Beatrice."

"But I will know. As will you. You are a cleric in the Orthodox faith. I do not proscribe to any religion nor do I wish to. And I will not live a lie, nor shall you, Yvgeny Thatcherev. My morals may be questioned, but never my ethics."

Yvgeny looked into that lovely yet serious face. He did not see the lines beginning to crease her cheeks or the touches of grey streaking the fair hair of his beloved Beatrice. He saw only the beautiful woman that he had fallen in love with so many years ago. What he also saw on her face was the look of resolve; a look that he knew signaled an unshakeable conviction to her beliefs. And with his acknowledgement of that look, he knew that any further argument was pointless.

"We shall enjoy these last few months as never before, my love." He placed his arms around her, pulling her close, that voluminous brush of beard that had been so strange when they had first met now instilled within her a warmth, a feeling of comfort. The very thought that she would not feel that soft brushing against her neck made her heart sink, but it also made her wonder how Abigail would react to such devastating news. She had always had in the back of her mind the idea that perhaps now was the time for Abigail to see all these places that fascinated and intrigued her, those places that, when Yvgeny described them, created visible portraits in her brilliant daughter's mind.

"I want to ask a favor of you Yvgeny."

"Only name it and it is yours."

"When you go, I want Abigail to accompany you."

Yvgeny was more than a little surprised by this request. The look of earnestness on her face confirmed her words, and he considered for a moment.

"I do not see many complications with taking her to Moscow. I have friends who would be more than happy to look out for her while I attend to my duties. However, I am concerned for how she may feel about this ... and how you will deal with her absence."

"I will be fine. Oh, yes, I will miss her incredibly, and I do not mean to suggest her departure be permanent, of course. I see this as a perfect opportunity to broaden her horizons. She is at an age of decision and, while I am not ashamed of my vocation, I do wish for her to seek out her own path rather than relying on the pleasure of men as her means of employment. That, Yvgeny, is something that I believe should be exclusively reserved for the one young man fortunate enough to take her hand. If she is as much like her mother as I believe her to be, he will be a fortunate man indeed."

Yvgeny smiled broadly at this comment and nodded in response. While they were very different in many ways – Beatrice the savvy businesswoman and Abigail the woman of art, culture and gentility – they did share many common traits that went beyond mere build and appearance. Beatrice had shielded her daughter from actively participating in the family business, though the men of Bristol, both young and old, could not help but sigh at the sight of her loveliness. While her nose was usually buried in a book, Abigail was very much aware of the effect that she had on men. And she appreciated that fact. Like her mother, she was a merciless flirt and knew exactly what to say or do to keep men coming back for more. The difference was that Abigail left them at the threshold of the front door. Beatrice invited them in, picked their pockets clean and left them apologizing for not having brought more for her to take.

Abigail also possessed her mother's unique moral outlook. Sex and intimacy, both reasoned, were the things that made humans so distinctly different from any other creature on earth. This was something to be celebrated, appreciated and practiced, not treated as some horrid "duty" reserved for the sole purpose of procreation. However, Abigail hadn't yet found any man interesting enough with whom to share this philosophy, though she did harbor a secret attraction that had as yet escaped even her mother's most perceptive eye. Other than Yvgeny, she had never met a man that challenged or fascinated her enough to explore the more intimate interactions. And Yvgeny was out of the question. While Beatrice never confided her true feelings for the regal Russian giant, Abigail was very aware of the depth of her mother's love for him. It had not escaped her that the most notorious madam and prostitute in southern England had shared her bed exclusively with one man for the past six years. She wondered if Yvgeny knew. Knowing her mother, it was unlikely she would ever confess such to him.

True to Beatrice's prediction, Abigail was overjoyed at Yvgeny's offer to travel with him to Russia. It saddened her to know that the love of her mother's life was leaving for God only knew how long, but, even without asking, she knew that this was how it had to be for Beatrice.

III

Perhaps it was because Parker House occupied such a tawdry subsect on the fringe of Bristol society or, perhaps it was because beyond its walls there was no sanctuary afforded to these ladies of dubious virtue. Or, more likely, it was because each woman who had taken refuge within the confines of the brothel felt a measure of maternal stake in the life of the teen mistress that news of Abigail's journey and Yvgeny's possible permanent departure was greeted with sadness, anger and protest. Abigail and Yvgeny brought a sense of unexpected normalcy to this most abnormal of residences, and in the weeks leading up to the inevitable departure, the women conspired, pleaded and gnashed, sometimes individually, sometimes collectively, protesting this uninvited disruption of their status quo. Knowing her prostitutes as well as a reverend mother knows her nuns and novices, Beatrice patiently heard out each protest, every rationalization, every portent of doom patiently and firmly, assuring each of her ladies precisely as required to assuage her fears and disappointment. She expected no less of her girls. While she was the madam of the brothel, in so many ways, her daughter had become the mistress, the source of reverence and the reason for obedience. Likewise Yvgeny, though not playing any official role in Parker House, gave the women a sense of comfort and safety, not only because of his imposing physical presence and influence within the business community – the primary source of income of Parker House – but he also provided what was, to many, the first semblance of a father figure on which they could count. Parker House was more than a brothel and place of employment. To these ladies, it was home, and the pending departure of the father and child figures was viewed as the tragedy of a broken family.

What Beatrice didn't expect was the calm acceptance of Abigail's departure by perhaps the two most vulnerable members of the household: Nettie, the African housekeeper, and her son Caesar. Despite the closeness Abigail felt with each of the ladies of Parker House, in so many ways the teenaged former slave and her child were Abigail's closest family members. In the few short years since Nettie and Caesar had arrived at Parker House, they had become the purpose for Abigail's existence. It was Abigail who had taught them both English. It was Abigail who had taught them to read and write. It was on Abigail's lap that Caesar had sat while her hand guided the young boy's fingers over the surface of the cast iron globe that showed him where he had come from, where he was now and where Abigail was about to venture. It was Abigail that instilled in Caesar a fascination with ships, seas and the brave adventurers who commanded them. While plying him with the classics, she had been wise to select tales of expedition and warfare ideal to inspire the imagination of a young boy.

Abigail, Nettie and Caesar had been almost inseparable since the two young Africans set foot in Parker House, and Beatrice expected the most expressions of concern from them. But, rather than comforting Nettie and her child, it was Nettie who provided comfort to Beatrice and Abigail, assuring them both how significant this trip would be for Abigail's continued growth and maturity.

"You be worryin' too much, Ma'am," Nettie chided Beatrice one evening when she found the lady of the house quietly weeping on the back stairs leading from the residence to the kitchen and servant's quarters.

"But it is so far, Nettie," Beatrice exhaled as Nettie patted her employer's hand. "So much could happen across so much water. She's so young! And ... Yvgeny!" The fresh thought of forever losing her most beloved brought a fresh stream of tears, and she buried her face her hands.

Nettie took one finger and placed it to Beatrice's chin, lifting it and moving Beatrice's hands as she dabbed her employer's eyes with the hem of her simple cotton dress. "Dere, now, Mistress Parker. You be tinkin' bad thoughts for no reason. Master 'Geny ... he's a holy man and god be watchin' him. He done heal Mistress Abigail once already. He protect her always. And ...," Nettie leaned in to whisper conspiratorially to Beatrice, "In no time short ... he bring her back to all of us. To you."

Yvgeny and Abigail booked passage aboard a Dutch merchant ship setting sail just before the Spring tide of 1679. The day found the Bristol quay crowded with merchants and stevedores and well-wishers for travelers, though the dozen or so gathered around Abigail and Yvgeny found themselves given a wide public berth by many of the same men who paid handsomely so frequently to crowd them privately. Abigail kissed and hugged them all, saving Nettie and Caesar for last.

"You take care of them, Nettie," Abigail whispered into the young African woman's ear as she hugged her.

"Don't you worry Mistress," Nettie replied, pulling Abigail back to face her, reminding her of her public obligations. "You just remember your place, now. Dis is your home. Dis is your family and dese are the people who will always love you."

Abigail studied the face of her closest friend, her sister, and squeezed her hand. She felt a tugging at her skirt. She smiled and bent at the knees so she could look eye level into Caesar's face.

"I have something for you, Mistress," Caesar said as he handed the book to Abigail.

"Oh, Caesar!" she replied as she studied the letters etched into the cover. "This is your buccaneer book. It's your favorite. Besides, I'm not going to America, remember?"

The six year old boy with the very serious face looked her dead in the eye. "There are pirates everywhere, Mistress. Best to know what to look for should you find one."

Abigail smiled as she stroked a finger along his cheek. "Good advice, Caesar. And, likewise, one never knows when one might encounter a king," she replied as she winked and kissed his cheek.

"Sometimes, they're one in the same, Mistress" Caesar stated seriously, though his face betrayed the slightest hint of a smile as Yvgeny took her arm and led her up the gangplank.

And thus, after the docks of Bristol's waterfront had disappeared from sight, Abigail retired to her stateroom to be once again regaled with Alexander Exquemelin's accounts of piracy and pirates, just in case Caesar was onto something. The young sailors on board sighed with disappointment as she disappeared between decks, but the British captain and Yvgeny quickly let it be known that the beautiful blonde, the one that forced them to double up in the crew's quarters, was strictly off limits. One look into the dangerous eyes of the giant Russian was all the warning the men needed. Abigail spent many hours of the long voyage in her cabin reading and conversing with her beloved stepfather, eager to arrive in this exotic land she had heard and read so much about.

Making port at the ancient city of Constantinople, the birthplace of the Eastern Orthodox faith, Yvgeny took Abigail on a brief tour of the magnificent old city, the highlight of which was a visit to the Cathedral of St. Sofia. Built by Constantine after his conversion to Christianity, it was one of the holiest sites in all of Christendom. As he described the importance of this holy edifice to his national and religious history, Abigail was stirred by a desire to be closer to this man who was, in all but blood, her father. While not raised with a respect or attraction to the ethereal, at this moment, in this place, it seemed only natural that she wished to feel the joy so obvious in Yvgeny's expressions. She turned to him, placing her gentle hand upon his strong arm. This gesture, so meek yet powerful to Yvgeny, removed him from his religious ponderings and refocused his attentions to that sweet face that gazed up at him with a look that took him back to the first time his gaze had fixed on her young, innocent, deathly-ill eyes that had stolen his heart.

"Yvgeny, I wish to ask a favor of you," Abigail requested seriously. "You know I have never had much interest in things religious, and yet you have always been such an incredible inspiration to me. I want to feel what you feel right now. I want that connection to you and to your people and to your religion in ways I just can't quite explain. Can you teach me what I need to know to practice your faith?"

Yvgeny was obviously very touched by the request. As a cleric in the Russian Orthodox faith, it was always one of his greatest desires to be sought out as a source of religious inspiration or conversion. Yet he felt it was critical that Abigail be moved, not by her love for him, but by a love for something greater.

"Oh, my sweet child," he said. "You cannot know how much joy that brings me to hear that you wish to share this very personal connection to me. But I think it is important that you get to know my country and why our faith is so important. Then, if you still wish to pursue the studies of my religion, you will find no more eager a teacher than I."

Abigail studied that big, broad, hairy face and its gentle sincerity and realized that what he said was true. She would continue on her journey with him to Russia, grow intimate with its people and culture, and perhaps before departing Yvgeny's beloved homeland she would broach the subject again. In the meantime, they stood together silently, drinking in the beauty and majesty of this most sacred icon of Russian Christendom.

The next leg of the trip carried them across the Black Sea and up the Dnieper River to Kiev for the final overland journey to Moscow. At long last, they arrived at the German Suburb, just outside the Russian capital of Moscow. Abigail was brought to the home of Dr. Robert Benyon, an Englishman who had served as Court physician to Tsar Alexi and now to his ailing son Tsar Fedor. Dr. Benyon and his now deceased colleague, Dr. Samuel Collins, had been instrumental in bringing modern medicine to Russia. It had been Dr. Collins' elixir that had saved Abigail's life, and Dr. Benyon headed the Russian Apothecary Board that had made this same elixir a savior of thousands of Russian children since. It was agreed that, for the sake of discretion and to conform to Moscow's prohibition of foreign residents, Abigail would be housed with the doctor and his family, who enjoyed respectability among the Russian nobles. Abigail was gratified to get to know one of the brilliant and adventurous doctors who, through their elixir, had most likely saved her life as a child. Through Dr. Benyon, Abigail quickly assimilated into the cosmopolitan European life of Moscow's suburban society. Her association with Yvgeny further enhanced her status among both Russians and Westerners. That, combined with her flawless command of the Russian language, quickly made her a favorite of the social gatherings of the Moscow privileged.

On one such occasion, Yvgeny introduced her to Vasily Golitsyn. As the principal advisor to Tsar Fedor and a respected and immensely powerful boyar from one of Russia's most prominent families, Golitsyn was the most influential man in all of Russia. His taste for everything Western included European books and works of art, considered sacrilegious to many of the more traditional of the Russian Orthodoxy. One of the more important aspects of his westernized beliefs was that the old systems of serfdom and cruelty were in desperate need of reform. What Abigail found particularly fascinating about Vasily was his belief that women should be shielded from the battering from their husbands – a radical view, not only in the very patriarchal Russian society, but throughout the rest of the "civilized" world where women, particularly wives, were mere property of their husbands and thus subjected to any number of cruelties. Vasily took a special interest in the young woman from England who, rumors suggested, was the adopted daughter of his new trade administrator. Many times he sat and conversed with the very independent thinking woman who, to his pleasant surprise, was well versed in things Russian. His interest in Abigail led him to committing what could have spelled his political doom and a radical change in Russia's future.

In the Spring of 1669, Tsar Fedor was entering his third year of rule over all Russia. At seventeen, the young Tsar suffered from a variety of maladies, kept in check by the dutiful Dr. Benyon. He had learned, through Vasily and others in his court, of the visiting young English woman, rumored to be the stepdaughter or, more scandalously, the young English mistress of Yvgeny Thatcherev. On one of Dr. Benyon's numerous visits to the royal palace to treat the frail ruler, Fedor inquired of the young woman. Feeling it best to remain circumspect, Dr. Benyon offered little information about his houseguest except to say that she was a learned young lady. To Fedor, this signaled the potential of nobility, having never known an educated common woman, and he questioned his aid Vasily about her. Vasily could not confirm noble ties, and he conferred with Yvgeny of her background. Not willing to cast dispersions on either of the women he most treasured, Yvgeny stated simply that the child's mother was a woman of means in Bristol and that he believed she was widowed prior to the birth of the girl. Fedor pressed, and finally Vasily arranged a meeting between the young Tsar and Abigail.

Fedor reacted instantly in breathtaking awe to the beautiful Abigail Edwards of Bristol. To his astonishment, Abigail practiced the rituals of royal introduction as if she had been bred to the boyar class. Certainly, Fedor reasoned, this woman had to be of nobility. He was immediately taken with her, and Abigail in turn was impressed by the teenaged Tsar who, despite his power and youth, proved to be much more sensitive than one would imagine. They spent much time in that first meeting, sharing philosophical views and ideas. He was impressed by the depth of her intellect as well as her beauty and indicated that he wished to spend more time with her in the future. To Abigail, who had finally met a man that challenged her mentally and excited her physically, encountering someone like the Tsar of Russia was the culmination of all of her dreams.

Shielded by her youth and hosts, Abigail was naive to the political storm that was swirling around them. One of the keenest of observers to her presence was Fedor's sister, the shrewish Sofia. Unlike most Russian women of her time, she had been tutored and educated along with her brothers. Sofia had designs on the throne, but her ambitions were thwarted when Fedor had refused to have their father's second wife Natalya and her son Peter exiled. The only other surviving brother, Tsarevich Ivan, was mentally retarded and posed no threat to her lofty ambitions. Sofia held little sisterly concern for Fedor's health. Her hope was that the weakling would die soon and thus provide her an opportunity to do away with those who threatened her rightful place as Tsarina of Russia. And bit by bit she had worked to isolate Fedor, such as engineering a revolt by members of the palace guard. While he did retain his crown, it came at the price of the life of Artemon Matveev, Fedor's favorite tutor and chief advisor, who met his demise by being hurled onto the spears of the rebel battalion. It made the role of advisor to Tsar Fedor the least desired role in the Kremlin.

Of highest priority to the ruling class was finding an appropriate bride for Fedor. Those closest to him knew that there was very little likelihood of his living a long life, and it was critical that someone be found to bear his heir. The more westernized of the inner circle of the court noted the attraction he held for the beautiful English woman. If she could be confirmed as nobility, perhaps their search was over. A council of boyars summoned Yvgeny Thatcherev to their court to discuss the matter. Central to his concern was protecting the reputations of Beatrice and Abigail, and, as the noblemen probed him for information, Yvgeny was forced to lie about the history of the two women he loved most. Yes, the woman was educated. No, she was not of nobility. Her father was a merchant who had died prior to her birth. No, he was not married to her mother but, yes, he did love her. The boyars convened privately and determined that Abigail Edwards was not a suitable bride for Tsar Fedor. Among the boyars that convened were a few whose loyalties were to Sofia. She was immediately informed of the status of the English woman and sighed with relief, knowing that a marriage between the two would never be sanctioned. For the time being, she could rest assured that the odds were stacking against her sickly sibling.

Despite the protests of the boyars, Fedor insisted on continuing to see the lovely Abigail, even after they had selected what they believed to be a perfect bride for him. Often, Abigail would come to the private family quarters of the Palace to dine with Fedor, Ivan, their stepmother Natalya and her precocious eight-year-old son, Peter. Sofia, having made an enemy of Natalya Naryshkina, was banished to the women's quarters and forbidden from participating in family activities. The Miloslavskaya family, Sofia and Fedor's maternal line, was incensed that they were excluded from the privilege of royal favor in lieu of Fedor's recognition of the rights of the Naryshkina line, his stepmother's family. Alexi had always enjoyed the respect of his eldest son. As such, Fedor honored his father's wishes, including his bestowments to the Naryshkina line and all the wealth and patronage associated. Natalya had taken to her role as stepmother to Alexi's sons with earnestness and, except for Sofia whose disdain for her father's new wife was palpable, treated his children as if they were her own. She was incredibly attentive and patient with the mentally deficient Ivan, who particularly needed a gentle and loving hand. Through Abigail's intimate association with the royal family, she learned of the unique but precarious balance of power that was Russian royalty.

On one particular evening, as the family had retired following a particularly sumptuous meal, Fedor and she adjourned to his private chambers. The drafty, darkened rooms of the Terem Palace glowed with the combination of firelight and the sparkle of love struck glances. There they sat and talked for hours about the world and its mysteries. There was a brief moment of silence as the two sat side by side. Fedor glanced over at Abigail, who returned his gaze with curiosity.

"May I make a confession to you, Abigail?" Fedor asked, more serious than was his usual demeanor.

"If you feel that I am the appropriate person to whom you should confess something, then please do," she replied hesitantly.

Fedor smiled. He knew that hearing the confessions of the Tsar, no matter how intimate one's relationship, was never a simple matter. He appreciated that his dear friend Abigail had quickly become his most trusted and intimate confidante. While that may have been a role greatly sought after by his consorts and advisors, it likely was not the most desired position for a teenaged English girl with a boy who was obviously attracted to her.

"Since meeting you, I cannot tell you how strangely wonderful it has been – to feel as good as I do. I have never been healthy, and it is no secret that many have wished that I had expired before my father did. There are many, some very close to me, who wish that my health was now as it was before you came into my life. When you are with me, whether in a crowded room or in a place such as this, where you and I are alone, I feel so," he paused, searching for the word. " … alive. You do something for me that the best physicians of Russia and all of Europe cannot do. You make me want to live."

Abigail sat silently and pondered this confession. She had noticed how Fedor seemed not as sickly as Doctor Benyon had frequently suggested and considered that good medicine had been the source of Fedor's apparent rejuvenation. She had never dreamed that the reason why this supposedly sickly king was now so vital was because she was, in essence, his healing balm. Yet was that really surprising? She, too, found herself a little more excited, a little more rejuvenated whenever she knew she was to be with him. At first, she had attributed it to the logical flattery that would accompany being in the presence of a king, but it wasn't his royalty that so impressed her. It was his kindness and gentleness that held her attention for hours on end and made her count the minutes until she would be by his side again. But this was foolishness. Fedor was the king of Russia, and at that moment the most attractive women throughout the kingdom were being summoned to Moscow to partake in the traditional bridal selection. Unlike the other kingdoms of Europe, Russian's kings and princes did not marry foreigners, even royal ones, as a means of integration into greater Europe. According to Russian custom, Fedor could choose any bride he wished, just so long as she was Russian. Abigail knew this was how it was and this reality struck her both painfully and poignantly.

"Fedor, I cannot tell you how much all this time we have spent together has meant to me. In fact, I am always a little shocked every time I receive a summons from you requesting my presence. It is obvious that I greatly admire and respect you and your family. The very thought that I, a simple girl from England, would ever get the chance to share so much time with such a powerful person is beyond reckoning. You cannot know how happy I am hearing that your health is on the mend, and I cannot tell you how flattered I am that you would suggest I somehow affect you in that way." She sighed and looked away. "But even if it were true, it would be for naught."

"And why so? I am the Tsar, and that affords me the ability to decide what is good for me, because what is good for me is good for Russia. And you, my dear Abigail, are good for me."

"Your words are sweet and yes, I will confess, they make my heart flutter, Fedor," she replied. "I have only met one other person who impresses me and inspires me so much. But you see, that relationship has spanned the last twelve years of my life. It has saved me. It has protected me. What you say now, to me, were it true, would spell the doom for all of us. You are the Tsar of Russia, Fedor, and your life is not your own."

Abigail's words to Fedor pierced his heart like an ice dagger. While what she said was the political reality, at this moment it had little bearing on his feelings. In her, he had found everything that made life joyous. While he owned his crown by virtue of royal birth and from the support of the ruling class, in this significant aspect of his tragic, pneumonic life, neither birthright nor politics would dictate to him what his heart said was most important.

"I have made a decision, Abigail," he said. "I have let so many decisions be dictated by the will of the boyars. But I have no desire to let them tell to me whom I must marry. It may surprise you to know that I have discussed this at length with Natalya, and she feels that what is best for Russia is what makes its king most happy."

Fedor took her hands in his. He looked deeply into her eyes.

"And what makes me most happy," Fedor smiled, bending his face to her face, his lips gently pressing to her lips in a brief but life changing moment. "…is you."

At last, Abigail Edwards knew she'd found the man for whom she had secured her virtue. While the words Fedor spoke may prove to be nothing more than the futile wishes of a lovesick young king, at this moment Abigail's heart let her believe his words were true.

Her eyes never left his as he guided her into the royal bedchamber.

Abigail's surrender to Fedor was both wonderful and dangerous. There was no denying how they felt about each other, yet there was the reality that, despite his protest to the contrary, such decisions as marriage were not wholly his own. While her heart had and would say yes to Fedor a million times over, her practical mind sought out the advice of someone who could honestly tell her how realistic this fantastic dream of hers and Fedor's could ever truly be. Abigail frequently confided her affection for the family and Fedor to Vasily Golitsyn, whom she felt was most instrumental in her meeting Fedor and considered him to be a true friend and confidant. Vasily was a good ear and seemed earnest in his concern for the well being of his Tsar. It was because of such confidence that, in late August of 1679, she revealed the truth of her background to Vasily. Vasily listened intently, the shock of her confession not betraying any expression on his face. He smiled and patted her hands.

"This ruins everything, doesn't it, Vasily?" she asked, feeling she knew the answer even before he gave it.

"Fedor is right when he says that what is good for him is good for Russia, and it is obvious, Abigail, that you have been very good for him, for no one has ever seen him in such good health and spirits. But I cannot answer this question myself, and if you will trust me, I will confer with people whom I trust about how we may make this fondest wish of your two young hearts a real possibility."

Abigail was shocked to hear that there was even the smallest bit of hope, and on the trip back to Dr. Benyon's home she felt as if she were being carried on gossamer wings.

"Is it as serious as we thought?" Sofia inquired as Vasily slipped past the retinue of Strelsky guard that kept Sofia sequestered in her private quarters.

"Oh, that and then some," Vasily replied, smiling and shaking his head. "It seems our two young lovers feel themselves to be star-crossed. The problem is her star shines brightest in an English bordello!"

"A brothel?" Sofia asked in amazement. "It's bad enough to hear that she's low-born, but are you telling me she's a common prostitute?"

"No, actually, it seems she grew up in one. Apparently her mother has the same bad habit of choosing men way above her station."

"And what about Fedor? Does he know?"

"It appears she's confessed everything to him, and it also appears that he doesn't care. Perhaps that will explain why the chambermaid is so impressed by the quantity left behind in his sheets. It seems as if our boy king's manhood is in the hands of a professional."

Sofia was beside herself with joy, and as she watched Vasily undressing, she could only imagine how much this would astonish the boyars when they learned that their Tsar was in love with an English whore. She smiled as Vasily climbed into her bed. Her handsome and charming noble was not beneath her station literally, but the very fact that they, too, were no better in their illicit relations made feeling the press of his naked body against hers that much more delicious. As he slowly entered her, her hands came to his shoulders, and pulling his ear down next to her mouth she whispered, "Treat me as if I were an English whore, Tsar Vasily."

Sofia was enthralled to learn of her brother's indiscretion, and she believed that the best course of action was to publicly expose his dalliance. Public knowledge would ruin him and force his abdication from the throne. Vasily, on the other hand, saw it as an opportunity to assert control over Fedor.

Yvgeny was in the study of his small Moscow apartment when, well past midnight, he heard a knock at his door. It was unusual to hear a summons so late at night, and it was seldom good news. With trepidation he opened the door and was surprised to see Vasily Golitsyn.

"Vasily! To what do I owe the pleasure so late in the evening?"

Vasily took the invitation and entered Yvgeny's apartment. He looked about to see how simply the man lived. Having carefully investigated Yvgeny's financial dealings, he knew how wealthy this simple Orthodox priest had become, and yet he chose such humble surroundings. Vasily perused the small space which contained few personal items revealing the life Yvgeny had made for himself in England. Stacked on every surface were countless volumes of books.

"How do you get the time to read so much, Yvgeny?," Vasily inquired as he took a chair at the simple wooden table that Yvgeny began clearing of books.

"I make the time, Vasily. It may come at the price of sleep. I limit my social schedule, but I must always make the time. But … you're not here to discuss books," Yvgeny stated flatly as he placed a bottle of bread wine, a most Russian of concoctions distilled from the region's finest grains and the recently introduced English potato, between them.

Vasily smiled, for now, other than books, he saw Yvgeny's one extravagance. The ornate blue bottle with the blue label told him that the Orthodox priest may not have been selective in the company he kept, but his taste in tipple was superior.

"I must say, Yvgeny, you men of Pskov are unequaled in two things – masonry and bread wine."

"You forget the third thing, Vasily. The men of Pskov are unequaled in our progressive views. Perhaps it is those long, snowy winters that give us time to reflect on our lives, to think about the future of Russia, for while you in Moscow spend your time in idle banter and endless parties, we are left with our spirits, our books and our silent contemplation. But you did not come here to talk about bread wine and masonry either, Vasily."

Long ago, Yvgeny had learned never to drink vodka, particularly Pskov Blue Label, when he was in a bad mood, but before Vasily Golitsyn had left his humble apartment, he had removed the cork from a third bottle. Golitsyn told all he knew of the young beauty from Bristol, from her tawdry beginnings to the evidence of her recent intimate encounters with the Tsar of all Russia. Yvgeny had always viewed Vasily as a friend, but now he was seeing a side of the man that he didn't like and feared. What he liked even less was the ultimatum. Vasily was prepared to go before the boyars in the morning and reveal all that he knew. That would effectively ruin Yvgeny, having lied to the nobles about the woman whom he had brought to their country. It would particularly destroy the young lovers and force Fedor to abdicate the throne for having taken up with the bastard child of an English whore. All would be spared the ugliness if Yvgeny agreed to take Abigail away from Russia and never return. Yvgeny was quick to see that there was no future for either him or Abigail in his beloved native country. Vasily provided details of passage he had arranged for a departure in the morning, and Yvgeny agreed to be aboard the carriage with Abigail.

At sunrise, Dr. Benyon was awakened by a persistent knocking. His alarm at seeing Yvgeny so early in the morning was only amplified by his demand to see Abigail immediately. He knocked at her bedroom door and entered. She still lay slumbering, as peaceful as the first time he had seen her sleep. His heart ached as he stared at her for a moment, wishing sorely that he had some magic elixir that could save her from the pain that he knew she was soon certain to endure. Gently, he roused her from her peace.

The look on his face said volumes. "My sweet Abigail," he sighed as he brushed the hair away from her face, "I am afraid it is time we return to Bristol."

The tears that began streaming down her cheeks broke his heart in a way that no potion could ever cure. "Do I have time to say good-bye?"

"No, my precious girl." He replied sadly.

Before the sun had a chance to fully greet the citizenry of Moscow, a carriage heading southwest towards Smolensk was viewed from the apartment window of Tsar Fedor. Standing at the window, the young king felt a horrible pain gripping his chest. Vasily Golitsyn smiled as he summoned Dr. Benyon to the Kremlin.

As the merchant ship sailed into the expanding harbor of Bristol, Abigail Edwards had finally developed the strength to leave her quarters. For the past few weeks she had been quite ill, and Yvgeny Thatcherev had posted an ever-present vigil on the young woman who, in every respect but biological, was his child. He was later relieved to discover that he wasn't about to lose yet another loved one to illness. He was on the cusp of experiencing a joy he never expected to feel in his long, sad life.

Grandfatherhood.

Chapter 1

Bristol Beginnings
1680 – 1685

I

Early spring in Bristol was often difficult to discern from winter. In 1680, rain and cold had been persistent throughout all of March, and the citizenry were pleasantly surprised to experience an uncharacteristically warm day on April 1st. Indeed, it was a truly Good Friday.

Every window in Parker House had been opened to allow the sweet-smelling, warm air to circulate throughout. Yvgeny Thatcherev had been up since before dawn and was anxiously pacing the floor in his private study. He prided himself on usually being a reasonably sober man, but at 9:30 a.m. he was on his fifth glass of bread wine and dismayed that it was doing little to calm his nerves. Until about an hour ago, he had been upstairs in the last room of the private wing. Abigail had awakened the entire house at around 4 o'clock with a loud, disconcerting moan that brought Yvgeny running, wearing nothing more than the glow of lantern light. The sight of the hairy, bare-assed ex-Muscovite holding the glowing vessel with a petrified look on his face was humorous enough to momentarily take Abigail's mind off of the dreadful pain she was feeling in her mid-section. But only momentarily. She had awoken to find that her water had broken, immediately followed by the first of many contractions signaling the start of labor.

Calmly and efficiently, Nettie, the Parker House housekeeper, strode past the naked Orthodox priest and, in her typical nonplussed fashion, took control of the events unraveling in these early hours. Caesar, her seven-year-old son, was right behind her and, like his mother, a picture of calm. She turned to her boy and told him to fetch the standard water and clean sheets.

Yvgeny was paralyzed by the sight of Abigail's naked midsection, fully visible as she had whipped off the covers and hiked up her nightgown upon awakening. Nettie whispered softly to Abigail, providing a measure of comfort as she helped her stand so she could strip off the stained sheet in one quick snap and replace it with one handed to her by her capable son. Her hands gently pushed up the damp nightgown, smiling as she rubbed the protruding stomach, and lifting the garment over the long blonde tresses of the expectant mother's head, placed Abigail back in bed between fresh linen.

"Thank you, Nettie," Abigail whispered, feeling instantly calm now that Nettie had taken charge of this most alien of experiences. If anyone could be trusted to get her through these next few hours, indeed a lifetime, it was certainly Nettie. The ever-serious African woman offered a soft smile and a wink that only Abigail could see as she tucked the sheets about her.

Beatrice Parker reached Abigail's room and threw a robe over Yvgeny's shoulders as she took the lantern away. He finally became aware of his nudity and quickly covered himself.

"We are very close, Abigail," Beatrice intoned as she stroked her daughter's forehead. Footsteps could be heard as the other ladies of the house, many of whom had just settled in for slumber after a busy night, came running. The spacious room quickly filled up, and the cacophony of excited voices filled the air until Beatrice was forced to shout to gain a semblance of order. "All right, ladies. As excited as we all may be, there is nothing you can do here, and bedraggled ladies are not what men expect to see at Parker House. Now, go back to bed, and as soon as anything of importance occurs, I will most certainly notify you. Shoo!"

This, of course, was a futile order, as the ladies continued to mill around the hallway of the private quarters. Yvgeny sat beside Abigail, holding her hand, stroking her brow, giving her water and acting more the expectant father than step-grandfather. At first, his presence had been reassuring but, as the morning began to drag on and he began to pace the room, in general getting under foot, Abigail asked him to open the window as it appeared to be a lovely day. He did so and, seeing an opportunity to keep him busy, Beatrice ordered him to do likewise for every other window in the house. This was no small task. Among the three stories, Yvgeny had some sixty-five windows to break loose, as they had swelled tightly shut throughout the long, dreary winter.

"But Beatrice – Abigail needs me here!" Yvgeny protested.

Beatrice stretched fully erect, looked up into Yvgeny's face and mused, "Pray tell, Yvgeny, for what?"

When he couldn't justify his presence, he bowed his head in resignation. He turned to Caesar and suggested maybe the men could be utilized elsewhere. Caesar looked to his mother for her assent, as this was Nettie's domain. Lowering her mouth next his ear, she whispered, "Keep him busy, but most important keep him away from dis room until I say different."

Caesar looked at Abigail, who nodded her head in agreement, and wordlessly he led Yvgeny out of the room. The Russian's natural strength and the extra dose of adrenaline rushing through his veins made short work of the task, and as he was making his way back up the stairs he felt the tug of Caesar's hand on the tail of his robe. The imposing four-foot-six Caesar was taking his charge seriously, and shaking his head, not willing to renege on his duties, his expression made it crystal clear that there was no way he was going to let this man, two feet taller than he, go anywhere near the birthing chamber. Long ago, he had learned not to question anything his mother requested of him, and this day was going to be no exception. Despite his love and admiration for the man he considered to be his savior, orders were orders, and Yvgeny found himself being muscled by a strong-willed seven-year-old

With resignation, Yvgeny led the way to the study. Hoping to find something to occupy his time, he pulled out books and maps, finding nothing of interest except his Blue Label bread wine, though Caesar seemed fascinated in everything. Five glasses later, Yvgeny was still pacing. Time seemed to be dragging on endlessly, and whenever he attempted to leave the study, Caesar's ebony visage could be seen peering at him from over the globe on the oversized desk, shaking his shaggy head.

Since returning from Russia, Yvgeny had taken up nearly permanent residence here at the most notorious residence in Redcliffe. While he owned a home less than half-a-mile away across the bridge in the central district of Bristol, he rarely stayed there as, invariably, he would end his evening in the arms of his beloved Beatrice. Yvgeny's omnipresence had caused a swirl of gossip among the town corporation, particularly since he had returned with a soon-to-be-obviously pregnant Abigail and an apparent censure from the Russian government. The most titillating rumor circulating was that he had conducted an untoward relationship with the daughter of his long-time English lover. The fact that he was ever present only fueled the fires of fantasy and tawdry speculation as to what was really going on in the private bedchambers of Parker House.

The other rumor, vigorously denied by Sergei Evanovich, the new emissary of Russia, was one a little closer to the truth. British merchants returning from Moscow were quick to note that the beautiful Abigail Edwards had been keeping company with someone in the Royal Palace. As almost everybody knew that Ivan was mentally deficient and Peter was a mere boy, the only logical conclusion was that she had been occupying her time with Tsar Fedor. One merchant, who had witnessed Fedor's Royal wedding just weeks after Abigail's departure, noted how sickly and unhappy the ruler appeared. Evanovich did his best to dismiss the innuendo, claiming that the Grand Tsar of all Russia would never take up with a foreign commoner, particularly the daughter of an English prostitute. Still, not even Evanovich could explain the sudden retirement of Yvgeny Thatcherev, a man who, less than two years ago, enjoyed enviable status in the eyes and ears of the Russian kingdom in southern England.

While they whispered and gossiped over their ales at Peal's Tavern, the merchants of Bristol would never turn down an opportunity to do business with the man. Yvgeny Thatcherev was, above all, a man with vast connections and a savvy entrepreneur to boot. For years, he had been advising Beatrice Parker in her business affairs. Yvgeny served as her official proxy, investing her money in a variety of ventures, many of them local and critical to the Bristol economy. The men of the town corporation silently begrudged yet readily accepted this infusion of hard currency, since frequently Beatrice Parker had more cash on hand then they had credit. Ironically, Beatrice was investing the money that these very same men had freely showered on the ladies of Parker House, thus owing to their own shortage of funds and the need for additional investors.

As banks had yet to make their way to the seaport town of Bristol, and as Beatrice Parker's primary enterprise was virtually recession proof, the threat of robbery had always been a prevailing concern, thus the need to find creative ways of disposing of ample stores of cash. Other enterprises, particularly those with foreign merchants and shipping companies, were so lucrative that the risk of piracy or theft by less successful merchants required a level of secrecy and security which kept even the most connected of Bristolians ever wondering what the wily Russian was up to. Yvgeny took strange and dramatic steps to keep his most profitable ventures out of the purview of the men who posted their vigils in the taverns adjacent to the Bristol docks.

Since his banishment from Russia, Yvgeny had commissioned the construction of an underground storage area accessible by ramps and stairs that descended into the basement below Parker House. To give more room to the storage area, Yvgeny instructed the builders, much to their surprise, to extend the construction beyond the property line and out under the street. The area of Redcliffe was already a vast wyvern of caves which had been excavated by artisans and craftsmen who mined the fine red sandstone for glass, making the task easier as small chambers were widened, connected and in some cases sealed with iron bars to keep out the curious local tunnelers. Initially, he had thought to build a separate structure away from the house, on the adjacent land to which Beatrice held deed. But wishing to keep his deals close to his breast, Yvgeny opted for subterranean, an idea which caught the attention of many of his fellow traders as a practical warehousing solution for the homes stacked cheek by jowl along the quays. His needs for storage space were dictated by the fact that Yvgeny and Beatrice, shrewd business people that they were, frequently opted to buy unusually large quantities of goods, which meant that they could get products for ridiculously low prices. Likewise, the two became a sort of clearinghouse for the unsold wares of other merchants. In the beginning, the town corporation saw them as fools who would literally buy anything, provided it was in quantity. Yvgeny and Beatrice, however, saw things differently. When a merchant made the unfortunate choice to purchase goods that wouldn't sell, he would willingly take pennies on the dollar to unload it, and the product would be wheeled into the expanding underground labyrinth of the Crazy Russian and the Whore, who would sit on it until there was an immediate need for it. And for a price significantly greater than what they had paid for it, the goods would be loaded aboard ships and en route to the desperate buyer faster than any craftsman or farmer could possibly produce it.

The truth was neither of them needed the money as badly as the typical merchant, who would usually have his fortune riding on every transaction. Even more than the financial rewards, Yvgeny was a man who thoroughly enjoyed the art of doing business. By day, he could be seen trolling the shops and meeting places of the town's merchants. He would venture out to the quays to chat with the captains of ships to hear the news of the world and the endless gossip and stories they had to tell, and on those strolls he always brought along a bottle of his Blue

Label Bread Wine, which would warm the belly, loosen the tongue and make Yvgeny the most pleasant of company to keep. In the evening, he would retire to either the private study or to the drawing room of Parker House to greet the men who had personal business of their own to transact. Wherever Yvgeny was, he drew attention with his wispy beard, an uncommon sight in late 17th century England, and his long black hair which, unlike the periwigged gentility he entertained and dealt with, was actually attached to his skull. To the gentlewomen of Bristol, he was the enigmatic giant who had taken up with that loathsome woman on the wrong side of the Redcliffe Bridge. To the men, he was a valuable business resource and the envy of those who so readily parted with their money to his obvious enrichment. His presence in Parker House had taken on a whole new meaning. Before Yvgeny, some of the less reputable guests felt no reservation of demanding more service for the money they paid. With Yvgeny in residence, the women of the house felt more confident to say no to customers who insisted on more than they had paid for or who demanded pleasures outside of the lady's proffered repertoire.

In short, Yvgeny Thatcherev was a man who took and maintained control over every situation he was involved with – everything, that is, except for the event that was transpiring upstairs. And suddenly, the activity rose to a new level. He could hear rapid footfalls and shuffling in the quarters above and muffled cries of agony. Yvgeny craned his massive head to listen more intently, and for what felt like days he anxiously subdued his instinct to rush upstairs.

"Caesar!" Nettie summoned from the upper reaches of the house. Yvgeny looked at the young boy, who shrugged his shoulders and dutifully responded to his mother's beckoning. Now he was alone and feeling very left out, for a game was afoot, and instead of being in the middle of the action Yvgeny was left with his bread wine and his books and a wild streak of imagination which was insisting that something had gone wrong. Hushed voices could be heard on the landing at the head of the stairs, and a panic began to ensue as every worst case scenario began to rush through his head.

And then, finally, virtual silence.

He slowly made his way down the hall and stood at the foot of the stairs, his hand gripping the railing, waiting for word from those who had denied his attendance. At long last, Caesar appeared at the top of the staircase and beckoned for him to come.

He felt as if lead weights were tied to his feet as he slowly made his way to the top of the stairs. The main hallway looked miles long and the journey interminable as he plodded steadily toward the last doorway on the right. The ladies of the house were congregated outside of Abigail's door, and they all turned to see the large Russian nervously approach them. They made a path for him to enter the room where he saw a much disheveled Abigail laying silently where he had last seen her.

This time, however, she had a look of contentment as she stared wonderingly down and melodically whispered to the sizeable bundle she held in her arms. Yvgeny Thatcherev felt his heart pounding, and he now recognized the proud smile on Beatrice's face as she stood at the foot of the bed, herself somewhat bedraggled. Nettie, who had midwived this long, agonizing labor of love, stood to the side with her son as witness of one of the most joyous events of their tragic lives. And they, along with the women of Parker House, stood mute as the one man they all truly respected approached this beautiful child, holding yet another beautiful child.

As Yvgeny grew closer, he could hear the words passing from the gentle lips of Abigail. The words were familiar, in the ancient language of his country, and they were sung in a sad and melancholy tone. They told the story of how a princess had stolen the heart of a giant from the snowy north. She turned to look at her adopted father, a radiant smile forming. Gingerly he sat beside her, placing an arm around her shoulder, and looked down at the child she held. The first thing Yvgeny noticed was the generous patch of black hair and the olive colored skin.

"It is a boy?" Yvgeny confirmed hopefully.

"A very large boy," Abigail replied.

"He looks Russian," he commented proudly as his eyes began to mist. "He looks ... like a king."

Abigail carefully handed the sleeping boy to Yvgeny. He cradled the baby closely to his chest and gently began humming the song that his mother had been singing.

"He is a Russian and will be a king, Yvgeny Thatcherev. And he should be named accordingly," Abigail stated.

"You are going to call him Fedor?" Yvgeny inquired, wondering to himself what kind of scandal that would create with Sergei Evanovich.

"No, I am going to name him after the most regal Russian and greatest man I have ever known. His name will be ... Yvgeny Thatcherev Edwards."

Yvgeny looked up in mild surprise. He noted the smiles on every face in the room. His eyes fell at last onto Abigail who looked even prouder than she had a moment ago. The big Russian flushed for the first time in anybody's memory. He lowered his eyes to the slumbering baby boy who began to stir and slowly opened his eyes. They were deep and dark and spoke of intelligence and the wisdom of monarchs. The boy was intently studying the face of the man who held him, and one tiny hand reached out to touch the great beard that hovered above. Closing a fist around a generous portion of that silky mane, the baby silently drifted to sleep.

"No great man ever need live in the shadow of another. We will call him Thatcher," Yvgeny declared as he stood and gently rocked the baby, returning to the haunting lullaby.

II

The masters of Parker House were always a sight to behold. It was obvious to anyone who saw them that these two were permanently bonded to each other, a fact that had become shiningly obvious to the women of the house from the very moment Yvgeny and Thatcher had laid eyes on each other. While Caesar had enjoyed the company and tutelage of the old Russian diplomat, he, too, realized that a new relationship had developed in this house of women. More than anything else, he saw something happening to this aging Russian that was new. It was joy. And Caesar knew that if anyone deserved joy, it was this kind, gentle man who had saved him and his mother. One might expect that jealousy would creep into the mind and heart of this stolid and stoic young boy, who owed his continued existence to this rare man among men. But he knew that his role, now and forever, was to be a protector and guardian to these two Russians. His first sight of Thatcher would be forever etched in his mind, and he realized his fate was sealed. Until his dying breath, it would be his responsibility to keep this chubby bundle safe, for he was more than the child of his mistress. Thatcher was, in all but blood, his little brother, a point that had been reinforced throughout the long pregnancy by both Abigail and Nettie.

Unlike most businesses, there were very few occasions that Parker House was closed. Most holidays, in fact, were usually some of their busiest evenings, particularly if part of that day had been spent in pious observation or in the company of large, annoying families. It was a little disconcerting for the men of Bristol who strolled up to the door of the house on the Saturday prior to Easter Sunday of 1680 to be greeted by a hand lettered sign, pointedly stating that the residents were not entertaining. Each man shook his head in mild despair, having carefully crafted excellent reasons to abandon the family in the midst of Easter celebration, and instead having to settle for a pint in commiseration at Peal's Tavern. About the only Bristol merchant not distressed by this unusual change of routine was Keith Peal, whose enterprise lay a few hundred feet from the front door of Parker House. Having discovered early on that the brothel was closed for God only knew why, he forestalled his plan to take off early, realizing that the soon-to-be dejected were going to have to find somewhere to kill an hour or so and part with a bit of coin.

Two men with plenty of time on their hands were Johann and Derek DeBeers, captain and first mate, respectively, of the Dutch trader *Orangeman*. A year before, their freiboat had departed Amsterdam with a hold full of woven cloth, sailing directly for the West African coastal island of São Tome, a slaving way station. There, they had traded the bulk of cloth goods for a boatload of captured Africans and immediately set a course for the island of Curaçao in the Dutch West Indies. Once again, they traded their cargo of slaves – a highly prized commodity to the plantation owners, having already decimated the indigenous Indian population who had served in the same capacity as their African replacements – for sugar and cocoa. They next set a course for the English colony of Charles Towne in Carolina with their latest cargo and the remainder of their cloth goods. There they filled their holds with tobacco and set sail for Bristol where they would trade that highly profitable leaf for a price proportionately greater then they had paid for their original cloth goods. Having reached the English port on Easter Saturday, they intended to lay over for the weekend and secure a profitable cargo to carry back to their homeport. In the meantime, they were eager to spend some of their earnings on the highly touted women of Parker House.

Paying no attention to the sign tacked to the door, Johann began knocking persistently with his fist after no one responded to the first subdued tapping of the brass ring. After several minutes, they at last heard the inside latch release, and Johann looked to his younger brother, gently jabbing him in the ribs with an elbow, and smiled triumphantly. Both were slightly disappointed to be greeted, not by one of the lovely ladies of the house, but instead by a petite black woman, whose expression bore displeasure at their presence.

"I am sorry, gentlemen, but da house is not receivin' guests today," Nettie stated as politely and firmly as she could gesturing at the sign she had written and posted on the door.

"What do you mean you are not receiving, woman? We are old and loyal customers of Mistress Parker. You tell her that Johann and Derek DeBeers are here, and we are expecting the normal courtesies," Johann demanded flippantly as he pulled his brother past the maid and walked into the foyer of the house. He removed his hat and held it out absently, expecting the woman to take it. It took him a moment to realize that she had no intention of doing so.

"Please, gentlemen, we are observin' da holy days dis weekend and are not entertainin'," she stated again, somewhat pleadingly as she tried not to yield to the displeased eye of the older DeBeers.

"Listen, you kafir woman, either you tell Mistress Parker that we are here, or I will go upstairs and tell her myself." Johann started to make a move toward the stairs, but the tiny Nettie intercepted him.

"Gentlemen, I am under strict orders to allow no one in da house or up dese stairs. Now please leave or I will be forced to make ye leave!" she said as sternly and fearsomely as she could muster, her face a picture of unflinching determination.

Johann and Derek looked at each other and laughed in amusement at the brave words from the tiny women before them, one hand on her hip and the other thrust into a deep pocket of her apron.

At that moment, Yvgeny and Caesar were in the basement of Parker House, rummaging through the multitude of casks and crates, oblivious to the confrontation occurring directly above them. They were looking for one particular item Yvgeny had purchased a few months earlier when they heard the screams coming from upstairs. For the moment, Yvgeny forgot his fifty-plus years as he leapt over the variety of obstacles between him and the stairs, beating the athletic seven-year-old up the steep flight by three long strides. When he emerged from the cellar door, he nearly slipped in a puddle of blood that coated the floor. He reached out to grab the body that was crouched nearby, using it as a brake.

"He made me do it, Master Thatcherev!" Nettie screamed in sheer panic.

Yvgeny looked up to see Nettie's usually immaculate white apron splattered with blood. The knuckles of her dark skinned right hand were white as she tightly gripped a large butcher knife, red ichor dripping from the blade. He could hear commotion upstairs and looked to see Beatrice and a few of the women quickly descending.

"Go back upstairs," Yvgeny commanded as he straightened. They stopped in their tracks, all eyes on the figure kneeling before the expanding crimson pool. "Do as I say! Go!"

The ladies saw the seriousness in Yvgeny's face and reasoned that it was best to comply with his demand. Yvgeny turned his attention back to the scene.

"What happened, Nettie?" Yvgeny inquired, as Caesar came to his mother's side.

"She cut off my brother's fingers!" Johann screamed as he kneeled next to his brother, who Yvgeny could see was holding his bloody, shaking, mutilated hand in front of him. "That damned slave cut off his fingers!" Johann repeated in shocked panic.

"Dey would not leave, Master Thatcherev. Dey demanded to go upstairs. He slapped me. I ... I could not let him go upstairs! Not with Mistress Abigail ... and da baby."

Yvgeny stood, walked to Nettie and removed the knife from her grasp. She looked up in terror. "Take your mother to the kitchen, Caesar. And wait," Yvgeny stated evenly and without malice.

She hesitated and slowly surrendered to her son as he guided her away. "Dey would not leave. I asked dem to go and dey would not."

Yvgeny returned his attention to the two men. He removed his crisp, white shirt and wrapped it around the disfigured appendage as Johann stared on, helplessly.

"That damned kafir will hang, I swear she will," Derek sputtered, still in shock.

"Nothing of the sort will happen," Yvgeny stated as he wrapped the bandage tightly around the stump. "You two are fortunate that you are still alive."

Derek looked up at Yvgeny, his face a mixture of horror and hate. "That slave wounded me. That means death."

Yvgeny looked down at the terror-stricken individual whose mutilated hand he easily covered with his own mammoth paw. His face flushed with fury as he stared at this trespasser and effortlessly clamped down. Unbelievable agony seized the Dutchman who let out a high pitched squeal.

"How dare you issue threats after barging into this home uninvited. I should kill you right now for threatening the safety of the ladies here," Yvgeny stated, remarkably even and controlled.

Seeing the grip that the big Russian had on his brother's injured hand, Johann seized the moment and, with all the force he could muster, delivered a punch that would have leveled a lesser man. The blow landed squarely on Yvgeny's exposed cheek, which recoiled slightly from the impact but did little to throw off his center of balance. Without looking up, Yvgeny simultaneously tightened his grip on Derek's hand and swung the back of his free hand toward Johann's face, sending him sailing and then crashing against the heavy front door. He lay there, stunned and unmoving.

He turned his attention back to the man who was yelping from the crushing pain. Yvgeny was a picture of ferocity, and he grabbed a handful of hair, pulling Derek's pain-streaked face within inches of his own.

"You should consider yourself quite fortunate today," Yvgeny stated in a quiet, menacing voice. "The woman was kinder than I would have been. Had I answered the door, you and your brother would have been carried out of here leaving your entrails mixed together on the floor. Now, if you say one more word or issue one more threat, I will gut you like a fish." To make his point, he released the hair and pressed the bloody knife against Derek's heaving stomach, and with this Yvgeny achieved the silence he demanded.

The look on the Russian's face, combined with the utter pain he was feeling, was more than Derek's bowels and bladder could bear, both releasing and fouling the clothes he wore and the floor he knelt on. Yvgeny perceived the unmistakable odor, his face now bearing an expression of disgust as he slapped the Dutchman's face. The hand holding the stump kept Derek from skidding across the foul floor, and Yvgeny transferred his grip to the nape of the man's neck as he stood and strode to the door, dragging Derek behind. He opened the door that wasn't blocked by Johann's crumpled body, grabbed the dazed brother and dragged his captives outside.

He made his way towards the center of town, towing both DeBeers brothers like baggage. As he passed Peal's Tavern, the men who had congregated inside streamed out, having viewed the big, shirtless Russian trailing the two Dutch traders behind him. Like rats to the piper, the men of Peal's fell in behind and followed him to the home of Doctor Fenton. The crowd stopped at the gate as Yvgeny Thatcherev carried his charges up the small walk, kicking the door with his foot to summon the doctor inside.

Doctor Fenton was a little shocked at the sight of the bare-chested Russian and the two battered men. Behind them, he viewed the group of onlookers watching with rapt interest, having found something to rouse them from their drinking boredom.

"This one is in need of your services, Doctor," Yvgeny ordered, indicating Derek, the ad hoc tourniquet having turned the white shirt into a dripping red mass. "This one I am taking to the sheriff." He indicated Johann. "I will have someone around to collect him once he has been treated."

"What happened, Yvgeny Thatcherev?" Doctor Fenton inquired.

"Trespassers. Possibly thieves."

"Master Thatcherev, I know these men. They are of good character, I assure you. Certainly, whatever they may have done, this matter can be quickly clarified."

"I will leave that up to a jury," Yvgeny replied, hauling Johann DeBeers by the collar as he returned to the street, a path rapidly forming in front as men moved quickly to give the huge Russian space. He didn't have far to go as Bertram Hughes, town sheriff, was rapidly approaching from the gatehouse that served as his office and gaol.

"This man is a trespasser, Sheriff. I release him to your custody."

"We were not trespassing, sir. This man's slave cut off my brother's fingers. It is she you should be taking into custody," Johann protested.

"And as you can see, he is a liar, too. I have no slave."

"The African woman – at Parker House!" Johann insisted.

"She is a freed woman who was protecting the household in which she is employed."

"Yvgeny Thatcherev, is this true? Did she injure someone?" Sheriff Hughes inquired.

"At my behest, Sheriff. As you know, we are closed for business today. This one and his associate broke into the house and threatened the women. She was protecting those she serves." Yvgeny released Johann, who began rubbing his throat where the material had been choking him.

Sheriff Hughes looked a little befuddled but equally intimidated by the angry Russian. "Very well. You come with me and I will hear your side of the story. Yvgeny Thatcherev, you are inappropriately attired for public view. I suggest you return to ... where you came from and put on a shirt." Sheriff Hughes led Johann DeBeers down the street toward the jail, and Yvgeny Thatcherev did as he was instructed.

When he returned to the house, two of the ladies were already busy at work cleaning the pool of blood and human waste from the foyer. Neither said a word as Yvgeny entered and immediately went to the kitchen. Beatrice and Allison Simms were there with a very flustered Nettie, who was still in a state of panic, despite the attempts of the women and her son to calm her. They all looked up as Yvgeny entered.

"Yvgeny! What did the sheriff say?" Beatrice asked immediately.

"Not much of anything. He took the uninjured one into custody."

"Master Thatcherev, I did not mean to bring trouble ..." Nettie began.

"No, Nettie. You did what was right. They had no business coming in as they did."

"But I injured a white man!"

"On my orders."

"Still, I am an African. I will be punished."

"We will see when the trial occurs. Until then, I commend you for protecting your home," Yvgeny stated with finality.

There never was a trial. The town corporation met privately with Yvgeny and disclosed that, for a price, the matter would be settled. On the Monday following Easter, two hundred crates of pots and pans were loaded aboard the *Orangeman*, en route to the warehouses of Amsterdam, courtesy of Yvgeny Thatcherev and Beatrice Edwards. Inside the pocket of the new coat, rush ordered for Derek DeBeers by

Yvgeny Thatcherev from one of master craftsmen of the Bristol's Merchant Taylors Guild, was a fortune of much greater value than the house wares that filled their hold – uncut Russian diamonds. A high price, but one more lucky stroke for Nettie.

Four years earlier, Yvgeny Thatcherev had gone against all of his instincts and purchased his first and only slaves. At sixteen, Nettie had been sold to Dutch slavers by members of the tribe that had conquered her village in the northeast of Madagascar. Three years before, as was the custom of her people, she had been married to Najas, a young tribal chieftain of the Antankarana Malagasy tribe. Herself from a good family, they had paid three dozen zebu as part of the dowry to be betrothed as the first wife of this promising young man, whom many had believed would lead his people to a new era of greatness. The coastal tribes had been seduced by the trinkets, muskets and gunpowder of the steady succession of European adventurers who had come to these shores intent to whisk away its resources and lay claim to the lands and the people who occupied them. Najas believed that his people's best hope was to hold onto their traditions and resist the overtures of the white men with all their might and power.

That final week in Madagascar was a horror Nahtee would relive in her mind forever. She had listened at the edge of the council fires as her handsome, wise husband had once again spoken to his people, exalting the legacy of their ancestors. The Betsimsakara tribesmen who had come to entreat on behalf of their Dutch trading partners voiced their disagreement, ridiculing Najas for wishing to hold on to the ancient ways in a world changing around them. Their leader, Panjaka, a large man whose numerous scars denoted his ferocity as a warrior chieftain, made his case to these primitive forest-dwelling Malagasy, telling them of all the white men had to offer. He stood before the fire, the orange light amplifying the depth of the scars that crisscrossed his neck and face, his eyes wide and wild as he stared across at Najas.

"You cannot fight the future, Antankarana, for the future is here, and you will either become part of it or be swept away by it. Join us, and we can take on our enemies and rule this land."

Najas sat next to his chiefs, who turned to him for guidance. His elbows were on his knees, his fingers interlaced, as he placed his chin on the bridge of his hands and studied the Betsimsakara warrior. "Rule this land? You rule nothing. You are a servant, a mere messenger of your betters. But we are Antankarana, and we have no betters. You are a servant and always will be. But we are Antankarana, and we will not be slaves."

The elders considered their young warrior's words, praising him and heralding him as the true future of the Antankarana. The Betsimsakara walked away in disgust, overpowered ... for now. While Nahtee's three-year-old son could not understand the significance of his father's words and the praises heaped upon him, Chasaa could sense the pride his mother felt for this man who had wrestled and played with him as they strolled back to their large square hut in the center of the village.

The loud explosions so unfamiliar to these primitive Malagasy ears were shocking and frightening as they pierced the pre-dawn silence. The boy and his mother awoke with a start, hearing Najas order them to stay inside as he rushed out the door. Chasaa could not help but be curious of the horrifying sound penetrating the thin walls of the wood hut, and he raised his head high enough to peer out of the window in front of him. What he witnessed was something strange and terrible, yet fascinating. The Antankarana warriors rushed with fury, bows, arrows and spears in hand, toward the frightening sound, and Chasaa could see bright flashes, like thunderous fireflies, in the woods at the edge of the village. His father was at the front, fearlessly charging, spear in hand, toward these strange invaders. Many stories of his father's bravery had been told around the fires, but to actually witness his terrible talent was remarkable. Antankarana men were reputed for their hand-to-hand combat skills, and once they closed with these terrible intruders, certainly the invaders would discover how foolish was their foray into an Antankarana village.

But something strange was occurring. With every bright flash and terrible thunderclap, Chasaa could see brave warriors collapsing to the ground. Did these terrible noises somehow render these Antankarana men into fear-driven paralysis? Why were they falling, when no spear or arrow had penetrated? Chasaa was confused to see his father faltering in his steps. With another round of explosions and flashes, Najas at last collapsed to the ground, just as so many others had. Chasaa could now see, slowly advancing from the woods, their guests from the night before stepping into the village clearing, each of them bearing large, blunt sticks. Nahtee lifted her head as the sounds of explosions were replaced by the wailing of dying men. She was horrified to see her son, his hands clasping the windowsill, witnessing the battle with rapt attention. She looked out and she saw the distinctive shape of her beloved husband, his hands pushing against the earth as he attempted to rise. He was being surrounded by these men carrying their sticks, and Nahtee could barely contain her scream. But at this moment, she knew her responsibility was to shield the eyes of her ever-curious son, so she pulled him down to the ground and whispered for him to remain silent. It took all of her strength not to bolt upright as she could hear her husband's agonized moans.

Seconds crept into minutes, minutes dragged into what seemed like hours until the invaders began searching the huts for captives. The sun was beginning to burn off the morning mist as she made every attempt to cover herself and her son with the brilliantly colored woven blanket she hoped would serve as even the most meager form of camouflage. Though young, she knew what fate awaited them if they were discovered.

She heard the sound of footfalls outside her hut and covered Chasaa's mouth to stifle any sound of breath, but her attempt to conceal their presence was for naught as the fibre blanket was snatched away. Four great hands grasped her as another pair grappled her son, tearing him away from her, and for the first time Nahtee screamed. As the boy was dragged from the hut, those four hands tore at her clothing, and a day of unspeakable sexual violation ensued, for her and every Antankarana woman and girl. Chasaa was herded into the center of the village with all the other young children, where each of them was wrung by the screams of rape from their mothers and the dying anguish of their fathers. To his grim fate, Chasaa was placed a mere few feet from where his father was now tied, hand to feet, his broad, sweaty, bloody chest coated with the rich brown earth beneath him.

"Give the order for your people to surrender now," screamed the scarred Betsimsakara chieftain, who had retrieved a smoldering stick from the night's previous fire and was using it as a spear to pierce into the young chief's bloody back.

"I will never surrender my people to slavery," screamed Najas.

"You prefer all your people die today, Najas?" Panjaka inquired as he drove the burning spear into his victim's scrotum sack.

"We are Antankarana Malagasy, and we will never be slaves," Najas screamed back, in both torment and defiance. It was at that moment that he saw the face of his petrified young son witnessing the painful murder of his father. "We are Antankarana Malagasy, and we will never be slaves," he repeated, this time more softly, not to his torturer but to his young son, whom he viewed with awe and fear for the future he would never share with him. Through his pain he smiled one more time at Chasaa, and with his last breath screamed: "Fight with all your will, Antankarana! You are the greatest of all Malagasy, and we will never surrender to these vermin who kill us today!"

And with that, the fire-bearing Malagasy shoved that smoldering staff directly into Najas' mouth with all of his might, driving it deep into the throat of the once and future king of the Antankarana.

Throughout the day, Nahtee kept her thoughts fixed firmly on her son as she maintained a death grip on that woven blanket. She remembered how lovingly her grandmother and aunts had made it for her, utilizing the strong fibres of the vines that clung to the trees of the forest. They were so rough and prickly when first picked, yet through loving and gentle care they were chewed and softened, and then when they were malleable and flexible, woven into a strong but soft covering and given to her on her wedding day. She and Najas had made love under this blanket, and her son had been wrapped in it at birth. But now, as the darkness gathered, this last anchor to a quickly disappeared past was like the village – tattered, torn, destroyed and soon to be forgotten. When at last she ceased to serve a purpose to her attackers, she was cast aside like refuse and began slowly crawling from the hut to the knot of children, where she found Chasaa studying the violated corpse of his father. She had meant to bring the blanket to wrap her son from the gathering chill, yet in her short journey she had released her grasp. Wrapping her arms around her child, her body shielding him from the sight of Najas and burying his head into her naked breasts, she at last succumbed to her pain and exhaustion.

She was barely conscious of when she and the small cadre of women and children began their forced march from the village. After long days of endless walking with neither food nor water through the forests that at last gave way to jungles, they would finally be allowed to collapse, exhausted, along the side of the trails when the darkness made it impossible to walk another step. The horrors that they had confronted the day of the attack were revisited every night with the women and girls and, in some cases, the young boys. When it seemed as if this trek through the unknown would never come to an end, Nahtee began to hear the distinctive yet unfamiliar sound of crashing waves, and before long their feet emerged from the tangled undergrowth of the jungle to the loose sand of the eastern shores of Madagascar.

Nahtee had never before seen fair-haired and -skinned men in her young life. But as the sun began to rise and the small group of Antankarana war spoils emerged into the shining sands of the seacoast, she witnessed for the first time these legendary Europeans. Though her husband had long warned of the dangers of these silver-buckle-shoed men of ruthless commerce, for just a moment she felt a sense of optimism that perhaps they would rescue her and her tribesmen from their plight. That hope rapidly diminished as she and Chasaa were herded down the beach into a long line, where their captors began attaching shackles to their feet and hands, then chaining them in a long line to one another. One by one the Antankarana were forced into the pounding surf until the water came nearly to the chins of the children. Women and older siblings reached out to the little ones, attempting to lift them high enough so their heads would be above the crashing waves, for it seemed as if these Europeans were intent upon drowning them. Chasaa was big for his age, but not big enough to keep his head above water, and Nahtee dipped into whatever reserve of energy she had to lift her son's head higher than her own. She was certain they were being led to their death, and she took one last gulp of air as she continued to be pulled along. Her head went under water, and with her eyes wide open she could see the row of survivors being plucked from the water ahead of her, their bodies whisking skyward. Her lungs were aching for air, and she had to fight the instinct to hold on firmly to her son as his tiny body torpedoed skyward. When she felt she could no longer hold her breath, rough hands at last plucked her from the sea. Hand over hand, she was lifted by a steady line of rugged, tan-skinned seamen, who as quickly dropped her body onto the deck. They had no time to rest as they were immediately prodded into the hold of the ship. Before disappearing into that dark, dank hole, her eyes took in the last view of her homeland and, only a few hundred yards away, the opposite shore of a place these Europeans called St. Mary's Island.

The voyage was a whole new hell unto itself. Dozens of her tribe members and dozens more dark-skinned Malagasy were crammed into the narrow space that would serve as their home for many months and many thousands of miles. The putrid stench, stifling heat and absence of water and food were cruel and inhumane by degrees unspeakable. Nahtee focused on protecting her child and resigned herself to this hellish fate for however long it lasted. But she was horrified to find that, throughout this long, gut-wrenching voyage, the emaciated, half-starved, filthy women such as her were still to be treated as objects of desire by the crew. She could not decide what was more despicable:

those who would rape her in the presence of her young son; or those who would unshackle the chains, pull every woman out of that fetid hole and pass them around like so many drams of rum, only to throw them back into that pit, violated, shamed and counting the seconds until the next inevitable violation.

The tortuous journey around Africa's Horn found Nahtee and Chasaa in much smaller company as countless of their fellow captives had perished from the weeks of malnutrition, thirst, abuse and the ceaseless battering of bodies slammed against rough hewn wooden pallet above and below them with every pitch and yawl of the ship. Pressed against the hull, Nahtee had to tear off a small piece of her sparse fabric to plug into an unsealed joint between two ship boards which squirted sea water with ever roll. At last they had reached calmer waters and the shuffle of feet on the deck above sent a small shudder of optimism that perhaps their trip was coming to an end. More feet and the rattle of keys could be heard shuffling within the hold. Row by row, the white men checked their cargo and, here and there, unlocked a row of chain. Nahtee had hoped that perhaps they would get a chance to breathe fresh air on deck but the sailors had no interest for the living and seemed only interested in unceremoniously discarding those who had died during the passage. Nahtee didn't need to remove the bit of cloth to know what was causing the splashes and thumps off the side of the ship as many of her countrymen found their trip coming to an end in a watery grave. But soon she perceived other sounds as the ship slowed and the anchors splashed heavily. With this Nahtee did remove the bit of cloth to peer out of the crack and breathe a few mouthfuls of fresh air. Through the narrow gash she took in the sight of her first European building. It was a huge fortress like structure, much bigger than Nahtee could imagine any tribe could ever need. Nahtee had difficulty understanding the strange tongue of her Dutch captors but two words, Elmina and Guinea, came up time and again as they drew nearer to land. Perhaps this was to be their new home, she thought and was about to suggest that to her son when she beheld the masses of more black people, in chains, methodically being scurried in a long line through a portal in the castle wall and loaded aboard the boats tied alongside the castle quay. And in no time the little bit of space that had been made possible from the removal of the perished was quickly refilled with more shackled souls, and for weeks more the abuses resumed. In that last leg of the trip from the Guinea Coast to the slave pens of London, neither Nahtee nor her son possessed the strength, or curiosity which comes from optimism, to take in the crush of buildings and humanity that was England's capital city.

Edward Colston had been eternally grateful for the confidence Yvgeny Thatcherev had placed in him. The Colstons were one of Bristol's most prominent families long involved with colonization, and Edward's father William was particularly respected for having been instrumental in the initial settling the Labrador colony. His pedigree and a well worded letter of introduction to the Russian trade minister's contacts at London's Mercer Company netted the 18-year-old Edward an apprenticeship with one of England's oldest and most prestigious trading companies. Edward was bright and ambitious and, in no time at all, had become instrumental in trade with Portugal, Spain, the Netherlands and most recently, Africa. It had taken a bit of coaxing but, at last, Colston had convinced his Russian mentor to visit him in London where, not only could he show off his spectacular home but also perhaps, intrigue this ear of Russia with a lucrative new venture.

"Slavery?" Yvgeny replied with more than a bit of disdain. "Two thoughts immediately strike me. One, as I understand it, this horrid trade is the exclusive domain of the Royal Africa Company. I don't see a respected firm like Mercers dirtying their reputation with such a venture. Secondly, if you know anything about me, dear Edward, you should know of my disdain for the industry of human bondage. My advice, dear boy? Steer clear of the business of slavery. No amount of perfume can take away that stink." Such a reaction surprised Colston who assumed that someone who spent an inordinate time in a brothel would be the last to moralize about flesh peddling. But, involuntary servitude had nothing to do with life in Parker House, and the thought that there were people bought and sold like cattle infuriated Abigail who, at thirteen, would be inconsolable until she saw such a place for herself.

It was as horrible as she imagined and even more so when she took in the sight of the emaciated girl and child lying in soiled hay straw. Though near death, to their owners of the Royal African Company, they were still a marketable commodity and, should they survive the final leg of the journey, would be tasked to increase the profits of the planters who would buy them to tend their fields or, if among the lucky few, keep their hearths. It was an unusual request but not one to be ignored, as it bore the seal of the Duke of York, to sell this woman and child to the bearded Russian and the insistent child who brought an air of discomfort to the Colston home. As soon as Nahtee and

Chasaa were strong enough to travel they were bundled off to start a new life in Bristol.

Abigail made it her personal mission to nurse them back to health. The trauma of the invasion, the crossing and the unspeakable violence they had endured made it difficult for either Nahtee or her child to trust or communicate with this fair-haired European girl. Yet as health and strength returned, an inexplicable bond developed between the two girls. Nahtee began to realize that, despite the circumstances that brought them here, in truth she and her child were quite fortunate, in comparison to the likely fates of her tribespeople. It was difficult for Abigail's English ear to decipher how the woman and child were named, so Chasaa and Nahtee, formerly of Madagascar, were now to be known as Caesar and Nettie of Bristol. Abigail offered them emancipation the moment they were strong enough to leave. However, frankly, Nettie and her child had no place else to go. Abigail convinced Beatrice that they needed a fulltime housekeeper, and Nettie and Caesar moved into the rooms next to the kitchen. She was paid a small wage, with the hope that one day she would have enough money to buy their way back to Madagascar, provided there was still a Madagascar to go home to.

Nettie was invaluable to Parker House and priceless to Abigail and her newborn child, and it was for these reasons that everyone desperately defended and protected her. The bond between these two young women was beyond understanding to anyone but the two of them, and even if it had required parting with every crate in their warehouse, that price would have been paid without question.

Though it had been Nettie's intention to stay at Parker House only long enough to earn money to go back to Africa, over the years she had come to realize that nothing waited for her there, and Abigail and Yvgeny determined that the one person who could be counted on to be a permanent fixture in Thatcher's life would be Nettie. So the following Saturday, the sign that had sent the men of Bristol reeling the week before was tacked to the door again. The ladies of Parker House made themselves busy, unshuttering the windows and bedecking the foyer, staircase and parlor with as many candles as they could find. Yvgeny and Caesar created a makeshift altar and baptismal font, for this was Bright Saturday, the day on which the Russian Orthodox Church celebrated the resurrection of Christ, and today the brothel was metamorphosed into an ad hoc cathedral. In due pomp and circumstance, the newest member of the household was to be baptized into that great faith.

To prepare her for her role as godmother, Nettie had been schooled in the teachings of the church earlier in the week, and she and Abigail had been baptized that morning in an abbreviated ceremony. Yvgeny had not asked Nettie to renounce the true feelings of her heart, which clung to the ancient beliefs of her native people, but he knew she would aptly fulfill her duties without sacrificing her true faith. For her part, Nettie understood the need for these Europeans to seek out and acknowledge the omnipotence of these three men who are one and, in respect to their needs, she agreeably went along with the ritual.

Abigail watched with wonder as her son, nestled in Nettie's arms, took in the bright lights, the strange smells of the incense and the somber tones of his chanting grandfather, and she felt a flush of joy and pride. Her joy was for knowing that her son was receiving a blessing and anointing to God that she herself had been denied, partly because the Church of England refused to acknowledge bastard children and because Beatrice gave little concern for such traditions. The pride she was feeling came from the knowledge of how pleased Yvgeny was to perform these rituals. But her biggest surprise came when her dear friend Nettie recited the Nicene Creed in Russian.

As Yvgeny took his grandson for his immersion, Abigail leaned in. "You didn't have to learn it in Russian, you know," she whispered as she squeezed Nettie's elbow in gentle thanks.

"It's not like it was any harder dan learnin' English, and it's not like I'd heard it in dat tongue either," she replied.

In truth, Yvgeny's baptism of her daughter and grandson could not have made Beatrice happier. Her disdain for religion stemmed from the church's refusal to baptize her daughter so many years before. She was quite happy to see Abigail finally receive official recognition in the eyes of God, if indeed he really existed. She had come to doubt his existence due to the ungodly treatment she had experienced at the hands of most people she encountered during her childhood, and the church was no exception. Yet how quick that pompous ass Vicar Tomkins was to request her to perform her own special rituals. It convinced her that no god could possibly exist that allowed these two-faced bastards to get away with what they did. As she witnessed the pleasure Yvgeny obviously derived from baptizing these three – a man who was slow to judge but quick to love – for a moment, she was ready to believe that there truly were real men of a real God.

The remainder of the service seemed to pass by quickly for the old priest who, following the final blessing of the assembled, lovingly hugged each and every woman, and heartily shook Caesar's hand, undaunted by the tears of joy that filled his eyes. At this moment, he felt more complete, more whole than he could remember. His daughter and grandson had been introduced into the mysteries of his faith, and the woman he loved most had expressed an unexpected openness to his belief. These truths, combined with the love and enthusiasm of all who had shared in the experience – these fallen women whom religion and society ecstatically reviled; this African woman and her child who had been condemned to a life of slavery and a denial of all they knew and believed and yet somehow joyously participated in this alien, arcane European ritual – made Yvgeny realize that he was among the truly blessed.

III

The next seven years were ones of utter happiness for the residents of Parker House. It was decided that Yvgeny need not, for the sake of appearances or for any other reason, maintain a separate residence, and in the Summer of 1680 he sold his home to the Church of England for a sizeable profit, providing Hubert Tompkins with a greatly enhanced rectory, and moved in with the ladies.

While lovingly attended by all of the women of the home, particularly his mother, grandmother and Nettie, who happily took to her role as his nurse, Thatcher Edwards could most frequently be found in the company of his grandfather and the ever-vigilant Caesar. As an infant, Thatcher would spend the greater part of the morning with Yvgeny, who would bear the heavy child with ease in one arm as he attended to his rounds with the merchants and traders. As soon as he was able to walk, Thatcher was constantly at Yvgeny's side along with Caesar, usually in matching attire, as they watched the ships sail into the harbor and met with the captains to discuss the contents of their holds and to listen to the news of the world. Thatcher would most often be found at the elbow of his stately grandfather whenever the gentlepeople of Bristol encountered him. His fingers gingerly laced behind his back, his chin pointed, his face a carving of dignity, he was forced early on to make long yet graceful strides to stay abreast of the

Russian giant he accompanied. The two seemed to always be in conversation, surveying the people and town with an air of propriety.

In the afternoon, following the midday meal, the three would retire to the study to pore over maps, or Yvgeny would pull down one of the countless books from the wall and regale the two boys with some wondrous tale or legend. Oftentimes, one woman or another would enter the study to find the two dark-haired gentlemen snoozing away, the smaller on the lap of the elder, with a book resting on the cushion beside them while the ever vigilant Caesar would be at the desk studying intently the vast collection of Yvgeny's maps and charts.

Near dusk, they would change into evening attire and join the ladies for dinner, as this was their family time before the first of the customers would arrive. If time allowed, the ladies would prompt Thatcher to give a recitation or perhaps a bit of drama from the Bard or, his grandmother's personal favorite, a reading from playwright Richard Edwardes. Before the first rapping of the brass knocker, the ladies would be shooed upstairs and the oversized dinner table cleared as the masters of the house adjourned to the parlor to meet and greet the gentlemen who had found some pretext to visit with Yvgeny to mask their obvious reasons for making their way to Parker House. Caesar, at twelve, already stood nearly six feet tall and kept a watchful eye from his post at the door. As Yvgeny and Thatcher became inextricably linked, one could not help but notice the vast similarities. While there was the black hair and olive skin to consider, most amazing were the mannerisms young Thatcher began to assimilate. Like the older Russian, young Thatcher created a presence when he entered the room. He possessed an air one could mistake as an attribute or aping of breeding, but it was something more ... something majestic. While his grandfather had been instrumental in instructing him in gentlemanly manners, there was something about him that went beyond mere etiquette, quite obvious by the time he was old enough to speak and frame coherent sentences. There was a quality that forced men to render a respect and deference that they usually reserved only for their societal betters. While one could say it was out of respect for Yvgeny, the truth was that one forgot he was in the presence of a bastard child of a brothel-keeper's daughter when Thatcher made his appearance. When on his home turf, within the Parker home, the young Thatcher civilly asserted dominance which Yvgeny seemed quite happy to defer.

Clad in the matching black breeches and waist coat of his grandfather, Thatcher would walk purposefully into the parlor beside him as all of the men seated there would rise and direct their attention to the two masters of the household. In turn, each gentleman would be greeted by both, made comfortable, and conversations would turn to matters of business.

"I see, Mr. Sneeden," Yvgeny began one particular evening, "that your shipment of porcelain from the Orient is nearing Bristol."

"And where did you hear this?" Eric Sneeden replied, a little perturbed yet not particularly surprised that Yvgeny Thatcherev seemed more apprised of his cargo status than he.

"Oh, you know how sailors talk. Captain Van Reuten of the ...," Yvgeny paused for a moment, his eyes fixed on the ceiling as one hand stroked his beard, intent on trying to remember the name of Van Reuten's ship.

"The *Astral Plain,* grandfather," Thatcher intoned emphatically. Yvgeny looked down proudly at his young grandson, whose contemporaries were still struggling with the alphabet and learning to count to fifty. Not only could the five-year-old effectively communicate with concise speech, he was mature enough to have learned to pay attention, to read and memorize ship names, and to heed the words and actions of the men who captained and worked aboard them. Yvgeny gently patted the boy on the head and smiled warmly at him.

"That is correct, Thatcher, the *Astral Plain.*" Feeling the need to further show off his grandson's intelligence he asked, "That is a ship of Bristol registry, is it not, Thatcher?"

"No grandfather. Rotterdam. Don't you remember? He was carrying twenty tons of whale oil to Bristol that he was trading for copper goods here to transport to the American colonies to exchange for timber. It was in Amsterdam that he saw Captain Wert aboard the *Tidewater* and where he learned of the shipment of porcelain and how Mr. Sneeden had definitely paid too much for the quality of porcelain he was receiving."

All of the gentlemen in the room shifted nervously, a few coughing and turning their backs on Mr. Sneeden so as not to have to acknowledge his embarrassment at the boy's detailed candor. Sneeden, somewhat flushed at the boy's innocent pronouncement of his foolishness, gave the appearance of a man who would gladly choose to be anywhere but where he was. But his embarrassment ran much deeper than the out of turn speaking of a mere boy. Moments before arriving at Parker House, Mr. Sneeden had been boasting of the very shipment that the boy had revealed to be a foolish venture. Sneeden, typical of many of the merchants of Bristol, had staked a sizeable percentage of his fortune on this, what he had believed to be, the trading venture of a lifetime. He had revealed to his Bristol colleagues, quite boastfully, of his savvy business venture in an effort to drum up partnerships prior to the ship making port in Bristol, thereby defraying some of his initial costs and, hopefully, netting a sizeable profit even before the ship's contents had been made available for public sale. And indeed, a number of the wealthy men who had gathered that afternoon in Peal's Tavern had expressed an interest in buying shares of his load. What unsettled Mr. Sneeden was that, while he had revealed the point of origin of his purchase, he had intentionally failed to reveal its contents, meaning that Yvgeny Thatcherev truly must have contacts that the rest of the Bristol merchants could only dream of having. But now with this insinuation of a bad purchase, it was very unlikely that Mr. Sneeden was to achieve firm commitments from these men who had, only shortly before, expressed an interest in his merchandise. A gentlemen's agreement, after all, held little water if contracts had not been signed or the haze of the alcohol had not at least had a chance to wear off.

Of course Sneeden couldn't possibly chastise the young boy for having innocently repeated what he had heard old men discussing. Above all, Yvgeny had permitted Thatcher to make his pronouncement to demonstrate the point that the boy should never be dismissed as a mere child. Of course Yvgeny never admitted to it, even when Sneeden took him aside to tactfully relate his misgivings of allowing the child to make such a blunt statement in the presence of the two men's peers and business associates. Yet he gladly accepted Yvgeny's ten pence on the pound proposal to take the entire stock of porcelain off of his hands, sight unseen. But Sneeden could not help but feel quite exasperated as he viewed the young boy, who at first appeared to be studying the large globe on the opposite side of the room, look up as the deal was sealed, an expression of devilish satisfaction in his eyes and a smile on his lips that confessed his proclamation had not, perhaps, been an innocent slip at all.

Several days later, many of Bristol's most influential merchants appeared at the docks to watch the arrival of the *Tidewater*. A group of the men who had been present at the time of Thatcher's revelation were gathered together, taking great sport in the absence of the approaching ship's former customer. Each congratulated himself at not having fallen prey to Mr. Sneeden's desperate pleas to make good on their agreement to purchase shares of his cargo. Perhaps, they had reasoned, Thatcherev was wrong or, even worse, intentionally misleading them so that he could make a ridiculously low offer and steal the cargo out of their hands. But while all were willing to concede that Yvgeny Thatcherev was a savvy businessman, none would dare question the former priest's integrity. After all, they argued, it wasn't Yvgeny who had made the comment. Rather, it had been his precocious five-year-old grandson, merely repeating the words of Captain Van Reuten. And, as every smart trader knew, a sea captain is more often than not correct in his assessment of the condition of cargo, whether it be aboard his ship or someone else's.

It was Mr. Duncan who first spied Yvgeny, Thatcher and guardian Caesar strolling down the quay, obviously rapt in conversation. This frequent sight – the old Russian emissary, the young dark-haired bastard child and the abnormally tall African teenager – had often served as a focal point of speculation and discourse among the men who gathered at Peal's Tavern. Yvgeny and Thatcher were in constant and animated conversations as they strode the streets of Bristol. What could the ancient former diplomat and a five-year-old child possibly have to discuss that would be so obviously of interest to both parties? About the only other man who could have possibly given an answer was Sergei Evanovich, as so often the intense conversations were conducted in Russian. That was, at least, until the two could tell that Sergei was within earshot, at which time the conversation would switch to Polish which, Sergei painfully confessed, he never had been inclined to learn.

The men watched as the three slowly made their way to the end of the dock where they patiently stood and waited as the *Tidewater* turned and positioned herself alongside, her crew scrambling to throw down the mooring lines to the gangs who gathered to tie them fast. Almost instantly the gangplank was put in place, and Yvgeny and Thatcher strode up the ramp as if they owned the ship while Caesar took his post, arms crossed, at the entrance. Captain Wert, who had been standing at the starboard side of the craft intently seeking out someone along the dock, looked a little confused at first when Yvgeny Thatcherev, a man whom he had known for over a decade, strode up to him and offered his hand. Captain Wert followed the lead and repeated the gesture to the young boy. After a moment of conversation, Yvgeny produced a neatly folded sheet of paper from his pocket, handing it to the captain. Wert read the document for a few moments and then returned it to Yvgeny, who handed it to Thatcher. The young boy carefully refolded the paper and placed it in his own pocket. After another moment of conversation, during which Thatcher indicated the ship tied to the opposite side of the dock, Captain Wert ordered his first mate to escort the two to the hold. As they disappeared, Mr. Duncan, a dealer in cooking ware, broke from the group of Bristol merchants and sidled toward the ship Thatcher had indicated. He caught the attention of Moses Harrigan, the first mate standing at the gangplank. "Excuse me, Mr. Harrigan. Are you to be taking aboard a cargo from the *Tidewater?*"

"That I am, Mr. Duncan," Harrigan affirmed.

"And how long ago were contracted to receive the goods aboard?"

"Oh, I guess it has been almost two months since arrangements were made."

"I would guess that Mr. Sneeden had originally contracted your services."

"No sir. These arrangements were made by Mr. Thatcherev."

Mr. Duncan had good reason to be confused, for Yvgeny had purchased the cargo from Sneeden only a week prior.

"And you were contracted to take only the items that were aboard the *Tidewater?*" he asked.

Well, Mr. Duncan," Harrigan responded, somewhat irritated as he was tiring of the questioning. "Nothing else has been loaded aboard and I do not see anything else alongside my ship that needs to be brought below deck, so I'll leave it to you to discover the answer to that question yourself."

Duncan returned to the group and imparted what he had learned. As he was giving them his account, Yvgeny and Thatcher emerged from the hold and proceeded down the ramp. The conversation of the men stopped as the two approached, Caesar falling in behind as usual, while the crew of the *Tidewater* began swinging nets full of crates and barrels across the dock via block and tackle to the crew of the *Whisper*. In his hands, Yvgeny Thatcherev held two ornate porcelain figurines. One was that of a pristine statue of the rotund Buddhist prophet whose body was covered in a fine gold leaf. The other was of a Madonna cradling an infant Jesus. The features of mother and child were outlined in gold and silver, and in the hands of the baby Messiah was clutched a huge heart shaped ruby which looked to be of approximately thirty carats. All of the men stared in awe at the two religious figurines.

"It never hurts to have as many deities around as possible, particularly when they are so lovely. Would you not agree gentlemen?" Yvgeny stated as he and the two boys headed down the docks toward Parker House.

That evening, *The Whisper* set sail for Boston.

IV

The lesson Yvgeny Thatcherev hoped to impart to the men of Bristol that bright spring morning in 1685 was that young Thatcher Edwards, under the careful tutelage of his grandfather, would very likely become a formidable man of business in years to come. Yet behind the closed doors of Parker House, in the private study where only the residents of the most infamous address in Bristol resided, another side of the boy was being developed. While it was true that the greatest amount of his time was occupied by his grandfather and the spirited games of combat he and Caesar played, the women of the house were insistent there needed to be more to his life than ships and commerce.

Due to the business nature of the residence, which required that most of its residents were awake until the wee small hours, early morning usually meant waking at 10 o'clock or so. Nettie would do the honors, first waking Abigail, who would rise and dress as Nettie popped next door and roused Thatcher from his sleep. As Nettie was helping Thatcher dress, Abigail would be running a brush through the long strands of her golden hair. It was critical to her that she always look her best for her son in the morning. Some could dismiss this as sheer vanity but, to Abigail, it was important to her that the picture she painted of women for her son was that of refinement and elegance, which, for Abigail, was as natural as breathing was for others.

She would usually enter her son's room as Nettie was nearly finished dressing him. She would always compliment the handsome man she viewed, partly out of motherly duty and for the simple fact that Thatcher Edwards was, even as a very young man, a dashing fellow. While most outsiders noted the similarity between he and Yvgeny, no doubt because their common Russian ancestry afforded them similar features, Abigail saw the striking resemblance between Thatcher and someone else entirely. To her, the resemblance was almost uncanny and very indicative of their common family line. At five years of age, Thatcher was already taking on the prominent facial characteristics of the Romanovs, and, in truth, he bore more similarity to his uncle Peter than to his father Fedor. If Fedor had known he had a child, and if he had lived, he would have been proud to see what his only living heir was growing to become – strong, tall, dignified and, thank God, in perfect health. Here, in the morning hours, as she watched her child being dressed by a loving attendant, it often broke her heart that she was unable to reveal the truth of his heritage. While she believed that someday Thatcher should know the story of his lineage, the need had not yet arisen. Because he had Yvgeny, he had never had a need to know of his male parentage. But what would happen when his grandfather, a man who was approaching the twilight of his existence, was no longer there to serve in the role of surrogate father? The very thought that one day the man that meant the world to her son would be gone was one of the few things that could bring tears to her eyes. But she could cheer herself, at least somewhat, knowing that Thatcher was born with something she had attained only after Yvgeny had come into her life – a man that loved and cared, unconditionally, just as a father should. How many legitimate children in Bristol, in the world, could lay claim to a man such as that?

Together, mother and son would descend the staircase and enter the dining room where Nettie would have already laid out a sumptuous breakfast. Following eggs, bacon, biscuits, and whatever else Nettie had found that sparked her interest, Abigail and Thatcher would retire to the study where she would usually have a few books set aside. The daily regimen included his reading from a variety of literary works, sometimes in Russian, Polish, or Latin. It was vital to Abigail that he be versed not only in the language of his paternal ancestry but also languages that most effected that region. While it was probable that he would never see the land of his father and grandfather, to her it was only fitting that Thatcher be able to read and write the languages of the mysterious land of ice and snow. She also stressed the importance of his deep assimilation into the culture of his native country. The works of Chaucer and William Shakespeare flanked the walls of the study and, with respect to the latter, Abigail thrilled in her son's ability to bring life to the words of the Bard. Thatcher seemed to take to the melodious flow of the playwright's meter. Very often, during readings of Shakespeare, the women of the household would quietly steal into the room, thoroughly impressed and entertained by the natural, theatrical flair that Thatcher demonstrated in his performances.

On the nights when foul weather limited, though never entirely halted, the flow of gentlemen callers, the uncommitted ladies of the house would retire to the study as Thatcher, the consummate entertainer, regaled them with ranting speeches in rhymed couplets from any number of English playwrights, ranging from the elevated to the common, acting out the scenes with extraordinary panache. One such evening Nettie, who normally would be seeing to refreshments for guests or catching a few winks, leaned against the door jamb to listen.

"But that the dread of something after death,   the   undiscover'd country from whose bourn no traveler returns, puzzles the will, and makes us rather bear those ills we have than fly to others that we know not of? Thus conscience does make cowards of us all;   and   thus the native hue of resolution   is sicklied o'er with the pale cast of thought, and enterprises of great pith and moment with this regard their currents turn awry, and lose the name of action." Nettie had never seen a professional theatrical performance, but it was clear that her godson had a flair for this, and she took great pride in his maturity. But suddenly, she was struck that a very important aspect was missing in Thatcher's life. She chastised herself for not having realized it earlier. Because he was born into a life of privilege, Thatcher had never known what life was like for the rest of the world. He was catered to hand and foot, and for him things magically appeared – a sumptuous meal, stylish clothing, and captivating luxuries. As the men who patronized Parker House were Bristol's most illustrious, Thatcher had little clue that there were less luxurious places in this lovely coastal town, where people dirtied their hands to eke out a living and human beings were bought and sold for more than an hour at a time. She realized that she also could contribute to his education.

The next morning, on the day of Thatcher's seventh birthday, Nettie woke at the accustomed break of day. Despite her years of residence in Britain, her African habits were still greatly ingrained. As the first hint of sunlight would filter through the sheer curtains covering the window directly across from her bed, she arose, paying appropriate homage to her ancestors, and quickly dressed in her simple cotton shift and headscarf. Typically she would rouse Caesar who would sleepily accompany on her morning rounds. But instead she made her way up the stairs to the family chambers and found Thatcher sound asleep, not expecting to be awakened until breakfast was ready. Nettie sat on his bed and gently shook him.

"Wake up, Tatch," Nettie prodded as she gently shook him. The room was darker than usual and he cracked open his eyes sleepily.

"Is something the matter, Nettie?" he queried.

"Nuttin's wrong, Thatch. Just gettin' your day started a little early. Come on. Get dressed" she commanded, standing the boy up. "You can help me do some shoppin'. See how Nettie does business. Maybe even you learn sometin'."

Though Caesar's duties required that he lock the door and seal the house upon the exit of the last of the customers, without fail he would accompany his mother to the market each morning, happy to spend this time with her and help her carry her purchases, no matter how few hours of sleep he had managed to get. When Caesar's door swung open this morning, he was surprised to see the sleepy-eyed Thatcher coming down the stairs.

"What are you doing up, Thatch?" Caesar inquired as he hitched up his drawers.

"Tatch has decided he's goin' ta go shoppin' wit' Nettie dis mornin', son," she replied, smiling at her drowsy child. "Why don't ya take advantage of dis opportunity to get a few more winks o' sleep?"

Caesar was about to protest, but the look that Nettie gave him told him that this unexpected break of good luck was important to her.

"Do you want me to come along, Thatch?" Caesar inquired of his seven-year-old charge.

"No, I think that you should do as your mother suggested and get a little more sleep. I think I can sufficiently take care of Nettie for a change."

Caesar gave a somewhat crooked smile and then replied, "I'm not worried about Nettie. We know she can take care of herself. My question is, who's going to look out for you?"

"I'm fully capable of taking care of myself, Caesar. You act as if I still need a nursemaid. I am seven, you know."

Caesar gave one more look to Nettie and Thatcher to confirm the seriousness of their words, flashed a rare full-toothed smile at the thought of a little more sleep, and returned to his room with a muttered, "Happy Birthday, big man. Nursemaid, indeed."

Nettie grabbed Thatcher by the arm and led him out the door, oh, so pleased when he refused to exit until the lady had passed first.

Despite the hour, the open-air market was bustling with a wide variety of individuals. Along with the expected merchants and farmers hawking their wares and goods were a mixture of domestics, like Nettie, along with a rough assortment of characters which Nettie pointed out were the cooks and quartermasters of the numerous ships that dotted the harbor. But as well as these fascinating people, Thatcher got his first look at those who were the extremely and desperately poor. Children his age and younger trailed them, begging for money, whatever they could panhandle from those trying to conduct business in the market. Nettie kept her eyes straight ahead, but Thatcher could not help but study the faces of those dirty children and the number of invalids who seemed to have nothing. What was most amazing to him was the utter disregard and contempt the merchants and the shoppers seemed to have for these very least of people.

"There are so many, Nettie," Thatcher commented.

"Da poor will always be among us, Tatch. Da sad ting is, it seems like dere are more of dem every day."

Thatcher was intrigued by the hub of activity and cacophony of noises, fascinated by the long tables loaded with fish, grains, vegetables, slaughtered meats and, to Thatcher's curiosity, precious goods of endless variety. But what he found to be most curious of all was the petite black woman who tightly held his hand. While he had always loved and respected her, what caught his attention was the sense of majesty she possessed as she walked amidst the throng of customers and vendors. Unlike the other blacks, who made great effort to avoid contact with the whites that mingled in the marketplace, Nettie made no effort to avoid brushing the Europeans who, like she, were there in search of great deals. If anything, Thatcher noted, the whites made room and apologized as Nettie made physical contact with them. Likewise, the merchants, normally a commanding and rude lot, seemed to render a more respectful tone and look in the presence of the little African woman.

"Good mornin', Mistress Edwards!" This greeting at first caught Thatcher by surprise. Never before had he heard Nettie addressed by anything other than her first name. He had never given much thought to the idea that she had any other name but Nettie. He was pleased to see that she shared the same name as he and his mother. Why did no one ever tell him that she was his aunt ... or sister? It had always confused him that his grandfather's last name was Thatcherev, that his grandmother's name was Parker and that his mother's, like his, was Edwards. Not wishing to appear stupid, he had never given into the impulse to ask why. And once again he would never bother to ask why it was that Nettie bore the same last name as he and his mother. He could not know, for no one bothered to tell him, that Beatrice Parker had, in a moment of impulse, informally adopted Nettie once the bond between her and Abigail became so inextricable.

"Good mornin', Mr. Stivers," she replied as she examined the vegetables displayed along the back of his cart, picking up a cauliflower and setting it down disapprovingly. "I see dat your vegetables did not fare da winter well," she continued preparing to move on.

Seeing he was about to lose an important customer, Mr. Stivers looked around conspiratorially and then waved her to the front of the carriage. Nettie tugged Thatcher by the hand, and they followed to where Mr. Stivers stopped before a small collection of boxes covered by a tarp. Looking once more to see if anyone was watching them, he peeled up a corner of the canvas and revealed a box of very fresh cauliflower. "I have a very small parcel of vegetables that were spared the ravages of the winter and spring frost, Mistress Edwards. As you are such a good customer and all, I will only ask for 25 pence a bushel."

"You're sellin' your other vegetables for ten pence."

"Aye, but look at the quality, Mistress. Surely I will make no profit this season on my crops. I only ask what's fair."

"Mr. Stivers, you insult me. You know dat your other vegetables are only worth about five pence a bushel. I will pay ten for these."

"But Mistress Edwards. Ten pence ..."

"Is fair," she stated finally. "I will take all you have of dis quality. You may deliver it to da rear door, and I will pay you as soon as I examine each and every one of dem." Nettie worked her way back to the front of the cart and began picking out the better vegetables from the ravaged crop. She paid Mr. Stivers and then said, "Ye know what to do wit' dese."

Without another word she walked away to another stall hung with freshly butchered meat. Rather than walk to the front of the stall, she circled around to the back where she examined a steaming pile of entrails. Meticulously she picked up a long intestine, squishing one end, and examined the refuse which exited. Thatcher was fascinated. She walked away from the stall as the merchant was emerging, ignoring his greeting and plea to return. She could see Thatcher watching her with a questioning look.

"Wormy," she answered as she continued walking to yet another meat merchant and another until she seemed satisfied.

"Good morning, Mistress Edwards," stated a butcher who responded to her gesture.

"I want da rear portions of dis pig," gesturing to a pile of guts, "and da dressed portions of dis lamb," indicating another. "Dose five hens and dat big young cock."

"Yes, Mistress," responded the merchant without feeling the need to ask instructions or to talk price. His long experience told him that it would be a mistake to send over anything other than the meat she had specified, not if he wanted to keep her regular business. As Nettie was issuing her commands to the butcher, Thatcher watched as Mr. Stivers carried a box containing the vegetables Nettie had picked out to a knot of children who had been hovering not far from the stands. Mr. Stivers set down the box as the children and the ambulatory poor people tore into the case of overflowing food, ravenously consuming what might be the only fresh food they got all day. The best these poor people could usually hope for was to eat the rotten cast-offs that no one else would dare buy, but Nettie, despite her admonition that poor would be omnipresent, demonstrated that that doesn't mean you don't have to care.

Thatcher began to see and could not help but be impressed by the obvious respect that all in the marketplace gave to the tiny black woman and by her apparent savvy handling of transactions, as well as her humble demonstrations of compassion. He beheld facets of the woman few within the home had ever witnessed. But his attention was continuously drawn to the stalls in which Nettie seemed to express no interest whatsoever. The keepers of these shops were obviously cut from a very different cloth than the farmers and merchants that manned the booths that held Nettie's focus. Typically the merchants here in the open-air market were merely poorly dressed versions of the men his grandfather transacted with on a daily basis. An obvious exception was a collection of a dozen or so men who, for the lack of a better word, were the most roguish collection of individuals that Thatcher had ever seen.

The fact that the men were sailors was plainly obvious by their sun-baked, leather-like skin and their salty manner of speaking. But, unlike the seemingly dispirited lot that traditionally manned the merchanters, these men possessed an air of malicious glee seldom seen in the faces of the run-of-the-mill able-bodied seamen.

"You missy, come view my collection of fine Spanish silverware," commanded one hearty fellow who clutched an earthen decanter in one hand as he waved a handful of weighty looking utensils at a meek young woman, who moved just a little faster as she realized that she was the object of the barker's attention. "Oh, missy! What a fine dowry my silver would make for the plucky lad who will beg your father for your hand." He continued undaunted, momentarily enjoying the pert little derriere that jiggled pleasingly as she made a hasty retreat. A salty smile splayed across his face as he pulled long from the bottle and acknowledged the jocular approval of the sight from his cohorts.

And yet, just as quickly, the woman seemed forgotten as a larger, more robust lady slowed, drawing near the table and feigning mild interest in a silver tray which rested on the rough hewn platform.

"Aye, dear mistress, you do have a fine eye," the gangly individual purred as he picked up the tray to display it for her examination. "Notice the fine details, lovingly carved by the disreputable papist craftsman who fashioned her," he extolled as she barely concealed her impression.

"What are you asking for it?"

"Ah, to such a lovely lady as yourself I would gladly sacrifice any profit I should make simply to see the smile of your eye present itself on your lips. Thirty Guineas."

"Thirty Guineas? Why, I can get similar quality from the reputable shop keepers for twenty."

"But, beautiful mistress. Such one of a kind artistry, such detail. And from a Spanish craftsman who, I would imagine, this very minute burns in hell for his sacrilegious beliefs. Perhaps, for you, I could part with this treasure for five-and-twenty."

"Twenty and not a penny more."

"Ah, it pains me, lass. Not only shall I not take a profit, I shall indeed suffer a loss at that price. However, for the pleasure of your smile, and perhaps the thought of your womanly form to carry me through one of my many lonely nights at sea, I could sacrifice it for twenty."

The woman was unable to contain her satisfaction at having successfully dickered for the object. The merchant looked expectantly into her face, as if hanging on the hope of her satisfaction, and he clapped his hands in joy at receiving the smile he had so desperately hoped for. The woman drew some coins from the purse she held and passed them to the seaman. She did not resist when he gingerly touched her hand and drew it to his cracked lips for a kiss.

"Perhaps, my lady, we can take this fine treasure you so successfully pirated from me and together we can find a suitable place in your home to display it. After all, bearing such a rare item, you should be escorted, pray some disreputable individual divine it from your lovely grasp." All the time as he spoke he moved around from the table and began to draw the woman away, and she, while mildly blushing, gave no resistance.

As pirate and his quarry departed, Thatcher noted as the man's comrades took great pleasure in watching their cohort walk away not only with the woman's money but, very likely, food and carnal company. They jabbed and elbowed each other conspiratorially. Thatcher was about to adjourn from the area when he noticed one of the men reach into a crate and extract a tray that looked to be an exact replica of the one that was just sold. The toothless old man took the other's place at the table and bellowed, "One of a kind treasure from Spain!"

For a moment Nettie had been caught up in a price negotiation for fresh Virginia tobacco to refill the pipes of the brothel den. As such, she had not noticed Thatcher drifting away from her and the tables of respectable merchants. The small group of swarthy seamen and their hodgepodge of Spanish goods were of great interest to Thatcher as he made his way to their stand to examine more carefully the Papist pieces of art.

The sun was barely up, and Roger Ayerly was already three sheets to the wind when he noticed the nattily dressed young man approaching him and his comrades. The very sight of the likes of him and his kindred was more often than not an excuse for a mother or nursemaid to grab tightly the hand of the curious youth whose view may fall in their direction, yet this well-heeled young lad seemed neither horrified nor cowed by the horde of the underclass that he so fearlessly approached.

"So, lad," Ayerly bellowed at the dark-haired dandy, who began examining the silver and copper ware carelessly scattered across the table. "Ye come to sign up for our next sail? We are always on the lookout for slight young lads to serve as powder monkeys and cabin boys."

His collection of comrades laughed. The sight of a boy such as this, dressed head to toe in black with buckles, was always a source of amusement to such fellows. Having mostly grown up in the less-heeled districts of the towns and cities of the British Empire, many had never quite gotten over their disdain for these dandy lads and their imperial airs – the markings of future Royal Navy Officers, a class to a man disdained by anyone who ever turned a capstan.

"You say these wares are Spanish?" Thatcher questioned as he examined first a tray and then a silver goblet, turning over each piece to examine the maker's mark affixed upon the bottom.

"Aye, lad," Ayerly replied. "We are fully commissioned privateers who brought down yet another Spanish infidel ship, sending those heretics to the bottom of the sea and liberating their unholy cargo in the name of King William, our Protestant protector."

"Then would you please explain to me why this maker's mark at the bottom bears the distinctive symbol of Chattley of Waterford?" said Thatcher. "I did not know he was a Papist."

Ayerly was a bit taken aback that anyone, particularly a mere boy, would bother to take notice of the small symbol indicating the craftsman who had fashioned these pieces. To be quite frank, he never bothered to examine anything other than the obvious coin value these metal pieces could potentially generate. The fact that a precocious child would not only question the veracity of its origin but also dare do it in the face of this motley crew sparked his ire.

"Now see here, boy. Obviously you don't know fine Spanish goods when you see them, and the fact that you're calling me a liar prompts me to want to tan your hide with the backside of this tray and leave that maker's mark impression upon your arse!" Ayerly fumed as he moved around the table toward the boy. Thatcher was neither frightened nor impressed by the brigand's attempt to change the subject in such a threatening manner.

"Well, sir," he stated matter-of-factly, perhaps a little more arrogantly than he should under the circumstances. "The only thing I can suggest is that perhaps next time you should more carefully assay the contents of the ledger from your supplier so anyone with a merchant's eye could not so easily call you on the source of your product."

Ayerly had to take a moment to discern whether or not the boy was calling him a liar or an idiot. But either way, he wasn't about to take such guff from a snotty dandy-boy as this one. As he snatched up the tray and began to march menacingly toward Thatcher, he was caught unawares when a pint-sized black woman swung a basketful of eggs at his head. The roar of laughter from his comrades, combined with the heavily accented rebuke from his assailant, momentarily set him aback.

"…to tink, ya big dirty man, be treatnin' to rough up a young boy, who come to see ya tings," Nettie chastised, swinging the basket of broken eggs once again against his head.

Thatcher reached for the yolk-soggy basket and took it away from the fuming Nettie, attempting to calm her. "Now, Nettie, you must understand the fellow's intentions. He was merely trying to correct me on a fine point of Spanish craftsmanship, and I think you misinterpreted his passionate defense for the quality of his product."

Thatcher retrieved a silk handkerchief from his jacket pocket and reached up to wipe a bit of yolk and shell from the brow of the grizzled bear of a man, who had just had his ass handed to him by a tiny African domestic. Ayerly looked down at the nonplussed little gent, who stared up at him with a slight hint of amusement, offering the soiled fabric to complete his task of cleansing.

"As I said, sir, it is always best to make a careful assessment of the products you market. One never knows when someone may call him upon the source and quality of the item. I apologize for any misunderstanding, but I wouldn't give you more than three pence per item, and that is if I were feeling generous."

Thatcher genteelly took Nettie's arm and led her away from the cacophony of the roaring seamen, guiding her back to the source of the lost eggs, which would be much needed to sate the ladies' appetites. Ayerly watched as the young boy led the small woman away with a growing, albeit grudgingly, sense of humor. He was about to turn back to face the chiding of his compatriots when he noted the well-dressed young fellow cast a glance over his shoulder in his direction, giving him a much amused, self-satisfied smile.

The experience in the marketplace with Nettie was the first of many to come over the next few years. It demonstrated to Thatcher that he was in a household of a rarified class of individuals who seemed to understand that life was a series of transactions, and inevitably someone must come out on top and someone must lose. It was interesting to ponder the fact that virtually every person in that household was a gifted and wily hawker of goods, be they fleshy expanses of bosom and thigh or crates of porcelain destined for distant ports.

As the ladies of the house and the aging Russian went to elaborate measures to celebrate the dawning of his eighth year, showering him with gifts and endless supplies of love, Thatcher's mind kept returning to the marketplace. While there was no doubt he was impressed with the savvy marketing prowess of his lovely caretaker, a different yet totally compatible skill as daily demonstrated by his grandfather, his thoughts kept returning not to the stalls of meat and vegetables but to that rogue collection of carefree individuals. He had heard often of the tales of freebooters and pirates who made a living sacking honest merchants, and he had heard of how others were always so willing to give little regard for the source of the underpriced goods they were buying. But until that day, he had never seen up close that here in Bristol they, too, seemed to hold a place in society among the merchant class. It was a thought that would intrigue him for the rest of his life and set him upon a course where his natural business acumen, his flair for the dramatic and his fearless, adventurous nature would forever stamp his name upon the annals of history.

A name he had not yet taken.

Chapter 2

An Awakening to New Worlds

1686 – 1687

I

If there was a quality one could never attribute to Thatcher, it was loneliness. Having days filled with rigid instruction in the practical arts by his mother and the afternoons with the business arts by his grandfather, the long evenings as host to a bevy of mercantile beauties, plus the constant presence of his adopted older brother and friend Caesar and the ever-doting Nettie, Thatcher was not wont for attention. Thatcher's home and lifestyle earned him the honor of being truly one of the most pampered boys in town. Yet there were times when it seemed that the books, the ladies, his grandfather and Caesar just weren't enough to keep his mind from searching out something that could possibly be missing in his life. From an outside perspective, it was easy to see what was missing. Thatcher had a lot of family and business associates, but he had no friends his own age. While he could hold conversations on a variety of subjects with the best of them, and his name never ceased to come up in conversations at Peal's Tavern, and in hushed disbelief in the finer parlors of town, Thatcher had little knowledge and experience of what it meant to be a boy.

Caesar had entered his teens just as Thatcher had reached his seventh birthday. While Caesar was always quick to indulge Thatcher's fancies and the two were masters of their gallant wooden sword battles, Caesar was outgrowing the desire to play. Always very serious by nature, the brawny African viewed these games of warrior chivalry on an entirely different level then his constant companion. While Thatcher enjoyed the robust sword play, it always seemed to him as if Caesar were in training for some mythic battle. It did make their games interesting, and on more than one occasion even a wooden sword could deliver a painful blow, to which Nettie would lovingly render treatment to Thatcher and a Malagasy tongue-lashing to Caesar. Thatcher actually liked rough play, and more often than not he'd chalk up one of Caesar's crushing blows with a grimace and a carefully masked limp. But those times when he couldn't hide the bruise or wound, Nettie would make much ado about nothing. Thatcher found himself constantly having to defend Caesar's choice blows as the stoic teenager seldom refused to speak a word in his own defense. It was simply contrary to Caesar's nature to make excuses.

In the summer of 1686, Yvgeny, Thatcher and Caesar were on one of their routine daily constitutionals along the docks to catch the latest news from the ships returning from sea, to ferret out potential opportunities and perhaps to pass along a little good natured misinformation. As the three made their way to the end of one of the newly expanded quays, Thatcher's studied eye made out a set of sails on the distant horizon, tacking into the wind toward the narrow and tricky channel leading into Bristol Bay. He shaded his eyes from the midafternoon sun so he could make out the approaching ship. He could tell she was a big one: three masts and a full splay of sheets, with a captain who knew how to use her sails to combat a wind committed to barring his entry into the harbour.

"Do you recognize her, Thatcher?" Yvgeny inquired, his eyes not sharp like those of his young protégé.

"She's a big one. Looks to be a Snow, but I've never seen one with quite that shape," Thatcher responded, watching the meticulous play of line and canvas as the big craft defied the assaulting wind and glided smoothly into the channel of the River Avon and began its port tack into the River Frome. His rapt attention with the approaching ship made him completely oblivious to the young boy who sidled next to him, likewise shielding his eyes to take in the sight of the harbour's new arrival.

"She's named the *Elizabeth*. She's my father's ship," Woodes Rogers, Jr., chimed in, with obvious pride. "Isn't she a beauty? They just finished constructing her in Liverpool, and she's right on time, just as promised."

Thatcher's study of the approaching ship was momentarily distracted as he took note of the smallish, high-voiced boy, who had come to view the arriving ship with them. He raised his eyebrows at the dandy-dressed lad, mildly smirked then returned his attention back to his ship gazing.

"So Captain Rogers is finally replacing one of his broken-down old tubs, is he?" Thatcher stated to no one in particular.

"Well, it's long past time he started spending some of the money he's made on a decent ship," Yvgeny responded with half chide, half muse of a future customer.

Captain Woodes Rogers was one of the most respected mariners in Bristol. Having relocated his family and business from the small port town of Poole, a half day's sail southward, he has become quite rich and well connected and reputed as one of the busiest captains in southern England. Rogers had grown wealthy by risking the dangerous waters of the Grand Banks where his ships transported vital fish stocks and whale oil harvested in the North Sea and bargained for on Water Street in St. John, Newfoundland. Henry Cabot had set sail from Bristol in 1497 and laid claim to the land as England's first colonial possession in the New World. But as England, France and Holland all lay claim to these fertile waters, top dollar could be fetched by captains brave enough to ply the rough seas. And brave was an apt description for Captain Rogers who would venture to St. John every summer to make repeated trips loaded to the scuppers in oil and cod. But, even more than brave, Woodes Rogers was reputed for his tight fisted nature and had relied for years on some of the most dated ships to grace this busy port. Few sea captains were moneyed enough to own the ships they mastered; the best ships in port were often owned by men who had never been to sea. Captain Rogers, however, was one of those rare captains who owed his fortune and the ships he sailed to his own hard work.

Yvgeny had had numerous professional dealings with Captain Rogers. However, Rogers' strict, uptight, and religiously zealous nature held Parker House and its form of mercantile in terribly low esteem. Yvgeny could tolerate the moralizing of good Christian men only so much, particularly when he knew that not long after their finger wagging speech-making he would be entertaining them in Beatrice's parlor, followed by a less than pious transaction with one of the ladies upstairs. Woodes Rogers, on the other hand, was the classic upstanding prig who reserved his moralizing for sacred settings and stanched his preachiness when conducting matters of business related to ships and cargo. The Bristol merchants had heard tale that the senior Woodes had been busy commissioning the design of a ship that would provide him new business opportunities and, judging by both his command and the vessel he plied, the Rogers family could be obtaining a new level of wealth in short order. Even Yvgeny himself began to calculate usages for this new herald of the Bristol quays.

"She's his pride and joy," Woodes breathed, a bit of puff coming to his narrow chest. "It's my hope that one day Father will actually let me join him on his cruises."

Thatcher sized up the pint-sized boy. While both were about the same age, Woodes Rogers, Jr.'s tow head reached just about to Thatcher's shoulder as he stood alongside him. While it was true that Abigail went to great pains to assure that Thatcher always presented himself as the properly dressed little gentleman, at this moment he took great relief in knowing that at least his mother didn't require him to wear knee-pants. Perhaps it was that Russian influence, but as long as he could remember Thatcher was turned out to appear as a young man, not as a young boy. Woodes's attire may have been fitting for the salons of the upper crust but certainly not appropriate for the rough and tumble world of the Bristol quays. The puffy lace collar was a distracting sight to Thatcher as the harbor breezes beat them mercilessly against Woodes' pale face. It amused Thatch to think, had Yvgeny not been such a strong influence in the house, perhaps he himself may have been forced to dress in such silly and god-awful clothing. Yet one more reason to thank God for the likes of Yvgeny.

"So, you have an interest in taking up the family business, do you?" Thatcher finally inquired, after studying the petite boy.

"Oh, sailing is such an important part of our family legacy, going back generations. It seems there has been a Rogers at a helm as long as there has been England. I could think of no other avocation for which I am more suited."

"Well, perhaps once you're out of knee-pants," Thatcher jested. "I'm Thatcher Edwards."

"Oh, yes, I know. I have seen you down here on the docks. Father has spoken of you and your grandfather many times."

"Unkindly, I am sure," Thatcher responded. The lack of reply from Woodes Jr. confirmed the obvious. He turned back to watch the ship.

Captain Rogers' crews warped the *Elizabeth* as expertly as if they had been sailing her for years. Her massive starboard bow and stern lines grew ever taut across the short gap that separated the ship from the wharf and, in mere moments, her massive hulk lay within gangplank's distance. By this time, a sizeable assemblage of the Bristol merchant class had made their way to the quay to greet Captain Rogers and his impressive new craft. Making her way through the gathering crowd was Mrs. Rogers surrounded by a well heeled entourage of ladies, dressed in their Sunday fineries. Her rapture at the arrival of her husband was quickly subdued as she took in the sight of the company her son was keeping. She hastened her step to reach him before the

THATCHER Chronicle One | 75

captain could disembark from his lovely new acquisition, towing Mary, Woodes' little sister, behind her like a doll.

"I told you to wait in the parlor until I was ready to come down here to greet your father," Agnes Rogers chided young Woodes Jr.

"I could scarcely wait, Mother, once I spied her sails in my glass," Woodes replied in self-defense. "Besides, it's perfectly safe when I saw who else was down here. Mother, may I introduce Thatcher Edwards?"

"I have no desire to make the acquaintance of ... Master Edwards," she replied icily, her moral superiority sounding like a trumpet to the three denizens of the den of iniquity she so impugned with her every thought.

"Well, I do.," seven year old Mary Rogers contradicted as she sized up her brother's companion. Every girl in Bristol had heard the name Thatcher Edwards and, even at seven, it was obvious the precocious waif, a year her brother's junior, was quite pleased to make his acquaintance. "No, you don't, young lady," she chided Mary. "And neither do you. Come, Woodes," she insisted, grabbing his hand roughly and pulling him toward the gangplank to greet the arriving Captain Woodes Rogers. Both Woodes and Mary watched Thatch as their mother sped them as far and fast as she could.

Yvgeny placed his hand sympathetically on Thatcher's shoulder as a measure of sympathy for the woman's common rudeness. And common it was, for while the men and merchants of this seaside hub of enterprise were more inclined to be polite to the young business prodigy, whether they approved of his upbringing or not, the proper ladies of Bristol were never disinclined to air their disapproval of the bastard of the brothel. While the English may be reputed for their civility, it seemed as if there was almost a moral obligation to wag a finger or tisk a tisk toward those who practiced or otherwise profited from the sensuous arts. Though Thatcher had no say so as to the circumstances of his birth and upbringing, the very fact that those wretched women, Beatrice Parker and Abigail Edwards, allowed this shameful child to be on public display as if proud of their licentious behavior and one of its obvious end results was more than these paragons of morality could bear. What made the proper ladies of Bristol even more uncomfortable was that Thatcher Edwards was, without a doubt, the most handsome young fellow any of them had ever encountered. Keeping their children, specifically their daughters, far away from that house, those women and this handsome boy was a full time campaign. Few things would raise the ire and fear of a proper Bristol woman more than to hear the whispers and giggles of pubescent girls commenting on the attractiveness of this obviously immoral boy.

Thatcher needed neither sympathy nor explanation from his grandfather. He had grown accustomed to the lifetime of public scorn and disdain of proper folks and chalked it up as an occupational hazard, whether it was his occupation or not. He watched as the Rogers family made their reunion, and Captain Rogers received the praise and congratulations from his present and future customers. The Captain looked down from the main deck to see Yvgeny and the boys where they had stood to witness his arrival and tipped his head in acknowledgment. Yvgeny returned the nod and led Thatcher and Caesar away from the crowding wharf toward the infamous house at the end of Guinea Street.

The image of the lovely Snow was firmly fixed in Thatcher's ship-crazy brain. While he had always appreciated the business of trade that required his close proximity to ships, his fascination with them extended far beyond simply acknowledging them as a means of commercial conveyance. The hundreds of yards of canvas, miles of rope and dozens of block and tackle always seemed to grab his attention. While he was able to quickly calculate the volume of a hold by judging her length and breadth, it was the sight of holy stoned planking that seemed to fascinate him most. Caesar shared this fascination with these lovely vessels; however, it was less the splay of canvas and more the map and compass that held sway over the teenaged African boy. While a nightmarish period of his early life had involved such massive crafts, having traveled to these shores as mere cargo, he never failed to be seduced by the thought of the distance ports such mighty vessels made call. To him, the ability to read the sun and stars, to calculate the wind and to gauge all the elements involved in navigation captured his imagination as few things did. On this subject, the normally quiet young man could talk for hours, and with Thatcher he often did.

And they were doing just that after watching the arrival of the *Elizabeth* when a light rapping was heard at the kitchen door of Parker House. Thatcher and Caesar were rapt in talk of knots and tonnage while polishing off a large plate of warm jumbles, fresh from the oven, as Nettie chopped vegetables on the sideboard. She answered the unexpected knock and was surprised to see the slight, blonde boy standing at the door.

"Beg pardon, ma'am," Woodes Rogers, Jr., whispered to the equally slight woman, his eyes focusing on the knife she held at her waist. "I'm calling on Master Edwards, if you please."

Nettie let the door swing open to show Thatcher and Caesar enjoying their snack. Woodes gingerly brushed past Nettie to settle on a stool adjacent to the table.

"Don't you think you've a tanning warranted should your mother discover where your feet carried you?" inquired Thatcher.

"I'm sorry about that. My mother is very selective about whom I choose as company, but then again she's yet to find anyone who meets her approval. Might I have a sweet?" Thatcher pushed the plate of treats toward Woodes, who daintily nibbled on an end. He and Caesar sized up the wisp of a boy, silently appraising their unexpected guest. "I believe I overheard you boys talking about the proper application of lateral tacking in the high seas. My father says one of the errors so many captains make is thinking you can fight the wind rather than yield to it," Woodes offered between bites.

That evening, there in the kitchen of the Parker House, as the ladies of the home prepared to receive a parade of gentlemen whose only interest in sailing was the cargo it conveyed, three young future seamen stayed rapt in attention, discussing the proper application of line and sail, though none but one had ever been aboard a ship in full sheet, and he as little more than merchandise. Abigail and Beatrice, along with the other ladies of the house, could not help but steal peeks through the kitchen door at the three young men spinning yarns as if old sailors. And it was with a bit of regret when at last Yvgeny entered the kitchen to inform his charges that the hour grew late and, well, business was business.

When Woodes Rogers slipped quietly through the kitchen door of his own home and up the servants' staircase to steal into his bedroom, he was thrilled at the notion that at last he had a friend of his own. As an awkward boy who lived with the reality that he was the son of a sailor and under the constant attention of a domineering yet doting woman with ambitions, Woodes Rogers had spent a lonely life in the company of only the most carefully scrutinized of guests, and virtually none of them were children. While he knew that his new friend was precisely what his mother had so stridently fought to shield him from, he also knew that at last he had found someone with whom he had a common ground. He could not know that as Thatcher went through the nightly ritual of changing dress appropriate for greeting his salacious guests, almost the same notion was running through his head. Time would tell whether the bond of their mutual interests could overcome their distinctive differences.

II

There was no denying the level of Russian pride that permeated throughout Parker House, as evidenced by the countless Cyrillic tomes in the library and the constant Muscovy chatter between the old man and his young colleague. But there was also an official boycott of discussion with respect to Thatcher's obvious blood connections to that great and vast country. As Thatcher became more proficient in the language and more involved with the day-to-day activities of his grandparents' enterprises, he often rummaged through old documents stored in the basement pertaining to his grandfather's dealings throughout the decades. While he was aware that Yvgeny had come to Bristol as an official emissary of Tsar Alexis in 1668, Thatcher was curious as to what had led to the severance of his official role. While his grandfather still had numerous dealings with a variety of Russian enterprises and maintained an active working relationship with Sergei Evanovich, the emissary who had replaced him, any conversations that led to that last trip to Russia in 1679 were virtual taboo. While discussions of Russia were necessary from time to time, events transpiring there of a political nature seemed to make Yvgeny uncomfortable. In the recent correspondences he had read from Yvgeny's contacts in Moscow, Thatcher learned that Russia was undergoing many changes. At this point in her history, Russia was on a course that would either propel it to preeminence in the modern world of the West or send it reeling back into the Dark Ages, an era from which Alexi and Fedor had fought so desperately to drag it.

After the death of Tsar Fedor in 1682, his sister Sofia proclaimed the role of Regent as the rightful heirs to the throne were incapable to assume governance. Her younger brother Ivan should have technically worn the crown, but the namesake of Ivan the Terrible was most terribly afflicted with mental retardation and would never be allowed to ascend unsupervised. Peter, her half brother, was a mere ten-year-old boy. While it wasn't uncommon for young children to ascend to the throne, the very powerful Imperial Guard, known as the Streltsy, were adamant that Sophia serve as Regent until Peter could be of an age to rule. It was an uncomfortable arrangement as Sophia, the eldest surviving child of Tsar Alexi, should by all rights ascend to the title of Tsarina, but powerful conservative elements, under the sway of the Orthodox Church, refused to allow a woman to rule over mother Russia. Had Sophia had her way, the sickly Ivan would have met with an untimely accident, and all members of Tsar Alexis' second family, Peter in particular, would have been executed, thus stanching all resistance to her rightful ascent. However, factions of the boyar royal class loyal to Peter's matriarchal line had built in safeguards to protect him by placing him in virtual isolation and out of Sophia's reach. It had been agreed to that when Peter reached his eighteenth birthday, the role of the Regency would be retired and Peter would take his rightful place as co-ruler of all Russia with his brother Ivan, provided, of course, Ivan lived that long.

Sophia's long time lover and chief advisor, Vasily Golitsyn, advised her that it was best to keep Peter occupied and away from the Kremlin, and so they indulged the boy's fascination with navies and armies and allowed him and his mother to go into virtual exile at Alexis' hunting lodge a few miles northeast of Moscow. Preobrazhenskoe sat along the idyllic Yauza River, where Peter filled his time creating his "boy army" of young nobles and all the recently dispossessed servants and advisors to his dead brother Fedor. Martial games occupied much of Peter's time, and in the warm months he and his retinue would relocate some 80 miles northwest to Lake Pleschev, building ships and studying naval tactics. What Sophia did not realize was that Peter, now in his teen years, was learning valuable lessons of command being passed off as child's play. And as Peter approached his maturity, he began to fathom his sister's plans to deny him his rightful assent. Eventually loyalties tilted in Peter's favor, and at the end of the day, despite her intelligence, power, command and calculation, Sophia could not muster the support necessary to maintain her dominance of the motherland. In August 1689, after a bloody attempted coup, she crossed the threshold of the Kremlin for one last time to begin a life of solitude behind convent walls.

Caesar glanced at the clock on the mantel to note the time. It was unusual to hear a knock this time of day, still hours from when they would receive their honored nightly guests. He opened the door and was surprised to see Sergei Evanovich, dabbing his temples with a handkerchief despite this being an unseasonably brisk, overcast December afternoon.

"I wish to speak to Yvgeny Thatcherev. If you would, please tell him Sergei Evanovich has urgent business on behalf of the Tsar of Russia," he stated formally. Sergei waited nervously as Caesar disappeared down the hall, where he could hear the large African male repeat his proclamation. Moments later Yvgeny appeared. His face betrayed the many different thoughts running through the old Russian's brain, and wordlessly he motioned for Evanovich to follow him to his study.

Thatcher had been in his room in the private quarters of Parker House when he heard the knock at the door, which oddly always rattled the window nearest to his bed. He reached the head of the long sweeping staircase that spilled out onto the entryway just as the door to his grandfather's private study banged shut. He caught Caesar's eye at the foot of the stairs.

"Sergei Evanovich," Caesar reported.

"He rarely comes here. I wonder what he wants?"

The two paced anxiously, awaiting word from Yvgeny. As the uncharacteristically shut door swung open, they could sense the nervousness of both Evanovich and Yvgeny as the emissary nodded his head in acknowledgement, passing reticently back through the front door Caesar had opened for him.

"Problems in Russia, Grandfather?" Thatcher asked as pointedly as he could under the circumstances. Yvgeny studied his nine-year-old grandson who was studying the Russian's face for any clue. Yvgeny realized that perhaps his nervousness was showing and tried to ease into an open smile, the type that broadened his already voluminous hirsute face.

"Well, it seems that Tsar Peter has finally ascended to his place upon the throne, along with his brother Ivan, of course. Sergei thought I should know that with respect to my business in Russia," Yvgeny replied, attempting to dismiss the importance of the visit.

"Well, why would he then request to see you on urgent business of the Crown if it was merely a bit of news from abroad?" Thatcher further inquired.

"You know us Russians, Thatcher," Yvgeny rationalized. "We always have a flair for the dramatic, and news from home is always an occasion for drama." He placed a large hand on each boy's shoulder. "Come, now. Let us adjourn to the study, and let me tell you a story about a place called Crimea." Yvgeny led the two boys into his well-stocked repository and spent the day discussing this beautiful place and the significance of Kiev.

"No!" Abigail wailed, followed by the hushing beckon of her parents. Since Sergei's visit the previous day, Yvgeny had dreaded this moment, and he and Beatrice had spent most of the night in discussion, reading and re-reading the sheaf of documents the trade emissary had delivered to Yvgeny, the ones with the Royal Seal of the Tsars of All Russia.

The sound of his mother in distress wrenched Thatcher from his sound sleep, and he was in the corridor in seconds, pounding on her door. He was a little shocked to see Yvgeny answer, with Beatrice sitting on the bed comforting her daughter, who was desperately trying to control her sobbing.

"What in God's name is going on?" Thatcher demanded of his grandfather, who began to lead him back to his room. At the same moment Nettie arrived, dashing up the private staircase, a look of concern on her face as well.

"Do not worry Thatcher, Nettie. Everything is all right. Your mother is just a little concerned with some news from home. Here, get dressed, and we'll meet you in the dining room to give you all the details." Yvgeny handed Thatcher off to Nettie, who searched the cleric's face for a hint of what was afoot. Though he smiled, his bloodshot eyes betrayed the sleepless night and a matter of much gravity. She could also tell that right now Thatcher needed a calm and assuring Nettie more than anything.

"Come now, Tatch. What kind of appearance ye presentin', runnin' 'round da household half-naked? Come in, Nettie get ye dressed." She led the boy in and closed the door as Yvgeny returned to Abigail's room.

She had grown quite flushed with the sobbing and had a look of abject terror on her face. Beatrice did all she could to calm her daughter, but she knew there was no consoling her, as an old wound had just been reopened, and there was a great fear that this time it would not mend. "It is absolute madness," Abigail insisted. "You are no longer a functionary of the court and there is absolutely no way they can make this demand of you!"

Yvgeny sat down on the bed next to Abigail, placing an arm around her as his other big hand brushed away the hair from her brow and the steady stream of tears coursing down her cheeks. He tried to smile as reassuringly as he could but realized any pretense of normality was not only an exercise in futility but also a lie he was not prepared to tell his child. He lifted her chin so his eyes could look into hers, now as red-rimmed as his were from a night of tossing, turning and pacing.

"My love, of course they can," he replied as softly and sincerely as he could. "I am a Russian, a boyar, and an Orthodox priest, and he is my Tsar. He has every right to demand anything he wishes and expect me to comply. If nothing else, he knows my Russian heart and my commitment to my country, so yes, he has every right to insist."

"Well, he can insist all he wishes," Abigail fumed. "It doesn't mean you have to comply. We've done all we've been asked to do. You were stripped of your titles and told never to return. Now they expect you to come back because the new Tsar demands it of you? I say no!"

"You know, Abigail, I spent all last night with Yvgeny, saying exactly the same things," Beatrice commented, attempting to console her outraged daughter. "But there's one thing you and I both know about this man, and one of the things we've always loved about him is his commitment and honor. We have been so fortunate these many years to be recipients of his love and devotion. It has spoiled us. It has spoiled me, because I never thought that I would love and need someone as I do him, but I always knew, and I feared that a time such as this would come. What you don't realize, my love, is when he took you to Russia, my greatest fear was that you would return home alone, or that neither of you would. But despite it all, I was given the gift of both of you, safe and at home with me." She smiled and hugged her daughter closely to her. "And then, there's Thatcher. What an unexpected gift!"

Abigail was not about to let her mother penetrate her softest side and tamp her steam so quickly. "And all the more reason why I say no! That boy will be absolutely lost without Yvgeny. He's reaching such an important age in his life when more than ever he will need his grandfather. Perhaps if he had been raised without him it would be one thing. But Yvgeny is the most important person in his life, more than me I must sadly admit, and more than you and this house and these women."

Yvgeny grew visibly uncomfortable with this thought. It had never been his intention to be anything more than a supporting role in the boy's life, but it was true. Thatcher was so much more than just a grandson. He had become an important comrade. Thatcher embodied everything that he had hoped his own Nicolai would have become had he lived beyond his five short years. He never talked about his lost children to anyone, not even his beloved Beatrice or Thatcher, particularly so with Thatcher, as too many times he looked at that strong, beautiful boy and saw little things that made him think of the son he lost so long ago. Anytime Beatrice had attempted to broach the subject, the overwhelming sadness was just too much to bear. She had met this man because he saw a chance to save a child when he had not been so fortunate to do likewise for his own. As much as Yvgeny Thatcherev had been an open book to her, this was a threshold neither one of them could cross, because the loss had been so devastating that its pain had never gone away.

"I don't know how we're going to tell him," Abigail breathed at the thought of his reaction to this news. "If there were some way we didn't have to ..."

Yvgeny turned to her, taking her hands and lifting her to a standing position, once again brushing her lovely golden strands away from her face and kissing her cheek. Instinctively, her little hand curled in that long strand of beard that provided her comfort in a way she could not explain. He smiled as he felt the slight tug, reminiscent of such a distant time. "Leave that up to me. He understands a man's need to do extraordinary things for family, business and country. I'll tell him in a way he'll understand. Now, there is an expectation we have always met when it comes to appearances before that boy."

Taking Yvgeny's cue, Beatrice retrieved her daughter's dress for the day. Sitting her at the vanity and brushing her luxurious golden locks, she began to lovingly prepare the future mistress of the house for a trying day, taking the chance once again to be a good mother to the beloved daughter who needed her. Yvgeny exited the room and cleared his throat. Gaining his composure and confidence as much as he could, he proceeded downstairs to the family dining room, where a much concerned Thatcher was sitting, breathlessly waiting for some bit of news about this morning's break in routine.

"Ah! There you are, Thatcher," he announced brightly. "Your mother and grandmother will be down momentarily. Both said they are so sorry to have begun the day creating such concern, but all is resolved, and we've much to do today as the *Diogenes* makes port this afternoon. I think that Albert Hutchins is very close to making a firm commitment, and we can unload that entire lading on him without having to pay a farthing in drayage. Now that would be a good day, don't you think?" Yvgeny was making every attempt, albeit futile, to restart the day as normally as possible. Thatcher was having none of it.

"What news from Russia would so greatly distress my mother?" Thatcher insisted.

To know Abigail was to know a picture of absolute composure. Since she was a small child, she had always embodied the quality of one not easily ruffled. While no doubt an aspect inherited from Beatrice, who herself was one of the strongest individuals anyone would likely meet, it was that regal quality, that assurance, that nothing or no one dare harm or threaten her, that made all of them – Beatrice, Abigail and Thatcher – forces to be reckoned with. It was quite uncharacteristic for Abigail to raise her voice. Yvgeny had always teased her as being his "quiet storm," as nothing was more dangerous or threatening than when Miss Abigail Edwards became quiet. While not prone to violence, her razor sharp tongue combined with her stunning intellect made a reproach from her more painful than a block and tackle upside the skull. It was no wonder that Thatcher was alarmed to hear his mother raise her voice so insistently, and Yvgeny's obvious attempt to avoid the subject only made Thatcher more concerned.

"Well, my boy, we'll discuss this in more detail when we're all together, but I assure you that there's nothing to be concerned with." Half whispering, Yvgeny leaned in conspiratorially. "You know these women. They don't take 'no' from us so easily, and if they could have their way we would never leave the house. They worry so much over nothing."

On this subject, Thatcher could heartily relate. While Abigail and Beatrice were no strangers to requirements of business, it was difficult for them to comprehend that sometimes men just needed to get out in order to get things done. Perhaps it was because they were in the business of hospitality and had been blessed with Nettie and Caesar, who took care of all those little day to day essentials thoughts that seldom entered the minds of the ladies, that they could not relate to the idea that sometimes men needed to do things that may not seem germane to business yet were essential in order to maintain one's standing. This would sometimes be as minor of an event as grabbing a pint or two at Peal's and speculating about the conditions of the winter to come, or indulging in a game or three of Whist, and, while at it, perhaps imbibe more than the originally anticipated pint.

Thatcher was almost satisfied with that relatable aside until he saw his mother's face as she made her way across the foyer, attempting desperately to look as if nothing was wrong. One other aspect of Abigail he knew as well – when his mother was angry, she stayed angry until she was damn well ready not to be angry any longer. She was a study in subtleties, and there was no amount of nuance in her expression at this moment. She was making every effort to appear just as Yvgeny appeared, as if nothing at all had transpired, but she was having little success.

"Well, I'm not exactly sure how long you all expect to keep this little charade going, but I for one would appreciate if someone would tell me what has happened," Thatcher demanded, not even waiting for his mother's derriere to touch the chair he held for her. Abigail and Beatrice shot a look at one another, having convinced themselves that Yvgeny would accomplish his goal of taking the edge off the moment and surprised that he had not accomplished it. Yvgeny realized that there was no getting through breakfast before he would have to make an explanation to his grandson.

"You are absolutely right, Thatcher. You are a vital part of all that goes on within these walls, and it not fair of us to keep you in the dark any longer." Yvgeny reached into his jacket pocket and withdrew the royal proclamation. He handed the ornate sheaf of documents across the table to Thatcher, who began reading the elaborately flourished Cyrillic characters. All three sat quietly as Thatcher perused the pages, pausing a little longer than expected on the last page, which bore the point of the document and the elaborate signatures of Peter and Ivan, co-Tsars of Russia.

"They are calling you back to Russia?" Thatcher quizzed, looking straight at his grandfather, an indecipherable look on his face.

"For a short while, Thatcher," Yvgeny replied, somewhat dismissively. "With the changes at Court and Peter assuming more responsibility on the throne, it is of vital interest for him to gauge Russia's relationships abroad."

"But that is what Sergei Evanovich is for, is it not?" Thatcher probed.

"Yes, this is true. Sergei and I will travel together. You must understand, Thatcher, that as capable as Sergei may be, there is much about Russia's dealings with England that goes beyond mere reports. I have an insight to this relationship that the Tsar feels is valuable, and thus he is requesting my return. But again, as I say, it will only be a short while."

Thatcher looked back down at the pages. "Well, then, I will go with you," he insisted. "I have long wanted to see Russia and have always hoped an occasion would rise where you would take me. This seems ideal, don't you think?"

The silence in the room was palpable and thick as the fog on Bristol Harbour. Simultaneously Abigail and Beatrice grew a shade paler and dared not breathe for fear that Thatcher would read something in their sighs.

"Ah, my boy, I sat up all night trying to figure out how we could make this work, and as much as your mother and grandmother would love it, I honestly need you here. In fact I think it is a great test of your capabilities to assist your grandmother in managing our affairs. Besides, I will be so busy that I fear our time together would be limited, and rather than enjoying the beauty of Russia you would find yourself confined to a dank shuttered room for days at a stretch. But I promise you, at another time, we will discuss traveling throughout Russia and all those places we've talked about."

While the women were expecting him to be disappointed, they could never have prepared for what Thatcher said next. "Well, actually, grandfather, I really don't think that is an option, is it?" Thatcher insisted, waving the document he held in his hand. "According to this, you have been instructed to bring with you all Russian citizens. I believe that includes me, does it not?"

This was one of those absolutely rare occasions when everyone in the room, save the nine-year-old with the insistent expression, was absolutely speechless. Each knew that not once had there been a discussion identifying the paternal parentage of Yvgeny Thatcherev Edwards. Having grown up in a home of libertine morals, there was no reason Thatcher would ever have any reason to believe that his father was anything but of domestic origin. Yet here was this boy delivering to the adults who had so meticulously sheltered him from the truth the evidence of his knowledge. The pressing question on everyone's mind at that moment was, did he know the truth? Or was he merely guessing? And if he wasn't guessing, exactly what did he know? For all the boldness so characteristic in the three adults around the table, not one was brave enough to advance the question, and yet Thatcher had thrown down a gauntlet, and somebody had to pick it up and respond convincingly.

"Thatcher, you are English born. You were born right here in this house. You've heard that story many times, told many different ways by everyone in this home," Yvgeny stated as coolly and matter-of-factly as he could. "While I am proud to think of you as my grandson, you know that this is merely an honorary title, don't you?"

"Oh, grandfather, this I know well. My mother has only known one father in her life, and that has been you, just as I have only known one grandfather. We've never concerned ourselves with blood ties, and at this moment that is not the issue. What is the issue is that Tsars Peter and Ivan have requested you bring with you all Russian subjects, and as Sergei Evanovich has already received his own commission it is safe to say that in the eyes of Russia there are more than the two that I know residing in Bristol. What other subjects could they be speaking of?"

Thatcher could tell that this line of interrogation was creating an air of uncomfortability unfamiliar to the very open dialogues and discussions that were legend in Parker House, and in that unsettling silence, all of his speculations were being confirmed. It was true that no one had ever discussed his father, either in conjectural terms or in fact. But Thatcher was an exceptionally bright boy. While one could attribute much of his personality and habits from his studied tutelage under Yvgeny, there was no denying the fact that, as he wandered the lanes and docks of Bristol, he had yet to encounter anyone of English stock to whom he bore the slightest resemblance. The closest proximity to a physical representation of what Thatcher was and was to become was embodied in that giant Russian for whom he supposedly shared no blood line. He had heard chatter on occasion of suggestions that an elicit liaison between Yvgeny and the teenaged Abigail had occurred, but anyone who understood the relationship between them would have to immediately dismiss that as so much folderol. Still, there was no denying that Yvgeny Thatcherev was the most apt model of Thatcher's potential paternal parentage.

This day was one all knew would come. The hope had been that it would occur at a time when Thatcher was a bit older and mature enough to handle those bits of truth they were willing to reveal. Likewise, it had always been hoped that, as a father discusses the fundamental differences between men and women to his ripening young son, a conversation not likely to be necessary in Thatcher's case, it would occur at a time more of curiosity and less of gravity. If there ever was a demonstration of Mr. Newton's recently published theory, this would be one of those times. There was no doubting that Thatcher's challenge required a response, and yet it seemed as if each of the three were hoping to defer it to someone else to say it. While it may have been easy to succor the boy with a lie, that would be totally uncharacteristic for any of them to do. Despite how others may perceive their nontraditional views on sexual mores, dishonesty was something held in great disdain by all members of the house. Their relationship was based on trust, and duplicity would sow such seeds of dissention that candor was essential in being able to effectively coexist. So, while a lie this time would seem justifiable under the circumstances, it was an act of which none were capable. Thus, the heavy air of silence.

"When I was but a teenaged girl," Abigail began, her eyes now fixed to a point on the plate before her, "I accompanied your grandfather on what was to be his last trip to Russia. It is true what you think. I did meet a man in Russia that grew into a love that was not to be. While I cannot explain it, likewise I cannot regret it, because without it we would not have you. So yes, it is true. Your father was Russian. But your home always has been and always will be England. Thus, whatever this decree may suggest and no matter your paternal line, you are not a subject of Russia."

Thatcher took in the words his mother spoke to him and felt a sense of both relief and sadness that his speculations were true. He considered for a moment, looking up to take in the awkward expressions of his beloved family. "If what you say is true, then even though my home and birthplace are England, it is likewise true that I am a child of Russia as well, and it is only logical that I help my grandfather fulfill the command of his Tsars and accompany him to Moscow."

Abigail looked up from her fixed gaze upon the plate into the face of her son, betraying an expression of utter horror. "Thatcher, you must understand that there were complications and ramifications for my indiscretions. We vowed, Yvgeny and me, that when I left Russia it was on the strictest terms that we never return."

"Mother, that was a different time under different circumstances. The fact remains, Yvgeny's king is calling him and all Russian subjects home. Whether you want to admit it or not, I am one of those subjects and have a duty to accompany him as deemed by our tsars."

The path of this conversation was taking a turn Yvgeny did not care to follow. "I should tell you, Thatcher, that all of this is moot. Just this morning, I was discussing with your mother and grandmother my choice not to return to Russia. You see, I must confess that when I was stripped of my commission, after my initial disappointment and anger, I was quite relieved to be free of the responsibility. In fact, had I not been stripped of my title, I had been seriously contemplating resigning my commission as I had grown to see England as my home. So really, we need not further discuss this. I will notify Sergei Evanovich that I am not going to respond to this request as I have so many responsibilities here." And with that, Yvgeny was hopeful that he was putting the issue to rest. Both Beatrice and Abigail breathed an audible sigh of relief that Yvgeny was putting his loyalties to his family and grandson before the Tsars of Russia.

"And with that, Thatcher," Beatrice chimed in, "your grandfather and I have also been discussing other opportunities that would give us a chance to travel throughout the British Isles more extensively, and possibly the Colonies. And one of the things that was most important to us was the opportunity to show you more of England. We felt these plans would be jeopardized or at least curtailed should Yvgeny return to Russia, and now we will be able to put those plans in motion. Do you not think this is an ideal opportunity? Abigail?"

Abigail looked at her son, and her mind was virtually tripping over the affirmations she wished to give to her mother's wise suggestion, but his expression forced her to give pause to the thought. "What do you think of that idea, Thatcher?"

"I think that for the first time in my life my family is lying to me. That Yvgeny would abandon his responsibilities to his country ... that my grandmother would concoct some elaborate scheme to distract me ... and that you would be party to a deception is something that greatly distresses me. It leads me to the question: what are you protecting me from? And when did we resort to cowardice in the face of threats?"

It was difficult to be called a coward by anyone, but especially so by a trusting nine-year-old. Each of them could feel a pang of shame in Thatcher's suggestion that they were retreating in the face of adversity.

They had always taught him to hold his head high and be proud of himself, no matter what others may say, and yet the outcome of this decision could forever shatter their credibility in his eyes. While to many that may have seemed trivial, to these people of Parker House, Thatcher's sanction was one of the most powerful and driving forces of their bizarre, untraditional existence.

Thatcher once again held up the documents. "We have been commanded by the Tsars of Russia to return to our homeland. We travel under royal seal. How many more could lay claim to such security?"

"Is this what you truly want, Thatcher?" Abigail asked, the weight of the world resting heavily upon her shoulders.

"It is what has to be, Mother," he replied, taking her hands in his and looking deeply into her eyes.

She sighed, gave a painful smile and turned to look at her mother and adoptive father. Both looked at each other, then back at her and nodded in agreement. She returned her gaze to her son and replied, "Let me tell you about your father ..."

III

There was much debate circulating in Parker House as to how quickly Yvgeny and Thatcher should depart for Russia. Winter was setting in, and travel into the Black Sea and up through the Dnieper River could be treacherous. Beatrice and Abigail were insistent and pleaded that they wait until spring before venturing out, but after conferring with Sergei Evanovich, who himself was concerned with how things were shaping up in Russia regarding his future, he convinced Yvgeny to join him as they sailed in the week leading into the New Year.

There was much disagreement over the decision to leave Caesar in Bristol. While it was true that any number of ruffians could have been contracted to serve as protection to the ladies of Parker House, Yvgeny felt he could trust the care of these women to no one more suitable than Caesar. To the guests who called on Parker House, Caesar's presence was well known. Typically the one responsible for answering the door and initially screening would-be customers, he would show the guests into the parlor where Yvgeny and Thatcher would provide conversation until a fitting hostess would join the repartee. While Beatrice and Abigail would fill the hospitality roles, it was made quite clear that, in the absence of Yvgeny and Thatcher, Caesar was to be the master of the house. While none doubted his capability to protect the lives and property, there were concerns that a freed slave serving in the role of master could present unique challenges to the genteel merchants and seamen who patronized the manor. Also, unlike Yvgeny and Thatcher, Caesar was a man of few words. Not that he couldn't effectively communicate, but his body language and imposing appearance could be a tad stress-inducing to the patrons, who came to Parker House for the sole purpose of relaxation. Caesar himself made this point and would have been happy to have served merely as a source of security, but neither Yvgeny nor Thatcher would have any of it. In truth, had he his way Thatcher earnestly relished the thought of his closest comrade joining him on this venture. And while it was unspoken, there was the very real possibility that neither he nor his grandfather would return. Thus with much trepidation, Caesar assumed his role as master of Parker House.

In January 1690, the trio of Russian pilgrims departed their Bristol home, plunging headlong into the rough, frigid waters of the wintry north Atlantic. As he had done a decade before upon reaching the storied city of Constantinople, Yvgeny shepherded his young grandson to the most holy sites and inspirations of the Orthodox Church, most importantly, of course, St. Sofia. At the Port of Kherson on the Black Sea, they transferred to the Dutch merchant vessel *Friesland*, captained by none other than Johann DeBeers and his seven-fingered brother Derek. Apparently the years had been good to them, no doubt from the assistance of the gifts they had received for not pressing charges against Nettie and agreeing to trade outside of Bristol. Derek was initially adamant about not admitting aboard Yvgeny and the apparent reason for his three missing fingers, but their trade along the Dneiper was lucrative and their contracts with their Russian associates too valuable to offend the proclamation-bearing Russians.

The full force of winter could be felt as the *Friesland* began its northward journey, winding through the heart of the Ukraine. Despite the tensions that existed between the DeBeers and Yvgeny, Thatcher could not help but be fascinated by this quick, compact ship sailing effortlessly up the near-frozen Dneiper River. He spent as much time as he could on the deck and amongst the sailors. He was even able to warm up to the ten-fingered Johann, who was appreciative of Thatcher's interest in navigation and application of the astronomical compendium and horary quadrant, which became necessary in the wider bodies of water. Thatcher had used his time crossing the Mediterranean learning how these devices operated in conjunction with the compass and thus seemed quite versed in their application to the elder DeBeers.

At long last, the *Friesland* reached Kiev, and the masses of envoys began their long overland journey east through the treacherous Tatar infested countryside of Ukraine. Thatcher marveled at the ancient wood structures and plethora of onion-domed churches that lined the way to Moscow. As they plunged east into an endless sea of white and frost, he could not help but wonder how people could eke out a living in such frozen conditions. The carriage finally reached the teeming metropolis of Moscow, where the streets coursed with an energy and life unexpected. And to Thatcher's ear, the cacophony of Russian language and the splay of Cyrillic lettering denoting the various shops along the broad avenue were pleasant and comforting. But he was not prepared for the amazement he would feel at his first view of the Kremlin. Its massive domes, spread out over blocks of Moscow's heart, were bordered with large stone walls and heavy iron gates. He marveled at his first sight of Red Square, which stretched the entire length of the Kremlin, and the twelve domes of the Cathedral of St. Basil the Blessed. Despite the long trip, Thatcher was anxious to begin exploring this marvelous city of white snow and colorful buildings and reached for the door as the carriage came to a stop at Red Square. Yvgeny tugged on Thatcher's heavy coat, halting his egress as the door swung open and Sergei Evanovich disembarked, Yvgeny closing the door behind him, to the dismay of the curious Thatcher.

"You will have them deliver my bags to my home on Stremskypoya Street, driver," Sergei instructed then looked into the carriage. "I will make my appearances and inform them of your arrival, Yvgeny. May I recommend you don't tarry too long?"

"I am merely going to get the boy settled and plan to make my presence known in the morning, if you would be so kind to inform anyone who may inquire," Yvgeny replied.

With that, Sergei waved the driver off who turned left along the road bordering Red Square, then turned left once again, making his way out of Moscow. Thatcher continued to take in the view of the massive facility disappearing behind him, then turned to Yvgeny.

"So we are heading to your home now?" Thatcher inquired expectantly.

"Actually, no, I have arranged accommodations for you elsewhere for the time being. It is only so I can get my quarters and affairs in order to make you more comfortable," Yvgeny replied calmly. The carriage continued its trip east until at last they began to enter another town on the outskirts of Moscow whose appearance bore no resemblance to the ancient metropolis they had just departed. As if suddenly transported back to the England he had left weeks before, they entered wide tree-lined avenues with structures unlike those which he had viewed in his travels through Ukraine and Russia. Russian structures were primarily constructed of wood and designed to withstand the harshest of winters. Except for the most beautiful of spring and summer days, they remained sealed and shuttered, a practical design to retain whatever warmth those drafty houses could. But here, two- and three-story homes displayed massive windows bare to the elements, and traveling down a wide boulevard they passed snow-covered squares with impressive frozen fountains. These stately buildings with their columns and cornices and the western-style carriages coursing along snowy boulevards made Thatcher feel as if he had suddenly been transported back to Bristol. In springtime the squares would bloom with grasses from home, framed with precisely measured gardens designed in the English style and as different from Moscow as imaginable. This was the area known as the German Suburb, where a broad collection of soldiers, merchants, craftsmen and a variety of sundry specialists from all throughout Europe – having been barred residence within Moscow proper – had developed their own culture unique to their expatriate experience.

The livery at last stopped outside a beautiful English home. As the footman escorted Yvgeny and Thatcher from the carriage, the two stately doors of the mansion swung wide as Dr. Benyon, physician to the Tsar, appeared, wrapped in large heavy furs and an ermine hat. He made his way down the freshly cleared walk and greeted his old Russian friend with a hearty, magnanimous hug. Yvgeny wrapped an arm around his old friend. "Thatcher, I want you to meet a very old and dear friend, Dr. Robert Benyon. Doctor, this is my grandson, Yvgeny Thatcherev Edwards."

Thatcher stuck out his hand to shake the doctor's, marveling at the strength of the old man's grip. "It is a pleasure to finally make your acquaintance, Doctor. My grandfather has regaled me with many tales of you two and your long-abiding friendship."

As he shook his hand, Dr. Benyon could not hide his expression of amazement at the appearance of the nine-year-old Thatcher. His resemblance to another young man who had been in his care as a child and whom he continued to serve today was uncanny. That thick black hair, olive complexion and prominently Romanov brow made it painfully obvious which bloodline coursed through his veins.

"It is an absolute pleasure to make your acquaintance, Thatcher," Dr. Benyon replied, a twinge of nervousness striking him as he took in the image of the boy. "I knew your mother many years ago and was so happy to have her here as a guest."

"Which is what we're arranging now for you, Thatcher," Yvgeny interjected. "Dr. Benyon has graciously offered his home to you until I get settled. Come, let us get out of this cold, shall we?"

They settled in for the evening as Dr. Benyon regaled Thatcher of tales from his mother's visit and the joy she had brought to his home. Yvgeny likewise tapped the vast knowledge of Dr. Benyon to catch him up on events since his departure. He learned in detail about the period of Sophia's rule and the struggles within the boyar class. Yvgeny was surprised to learn that Peter, while taking control of the throne, was seldom found in the Kremlin but had taken up residence a bit further down the road at Preobrazhenskoe, the hunting lodge of Tsar Alexi. While he could be cajoled into returning to the Kremlin to conduct official business, at the conclusion of his day Peter would immediately mount his horse and, with the two hundred or so of his faithful retinue typically referred to as the Jolly Company in tow, sprint to return to his riverside home.

After a marvelous dinner, Yvgeny escorted Thatcher to his room where the two sat down for a very serious conversation. "My boy, I need for you to do me a favor and ask no questions. Only realize what I ask is vital," Yvgeny began.

"Anything, Grandfather," Thatcher replied without hesitation, realizing his response was a commitment to whatever his grandfather was asking.

"Tomorrow morning, I will go to the Kremlin to present myself first to the boyars and eventually to Tsar Peter. I do not know how long this will take, perhaps a day, perhaps a week, maybe longer. What

I need for you to do is to stay here until I come for you. It is very important that you do not inquire of anyone where I am or what I am doing. When I have conducted my business, I will come for you, I promise. But for the time being, I need you to stay here and trust me. Will you?"

"I have always trusted you, Grandfather, and I will always do what you say. But may I ask one question?" Thatcher queried.

Yvgeny smiled and replied to this most minimal of challenges, which was a characteristic of his grandson, "One question, Thatcher."

"Will you come back?"

Yvgeny thought for a moment, heavily aware of an urge to lie but knowing he could not. He smiled gently and replied, "Hopefully."

Thatcher could never know that in the weeks before they sailed for Russia, Yvgeny had plotted a meticulous plan to protect his grandson in the event things went very badly. Dr. Benyon had daily business at the Kremlin and an unrivalled network of contacts that would keep him abreast of Yvgeny's status. The moment any threat came to light, Dr. Benyon had arranged for a secret evacuation of Thatcher from Russia. Rather than taking the anticipated southern route to Kiev he would be transported north to the Gulf of Finland, where a ship was standing by to carry him back to England. It was hoped these precautions wouldn't be necessary, but with the state of things now occurring in Russia, there was absolutely no telling how threatening Thatcher's presence could be. Thatcher watched from the window as his grandfather exited the grand English estate in the heart of Russia and disappeared into the night.

Yvgeny woke early the next morning in his long shuttered home in the heart of Moscow. It was dusty and reeked of mildew and years of abandonment. Despite the harsh chill of the Moscow weather he reverted to form from his many decades in England by immediately unshuttering his windows to take in the sight of an absolutely glorious day. A fresh blanket of white covered the streets of the city, yet the sky was so blue as to make Moscow's standard grey appearance almost unbelievable. He looked across the cityscape toward the unmistakable landmark of St. Basil's spires. Dressing quickly and retrieving his papers, he began the twenty-block stroll and the steep climb of the prominent hill that led to the gates of the Kremlin.

The Streltsy guard who received him at the well-fortified gate reviewed the royal summons presented by him, then conferred with his Officer of the Day. Reviewing the documents himself, the young captain led Yvgeny through the crowded courtyard, past the copious collection of government and service buildings and between a collection of churches and chapels that filled the center of the massive royal complex. They entered the ornate chambers of the Palace of Facets and Yvgeny was graciously requested to be seated until he was called upon. The young captain retained the documents, carrying them with him as he passed into an anteroom and disappeared for some moments.

It had been a long time since Yvgeny had been inside this sumptuous palace. He thought of the occasions he had entered the Terem Palace, the private quarters of the Romanovs, where he had dined with Abigail and Tsar Fedor in much happier times. He reflected on that era, when life seemed to hold no limitations and his beloved Russia was entering a new phase of its long and magnificent history. He had tried not to give it thought, but he wondered whether this new Tsar would honor Alexis' vision as intently as Fedor and Sophia. He was lost in his thoughts when a retinue of Streltsy guard appeared in the chamber. The young captain politely requested him to please stand and follow him. The guard flanked them both as they proceeded deeper into the palace. They traveled down the long, lavish hall leading to the throne room then abruptly turned right down a side passageway and into a vast chamber. There, behind a massive desk, sat an old and familiar friend that at one time had been a source of comfort and friendship to Yvgeny. Tikhon Streshnev put down his quill and rose to cross the long room and greet his old friend from the past.

"Yvgeny Thatcherev! My, it has been so long since I have seen you! England has been good to you, no?" Streshnev smiled and vigorously shook his hand, conducting him to a comfortable set of oversized chairs next to a roaring fire. Yvgeny was surprised to see that Tikhon had survived the recent disturbances where his loyalties to the Tsar were called into question, yet somehow he had managed to survive the purges of Sophia's most loyal to rise as one of the most powerful men of Russia in his position as Conductor of All Home Affairs.

"I must confess, Streshnev, that I have grown very fond of England and much in love with my adopted home of Bristol," Yvgeny replied, taking a seat and the offering of hot tea.

"There were many who did not believe Yvgeny Thatcherev would return to Russia, but I knew you would. This is your home, and you are a loyal subject of Russia."

"I must again confess, Streshnev, that I had to give much thought to the request, but it is difficult to refuse an order from your Tsar, no matter how deep your trepidation."

Streshnev studied Yvgeny for a moment and smiled a broad smile. "But you are here and that is all that matters. And I know that Tsar Peter – and of course Ivan – are anxious to see one of their oldest and most trusted emissaries."

"Former emissary, Streshnev," Yvgeny corrected.

"Yes, yes, of course. I met with Sergei Evanovich when he arrived yesterday, and I was disheartened to hear that you were not with him. I had feared you weren't coming and would have been wrong about you."

"I had business to attend to before making my presence known. I apologize for any inconvenience."

"No inconvenience, Yvgeny. Our beloved Tsar Peter will be making his way in from Preobrazhenskoe ... in good time. He is so much like his father, with his love for that rustic lodge, so much more than the splendor of the Kremlin. In the meantime, Yvgeny, tell me all of what has happened in England since you departed."

While Yvgeny Thatcherev nervously pondered his fate in Moscow, Peter Ivanovich, Tsar of all Russia, was slowly waking after another long night of drinking, something he would much rather continue than attend to these affairs of state that dragged him into those stifling walls of the Kremlin. General Patrick Gordon, formerly of Scotland and in service to the Russian Tsars extending back to Peter's father Alexis, picked his way across the crowded dining chamber, stepping over the mass of men and women of questionable virtue still splayed where they had collapsed drunkenly on the floor. He stopped before Tsar Peter, who was half-sitting in a planter. Peter buttoned his trousers and moved aside the bare-breasted young German woman sprawled out next to him to find his missing shoe, then resentfully surrendered to the dutiful attendants who were making their best effort to properly dress him before his public appearance. Some of those in attendance began to stir, aware that their Tsar was on the move, his head now pounding from alcohol, tobacco, music and women indulged   to excess. One by one, the Jolly Company began to prod and poke one another into some pitiful semblance of life, themselves re-clothing from various states of undress.

"My apologies for having to roust you at such an ungodly hour, sir," Gordon offered, glancing at the clock upon the mantelpiece. It was nearly ten a.m.

"So is he here?" Peter mumbled as his attendants affixed his black tunic and made an attempt at a polish of his boots and smoothing of his trousers.

"He is at this moment with Streshnev," Gordon replied, helping Peter with his sword.

"And the boy?" Peter further inquired.

"In the German Quarter lodging with Doctor Benyon," Gordon answered.

"Well, then, for God's sake, let's get this under way," Peter commanded as his half-sodden retinue filled in behind him. They stumbled out of doors to the rows of freshly saddled horses, and bit by bit their brains began to emerge from their drunken stupor. By the time they had mounted, Peter's Jolly Company resembled the honor guard that had so frightened Sophia into surrendering her crown. The retinue galloped west, quickly reaching the German suburb en route to Moscow. When they reached the stately home of Dr. Benyon, Peter drew his black stallion to an abrupt and slippery halt, his companions following suit. At an upstairs window, a small dark-haired boy gazed down on the scene, no doubt drawn to the thunderous approach of two hundred horses hurtling down the wide boulevard. Their eyes locked for just a moment and then Tsar Peter doffed his tricorner hat and bowed every so slightly in salute to Thatcher Edwards. He smiled and then, as quickly as they had appeared, the company continued their mad charge toward Moscow.

From the 65-foot walls surrounding the Kremlin, the Streltsy guards observed the approach of the monarch, setting flag bearers to raise the standard of his presence and bell ringers to announce Peter's arrival from the triple stand of towers, sending lazy clerks and slovenly soldiers to the ready as the Captain of the Guard began his trip back down the long halls of the Palace of Facets to inform Tikhon Streshnev.

"Well, my dear Yvgeny, it appears our Tsar has arrived. Perhaps if we move quickly we can beat the Director of Foreign Affairs. He is usually the first to the chamber, and we do not want to have to wait for an endless parade of diplomats and foreign officers presenting credentials"

The very fact that Streshnev was making every attempt to put Yvgeny at ease actually had the reverse effect by compounding his discontent. He had fully expected that his days would be filled passing through the layers of petty functionaries and a gauntlet of boyars and God knew how many others who stood between the Kremlin Gate and the Tsar. Being as he no longer had any official title and, except for his dealings with trading partners throughout the city, he had had virtually no contact with official Russia for ten years, he was surprised by the royal treatment. Now, as he was once again joined by those same two ranks of Palace Guard conducting him and the Home Minister to the Throne Room, he found a new sense of discomfiture as it almost seemed as if he was being disposed of rather quickly. Out in the courtyard, Yvgeny could hear the din of men and horses arriving outside the Palace doors and could sense the general hubbub ensuing as his guard came to a halt. With confident steps, eighteen-year-old Peter the Great strode past the masses bowing in supplication before him. Both his age and years away from court had slowed Yvgeny's responses, and it took him a moment to realize that the monarch was now in his presence, and he was the only person still on his feet.

Peter could not help but notice the old man, the only one not yet on his stomach. He watched as the graying Russian slowly moved to demonstrate appropriate fealty to his Tsar. Peter stopped in his tracks, impeding the massing pack behind him who began to bunch up into one another not anticipating the Tsar's sudden halt, a sight and sound very amusing to the hung over monarch. He stepped over the first rank of prostrate subjects and caught Yvgeny at his shoulder just before his head could bend in appropriate respect.

"Yvgeny Thatcherev! I do remember you and your kindness to me and my mother. We have much to discuss, and I am glad you came." Peter's mannerisms and expressions, his words rolling with the confidence so reminiscent of his own grandson, both honored and frightened Yvgeny to the very core of his being. The Tsar's dark flashing eyes and mischievous smile would, in other circumstances, have put him at ease, but at this very second Yvgeny wished he had been a little faster to his knees so as not to draw the unnecessary attention. Peter smiled again, clicked his heels and mounted the four flights of stairs to the Tsar's Chambers to begin what he hoped would be one of his less mundane days astride his throne.

Much to his frustration, Tikhon Streshnev was beaten to court by the Foreign Minister as they joined a crowded anteroom. For what seemed like hours, he conducted the steady stream of commission-bearing diplomats who were paraded in to offer their credentials and the great wishes of their king for a long and successful rule of the Tsars, followed by an update on every aspect of their foreign policy with every nation as timely as the most up-to-date dispatches could reveal. At long last, Home Minister Streshnev was admitted to the Tsar's Reception Chamber and slowly and graciously made his way to the feet of his monarchs. Suddenly and unexpectedly, Peter breached protocol to interject before Streshnev could begin dispensing the day's business.

"Dear brother Ivan, as I know Minister Streshnev has much business to bring before us, it was my hope you would not mind if we take a somewhat different tack today. As you may have heard, we have guests. Would you mind, dear brother, if we make a slight change to the schedule for today?" Peter begged as respectfully as he could. Ivan's continued blank expression was all the agreement he required. "Good, then. Minister Streshnev," Peter redirected, indicating for the Minister to rise, "if you would, please."

Streshnev rose to his feet, bedecked in all of his Russian finery, and bowed slightly at the waist to his two Tsars. "Oh, great kings of all Russia, you have charged me with recalling key members of our great Empire who have ventured far and wide on our behalf and now return to kneel before you as a demonstration of their loyalty and fealty. Today one such great citizen of Russia has returned with love and worship. If you will permit me, I wish to introduce Yvgeny Thatcherev, former Trade Minister to Bristol in Great Britain."

Peter waved his hand to indicate his approval. Backing the entire distance of the magnificent Cross Chamber, Streshnev reached the Captain of the Guard who stood poised at the door and beckoned for him to admit Yvgeny. In seconds, the guard returned with Thatcherev. At the moment they fell under the gaze of the Tsars, both men bent deep at the waist and advanced in measured pace to the thrones, where they sank to their knees in fealty. As both men's faces were directed to the floor, Minister Streshnev began the introductions.

"My beloved kings, may I humbly present your loyal servant, Yvgeny Thatcherev of Pskov. Bow down in supplication to your lord, Yvgeny Thatcherev," Streshnev commanded. Yvgeny followed the ancient traditions, flattening himself before the Tsar in reverence, a position he had been unable to achieve quickly enough for good order a few hours before.

"Arise and be acknowledged, Yvgeny Thatcherev of Pskov," Peter commanded, extending his hand and the royal ring to be kissed. Yvgeny immediately offered the expected response and was surprised by the almost automatic repeat performance from the somniescent Ivan. In the ten years since he had last seen Ivan, the frail and feeble boy was a mere shell of himself. While his infirmities had been obvious even then, there was at least a hint of life, particularly in the presence of his stepmother Natalya. Now Ivan was little more than a wax caricature of a monarch. Yvgeny stood, placing himself squarely between the two monarchs, his head bowed and eyes to the ground in continued supplication.

"Let us look at you, Yvgeny Thatcherev of Pskov," Peter requested, his finger directing the raising of the old Russian's eyes to his. Yvgeny could now see that the cavalier figure that had strode past him earlier, the brash horseman, had been transformed into the very image of a king. Despite the obvious physical differences of the commanding Peter and the pathetic Ivan, both were dressed in the traditional long cloaks and embroidered garments of traditional Russia. Each wore a long heavy majestic robe of ermine, billowing out from the voluminous seats of their matching thrones. Heavy gold crowns bedecked with numerous jewels, symbols of Russia's mineral wealth, topped their long-wigged heads. But even more notable was the countenance of the young monarch, who at this very moment emanated all the majesty and greatness of the beloved and departed Alexis. Ivan, on the other hand, bore none of the countenance of royalty. His stare was vacant and his nearly transparent skin was lined with thin blue veins. An attendant stood at the ready to remove any trace of spittle that could not be contained within his mouth.

"It has been quite some time since my brother and I had the honor of your company, Yvgeny Thatcherev," Peter began. "It is my understanding you chose to surrender your official duties to return to England, no doubt to take advantage of your vast network of trading partners. Is this not true?" Peter inquired almost innocently.

Thatcherev pondered the question for a moment, deciding how best to proceed with such a direct and obviously misleading question. "It was truly a joy to have been honored in the presence of the royal family, both here in this majestic hall and in your private quarters. It had been my great joy to serve as this kingdom's envoy of trade to one of the many ports where my majesties honored them with the riches of our nation. However, as my duties could best be served in an unofficial capacity with the great assistance of your new envoy, Sergei Evanovich, I was pleased to do whatever I could to assure the continued success of Mother Russia," Yvgeny replied carefully.

"Tsar Fedor was always quite impressed with your capabilities on our behalf, Yvgeny Thatcherev. He was most impressed with your ability to work among the westerners and still maintain your Russian values. As I remember it, on your last visit you honored us with the presence of your adopted daughter, is that not true?"

"Yes, my Tsar. Her mother thought it would be of benefit to her education to see the magnificent homeland, which I proudly served."

"And your daughter – Abigail her name was, I believe – is she well?"

"Yes, your majesty. She and her mother are well and attending to our affairs in Bristol."

"I imagine she has become a quite capable young woman, Yvgeny Thatcherev. It is a shame she could not join you on this journey. Our entire family, particularly the former Tsar himself, Fedor, was quite enchanted with her."

"I was not bold enough to assume that such an august request referred to a family journey as your commission cited specifically my immediate return. As you know, Tsar, she is not a Russian citizen."

"This is true. She is certainly most English."

"Precisely, your majesty. That is why I took your summons as specific and responded to it post-haste."

"And yet you did not travel alone, did you, Yvgeny Thatcherev?" Peter toyed, a mischievous smile curling up on his lips.

"No, your majesty, I traveled in the company of Sergei Evanovich and another young Russian citizen." Yvgeny felt a cold chill creep up his spine.

"Yes, Yvgeny Thatcherev. I know about the young man of whom you speak. I saw him at the window of Dr. Benyon's home in the German Suburb as I was passing on my way here."

The cold chill overtook his entire body as Yvgeny Thatcherev's concern for his grandson for a moment overtook his sense of courtly decorum and his eyes firmly locked upon Peter's in a gesture many could mistake for insolence. Peter returned the gaze but his eyes softened at the expression of concern from the proud old Russian.

"He seems to have a great interest in horses. I think it was the sound of my retinue that attracted his attention to the window, as he seemed to take in the display with true boyish curiosity. As my dress was somewhat more casual than now, I'm not certain he recognized me. But I certainly recognized him."

Struck by the certainty of Peter's knowledge, Yvgeny struggled to find his voice. "He is a fine boy, your majesty, and as proud as he is of Russia, the homeland of his grandfather, your humble servant Yvgeny Thatcherev, he is purely a product of England and has a great future there."

"I'm sure under your tutelage he has become an amazing young man, Yvgeny Thatcherev of Pskov. In honor of his mother, whose company we so greatly enjoyed, it would be my great pleasure to get to know your grandson."

Yvgeny blood froze in his already chilly veins, and it took him a moment to respond. "Your majesty, no mere English boy could expect such a great honor from two such magnificent and no doubt busy Tsars. Certainly, while he would be most eager to comply, we do not wish to impose upon your majesties' precious time."

"Oh, but certainly, Yvgeny Thatcherev, I can and will make time for the child of someone whom our beloved departed Tsar Fedor so greatly admired. Thus it is settled. You and this young man ... what is his name?"

"Yvgeny Thatcherev Edwards, your majesty," Yvgeny replied, making certain to emphasize all three names clearly.

"Ah ... and so he takes his grandfather's proud name, and yet retains his mother's last name. Such western things are fascinating to me. Well, then, the two Yvgeny Thatcherevs will join me this evening at my home at Preobrazhenskoe. Minister Streshnev, if you please."

The Minister had been observing these exchanges quietly and intently, attempting to read the expressions and mannerisms of his monarch and former charge. There were times when it was difficult to interpret the Tsar's playful nature. While there had been rumors surrounding the return of Yvgeny Thatcherev, who had hastily departed Russia under suspicious circumstances, and his grandson, there were no official statements or suggestions that they should be of any circumstance to Peter or his family. Having been an intimate member of the Naryshkina household, Streshnev could never recollect any correspondence to or from Yvgeny Thatcherev of a personal nature, and while talk among the boyars had suggested his dissatisfaction with Fedor's matrimonial selection, none but the most intimate of whispers had suggested the two instances were in any way connected. No doubt these exchanges would fuel the rumors that had been whispered in the days of Tsar Fedor and would likely spark what should have been a long dead ember of gossip.

"Yes, your majesty," Streshnev replied, his head again respectfully bowed.

"Please have our guest escorted to Dr. Benyon's home, and have him and his grandson delivered to me this evening. We welcome you back to your home, Yvgeny Thatcherev, and trust you'll have a long productive stay amongst your people. Until this evening."

He and the automaton Ivan both extended their rings to be kissed, and Yvgeny Thatcherev and Minister Streshnev began their long slow bows out of the chamber. In moments, the two found themselves ushered into a royal carriage, escorted by their guard. As the coach began to roll out of the courtyard, two rows of horsemen dressed in the unique design of the Preobrazhensky Regiment fell in file along the lines of Streltsy who accompanied the carriage on foot.

Thatcher had passed the hours in the Benyon mansion with a book of Russian history, commissioned by Tsar Fedor the year of his death. The beautiful language penned in majestic Cyrillic calligraphy was accompanied by ornate plates bearing paintings of the beautiful Russian landscape and members of the Romanov family. One painting specifically held his fascination. The picturesque background depicted a sprawling wooden cottage set beside a meandering river, but it was the distinctive face of a boy standing in the foreground that intrigued him. For there, staring off the page, were the piercing eyes, the thick dark hair, the regal nose and defiant chin that had looked back at him from the mirror for years.

His rapt attention was broken once again by the sound of many hooves approaching down the lane. This time, rather than peering through the window, Thatcher went to the door that opened into the snow covered English garden separating the house from the street. He was amazed to see this time a smaller company of horsemen, flanking a row of marching soldiers who escorted an ornate carriage being pulled by a team of horses as white as the snow on which they trod. The distinctive symbol of the Romanov family was emblazoned on the side of the carriage, and he was a bit taken aback when the assemblage stopped at the gate of the Benyon home. The young officer who had been astride the lead horse affixed to the carriage dismounted and walked back to its street-side door. An impressive gentleman emerged, dressed in a dark fur robe, and behind him was his grandfather. The horsemen and soldiers formed a corridor from the street to the front gate, the young officer trailing Streshnev and Yvgeny as they walked toward the house. The old Minister looked up at the young boy standing in the doorframe, and his jovial expression changed abruptly to one of uncomfortable surprise. Thatcher walked down the steps, meeting his grandfather halfway down the walk. Yvgeny maintained a calm expression and walked briskly to his grandson, placing his arm around his shoulder to introduce the Minister.

"You have returned much sooner than you had suggested, grandfather," Thatcher stated as Yvgeny led him to meet his old friend and escort.

"Ah, court business moved much quicker than I had expected, my boy. Yvgeny Thatcherev Edwards, it is my pleasure to introduce a very old friend, the Home Minister for all of Russia, Tikhon Streshnev. Dear Minister, my grandson and namesake, Yvgeny Thatcherev Edwards."

Streshnev had to fight the instinct to bow supplicant there in the snow of that German Suburb sidewalk, but remembering his place both as a servant to the Tsars and a leader of his people, he buried his urge and stuck out his hand in greeting to the boy. "Yvgeny Thatcherev Edwards, on behalf of my kings, the Tsars of Russia, Ivan and Peter, we welcome you to our homeland and request your presence at the private estate of Tsar Peter."

Thatcher turned his widened eyes to his grandfather, a million questions on his face. "Tikhon, perhaps I should take young Thatcher inside and find him some appropriate dress for our appointment. Will you please excuse us?" Yvgeny asked.

Streshnev nodded agreement, then conferred with the captain of the guard. As Yvgeny led his grandson to the house, half the assemblage of foot soldiers made sentry outside the gate while the other half fanned across the snow of the frozen English garden to take up their post at the back door.

It had long been known that outside of court Peter favored western dress. Thus as they had done for so many years, grandson and grandfather donned their heavy black wool tunics, black wool breeches and heavy black buckled boots. Because of the frozen weather, they added to their ensembles two large matching black bear coats with hoods to shield them from the Russian cold. In the short time they had together, Yvgeny did his best to fully inform his grandson of the events of the day while at the same time reassuring him with his normal dose of skepticism.

As the winter sky began to grow dark, a great thunder of hooves once again heralded the arrival of the Jolly Company, and again the retinue paused outside the Benyon home, all carriages and traffic coming to a halt for the king's accompaniment. Thatcher peeked from his window and could see Peter conversing with General Gordon, the captain of the horsemen who had accompanied the carriage. They and a number of riders in the company seemed to be laughing about something and having a jolly time indeed. Joining their comrades, the escort cavalry remounted their horses and together they all stormed in the direction from which they had come earlier in the day.

The captain of the Streltsy guard summoned his charges, and when Yvgeny and Thatcher departed Dr. Benyon's house, they found the two rows of guards now stretching from the door of the home to the door of the carriage. The captain fell behind the two of them as they made their way down the rows of Russian soldiers. He reached around to open the door, extending his hand to assist their climb into the high rise carriage. Fully expecting the soldiers to once again fall in alongside, Yvgeny was surprised when the Streltsy turned and began marching back in the direction of Moscow. With a click of the reins, the carriage proceeded unescorted the short distance to Preobrazhenskoe as the beauty of the German Suburb fell behind them.

In short order, the carriage came to a halt. Rather than a disciplined captain to open the door for them, the footman who had ridden silently at the back of the carriage appeared, handing the two men down to face Preobrazhenskoe. Thatcher recognized the simple riverside structure, which stood in dramatic contrast to the ornate and regal citadel of the Kremlin, as Alexis' hunting lodge from the picture in his book. He was surprised not only by the simplicity of the structure but also by the fact that no guard or security was to be seen anywhere upon the grounds. The massive barn overflowing with sweaty horses and the loud din emanating from the shuttered wooden house indicated a very heavy presence of life as the two stood, staring at the front door, awaiting some sort of escort. After a moment of stark realization that no one was coming, they mounted the steps and lifted the simple wooden door handle of the rambling hunting lodge.

The two entered and were met by a cacophony of life and firelight. A laughing young man, whose whole duty seemed to be to make sure that no one crossed the threshold without a tankard of ale, offered greetings and waved at the impossible to ignore assemblage of Russian and European men, some still decked out in various pieces of their black uniforms, and a bevy of beautiful German, Dutch, French and English women. While no strangers to bawdy environs, the two were absolutely overwhelmed with the chaotic joy permeating the entire structure. Their eyes swept the crowd of soldiers and hard-drinking women, hoping for a sign of their host. Off in the corner was a collection of musicians, whipping off a wild German reel. And as their eyes fell upon the mirthful troubadours, at last they spotted Tsar Peter. Rather than sitting at the head of some lavish table holding court, the king of all Russia was swinging violently with two large mallets, beating briskly in time with the music on the sheepskin-stretched head of a drum. Pounding away with abandon, he appeared more a mere boy playing a cadence to war rather than the most powerful man in all the frozen north. When he finally noticed his guests, he stood up, screaming above the chaos to get the attention of his Jolly Company.

"Men! Men! You drunken bunch of sots, be quiet for a moment," he shouted, throwing one of the mallets at a particularly noisy group. "I have been telling you all for quite some time of the lovely guest my brother, our beloved Tsar Fedor, entertained some number of years ago." The noise began to rise again as the assemblage toasted their approval of a story they were all quite familiar with and seemed to take quite a bit of joy in its reference. "All right, all right. Now, as many of you know, we are here for a number of reasons. One is to celebrate the upcoming birth of my child. And the other is to welcome another child into our fold. For my friends, standing before you is the very offspring of that enchanting young Englishwoman who graced our country with her presence and then, alas, stole away. My friends, may I introduce to you Yvgeny Thatcherev, our former emissary, and his grandson, Yvgeny Thatcherev Edwards!"

The din immediately returned tenfold as Peter's Jolly Company toasted the arrival of two prodigal sons. The old priest was quite overwhelmed with this totally unexpected display serving as an introduction of his young charge to the Tsar of Russia. Not wishing to show his unease, he raised his tankard in acknowledgement and waved it to the celebrating assemblage. Thatcher, on the other hand, betrayed a completely different countenance. What would seem to be an overwhelming introduction into a bawdy company of hard-drinking men, one of which was not only his uncle but the king of Russia, for some reason felt quite comfortable and natural. He raised his cup, not to the assemblage but to his host who was studying him with a very curious eye, and paused with his vessel outstretched to Tsar Peter as the crowd slowly dulled to silence.

"No, to you sir!" Thatcher stated simply as he drank down a healthy gulp of the bitter German beer that filled the tankard. His action, bold, fearless and absolutely appropriate, sent Peter into roars of approving laughter as he pushed his way over a table of men who sat between him and his guests. He placed a firm, rough hand on each shoulder, gripping them like iron, smiling and laughing with abandonment.

"My God, Yvgeny Thatcherev, if he isn't a handsome boy," he roared to the approval of all in accompaniment.

"Well, there's no point in standing on ceremony. Tsar Peter, let me introduce you to my grandson," Yvgeny pronounced proudly.

"Thatcherev, there are no Tsars here, only men who drink and women who serve them. Tsars reside in palaces. Do you see any palace here?" He turned and looked at the tall boy and smiled with a sense of absolute familiarity. "You will find we don't stand on much pretense around here, and titles are left at the door. So young man, what should I call you?"

"Thatcher. They call me Thatcher. And I should call you ... Peter?" Once again, Peter howled at the boldness of the boy, who seemed to fall right in with his company. He grabbed their hands and led them wading through the mass of humanity to an enormous roasted pig spread across the entire length of a table. He gestured them to sit down and from out of nowhere produced a huge curved knife that for just a second sent a shot of alarm through Yvgeny. His fears were quickly allayed as Peter thrust the knife deep into the pig, wedging off huge handfuls of hot, dripping pork for each of his guests. Yvgeny Thatcherev and his young grandson would find themselves being severely chastised for their manners by Beatrice and Abigail were they to witness this display of barbarian vulgarity as the three bit into huge hunks of flesh, washing them down with ample mouthfuls of bitter German beer.

During the early parts of the evening, Peter seemed to give no acknowledgement of the two, other than as new faces amongst a common assembly. Buxom young women continued to bring out ample supplies of ale, pig and breasts, as well as to refill the pipes with much-coveted Virginia tobacco. The loud conversations that filled the room as heavily as the clouds of smoke took on a variety of natures, including the state of trade, wealthy new lands to exploit and seemingly inappropriate jesting at the expense of the Patriarch and the boyars, where no amount of taunting and mocking was censored. Alcohol filled the senses of the assembled company, including the nine-year-old boy who was no stranger to drink but had never sampled quite so potent and bitter an ale. He and his grandfather fell right in with this company as if they were born to it.

As tables were cleared and tankards took a place upon the floor, rubles were pulled from pockets as violent games of ninepin began to ring throughout the chamber. When a buxom, raven-haired beauty placed herself firmly on Yvgeny's lap and pulled his face into her chest, certainly he could be forgiven if he could not help but to rub his pork fat-filled beard vigorously into that canyon of cleavage. And all around them, young maids relinquished their responsibilities of serving meat and beer and found themselves replacing the pigs upon the tables and serving themselves. Tolerance of such behavior seemed out of character for these two, for as masters of the brothel they would never permit these breaches of protocol from their own customers and would cast a man into the alley to sleep with the cats and vagrants were he to display such vulgar behavior. And yet in this cloister of men in this country where women were much more subservient than even the most patriarchal of Europe, the Russianness in Yvgeny and Thatcher seemed to rise up from a depth long buried amongst the English gentility.

As the night grew long and alcohol and sexual exhaustion began to waylay many of the assembled, Peter pushed aside a particularly winsome lass, who someone had mentioned was French, and hitched his drawers to seek out his guests. To his dismay, but not to his surprise, Yvgeny had succumbed to the stimulation of the evening. Trying diligently to be a good protector and guardian of his grandson, somewhere in the night he had opted for posting vigil from the floor under a table, no doubt guarding the sheep he was counting. Thatcher, on the other hand, had found a different interest, enjoying the rapt attention the ladies seemed to have for his curly black mane, a twosome of which were gyrating away as he took his place joyfully upon the drum. The sight overwhelmed Peter with pleasure, and he clapped his hands against the tankard he held, spilling beer with every beat. He gave a playful squeeze to a breast of each beauty entertaining the boy and pulled him away to engage him in conversation.

Peter grabbed a decanter of bread wine in one hand as he wrapped his arm around the boy with the other, leading him to a table a bit away from the drunken din. He pulled out his sword and cut off the end of the bottle, spilling a few drams on the floor. He took a long pull and passed it to the nine-year-old. Without hesitating, Thatcher mimicked his uncle, but despite his brave exterior he could not help but let out a furious cough from the potent clear elixir. Peter laughed, slapping the boy heartily on his back.

"Well, it is good to know that there may be one thing I am not bested at by a nine-year-old," Peter roared, taking another solid pull of the bottle. "So, Thatcher, what do you think of all this?"

Thatcher thought for a moment and smiled. "I guess, Peter, it is everything a boy could ask for. I thought that the Kremlin was your palace but, seeing the life you lead and the company you prefer to keep, I think your father's hunting lodge is a fitting place to play."

Peter smiled. "Ah, so you are a smart boy. But Preobrazhenskoe is more than just a hunting lodge, Thatcher. Because it was his favorite retreat away from the boyars and functionaries that made the Kremlin a beehive of activity, Preobrazhenskoe was Tsar Alexi's favorite place to meet and entertain ambassadors and emissaries from throughout the known world. This," Peter gestured, "was his favorite place of all. This was the Comedy Horomina, Russia's very first theater. Because acting was unheard of in Russia, my father imported German actors to perform on his stage. With them he created a theatre school where German and Russian children learned the craft. You are cultured boy. Of course you are familiar with the theatre. I'm sure you have seen the plays of Shakespeare."

"My family is partial to Richard Edwardes, actually," Thatcher responded. "Though, I do like the words of Edward Dyer." Thatcher paused for a second. "'My mind to me a kingdom is, such present joys therein I find. That it exceeds all other bliss, That earth affords or grows by kind, Though much I want that most would have, Yet still my mind forbids to crave.'"

Peter stood and applauded. "Very impressive Thatcher. You are a perfect fit with my Jolly Company. You see, all these young men were actors and performers with the Comedy Horomina. That is, of course, until my father died. And because it brought him so much joy and Russia a little closer to being like our western neighbors, my sister Sophia had it shut down and all Romanov life, official or otherwise, confined behind the walls of the Kremlin and my mother and me with these ne'er do wells to fend for ourselves at Preobrazhenskoe. To some the Kremlin it is a fortress. To me it is a prison. But you, Thatcher. Your mind is your kingdom. You are a man who can be content anywhere."

"The prerogative of being the Tsar of Russia is that you can choose to rule from wherever makes you happy. Preobrazhenskoe and your Jolly Company make you happy. Who has the right to judge you?"

"It does make me happy. Ever ramshackle, noise filled inch of it. But not what you would expect from the king of all Russia, would you Thatcher?"

"I have found that there is a bit of boy in the most regal and elegant of men. From what the ladies of my home tell me, it seems that even the most sober vicar craves infantile playtime and is willing to pay well for it. Why should the Tsar of Russia be any different?"

Peter studied the boy, looking for a hint of disapproval, condemnation or subtext to his words, but those bright eyes revealed only a young man who knew and had seen more than his youthful eyes should reveal. In that expression, Peter saw much of himself in Thatcher. "So what are your thoughts on my country, young Mr. Edwards?" Peter asked, truly curious to know what this very candid young man had to say on the subject.

"I find Russia a study in contradictions." Peter took that in for a second and gestured the bottle at Thatcher both to take a pull and continue with his observation. "I see a deeply religious country and a very serious people who desperately want to break out and enjoy life. Everyone I've met in your country is very polite and very suspicious, yet like the weather itself very cold and beautiful. I can't help but believe that there is a warmth and a fire awaiting some sort of ... spring."

"I like the way you see my Russia, Thatcher," Peter replied, nodding his head and taking another long draw from the mutilated bottle. "But I think to know Russia is to see it in those moments immediately when the long winter had yielded to the insistence of the sun, and spring comes whether winter likes it or not. Then, Thatcher, then you truly see Russia."

"I think that is one of the reasons why my grandfather holds so firmly to his religious traditions, for as you describe it, it seems that the rising of his soul melts away any coldness of his loneliness and yearning for Russia," Thatcher offered as much to himself as to Peter.

"Ah, so he is still practicing Orthodoxy? I would have thought by now, in all his years in England, he would have yielded to the insistence of the Protestant faith," Peter replied, a little surprised at this revelation.

"Yvgeny is like Russia, a study of contradictions. While he can at one moment glory in the rituals and traditions of his religion, in the next moment he can revel in the writings of the free thinkers who challenged the slavery of Orthodoxy. I think it is the conflict that most appeals to Yvgeny, less than the resolution to be found in the dogma. Then again, he has been a great missionary on behalf of the Russian Orthodox faith, for both my mother and I have been baptised in your traditions."

"And this was your choice, Yvgeny Thatcherev Edwards?"

"Well, the choice of my baptism was of course my mother's. Hers, on the other hand, was of free will. I think her time here in Russia made her find something that she could believe in, and while not as Orthodox as either my grandfather or mother, I must say I do find the rituals fulfilling."

"And of your father, Yvgeny Thatcherev Edwards – what do you know of him?"

This was a question that Thatcher had known would be coming at some point, and he had carefully rehearsed his speech for such an occasion that was neither a lie but at the same time certainly not the blatant truth. Yet at this moment, he did not feel like standing on pretense. "I know that my mother loved him as no man before and no man since. I know that in England she had a body and mind, but with him she found and lost a soul." Thatcher let that sink in for a second, staring intently at the man that could likely be his executioner. "I know that my mother never got over him, and she never got over this place. She may have tried to dismiss it as the awakening of a young girl's love, but I know that had she been able to stay here with him, he would be alive today, and she ..."

"She would what, Thatcher?" Peter insisted.

"She would be happy. My mother has done all she can in our unique world to make me as happy as possible. But I think it has come at the price of her own happiness."

"I remember your mother well, Thatcher. She was not the first foreign woman to turn the heads of Russian men, but I can tell you she was one of the most memorable. And I'm not telling you anything you don't know, but it's not just her beauty and elegance. There is a something to her I can't quite explain."

"I can tell you, Peter. It's because no matter how many people may be in a room she has the capability of making you feel as if you are the only one there and the only one that ever mattered. This is a fact any man who has known her can attest, most assuredly that old man there" indicating the snoring Yvgeny under the adjacent table, "and me, and I guess most importantly my father."

"And me," Peter added, finishing the few drops of one bottle and drawing his sword to cut off the end of another. "You know, Thatcher, I was about your age when I met her. I can tell you in those times her kindness to my mother and me was much appreciated. I mean, not that anyone was cruel or malicious – no one would be that way to us. We could always count on the gushing attention from anyone who came within our presence. But it was her interest in whomever she spoke to that really set her apart. I mean, I knew why she was there and why she always came and why she always stayed. But it was those times when she would sit and talk with me out of the earshot of my mother and the guardians and my brother, where she'd sit and listen to me. Those eyes, Thatcher, your mother's eyes are so warm. I was so sorry to see her go, but as you can guess there were complications."

"There are always complications, Tsar Peter. I think we cannot help ourselves but complicate the most simple of things. But I guess in the end are we any better, beyond our simplicities?"

Peter's head turned to look into the face of Thatcher and for the briefest of moments he saw a ghost. "You know, I have heard such a very similar thing said before. Do you know where you heard it?"

Thatcher thought for a moment, and replied, "No, not that I can recall, Peter. It just came to me."

"I can tell you where I heard it. I could not have been more than, what, three years old I would guess. Yes, I must have been about three, because it was the one and only time that my father ever had the chance to take me falconing. We came here after we had tramped after his falcons all day long. And he was sitting here at this table, cleaning rabbits. It was just the two us. And my father was very happy and contemplating his life beyond the throne. He did not look like the Tsar of Russia. He looked like any common man who had successfully hunted for his supper, and I remember he said to me, 'Life is so complicated, Peter, and really are we any better beyond our simplicities?'" The two sat for a moment as the noise began to die down around them. The Jolly Company had accomplished their goal and had become the Sodden Company, and one by one each had fallen off to enjoy the embrace of Bacchus. "Yes, Thatcher, I want you to see my Russia when spring bursts forth. I think it's something you owe yourself. No, I think I owe you. You will stay to see the arrival of my son, of my child, the heir to the throne. I want to show you my boats and my armies. I want you to see what Russia is and what it is becoming. Will you stay?"

Thatcher didn't require even a second to think about it, though he knew he may have quite the task of convincing Yvgeny that not only was this a dream come true but a continuation of his Tsar's command. "I would love to see your boats, Peter. I would like to see your Russia because I know there's so much to see."

"It is not just my Russia, Thatcher. It is the Russia of your father and all of his ancestors and the blood that has been spilled to build this magnificent kingdom. So I must ask you again, Thatcher, has your mother told you much about your father?"

"She has told me all she could relate about those brief six months she was allowed to be in his presence. And of course there is what I have been able to piece together from all I have read."

Peter smiled, filled two cups and took a long pull of his tankard. He smiled, than put a hand on his nephew's shoulder. "Well, then, Thatcher, let me tell you about your father ..."

Yvgeny woke some hours later from his curled position underneath that rough-hewn table, still dripping with beer and pig grease. Some chesty wench had curled up beside him, unbuttoned from stem to stern, and seemed not the least bit concerned when his sore body and brittle bones attempted to climb over her. What a sight it must have been to see the old cleric crawling head first from between the legs and from beneath the table, the sufferings of his body and the ravages of his mind turning his face into that of a suffering newborn child. It took him a moment to recollect his surroundings, and he was suddenly struck by a rush of panic as he searched the room, looking for his grandson. A loud explosion from outside the lodge sent courses of adrenaline rushing to his previously feeble body as he scrambled out the door in fear and desperation.

Peter and Thatcher were about a hundred feet away from the house as the boy was lifting a heavy musket, trailing a flying bird just flushed by a pack of hounds. Once again a loud explosion emitted from the ponderous weapon on the young man's shoulder, yet despite his best effort the barn raised grouse continued on with his desperate flight unscathed. Yvgeny trudged quickly across the frozen snow-covered ground and joined the young hunters.

"... and you must remember it is critical that you take into consideration the slight delay of the slow match as it ignites the powder. You must lead the bird," Peter instructed, his tone a measured patience as he took great joy in beginning the martial instruction of his young nephew.

Thatcher looked up to see his grandfather and waved a hand in joy to see him. "Good morning, Grandfather! Uncle Peter has been trying to teach me how to use this musket to bring down a bird. He makes it look so simple. Look! We've already bagged four this morning."

The shock of Thatcher's cavalier salutation of the Tsar of Russia took Yvgeny by surprise at this way-too-early hour of the morning, relatively speaking. He noticed Peter's expression bore a hint of satisfaction at the obvious progress made over the course of a drink-filled evening.

"Good morning, Yvgeny Thatcherev. My, but I thought you would sleep the day away. But then again, you looked so comfortable curled up with the ever-accommodating Heloise. No one could in good conscience wake you. I am surprised, Yvgeny Thatcherev, that under your careful instruction you may have taught this boy much, but you failed to instruct him in the most Russian of arts ... the downing of defenseless birds! Pray tell, why have you shirked on your responsibilities to my nephew?"

Yvgeny was speechless. To be chided first thing in the morning with swollen joints, a pounding head and hair and beard filled with the most devilish of offal by his grandson and the Tsar of Russia was just a bit too much to comprehend. He stood there assessing the two, standing side by side, each with a hand cocked upon his waist, staring with rapt amusement at the old Russian cleric.

"Have you forgotten how to fire a musket, Yvgeny? If I remember, the priests of Pskov claimed their prowess in arms as a hallmark of their order. Am I wrong?" Peter gently chided, handing a freshly loaded musket to Yvgeny.

Yvgeny once again assessed the two and lifted the loaded weapon to his shoulder. "And what shall I be downing today?"

Peter waved his hand in the air, and from behind a snow-encased wagon the distinctive flutter of wings could be heard. The handlers released a quail that had been lovingly raised better than the average Russian for the purpose of Peter's entertainment. Despite his aching head and the many years that had passed since he had hefted a weapon, there was a moment of pride that took over Yvgeny as that unmistakable sound of a bird in flight rang in his ears. He guided into his periphery and, as Peter had just instructed Thatcher, the barrel trailed out in front of the fleeing quail as the slow match ignited the charge, exploding and hurling the iron shot on a perfect trajectory to fell the prey. As Yvgeny's eyes tracked the downward spiral of the slaughtered bird, the handlers who had seconds before released it quickly made their way across the snow to retrieve the prize. Yvgeny turned to Peter, handing him back the spent weapon, a slightly cocky smile crinkling the corners of his voluminous, greasy moustache.

"Perhaps, when I have a chance to re-attune my reflexes, I will be able to more effectively demonstrate the validity behind the boast of the priests of Pskov," Yvgeny commented, noting the amazement of Thatcher and Peter.

"So we've spent the evening talking, and young Thatcher and I agree that he must allow his Russian side to fully manifest. Therefore, with your permission of course, I have made arrangements for Yvgeny Thatcherev Edwards to take boarding with a trusted member of my foreign guard. I am sure there is much you wish to do while you are back home, and Dr. Benyon is a fine man; however, perhaps a bit too staid for the curious mind of such a boy as he. Would you permit Thatcher this opportunity?" Peter asked quite politely, but under the circumstances most pointedly.

"Grandfather, you were telling me how you were so looking forward to returning to Pskov to visit old friends, and I promise Dr. Benyon will know of my whereabouts at all times." Thatcher's face was virtually pleading. While Yvgeny could not measure the tone of the conversation the night before, it was obvious that these two had struck some sort of accord. Still, there was no telling how the blush of this new toy could in time fall out of favor with the youthful Tsar.

As if reading his mind, Peter offered, "Yvgeny Thatcherev, as long as you and your grandson are on Russian soil, you are under the protection of Tsar Peter Ivanovich, as if you need to be reminded."

Yvgeny nodded his head in resignation that neither Peter nor Thatcher would take no for an answer. And as they talked, a small platoon of Peter's most trusted company was arriving at Dr. Benyon's home to remove Thatcher's personal effects. In his hand, Dr. Benyon held a note, penned by his Tsar, thanking him for his care and discharging him of any further responsibilities for his young guest. The three walked to the lodge where they dressed and roasted their freshly killed birds for their noonday meal. Following lunch, the carriage which had carried them to the lodge returned, and Yvgeny Thatcherev bid good-bye to his grandson for what he hoped would be a short separation. He looked out the rear of the carriage where a footman crouched underneath the opening, and over the top of his hat he could see the two waving at him.

After watching the old man disappear down the lane, Peter and Thatcher walked to the stables where matching black mounts had been saddled in waiting. They whipped the horses into a full run, proceeding along the twisting trail beside the Yauza River. Their path would carry them back to the German Suburb, bypassing Dr. Benyon's stately residence, and bringing the two foam flecked horses to a halt in front of the residence of Edmund Drummond. Like so many of his countrymen before him, Edmund Drummond had escaped the highlands of Scotland during the great purge of Bloody Lord Oliver Cromwell. Having fought on the side of King Charles I, there would be no refuge of safety in all of Great Britain for any Scotsman or Catholic after Cromwell had taken the Papist head of King Charles. Tsar Alexis had been a close friend and intimate of Charles, and his anger at the beheading of the sovereign of England created a rage in him that nearly led to the expulsion of all English on Russian soil. In Moscow, more specifically the German Suburb, Scottish Jacobites were offered safe refuge under the protection of Alexis and welcomed into service on behalf of Russia.

Edmund Drummond departed his home in Inverness, leaving behind his wife, children and lands, to take up exile with his fellow royalists in the frozen expanses of Russia. Unlike many Europeans, Scots had fewer problems acclimatizing to the harshness of the Russian winter, having endured countless generations in the freezing reaches of the Scottish highlands. He had always wondered what made his father William desire to return to the English colony of Albemarle in Virginia with its sweltering heat not fit for Scotsman or beast. Granted, initially, he had little choice in the matter as he had sailed as an indentured servant, leaving his young wife and son alone to fend for themselves. His father had chosen to stay in the colonies where he rose to become a justice of the peace and sheriff and quite astoundingly, the first ever governor of Albemarle Sound when Virginia Governor William Berkeley so appointed him at the behest of the Lords Proprietors. Edmund had always hoped his father would send for him. Like his father and countless Drummonds before them he had mastered the forge and pounded the steel into some of the finest weapons of war. But that call never came and like a good Catholic he had followed his king into battle to its bloody conclusion. His skills as a master swordsman and former officer in service to King Charles made him a much sought-after commodity to the burgeoning Russian military. Serving under the command of General Gordon, he was set to improving both the mastery of swordsmanship and working with the Russian craftsmen to make improvements to the primitive cutlery of the Russian arsenal.

Edmund Drummond would gladly do whatever his Tsar commanded. He was much taken aback, however, when Thatcher Edwards was introduced to him, and both were informed that the boy was to be in his care and under his training for the foreseeable future. Only hours before, he had made his way home from the night of revelry, where he noticed how these two had seemed to form an immediate bond. There was no doubting that their young Tsar had taken a liking to the boy, and many speculated what the final disposition of this young new "visitor" would be. Edmund Drummond had bet that Tsar Peter would not muss a single hair on the boy's head. Having been in Russia now since before Peter was born, Drummond knew the character of Tsar Alexis, who had taken him into his foreign guard and who had retreated to Preobrazhenskoe and began the tradition of bonding with his foreign soldiers. When Peter was born and his fat little naked body was displayed for the first time by Tsar Alexis, there was a look that the king of Russia gave when he stared at that pudgy infant, and that look had been seen in the face of this Tsar when he sat upon his horse, looking up in the window of Dr. Benyon's house.

"I think Peter up there has taken a shining to the lad," Edmund Drummond commented to General Gordon.

"I don't know, Drummond," Gordon replied. "Peter is still feeling a little nervous about potential usurpers to his throne. I don't feel as confident as you do about the fate of that wee bairn."

"Fifty rubles and a new sword says that boy is a twinkle in Peter's eye, General."

"What, you'll make me a new sword if he kills the kid?"

"I'll make a hilt out of his jawbone if he does."

"You've got yourself a wager then, Drummond."

The fifty rubles that General Gordon had dropped off that morning gave Drummond a true sense of satisfaction. But it also made him just a bit nervous when he was informed that he was taking on this new boarder.

"So, Colonel Drummond," Thatcher queried as he was shown to the well appointed guest room he was to occupy in Drummond's house. It was a very masculine room, but not in an overly manly sense, for while it had weapons – guns, pistols, swords – Thatcher could not help but note how each of them had been made for what appeared to be a smaller grip, for the swords were not as long and the pistol guards not as wide as the full sized versions. "I hope I'm not putting anyone out of his room."

Drummond shook his head. "No, lad, no one lives in this house but me. When I built it, it was my hope that my wife and children would join me here in Russia. This room here I built for my son, Robert. Unfortunately, he and his two sisters and my wife fell under Cromwell's sword. So, they never made it to Russia, and I never had any reason to go back to Scotland. You're the first person to occupy the room, boy." Drummond walked to the wall where two sabers of approximately two-thirds dimension hung, crossed, and removed one. He handed it to Thatcher, who felt its weight and grasp. Indeed, it was a young man's sword, yet it possessed all the lethality of its full-size cousin. In the right hands this could be deadly. Drummond looked as the boy admired the sword and smiled with satisfaction. "I'll teach you how to use that thing like a real cavalryman. And when you get expert at that," he commented as he reached from the opposite wall and took down a much more primitive and likewise more lethal battle-ax of the same scale, "I'll teach you how to heft this thing like a Highlander."

IV

As the stubbornness of winter gave way to the persistence of spring, Thatcher began to absorb this annual rite of Russia, where the landscape arose from its colorless hibernation to the brilliance of rainbow-strewn beauty as the snows yielded to the upthrust of grasses, providing a firm and nutritious footing for the eruption of countless sprays of early spring flowers. The sun began to shine persistently longer and longer each day, and the thick blankets of snow slowly began to melt, coursing across frozen planes and ice covered lakes and rivers. Their constant movement and rising temperature slowly but surely began to first crack and then break the thick sheets of ice that had brought these massive bodies of water to a standstill. These movements of ice and fillings of streams and rivers signaled the movement of nautical traffic, first in narrow channels and then in broadening rivers, allowing merchants, farmers and peasants at last to begin to use these traditional routes to move their goods to markets near and far.

While Thatcher began to settle into his new routine of training and appreciation of the annual re-birth of Russia, Yvgeny began his journey north some five hundred miles to his beloved hometown of Pskov. Unlike the merchants who waited in great anticipation for the melting of the snows, Yvgeny in contrast hoped that the ground that traveled beneath the skids of the sleigh in which he rode would continue to stay frozen for at least the length of his trip. To Russians, ice and snow were not curses but much-desired means of smooth travel throughout the rural hinterlands that composed the vast majority of this extensive nation. While spring brought a colorful beauty to the landscape, melted ice and snow turned slick sheets of ice into impassable bogs of mud, making travel both filthy and multiple times longer. To his great joy, snow still fell as the old cleric's weeks-long journey north at last came to an end.

The driver carried him through the picturesque city as he enjoyed the peals of noontime bells, seeming to extend a personal welcome to one of its long-lost sons. His eyes beheld the ancient wooden structures, still shuttered against the onslaught of winter cold as he passed through the silent streets. He craned his neck to take in the familiar landmarks of a much happier time in his life and reveled in the joy he felt as he remembered when he and his beloved Katarina would enjoy long walks into the village to watch their sons frolic on the green. He felt a stab to his heart as he remembered that last winter and the promise he had made to his deathly ill Nicolai, that as soon as spring had come they would once again walk to play among the ancient trees of the frozen forest that stood as sentinels on their jaunts to Pskov. Spring was still long to come when first Nicolai, then young Steven and finally his beloved Katarina succumbed to the cough that strangled them. The season took on a totally different meaning as the retreat of winter would at last require him to bury his entire family within the freshly thawed earth of the cathedral cemetery. On the day he buried them, he walked away from Pskov, swearing he would never return. Yet now as the driver halted outside that same cemetery, for the first time he would allow himself to let his tears flow freely and join the snow that encapsulated their graves.

Pskov was an ancient place with families long devoted to loyal supplication and reverence to their ancient practices. As he had been preparing for midday service, Marcellus had noticed the sleigh bearing the signs of distant travel pull past the cathedral and stop at the gates of its cemetery. While visitations to these sacred grounds were not uncommon, the figure that exited the sleigh moved with a cadence familiar to the Metropolitan. His duties distracted him from further inquiry, and he proceeded with services giving no further thought to the visitor. It was later that one of his altar boys reminded him, reporting his concern for the pitiful condition of a man he had seen in the cemetery. Marcellus donned his heavy outer coat and made his way across the grounds to inquire if his assistance was needed, but once he recognized the location where the weeping figure lay prostrate, he knew well the mourner. Rather than disturb a long overdue reunion, Metropolitan Marcellus left Yvgeny Thatcherev to his grieving, knowing that in a few days he would visit his old friend at the long-abandoned home on Lake Pskov.

It was nearly dark when Yvgeny Thatcherev at last stood at the doorway of his home along the banks of Lake Pskov, which he had loved and cherished so much. He had built it as a wedding gift for Katarina, at first just a simple structure with a room to enjoy a roaring fire and her simple yet sumptuous meals, and another room where both of his sons had been conceived and born. With each spring, Yvgeny would add another room, first one for each child and then another to contain his vast collection of books, and at long last that room that faced the east where Katarina would spend her days lovingly creating clothing for her constantly growing boys. That last winter, before the cough, he had made plans to add one more room to the home that would hopefully welcome the daughter she'd always wanted. If the snows melted early, he would have just enough time to frame and enclose it before she arrived. He stood at the door, not knowing how much time had passed, as he reminisced about a future that never occurred, fearful of what he would see and remember as he crossed the threshold. At last, he found the strength and pushed up the firm wood handle, pressing his weight to the door to force the long frozen hinges. The last few rays of sun fell upon the long-abandoned room, still adorned with the furnishings as they had lain the day he walked away from the cemetery. Throughout the night and into the next long and lonely days, Yvgeny Thatcherev would begin to set his home back in order, not to create a place of comfort but to allow him once again to be surrounded by the beauty and welcome the ghosts of his family who had never left.

Yvgeny spent nearly a week confronting his ghosts and falling into his routine of sadness and joyous reminiscences. Once he had made the main room livable, he opened new wounds as he finally cracked the door to the bedchamber of he and his wife. He forced himself to open the drawers, closets and boxes, still filled with the tattered remnants of his once-happy memories. Though he knew his imagination yielded, he could almost swear that he could still catch just the slightest whiff of his Katarina's hair she had so lovingly washed with the flower oils and herbs that grew along the banks of the lake. His home was like a time capsule, and to his great surprise he found a huge cord of wood still stacked along the rear wall, allowing him to fill the room with light and warmth despite the coldness and darkness that filled his heart. He could not bring himself to set into shape the rooms of his two sons and had yet to venture into them. Instead he turned to his study, still filled from roof to floor with the freeze-dried books he had so lovingly collected. While paging through one of his favorite volumes of Polish poetry, he was surprised to hear a knock at his long-forgotten front door. As the smoke billowing from the chimney betrayed the presence of someone, he knew he could not just sit silently and pretend as if the home remained empty and forgotten. He finally mustered the courage and crossed the main room to open the door. Standing there in the entryway was someone he never thought would still be in Pskov, and yet his heart filled with joy to see his old friend Marcellus.

"And so you thought you could just steal into Pskov and not look up your oldest and dearest friend, Yvgeny Thatcherev? Shame on you!" Marcellus chastised as he was taken into a huge bear hug by a weeping Yvgeny.

"Marcellus! My dear brother, I did not know you were still in Pskov. I could not have hoped it. Oh, my, how so much time has passed. And you are looking old!"

"Ah, I'm looking old. At least my beard hasn't gone completely grey as yours has, Yvgeny Thatcherev," he said as he strode into the house, its warmth prompting him to remove his great coat and in the process revealing his clerical gown, betraying his ascension to position.

"Well, if there isn't a God in Heaven, for before me stands a miracle today. And who on the Synod did you have to bribe to be elevated to Metropolitan?" Yvgeny admired while teasingly mocking one of the most deserving men he had ever known for such a position.

"Oh, this," Marcellus offhandedly acknowledged. "I had no other clean clothes, and so I figured I would don this old thing. Do you like it?"

"Like it? I just want to know where the naked fellow is that you stole it from. Don't you know they can punish you greatly for imitating one so close to perfection as the Patriarch?"

"Oh, His Holiness was more than happy when I was willing to accept my humble service far enough away from him that he would not have to deal with my outrages," Marcellus sighed as he collapsed onto the broad sofa, helping himself to not the first bottle of bread wine of the day.

"I can only imagine what it must have been like when the Synod put forth your name for Metropolitan. I'm sure Joachim thought the heavens themselves would open and the seven seals would immediately be unleashed upon all of greater Russia."

"It is amazing how comforting Sophia was under these circumstances. You can imagine my surprise when she came to my defense. Who would have thought that such a heretic as I would receive the favor of the Tsarina? My only guess is that Vasily Golitsyn saw greater utility with me here out of the way and not underfoot in Moscow." Golitsyn's name sent an obvious stiffening to the Yvgeny's spine, noted by Marcellus. "Oh, yes, I had heard that Golitsyn may have been involved with your hasty departure from Russia. I had inquired as such in my letters, and yet you never answered them. So now that you're here, you can answer my questions personally."

And through the night, the two old friends, the prodigal Orthodox priest and the Metropolitan of Pskov, talked of the previous ten years, both in Moscow and in England. As one of the leaders in the Reform Movement, it was only a shade of parody that Marcellus had often been considered to be a heretic. One of the most educated of clergy to fill the ranks of the Orthodoxy, Marcellus was one of those rare breed of churchmen who viewed the world not as a scourge to be avoided but as an opportunity to both modernize the church and spread the message of the Russian Orthodox faith.

The surrender of winter gave with it not only a rebirth of a snowbound Russia but also brought with it a new life, one that should have been holding Tsar Peter's attention much more than it was. As he began to build his acquaintance with Thatcher, he gave scarce attention to the fact that his much-despised wife, the Tsarina Eudoxia, a woman selected for him by his mother and the boyars, seemed to force an early spring as she gave birth to his son in the final days of February. At nearly two years older than her husband, Eudoxia was a very pretty girl from a proper family who would likely bear him good heirs. To the boyar class, she was a catch. To Peter, she was as boring as drying paint. What had first been a general indifference to his bland and uninteresting queen in time became an absolute revulsion. Her conversational skills were minimal, her interests were superficial and her lovemaking was as bland as her name. That the young Tsar had other interests besides making an heir with her was a constant source of annoyance and one more reason for her insufferable whining, which made Peter grow to hate the very sound of her voice. To no one's surprise, Peter was nowhere to be found the day the heir to the throne came into the world.

It had only been two weeks since his arrival, but already Yvgeny Thatcherev Edwards had fallen into a very comfortable and pleasant routine. After a long night of drinking and carousing with Uncle Peter and his Jolly Company, he would finally collapse, drunk and exhausted, only to be roused by either General Gordon or Edmund Drummond to begin a long day of martial studies. Thatcher became quite proficient with the musket, and the heavy Russian swords, though at first difficult to swing and effectively control, became more capable in his hands as his muscles began to build in his chest and arms. But the one weapon Thatcher most enjoyed and quickly excelled at was the pistol. One could say the size of the weapon was easier for a nine-year-old boy to handle, but it was something more. He had learned to swab and prime and re-load his shot quickly, affix the slow match to allow for more accurate discharge and less misfire, and he amazed his instructors at his capability to deliver deadly fire. While it was typical for the process to take long enough to allow only two shots per minute, Thatcher's capabilities allowed him to get off a third shot and be priming his pistol for a fourth round with time on the minute glass to spare. Peter was so impressed with Thatcher's mastery of the pistol and his obvious affection for the weapon that he had designed a special holster the boy wore across his chest, capable of holding a brace of three. He always found it quite amusing how Thatcher would take his position before his target, assuming a sidelong pose to make a smaller target, while drawing each weapon, each smoking with their own active slow-match, and in rapid succession fire each pistol one by one with deadly accuracy. It was during one of these sessions of target practice when a Streltsy guard appeared, galloping across the field. He came to a screeching halt about twenty feet away from the Tsar, dropping to his knees as part of his dismount and begged the Tsar's forgiveness for the interruption, but he bore an important message from the Tsarina.

"I am pleased to inform you that this morning your son, the future Tsar of Russia, has been born. The presence of your company is requested to herald this magnificent new dawn for Russia. Much love and affection, Tsarina Eudoxia," the guard repeated accurately and carefully the message dictated to him by the Tsar's mother Natalya.

"Well, Thatcher, I guess congratulations are in order. It seems as if I am now a father." Peter began casually swabbing his pistol. "What say we get off a few more rounds of practice and then let's go take a look at your cousin, shall we?"

About an hour later, as news of Peter's heir began to circulate throughout Moscow, an impressive contingent of the Jolly Company met up with Peter and Thatcher to escort them to Terem Palace.

Thatcher was surprised when, upon arrival in the courtyard, his uncle took him by the arm to lead him to the private chambers of the royal family. Such fears had been relayed previously by Peter's mother Natalya, who was concerned at the obvious growing affection between Peter and Thatcher. While she, too, had had a genuine affection for Thatcher's mother and could well remember the effect her presence had on Fedor, the facts were that Fedor was gone, Sophia was in exile and Ivan would never fully claim his title to the throne. Their family, the Miloslavskayas, no longer had any legitimate claim to the ascendancy, and yet here was Peter, parading around one of Fedor's good moments as if he were an actual member of the lineage. Her disdain of Thatcher's presence was palpable the moment Peter entered the room, trailed by his nine-year-old mirror image. To actually ferry about not only a look-alike but a blood connection in the face of his mother, wife and child was more than she could bear.

"How dare you bring him here at this most precious and critical time, Peter!" his mother whispered with an echoing resonance.

Peter ignored her, after giving her a glancing kiss on her cheek, as he made his way past his mother, completely ignoring Patriarch Joachim and the voluminous retinue that accompanied him, and finally to his wife's bedside. Her pitiful expression for some sort of sign of approval and concern from her husband was unsatisfied, as Peter scarcely acknowledged her presence, taking his child from her arms for a closer examination. The baby was tightly swaddled to protect his newborn skin from the omnipresent chill that wafted throughout the dank palace. Peter undid the swaddling, casting it upon his wife's bosom, and held up his naked, chubby, dark-haired son for a much more careful look. He studied first the hair, the eyes and the nose, and at last the penis. And then, as if confirming something that had been in doubt, he pronounced, "Yes indeed, without a doubt, a Romanov." He clasped the baby to his chest with one arm and strode to where Thatcher stood at the threshold of the door. Once again he held out the child, as if it were some game he had just bagged and asked in his most innocent and boyish way, "So, what do you think?"

Thatcher had to admit that the sight of the boy and his presence in this less-than-friendly environment made him somewhat uncomfortable. Yet the expression on Uncle Peter's face, sincerely wanting to know Thatcher's opinion, made him give the only answer that seemed appropriate at the time. "He looks like you." While not huge on sentiment, it was exactly what Peter needed at that moment.

"Yes, he does. And good thing. It is time that new life came to the Terem and, with this day, hopefully, a rebuilding of the Romanov name. As such a boy needs a name befitting as ours, and I name him Alexis Tsarevich, Prince of Russia."

"Tsar Peter, you know this is not the time or place to pronounce a birth name," chided Patriarch Joachim, as his minions murmured amongst themselves for this breach of royal and sacred protocol.

"Well then, Patriarch, I guess you need to pick that time and place. I'll leave that to your capable hands. As for me, I have celebrations to plan." And with that, he handed the naked baby to the Patriarch, who at that moment was baptized with a firm and steady stream of urine from the infant. Peter and Thatcher departed the chamber, rejoining their comrades in the courtyard. They sent up a resounding cheer, and as a body their hooves could be heard echoing off the ancient sacred walls of the Kremlin at their departure.

Word of the birth traveled quickly through all the corners of Russia and within days had reached Pskov. Marcellus had performed miracles with Yvgeny's spirits. Upon hearing the news of the arrival of Alexis, Marcellus and Yvgeny set aside their reunion and the healing of the prodigal cleric and began their long journey through the muddying roads south that would carry them to Moscow. They had arrived only a day before the March 10th celebration, one of those rare moments when all of Russia collectively joined together in sacred reflection and copious alcoholism. Throughout Moscow, the church bells pealed day and night to christen the name Alexis Tsarevich. As official Russia went about their task of planning their corresponding celebrations, Peter and his Jolly Company had set about their own important tasks to add a certain flair Russia had never before seen. Peter decided that he and his company would go to great measures to make sure that this celebration was one that all Russia would remember for a lifetime, though few of the hundreds of thousands who had flocked to Moscow could know that Peter was also commemorating another young life for whom he had developed a great affection.

To the curiosity of the citizens of the capital city, a steady stream of wagons was dispatched from the armory of Moscow en route to Preobrazhenskoe. In the fields adjacent to the lodge, Peter commanded his ragtag battalion of munitions men to set about an awe-inspiring array of demolitions and incendiaries, in a manner one would expect to be part of some upcoming major military campaign. Day and night and wagon after wagon, the meadow was transformed into a veritable arsenal. When it seemed the work and the drinking that accompanied it would never come to an end, the products of their labor were loaded aboard the wagons, and a convoy of laden carts made their way to the center of Moscow. One could only imagine the level of discontent and concern that crossed the minds of the gathering masses, as they observed the meticulous layout of this strange and fascinating compilation of pyrotechnics that was assembled and arrayed throughout the entire day. There in the middle of all the activity, among all those men who carefully laid out the stockpiles of explosives, raced Peter, directing the assembly of this mad display until the last rays of light fell upon the breadth of Red Square. It had grown eerily quiet when at last the massive confusion came to an end. All of official Russia had assembled outside the walls of the Kremlin to view whatever spectacle was to come. Standing there in the center of Red Square was their monarch Tsar Peter, illuminating the pitch black with a single torch, and as the hundreds of thousands had hushed to an absolute silence, Peter dropped the torch ... and ran.

Patriarch Joachim, sitting upon his throne in the shadow of the Cathedral of Annunciation, furiously began to cross himself and pray for salvation as the very mouth of Hell opened before him. Gasps of fear and abject terror waved through the assembled throngs of peasants, priests and royals, as for the next five hours the skies and grounds of Moscow burst into flame, fury and explosion. And no matter how he tried, Patriarch Joachim could not bring to a stop any number of Peter's company who raced into the belfries, pulling the bells to serve as a manic accompaniment to the fireworks. While Peter had played with skyrockets before, it was inconceivable that those years of war games could lead their monarch to such a God-forsaken display as missiles and flash pots and small kegs of gunpowder sailed skyward, lifting higher, threatening to set the skies of Moscow itself aflame. While others screamed and scattered for cover, Peter and his Jolly Company, along with their deranged band of minstrels, struck a tune and whirled like Dervishes in the cacophonous display. Even when a five-pound rocket misfired and hurled to the ground, striking a boyar in the head and killing him, the band played on.

Thatcher had spent the last two weeks virtually sleepless helping his Uncle Peter realize his pyrotechnic fantasy, and he sat upon an empty gunpowder cask, a bottle of bread wine freshly decapitated, as he marveled at the joy and unbridled passion of his uncle. At some point during the festivities, Thatcher caught Peter's eye, holding his infant son amid shower-spraying skyrockets. He could see his Uncle Peter attempting to yell something across the thundering gulf, and he rose to move a little closer, straining to hear what he had to say. Finally, after many attempts, he heard Tsar Peter, accompanied by manic laughter, scream, "Happy Birthday!" as he danced among the flames.

Peter's shenanigans portrayed a young man who was still insistent on playing boys' games, and most feared he had no intention of taking his duties to the State seriously. In truth, Peter had begun to seriously reflect upon the future of his child and his kingdom. Not long after the fireworks display, as his merry band continued their bawdy celebrations on the banks of the Yauza, news came that Patriarch Joachim had died. His passing, while a serious and officially sad time for all of Russia, was to Peter an opportunity to redefine the Orthodox Church for the next century, and as the body of the Patriarch lay in state in the Cathedral of the Annunciation, the competing factions of the Church began their warfare for Peter's attention in the selection of the new Patriarch.

These were exactly the aspects of state that Peter despised, and while the official body of Russia waged a war of words and ecclesiastical damnation upon one another, Peter took the signs of spring as his cue to flee Moscow. In tow was his unrecognized nephew, who had just turned ten the day before Peter and his retinue made their way to Lake Pleschev. There each day, at the first rays of dawn, Thatcher would join Peter and his boat builders as they went about the task of repairing the winter's damage to Peter's beloved vessels. The workmen spent all day long sanding and painting the hulls, repairing the keels and sealing the seams to make them seaworthy. And when torchlight failed to illuminate the work effectively, they would turn to their bottles and food and celebrate this magnificent landscape of Russia. For days they worked to make the crafts seaworthy and to prepare rigging, masts and sails. At last Peter and Thatcher led their little flotilla across the vast body of the magnificent lake, where uncle and nephew honed their skills at navigation, far beyond the sight of land. Plying the winds all day, they would at last drop anchor at night, tracing lines to connect the stars that formed the various constellations. Thatcher had always been enamored by the image in his head of Russia, and for the first time he felt the longing pangs of falling in love. The long and glorious days aboard that sailing craft honed the burgeoning talents of the Tsar and his apprentice seaman.

Second only to sailing these boats was the unslakable passion to build and maintain them, for every time they approached the land the ships would be hauled back onto shore and tools were applied to every square inch of their keels to assure a smooth finished bottom. Thatcher had to laugh, for as much as he knew his Uncle Peter loved the sight of sails and rigging, he could not keep his hands off a freshly sanded underside.

"I'm not much to give advice, my friend," Peter mentioned one night as his hand ran slowly along the freshly finished hull of one of his beloved boats. "But know one thing – no matter how tight your sails or skilled your crew, if you don't take care of your bottom you drag the sea behind you. Always, always, always keep your bottom clean."

Their unquenchable passion for the sea and the boats that sailed upon them would obsess Peter and Thatcher for the rest of their days. Peter's fixation with his navy was not only a desire to master the seas. Even in the worst of weather, few places made him feel more calm than when his boat was far from shore, and it felt to him as if the world was nothing but water and he its monarch. It was here he did not have to listen to the demands of Moscow or the remonstrances from his mother or the whining of his wife. Here he was not Tsar of Russia. He was King Neptune. And he was both servant and master of all that he surveyed.

But as much peace as he found at sea, Peter realized that he must truly seize the reigns of his monarchy and fully assume his role as commander in chief. He became determined to prepare Russia for the day when it must reach beyond its borders by land, and to do that he must prepare his land forces for the wars to come. As such, Peter's boy armies had become his real armies, and it was time to put his armies to the test. Despite the peace he found at Lake Pleschev, he made his way back to the Yauza River to begin planning for war games.

He had spent countless hours in the company of General Gordon and his foreign regiment discussing military tactics and the latest technologies to be found in the great armies of Europe, and Peter formulated an idea to apply these new technologies amongst his most trusted troops. He took his Preobrazhensky Regiment and set them in mock conflict against a fortified encampment containing his Semyonovsky Regiment. Both sides prepared vast quantities of hand grenades and fire pots constructed of plasterboard and clay, no less dangerous than their actual counterparts, with the intention of testing their capabilities of assaulting a fortified encampment. Edmund Drummond had drilled Thatcher rigorously to be a master of combat arms, so Peter's nephew took his place as a soldier in the

Preobrazhensky Regiment and practiced his role of applying lethal fire against the fortified position. Throughout the summer, day after day, the troops underwent intensive training and practice for this mock assault. On October 6th, the armies began their two days of furious battle. Thatcher had greatly enjoyed being a young gunner and was overcome with exhaustion at the end of the battle. But like everyone else who had taken part in the violent display, he was in shock when Peter, himself wounded from an exploding clay pot, screamed his discontent with the outcome and ordered the battle be fought again.

Summer had given way to the violent rains and treacherous winds of the Russian autumn, but three days later, they waged the battle again. Unlike the first time, this mock battle delivered real casualties as Prince Ivan Dolgurky, who was shot in the arm, died from infection nine days later. General Gordon, himself a veteran of many military campaigns, was severely burned and spent a week in bed recuperating. And as Peter assessed this round of battle, bleeding and burnt from numerous wounds, he sat upon a hillside surveying the destruction and smiled to himself that one day his armies would stand up to any foe and destroy them. His eyes scanned his fatigued, filthy and injured men with pride and sought out that young protégé of his, who had come to Russia a mere merchant's grandson and was leaving it a warrior. And leaving it he was.

Yvgeny had joined the men in encampment, providing a sense of spiritual guidance for the harrowing experience, and watched as Peter waved for Thatcher to join him on his hillside repose. He had long wondered when Peter would grow tired of his playmate, and as the smoke still billowed over the battlefield, he watched the two conversing on the hillside.

"You have proven to me how very strong and ferocious you are, Thatcher," Peter confessed as he wrapped his arm around the boy.

"I never thought that my trip to Russia would find me out in her distant fields, practicing the art of warfare with her Tsar," Thatcher confessed as he took in the bloody vista.

"I can honestly say, Thatcher, that had Fedor lived to see you grow up, had he had the chance that I had, to see all that you are capable of, I know he, too, would feel as I do right this moment. Not just pride ... but fear."

Thatcher listened, thinking about what his uncle had said, and while sensing the ominous quality of his statement, he likewise felt a bit of arrogance learning that he could make this Tsar of Russia nervous.

"Tonight you and I will drink a few last toasts together, Thatcher. And once again, I will tell you more stories of the not-so-Tsar-like things your father did when he was a boy. It is good to know how human a Tsar can be and how we all wish that we could forever stay boys. But that's the sad part. One day we must grow up to be men, and not only protect our countries but protect our thrones. And the greatest threat to my throne and my son's future is not Poland or the Ottomans or the Swedish or the Danish who threaten my borders. It is the knowledge that out there is a young English boy who calls himself Edwards, but in truth he is a Romanov."

The Russian fall sun rose early in October in its last attempt to seize and hold the day that in short order would be a losing battle. But the sun was still slumbering as the old Russian cleric and the young English boy departed the hunting lodge along the Yauza River, heading southwest across the dangerous frontier of Ukraine to the port of Kiev. While that threat had been present when they had arrived eight months before, on the return trip it was a little less disconcerting, for under the heavy black coat Thatcher wore to shield himself from the pre-dawn cold resided a bandoleer containing three braces of pistols, fully armed and ready to face whatever Tatar threat may come. The future of Russia now lay in the hands of Peter the Great and his vision for a vast, expanding and modern Russia.

As their ship sailed down the Dneiper River and they crossed the Black Sea and Bosporus, across the Aegean and the Ionian and back into the Mediterranean, Thatcher and Yvgeny recounted again and again the tales they would never be able to tell to the women who awaited them back in Bristol. For as that merchant ship exited the Straits of Gibraltar and began her northwest course across the English Channel, the two made a solemn pact to one another that the life they had led was one that only a Russian would understand.

And what happens in Russia stays in Russia.

Chapter 3

A Forging of Rivalries
1688 – June 1696

I

During Thatcher's year in Russia, Woodes Rogers would have been a lonely and friendless soul had he not found a place of shelter to bide his time until his friend returned. His mornings were occupied with the various tutors Mrs. Rogers had so carefully procured for her son's education and betterment. In the afternoons, on those rare times when Captain Rogers was in Bristol, Woodes could be found at the docks, entertaining himself by playing captain of his father's ship, gently pitching with the flux of the tides yet safely fastened to the wharf cleats. More frequently, when Captain Rogers was at sea, Woodes would finish his lessons and sneak down the back stairs of his High Street home, stealing across the Redcliffe Bridge and into the marketplace where he could easily get lost in the crowd to mask his trail to Parker House.

Almost like clockwork, Nettie would hear Woodes's soft tap on the kitchen door. Uncovering the muffin she had set aside for him and pouring him a hot tea, she listened to him talk about his lessons for the day. Because of the absence of his principle charge, Caesar would eventually join Woodes, and the two would make their way down to the docks to watch the ships and their cargoes come and go. Because of the age difference and the obvious complications of race, the relationship between Woodes and Caesar could not actually be described as friendship; rather, Caesar dutifully accepted his role as an unofficial bodyguard for Woodes who, without appropriate accompaniment, had no business being on the Bristol quays. Despite the prominence and esteem held for the senior Rogers by all who made their livings along the docks, such respect was not automatically bestowed to his namesake. The working class youths – who picked up extra ha'pennies toting loads to the merchants' fashionable underground storage facilities – made sport in loathing dandy boys like Woodes. On such trips to the wharves, it wasn't uncommon for him to encounter one of these common gents who viewed the sight of Woodes Rogers as an opportunity to vent every hostility they felt for the privileged class. On those occasions when Caesar was about, these energetic lads would tend to give Woodes wide berth. But when he dared to venture out alone, it wasn't uncommon for Woodes to show up at Nettie's door with a bloody nose and a swollen eye or a tattered piece of clothing. She would shake her head, then skillfully and quickly mend the offense so Woodes would not have to explain to his mother the general lack of respect routinely dealt to the son of Captain Rogers.

Caesar saw a need to educate Woodes on a few basic points of self-defense. While the slight lad was enthusiastic, his lack of coordination made Caesar's task more complicated than he had hoped. After months of near futility, Caesar gently suggested that perhaps the best thing for them to do would be to work on Woodes' running skills. Caesar did derive certain benefits from the relationship as well. Woodes was a brilliant and well-educated boy, and he seemed to take great pleasure in imparting those things he had learned throughout the day ... ad nauseum. But to Caesar, Woodes' endless prattling was in its own way very comforting, as it reminded him of the enthusiastic chatter that was part of Thatcher's personality as well.

When word was received that the *Neptune* had been spotted exiting Gibraltar, Caesar and Woodes were animated to know that soon their friend would be returning. On a chilly December afternoon, almost a year to the day from making their leave, the merchant vessel loaded with carpets from Constantinople, gathered from throughout the farthest reaches of the ancient Silk Road, made its entrance into Bristol Harbour. While discretion had been the hallmark of Parker House, that afternoon the twenty or so ladies of that storied institution stood wharfside, decked out in their fineries awaiting the return of the two beloved men. Standing at the front of the throng, Beatrice Parker and Abigail Edwards were flanked by Masters Caesar and Rogers. When Thatcher and Yvgeny appeared at the gangplank, two things were immediately quite obvious. The cold winters of Russia had taken a toll on Yvgeny, whose beard and hair were much greyer than they had been upon departure; and Thatcher, who had turned ten in a most celebratory fashion, was at least a foot taller, his hair longer and his chest fuller. While he continued the tradition of matching his grandfather article for article in dress, including the heavy bear coats and ermine hats on their heads, Thatcher and Yvgeny departed their commonality on one fine point: countenance.

As soon as their feet hit the dock, the two men were surrounded and nearly tackled to the ground by the loving assemblage of women who assaulted their faces with kisses while simultaneously peppering them with questions and compliments, so much so that it all seemed to ring in one furious din. Beatrice and Abigail were both beside themselves with joy, and Yvgeny was in tears, smiling and laughing at having finally returned home. Thatcher, on the other hand, was much more subdued. As his mother took his face in her hands, kissing him long and hard at the gratitude of having her son home, she was a bit surprised to find her son so distant and preoccupied. He smiled and kissed her and his grandmother and was nearly toppled over by the overwhelming embrace of Caesar and more gentle hugs of Nettie and Woodes. Still there was something about Thatcher that seemed less than happy to be home. Abigail, ever sensitive of her son, chalked it up to the long trip and many experiences from his journey. As she held his arm leading him back to Parker House, she whispered in his ear how absolutely grateful she was that he was home safe with her again.

Thatcher's restlessness was apparent the moment he returned home. The women of Parker House had planned an elaborate homecoming celebration, including all of Yvgeny and Thatcher's favorite foods. Beatrice, Abigail and Caesar felt that this was one of those rare occasions that Parker House should be closed for business and had made the point of letting the assembled at Peal's Tavern know that they would not be receiving guests for the evening. Caesar's pointed delivery of that message and memories of what had happened a decade before quickly cooled all protests of dissent, and a general wish of welcome home was sent by the disappointed gentlemen to the returning Russians. In the year that he had been gone, Thatcher had developed a lusty appreciation for a good party, and he did all he could to affably accept the loving embrace of the women in the house. Abigail was a little surprised, however, when her ten-year-old son put aside his punch for a large tankard of Yvgeny's private stock of Pskov Bread Wine. Her motherly instinct to chide was quickly suppressed by a warning look from Beatrice to let it be. Beatrice had lived with a Russian for over twenty years and knew that to them bread wine and celebration were synonymous. Despite her concerns, Thatcher never betrayed any signs of overindulgence throughout the evening, and he took each question and request for his time very graciously, albeit none too enthusiastically. While the women had planned this celebration as their time with Thatcher and Yvgeny, they had to compete for the returning men's attention from the other two males in attendance. The normally reserved and quiet Caesar could not take his arms or eyes off Thatcher, and while many knew the genuine affection between the two, none had realized how lonely he had been without his dearest and closest comrade. He had performed so admirably in the absence of Yvgeny and Thatcher that the house had been peaceful and quiet and without incident throughout their entire departure, mostly due to Caesar's vigilance and calm power. While all had grown to appreciate Woodes Rogers's presence and to see him as the cute, precocious boy he had become, it was obvious that he was holding his friend in a very strange esteem. Like Caesar, none could know how much he had been lost without his friend, and both peppered him with questions which held absolutely no interest to the ladies of the house. Sometime in the course of the evening, Thatcher had gone missing, and Abigail grew concerned that her son was nowhere to be found. Yvgeny suggested the boy would turn up eventually and was merely trying to process the overwhelming sensations that were assaulting him upon his homecoming. A few moments later, Abigail noticed Allison Simms coming down the stairs, with Thatcher in tow a few seconds behind. His sudden reappearance was a point of curiosity to Abigail.

"I was worried. I looked for you and I couldn't find you anywhere." Abigail gently rebuked her son, wrapping an arm around him and running her fingers through his long black hair.

"Well, mother, I have missed my bed for this last year and thought I would stretch out to see if the goose down still felt the same," he replied, giving her a little smile and a kiss upon her pale cheek. "I have missed many things, Mother, but most of all I missed you."

Abigail embraced her son whom she had so feared she would never see again. Thatcher had always been so big and mature for his age, but while only ten he had an air about him that was inexplicable. Now that he had finally taken off that big heavy bearskin jacket, it amazed her how much her son had filled out. His chest and arms were a mass of coiled springs, a physiological aspect one would not expect from a ten-year-old. But what most surprised her was when she took his hands. Having lived a gentrified life free of physical labor, she was shocked to find his palms so callused and rough, laced with a small series of scars, healed gouges and nicks to the skin. It was as if she were looking at the hands of a seasoned sailor rather than those of the privileged boy who had left her just a year before. She looked in his eyes questioningly, and he smiled as gently as he could, hoping to allay any fears.

"Russia is a very cold place, and if you are going to get along with the locals, you must demonstrate your capability to pitch in," he offered.

This wasn't the first time his rough hands and strong physical body had been inquired upon this evening. Alison Simms had been present the day Thatcher had come into the world. At sixteen, she had come to Parker House, having been ejected from her home after her father had caught her surrendering her virginity to one of the laborers on his Chippenham farm. Well, actually, not her virginity precisely. That had been lost sometime previous. She had hoped that a claim of first time would spare her the humiliation and fear of being tossed out, but her father was inconsolable, and she found herself homeless with no marketable skills except for those she had developed on her back. Having always been an adventurous girl, she figured this would be the perfect time to at last see London, to the east, but penniless she hitched a ride with, and on, a carriage driver who was on his way west to Bristol to pick up a fare. She had thought, perhaps, she could use her talents to amass enough money or to persuade a London-destined traveler to take her to her desired destination. As a pretty girl with a valuable repertoire, her ability to attract a customer or two immediately was not an issue. Having performed a much desired unnatural act for the few farthings in a fellow's pocket, Allison was intrigued when he suggested, as he hitched up his drawers, that such talents could be quite profitable in the right setting. And thus she was directed to Parker House.

Beatrice Parker had made it clear that she was not running a shelter for wayward girls or a reformatory. Parker House had become quite profitable by featuring exquisite young ladies who had not only talents between the sheets but likewise brains in their heads. As she served a prestigious and moneyed clientele, it was not her desire to pick up just any young woman with the capability of providing relief to her customers. Rather, she had built her reputation upon giving her customers the illusion that such practices and favors granted were an exception, not the rule, of the ladies of Parker House. One obvious drawback, of course, was that from time to time her best girls had so effectively filled the fantasies as well as the hearts of some of her distinguished patrons. With the proper dowry, she would release the girl from her contract with her best wishes and turn to the task of filling the vacated room. Such was the case when Allison Simms appeared at her door in her rural finery. Yvgeny had shown the young lady to the chairs in the hall and sought out Beatrice, who had been occupying herself throughout the morning with her ledger sheets. The sheepish expression on Yvgeny's face told her that the knock at the door had obviously been for her.

"There is a young lady in the hall who had inquired for the mistress of the house," Yvgeny offered.

"And did she happen to mention what she was selling?" Beatrice inquired.

"I'm not quite certain, but I believe she is selling herself. I think she mistook me as the Master of the house. I merely mentioned I was using the library."

"Well, Yvgeny Thatcherev, under the circumstances, were she selling would you be buying?"

"Ah, my lovely Beatrice, as I have you I'm no longer a man with money in his pocket," Yvgeny offered as gallantly as he could. "But of course, if I were a man of such means and interest, I can tell you I would have made good use of that library."

The immediate impression of Allison Simms was not positive to Beatrice. It was obvious from her clothing and the way she sat on the chair, legs spread with a hand resting between them, that she was not a woman of breeding. Allison could tell immediately that Beatrice was not impressed.

"Good morning, I'm Beatrice Parker, Mistress of this household, and I wish to thank you for visiting, but at present I'm not in need of your services," Beatrice offered, extending a hand both to greet and to show Allison to the door.

"Mrs. Parker, my name is Allison Simms. I know my attire may not be fancy and perhaps my carriage not quite erect, but, you see, only yesterday I was kicked out of my home with not a penny to my name and only these clothes which I was able to put back on before my father ejected me from his property. I can see this is not a house of charity, and perhaps my exhaustion from a long night of travel and services rendered to bring me to your doorstep gives a bedraggled impression, but ma'am, I do clean up well."

"Well, young lady, sad as your story is, at the present I've a full house, save one young charge who went and got herself married. Now, if you need a few farthings to get you down the road, I'd be more than happy to offer that courtesy from one professional to another. But you sound as one who is seeking a grub stake and passage to London, and I don't need to be renting my room at this moment." Beatrice lifted her skirt a few inches and retrieved a pound note from a garter just above her ankle and handed it to Allison. This was more money than Allison had ever seen in her life, and her instinct was to take the offering, thank the good woman and see how quickly she could charm her way aboard a London-bound carriage. But instead, she took a moment to study Beatrice and then take in the opulent surroundings in which she stood.

"Missus, I'll confess that I don't expect I'll get too many offerings of a pound note again anytime soon. Which leads me to wonder if you have the capability of offering this as charity to a stranger, how much more can a girl like me with truly astounding skills be able to make for you?"

Beatrice smiled and led the girl to the study where, after quickly demonstrating the acceptable way to sit, she inquired upon her sexual history. To her pleasant surprise, she discovered the extensive and enthusiastic capabilities the young woman had mastered. There was one thing she understood about farm girls – their curiosity was only bested by their enthusiasm. That evening, after passing along a few talking points so as to be able to engage her customers with at least a facsimile of small talk, Beatrice Parker introduced Allison Simms to that evening's assemblage, and then offered up the infrequent but much anticipated game reserved for new girls the customers affectionately called Dibs.

What was expected to be a short-term, mutually profitable contract had persevered for twelve years. One of the things that had kept her around for so long was the feeling of being part of a family, punctuated by that joyous occasion ten years before when Thatcher Edwards came into the world. To all the ladies of the house, Thatcher was in many ways their baby and later their little boy. In his young life, Thatcher had been the source of amusement and entertainment and pure agenda-less flattery and joy. But as he began to grow up, all the women speculated what a handsome and dashing figure he was going to make when he became a man. And many of the ladies opined as to which one of them would be the first to help him along that path.

Thus, it was with pleasant astonishment when Allison noticed Thatcher appraising her on the dock. She so dearly loved the boy, and at first read it for having missed his dear Auntie Allison. However, she was quite a bit surprised when she discovered that the hand upon her ass was not the stray graze of one of the ladies but that mischievous handsome lad who had just returned home from the sea. When she looked to confirm her suspicions, she was greeted with a flashing smile and a growing awareness that young Thatcher was becoming a man all too quickly. As the party ensued, and each took their turn to give him hugs and kisses and welcomes home, that same smile was on his face again, only this time when Auntie Allison leaned in for a hug Thatcher's eyes first took in her impressive expanse of décolletage and then his mouth found her ear and whispered, "How I've dreamed of once again seeing those beautiful breasts, Allison. The only problem is that they're still clothed."

She looked at Thatcher in shock as his head nodded toward the stairs. Her instinct was to chide the young boy for being so fresh, but her curiosity got the best of her. She glanced around to see if anyone was looking, then stole up the stairs and lingered in the hallway leading to the private quarters. She thought of her excuse should Abigail, Beatrice or Yvgeny appear instead, but her heart began to race a bit when she heard those heavy boots making their way up the last few steps. Thatcher strode imperially down that long corridor and seemed as if he were going to walk right past her when he stopped before her, pressed his body against hers, kissed her full and furiously upon her mouth and said, "Good."

She was half in shock when he grabbed her hand and pulled her down the hall and into his room, swinging her onto his bed as he shut the door. She took in the sight of this English boy dressed head to toe in black, cloaked in bear and crowned in ermine. She had wondered why he had kept that heavy coat on as well as that silly hat, but she figured he was showing off his Russian finery and wasn't quite prepared to part with it. Or, she hoped, perhaps he was seeking an excuse to go to his room and remove it, giving him a good cover story. Whatever reason, he took that hat off, its fur matching the color of his long black hair, and then removed that big heavy coat. She found herself giggling just a bit as his expression bore that of a man who was trying to be impressive, and she had to keep reminding herself that she couldn't keep reminding herself that he was only ten. But as that jacket came off, her mouth was a bit agape as she took in the sight of her beloved baby boy Thatcher cloaked in a bandoleer of pistols, as if he were preparing to go to war.

"Thatcher, look at you, what cause do you have to be wearing guns in your mother's home?"

"You must understand, Allison, there are brigands on the high seas, and a man must be prepared for whatever action may call."

"Oh, and so you're gone for a year and now you're ten, armed to the teeth, and likewise a man, are you?"

Thatcher undid his brace of pistols, his most prized possession from Russia, and walked slowly to the edge of the bed where Allison lay, amused and quite breathless. "My beloved Allison Simms, it is neither a gun nor age that makes the man. I guess perhaps I could try to explain it at length what I mean, but rather let me show you." As Thatcher undid his tunic, and the cotton shirt beneath it, she had to admit that she hadn't seen many ten-year-olds with the chest this boy was portraying. While she was curious to see just how far Thatcher's little game was going to go, she was a bit surprised – no, absolutely shocked – when Thatcher began to peel off layers of skirt and petticoat, his rough and callused hands sliding along her bare legs as they found and expertly worked laces and braces, and she knew in good conscience that she should stop him somewhere along the way. After all, she was Auntie Allison. And yet, when his head disappeared underneath her petticoat and those boyish lips found her girlish ones, she knew she would need more time to find an adequate protest. The best she could offer at that moment was, "But Thatcher, I was at your christening."

"Yes," his slightly muffled voice responded. "I've heard."

Allison Simms knew that things around the Parker House were going to get very interesting, and while there was a great desire to brag that she had been the first, she knew that upon its revelation she would have to share. So for the time being, mum was the word for as long as she could keep her tongue ... and his.

As much as Abigail wanted to monopolize her son's time, she knew his return was going to make many demands upon him, and she opted not to protest when Thatcher, Caesar and Woodes disappeared up the stairs, running like boys off to some game. He spent the evening regaling Caesar and Woodes about Russia and its army. They thrilled over the fact that Thatcher had learned how to fire guns and use real swords, rather than the wooden ones they had played with before he left. With Thatcher's return, the three became inseparable. Since the incident at the rogue's gallery in the marketplace three years before, Nettie had beseeched Caesar to take on an even more prominent role in Thatcher's life, and now, though Caesar was still seven years older than his brother, this change in attitude and experience made it much easier for them to relate to one another. Thatcher wasn't the dandified twit so suggested by that pirate in the market. On the contrary, another commonality between Thatcher and Caesar was that both spawned from a warrior culture, and this was why so often, during their sword play and bear cub fisticuffs, the two boys would take their games to a very violent level. Yet there was no malice in their intentions. Rather it was as if two warriors were sparring to prepare for great battles to come.

II

It was an almost imperceptible transition, yet somewhere over the next few years Thatcher and Woodes matured into young men. Along with Caesar, each was an outcast in his own way, and as such they formed a tight coalition, bent on protecting each other and preparing for their future lives as nautical men. And it was quite the sight to see: the dark haired Russian, growing long, lean and tall; the African guardian, who towered over his brother by inches all throughout his life; and Woodes, still dressed in the fineries of genteel Bristol, who finally began to sprout and grow stronger, though his boyish face and fair hair remained an unchanging fixture.

While quick to join them and their pseudo-swordplay, Woodes was less inclined to participate in the new level of violent contest that arose between Caesar and Thatcher. On many an evening, as the sun was waning on the River Avon, Thatcher and Caesar would saunter to Redcliffe Back, the docks adjacent to where the main river and its manmade channel split. They would doff their tunics and circle each other like hunting lions, delivering bruising blows to one another, though afterward, each would laugh and brush away whatever sweat or blood resulted from their violent workout. No amount of chiding or lecturing from Yvgeny or the ladies of the house could stop these two from continuously attempting to physically best the other.

These frequent strange rituals of fisticuffs did not go without notice to those who worked along the waterfront. During one of those nightly blood-drenched dances, a visitor to Bristol took note of the two young men squaring off and delivering some of the most crushing blows he had ever seen – quite a hallmark indeed, as he made his living finding such young men to put their talents and physical toughness to work for profit. Artemus Grey was a modern-day trainer of gladiators, only now those whom he recruited need not fear lions or swords or a thumb-down ruling from a king or a crowd. The fate of these modern warriors was solely sealed by their capability to stand up against another likewise trained young man and be successful enough to walk out of the ring under their own steam. Few were the men who entered the ring and did not at some time in their career finally fall fatally prey to someone stronger, younger and more determined to carry the day. Artemus stood and watched the sun slowly set that spring day in 1693, as he witnessed the two dark-skinned men batter each other to a pulp. Finally the lighter-skinned man delivered a stealthily driven haymaker that swept the heavily muscled African off his feet. Caesar had known to watch out for that surprise left Thatcher had added to his repertoire. But that chain of right jabs had distracted him just long enough for Thatcher to present the coup de grace that nearly spun his head off his neck, sending a fine mist of blood spraying from his mouth as he hit the ground in a spread-eagle pose. No sooner had his shoulders hit the hard wooden surface of the wharf than Thatcher was on both knees, lifting his sweaty sparring partner at the neck and slapping each cheek.

"I need to remember that left," Caesar choked out, half laughing, half panting, as he cleared a wad of blood coated mucus from his throat.

"You need to remember to keep that right hand up, or it'll get you every time," Thatcher replied as he lifted Caesar to a seated position, his back resting against a rough dock piling, and brought a tankard of beer to Caesar's mouth. His brother snatched the mug from his hand, resolute to demonstrate that he wasn't that helpless.

"You two seem to have a pretty strange way of expressing affection, I must say," Artemus offered as he approached them.

"Ah, 'tis only our way of making sure each one of us has the other's back, sir," replied Thatcher as he took a deep pull of the slightly bloody mixture in the pewter container.

"So have you two resolved your differences, or shall we wait to see who needs to be carried off to the coroner?" probed Artemus, as he sat down on a box next to the two pugilists.

"There is absolutely no malice of intent, I assure you, sir," defended Thatcher to the overly curious older man who, like him, seemed to possess a boldness that restricted his capability of keeping his nose perhaps closer to his own face.

"Our calling requires us to be capable in ways such as this," Caesar offered in a rare exchange with a stranger. "This is the only way we know we can protect each other."

"I know men who must possess violent talents as part of their vocation," Artemus said. "In fact, some do nothing more than what I've been watching you do for a very long time ... and make quite a bit of quid in the process."

"Yes, I have heard of professional pugilists. I must say that despite what you may have just witnessed it would seem strange to me to intentionally have my body inflicted with harm for the entertainment of others. There are many more ways the body can be used for vocation and entertainment, don't you agree, sir?" offered Thatcher as he stood and offered a hand to help Caesar rise.

Artemus chuckled. "Well, gentlemen, I don't know if watching another fellow pugilist demonstrate his skills would be of interest to you, but I would be most pleased if you would be my guests as I am off to meet with my protégé this instant. He is preparing now for a contest this evening, and again I would welcome you as my guests if nothing more than to intrigue you with a prospect."

Thatcher glanced in the direction of the setting sun and gauged that the services for which they so heartily trained would be required shortly. "As intrigued as I am by the notion of meeting your charge, alas the sky tells me that we are short on time and must make ourselves more presentable for our avocation, sir. Another time, perhaps?"

Artemus rose, offering his hand to both Thatcher and Caesar and indicating the warehouse where he and his fighter would be holed up the next few days – provided, of course, his partner survived the night – and bid them farewell. While he had guessed much about these two, the fact that they were obviously not enemies and shared a bond of intimacy might have been strange to most but was quite recognizable to Artemus. There were those who thrilled for combat. While most would fight out of sense of self-preservation, there were a rare few who viewed pain and suffering not as something to be avoided but something to be mastered. It was a hardening of body and of spirit. It was primitive and one of the reasons why humans had developed the capability to stand up to much bigger predators and lived to tell the tale by cook-fire. Society had worked hard to convince men that violence was something to be avoided, and yet the truth was that violence, like sexual passion, was the most human of qualities. Successive generations of genteel living had bred away the impulse that made one relish the delivery of fist to face. But among a select few, no amount of chiding or breeding could take away what was most base and most real about mankind – its exceedingly violent nature. Rather, as Artemus in his many years had come to realize, men practiced violence in a more civilized manner, affording him an ideal opportunity to cash in on those basic desires.

The storms of the previous day had forced the *Charles II* to belay its arrival in the town of Bristol the evening before. As was the daily custom, Yvgeny, Thatcher and Caesar had made their way to the quays, this time to await the arrival of a dear old friend and trading partner of the aging Russian. Yvgeny had turned 63 in the winter, and Thatcher was beginning to see the signs that his beloved grandfather was betraying the ravages of age. There was nothing painfully obvious about these differences; merely a slowing in the gait and a tendency to lose track of whatever conversation they had been engaged in moments before. There was also this tendency for dear Yvgeny more frequently to revert to his native Russian, as so often he had to reach for the English word for an important point he was trying to communicate. The three had waited on the dock in the pouring rain, looking out to the west and, after a while, surmising that the much anticipated guest would be delayed in his arrival. Delays were par for the course to those who made their living from the sea trade. Yet for some reason, this delay seemed to bother Yvgeny in a way Thatcher had never witnessed before. The countenance of disappointment hung heavy as the three returned to Parker House. In the evening, holding court in his traditional comfortable caquetoire chair, Yvgeny was less conversational than usual, and Thatcher found himself more and more chiming in to questions posed to the old Russian, who seemed lost in his thoughts. At an appropriate moment, when their guests were all being otherwise entertained, Thatcher drew a chair next to Yvgeny, priming and lighting his pipe for him.

"You seem terribly troubled, Grandfather," Thatcher probed. "It's not like you to become so disappointed at the delay of an arrival. Is there something pressing?"

Yvgeny took a deep draw from his pipe, the yellow-tinged curls of smoke wafting elegantly around his grey-bearded visage, as he pondered the musings of his grandson. "Captain Gibson is an old friend of mine, and I was so looking forward to catching up with him this evening."

"Well, grandfather, I am sure he will arrive tomorrow or the next day, and you two will have plenty of time to catch up. But, this isn't what's troubling you, is it?"

"Only partly. I have been waiting for a dispatch from the Colonies, and I'm certain Captain Gibson is carrying it with him. I was anxious to receive a reply to an inquiry. I was hoping it would arrive today. That's all."

"Is there anything to be concerned with, Yvgeny Thatcherev?" Thatcher posed, as he had so often when his grandfather had been holding out on him.

Yvgeny smiled and pulled his grandson closer to him, kissing his forehead as he had done so often when he was a child. While he would never actually admit it, Thatcher considered this one of Yvgeny's most endearing qualities. As Thatcher had grown older, Yvgeny had grown more reserved with his affections as if to signify the impending adulthood of his grandson. Thatcher and Yvgeny had a relationship that extended beyond paternity, and he was now his grandfather's closest business intimate, even more so than Beatrice. It may also have been the change that Thatcher had undergone during his time in Russia. Yvgeny had thought it would be his duty to protect his grandson, but it was obvious that there was nothing Yvgeny could do to protect Thatcher. In the end, in truth, he was fighting to retain his importance in the young boy's life. This change of relationship had created somewhat of a gulf, so when Yvgeny showed this little bit of affection, Thatcher thrilled that for just a moment Yvgeny was being his lovable grandfather again. When Thatcher had first noticed the changes in his grandfather and in their relationship, he queried Yvgeny as to the reason. The old Russian had looked pained yet resolved by the inquiry. He explained to Thatcher that, more than ever, he needed his grandson's brain and not his love. That response had hurt Thatcher in a way he couldn't explain, but he would do anything his grandfather required, and if that meant pulling back from that childlike affection and assuming more of an adult role, then that was a duty he would perform to his utmost.

The next morning, Thatcher heard an insistent knocking, much earlier than he had hoped to hear one. He opened the door to find his grandfather fully clothed and insisting they must get an early start on the day. It was good fortune that Marilee Thompson had thought it wiser to climb back under the sheets rather than answer the door as she had intended, and Thatcher quickly pulled on his breeches, his shirt, his jacket and his highly polished boots, giving Marilee's ample left breast a gentle and grateful kiss as he rushed out the door to meet his grandfather.

Yvgeny was demonstrating a strength he hadn't in a long time as he bounded two at a time down the long staircase. It never ceased to amaze Thatcher how Caesar seemed to know his footfalls, for he was already dressed and at the front door waiting. The three marched down Redcliffe Street with Yvgeny in the lead, his long strides like the days of old. As they reached the quay, Thatcher could see the crest of sails of the *Charles II* now entering the port. The look of anticipation on Yvgeny's face both amused and concerned Thatcher, as he had rarely seen his grandfather demonstrate anything but absolute calm under even the most trying of circumstances. This must have been what he was like some thirteen years ago as he had so often heard in the re-telling of the stories of his day of birth. Yvgeny had to be convinced repeatedly by both Thatcher and Caesar to stand clear as he was constantly getting under foot of the stevedores attempting to grapple with the lines to bring the massive ship to port. From the quarterdeck, Captain Gibson stood by the harbor pilot who was making his final adjustments to the rudder to secure the ship to shore. On his face was painted a smile of sheer amusement as he witnessed his old friend and trading partner pacing the length of dock. The captain directed the lowering of the gangplank and made his way to portside to greet Yvgeny, who was attempting to mount the entry platform even before it had firmly come to rest.

Yvgeny's long left leg had cleared the gunwale just as Captain Gibson reached him. Extending out his weathered, tanned hand to the Russian, he was greeted with a bear hug that nearly took the breath out of him. "Do you have something for me?" Yvgeny asked with some urgency.

"Ah, yes, my friend. The packet is in my cabin," Captain Gibson responded, gesturing for Yvgeny to follow him. Yvgeny turned back to Thatcher and Caesar who had, by this time, caught up with him. They were taken a bit by surprise when he asked them to wait on deck.

Now it was Thatcher's turn to pace anxiously until the two old men emerged some time later from the darkened confines of the ship. Yvgeny reached out to his grandson's arm, beckoning him forward.

"Yvgeny Thatcherev Edwards, I wish you to meet one of my oldest friends in England, Captain Charles Gibson. Captain Gibson, my grandson, Thatcher Edwards." The two reached out and vigorously shook hands.

"It is a pleasure to finally meet you, Captain Gibson. My grandfather has told me so many stories about those early days and how helpful you were in establishing his prominence to the court of Russia," Thatcher offered, genuinely pleased at meeting his grandfather's old friend.

"Thatcher, I need you and Caesar to do me a favor. Please conduct the good captain back to the house. You've been at sea long, Captain?" Yvgeny asked.

Gibson smiled and replied, "A few months, old friend. If you promise there's more of this," indicating a decanter of grain wine Yvgeny had presented to him, "your grandson can conduct me anywhere you please."

Yvgeny smiled back. "Oh, I'm sure we can find many things to cater to your needs, my good friend. Thatcher, would you arrange that as well?"

"Why, of course, Grandfather. But you are not coming?" Thatcher quizzed.

"I shall be along shortly. As for now, my friend, I put you in the good hands of my most trusted business associate, and I trust we will catch up later."

Without another word, Yvgeny quickly exited the ship and ventured off into the waking village of Bristol. Captain Gibson turned to the young man and inquired, "I will not be imposing, will I?"

"Captain Gibson, you will find all the accommodations of Parker House at your disposal. Whatever your needs, sir, I am sure we have what you may desire."

Captain Gibson gave a big smile, patted Thatcher's shoulder and commanded, "Well, then, lead the way, good man. Oh, but first ... Mr. Avery?"

From the starboard approached a broad, powerful man. First mate Avery stood before his captain, somewhat peeved at being called away from preparing the ship for unload, a task made more urgent as they had lost a day in port to a storm. "Aye, cap'n."

"Mr. Avery, I will be leaving the ship for some time. Please make sure all arrangements for offload are completed and that all cannon and armament resupply begins immediately after we've cleared all cargo and passengers."

"Offloading will begin immediately, sir. As soon as the cannon and supply arrive, we'll immediately get 'em placed and stowed, sir. Is there someplace I can find you should we need you?"

"Parker House," Thatcher indicated to the rough looking seaman who would take command of the ship in the captain's absence.

Mr. Avery sized up the young man and his African accomplice and bid "Aye, aye" as the captain disembarked. That the captain would immediately depart the ship the moment they arrived and when they had such pressing business in port was of no surprise to Mr. Avery. Having served with the captain for many years, Avery had come to realize that his captain placed his priorities upon locating the first punch house he could find ashore. This fact was one of many that disturbed and irritated Avery and many of the crewmen aboard. It was the reason why the captain had not seemed able to get his bearings in very familiar water and make port last night rather than sailing aimlessly outside the Bristol Channel. Much grumbling had been heard below decks, and few of the crew were pleased with the notion that their next duty was to play escort to their previous enemy, the Spanish. While retooling to serve as a man-of-war for the British Empire might be considered honorable work by some, this crew had no love for either the Spanish or the low wages offered by England for escort duty. To Mr. Avery and many of the crew, it was a waste of good cannonade to have it employed protecting Spanish ships rather than raiding them of their plate and sending them to the bottom. Perhaps those crewmen hesitant to go "on the account" would be more encouraged when, yet again, their captain spent the afternoon in a drunken stupor while they sweated and toiled to make the ship ready to protect their recent enemy. It was really only a matter of time ... and opportunity.

III

If one were to observe Nettie on a typical day, he would almost swear the woman never slept. From the break of day, when she conducted her business in the marketplace, to late at night, when she collected the soiled sheets, whether doing it herself or supervising others, Nettie was always on the go. Sumptuous food seemed to flow from the kitchen at all hours of the day, as the ravenous appetites of teenaged boys and busy ladies were constantly in need of sating. Small gangs of cleaning women scoured the three story building from top to bottom during the daylight hours. And acres of laundry bounced from the lines in rhythm to the Bristol winds.

Beatrice Parker was fastidious about cleanliness, not only for the home but for those who lived in it. One of the strangest features of the home was a room beneath the staircase, always an object of curiosity to visitors, which was devoted solely to the purpose of bathing. Beatrice had installed a series of large basins capable of holding an entire human body in which said individual could be fully immersed and generous portions of soaps applied for thorough cleansing. The very thought of such a room was as scandalous as the practices of the house itself, as even the most gentrified of English people of the era routinely bathed semi-annually at best and then at great protest. Such was the feeling of most of the girls the first time Beatrice laid down to them the ground rules of cleanliness. While the demands of performance and openness to repertoire were taken in stride, to be asked to immerse themselves daily with soap was much more than some of them could handle. But to those who became accustomed to the process of ablution came also an increase in vigor and decrease in ailment, and this went to the heart of why Beatrice stressed cleanliness. The less-than-hygienic women who were contracted to fill those tubs and basins could barely contain their outrage at the thought, but the steady quid and guarantee of seven days a week of employment made them screw up their disdainful noses and go begrudgingly about their task of filling and emptying these bathing tubs in silence. It did, however, make conversation in their filthy homes with their filthy husbands and filthy families much more intriguing and certainly titillating.

But Beatrice's obsession with cleanliness was not limited to the ladies and the house exclusively. She was adamant that good hygiene be practiced by her customers as well. As a consummate reader, Beatrice realized that the greatest threat to her home was that which was brought from the outside world. The whorish nature of her customers was obvious, and unlike their spouses she was not foolish enough to believe that these men were exclusively loyal to her ladies. Thus, new customers to Parker House were taken aside to be enlightened to the house requirement of a strange and discomfiting practice – the wearing of condoms. When gently explained by Beatrice or Abigail in such a way as to make the process of affixing the item less uncomfortable than imagined, the regular customers took this peculiarity initially with resignation and eventually with great anticipation. Since reading Gabriele Falloppio's *Anatomy*, Beatrice had become a strict advocate of his theories on cleanliness and his treatises on baths and purgatives. Most fascinating to her was his thesis on clinical trials he had conducted on condoms to combat the spread of syphilis and unwanted pregnancy. As the women of Parker House could otherwise be rendered unserviceable, Beatrice was adamant that her house and the ladies employed there would not be side-lined with macho insistence and revulsion to good hygiene.

Promptly at six, all the residents of Parker House met in the great dining hall where Nettie would provide a lavish dinner to make sure that the ladies had full stomachs in preparation for a busy and long night of work. By seven, the cleaning women having finally departed, the house set in order and the rooms prepared, with clean sheets and an ample stock of sheepskins, the ladies would return to their rooms to apply final dabs of ablutions as the first of the guests would begin to arrive. And the guests were always like clockwork. As the Bristol gentry completed their dinners, it was a common custom for the gentlemen to meet and stroll through the business section of town to walk off their own heavy meals. Of course, when they turned the corner out of view of their wives, they would pick up their pace and cross the High Street Bridge into Redcliffe to darken the door of Parker House. While time was short and purpose was known, these elaborate rituals of asking for the master of the house, the escorting to the parlor, the light conversation of business and news of the world, to the accompaniment of good drink and smoke, were essentials so that no one felt barbarous in the process. The ladies would make their way into the parlor, pick up on the threads of small talk, and when an appropriate number of moments had passed and excuses made to bid adieu to the company, the gentlemen would quickly proceed up the stairs with their lovely attendants and in short order be happily escorted back to the door. It was common for groups of these gentlemen to come together and depart together so their stories were straight and less likely to create a stir among the gentle wives who had spent the last hour or so preparing their children for bed. And as they strolled through the business sector and back to their homes, they would greet their fellow businessmen and the most recent arrivals from sea passing in the opposite direction.

And such the process would continue as first the married men, and then the single merchants, and finally the contingents of sailors and their officers would pour from the numerous taverns and public houses of Bristol to begin their ritualistic stroll to Parker House. Usually the late hours were reserved for those poor souls who could not sneak out of their homes earlier or, the most sad and pathetic lot of all, the lovelorn. From these last two groups of customers the fortunes of Parker House were built, for those who could not abide themselves with stiff drink to get to sleep or those smitten by the charms of one particular lady were always willing to pay a premium to be the last in line for the evening. Around two or so, as the last of the customers bid adieu to Thatcher and Yvgeny and Caesar, Nettie would begin her late night process of stripping the sheets and laying down fresh cover so the ladies of Parker House could sleep without the scent of their customers still in their nostrils and pillows. While Nettie may have appeared to be in constant attendance throughout the day, she would steal off to her room during the height of business and log in her most solid hours of sleep. Those hours when Parker House was closed for business and all lay slumbering, Nettie would begin her baking, stealing a brief catnap as her bread rose, then start the day anew. Such had been Nettie's life years, and though it may have appeared sheer drudgery to an outsider, to Nettie it was utter contentment. Taking care of such a large and busy home for such loving and appreciative people was not just her job. It was her role in the family – and handsomely profitable as well.

Periodically, there were interruptions to the system, as was the case when Yvgeny's old friend Captain Gibson came through the door at seven a.m. Nettie was happy to serve him breakfast and make him feel at home. Thatcher had likewise procured other diversions for the captain, and he had disappeared upstairs hours ago with Marilee and a bottle of Yvgeny's finest bread wine and had yet to return. But this interruption to her system wasn't what concerned her. For as long as Nettie could remember, the boys had spent their mornings with Yvgeny, but he had not returned with them from the docks. Thatcher and Caesar's concern as the day went on was palpable. Finally, as dinner was just about completed, the front door swung open and Yvgeny appeared, hurriedly making his way to his spot at the table. He began digging into the remaining portions of lamb and sweet potatoes and a diminished pile of fresh bread as if his absence were merely a figment of their imaginations.

"Grandfather, you've had us worried all day. We walked out the door at six o'clock this morning – here it is almost seven and you finally return. Is there something afoot?" Thatcher queried, a bit put off by his grandfather's cavalier return.

Yvgeny finished chewing a mouthful and replied, "Yes, I know my boy. It's been a very busy day, and I am sorry to have caused concern.

We will discuss it at great length later this evening. But we have such a short time before our guests arrive. Speaking of guests, where's Captain Gibson?"

Marilee smiled and shook her head. "I went upstairs to roust the gentleman, to invite him to dinner, but he wasn't having it. After taking a second helping of me, he went back to sleep."

"Then I guess I had better see if I can entreat him to join us," Yvgeny announced, piling some bits of the left over food on a plate and heading for the stairs.

Like clockwork, the doorknocker resounded promptly at seven, and Thatcher began to greet the evening's guests. In short order, Yvgeny brought Captain Gibson to join the gentlemen in the parlor, and he began to regale them with tales of the sea and the important job he was about to undertake.

"So Captain, I'm sure you must have a bit of reservation having to now provide escort duty for our former enemy," probed one of the merchants.

"I have been sailing long enough to know that no enemy or friend is permanent. I am sure in no time we will once again be viewing Spain as the Papist infidels they are. But for now, my king feels it critical we protect our new ally from the depredations of piracy, and I fully intend to stand and deliver."

"And what of your crew, Captain Gibson. Are they likewise as malleable?" asked Thatcher, who was quite intrigued by the line of questioning.

"Well, you can imagine that having just come off privateer duty and the obvious difference in pay, it is never well-received. But they are a good crew and my first mate, John Avery, has the loyalty and fear of his men. I'm sure whatever misgivings they may have he'll promptly put asunder."

As the ladies of the house began to filter into the parlor, escorting away men whose depth of commitment to the conversation was waning by the second, Yvgeny and Captain Gibson stole off to a corner and seemed rapt in conversation. Thatcher could pick up pieces of their discussion that seemed to focus on shipping and the Colonies, but nothing substantive to be able to put together the clues of Yvgeny's disappearing act. As the night continued on and the various waves of customers passed in and out of the front door of Parker

House, Thatcher's thoughts were distracted by the arrival of Artemus Grey. In tow was a young man in his twenties who, like Thatcher and Caesar, bore the marks of fresh battering. Despite the obviously painful cuts and contusions which crowned his cheeks and forehead, he seemed to be in lively spirits.

"Ah, there you are! These are the two young men I was telling you about, Jocko," Artemus began as he pulled his companion to where Thatcher and Caesar were standing. "Unfortunately, I did not get your names."

Thatcher smiled and offered his hand to both men. "You'll have to forgive me for my rudeness. My friend and I were pressed for time and were too impolite to make proper introductions, though I must commend you, sir, for figuring out where to find us. I am Thatcher Edwards, and this is my brother Caesar," Thatcher offered, as all men took a round of hand shaking. The obvious reference to Caesar as a sibling was received with a bit of surprise by the two men.

"And I did not introduce myself either. My name is Artemus Grey, and this young man is my protégé, Jocko McMullan. As you can tell by his obvious badges of honor, dear Jocko is the young man to whom I referred earlier today and, I am happy to report, champion of tonight's festivities."

"Artemus was tellin' me about ye two lads and the serious thumpin' ye were giving each other. And ye say ye're brothers?" Jocko pressed.

"Different mothers," Caesar offered.

"Yes, Artemus was telling us that apparently you two travel about and pick fights for profit. I could not tell from your face that you were this evening's victor, but I'll trust your standing here that there must be truth to that boast," Thatcher offered.

"Oh, this? Ye think this is bad? One fellow had to be carried out and the other is, I believe, still lyin' where I dropped him, poor man, God love 'im," Jocko replied with a big smile betraying the absence of a number of teeth. "But I'm lookin' at these bruises here on your face, my friend. Seems one could wonder the same thing about ye," Jocko continued as he touched the soft spots on Thatcher's face.

"Well, the difference is, my friend, my brother and I simply keep each other in shape. We're not trying to earn bob battering each other for other people's entertainment," Thatcher replied.

"Gentlemen, the way I see it is that you two seem to take an awful lot of pleasure in seeing how much pain you can take and receive," replied Artemus. "Jocko's no different. He just knows his value, which, as well as making your acquaintance, is what brings us here. I wish to treat my good friend to the best the house has to offer." At that moment, the lovely Allison Simms entered the room, offering smiles all around and offering extended eye contact with Jocko.

"Best is a relative term, but I can assure you whatever it is that Mr. McMullan seems to enjoy – beyond being beat half to death – any of my fine lady friends will be happy to provide. But before I introduce you to the ladies, let me introduce you to the Lady of the House." And as if on cue, Beatrice Parker, still ravishing in her fifties, glided through the room with absolute poise and dignity to join the men with her grandsons. The news of new guests always reached Beatrice in short order, and she made it a point to personally greet all new customers.

"Mr. Grey, Mr. McMullan, it is my pleasure to introduce the enchanting mistress of Parker House, Beatrice Parker," Thatcher stated, as Beatrice elegantly offered her hand to both men. She surveyed the one with the nasty cuts and bruises on his face, giving a quick look to her grandson. "Grandmother, Mr. McMullan here is a professional pugilist and is flush with cash from his victories."

"It's a pleasure to welcome you gentlemen into my home. Mr. McMullan, I trust you don't seek such physicality in your female companionship, do you?"

Jocko smiled and slightly blushed at the overtness of the woman's comments. "No ma'am, after what I do for a day's pay, what I'm seekin' is a much more gentle touch."

Artemus surveyed the beautiful Beatrice Parker, the question running through his mind as to whether or not this finer vintage was on the menu. "Mistress Parker, Artemus Grey. And let me tell you what a lovely home you have and how lovely you make it seem," he flattered as he took her hand for a kiss.

As if reading his mind, Beatrice replied as sweetly and kindly as possible, "Mr. Grey, your kind words are much appreciated and make this old woman's heart skip a beat. May I suggest you save them for one of my dear ladies who are so taken by the flowery words of handsome, seasoned men." Now turning to them both, "We welcome you to our house and are certain you will find everything to your liking. But my first question: are you familiar with the application of a sheepskin?" Beatrice took each of them by the arm and led them to a quiet corner.

The brisk pace of business made the evening pass quickly, and later, as Artemus Grey and Jocko McMullan took in the last few moments of their visit to Parker House, enjoying a fine brandy and pipe of tobacco, Artemus proceeded with his pitch. "Now, boys, I understand you may have misgivings about our chosen profession, much as I'm sure others have misgivings of yours. But in truth, we're both in the same business. People seek distraction from their mundane existence and find it in watching and participating in intimate grappling between two people. What I ask of you is nothing more than the opportunity to let you fellows conduct your pastime in an atmosphere more conducive than the docks. Dear Jocko here was like you – a real scrapper who fought just because he liked to see if he could stand up to bigger fellows. And he did. But all he had to show for it was bragging rights and busted noses. Now, not only does Jocko get hurt less, but he provides a valuable form of amusement and is appropriately compensated for his effort. May I, if nothing else, ask you to come down and see what we do and how Jocko is able to so effectively practice his craft with such lethal talent?"

Thatcher and Caesar looked at each other and silently appraised the offer. Wordlessly they reached an agreement. "If for no other reason than curiosity's sake, we welcome the opportunity to watch Jocko do professionally what we do for mere amusement," Thatcher admitted.

"Gents, come down tomorrow and watch as I put a fellow through his paces for practice. Right now he's preparin' to take on matches of his own, and it's a good opportunity if nothin' else to see what good trainin' can do for ye," Jocko stated, pleased to hear that the two were taking them up on their invitation.

Caesar and Thatcher showed their guests to the door with assurances of tomorrow's attendance. With the last of their guests now gone, Thatcher sought out his grandfather who had retired to the study with Beatrice and Abigail.

"Ah, have the last of our guests taken their leave?" Yvgeny inquired as Thatcher and Caesar entered the library.

"We'll go take one last tour upstairs in a moment to make sure the lovelorn have been shooed," Thatcher said. "But now, Grandfather, I think it's time you let me in on what has kept you preoccupied all day."

"I was just discussing that with your mother and grandmother. And I'm sorry that I appeared so secretive today. But big changes are about to occur, and I wanted to make sure the ladies were fully comfortable with the decisions about to be made. You remember a few years back, just before we went to Russia, when I told you that your grandmother and I were looking into other enterprise opportunities?"

"Yes, Grandfather, but I thought you were merely trying to distract me from considering the trip to Russia," Thatcher replied.

"In some small measure, perhaps I was, but your grandmother thought there were other opportunities we have been overlooking and limiting ourselves due to the unique nature of our primary enterprise."

To Thatcher, this primary enterprise, this house, was what he had known all his life, his mother's life as well. While others may have had their judgments and cast aspersions with regard to it, Parker House was one of the most profitable businesses in all of Bristol. If nothing else, that was a testament to its viability and desirability. "Grandfather, you have taught me there are virtually no limitations to anyone smart enough and strong enough to take on any challenge, business or personal. I quite frankly don't see how our business here has in any way limited us from other very lucrative enterprises. Have I missed something?"

Nettie entered the study with a freshly tamped pipe, handing it to Yvgeny along with his nightcap glass of bread wine as Beatrice struck a match and lit the tobacco. He took a deep draw of the pipe, smiling at the ladies who, through these subtle gestures, always made him feel very much at home. "While it is true that we have done very well in a number of avenues, there have been doors closed to us by virtue of this house. There are many who point a finger and refuse to consider us as good business partners for no other reason than we provide a service that they deem immoral. But, despite the great life we've made, there are opportunities to make an even greater one, and with it a fresh start."

Thatcher looked to his grandmother and mother. Such a revelation cast the greatest dispersion on them, as they had spent lifetime in this vocation. These women had raised him to acknowledge the fact that men always craved the attentions of women and that a woman who understood her value and professed this trade not only empowered but likewise acknowledged the unique gift they had been given as sexual creatures, no different than those who paid for the service. "And how do you feel about this, Grandmother? Am I to believe that the business that has sustained my family for nearly thirty years is something to be shamefully abandoned?"

Beatrice moved to sit beside her grandson and put an arm around his shoulder. "Thatcher, I've never been ashamed of what we do for a living, but if I had been given the choice some thirty years ago to earn my living otherwise, without a doubt I would have taken it. I was able to raise my daughter and grandson very handsomely on the backs of other women. This was an acknowledgement of our capability, but it is not a limitation. What your grandfather is proposing is to make this a past to be put behind us and make a future where we do not have to create veils to mask our way of living."

Abigail came to sit at his other side. "Thatcher, we have worked so hard and faced the criticism of so many people for so long that I think what your grandfather is proposing would be best for all of us. It would give you a chance to apply that brilliant mind rather than having to flex that magnificent brawn. This is something I want you to consider, for all of us. For you and most especially for me."

"So obviously what you're proposing is taking us away from Bristol?" he asked, more as a confirmation.

"Oh, yes, very far away from Bristol," Yvgeny replied, taking the documents out of his pocket and handing them to Thatcher. Once again, mere sheets of paper stood to make a dramatic difference in Thatcher's life. He took a moment to read through them and then handed them to Caesar.

"So what's in Carolina?" Thatcher questioned.

"A wonderful opportunity to re-start a dying trade town." Yvgeny retrieved a map he had pulled out for just this occasion. Caesar and Thatcher joined their grandfather as he spread the rolled up parchment out on the table. "This is the Carolina coast. Here is the settlement of Charles Towne in the south. It is becoming an important trade port of the Carolinas. But notice this big, vast portion of protected coast behind these barrier islands that stretch all the way to the Chesapeake. Right here, in the middle is a river called the Cape Fear, and here at its mouth, settled some years ago, is a little town called Brunswick. It showed great promise that has not yet been realized. This commission, from the Governor of Carolina, will allow us to take over this port and potentially build a trade empire, taking crops from the land and sending them here to England. But not Bristol – London, where there is limited knowledge of Parker House and no limitation to the wealth we can achieve."

Thatcher studied the map. What his grandfather was saying made great business sense, but something even more important than the profit to be made troubled him. "But what of the house? And what of the ladies? What is to become of them?"

Of all the things that would concern Thatcher, Beatrice and Abigail had correctly guessed that this would be the one that would trouble him most. These women had been an omnipresent part of his life since birth, and while his relationship with them may have changed over the years, there was no doubting that his love for these women was incredible and passionate, as was theirs for him, reciprocated in ways not openly discussed.

"You know, Yvgeny thought we would be the biggest challenge on this issue, and we told him that in truth you would be," Abigail remarked. "And that has been one challenge he did not expect he would have to undertake. But it has been a huge occupation for him as well. Yvgeny?"

"While we have not yet discussed it with them, we have every hope that they will choose to join us in Carolina, not in their current profession but with new ones. Of course, they cannot just instantly have new careers, but that is why your grandmother and I are leaving first, to establish our home and business and to seek out opportunities for the ladies."

"So then we won't all be going together," Thatcher queried. "When were you and Grandmother thinking of going then?"

"I have spent the day making arrangements for your grandmother and I to sail to New York from Bristol. It was a challenge, but we've been able to secure passage in one week. We've chosen New York because, quite frankly, we don't want people knowing we're going to Carolina. To those who need to know, your grandmother and I are taking a trip to the Colonies as our honeymoon."

Yvgeny's statement took a moment to sink in. Thatcher looked at him and then at his grandmother, who had moved to her paramour's side. He then looked at his mother who was beaming. "Yvgeny Thatcherev," Thatcher managed, standing to confront the old man. "Are you asking for my grandmother's hand in marriage?"

Yvgeny's eyes twinkled as he sidled up next to Beatrice, placing one arm around her shoulder and taking her offered hand. "Only with your blessing, my boy."

IV

In truth, it had been Beatrice who had set the wheels in motion for this new and exciting venture. To a certain extent, she may have begun the process to fill those empty and frightening months her lover and grandson were in Russia. Every day, she had feared that word would arrive that Yvgeny or Thatcher had met with some unforeseen incident that led to their being jailed or dead. She grew particularly concerned when in mid-spring Sergei Evanovich returned to Bristol without Yvgeny and Thatcher. Though he brought with him letters that assured her they were both alive and well, neither she nor Abigail could stop discussing conjectures as to why the two had prolonged their stay in Russia.

Speculation was a common trait between Abigail and her mother on a variety of levels. As consummate readers and lovers of tales, they had shared a lifelong game of observing people and speculating their life stories. Most frequently in their adult years, to the great embarrassment of Yvgeny Thatcherev, they would speculate on the sex lives of their most loyal customers. But another form of speculation, which had proved to be quite lucrative, was one they shared with Yvgeny and their ability to see the potential of wise investments that had added greatly to the Parker House financial portfolio. It was Beatrice's desire to take her daughter's mind off the speculations about their family abroad that began her ardent quest to find something of a conjectural nature that would occupy their minds until the return of Yvgeny and Thatcher. This is how she stumbled upon the opportunities in the Colonies. After almost a year of separation and the return of the men, Beatrice and Abigail began to share with Yvgeny the results of their explorations. As mere women, they had reached their limitation of inquiry, and Yvgeny, quite motivated from the rationale of their argument, picked up the ball and began to inquire further. The ladies' research had carried them as far as the docks of New York, but Yvgeny decided he wanted to look further, and his deeper inquiries led him to Carolina. This shared project, which put not only commerce but also their family in a new light, crossed a threshold with Beatrice that made her feel closer than she could ever have imagined to the old

Russian. While the thoughts of some harm coming to her grandson gave her many a sleepless night, she would never openly admit that the thing that kept her wide awake most often was the thought that she had lost her Yvgeny. Their relationship had been one of great passion but unspoken commitment, and yet upon his return she very frequently found herself bringing up the subject of their future. To Yvgeny, these were words he had always hoped to hear her speak. While he respected her viewpoints on religion and its traditions, he also saw that in her was something that was taking this meaning of family to a whole new level. And that's when he asked her once again to marry him, expecting her to give it great thought and then, as usual, gently turn him down. But it was her instant "yes" that floored him. So while he began shaping up his plans and working to secure his commissions from the Governor of Carolina, he likewise began to send inquiries to someone whom he thought could best help him make her "yes" the most memorable "yes" of her life. His inquiry and appeal of assistance was met with yet another resounding "yes," and the letter from London which had arrived just days before the packet from Captain Gibson made him feel as if God's hands were in the works to make all of this possible.

It was just after dawn when the carriage from London arrived with its sole passenger, who disembarked at the front door of Parker House. The early hour and the knocking on the door rousted those who were already awake to race to answer it. While Yvgeny had long strides, Caesar had the advantage of ground floor quarters and youth. He opened the door and took in the sight of the slight, stooped unfamiliar gentleman, decked head to toe in layers of black tunic and possessing a long and wizened beard, just like Yvgeny Thatcherev. The old man smiled, taking in the sight of the large African who stood at the door and studied him carefully.

"Without a doubt, you must be Caesar," the old man offered as he stuck out his hand to shake that of one of the first Africans he had ever encountered. "I have heard very much about you from Yvgeny Thatcherev. Oh, my manners. Would you please tell him ...?"

"Marcellus!" Yvgeny cried at the top of his lungs, pushing past Caesar and embracing the old man like the brother he was. "My God, how old you've gotten! Where is that youthful vigor that I used to have to compete with?"

"Unlike you, Yvgeny Thatcherev, I don't have beautiful women to keep me young. My days are spent with old clerics addressing new ideas ... and old nuns," Marcellus joked, hugging his old friend. He motioned to Caesar, who took in the two chattering away in Russian. "You said he was a big fellow, but I did not realize this big," Marcellus said indicating the African who was gesturing for the two gentlemen to come in from the morning chill.

"It's a common trait of my people," Caesar replied in his perfect Russian. "Just like your people wear beards."

Yvgeny and Marcellus laughed and made their way in. Marcellus, giving a gentle punch to Caesar's chest and shaking his hand as if in pain, "You did not tell me he spoke Russian, too."

"Yes, but his Polish is atrocious," Yvgeny laughed as the two men walked in through the long hall of the main floor and into the kitchen, where Nettie was just about to leave for market.

"And this is Nettie!" Marcellus exclaimed as he took in the small black woman, studying the two men who were being awfully loud first thing in the morning and disturbing her peaceful hours. "And does she speak Russian, too?" he asked in his broken English.

"Nyet," Nettie replied as the two burst out laughing again.

"Nettie, I know you're heading off to market, but my dear friend Marcellus has been traveling all night long, and I'm sure he is starving. Do we have anything we could scare up for him to tide him over 'til breakfast?"

"Hello, Metropolitan Marcellus. I must say I did not expect to meet you, though Yvgeny has talked about you so much these last few years," she offered as she peeked into the stove that contained bread still baking. She looked at the hourglass sitting on the counter and opened up a decanter of her preserves and set it on the kitchen table. "Do either of ye learned men know how to read this?" she asked, indicating the hourglass. "When this sand runs out, the bread will be ready. Don't take it out before then, or it will be too doughy. Don't let it wait too long or it will burn."

Yvgeny smiled and hugged the saucy Nettie. "I think we can master an hourglass, Nettie, and while not typically part of our breakfast regimen, if you see some good fresh fish, I'm sure Marcellus would be extra pleased." Yvgeny gave a kiss on the cheek to his beloved Nettie as she shook her head and exited the kitchen. Nettie paused for a second at the door than gave another careful once over of Marcellus.

"You would have made a fine Patriarch, Metropolitan," she admitted nodding her head in affirmation as she exited the kitchen door.

"You would have, you know," Yvgeny added as Marcellus took up a stool and watched studiously as the sand ran down though the hourglass.

Marcellus smiled, not looking up toward his friend. "It was too soon for Mother Russia, Yvgeny. Change will come, perhaps in the era after Patriarch Adrian. But it most assuredly won't be someone like me, like us, with an affinity for barbaric tongues." When the final grains of sand had spilled from the top, Marcellus grabbed two towels and retrieved the perfectly baked bread and cut a huge chunk for himself and Yvgeny who passed across a glass of Pskov Blue Label. Marcellus smiled taking in his old friend. "To great things from Pskov," he toasted as he shot down the glass. "Now, hand me that jar."

It had been a long night for Beatrice and quite a few emotional days before it. She was much desirous of a long sleep, but the noise downstairs could not help but pique her curiosity. She dressed, pulled her hair together and made her way down the stairs where she could hear the noisy Yvgeny, laughing and shouting up a storm. She could also detect another voice, not familiar but obviously Russian. Silently and slowly she made her way down the hallway, trying to catch snippets of the conversation, though her Russian was not nearly as proficient as the younger members of the family. She stood for a moment outside the door, but her curiosity got the best of her, and she pushed it open to see two aged and bearded men sitting with a pile of bread, ever so slightly crisp, both of their hirsute visages smeared with Nettie's plum preserves. Yvgeny was on his feet like a shot the moment that Beatrice entered the kitchen, and his companion smiled the sweetest and warmest smile as she entered the room. She retrieved a cloth from the counter as she walked to her beloved Yvgeny, who had his arms spread out, covered with plum, and began dabbing at his hands and beard as she shook her head with annoyed amusement. Marcellus began wiping his hands upon his tunic, recovering them with preserves as he wiped them out of his beard, and both men stood there, smiling with love and adoration at the lovely and wondrous Beatrice Parker.

"My love, my dear Beatrice, I am so sorry if we woke you. I know you are so tired, but I am overjoyed that my dear friend has at last arrived from London." Yvgeny said as he embraced her gently with one arm, leading her to introduce her.

"Marcellus of Pskov. I would know you anywhere as you are my Yvgeny's salvation," she stated as she embraced the plum-stained old cleric as if he were a long-lost family member. "But what, pray tell, are you doing here in Bristol?" she inquired, the answer dawning on her as she asked the question.

Marcellus took both hands and placed them on her arms to study her and her lovely face, the face that was the true salvation of Yvgeny Thatcherev. "It was my good fortune that I was in London meeting with representatives of your holy Anglican Church when I heard that Yvgeny Thatcherev was trying to find me. It had fully been my intention to come here and surprise him, but how I was pleasantly surprised when a young messenger from my country's trade representative here in Bristol came to me and inquired on behalf of Yvgeny Thatcherev. And when I read his note, I knew my deep theological discussions with the members of the Anglican faith could wait a little bit longer." He looked to Yvgeny who likewise placed an arm on each of his two beloved comrades.

"When you said yes to marry me, I knew that you would never be able to marry in the Anglican Church, and you are too good for a civil ceremony. So I asked Marcellus if he would come to Bristol to join us in Holy Matrimony. And he said only on one condition: if you wish the same."

Beatrice studied the two men who were virtually beaming and yet seemed poised on bated breath for her affirmation. "How could any woman say no to such faces?" she said, gently tugging each of their beards, still flecked with remnants of plum.

It had been thirteen years since Parker House had undergone such a state of cacophony. Thatcher was overjoyed to see Marcellus here, and he and Caesar spent every spare moment running down the various requests put forth by Yvgeny, Beatrice and Marcellus. Abigail was in tears nearly the entire time leading up to the ceremony as waves of joy overcame her, reducing this typically strong woman to misty eyes every time she looked at her mother. Once again, that infrequent sign hung outside Parker House, only this time a select group of merchants and luminaries of Bristol had received invitations to witness the holy nuptials of Yvgeny Thatcherev to Beatrice Parker.

The appointed time for the ceremony had already long since lapsed, as both the bride and groom were still nursing painful headaches from the previous night's celebration. As was the Russian tradition, Yvgeny and Marcellus had been gone most of the day before, drinking pints and cups at Peal's, enjoying the conviviality of the merchants and rogues who had been benefiting from the steady flow of free drinks all day long. As the sun began to set, the two Russians and their motley assemblage of new best friends made their way out of Peal's and down the lane to Parker House. Yvgeny rapped thunderously at the door, where he was greeted by a sober and serious Thatcher, who stared disapprovingly at his drunken grandfather and this hoard of brigands who accompanied him and Marcellus.

"Good evening, dear Grandson," Yvgeny nearly shouted. "I have come to see my intended and demand you take me to her at once." This demand was trumpeted by the drunken assemblage behind Yvgeny, who seemed quite insistent that his demand be met. As the crowd got louder, Thatcher was joined by Caesar and Nettie, ceremoniously holding her hand inside her apron.

"Yvgeny Thatcherev, your drunken and sodden behavior shows you are absolutely unworthy to be married to my grandmother, and thus I will have to ask you please to leave as I'm certain she has no interest in seeing you in such a state," Thatcher insisted.

The crowd was not pleased with this answer and demanded that Beatrice Parker be brought forth to see her intended. Rather, their shouts did nothing more than beckon the ladies of the house to join the guardians at the door in their disapproval and disavowal.

"Dear Grandson, are you attempting to stand in the way of your grandmother's happiness? She has accepted my proposal of marriage, and I demand you bring my bride to me now!" Yvgeny shouted, greatly cheered on by his entourage.

Thatcher thought for a moment, studying his very drunk grandfather, and then reached a solution. "Your crosses. Yours and Marcellus'. Give them to me now as payment for bringing my grandmother, and I will consider your offer."

Marcellus and Yvgeny studied the large silver crosses around their necks, both possessing incredible spiritual and material value, and then looked at the boy showing discontent with his vulgar demand.

"Young Thatcher, we are men of the cloth, sacred representatives of His Most Holy Patriarch of the one and true Orthodox Church," Marcellus protested. "You would demand payment from your beloved grandfather and his dearest friend in order to retrieve your grandmother? Have you no shame? Have you no fear for your soul?"

"The crosses, gentlemen, or you and your mob must depart the premises immediately," Thatcher stated with absolute resolve.

The two old clerics looked at each other, shrugged, kissed their crosses as they took them off and handed them to this brigand of a grandson. He studied the two heavy crosses and then unceremoniously tossed them to Caesar.

"Very well, take the old woman," he stated cavalierly as Yvgeny and Marcellus acted like teenagers, racing up the stairs to the cheers of the crowd.

Beatrice Parker's scream could be heard resonating down the hallway, and Marcellus was in the lead, taking two steps at a time, as Yvgeny trailed with Beatrice Parker thrown over his shoulder. He stopped at the bottom of the stairs, took a long pull from a bottle of bread wine and gave a solid swat to Beatrice's derriere to the further cheers of approval not only from their Peal's posse but from all the people of the house. It absolutely amazed Thatcher how strong and vigorous his grandfather could be when properly soused and motivated, but Beatrice Parker kicked and screamed and laughed from her perch on Yvgeny's shoulder all the way to the clerk's office to file for their marriage license.

That night, Parker House was not closed, but in the spirit of the tradition of giving, all the ladies of the house were happy to give their all in the celebration by sharing themselves with whoever offered a hopeful inquiry. And now it was hard to believe that this beautiful house, so elegantly appointed in preparation for these holy nuptials, had been a scene of a virtual orgy the night before. The Orthodox marriage tradition was one of sheer beauty and a breathtaking experience for both the couple and the assembled guests. As Yvgeny and Beatrice recited their vows to one another and Marcellus intoned ceremonial chants, those assembled were invited to offer their own intonements and blessings for this sacred occasion. The room shimmered with the magnificent splay of candlelight, made more luminous by the billowing fragrant smoke that hovered throughout the chamber. Other than the two Russian clerics, none in the room had ever witnessed such a glorious and magnificent affair, tinged with both humor and mirth as an accompaniment to the sacredness of the event. At last, after the couple and all in attendance had once again been blessed, Yvgeny and Beatrice Thatcherev were introduced to all as man and wife.

Immediately the makeshift cathedral was converted into a dance floor, as a complete and authentic Russian band began to strike up a lively collection of the sad and lovely music of distant Russia. These musicians were a rogues gallery of men who made a living working the dockside trade and seafaring life, who by the strangest of miraculous coincidences responded to the beckoning of one Sergei Evanovich as he had spent the days leading up to the wedding prowling the waterfronts of Bristol, Gloucester, Cardiff and Swansea. To everyone's delight, Evanovich himself took the stage, booming in a magnificent bass that brought tears to the eyes of the most cynical guest. Simultaneously, great tables containing fish, venison and caviar were brought in to feed the assembled while great casks of bread wine were brought up from the basement of Parker House and uncapped to flow like rivers. While the reserved and dignified British in attendance were at first repelled and frightened by both the strange music and the bizarre dance steps that accompanied it, the bread wine proved a capable coaxing tool to prompt the revelers to the floor, and through the evening the lovely ladies of Parker House swung and danced and laughed, dragging the merchants and the seamen to the floor to join them in their poor imitation of these very complicated steps.

As the night began to wind down, Thatcher quieted the band and gained the attention of the celebrants. He had so enjoyed spending the evening filling his mother's dance card, and his heart was near busting with her beautiful smiles and laughs of sheer ecstasy. He could almost imagine what she must have been like at sixteen in the presence of his father, for as he swung her in his arms he felt an overwhelming sense of joy and happiness and fell in love with his mother in a way he couldn't understand. He held her as if she were his one true love. Calling his grandfather and grandmother to him, he beckoned for the attendants to make sure that every person in the room had a glass of champagne.

"To say this day was one I never thought I would see is paltry for how I feel at this moment. I have been blessed to be raised by a man who graciously accepted the role as my one and only grandfather. He has also been my closest friend and a man of whom I could only hope to be half the measure. My grandmother is a woman of rare qualities, who withstood the shame and scorn of polite society, rose above their pettiness and built this extraordinary home and the empire that radiates out from it. My beloved mother and I will never be able to express our love and joy for these two people, not only for this day for but every day they've given us. So I ask you to raise your glasses and celebrate the two most magnificent people to grace the streets of Bristol, and join me in wishing them health and a long life." Thatcher raised his glass, drinking its contents and shattering it on the ground at his feet. Abigail repeated it, and likewise Marcellus and all the Russians in the band. Following their cue, the celebrants downed their champagne and tossed their glasses to the floor as the room rang of shattering crystal. Yvgeny turned and kissed his lovely wife, they, too, finally drinking and throwing their glasses to the ground. But unlike all those who came to give their love and support on this very special and magical day, they watched as their glasses fell to the ground and remained intact. As the two glasses rolled along the stone floor, the strangeness of their shatter-free existence was only made more so as each glass rolled away from the other. There was a momentary silence as the crowd took in this sight, and instinctively Marcellus and the Russians in the band crossed themselves. But Yvgeny, who knew the gravity and superstition associated with the bad luck omen, reared back his head and gave his hearty laugh and kissed his beautiful bride and demanded the band play.

In three short days, the residents of Parker House gathered on the Bristol quays to bid good-bye to Yvgeny and Beatrice Thatcherev, who were off to the Colonies to create a new life for all of them. Yvgeny and Beatrice took Abigail and Thatcher aside just before boarding the gangplank that led them to the main deck of the *Holy Cross*. The four entered into a group embrace as tears flowed down all their faces, as once again they found themselves parting. Yvgeny took his grandson and held him at arm's length. It was amazing that at thirteen years of age Thatcher was nearly as tall as his grandfather. He looked into the eyes of his grandson and into the very heart and soul of the Romanov line. He thought how singularly privileged he had been to watch this dear boy grow up into the amazing man he was becoming. And while many may have thought he took on some other man's responsibility, to raise this boy and his mother, he could not think of a greater honor in his life. As he thought of all the pain and suffering he had felt at losing his first wife and children and the great sadness that had consumed his heart and mind at such a tragic loss, he would never have believed the absolute pride and joy he was feeling this very moment.

"As soon as we reach New York, Thatcher, I will dispatch a letter to you on the first ship sailing for England," Yvgeny stated emphatically.

"Grandfather, I will look on every tide for a ship bearing the assurance of the safe arrival of you and my grandmother," Thatcher responded.

"I know you are not as enthralled by this new chapter in our lives as perhaps the rest of us are, but I promise you, my boy, the life to come will so greatly supercede any expectation you may have of a life in Bristol. Our future lies across that sea."

They embraced and held each other for a long moment, the distances they had come with the aging of both men suddenly and momentarily melting away as the grandfather possessively held his grandson. Both had tears in their eyes, as at last the two were forced to come to grips with their separation, if only for a short time. Beatrice and Yvgeny at last yielded to the request of the captain to board, and they gave one final embrace to their children and accepted the good wishes of their strange and wonderful family as the *Holy Cross* began to pull away from the quay. The sadness of the departure became too much for Abigail, and in tears the ladies of Parker House led their mistress back to their home. Nettie held her dear, beloved friend and talked of tasty pies and treats awaiting them. Caesar, on the other hand, took his place alongside Thatcher, placing his arm around his brother's neck, and the two stood motionless until the *Holy Cross* finally disappeared over the horizon.

V

The weeks stretched into months as, every day, Thatcher and Caesar made it their ritual to go down to the Bristol docks to inquire as to the progress of the *Holy Cross*. Every day they would ask the same questions to the captains and sailors making their way into the ever-expanding quays of that growing port and always received the same answer. They expanded their questioning to the livery men and drivers of hansom cabs who plied their trade between London and all the port towns along the southern coast if any word had been heard of the ship that had last been seen over Bristol's horizon. And yet, like a phantom, the *Holy Cross* had mysteriously vanished in that stretch of broad water that separated Bristol from the bustling port town of New York. Thatcher had established a correspondence with the owners of the ship who, like he, had a vested interest in its safe arrival in New York. Carrying a full hold of coppers and crystal to anxious merchants in the colonies, they, too, had much riding on an expedient delivery of their cargo. The one difference of course was that there, in London at a coffee house where merchants gathered, they had succumbed to the newfound tradition of placing wagers on the safe arrival of their merchandise. What had begun in the coffee houses of Amsterdam was starting to catch on in London, where some clever businessmen were willing to stake the odds of a ship's safe arrival at its far-flung destination. For a small fee, usually a fraction of the value of the cargo and vessel, owners and merchants could wager a bet that their ship would not safely arrive. And were their cynicism to prove incorrect, they would be out a small amount of money. To those men who were willing to take those odds and guarantee that these ships would more likely than not arrive safely, their confidence in the masteries of the sea provided ample opportunity for profit for no other purpose than belief. However, if their faith was proven incorrect, then the owners of ships and contractors of cargo would be paid the amount of their loss. This strange and discouraging new form of venture capitalism was to eventually become one of the most lucrative aspects of the business of trade, and for England it all began in a London coffee house called Lloyds.

The growing frustration and concern that Thatcher was experiencing as he and Caesar took over the business of both Parker House and the Thatcherev holdings required an outlet that would let him vent his frustrations in some constructive manner. As they had promised, they visited Artemus Grey and Jocko McMullan down by the docks, where they had crafted a gymnasium in a section of a warehouse, wedged between vast quantities of shipping crates. Upon arrival that first day, they could see Jocko going through the paces with a modest-sized lad in his early twenties named Simon Cooper. While he had seen the man before working on the docks, Thatcher noted how meticulously muscled this young fighter appeared. As he and Jocko squared off, between a series of chalk lines indicating the area of combat, Thatcher and Caesar were amazed to see how both Simon and Jocko used their feet as much as their hands in order to jockey for effective scoring positions. Artemus Grey greeted the boys and offered them seats on a couple of empty crates.

"I'm glad you boys took me up on my offer, and you've come at a good time. Simon there has been giving Jocko a run for his money," Artemus explained. "Now you see these lines? Here, all around, they must stay within this area or it's a loss for whoever crosses."

As Artemus was explaining, Jocko closed in and delivered a crushing blow to Simon's chin, reeling him back. While he was off balance, Jocko delivered another painful jab to Simon's midsection, doubling him over. Like a cat, Jocko pounced, wrapping one arm around Simon's neck as his free hand delivered punch after punch to the young fighter's face. With each blow he walked Simon closer and closer to the line. Despite the profusion of punches, Simon's arms wrapped around Jocko's waist, making every effort to push back and break Jocko's hold. He gave one last powerful surge, making Jocko move ever so slightly off balance, giving him the advantage he needed to break Jocko's arm free from his neck. He stood with both hands outstretched, his swollen face a pulp of dripping blood. Despite his near blindness, he was able to deliver a couple of powerful stings to Jocko's chest, but his limited visibility prevented his seeing the solid right cross delivered squarely to his nose that sent him sailing off his feet. As Simon crumbled into a heap, awash in his own blood, two fellows standing a few feet back ran forward with buckets filled with Bristol Harbour water and heaved it on the downed pugilist. The gallons of foul liquid that covered him did nothing to revive him from the punishing and finishing blow, and Caesar and Thatcher rose to their feet to check on his condition. Artemus squatted next to the crumpled Simon and produced an egg, into which he punched a small hole, and waved it under Simon's nose. Immediately its foul stench permeated the air, and in mere seconds Simon began to wretch and cough, the pungency of that fetid container forcing him to gasp and vomit up his blood and noontime meal. The smell and the violent reaction that resulted from it nearly made everybody else reciprocate in kind as they moved away from the point of stench, all but Artemus who reached down and grabbed the blood- and vomit-covered fighter to lift him to a sitting position.

"There you go, Simon. A little bloodied but better for the lesson, right? I keep telling you, Jocko's hand to your midsection is going to be the death of you, and you cannot allow him to get you in that clinch," Artemus instructed patiently to the half-dead fighter. "I think that's going to be enough for you today. Boys, why don't you take Simon here and run him down to the end of the dock for a good dipping?" The two attendants nearly slipped in the mixture of bodily fluids and bilge water as they extricated the fighter from the warehouse. Artemus retrieved another bucket of water and spilled it over the mess to further dilute it.

Having caught his breath, Jocko made his way to Thatcher and Caesar. "Ye may not believe it, but Simon's come a long way. It took me nearly half an hour to get him to that point. He's gettin' better, and he's about ready to start takin' bouts for profit."

"I don't imagine he'll be doing any serious fisticuffs anytime soon," Thatcher commented, still flinching from the foul scent of that rotten egg and vomit still hanging in the air.

"Oh, you'd be surprised, my boy. He'll take today and lick his wounds, but tomorrow he'll be right back here facing his first challenge after a training run with Jocko," Artemus offered. "It's like you two, brawling like bear cubs, half killing each other, then off to a long night of work. Did that pain and suffering make you crawl off in a corner and die?"

"Well, I don't think we took quite the punishment he did, and besides I have responsibilities," Thatcher explained.

"And so does he. Tonight he's got ships to unload, and while not as grand and glorious as your life in that brothel, his responsibilities are no less pressing and his desire to fight no less powerful. That's the way of the fighter."

Artemus began his tour of his spartan but effective facilities. "Now see, one of the most important training tools we have are these swords," he indicated, retrieving a couple of wooden swords, not dissimilar to those Thatcher, Caesar and Woodes had played with as children. "Believe it or not, these swords help strengthen the same muscles that go into a good punch. And these," indicating a couple of lengths of wooden poles, "help you build a rhythm in your arms that give a fighter a fluid motion with both hands." He waved the stick like a dorry's oars, then directed them toward a large sack filled with sand and suspended from a rafter. "This weighs about the same as your average man, about nine stone. Your ability to strike this repeatedly without busting a wrist or hand gives you the ability to deliver crushing blows to a midsection that will wear a man down and bring him to his knees."

Thatcher and Caesar surveyed the simple yet logical devices Artemus had devised for Jocko's training. "But is it really any better than just fighting a man?" Thatcher inquired.

Artemus laughed. "Well, the only problem with constantly fighting a man fist-to-fist is that not every man is capable of standing up and coming back for more. Oh – and sometimes the man fights back."

Caesar examined the hanging bag of dead weight. "Well, that's the point, isn't it?"

Jocko took Caesar's point and nodded his head in agreement. "What brings a man to this game is his love for a good fight – an awareness that others with less skill are willin' to pay to watch him do it. You're right, the fight is everythin'. But the sufferin' is best minimized and saved for the payday."

"Well, obviously you're not doing this out of the kindness of your heart, Artemus. What's in it for you?" Thatcher inquired.

"You're right, Thatcher, I'm a businessman, and I'm in this to make a good living. With Jocko now, and Simon to come, and many men before them, I've made a pretty penny recruiting the fellows who think they know a good fighter when they see one. And other men who think they've got the strength and toughness to toe the line with the likes of a Jocko. So while you fight and train, I go find the type of men who enjoy a good fight and wager them my fighter against any they bring on. If my fighter loses, we go hungry. If my fighter wins, we share in the victory, fifty-fifty, right down the middle."

Thatcher considered for a moment more. "I guess I'll have to see that for myself, before I can fully believe it."

"I would expect no less from you, Thatcher Edwards. Come back here tomorrow afternoon, both of you. I realize you work at night, so I took the liberty of arranging two bouts tomorrow afternoon. The first will be with Simon and anyone willing to take him, and the final with Jocko and a fellow arriving from Dublin on a boat this evening – that will be a match to watch."

Jocko smiled and shook his head. "Old Artemus has been tryin' to get this match up for some time. He thinks that Englishmen will pay good quid to see two Irishmen beat the hell out of one another. And Mike McManus has yet to lose a match – sent a few of his adversaries to the undertaker as well."

"I keep telling you, Jocko ... keep him away from your left side and you'll lay him out like a side of beef."

Thatcher and Caesar hated to admit that they had had quite enough fight for the day, so they spent the afternoon watching Jocko work the poles and swords and bags, amazed how the hours of physical effort never seemed to wear on him in the least. What they did not realize was that Jocko wasn't showing off his capabilities. Jocko was facing the bout of his life, and that evening he would offer a few very special prayers to the saints to protect him from the Irish mauler Mike McManus.

And so Thatcher and Caesar fell into a new routine, one that would optimize the hours of their day and keep Thatcher distracted from joining his mother in her speculations of what had happened to Beatrice and Yvgeny. After breakfast, Thatcher would join his mother to go over the accounts of both Parker House and the Thatcherev enterprises. He had suggested that the way Abigail could occupy her time was to begin training the girls for basic new skills such as sewing and cooking, talents that could not only potentially net them new jobs but husbands in the New World as well. So as he and Caesar would head to the docks to catch up on the latest news of the world and invariably inquire after the *Holy Cross,* the ladies of the house participated in seminars of domestic endeavors, with Nettie or some outside expert hired to instruct them.

The Edwards boys had developed a habit of stopping by Peal's Tavern around midday for a pint and a light snack. It was here they developed a taste for a vile brewed concoction that would entice them for the rest of their lives. At first they had greeted the hot, bitter liquid with disdain, but upon experiencing its rejuvenating effects, they eagerly ordered up beans to be delivered to Parker House, where they worked with Nettie to develop the optimum method for roasting, grinding and brewing them. It wasn't long before Parker House began to be known as much for its coffee as it was for its ladies.

After lunch, it was off to Artemus Grey's where the two would follow the regimen of training and exercise that Artemus had laid out for them. For several grueling hours they would limber up with the poles, practice fencing and pound on the heavy bag, learning how to use weight and motion to protect their hands and wrists. Often Jocko would lead them for a run through the countryside to build up strength and endurance. Finally, they would undergo a light round in the chalked square where Jocko showed them how best to utilize not only their hands but their feet and the rest of their bodies to more effectively move in and out to deliver or thwart a blow.

Back at home, they were in much need of cleansing after their sweaty ordeals at Artemus' gymnasium, so they would join the ladies in the tubs below the stairs. As the definition of their muscles grew more and more prominent, the ladies of Parker House increasingly voiced their admiration and fell to the task of rubbing down their sore, aching flesh. The process so invigorated them that Thatcher suggested to Artemus he should find someone to perform the same function for Jocko, though the trainer admitted he wasn't fond of the idea of cutting into the profits. Much to their dismay, bath time would to come to an end and all would depart to change for dinner, followed by a round of that magnificent coffee to prepare them for the evening ahead.

Parker House's reputation, particularly after the wedding and its introduction to more of Bristol society and the good patrons of Peal's, was growing, and they found themselves having to entertain more customers than they had previously accommodated. Naturally, sherry, small talk and coffee could hold these gentlemen in waiting for a brief spell, but having to watch men more pressed for time than their desires could counterbalance led Abigail and Thatcher to discuss how they could make more productive use of the ladies' time. Meetings were held to poll the ladies as to the more effective and desired techniques to satisfy the needs of their customers perhaps a bit more promptly, and the most common answer that came back as the most efficient for those customers pressed for time was fellatio. Many of their customers were familiar and quite pleased with the method practiced and perfected by some of the busier women of the house. But, among the many good Quakers and Congregationalists who made up much of their clientele base, few had experienced anything beyond basic face-to-face intercourse. Add to that the extra time required to achieve a masterful position combined with the application process of the mandatory sheepskin, the foreplay could sometimes take more time than the actual act. Thus it was agreed that this efficient process of engagement would somehow be combined with the application of the house-required barrier and with it, it was discovered, customers could quickly leave Parker House both satisfied and educated. Of course, the initial introduction to these unnatural acts was met with a mixture of surprise and protest by its newest recipients; however, in time it was discovered that resistance melted and in time, it became an item of frequent request.

One evening, it was suggested that, like the noon-day quick snacks so common among the citizenry of Bristol, Parker House should likewise consider an abbreviated and economic entree of its own. Calculating the profit margins to be obtained made this an attractive consideration. However, the concern, of course, was Nettie's ability to supervise the daily revitalization of the residence and the demands that it could make on Caesar and Thatcher's time. It was suggested by one of the ladies, quite gifted and frequently requested for her fellatio skills, that, rather than investing the upstairs rooms for such rapid and brief encounters, instead perhaps one of the rooms on the lower floor could be employed for that purpose. There, with carefully positioned chairs so as to offer at least a measure of privacy, such tasks could be quickly practiced without the need of investing either a bedroom or a sheepskin. And thus the Parker House library took on a new function.

Caesar and Thatcher were happy to move their midday habit from Peal's to the library, where they could indulge their love for books and maps while providing a moderate sense of security for both patron and employee. They limited these hours from eleven to two so they would not miss out on their training regimen. There was initial concern that providing this new and abbreviated service could cut into the profits of nighttime business, yet to Abigail and Thatcher's astonishment, they were pleased to see that it nearly doubled the amount taken in from many of their best and most loyal nocturnal customers. And, as Nettie had discovered a process for making quick noontime snacks consisting merely of simple cuts of meat pressed between two pieces of bread, combined with a cup of coffee, the customers were doubly pleased and satisfied. This newfound approach to dining and the additional revenue it brought into the house was viewed as a great potential new venture when they relocated to the New World.

The weeks slipped into months and at long last years, as the dreams of a new life in the New World no longer seemed to captivate the residents of Parker House. One evening when business was rather brisk, a new face joined the cast of regulars that conducted their exchange at Parker House. David Mullins had the look of a seasoned sailor, one of those men of indeterminate age, with his dark brown leathery skin, his primarily eroded teeth and his land-borne stance which showed the uneasy sway of a man who spent his life at sea. Mullins could easily have been somewhere between his late twenties and early fifties. He had come alone to Parker House, no doubt intrigued by the word-of-mouth advertisement that spread along the waterfront of a house quick to exchange any man's gold for a momentary slice of heaven. The shoes he was wearing, something obviously new to him and one of the ground rules of patronage at Parker House, caused his feet to ache bad enough to distract him from his primary purpose for being there, and he sat in the corner to remove them, if just for a moment. Thatcher noticed the weather-beaten sailor perching next to the door that led into the kitchen, nursing his aching dogs, and smiled, knowing the source of the sailor's misery. He sat beside this new customer, who recognized the well-dressed young man from his earlier introduction as the master of the house.

"My apologies, guv'nor. Know ye have a rule about togs, and I promise after a moment of airin' I shan't make a step without the required clothing," Mullins offered in an effort to save the expected lecture.

Thatcher smiled and waved his hand dismissively. "It's fine, good sir. Feel free to cool your heels. I know how uncomfortable such a peril can be when you've spent a life without them. It may seem as a silly thing for a man such as you who comes here not to appear the country squire but to transact business for honest services. But it's a holdover, a tradition of sorts, from the previous master and mistress of the house," Thatcher replied.

"Ah. So you've taken over as the new owner, have ye?" Mullins remarked, impressed, noting the man's youth, envious of the wonderful way he had found to make a living.

"Well, actually, my grandparents still own the house, but we haven't heard from them in some time since they set sail for the Colonies aboard the *Holy Cross*," Thatcher replied.

The seaman stopped rubbing his feet as a disconcerted look came across his face. "The *Holy Cross* ye say? Sailed out of England en route to the colonies a few years past?" Mullins quizzed.

Thatcher's stomach dropped. He and Caesar had been querying sailors for so long that he automatically anticipated a negative response. "You are familiar with the *Holy Cross?*" Thatcher asked, leaning in close.

Mullins paused and then began to shake his head. His eyes bore a look of sorrow for what he was about to reveal. "Aye, young master, I knew the *Holy Cross,* I'm sorry to say."

Thatcher studied his face to see if this weathered seaman was merely spinning a yarn to appear to be a man of a rare knowledge or if he was speaking the truth, and his expression told Thatcher that finally, after three years, he had met someone who seemed to know what happened to his grandparents.

"It's been some years since I had made port at Bristol. 'Course, last time I left I never thought I'd be returnin'. I'd come here aboard the *Charles II*, sailing under Captain Gibson," he began.

"Yes, yes, we met that ship. Captain Gibson is an old friend of my grandfather's."

"Aye, was he, now? Well, I can tell ye, none of us were too pleased at the notion of giving up privateerin' to be a wet nurse to a bunch of Spaniards. The captain weren't too happy about it either, but he saw this commission by the Crown as an opportunity for greater things, did his best to quell the crew. What he didn't know was that the man who he needed deliverin' that line below decks as well as above was the man who hated this new responsibility more than any of us. When we reached Cadiz, Mr. Avery took the ship, set Captain Gibson adrift along with a few fellows more loyal than sensible. We knew there was only a matter of time before England and Spain were enemies again, so we decided to pick while the fruit was fresh and went about plunderin' every Spanish ship we could get our hands on."

Mullins looked down at his callused hands, seeming to ponder whether he should continue. He took a deep breath. "But we stopped being so particular what flag flew over a ship, and be it French, or Portuguese, or Dutch meant little to us. What mattered was what was in the hold. When a man stops lookin' at flags and makin' decisions as to who's an enemy or not, it's only a matter of time 'til you start going after your own, and we did. The Union Jack meant little by way of discriminatin'. The only thing that kept Avery from takin' down an English ship was how many gun ports she sported. And the *Holy Cross* had very few."

Thatcher finished off the half cup of coffee in his hand. "Go on, please."

"When we came 'longside her, we saw her as just another merchant, ripe for the pickin'. But she made Captain Avery angry when she decided to roll out her few guns and put up a fight. That's when Avery brought along our much bigger ship and sent one broadside after another into her until all that was left was a leaky, dyin' ship. I was one of the first to board her, 'cause we wanted to get what we could before she went to the bottom. We weren't surprised to find passengers and figured Captain would order out a longboat provisioned and loaded with payin' customers, but he was in a dark mood that day. After strippin' every bit of cargo we could get before her hold filled with water, Avery ordered the boats cut loose and brought aboard our own ship."

After three long years with no word, Thatcher had come to accept the possibility that his grandparents had been drowned in a storm, but there was always a sliver of hope that somehow they might have made it to some island and were, even now, awaiting rescue. These words dissected any hope he may have held.

Mullins cleared his throat and leaned his elbows on his knees. "I remember this old fellow, tall with a big beard, askin' us to take this woman with us. He promised she'd show us a helluva time and make our days at sea a little less borin'. Avery jes' laughed and told him Captain Gibson sends his compliments. Then he had a couple barrels of gunpowder placed aboard and gave the old man and his lady a choice – fire or water. We'd only pulled away just a few minutes when both them barrels exploded, and the *Holy Cross* was crucified." He straightened up and stole a glance in Thatcher's direction, then looked back down at his hands. "That was a bit too much for me. And the first moment I could spot land and felt I could make a swim out, I went overboard and took my chances with those sharks in the water rather than the ones aboard that ship. Been trampin' around since then, takin' whatever ship will have me and avoidin' Bristol at every turn. But here I am. Now all of a sudden my taste for a comely young lass don't seem so strong."

Thatcher finally had the confirmation he had been so desperately seeking. And while there was an instinct to want to throttle this old pirate for his participation in such a tragic loss of his grandparents, he tempered that against finally knowing the truth. He stood, taking Mullins by the sleeve, and led him quietly and slowly to the door. Caesar could see Thatcher escorting David "Darby" Mullins and stiffened, thinking he had an issue brewing. But Thatcher waved him off. Darby was thinking the same thing and was prepared to take a beating he no doubt knew the young man felt was coming. He was surprised when Thatcher stopped him at the door.

"I have been waiting for news for three years, news I came to think would never come, and I had to get it from someone who watched my grandparents die. There is a side of me that wants to take out everything I'm feeling on you, but at least you had the honesty to tell me. So I'm grateful and hope you understand that I think you've taken quite enough from this house as it is," Thatcher stated without emotion.

"Young man, I can tell ye I'm sorry I'm the one doin' the tellin', and if ye feel ye need to take it out on someone, I'm prepared to take what ye want to dish out," Mullins replied, resigned to the beating to come.

"No. I'll let someone else more prepared to deal with what I'm feeling suffer those consequences. Just so you know, that old man's name was Yvgeny Thatcherev, and the woman he offered up was Beatrice Parker Thatcherev, whose name graces this house."

"Not that it matters to ye, son, but my name is Darby Mullins, and I promise not to trouble ye again, for the first ship I can get to the colonies I'm leavin' the sea and takin' up the job of my father, woodcuttin'." Darby gave a look that showed his sorrow, both for his previous involvements and for the pain this boy was feeling right now, and he pitied the man who was going to one day have to pay the price for his sins.

Thatcher waited until the end of the evening and then took his mother in her room and closed the door. The pain of her wailing and sadness resonated against every wall and within every soul of the people who made up her family in Parker House.

Thatcher, on the other hand, never shed a tear and never demonstrated a moment of grief. What he felt instead was a rage that he demonstrated every time he and Caesar went for training with Artemus. While he always possessed the talent, Thatcher had never demonstrated the will to take his advanced skills into a public venue. But one night, just as they had finished training, Thatcher took Artemus aside for a private conversation. That discussion did not remain secret long, for all along the docks of Bristol word began to spread that young Master Thatcher Edwards would be taking on a brute of a pugilist who had been making the rounds in London. This was the rarest of occasions, a seasoned brawler with many victories under his belt taking on a young lad who had yet to wage one single bout. This practice, particularly among the fighting community of Bristol, had ceased after the brutal slaying of Simon Cooper.

The pairing of Cooper against an experienced fighter should never have occurred. His opponent had been a virtual wall with legs and arms, and though Simon was well disciplined and had learned many a valuable lesson in his training, he never had a chance to show his prowess. The more experienced giant had charged him like a rabid rhino, grabbing him and crushing his spine like a twig. As wagers were being paid off all around, after Jocko had taken out his that night, the general gentleman's agreement was made among the promoters that no longer would rookie pugilists be given the opportunity to face prize fighters and that no longer would a man who clocks in at twenty stone face off against a man half his weight. That agreement was now to be broken.

Try as he might, Artemus could not convince Thatcher of the dangers he faced in this ill-conceived match. But Artemus could not understand that this fighter's record, talent and size were nothing compared to his name: Thomas Avery. If Thatcher could not avenge his grandparents' death, at least for the moment, against the pirate John Avery, he could at least take out his rage on someone with the same name. Thatcher was adamant and Artemus was a businessman, and this unusual match became the more so when it was scheduled to occur at three a.m. on the Sabbath. While not the purvey of the genteel class, the participation of Thatcher Edwards waging a pugilist event on the Sabbath sent a clamor throughout the community, and a match between Thatcher and anyone at any time brought the brightest and richest of the community to the rough and tumble Bristol docks.

In the days leading up to the match, Parker House had done record business. As word spread throughout the countryside, it seemed as if every person who had ever done business with Yvgeny Thatcherev or Beatrice Parker, in one fashion or another, had turned out to wish the boy well, avail themselves of the house services and be on hand for this Sabbath pugilism contest. Thatcher and Caesar spent every available moment training and sparring at Artemus Grey's gymnasium, and while it was a little disconcerting that there always seemed to be a crowd on hand to watch the young Russian train with his African partner, Artemus Grey saw it as an opportunity to run up the box office and wagers, as a fever pitch seemed to take all the Bristol gentry. Pugilism, as a rule, was the sport of the working man, yet with its popularity growing throughout London, it was only a matter of time before communities like Bristol and the luminaries that led them would somehow legitimize this raw blood-sport as some genteel pastime.

Only two people whom Thatcher encountered over those days were not supportive of his dangerous endeavor. The first was to be expected, of course, in his mother. While Abigail knew very little about this avocation that occupied so much of her son and Caesar's time, she had heard stories of the violence and the fatalities, specifically in the case of Simon Cooper. At every opportunity, she would beg him to reconsider, fearing what her life would be if anything happened to her son. But as much as he tried to reassure her that he felt he was ready for this challenge, and knowing that he could not reveal his advantage gained in the fields of Russia, Abigail was inconsolable. He did, however, try to paint it as a bright spot when he reviewed the ledger sheets each morning that this little match-up of fisticuffs had been a very effective marketing tool for Parker House, though this did little to belay her fears.

The other person who demonstrated virtually no support for Thatcher's endeavor was his old friend Woodes Rogers. Since becoming teenagers, Woodes and Thatcher ran in very different circles. Having finally filled out and getting the chance to pursue the family trade, Woodes had become quite the toast of the ladies of Bristol and the daughters with whom they hoped one day pair to him. The same mannerisms that had prompted boys to want to pound upon him were now the ones that assured him invitations to the finest teas and socials throughout greater Bristol. And having spent much time upon the seas learning his father's craft, Woodes displayed that same quality that had made his father so wealthy – an abiding passion for the sea. Thatcher's encounters with Woodes were few and far between and most often on the docks, when Woodes was coming from or going to sea, and periodically at Peal's. But the encounters were casual at best and sometimes on the borderline of chilly. The day before the fight, when the men of Bristol were buying a round for Thatcher and Caesar, Woodes Rogers happened to enter Peal's to see his old friend receiving the adulation and praise of their mutual associates. Woodes was hallooed over to join in the celebration, but he declined, finding his comrades in a far corner to whisper and laugh about the outrageous display. It bothered Thatcher that his old friend could not even celebrate in this big moment for so many in Bristol, and three or four pints in he decided to ask him about it. Caesar gently attempted to keep him in his chair, but Thatcher was having none of it, and Caesar could do little more than remain a few paces behind in support.

"Well, Woodes Rogers. It's been quite some time since you and I have sparred upon the quay. How go things now as you assume your role as the future Captain Rogers?" Thatcher smiled, raising his tankard in mock salute.

"Well, Thatcher Edwards. My friends tell me your house of ill repute does banner business these days. I would think you scarcely find the time to demonstrate some other great prowess of yours," Woodes commented to the snickers of his friends.

"Ah, Woodes. You spent so much time watching me battle away with my dear brother here," indicating Caesar, "for free and for fun. I hear you're a sporting man. Let's say you be my guest so you can get a ringside view of just how powerful my prowess can be."

"While I'm certain yours will be the place to be both before, during and after your little barbaric demonstration, and while I'm certain many of our common friends will be there to put down money for, and against, you, I hope you realize that there's a little more than a slight wish by many that your arrogant ass hits the ground hard. Perhaps a fall will do you good," Woodes replied, turning his back on Thatcher.

Thatcher smiled, finishing his tankard and was about to walk off but stopped to put in a last word. "Woodes, barbarism is in the eye of the beholder, and though I know you've never had a strong stomach for blood, do not fear, my friend, it won't be mine they're seeing." With that, Thatcher turned around and, with Caesar's prompting, made his way to the gymnasium to sweat out the many pints.

On the night of the match, Caesar had gone to great lengths to try and convince Thatcher to take the evening off and spend his time concentrating on the fight, but Thatcher reckoned differently. He knew the receipts would be huge and the wishes many, and so he turned on every ounce of charm he had to greet every guest and to encourage vigorous wagering and a little extra something upstairs to make the night truly memorable. At two o'clock, it took absolutely no prompting to chase even the lovelorn out the door, for the men of Bristol had someplace important to be this late and electric evening. Abigail made one last appeal, knowing it was fruitless, but it was her duty as a mother. Thatcher lay on her bed with her, entwining her in his arms and assuring her of his confidence in the outcome. He stroked her hair and whispered in her ear all the things he knew that comforted her and she nestled in his arms, much like he had done when he was just a little thing, and let herself accept this inevitable event in her son's life.

Bristol at this time of morning was typically as silent as the tomb. This night, in the thousand feet from the front door of Parker House to the front entrance of the gymnasium, Thatcher could hear the cacophony of excited voices. All along the route, men of Bristol had hung back, hoping to catch one last glimpse of Thatcher before the bout to judge his composure and form the decision for their last bets. Artemus Grey was standing at the entrance of the gymnasium, anxiously awaiting the arrival of his fighter. Just a few feet behind him stood Thomas Avery's promoter who appraised the demeanor of his fighter's opponent, and what he saw was ice. In these days of early pugilism, there was little ceremony leading to the bout. Artemus Grey led Thatcher through the steamy, packed warehouse to the chalk-marked square that would serve as their battleground. For those who had been in attendance for the bout that killed Simon Cooper three years before, the similarities between this match up and that one were eerie. While Thatcher was tall and muscled, he was lean and limber but certainly not beefy. In contrast, Thomas Avery was a broad, hulking brute. It was easy to see why he had been so successful in so many matches. Thatcher could tell that Avery was not going to bring finesse to the ring, for the sheer size of his chest and arms and legs reminded him of a bull.

The rules were simple. The fighters were separated by less than a foot between them. Once each placed a toe upon a line scratched between them, the bout began. Avery walked to his place and put his toe immediately upon the scratch. Thatcher hung back for a moment, studying his competitor. The bull metaphor was complete as he heard Avery's breath permeating audibly across that small gulf. Avery remained nearly fully clothed, having removed only his jacket. Slowly and patiently, Thatcher removed his jacket and then his shirt, revealing his well-toned muscular chest and arms, turned to Caesar and handed off his raiment. His brother leaned in to offer one brief word of advice. "Do not play with him."

Thatcher smiled and patted Caesar on the shoulder, then took one long step backwards. Grazing the line with his toe, he swung with every bit of his weight into a smooth rocking pivot, planting a bone-crushing left fist into Avery's face. Avery's body position did much to absorb the crushing blow and keep him standing on his feet, but the punch let loose a mass of blood that sprayed up into his eyes. As he raised his hands to clear his sight, Thatcher laced his right arm into the crook of Avery's right arm, planting a foot behind his forward leg and with all his strength pulled the big ox over onto his back. Cartwheeling over the thrashing bull to remain free of his grasp, he managed another hard punch into the bleeding mass that was Avery's face. He moved to the edge of the square and was surprised to see how quickly Avery was able to heave his massive body to a standing position. Avery's grey undershirt was now covered in his own blood, and his torn nose seeped a continuous stream of red, yet he seemed undaunted, and he moved forward in big lurching steps toward Thatcher, who stood quite calmly, his hands at his sides, watching Avery approach. When it seemed he was about to be crushed by Avery's full weight Thatcher quickly dodged out of his way, causing the Goliath almost to stumble out of the chalk line. When Avery turned, Thatcher was standing at the opposite end of the square, smiling and beckoning him like a lover. Avery moved to the center and stomped his toe on the line where this little dance began and repeated a gesture to Thatcher to come and play like a man.

Thatcher put both hands upon his waist and slowly sidled up to his outsized competitor and then, when he was a mere few paces away, veritably leapt the chasm between them, bringing his right hand down upon Avery's thick massive skull. While it would not seem a very effective move, Avery did not have time to judge Thatcher's action, and as his hands lifted to stop the dropping competitor, he was not prepared when Thatcher's body swung not in front but around his side, as Thatcher used the fleshy expanse that covered Avery's kidney and let every bit of that momentum travel from his body through his fist and into that tender organ. Avery's right hand shot to cover that quickly injured vital, his body slightly canting and revealing his exposed chin, now pointed skyward as he winced with pain. Avery's left hand swing uselessly at the air as Thatcher bobbed down, clear of the swing, and popped back up on spring-loaded legs, his right hand grabbing Avery's shirt as leverage and his left fist connecting squarely underneath Avery's descending jaw, sending him sprawling backwards at an awkward angle to the ground.

The assembled mass went wild as, in less than a minute, the prizefighter from London lay flat on his back. Thatcher circled around Avery, watching for some sign of rousing, certain that this old and massive fighter still had quite a bit left in him. As expected, Avery did, and the sportsman in Thatcher wanted to give Avery that fighting chance, but this battle wasn't about sportsmanship. It was about representational revenge. And as Avery placed one palm flat behind him, attempting to rise into a sitting position, Thatcher reared back one heavily buckled boot and sent it careening to the top of Avery's head. The room grew quiet. Thatcher listened for that bull-like breath that had taunted him from across the line, but Avery lay silently on the ground, the blood from his face no longer pumping but merely oozing.

As it was obvious the bout was over, Thatcher returned to where Caesar stood, still holding his clothing, and slowly and elegantly put on his shirt and tunic. Avery's promoter ran to his fighter, rotten egg in hand. While those who were closest to the downed fighter may have responded viscerally to the stench, Avery twitched not a muscle. Artemus and Jocko slowly walked to where Thatcher stood, still finishing his final button-loops. While congratulations were in order, none of the four felt much like celebrating.

"I'll come by Parker House tomorrow to divide the winnings," Artemus offered in the most logical form of congratulations he could think of.

"Tell me, Artemus, were they betting more heavily for or against me, my kindred brethren of Bristol?" Thatcher asked as he studied the shocked faces of the many men with whom he did business.

Artemus looked at Thatcher as if he already knew the answer to that question. "Five times one against, my boy," he replied.

Thatcher smiled and patted his business partner on the shoulder. "Well ... show's them."

Thatcher and Caesar slowly made their way through the crowd. There were a few half-hearted congratulations as they passed, but for the most part the crowd stood still in shocked silence. The two made the long, apathetic walk back to Parker House.

And for the first time in a long time, Thatcher wanted to be alone.

VI

There was a general agreement among those who resided at Parker House and those who did business with Thatcher Edwards that the incident at the warehouse was best left undiscussed. To many of the men of Bristol who had watched Thatcher grow up from the miniature version of Yvgeny Thatcherev to the brutal and vicious man they had witnessed that memorable morning, it was difficult to fathom the sheer violence that resided under that calm, convivial exterior. While none could know, the gut-wrenching horror of Thatcher's first kill had consumed him and led to many sleepless and solitary nights, not the slightest bit betrayed by his business-as-usual nature. Mere hours afterwards, Thatcher and Caesar performed their customary survey of the ships recent to port to catch up on news of the world and to seek out great trading opportunities. They took their customary post in the library to study maps of potential enterprises while the ladies of Parker House served lunch. And in the afternoon they strolled down the quay to the warehouse district.

"I must confess I did not expect to see you today, Thatcher," Artemus stated, his surprise obvious on his face. He looked at Caesar, who maintained his sober visage, but he could tell there was a hint of concern in his expression as well. The spot where Thomas Avery had bloodily and brutally died still bore the outlines of human stain, though much scrubbing and water had been applied in the ensuing hours.

"Well, Artemus, one must always train for the next bout. I can't rest upon my laurels, can I?" Thatcher replied casually, his eyes fixed upon that killing corner.

"That is the fighting spirit, Thatcher," Artemus replied, somewhat soberly and without cheer. "Here's an idea … why don't you and Jocko go take a walk as Caesar and I retrieve the winnings and begin account?"

"Come on, sport," Jocko replied, giving Thatcher a smile as he wrapped an arm around his neck and led him out of the gymnasium. Jocko fully understood what Thatcher was feeling. While Artemus had borne witness to a number of fatal ends to fighters' careers and may have profited handsomely from it, he had never delivered the final blow that ended a man's career as well as his life, and Jocko had. Such a fatality didn't usually come so early in a pugilist's career, and the taking of a man's life, no matter how fair or likely, was never an easy thing upon a man's conscience. Those for whom it was easy found themselves less likely to have someone to support them in their corner.

The two had walked in silence for a good length, taking in the afternoon air of this polluted seaport. At last, Jocko stopped and turned to look his young contemporary in the eye. "Tell me how ye're feelin' now, Thatcher," Jocko insisted, a look of deadly seriousness on his face.

Thatcher looked down at the ground as he thought, and then looked up at Jocko. "In all honesty, Jocko, I really don't know how I feel. I know that if the situation had been reversed – and it was obvious that those who were in attendance thought it would be – I don't think that Avery would have shed a tear over my loss. And I am not one to shed tears over much of anything. Losing my grandfather and grandmother did not drive me to them. Yet last night, more than one fell, and I'm not exactly sure why."

"It's called humanity, Thatcher. Ye may enter the sport knowin' the consequences, but it don't make it any less real or less painful when ye see the results of it, especially when ye deliver it. And I'll be honest, the last thing ye need for the next few days is to bury yerself in trainin', thinkin' it will go away, 'cause it's business. But it ain't business. It's a side effect of it. And ye never want to get good at buryin' it and acceptin' it as just one of them things."

"But the last thing I want to do right now, Jocko, is sit at home and dwell on it. Because this isn't all I do, and dwelling isn't good for my other businesses. So, as much as I am hating everything about this business, I feel I have no choice but to treat is as business-as-usual. Do you understand?"

"Tell ye what, Thatch. Let's spend the next couple o' days on the heavy bag, 'cause the only one it's going to damage is you."

"You are the expert, Jocko. Lead on."

They returned to the warehouse where Artemus and Caesar sat on a couple of boxes and one between them, sorting through a stack of pound notes and a pile of farthing, guinea and pence. They watched as the two men entered, and Artemus was relieved to see Jocko nodding.

"So a couple o' days on the heavy bag, then?" Artemus asked, knowing Jocko's usual prescription.

As the weeks stretched on and the shock of the event was replaced by the day-to-day activities of Bristol life, only the most tired of whisperings continued, usually at Peal's from one who had been in attendance to one who had missed it. Thatcher and Caesar maintained their solid ritual, and it seemed as if life had gotten back to normal for Parker House and all its varied enterprises. But the routine was about to break, as one afternoon Thatcher and Caesar entered the warehouse where both Jocko and Artemus sat waiting for them.

"Good afternoon, gentlemen. I'm surprised to see you sitting around when there's training to be done," Thatcher offered gregariously.

"And good afternoon to you lads. Of course there's training we have to get done today, but first there's a bit of news we have to share," Artemus replied, gesturing for Thatcher and Caesar to join them.

The two sat down and Thatcher studied the troubled looks on both men's faces. "Well, what's got you two so hang-dog in expression?" Thatcher queried.

"There's much to share, and much change to come as a result of recent events," Artemus replied.

"Something of grave importance, it appears," Thatcher offered, sensing the seriousness of the moment.

"It seems as if this space we call our gymnasium has been leased to a company that requires it for storage. So it looks as if we've lost the location," Artemus explained.

"Well, that's not so severe. There's more warehouse space available," Thatcher dismissed.

"Apparently not to us," Jocko piped in. "We've spent the last few days tryin' to find a replacement location, and mysteriously no landlord is willin' to take us as a tenant. We thought that strange until we inquired further and have discovered that the powers that be in Bristol don't wish to gain a reputation as a center for pugilism and have made it quite clear that we need to find other accommodations, suitably far away from Bristol."

Thatcher thought for a moment and shrugged his shoulders dismissively. "Well if it's a matter of not finding a landlord, then I just happen to have the good fortune of money and property to do as I please. In the short term I can convert any number of the thousands of square feet I possess beneath the streets of Bristol to fill the immediate bill. But for the long term, there are a number of empty properties in our holdings waiting to be constructed upon and we shall build a facility much more suitable to our vocation than a filthy warehouse. Why, I can imagine a theatre, just as you've told me about in London," Thatcher reasoned, ready to dismiss the discussion. He caught the look between Artemus and Jocko and realized his solution to the problem was not going to be considered.

"It's not quite that simple, Thatcher. Very powerful people in this town, some who lost money on the bout and others with interests in London, including investments in your competitor, have made it quite clear that we are out of business," Artemus explained. "Which, to be honest, is fine with us. It goes along with plans we had made for the future that have been now moved into the present."

"Plans? You're telling me that you're just accepting these ultimatums and moving on with other plans? And what plans would those be?" Thatcher fumed.

"New York. Pugilism is becoming quite the rage throughout the Colonies, and with Jocko's skills and my contacts we have a whole new market to pursue, free of threat and ripe for the picking," Artemus said.

"And so how soon will you be putting this plan into motion?" Thatcher protested. "And when were you going to tell me?"

"We knew that there would be no consoling you on this subject, and we reached our final resolution this morning when we booked passage for New York, leaving on tomorrow's tide."

"Tomorrow. You're leaving tomorrow?" Thatcher was deflated.

"You might say it was suggested that it would be in our best interest to clear the Port of Bristol as rapidly as possible, and when we were offered these tickets as a subtle hint to go, we took them."

That night, Thatcher allowed it to sink in how truly powerless he was under the circumstances and how powerful were the opposing forces. Life was changing in Bristol and with that the realities of his position. As Yvgeny had so frequently warned would happen, he had bitten off more than he could chew, and now others were choking in the process. And so, accepting the situation, he treated his friends to a night on the House and escorted them to the ship that would carry them to America.

This change in their schedules forced a re-working of their days, and so Thatcher and Caesar adopted new habits to fill their time, much of it involving drinking and baths. And it wasn't an unpleasant alternative to their usual routine, but it left Thatcher and Caesar without a creative outlet to blow off a bit of their pent-up rage, despite the civil acceptance of their new reality. Late one Thursday evening, after several weeks of this idle life, Thatcher and Caesar had settled into a couple of comfortable chairs, enjoying a snack of coffee, tobacco and Nettie's bread and meats. The last of the late arrivers and lovelorn were enjoying their feminine repast when suddenly a scream was heard from upstairs.

Screams were not an uncommon sound at Parker House, but the masters were able to discern the difference between one of pleasure and another of panic. In seconds the long-limbed strides of Caesar and Thatcher made short work of the long flight of stairs. The ladies standing at the door in various states of dress indicated where the scream had come from. Having tried the door handle and finding it locked, Thatcher's heavy boot reacted in a flash, smashing the door of Abigail Edward's room. The sight of his mother, laying on her bed holding together the fragments of her evening gown, contrasted with the unexpected sight of Terrance Higgins, town exchequer and long-time trading partner of Yvgeny, Beatrice and Thatcher Edwards, standing there over his mother's bed. The look of terror in Abigail's eyes amplified as Thatcher crossed the room and took the middle-aged accountant's throat in his hand.

"Thatcher! Stop! Let him go. It was an honest mistake that went too far. Stop it now!" Abigail pleaded as she watched her son deliberately crush the windpipe of the defenseless erstwhile rapist.

On more than one occasion throughout the years, Mr. Higgins had been warned that his amorous observations and misanthropic asides about Mistress Abigail Edwards were breaches of house rules and good sense. He had pursued Abigail with amorous and sexual intent and had been gently but sternly rebuked by Abigail, Beatrice, Yvgeny, Caesar, Nettie, a collection of the women and Thatcher Edwards himself. To add insult to injury, Terrance Higgins owed his power, wealth and position to his privileged wife of twenty some-odd years. Her family traced their lines back to the twelfth century and the founding of Bristol, and their connections reached into every aspect of town and commercial life. These realities had kept Caesar and Thatcher in check for years and provided Higgins with latitude extended to virtually no one else. It had been hoped that the frequent rebukes had finally taken hold as Higgins had apparently developed a deep and abiding affection for the lovely Louise Ferrar, a dark haired ravishing French woman of Moorish extraction. Higgins had developed the custom of arriving many nights a week at midnight and depositing heavy amounts of his wife's gold for the pleasure of her lovelorn company. And tonight had seemed no different from any other night, Louise explained as the lifeless body of Terrance Higgins lay on Abigail Edwards' floor. They had been lying in bed when he had expressed an interest in one of Nettie's delightful snacks, and she had gone downstairs to get him his post-coital treat. She had made the mistake of being engaged in conversation with Sheriff Atherly, who had caught her as she was going up the stairs and had offered a bit of coin for a quick trip to the library. She had meant to be gone for only a moment and hadn't thought to close her door, and that's when Abigail Edwards must have been passing by. For when she returned to the room, her sweet and balding Higgy was gone. That's when the story picked up from Abigail, who spoke as if in a daze to all the ladies now crowded into the room.

"You know I usually don't come upstairs so early in the evening, but Louise came into the library where I was finishing up the night's accounts. I reckoned the Sheriff and Louise did not need an escort, so I came up to my room to get ready for bed. I saw Louise's door open but didn't think about anyone still being there. And so I continued on to my room. I was about to dress for bed when Terrance Higgins appeared at my door. He said that Louise had been gone for some time and was preparing to leave himself, owing to the lateness of the evening, but saw that, as I was unaccompanied, perhaps I would care for a little of his attention. I felt sure I would be able to talk him out of the room, and I felt that having reminded him of the agreements that we have reached and Louise's obvious affection for him perhaps it was best to say good-night. I was convinced he had accepted that, until he grabbed me at my waist and tried to kiss me. I shoved him away and told him quite pointedly that it was time to go, but he had this look in his eye, Thatcher, that he was finally not taking no for an answer. And when I went to open the door to show him out, he hit me very hard, here." She indicated a spot on her covered chest. "He must have locked the door then. The next thing I knew he was tearing at my gown. That's when I screamed, and he hit me again, probably out of fear. I shouldn't have screamed. I should have just dealt with the situation and then taken matters to the Sheriff in the morning. Why did I scream ..."

The obvious trauma and shock of first the attempted rape and then the death of her rapist at her son's hands began to set over her like a dark cloud. Because, unlike any other attempted rape by virtually any other man in town, this incident could not be rectified with the right story and the right amount of money. This wasn't Nettie with a knife, fighting off two sailors in the hallway. This was Thatcher Edwards, a killer of recent repute, who had taken the life of the husband of the most powerful woman in Bristol.

"You have to go, Thatcher, and you have to go now," Abigail stated with a quiet determination.

"No, Mother, I can explain this. This was self-defense. He has been warned more times than any man should be allowed to be warned, and he tried to rape you. And he may well have been successful if you hadn't screamed. It doesn't matter who his wife is, we have friends. We have justification and we have money."

"Are you aware of the words that have been spoken of you these last few weeks?" Abigail stated, a look of horror on her face. "Do you realize that there is not one bit of sympathy left for you or us or this family? Do you realize how hard we've all had to work, how much money has been spent just to hold our ground in this little corner of Bristol, and how much good will was pissed away when you decided you wanted to be a pugilist? No, this can't be fixed. There is no amount of money that can save you now. There's only one thing that can be done, and you must go now."

"Caesar, ye must go, too," Nettie chimed in. They all turned to see her standing at the door, making her way past them to inspect the very dead Terrance Higgins. "It will be no safer for ye than it is for Tatch, because they are going to make sure that someone swings for this if there's a man who can be hauled up on the gaols."

"Nettie is right," Abigail replied. "Caesar, you and Thatcher have to go now. You're going to need each other."

"That's lunacy, Mother. Who will protect this house? These women?" Thatcher protested.

"I will," Nettie responded, a look of deadly seriousness and determination in her eyes. "I have been protecting this house since before ye were born, and I will continue to protect everyone who lives here."

"You need to see someone, right now, who in many ways owes you his life," Abigail insisted. "You need to find Woodes Rogers."

"Woodes? Woodes Rogers is the last person in Bristol who would help me," Thatcher replied, anger in his voice at the thought of his former best friend.

Abigail pulled herself together and made her way to her table, pulling out a sheet of paper and her quill, and quickly wrote a short note. She folded it and handed it to her son. "Find him now and hand him this. He owes not only you and Caesar for all the kindness and protection you gave him. He owes me as well." Abigail placed the note in her son's inside jacket pocket and held him and kissed him very tenderly. "You have grown into a remarkable man, Thatcher Edwards, and I'm sorry I can't see the great things to come."

Nettie stood and looked into the eyes of her son Caesar. There had never been the demonstrated affection between them as there was between Abigail and Thatcher. It wasn't their way. It wasn't the way of their people. But she looked up into those dark, soulful eyes, grabbing his chin and forcing his eyes to hers. "Remember what your father said. Prison is no better than slavery. And you must be free for him."

Caesar looked at his mother, realizing that the secret he had kept for so long had never been a secret to her. She had fiercely fought to protect him and keep him from all the hells and horrors she had experienced, but he had not done so well in protecting her from his hell. All these years she had known what he had seen and had never said a word. "I will honor my father as I honor you with your wishes," he stated reverently to his fearsome, wonderful mother. He knew what he needed to do, and he grabbed Thatcher by the jacket and pulled him behind him. Thatcher stopped only long enough to enter his room and retrieve his most precious keepsake, his Uncle Peter's brace of pistols. They then made their way down the back stairs that led to the kitchen and out the back door.

The women of Parker House would bite their tongues as long as possible until the absence of Terrance Higgins became impossible to cover. There was hope that with a few hours of silence Thatcher and Caesar would be able to make a clear break from Bristol before the long arm of justice could catch them. It was getting close to dawn as they arrived at the Bristol quay where the *Regent* was preparing to set sail. As if fated to be, the one person whom they could see clearly in the pre-dawn light was Woodes Rogers, assisting the crew in preparing the ship for sail.

"Woodes," came a voice from the shadows that at first startled the young seaman. As his eyes adjusted to the dim light, he could make out the distinctive shapes of Thatcher and Caesar Edwards. He shook his head in slight disgust.

"A bit early for your daily stroll, isn't it?" he sighed.

"I do not have time to banter with you, Woodes. I need to ask you a favor," Thatcher replied, more serious with Woodes than he had been in ages.

Woodes noted the ominous tone. "I'm a bit surprised that you would be coming to me for favors, Thatcher Edwards. I cannot think of anything I have that would be of any use to you."

"You have this ship, and we need to be aboard it," Caesar replied.

"And I should, what, just hand you the tiller and say have a good cruise gentlemen? Please. I've much to do before she makes sail, and you're wasting my time with your silly chatter," Woodes replied, turning his back to both of them.

"You owe us this, Woodes," Caesar insisted, his body looming large as he came closer to the smaller teenager.

"I owe you? I owe you nothing. Your childhood friendship may have meant something to me at one time, but I never liked what you two have become and what you represent, and I don't think, whatever benefit I may have gained from knowing you then, that I owe you anything now."

Thatcher reached into his coat and withdrew the piece of paper his mother had penned. He hadn't bothered to read its contents but felt that it was the only thing he had to offer to make his argument. "She does," Thatcher said simply, handing the note to Woodes.

He took the piece of paper and moved a few feet away to take advantage of the lantern suspended from the gangplank. He read the few short lines Abigail had hastily penned and for a moment looked skyward and under his breath whispered, "Oh, Lord." He walked back to them, placing the note inside his own jacket.

"I will sign you aboard as able-bodied seamen, and you can remain below decks until we clear Bristol Harbour. But I shall need to sign you aboard under some names."

Thatcher and Caesar realized the break they had hoped for had come, and whatever Abigail's note had said had forced Woodes Rogers to yield to this request. Thatcher thought as Woodes retrieved the crew manifest.

"Drummond. Edward Drummond," Thatcher offered, giving silent thanks and tribute to his old German Suburb instructor.

"Johann DeBeers," Caesar replied. Thatcher gave him a look as if wondering why he would be choosing that particular name so reviled in the Parker household, the name of the man who had almost gotten his mother executed for the defending the house. Caesar leaned in to whisper to Thatcher, "He was the first white man I ever knew. He and his brother were part of the slave ship crew that brought me and my mother here."

Woodes wrote both names on the manifest and then directed them to the bottom of the ship at the rear of the hold. Before they could board, Woodes Rogers leaned in to Thatcher. "From this day forward, Thatcher Edwards no longer exists and will never be spoken of by my lips again."

As Bristol began to wake to a new day and the wagons of area farmers and merchants made their way to the marketplace, Mrs. Higgins awoke to find that, once again, her husband was not in bed where he belonged. In a few moments she would rise, hasten downstairs and summon the servant boy who would begin his common rounds of the taverns and public houses and back alleys of Bristol in search of her disreputable and drunken husband, who once more must have chosen the bottle over his familial responsibilities. As the boy began to make his appointed rounds over a well-tracked course, the *Regent* slipped her moorings and warped away from the Bristol quay. Woodes Rogers, Jr., walked back to his family home, feigning an illness that precluded him from joining their ship on its quest to America. While bringing great pleasure to his mother and great disappointment to his father when he failed to make his voyage, Woodes Rogers could not bring himself to spend the next many weeks at sea in the company of Thatcher and Caesar. For despite his name, his prestige and his family's wealth, deep down he felt they would always be his betters. Despite the pretenses and airs and self-righteousness of the Rogers name, they, too, were only human and driven by the same base passions that drove all men. The difference was they did so in secret, requiring other people of discretion capable of meeting those dark, deep desires in a manner by which they could maintain their pretense of piety.

Just as Abigail had so pointedly reminded him.

Chapter 4

Chasing Ghosts
June 1696 – March 1699

I

The hours slipped by uncountable to Thatcher and Caesar. The two had remained silent and motionless in the lowest and farthest reaches of the hold since boarding the *Regent*, making it impossible to get a fix on time. What they could tell from their shadowy hide-away was that the *Regent* had slipped her moorings, evidenced by the back and forth motion of the ship as it warped away from the dock. The subtle change as the ship passed from mild bay to the rough pitch of the rolling sea told them their voyage was well under way. They quietly debated when they should make their appearance. As they had been added to the manifest, no doubt eventually someone would be looking for them, demanding an explanation as to why they had not been on deck to bring the *Regent* to sea. At the same time, there was no telling whether the ship was being pursued or had actually been boarded by a search party seeking out the killers of Terrance Higgins. At long last, they heard noises in the hold, bringing Thatcher and Caesar to dead silence as they sat quiescent in their dark corner of the ship.

"I'm seekin' Drummond? And, uh ... DeBeers?" the voice said from the shadows. "There be those two men down here?"

The illumination of a wagging lantern could be seen slowly making its way down the densely packed cargo hold, and both men pressed themselves closer to the hull, not knowing who was seeking them out. From their secluded hiding spot, Thatcher could just make out the shape of the man holding the lantern and calling out their assumed names. It took him a moment, but at last he recognized the fellow.

"Drummond? DeBeers? I have been sent down here by Master Woodes, who gave me instructions to seek ye out when we had reached open sea."

Thatcher looked at Caesar, who was quite prepared to remain exactly where he was or put this fellow down and take their chances on deck. Thatcher indicated for him to relax. "Good fellow, Drummond here, with my friend DeBeers," Thatcher replied as he slowly rose from his hiding place within the shadows. He could see the nervousness on the man's face and the look of confusion when he recognized the dark haired young man.

"DeBeers?" Darby Mullins asked, looking at Thatcher Edwards, formerly of Parker House.

"Drummond. This is my traveling companion, DeBeers," he indicated as Caesar himself rose ominously from the dark corner.

Darby Mullins took this in for a moment. It wasn't uncommon for men to go to the sea under assumed names. Darby himself had traveled under a handful, but he was surprised to see the young man with whom he had spoken just weeks before at that bordello where he had, alas, left quite unsatisfied, both with his lack of female company and over the dismal news he had conveyed. While he had been waiting to catch a ship back to America, he had witnessed the fellow in his match against that Irishman from London, who returned to his home in a pine box. There had been much talk on the docks and in the taverns about that fight and the level of brutality demonstrated by the young brothel keeper. It had served as a warning to many, including Darby, who had thought to perhaps win his way into Edwards' good graces for a chance to try once again to transact much needed business. But whatever fire he may have had was quickly put out the night that fellow died most hideously in that warehouse. Certainly, it had been a fair fight as pugilist matches go, and there had been no discussion of retribution on the boy, so certainly that couldn't be the reason why he was here. Obviously, something else had transpired to make the fellow flee the most enviable job any sailor could imagine and slip aboard a merchant ship under an assumed name.

"Mr. Drummond ... and Mr. DeBeers, then. Master Woodes mentioned ye might need some orientation on this vessel, as perhaps yer skills may not be in line with the demands of a workin' ship. So I should ask ye candidly – do ye have any experience aboard a sailin' vessel?"

"Well, I sailed through Gibraltar and up to Kiev in the Ukraine a number of years back," Thatcher replied honestly.

"And I, too, spent time aboard a slave vessel from Madagascar to London," Caesar added.

While not necessarily dishonest answers, it did not quite paint the picture that Darby Mullins was conjuring. "And you, Mr. Drummond ... ye worked the tops?"

"No. I apprenticed for a navigator," Thatcher replied. "And I also have shipwright's experience, having apprenticed in a shipyard as well."

"I was cargo," Caesar replied. "But I apprenticed in navigation under an apprentice to a navigator."

"Well, perhaps the workin' of the lines and tops will be a great place to begin, and if the carpenter is seekin' a mate, yer skills may be put to good work, Mr. Drummond. As for navigation, those apprenticeships are typically held by the young men who come aboard as future officers. But we'll see what can be arranged." He took in the clothing of the two men, both dressed in black pants and tunics and heavy dark boots, no doubt great wear for a night of frolic on shore, but certainly not appropriate on the deck of a ship.

He brought them up into the crew's quarters, a packed, narrow space where seventy-odd men took shifts sleeping shoulder to shoulder in hammocks. As the first watch had just gone to racks, Darby found a spot for the two men to bed down near him and arranged to begin their rotations in a few hours when they could hopefully get lost in the confusion of leaving port. Having set sail in the first rays of dawn and completing the ship's company at the last moment, it was possible he could concoct an explanation as to why no one had seen these two in the last half-day at sail. He would work that out in the next few much-needed hours of sleep. Darby immediately fell into his hammock, which swung him to sudden slumber while Thatcher and Caesar made do across barrels and sacks of crew provisions.

The eight bells indicating a change of shifts was greeted with violent and vile cursing of the somnolent men piped to quarters. Darby rolled from his rack and nearly landed on Caesar. Thatcher and his brother rose from their less than satisfying sleep and followed their new mentor to the deck, where the cook had laid out a large vat of salted beef and rock hard biscuits, their meal of frequency over the next few weeks at sea. Thatcher assessed the grey, salty meat and broth and tried his best to bite into the unyielding biscuit, then followed Darby's lead by dropping the biscuit into the fetid broth to give it some measure of softness. The looks of the collection of seasoned, rough-hewn sailing men that made up their watch betrayed the inappropriateness of Thatcher and Caesar's appearances, no doubt much as Woodes must have appeared to those dockside ruffians in years past. But landsmen new to the sea were not an object of curiosity or an unusual sight to the men who made their living aboard merchant ships. England dealt with its most indebted of citizens by releasing them from the overcrowded prisons and selling their bonds of debt to captains and ship owners who were always pressed for able bodies. Their appearance aboard ship only signaled to the crew that until these landlubbers got their sea legs and a bit of rope burn upon their hands, they would be virtually useless. But while Thatcher and Caesar may have been new to sea life in the traditional sense, the crew was pleased to discover that what they lacked in finesse they certainly did not lack in strength. And, of course, there were whisperings among many of the crew who had been in and out of Bristol Port for much of their careers, who had seen the tall, dark-haired youth and his sizeable African companion mixing with their employers and contractors in a very convivial fashion. So many of their shipmates knew this Drummond and DeBeers to be *noms de guerre* for whatever purpose they had deemed necessary. And many wondered: this wouldn't have anything to do with that fight, would it?

From their spot on the main deck, Captain Walgrave and his first mate Mr. Harrington could be seen conferring with each other about the course and weather. The captain seemed displeased with the trim of his sails, and Mr. Harrington brought the crew's lovely meal to an end by insisting the watch re-sheet immediately. Thatcher and Caesar were about to follow Darby, but he stopped them, indicating they should remove their boots and tunics. The three then proceeded up the ratlines to the tops. While neither Edwards could consider himself to be afraid of much of anything, that first time climbing those interlaced sections of rope, traveling some one hundred feet vertically along a solid, creaking stand of timber mast affixed to a rolling ship, evoked a moment of discomfiture. As Darby rapidly snaked his way, moving not only vertically but also diagonally along the precarious route, it took a moment for Thatcher and Caesar to gain both their bearing and nerve, as every few seconds their line of sight pitched to a higher and higher degree. Darby waited for them at the cross tees of the mizzenmast as they slowly but surely worked their way to him. They climbed to that solid piece of wood that crossed the long and solid mast where Darby told them to spread out a little and grab a section of canvas held in place by small cloth ties. With their backs to the stern, Thatcher looked down to the tiny deck below him to see the scurry of activity as others ran to the lines and stays that held the present sheets aloft.

As they began to heave upon the line and the sails that currently propelled the ship forward began to slowly creak up, Darby indicated for Thatcher and Caesar to step off their firm wooden footholds and onto the thin piece of rope that swayed under their feet. The feeling of this taunt and strained fibrous step which swayed with the movements and weight of each man that stood upon it, plus the force of wind that wished to remove whatever slack remained, made both first-timers of the tops a little nervous and unsure. This was made even more so as Darby instructed them to release their hands from the canvas and to take a hold of those ties that held the furled sail by the slightest tug of a slipknot and told them to stand by until told to do otherwise. So, with their feet swaying, their bodies arching and their arms stretching, fingers grasping the ties as their hands held to the knot, they stood there until at last they heard Mr. Harrington scream from the quarterdeck, "Set sheets!" In unison the seasoned sailors grasped those strings and pulled with all their might, standing nearly upright as they held the loose strands in their hands. The lubbers, on the other hand, took a second more to grasp what was being asked, and Thatcher and Caesar, and the other pitiful fellow they had seen scrambling up the opposite ratline, followed suit as that massive mizzen sail and its hundreds of feet of canvas began to drop like a stone toward the deck. For just a second there was a noisy stillness as the sheets surrendered to gravity, but the tautness gathering on the lines that trailed from them and held by the men on deck gave the sheet no place to go but forward. And as the men below scrambled furiously to secure the lines to the stays, Thatcher could feel the gathering wind in his back and was awestruck at the vastness of white that began to billow, then curve before him. For just a second, the sight of those sails and that magnificent spread of white took him back to Russia, when the snows and skies had joined the ground in a persistence of monochrome majesty and everything he saw was a blinding white. Thatcher's reminiscences quickly lurched to an end with the surge of the ship as those huge canvases now gathered with the ocean's breath, and the cross tee and mast strained to maintain their purchase to the deck so far below as man and wood reacted to the insistence of a maddened sail that wanted nothing more than to move.

Thatcher and Caesar did not realize the importance of not standing totally upright with those strings in hand or the value to be placed in leaning slightly back as did the seasoned sailors, who rode this surge and held their strands of cloth as if the reins on a majestic coach and ten. For the lubbers, it was all they could do not to lose their feet and hands and crash the hundred feet to the deck below. The joyous smiles and the sinister laughs of these coachmen of the sea gave them their first taste of the great traditions of the masters of the waves. The rope beneath their feet once again began to strain as men worked their way out of the tops and back down the ratlines. Throughout the weeks to come, Thatcher and Caesar would grow intimate with that well-traveled, precarious path as they ascended and descended a dozen times a day to satisfy the demands of the captain and his first mate.

The crossing from southern England's Land's End to New York was a well-worn path, coursed by thousands of ships at any given time, though on these vast stretches of empty sea a man could stand at the tops and look for miles in any direction and see no sign of other sail, creating a sense of absolute and sheer isolation. As Darby had suggested, young well-heeled men of education and means joined the navigator each day at noon at the bow to take the readings of the sun and its meridian and to read the compass to make a reasonable estimation of the course of travel. Thatcher and Caesar, mere topmen, would often try to insinuate themselves near the assemblage of young gentlemen and the navigator, Mr. Toombs, who would explain the process and quiz his apprentices as to their estimations and application of these none-too-exact sciences of sailing. Along the larboard side, one of the crew would stand with a small log in his hand, a rope tied to one end with knots placed the length of a man's two-arm span, and at the navigator's command he would cast the log over the side. Next to him, another crewman would have an hourglass with precisely twenty-eight seconds of sand, and the moment the log left his shipmate's grasp, he would turn the glass as his partner would begin to call out each knot that slipped between his hands. As soon as the last grain had fallen from the top glass to the bottom, the timekeeper would scream "Now!" And the log man would grasp the rope with all his strength. In this year of 1696, this rudimentary method was the most scientific aspect of shipboard life as that precise count of knots timed with twenty-eight seconds of sand could give the navigator and the captain a precise speed at which the ship was traveling, given to them as nautical miles. With their calculations of the sun's position relative to the known noontime hour, combined with the speed of the ship and its hourly sounding and the direction of the compass needle, the navigator and the captain could fairly accurately determine their latitudinal position. In the middle of endless ocean, only the predictability of the currents and winds could give them reasonable assurance of that accurate course, as nary a landmark would be seen until the sight of the mainland was called from the crewman in the crow's nest.

One other thing that could be depended upon in these Atlantic summers was the very good likelihood that the beautiful blue skies could quickly grow dark with the gathering black clouds of the seasonal hurricanes. As the *Regent* had set sail from Bristol in the earliest days of summer, Captain Walgrave felt very confident that they would make New York Harbor before the summer storms. But as a seasoned captain and a man of infinite caution, he established a round-the-clock watch to man the crow's nest affixed to the top of the mainmast. As topmen, Caesar and Thatcher spent many hours between bells, their eyes cast to the distant horizons, searching for sail and storm. It was in these hours alone that Thatcher would let his mind return to the events of the last few years, beginning with Russia and carrying him to that morning when he felt Terrance Higgins' life come to an end in the palm of his hand. While prone to dreams of action and adventure, Thatcher had always envisioned himself to be not a man of violence but a man of business. Still, in his training under the man whose name he honored in this crossing, he had discovered, to his surprise, that no piece of business nor pleasure to be had at the fringe benefits of his family enterprise could quite compare to the joy he felt when he was participating in martial endeavors. Losing his grandfather had made business seem trivial, and he dealt with his grief and fear through the only other thing that made him feel truly alive. It was unfortunate that the thing that made him thrive was also likely to be the death of others, and he wondered which side of him would disembark at the Port of New York: the businessman, or the warrior.

It was on one such evening, as he reminisced in his private little spot perched high above the heaving deck, that off on the horizon a dark shape began to manifest. Its massiveness at first appeared to be that gathering line of dangerous cloud that he had been trained to watch for, but he paused for a second to clarify that which filled his vision, and he realized that his eyes were not beholding a gathering gloom. They lay for the first time on the destination of his new future. It was land.

He had heard so much about these colonies, this far off distant place that would propel England to become the most powerful nation in all of Europe. America was a place of dreams and ambitions and created thoughts within a man's mind, sending him in a tiny vessel across the vast sea to pursue his longing for wealth and all too often disappearing beneath the waves of these boundless seas long before that mythic shore would ever cross his vision. But unlike his grandfather and grandmother, Thatcher's eyes beheld that promised land, and for the first time in many weeks he felt the joy rise up in his soul and his lungs expanded, his hands cupped round his mouth, and in the most loud and furious tone he could muster, he screamed, "Land!"

No matter how much a man may love the sea, the promise of land was the greatest pleasure to fill the minds of this highly superstitious subset of humanity. Sailors, be they merchants or Royal Navy or pirates, lived for the sound of "Land!" And every hand raced to the bow to catch his first glimpse of that much desired sight that had been merely a fantasy for weeks. Though an easy crossing with only a few squalls and Royal Navy challenges, every man breathed a little easier that, in just a short time, his feet would once again be on dry ground.

As the *Regent* began her final approach into the crowded harbor of New York, she fell into a long line of fellow merchanters and Royal Navy warships jockeying for position into the limited dock space that was the burgeoning New York Harbor. The nimble *Regent* picked her way past the larger and slower ships of the Royal Navy and the big Dutch merchanters whose limited sail in such crowded conditions slowed them to a near crawl. While the collection of ships from all throughout the known world was impressive, what truly caught their eye was one massive ship, whose style and size reminded them of the vessels of old. The behemoth dominating their vision was one that depended not solely upon its massive spray of sail to ply its way through Long Island Sound but additionally two rows of great oars that moved in time to launch her forward. Thatcher and Caesar hurried to the bow to join the others, who had heard that this impressive galley, just christened in the shipyards of London, was making its way to New York. While they had expected to see her at port sometime during the summer as she was to call New York her new home, none had ever expected to see this unique feature, harking back to the ships of Rome and before, actually being employed for their amazement and entertainment.

"There she is, boys," Darby Mullins praised. "Ye're looking at the most modern ship to set sail from the Thames – the *Adventure Galley.*"

Thatcher studied this anachronism that many had said was a creation of folly, but seeing her under way, slipping easily past so many ships that had to run with the minimum of sail, demonstrated how brilliant the concept was. And he had to admit, it was impressive. While their crossing had been relatively uneventful and actually quite rapid as the winds had favored the *Regent* and closed the crossing to a mere thirty-four days, the *Adventure Galley* was designed specifically never to have a bad-wind day. Her crew could be employed to stretch her oars at times when the winds had trickled to nothing or when the waters were so shallow that sail could beach the massive hull, or on those rare occasions when one would require a silent and hasty retreat by night where the flutter of canvas could betray a surreptitious departure. This was never to be of a concern for the *Adventure Galley*, and speed and stealth were absolute necessities for her mission and the man who captained her.

Thatcher and Caesar, or Drummond and DeBeers as they were known by their crewmates, had melded with their fellow sailors, quickly shedding their landlubber reputations and demonstrating real potential as able-bodied seamen. Unlike so many ships where crews grumbled about the cruelty of their officers, the drudgery of the duty and their antipathy for the ship, the crew of the *Regent* was for the most part a happy one and intended to sign back aboard for her next cruise. Darby, on the other hand, had plans to put the sea behind him. He had saved enough from his last few cruises to buy a small dory with which he intended to make like a galleyman and row that tiny craft down the long coast of the colonies to Carolina. His first introductions to water were not the salt of the coast but the many tree-lined rivers which coursed the length of the Carolinas. He had spent much of the cruise telling Thatcher and Caesar about the many broad and calm waterways that stretched between the Chesapeake down to the much-fabled Cape Fear. His hopes were to return to his traditional vocation as a timberman, one of the many reasons why Carolina was such a coveted colony to a tree-sparse England.

When Darby's father had emigrated from Ireland in the 1650s, he never thought that his dirt-farm traditions would be transplanted by a career in timber. But the terms of his indentured servitude gave little regard for what he had done in the past, and his new master cared only about the tall loblolly pines, of which he was titled to tens of thousands of acres to farm. So Williams Mullins came to America to serve out his seven years of servitude, and by year five he knew that he would never be returning to Ireland. He had grown to love this dangerous, back-breaking work of felling trees taller than anything he had ever seen in his life to make way for the true cash crop to come: tobacco. When he met Mary Shannon, another indentured servant who had come to the New World to cook for this new generation of timber and tobacco men, William Mullins impressed her with his good nature and jovial spirit. Unlike the other bondsmen who could never stop talking about the treeless rolling hills of Ireland, William Mullins had fallen in love with that crowded sky that he saw as a challenge to open. As his term came to an end, he surprised Mary Shannon by asking her to be his wife. On the day her servitude expired, she took the Mullins name, and together they ventured south to the trading post of Nathaniel Batts, on the banks of the Chowan River in the northern reaches of Carolina. Batts convinced him that the vast array of tobacco fields to come needed clearing, and clearing meant a lot of timberwork. That timber could in itself become a cash crop, as settlers would need wood for homes, fires, wagons, canoes and barges. And so, William and Mary Mullins cleared their first few acres to build their own home, which would expand year to year as together they procreated ten Mullins children over the next decade. Their youngest, David, followed in the tradition of his six brothers and picked up an ax and saw the moment he could heft theit weight.

Every morning just before dawn, the Mullins men would climb into their dories and row down the broad Chowan River, enjoying the silence of the miles of tree lined banks teeming with limitless game, which would be hunted on the return trip home to grace the Mullins' table. The men would reach their designated stands, easily discernible in this early light from the clearings they had already meticulously manufactured, and begin the process of churning out dozens of perfectly straight stands of timber to be trimmed and rolled into the Chowan and floated to the mills downstream. While David was leaner than his brothers, he was no less capable in bearing his weight on either end of a saw or an ax, but David's slight build gave him one distinct advantage and a job for which few of his brothers wished to challenge him. As a tree was selected for its size and shape and height, David would strap on an ax and saw, and taking a section of sheet, he would wrap it around the width of the tree, throwing it a few feet above his head, then wrap his legs around the trunk and quickly scale its length, sawing off stray limbs as he climbed until he reached the very top. From his perch high above the ground, David was able to take in the endless miles of green that stretched to west, north and south. It never ceased to amaze him, having heard the stories of his treeless ancestors' home, how it appeared that all of Ireland could take saw and ax into hand and never fell all the trees that stretched beyond his vision. While all of this was impressive, what impressed him the most was his view to the east. From his perch, he saw a sight few men would ever see. From here he could see how the Chowan River widened into a broad bay, which was only a precursor for the massive body of water that extended beyond it, known as the Albemarle Sound. From here he could watch as ships slowly threaded the tricky channels, some bringing new settlers to the area, most coming for the tobacco and many for those endless miles of timber felled by the Mullins and their fellow woodsmen. As he would trim the tops of these great stands, sending their massive branches to the ground to be further reduced and cleared by his brothers below, David would take in his last view of those broad waters, then quickly shimmy down and watch in fascination as those mighty pines crashed to the ground to be trimmed and rolled down the mighty Chowan to those arriving settlers and waiting ships.

Darby followed the trail of those down-river logs one day aboard a dory with all the possessions to his name, primarily a few changes of clothes and his imagination. At fourteen, it was always easy to find apprentice work aboard a ship offering experience rather than wages. And with no questions asked, Darby found a new life at sea. But over the years, his fascination with the mariner's life had slowly but surely waned. He had never expected to be anything more than a simple seaman, plying an honest trade and traveling to far-off places.

But the nature of ships and the men who crew them was a careful balance of indulgence and cruelty. Every now and again one was fortunate enough to sail with a captain like Walgrave, but unfortunately he was an exception among captains. It often seemed that only the most malicious and cruel of human beings chose to make professions as merchant officers. Much of this had to do with the class structure, which made these typically English or Scottish gentry look down upon the common, lowborn men who toiled in the rigging. But there was a certain lot, specifically those who captained England's ships of war or those who had started their careers in such a way, that brought cruelty and disdain to new levels. These captains who could not keep enough of the crew loyal to them and their mission were easy prey for those who viewed their lot in life as nothing more than disposable chattel and who resented every aspect of that reality. This was the case of Captain Gibson who, while not particularly cruel, had truly been one of the most dismissive of men. It was his constant penchant for drink and his seemingly endless ambition that put him in that awful position in Cadiz that led to the taking of his ship. That he had let his first mate

Avery select the crew without so much as purveying the natures and histories of these men demonstrated Gibson's disdain for details and blindness to disloyalty. Darby had heard the rumblings start long before they made Bristol, first amongst the men below decks and then echoed and encouraged by the men who occupied the gunners' room, those officers whom one would expect would be loyal to their captain. Darby dismissed most of the discussion as the boastings of powerless men, but that night, when Mr. Avery cut the lines that held the anchors and floated the ship out of the port of Cadiz with Captain Gibson powerless and undermanned and, as usual, totally sodden, he did not sympathize with either the captain or his small band of loyalists. And he had been fine when the crew decided that Spanish ships and the African trade were to be their chosen quarry. That was how it began, as they slowly meandered through the waters off Spain, preparing to cross the doldrums that would take them down around the Horn to the east of Africa. But Avery belayed just long enough in those waters between Spain and the New World to realize how easily such a massive ship, so heavily armed, could opt to plunder any vessel it chose, regardless of flag. And when it was French or Dutch, Darby could justify it. But when the *Holy Cross,* blown southward by bad storms off the western coast of England, fell into Avery's crosshairs and no one dared say no to taking an English vessel, something changed in Darby. And when Avery broke with tradition, not giving the passengers a sporting chance of survival and instead giving them a cruel choice of ways to die, Darby was done. Now he was ending his nautical career with a good crew and a good captain. He would take a little of his money into New York, enjoy some lively spirits and sample the ample supply of Dutch prostitutes plying their trade on Beaver and Petticoat and then take the remainder of his money, purchase his dory and slowly row down that long coastline into those protected waters of the Albemarle Sound, back up the Chowan River, and see what progress the Mullins had made in clearing those endless trees.

Like Darby, Thatcher and Caesar would also pass on continuing with Captain Walgrave and his jolly crew. Rather, as soon as they could gather their pay and make their way to shore, they had a very specific mission in mind. Only weeks before they had departed Bristol, Jocko and Artemus had set sail for New York. Chances were good that they had made port just days before them. Knowing their habits, Thatcher and Caesar would search the small gathering of warehouses that were being expanded by the day to accommodate the steady flow of commerce. They would also search the long strand of taverns and public houses that filled both sides of Wall Street, for Artemus and Jocko would seek out those places where the men of commerce gathered. And like the sailors who had made port and were dying for a bottle and a brothel, so, too, would these men of commerce be seeking creative ways to spend the money rolling in on every tide.

II

Despite being one of the most prominent cities of the colonies, New York was a relatively small and dirty place. With barely five thousand residents, a fifth of them African slaves, and in transition from the Dutch majority colony that was New Amsterdam to a British plurality, New York reeked of that frontier quality where function was much more critical to daily life than form. The filthy streets, mostly mud and tended by pigs, still gave an air of the Dutch liberality rather than British austerity, as the women wore dresses more inclined to show a generous expanse of leg and bodice, with virtually no layers between them and the thin, white cotton that loosely clung to their bodies. This suited the merchant and pirate class well, as New York had become a Mecca for those who had gone "on the account," a euphemism for those who had chosen the piratical trade, and returned from their Caribbean and Atlantic ventures laden with merchandise to be sold at a fraction of its value. And it was because the trade was so lucrative that more enterprising rogues who demonstrated a penchant for acquisition could seek out merchants who saw great profit in funding future ventures. As much as New Yorkers loved pirates, pirates loved New York, where a fellow with a little gold and free time could find anything he wanted to fill his days and empty his pockets, thus motivating him to return to the sea to repeat the cycle.

In 1696, the hub of New York life was the tavern-strewn Wall Street, where legitimate and illegitimate trade was conducted in the shadow of ever-emptying casks of rum and ale. To Thatcher and Caesar, this was what Artemus and Jocko had been talking about – an environment ripe with cash-flushed men anxious to wager and hungering for entertainment. Artemus had spoken of one particular establishment, where the roughest of seamen easily mixed with a collection of rogue entrepreneurs, and they wasted no time locating it. Thatcher walked up to the barkeep and inquired as to its owner. He was directed to a table where an odd collection of gentry and rogue sat screaming at a cup and demanding it produce the dice they desired.

"Mr. Michael Hawdon?" Thatcher inquired of one particularly frustrated fellow, who was punishing the impudent dice for their refusal to obey his command. The questioned fellow did not bother looking up as he stared down at the six-sided ivories as if thinking they would change their mind.

"I'm Hawdon," the tavern owner replied. "State your business."

"I'm seeking out a fellow we both may know named Artemus Grey," Thatcher continued. Hawdon's expression changed immediately, hearing a name from the past and anticipating an opportunity to make back some of the money he had just lost.

"Artemus Grey is here?" Hawdon asked with newfound excitement as he turned to face his inquisitor and the ominous African fellow behind him.

"Well, that is what I was hoping you could tell me. We had been working together these last three years in Bristol, and they left a few weeks before us. He had mentioned yours would be the first call he made. Frankly, I'm surprised to hear he hasn't shown up here yet," Thatcher replied.

"If Artemus Grey had arrived in New York, I would know it. You say he left a few weeks before you?" Hawdon inquired.

"Well, I must confess, our ship caught very fair winds, so he may have lost some of the advantage, but certainly not all," Thatcher continued.

Hawdon sized up Thatcher Edwards and his stout companion. These fellows gave the impression of men of breeding and culture, yet they possessed an air more inclined toward the pugilist than the bettor. The New York fighting scene was still in its infancy and more a spontaneous outbreak than a planned event. One need only stand still for a short while and fisticuffs were certain to break out, but seldom would one have the chance to wager on the outcome before the bout was through. To hear that Artemus Grey was coming to New York meant great profit for this rambunctious lot of men, for both merchant and mariner could not wait to have their pockets picked by the bloody hands of boxers. Hawdon knew that he had a ground floor opportunity to seize the advantage in the fight game and wanted to make certain that these two young fellows knew who buttered their bread when they stepped onto the shores of the New World.

"Well, I'm certain the moment Artemus arrives, he'll be seeking out his old friend Michael. In the meantime, lads, have you found quarters?" Hawdon chimed.

"We've just arrived aboard the *Regent* and have barely been on shore for an hour," Thatcher replied.

"Then it's my good fortune you found me first," Hawdon beamed. "Above my tavern I have a few rooms usually set aside for the conducting of short-term lodging. I'm happy to make them available to you as my guests. But first, gentlemen, you've just arrived from sea. You need real food and drink, and perhaps a little companionship to welcome you ashore."

Hawdon led the two men to a table where an attractive amber-haired woman served them an endless supply of unsalted meats and delightfully soft bread. Meanwhile, Hawdon sent forth his minions to begin searching every tavern, bawdyhouse and alleyway within a horse's distance to find out what had happened to Artemus Grey and to let him know his friends from Bristol were waiting here for him.

Thatcher and Caesar were pleased to receive such a warm welcome. It seemed that dropping the right name with the right man had led to comforts they had not quite expected in this rough-and-tumble town on the river named for explorer Henry Hudson. It seemed as if their money was no good, for Hawdon waved away their sailors' pay and said they'd settle up down the road. And Hawdon's was a good place to be, for like Peal's it seemed to be the font of information of the comings and goings of New York port. Every sailor and captain seemed to have a relationship with Michael Hawdon and his lackeys. Of course, much of the buzz was about the *Adventure Galley* and her captain, who bore a fresh privateer's commission from King Charles. The captain, however, was having a difficult time recruiting able-bodied seamen. As their shipmates aboard the *Regent* were preparing to make sail for New Providence, many had been approached to consider signing aboard the *Adventure Galley*, but the unattractive wages being offered made them disinclined to spend months or possibly years at sea with no assurance of payment.

Captain William Kidd had ventured from New York as a successful merchant seaman. Well respected and likewise well married, he enjoyed the status as the wealthiest man in all of New York, having built a respectable business in commercial shipping and having married the richest widow in the colony. Though his earlier years were spent in less respectable aspects of the nautical trade, his reputation in New York was sterling. Through his contacts in England, he had gained an impressive array of backers who had given him carte blanche to build his dream ship while likewise finagling a king's commission to hunt pirates and the treasures they carried. On the surface, this sounded like an ideal opportunity for starry-eyed fortune hunters. But Kidd's backers were adamant about keeping the bulk of the proceeds for themselves, and they put Kidd in the untenable position of having to recruit sailors willing to commit for a share of future profits. While there were many men to be found in New York who had sailed under similar arrangements, the difference was they had been not employees working on commission but co-owners of a ship, where they equally shared in the profits and where the rules were certainly less stringent than those Kidd's sales pitch entailed. "No prey, no pay" was fine as a pirate, but as a pirate hunter it was not the least bit attractive.

July and August dragged on with no word of Artemus Grey, and Hawdon's hospitality was beginning to worry Thatcher and Caesar, for while both were good businessmen, they were also young men and the notion of "free" was too good to turn down. They liberally exercised that perquisite, never realizing that every single pence was being counted by the barman and the ladies who continuously offered up their goods. In early September, Michael Hawdon joined Thatcher and Caesar, both quite sodden and soiled at the table they had come to think of as their own, taking a chair and shaking his head.

"Well, Mr. Drummond ... Mr. DeBeers. It appears we have finally tracked down our mutual friend. I have had people from Boston to Philadelphia inquiring as to the whereabouts of Artemus Grey, and at last we have word. He is in New Providence. And he has no recollection of either a Drummond or DeBeers, which puts you in a very precarious situation. You see, I'm willing to extend hospitality for friends, but I have a problem with liars."

Thatcher and Caesar looked at each other, then around them. At every turn and exit, at every corner, Hawdon's men stood at the ready with truncheon, sword, knife and musket, to make his words more poignant.

"Mr. Hawdon, I should have told you our dealings with Artemus Grey were not under the names of Drummond and DeBeers, but I think identities mean little to you right now, am I correct?" Thatcher reasoned.

"Gentlemen, New York is full of men who go by many names, and I care less about your identities than those on the coins you hopefully have in your pocket right now," Hawdon intoned.

"I think I am safe in assuming that however much coin we have in our pockets won't come close to satisfying the amount you feel we owe," Thatcher replied.

"Yours is a safe assumption, Mr. Drummond, but I may perhaps have a solution that would solve both of our interests." Hawdon smiled.

Hawdon was a down and dirty businessman and not a marketeer like Artemus Grey, but he knew his audience, and he knew what they would find to be entertaining. Thatcher and Caesar spent the rest of the day holed up in a dingy shack close to the docks. They had left Hawdon's company, not with the lovely flaxen-haired whores they had been pleased to enjoy these many days in New York, but rather with two very large pug-faced men with loaded muskets. These fellows were pleasantly surprised to discover that their captives could, if nothing else, carry on a conversation with them in their own Polish tongue, which made the long wait less tedious. Outside the shack a gathering din of voices could be heard as the night began to fall and the sunlight that had filtered through the cracks of the building was replaced by torchlight. As the voices got louder and the flickering lights more bright, the latch on the shack opened and Michael Hawdon appeared, smiling with delight at what he had accomplished in so short a time.

"Good evening, gentlemen!" he announced. "As you claim to have been in the company of Artemus Grey, I'm trusting you managed to pick up a few skills. Otherwise, my customers will be very distressed at how short their entertainment will be. In a moment we'll be joining those anxious gents who've put forth a hefty coin to be sufficiently entertained. You two will take on a couple of fellows I've rounded up who may lack Artemus's training but no doubt have brawled and lived to talk about it. Whoever walks away wins. If it's you, your debt is settled and perhaps we can discuss future arrangements to our mutual satisfaction – or I'll bid you an adieu. If not, the gate I've collected more than paid off what you owe me – so either way, I win. Four men in, two men out. Simple. Are you ready?"

Thatcher and Caesar looked at one another and smiled. This was far less ominous than they had expected, and they at least had a fighting chance to walk away.

"You know all you had to do was ask, but we've enjoyed our time with the Stanaslavowicz brothers and their tales of Gdansk. It's really all quite fascinating. You should ask them sometime. Well, actually, asking doesn't seem to be your style, does it?" Thatcher rose and stuck his hand out to Michael Hawdon. "It's a deal, then. Mr. DeBeers? After you, sir." He gestured to Caesar.

"Oh, no, Mr. Drummond, after you," Caesar declined with a bow.

It was a good thing they had not grown too accustomed to ship board life, for in their weeks at sea they had adopted the lighter clothes and unshod feet of the professional sailor. But here in port they reverted to their custom of wearing their comfortable trousers, black tunics and heavy black boots, inappropriate for the New York summer but perfect for the presentation they were about to make. They donned their tricorner hats and audacious smiles and strode out side-by-side. They made their way through the odd collection of salty sailors and gentrified businessmen, all of whom shared the same bloodlust in their faces as they made their assessments of Drummond and DeBeers, late of Bristol.

When they reached their place of battle they noted the complete absence of lines, save one, which they would be required to toe. Facing off on the line and waiting were two very large individuals, each scarred, stripped to the waist and holding wooden cudgels. Thatcher and Caesar smiled, bowed at their competitors and slowly began removing their tunics, gently handing them to the Stanaslavowicz brothers as they removed their fine ruffled shirts. They placed the shirts in the brothers' hands, then took back their tunics and began rolling them into tight, taut lines, holding one end in each hand. Thatcher and Caesar took the most elegant swordsman's pose, holding those rolled heavy garments over their heads as if brandishing swords, and then, together, they stepped to the line and simultaneously snapped those tunics as if they were whips into the faces of their two beefy competitors.

This first strike did little more than get the attention of their opponents and the assembled masses, who thrilled to the sound of the whip cracks. Blood streaked from where brass buttons had torn open their cheeks, but this did not deter them as they charged forward with their lengths of wood, swinging wildly at the two men from Bristol. What they lacked in finesse they made up for in ferocity, and it was only a last minute sidestep that kept those heavy wooden rods from crunching bone on impact. The crowd made that small space even smaller as they crushed in to force the competitors into a more face-to-face competition. Thatcher wrapped his tunic around one hand very tightly, making sure those buttons stood up above his knuckles, and closed in on his foe, beating ferociously at the arm holding the stick until he dropped it. His hand no longer encumbered with his weapon, the ogre began punching and grasping, but Thatcher threw his body against the mass of on-lookers behind him, using their resistance to launch with all his weight at his opponent, delivering a bloody blow upward on the other fellow's chin. As his face went skyward, Thatcher whipped his sheathed hand like a knife across the man's eyes, the buttons gouging into that tender flesh like a saw blade

Caesar meanwhile used his length of tunic to whip mercilessly at his brute, repulsing him as dozens of little stings hit his face and brow. His opponent swung wildly, a few times glancing off of Caesar's massively muscled chest, opening little rivulets of blood. But Caesar was testing his assailant and saw the way he consistently swung, and he gave an intentional open that the fighter responded to, swinging the rod once again. This time, Caesar brought the tunic directly down upon the wrist of his antagonist, and the sound of the whip crack and the cracking of the wrist echoed nearly simultaneously. In a continuing motion, Caesar swung his tunic around the neck of the unskilled fighter, grabbing the extended end in his massive hand and twisting it. The human neck was not designed to go in that particular angle, and Caesar carried the fighter around his body, continuing the twist of the material one way as the man's neck went the other. Caesar's body followed him to the ground, and grabbing the hair of his opponent's head he continued the twisting motion until the pain-wrenched and shocked face was nearly one hundred eighty degrees from the way God intended it to be. Caesar's weight lay heavily atop the spasmodically twitching body, reacting in a fashion similar to those who met their demise at the end of a hangman's noose.

Caesar turned to see Thatcher, now studying his blinded opponent, and he had to wonder if Thatcher could be satisfied with a simple victory or if he would cave to his showman's instincts and give these bastards their money's worth. Caesar could not hear what Thatcher was saying as he leaned in to speak to his eye-gouged opponent, whose bloody fists covered his face. The fellow relaxed as Thatcher retrieved the truncheon that had been delivered against him and brought it down with great force upon his opponent's neck. The blind man collapsed to the ground in a flash while the solid wooden rod splintered in Thatcher's hand.

Unlike the crowd in Bristol, these New Yorkers were thrilled at a multi-death blood match and nearly stepped on the bodies of the losers to congratulate the victors. Thatcher and Caesar retrieved their shirts from the Stanaslavowicz brothers, shook out their wrinkled and bloody tunics and laid them over their arms. Hawdon pushed his way through the crowd and congratulated the boys, smiling and mentioning something about a great future together. However, these young pugilists were about to put their possibly lucrative careers on the back burner for something less straining.

Their friend Darby had done at least part of what he had said he would do, and that was to take the bulk of his wages and invest them in his dory. But his rowing trip down the coast was constantly put off by one more night, one more drink and one more Dutch prostitute, and he found himself lingering in the companionship of Thatcher and Caesar. In his meanderings about town, he came upon a list of Kidd's potential quarries, and he found himself weighing his own guilt and anger, considering one more mission before he could put the sea completely behind him. When he showed the list to Thatcher and Caesar, they, too, were in a quandary as to whether to follow their original plan or set out on a course of vengeance. For they knew Kidd's quest was to hunt down pirates, a task that did not inspire them, but one name on Kidd's list interested them all profoundly ... Captain John Avery.

Captain Kidd had watched this hastily assembled battle, and from the edges of the crowd he appraised the young fighters with admiration. He was in need of distraction as his attempts to flesh out his roster of crewmen had stalled. After church service at Trinity Cathedral, one of his boastful beneficiaries that kept him in good stead with the more religious citizens of New York, he had entertained a few of the colony's finer couples at his Pearl Street mansion. When the ladies took to the drawing room, the gentlemen took up their pipes and snifters of brandywine and meandered down to the warehouse district on the rumor of a good bout of fisticuffs. He was intrigued when he saw the two young victors working their way to stand before him.

"It is our understanding that you are assembling a crew to hunt pirates in the Red Sea," Thatcher offered with no introduction.

"Of course, gentlemen, we are seeking able-bodied seamen in our quest for England's most reviled pirates. And we are always looking for good men who can handle themselves in a conflict," Kidd replied.

"Well then, Captain, we'll be by your ship tomorrow to discuss the terms, as we understand you may be making modifications to your original agreement with your owners, making such a contract more to the liking of experienced seamen," Thatcher continued. Word had been circulating that Kidd, having had a difficult time mustering a crew to sail for such a small percentage of the take, was making a command decision to turn the bulk of their prizes over to the crew instead of the owners once they were at sea.

Kidd studied their faces and nodded. "Such rumors have the basis of truth, although I cannot officially confirm them."

"In that case, we take your meaning, our leave, and promise to see you tomorrow."

As they strode toward Wall Street, Caesar caved in to his curiosity. "So, what did you say to that poor man just before you murdered him, Thatcher?"

"I told him that a quick death is much better than a life of blindness and to simply accept his fate. I said that perhaps if he was right with God he would see Jesus soon. I understand that can be quite comforting to the dying."

"What about you, Thatcher? When it's your time to die, will the hope of seeing Jesus offer you comfort?"

"That's just it, Caesar. I don't plan on dying. I intend to cheat death, or at least take it on my terms."

Despite how things could have gone that evening, Thatcher and Caesar were wont neither for food, company nor shelter. With a mob following behind them and invitations yelled from every door, they encountered Darby, who had sworn he would be leaving on that morning's tide.

"When I heard that you two would be otherwise engaged tonight, I could not leave without makin' certain ye were safe. Am I to understand the party ye sought will not be arrivin'?" Darby asked.

"It appears our friends have opted for New Providence and so we, too, will be making leave of New York soon," Caesar replied.

"To New Providence, then?" Darby queried expectantly.

"No, my friend, to the Red Sea," Caesar replied.

Darby had hoped that, had his friends survived the night, they would go someplace other than New York or the Red Sea, for he felt a bit of responsibility for their decision. Reluctantly he resolved that he would put Carolina off for the foreseeable future. "Well then, my friends, it looks like it's going to be a threesome," Darby replied, as he declined their offer for a night of carousing and returned with a bottle to his dory to dream of pine trees.

The "help wanted" placards that had been posted throughout New York's tipling houses and the rumors of a new deal were much more effective than the Kidd's initial recruiting efforts. Thatcher and Caesar queued up with the long line of would-be crewmen. Rumors of the new pay structure had brought out not only professional sailors but also rough-edged rogues of the likes they would be hunting and New Yorkers seeking better pay than the meager wages paid by local merchants. Not knowing how things were progressing in Bristol, as no word had yet come from any ship sailing from that port of an ongoing manhunt for Caesar and Thatcher, it was decided that once again they would need to cover their tracks. So they determined that, should they encounter any merchant ship or man of war sailing out of their home port and casually reviewing the manifest, neither the name Drummond or DeBeers would appear to arouse suspicion. As they neared the gangplank, Thatcher and Caesar contemplated their new identities for the trip to come. Below them, they could hear the sound of splashing oars as Darby Mullins tied his dory to the dock, half drunk from a night of rum and Carolina contemplation and nearly slipping overboard, to the amusement of the men assembled. Caesar and Thatcher went to their friend to help him up the slippery and precarious footing of the slimy pilings that held the dock and dragged him in line with them.

"We thought you'd changed your mind," Caesar mentioned, as their sad friend joined them.

"Why not put an end to the sea and go home, Darby?" Thatcher asked.

Darby sighed and looked with resignation at his two shipmates. "Because as much as I would love to see the view from my trees, I more want to see Avery's face when ye introduce yerself to him."

The line traveled up the gangplank and across the broad deck of the *Adventure Galley*, down a long dark hallway that spilled into the sunlight-filled room of the Captain's quarters at the stern of the ship.

Sitting there at a table were Captain Kidd and his Quartermaster John Walker. The Captain surveyed the men who were signing aboard his crew and nodded with acknowledgement at the two pugilists who had honored their word and appeared to sign their names to his manifest. They stood in line behind a gentleman who gave his name as English Smith and cited his profession as former Sheriff. He made his mark and Darby advanced.

"Name," Quartermaster Walker asked without bothering to look up.

"Mullins. David Mullins."

"Profession?"

"Well, I've done many things, including woodcutter. But of late, able-bodied seaman," Darby responded.

"Make your mark here," Quartermaster Walker commanded as Darby made his mark.

Darby looked around the spacious cabin and back down the long dark hallway and then half-jokingly commented to the Captain and Quartermaster, "She's a mighty large ship, gentlemen. Think we might be able to find a bit of space for my little boat?"

Quartermaster Walker just stared at him, not amused. "Next."

Up stepped Caesar, whose *nom de guerre*, he explained to Thatcher, meant nothing. It just sounded Irish.

"Name."

"John Parcrick."

"Profession."

"Navigator's mate."

Captain Kidd and Mr. Walker studied the African making such a strange claim. Neither felt like challenging him at the moment. They would test his truth soon enough. "Make your mark."

Caesar took the quill and with an elaborate and flourishing hand signed the name John Parcrick as if he were born to it.

"Next."

"Peter Evans."

"Profession."

"Navigator's mate."

They looked at Thatcher Edwards – or Edward Drummond as they had remembered him the night before. Kidd nodded; Walker shrugged his shoulders and said, "Sign here."

And Peter Evans, a tip of the hat to his Uncle Peter, signed his name and disappeared from the official registry of Bristol citizens.

On September 6, 1696, the *Adventure Galley* set sail from New York Harbor with one hundred-fifty men aboard on the hunt for Red Sea pirates. As promised, four days later new contracts were drawn up and the men signed them, giving them the lion's share of any wealth to come. After an uneventful crossing and the propitious use of the sweeps through the doldrums, the *Adventure Galley* had the misfortune of encountering a flotilla of the Royal Navy. It was well known that life aboard a Royal Navy ship was the most brutal, de-humanizing process any man was likely to encounter, and thus the Navy was ever on the search for fresh able-bodied seamen to fill their sparse ranks. Either through depredation or scurvy or desertion, Royal Navy ships could seldom hold onto a company and looked for private vessels like the *Adventure Galley*, fat with sailors, for hands to press into service. Kidd performed his song and dance for the Commodore, making himself a good guest and skirting around the subject of the two or three dozen men the Commodore demanded he surrender. Kidd kept up his ruse and softened the Commodore by playing the happy drunken guest one evening, promising to deliver his crewmen in the morning. Perhaps Kidd was too convivial of a guest, or less a master masquerader and more an arrogant, sloppy drunk, for the officers of the fleet assembled at the Commodore's mess were left with an impression that perhaps Kidd was not the pirate hunter he claimed but merely a well-armed, well-manned pirate himself. And their suspicions were fortified when the *Adventure Galley* put to good use her secret weapon, and in the dark of night all the sweeps ran out and quietly rowed the hulking vessel as far and fast as they could before the stark revelation of day. The Navy ships gave chase, but the long night of furious rowing had given Kidd enough distance to avoid the pursuing fleet, and the Commodore continued south to the Cape of Good Hope to chase Kidd and to report their concerns to London.

Fearing the wrath of the Royal Navy, Kidd decided to bypass the Cape of Good Hope at the southern tip of the African continent, dipping farther south and forcing the ship to sail on an extra six weeks before sighting the coast of Madagascar and a chance to restock vital stores. The impressive ship had proven to be deficient in construction, as pumps had to be manned around the clock to keep the seawater from overwhelming the hold. Much of the crew was grumbling and many were sick by the time they reached St. Augustine's Bay on the massive island, a known haven for pirates and perhaps a chance to lift the spirits and prospects of Kidd's discontented crew.

For nearly a quarter century the western coast of Madagascar had been a veritable pirate haven when Captain James Misson and a rebel Dominican priest named Caraccioli led some 200 pirates in the founding and settling of Libertatia, an idealistic society of anarchists whose goal was to wage war against all states, liberate prisoners and slaves and royal prisoners pressed into naval service. Recent pirates such as Thomas Tew, John Ireland, Thomas Wake and William Mace were reputed to have fled the waters of the Atlantic to take up residence in the storied Libertatia and were specified in Kidd's commission obtained in Plymouth before he set sail in his custom made ship for New York. Hopes of capturing any of these legendary pirates fueled the imaginations and briefly lifted the spirits of the crew. But the bay was empty, offering no prizes for the tired and disgruntled sailors, and talk of mutiny began to grow.

Thatcher and Caesar, known to the captain and crew as Evans and Parcrick, had proven their navigational skills and in turn gained Kidd's trust. They were fortunate not to have contracted the bloody flux, a sort of violent dysentery that was waylaying so much of the crew, including Darby, and were charged with ferrying sick men to shore for recuperation and restocking the dwindling supplies of the *Adventure Galley* with fresh water and fruits and a peculiar type of local cow called zebu.

With the ship finally repaired, the crew refreshed and the sick either recuperated or dead, the *Adventure Galley* resumed its journey northward along the eastern coast of Madagascar to check every bay and waterway showing any sign of pirate life toward the Red Sea, where Kidd was anxious to find pirates awaiting the rich Moslem ships who plied those waters. His discontented crew was anxious to find any ship that would promise them treasure, and Thatcher's hope was renewed that they would capture Captain Avery, who had so successfully pirated these waters two years before. What he could not know was that Avery had deserted the Red Sea with his fat, rich catch and had made sail for New Providence where he applied for and received a Royal Pardon. In Boston he had found good markets for his ill-gotten gain, and with his Pardon still fresh in hand he retired to Ireland where he set up housekeeping under an assumed name, a free and filthy rich man.

Kidd was dismayed to discover that his bona fides were in question in this part of the world, so before long they abandoned the Red Sea for what they hoped would be riper pickings in the waters toward India. The noble notion of pirate hunting had ceased to be their motivating objective and, without exactly knowing how it happened, the crew of the *Adventure Galley* had seemingly evolved into the creatures they had originally set out to hunt. They did manage to capture two prizes, a French ship they renamed the *November* and the *Quedagh Merchant*, a beast of a ship sailing out of India and filled to the brim with treasures, but they also secured the wrath of the Portuguese merchant fleet in their questionable endeavors. So with a vengeful armada in pursuit, Kidd's small fleet split up with a promise to meet at St. Mary's Island off the coast of Madagascar. Captain Kidd took the fastest ship, the *Adventure Galley*, and carried the bulk of their catch to ensure the others show up.

Thatcher and Caesar had been appointed navigators aboard the *November*. This crew was made up primarily of malcontents, who immediately began to complain and accuse Kidd of saddling them with this unwieldy beast so he could make off with their cargo. As men stood in the tops watching the *Adventure Galley* disappear off their bow, they were convinced that rather than chase their Commodore, who had most likely abandoned and cheated them out of their rightful prize, the *November* should cut its losses, free itself from their priggish commander and go pirating on their own. Still well-gunned and with an experienced pirate crew, there were countless more vessels and European traders coursing these waters that would provide for an ample recompense for their lost prize. The most vocal in opposition to everyone's surprise, particularly Thatcher's, was Caesar himself. John Parcrick, the lone African to sign aboard the *Adventure Galley* in New York, had kept counsel with a small group of men, specifically this Evans and the Irish woodcutter Darby. Most had painted him as a loyalist to Kidd along with his friends and took his arguments to be nothing more than a foolish faith in a self-serving captain, and they made every effort to counter each argument that Caesar made. But the one thing that convinced them all of the reasoning of his logic was this:

"We've all suffered for the vanity of this Captain Kidd. And what do we have to show for it? This empty ship. I say we sail to St. Mary's and if we get there and there's no Captain Kidd, we buy or steal what we need to get us around the Cape and then we chase Kidd to hell. For if I am to be cheated by this rich Englishman, I will have, if nothing more, his head for a prize. Who wants his heart?"

These threats on Kidd were just the motivation the crew needed, and for weeks they pushed every foot of sheet they could in their driving quest, with Caesar as their inspirational leader. As weeks stretched into months, the only thing that seemed to keep the men motivated was the thought that Kidd had run off with their treasure and the very painful vengeance that would be brought on him and every ship that came between St. Mary's Island and New York Harbor. By the time they neared the Madagascar coast in May 1698, the *November* was practically falling apart. They limped into the harbor and, to their astonishment, there floated the *Adventure Galley*. A cheer went up from the crews of both ships as the *November* sailed through the channel. Anxious to get off this rotting tub and caring not what happened to the ship, they let her ram straight into the beach, not bothering to throw anchor lines, and went on the search for women and whiskey.

Thatcher and Caesar, with Darby in tow, made their first stop the *Adventure Galley*, where Kidd and his faithful were pondering the whereabouts of the *Quedagh Merchant*. The Captain congratulated them on their proven navigation skills. "We've been waiting for you for five weeks – and in the meanwhile waiting out the arrival of these rogues," indicating the other ship in the harbor. "She's the *Mocha*, and she's commanded by Captain Culliford, a pirate who's taken to the jungles to avoid facing his inevitable fate at my hands. But he's got to come back for her sometime. And when he does, he and that ship and whatever treasure he's hidden out here are coming with us. Now that you're all here, and with the *Quedagh Merchant* due any time, we've plenty of hands to face however many men he has hidden out there with him."

In truth, Culliford and his crew were not hiding at all, only taking in some rest and relaxation among the natives. Captain Culliford himself had taken his gold and marched four miles into the jungle to hole up at the reinforced and heavily armed settlement of an English trader reputed to have occupied one of the strongholds constructed by Misson and Caraccioli. He had nothing but time and expected many more of his Brethren of the Coast to come along any time and put this Kidd in his place.

And Caesar was quite content to wait himself. Long ago he had given up the dreams of returning to Madagascar to reconnect with the land of his father and mother, as now both pirates and Europeans overran it, tore it apart and greatly divided the many Malagasy tribes that peopled her. Still, his thoughts had been focused on this island for over a year, and now he was standing only days away from his ancestral home. The Madagascar of his youth was gone. But one thing remained, of this he was sure.

III

Through their alignment with Dutch and English slavers, the Betsimsakara people had grown powerful and dominant as they had maintained the advantage of musket and gunpowder. Back in Engand, while Caesar had let Yvgeny and Thatcher do most of the talking to the captains and merchantmen, he had made a particular point of staying abreast of the situation here in Madagascar, gleaning information from the crews of the slaving ships and those few slaves who had found domestic service in Bristol. While a diversity of Africa's people could be found in the kitchens, gardens and storerooms of the Bristol gentry, a steady stream of Malagasy people still accounted for quite a number of Africans pouring into London's slave pens en route to a life of back breaking toil in England's colonies. Of course the Royal Africa Company's most lucrative merchandise was a constant topic of the nightly patrons of Parker House, so many of them members of the Merchant Venturers Society who had been vocally protesting, plotting and scheming to break Royal Africa's monopoly of the slave trade. Edward Colston, the man who had conceded to Abigail Edwards' tear filled pleas to sell Nettie and Caesar to Yvgeny, had been leading the effort on behalf of the Merchant Venturers to make Bristol England's principle slave port, and his every machination on their behalf was discussed in the parlor of Parker House within earshot of Caesar. And from these people – Bristol merchants, crewmen who spoke English and Dutch and those Africans who spoke Malagasy – Caesar had been able to piece together a fairly continuous history of who held power in Madagascar. When he heard that Kidd's ship would be coming to St. Mary's, just a stone's throw away from the Madagascar mainland, the place where he, his mother and their village had been herded, the very beach where they had been nearly drowned as they were herded onto the slave ship, his purpose locked firmly in his mind. Now that they were here, nothing could stop him from accomplishing his solitary task. Right there, he could see that place, where the *Mocha* was tied, that was the place, and that was where his pilgrimage would begin.

Thatcher could tell that Caesar was definitely somewhere other than lost in gold fever and lust for Malagasy flesh. Since that moment on the deck of the *November*, when Caesar stopped being the strong, silent type, it was obvious that treasure and women were not his motivations for reaching St. Mary's. While Caesar wouldn't talk about it, it was obvious he was obsessed by something, but as of yet he hadn't uttered a word. Thatcher knew why this island was so significant to him, but he did not know that his friend had, for the last twenty odd years, carried a rage inside of him that defied description.

"So Caesar, we've time on our hands. Where shall we go now?" Thatcher asked his friend, joining him as he studied the nearby bank of the mainland of Madagascar.

"We, Thatcher?" Caesar questioned. "I don't think we are going anywhere. This isn't about us or Captain Kidd or white pirates. This is about me." In all his years, Caesar had always acted with others in mind, but this was a purely selfish desire that did not take anyone else into consideration – not entirely.

"You are my brother, Caesar. There is no you or I. There is always only we. So what are our plans?" Thatcher insisted.

A few strokes of an oar later, their mission began to unfold, as Caesar and Thatcher set foot on the mainland of Madagascar and began a long northwest march into what had once been Antankarana country. It was amazing to Caesar, having not trod this land since he was three years old, that he somehow knew exactly where he needed to go to find what he was looking for. For days, they walked until exhausted, then slept and walked some more. The coastal plains yielded to jungles and finally to those hardwood trees that told Caesar that he was getting close. Since he could walk, he had played around these trees, felt their distinctive rough bark, could hear the birds singing in their treetops, and he knew he was home.

His village was long gone. What hadn't been burned or pillaged by the Betsimsakara had since been reclaimed by the forces of nature. But Caesar didn't need objects to tell him where he was. These clearings and the waters that coursed around them, mostly mere streams, made it very easy for Caesar to orient and find the spot he sought. It was here, his mind told him, where he and the other children huddled in a circle, listening to and watching the death and agony around them. He sat down where he had sat as a child and stared at that spot just a few feet away where his father had been tortured and murdered. He didn't say a word, and Thatcher let him have his silence. Caesar let his mind wander back to that day, watching his father's agony and hearing his command that he would never be a slave, and through fate and his father's spiritual intercession, he was not. He took that moment to revere the spirit of his father and those dozens of men who had died here and thanked them for guiding him home. He then studied a tree just a few feet from where his father had died, a tree no doubt nourished by the blood of Najas and those Antankarana warriors. He stood and walked to that tree, cutting a single branch. He carved one end to a sharp point and then he began walking southeast.

Thatcher knew that this was Caesar's journey, and the greatest way he could respect his brother was to remain silent and let whatever was guiding Caesar speak. While good in navigation, Thatcher had been lost the moment they crossed that narrow channel and headed into Madagascar's interior, but he could tell they now seemed to be backtracking. Ever so subtly, Caesar altered his course, carrying them east, and north of the channel of St. Mary's Island. As they approached a particularly wide stream, Caesar stopped and listened, cupping his ear, drinking in the breezes. They began moving slowly south along that stream, and Thatcher did his best to mimic Caesar's steps. In the seventeen years he had known Caesar, he had grown proficient in mirroring him, and as they moved silently and stealthily into the growing tangle along the bank, Thatcher's nose at last picked up the distinctive scent of smoke. Shortly he heard the faint sound of voices. They were on their bellies now, creeping through the bristly undergrowth. At last Caesar stopped.

Across the stream they could see an encampment. At first, it appeared to be native, but as they looked closer they could see the telltale signs of the modern world. They observed shoes sitting outside a round hut, the flash of someone moving wearing a cotton shirt and breeches, a powder horn dangling from a branch. At last they saw guns propped up against a tree. While they had not come on this little journey completely unarmed, as Thatcher possessed his brace of three pistols and a knife he had bought from a trader back in India, they certainly weren't prepared to face a large body of men with muskets and ample powder, at least not directly.

The Betsimsakara slave hunters had become very accustomed to their tools of modern warfare. In fact, that was exactly what Caesar was counting on, as men with muskets eventually lost their ability to handle bow and spear. Likewise, they lost the one most important aspect of a Malagasy warrior – their stealth and suspicion. Being well armed with modern weapons tended to dull one's instincts and natural reading of the land, the wind and subtle changes in the forest around him. In their better days, the Betsimsakara would have sensed their coming hours ago, yet the casual appearance of the camp, the laughter, the tobacco as well as campfire smoke, showed an encampment of men who feared nothing nor possessed the good sense to fear what crept beyond their campsite. This was a small encampment, but what appeared to be a semi-permanent one as the structures had been in place for quite some time. The general trash strewn around betrayed men who had grown accustomed to European diets, perhaps periodically supplemented by a stray zebu or unfortunate lemur that happened to cross within musket range. But these men were hunters no less, only their quarry had changed from the animals of the forest and jungle to its people. Caesar knew he had to get closer, so he and Thatcher continued to wind their way through torturous bracken and down into the water, where they quietly slipped below the surface and dragged themselves along its shallow bottom. They proceeded a few yards south of the encampment and then onto the embankment, continuing their slow crawl to a point where they could observe their prey.

Now that they could see the entrances of the huts, they could sense more movement inside, and as they listened could hear the sounds of men taking great pleasure in taking women. Scanning the encampment, just at the edge of the huts they spied a small knot of children and young men with their arms tied behind their backs, sitting in a circle. It was easy to guess who the women inside the huts were. As they scanned the length of the camp, they confirmed that only three men seemed to be providing any form of security, and they were huddled around a fire where a very young and somewhat battered girl was serving them food from a pot. As their backs were to Thatcher and Caesar, this looked like the perfect opportunity to make a move against the three armed men, but something told Caesar to pause, and his caution was rewarded when a fourth man emerged from one of the huts. Caesar's eye focused on the man's face, studying it, remembering it. Those distinctive, albeit fading scars on his face and neck told him the voices had guided him correctly: Panjaka, the Betsimsakara chieftain who had betrayed his father. He studied that memorable man, his lumbering gait, as he strode to the fire laughing, and gesturing to one of the men to avail himself of the helpless girl he had just discarded. The fellow needed no convincing and disappeared into the hut. The chieftain was about to sit down next to the fire when a cool chill ran down his spine, and he turned to look exactly where Caesar and Thatcher lay staring at him. He paused for a moment, his eyes straining against the gathering darkness, eyes that in a different time would have picked up the obvious outline of two human forms waiting to spring. But his musket and the confidence that came from its mechanical power had dulled those senses to absolute blindness, and he turned his back and sat next to the fire.

Slowly Caesar stood, as tall and proud as he had ever been. Thatcher took his cue and did the same, retrieving one pistol for each hand from his brace, and the two began methodically striding toward the three by the fire. The walk became a jog and the jog a full run as Thatcher lifted his pistols fully outstretched. Caesar took his newly-fashioned spear, nourished by the blood of his father, reared back his arm and sent it flying straight and perfect into the back of the scarred man. Its impact forced him to let out a guttural groan, but not soon enough to give those men seated next to him time to react and raise their muskets before the tops of their heads were blown off by Thatcher's discharged pistol balls. Thatcher and Caesar reached the three men before their bodies had completely settled to the ground. Panjaka was injured but certainly not dead as Caesar put his foot against his back and removed the spear, looking down at the man, now paralyzed, blood bubbling from his mouth. Caesar's face announced to his victim that he was far from done with him and would no doubt return shortly. Perhaps the spirits of Panjaka's ancestors would be kind and allow him to die before the Antankarana returned.

Thatcher re-braced his pistols and shoved one of the Betsimsakara muskets between his chest and the holster. He grabbed the third musket and inspected it to make sure it was loaded and charged for the first hut, where he discharged it into the chest of the man who appeared at its entrance. He was able to grab the man's loaded musket from his dying hands and charge to the next hut as Caesar ran before him, tossing his spear into the face of a fellow who had raised his musket to fire. Thatcher leveled his newest musket at a target moving toward the river, blasting a hole in his lower spine and leaving him his third still-loaded pistol. He leveled it and pointed it at a shape that moved inside the third hut and had to check the squeeze of his finger to avoid sending a ball into the forehead of a teenaged girl. But the armed white man terrified her less than the black man inside the hut who was struggling to pull up his pants, and Thatcher sent that ball exploding into his crotch.

Caesar unsheathed his knife and dived headlong into the fourth hut, stabbing whatever object was attempting to move away from the entrance. His knife dove into the muscular shape repeatedly and severed the windpipe as he launched off the dying body and back out the entrance. While screams and voices could be heard still, they were more of a feminine and youthful quality, and Caesar turned in their direction, not seeing the encampment's one white member as he leveled a musket and fired it at him. He felt the hot blast against his back and a searing burn in his side, but his wrath and bloodlust were more powerful than any wound. He turned to face the white slaver, who was desperately trying to reload his musket. He had succeeded in pouring powder down the barrel and was fumbling with shot and wadding and his tamping rod, but in his desperate attempts to reload he knew he didn't have a chance when that large stalking African, knife in hand, reached him, grabbing a long lock of blond hair and shoving the point of the blade directly into his right eye socket.

Thatcher heard the shot and turned to see Caesar, who was framed in a billow of smoke, but as he was still standing and moving toward the shooter, Thatcher proceeded to the final hut. He strode confidently, the final musket crocked under his arm as one by one he reloaded his pistols, mechanically, with the amazing speed and precision of a practiced shootist. Standing at the entrance was a young woman, naked, shaking and soiled. Behind her was a very nervous Betsimsakara man, screaming in Malagasy a string of words too fast for Thatcher to comprehend. He was holding a knife to the girl's throat, his musket leaning against the outside of the hut. Thatcher proceeded with his march, his eyes locked on the young girl's, and said one word in Malagasy: "Bite." And without a thought, her mouth came open and clamped down on the wrist of the man who held the knife near her throat. The downward motion of her head was all that Thatcher needed as he sent a shot careening into the nose of the panicked young slaver. A second shot hit his elbow, forcing his arm in a reflex jerk away from the girl, and as he began his fall the third shot caught him in the chest. Though already dead, his assault was far from over as the young Malagasy girl grabbed the musket, pointed it at his flaccid penis and pulled the trigger.

Caesar retrieved his spear and walked back to where his first victim had fallen, crumpled by the fire. Panjaka's ancestors had been unkind, for while he lay dying his eyes had taken in the rapid and brutal destruction of his warriors and the Dutchman, who had been about to take custody of his property after one more round of usage. A generous hunk of flesh seemed to be missing from Caesar's side and blood streamed down his back, but his wound was certainly nothing close to fatal. That was the least of the Betsimsakara chieftain's concerns as Caesar came near him, leaning down to verify a semblance of life. Thatcher watched as Caesar studied the man and placed the tip of his spear inside that campfire. A few moments of turning within the hot coals heated that wood and charcoaled the end, now almost as hot as the flames in which it sat. Caesar rescued his spear, now smoking and slightly burning, as he hovered over the slaver's body. Panjaka tried to make recognition of the face that was about to send him to the realm of his ancestors, but he could not recall it from the thousands of his countrymen who no doubt wished such a fate on him. Caesar wouldn't let him go to seek out his ancestors without at least a little knowledge as he raised that smoking, burning spear to the face of the Betsimsakara warrior.

"We are Antankarana Malagasy, and we will never be slaves," Caesar demanded as he used every bit of strength in his body to send that spear through the mouth and deep into the brain of the Betsimsakara slaver.

It had been many years since the people of Madagascar had not feared they would find themselves loaded onto ships to suffer a life of slavery, but this group of children and women would have a chance to begin life again back in their forest. It was hard to blame them when they opted to dismember the bodies of the Betsimsakara captors and their young Dutch customer. Caesar made only one demand – that the chieftain remain exactly as he was, for out here in the wilds of Madagascar there were others who had been there that day when that small band of Antankarana witnessed the death of their chief. Caesar did all he could to wave off the attempts of binding his wound and the pleas of these women and children to stay and rebuild their tribe in his father's memory. It was a difficult refusal, as these were the children of other Antankarana tribes that had been running from the slavers for nearly thirty years, retreating into the caves where their dead had been buried in hopes that the ancestors would protect them. Those caves and endless wyvern of pathways leading deep into the rock were the last bastion of the Antankarana, and in time they would become a symbol of the destruction brought upon the people of Madagascar, delivered by ambitious, musket-toting countrymen in service to the imperial ambitions of Europe.

At last Caesar and Thatcher trekked back to the coast and to the channel that separated Madagascar from St. Mary's Island. They returned to a very different environment than that which they had departed. The *Quedagh Merchant* had finally arrived. The pirate Culliford had emerged from his stronghold, but rather than becoming Kidd's prisoner he had managed to convince the disenfranchised crew that he could provide a better life than this privateer from New York. After scuttling the *November* and commandeering most of the captured cargo, Culliford and his rogues sailed away on the *Mocha* with a volley of screams, laughs and taunts, leaving Kidd with fifteen men and two ships, neither of which were seaworthy enough to brave an Atlantic crossing.

IV

Every reason that Thatcher had chosen to leave New York for the wild waters of the Red Sea had sailed away, either with Culliford or a year before with the now-pardoned Captain Avery. He had left his home at the behest of his mother, who feared there was nothing she could do to protect her son from the full weight of the Bristol power structure coming down upon his head. But all his efforts - those months in New York with no word regarding his felonious flight; his unceremonious need to depart New York, wishing the destination was Bristol more than anything; and his current predicament, stranded halfway round the world with a broken ship and inadequate crew – would later prove to have been an exercise in futility.

In the pre-dawn light, the women of Parker House were plotting what to do with the stiffening Terrance Higgins. Abigail was for taking a forthright approach, marching down to the Sheriff's office and confessing to the murder of Terrance Higgins. She had the dress to prove an assault, but this idea was shot down as Nettie examined the crushed windpipe and asked exactly how Abigail's little hand could have done such lethal damage. There had been discussions of leaving him in an alley or on the docks to see if blame for his death could be passed on to some ruffian, but as the sun was already rising high in the sky, that plan became less plausible. Louise Ferrar had spent much of her vigil in tears, feeling responsible for the mess that had resulted from leaving Terrance to his own devices upstairs. She broke down some time in the dawning hours as she blurted "Oh, if only I had tossed him down the stairs." The words began to form an idea in Nettie's mind. The ladies carried Terrance Higgins to the edge of the stairs and unceremoniously dropped him. In a few moments, Nettie would "discover" the body and seek out Louise Ferrar to ask her what had happened to her beau. She would scream and both would flee to the Sheriff where Louise would concoct a story of Terrance's anger that she had taken so long in the study, how she had broken a house rule and let dear Terry stay the night so she might issue her apologies repeatedly. Louise was a very convincing young lady, and she was sure she could get the Sheriff on her side.

But how to explain the disappearance of Caesar and Thatcher? Would not even their best story point the finger back at them, abandoning the ladies of Parker House in the middle of the night under suspicious circumstances? Abigail marched down the stairs, stepping over the very dead Terrance, and made her way into the library to rifle through the copious notes kept by Thatcher of the comings and goings of ships. To her great delight, she found one that would serve her purpose. As Louise, Nettie and Abigail set off for the Sheriff's office, Siobhan O'Reilly, wearing something most plunging and using that amazing and memorable décolletage to be certain to make her presence well noted, hurried to the livery where she contracted a coach to London bearing an urgent note for Thatcher and Caesar. At the Sheriff's office, the contingent of Parker House ladies laid out their case to Sheriff Atherly. As what would be one of the worst of coincidences, just hours before, Caesar and Thatcher had received a note from the captain of the merchant ship *Gravesend* that bore news regarding their grandparents, prompting the boys to leave quite unexpectedly with the messenger returning to London. After the "incident," dear Siobhan had contracted livery to speed her to London to make Thatcher aware of the horrible situation regarding Terrance so he and Caesar could return and help these poor, defenseless women with this most horrible tragedy. Of course, Siobhan would be too late, as the *Gravesend* had set sail for America just hours before her arrival. She, of course, would bear a copy of the manifest showing that Thatcher and Caesar had indeed booked passage, something she could fairly well guarantee she would convince some bookish Dockmaster to manufacture for her. While this may not take the suspicion off Thatcher and Caesar, at least the authorities would start their search for them on the wrong ship.

Unbeknownst to the ladies, Terrance Higgins' absence had already been noted, as the young man from the Higgins' home who had been dispatched to seek out the whereabouts of his master had already stopped by the Sheriff's office. Sheriff Bertram Atherly damn well knew that Terrance had been at Parker House the night before and possessed a particular fondness for Louise. In light of recent events and the disappearance of Thatcher and Caesar, the ladies' story of their coincidental departure prior to Terrance's tumbling down the stairs seemed a bit hard to swallow. But Louise's ease of swallowing made the story somewhat more palatable. When reasonably satisfied with the ladies' stories and the firm conviction of Louise herself, Atherly accompanied the ladies back to Parker House to view the scene of the accident. Poor, dear Terrance lay very dead, with his head at a strange angle and a reasonable amount of blood at the foot of the stairs. What troubled him was the horrible discoloration at Terrance's neck, but one could reasonably assume that a fall could do such a thing. The unique location of Terrance's body was in itself a most delicate situation and one that needed to be handled with discretion. After leading all the ladies of Parker House into the parlor and accepting the wonderful cup of coffee offered by Nettie, he explained to the ladies that there was much to question here. As they were well accustomed to the needs of discretion, he needed them to likewise continue that Parker House tradition in this circumstance. Not knowing exactly what to do with Terrance at this moment, he accepted Abigail's offer of a fine Persian carpet in the basement with which to delicately wrap Terrance for proper temporary storage. Next he exited Parker House by the kitchen door, accepting Nettie's generous offer of a lovely warm bun enveloping a thick slice of ham, and took the route through the marketplace to the back door of the Higgins' home. The young servant boy, who had sought him out earlier and had just completed his rounds of Terrance's typical drunken haunts, led him to where Claudia Higgins sat in her parlor, a look of furious indignity on her face. The sight of the Sheriff only made her more so.

"Well, Sheriff Atherly, I'm sure you're here to tell me where that drunken sot of a husband of mine is sleeping off last night's tippling," she demanded.

"Good morning to you, Mrs. Higgins," the Sheriff began. "I have been searching for your husband, and indeed I have found him."

"Well, good. When he wakes up make certain to let him know that he can find someplace else to spend the evening, and perhaps this time he can try to do it sober," she snipped.

"Well, ma'am, that's the reason I'm here. It appears your husband met with a misfortune last night," he replied, holding his hat in his hand and looking at the floor.

"An accident? And where is he now, with the doctor?" she demanded.

"Well, no, madam, actually, Mr. Higgins has deceased."

A look of shock and horror crept across Mrs. Higgins' face as she contemplated that, despite her many wishes, dear Terrance had at last finally kicked the bucket. "Pray tell, what happened? Was he assaulted? Robbed? Was this some sort of act of maliciousness by brigands, ruffians, fellow merchants?" she queried.

Sheriff Atherly cleared his throat. "No, madam. It appears it was an accident. He fell down a flight of stairs and expired."

"Stairs? Which stairs did he fall down?" Claudia Higgins pressed further.

"Um ... the stairs at Parker House, madam," Sheriff Atherly confessed, feeling quite embarrassed and uncomfortable at revealing this very public secret.

"Parker House?" she fumed, standing up and crossing her arms, pacing back and forth as she repeated, "Parker House?"

"Yes, madam. He made the company of a young lady with whom he shared the evening. Apparently the house was dark, and he slipped on the top stair and met with his demise."

She ended her pacing and stepped into the face of the Sheriff. "And who knows this?" she whispered.

"Only the ladies at Parker House, and despite your misgivings with their particular trade, they are known for their discretion."

"And you're certain this was an accident and not perhaps something to do with that fellow who runs the place, that Thatcher Edwards?" she further probed.

"No, madam, I can assure you he was in London at the time, and a messenger has been dispatched to bring him back immediately."

"While this is horrible and a most inappropriate venue, I'm sure those people don't wish to have this made public any more than I do," she confessed.

"My thoughts exactly, madam. Perhaps, as we all see this was an accident, where the accident occurred is not as important as the sorrow we feel at his passing."

Of course, it was all quite terrible, this news of Terrance Higgins' sudden death. As the story goes, a carpet that Mrs. Higgins had ordered had arrived and was carried to the top of the stairs where it would stay until she decided where to place it. And dear Terrance, so distracted in his notes and papers that he was carrying at the time, exited the upstairs bedroom, not seeing that carpet lying at the top of the stairs, which he tripped over, tumbling to his most unfortunate end. All of Bristol's most luminary citizens and important men from throughout the region crammed into the narrow confines of Saint John's On The Wall Church to bid good-bye to poor Terrance as he was laid to rest in the family crypt in the vaulted confines below. And when lovely Siobhan returned from London, quite upset at having missed Masters Thatcher and Caesar by hours as they had sailed aboard the *Gravesend* for Boston, apparently having heard that there could be word regarding Yvgeny and Beatrice Thatcherev that required their immediate sailing, Sheriff Atherly was not the least bit pleased that he could not question these two men in conjunction with such a coincidental parting. But, as Mrs. Higgins and those who administered her family's estate wished to let the matter die, so to speak, he would make the point of interrogating the two the moment they returned from Boston, if only for his own curiosity.

These things Thatcher and Caesar could not know. Abigail Edwards had discreetly dispatched a letter to her son's attention in New York via Captain Steinbeck of the *Golden Cup* sailing from Bristol, informing them that they could return at any time as the matter had been very conveniently settled. But that letter would never reach them. As far as anyone in New York knew, Thatcher and Caesar Edwards had never set foot on their shores. And that letter sat unclaimed and unopened, first at the custom-house which in 1686 took responsibility for the collection of ship-letters, then forwarded to the post-office which opened a few years after the letter arrived to molder for a few decades until finally making its way to to the new post office opened in

1732 at Broadway and Beaver Street, where the envelope and the delicate wisp of a woman's pen faded almost to illegibility until 1753 when it was forwarded to the Postmaster of the Bristol Post office at 48 Corn Street by Benjamin Franklin, Postmaster of New York who, among the many tasks he undertook to stream line and make the post more profitable, was establishing a system of dealing with dead letters.

Something else that Thatcher could not know was that, as he sailed in search of his grandparents' killer, another flotilla was departing Novgorod and Pskov across the great Russian frontier for Livonia. On March 20, 1697, Peter the Great began his first great embassy to visit the most important capitals of Eastern Europe and then to make his way to England and Holland. Peter led a massive assemblage, posing as a mere ambassador in an effort to travel throughout the continent incognito. While diplomacy was his motivation for visiting the region's great capitals, his reason for traveling to Holland and England was to master for himself the advanced shipbuilding technologies of these two great sea powers. But there was another agenda for wanting to go to England, and that was to see for himself how his nephew was faring.

Before departing Russia, Thatcher and Peter had made an agreement that his illegitimate kinsman would never again cross Russian soil. But that deal wasn't made the other way around, for Peter had greatly enjoyed the company of the bright and very Romanov Thatcher Edwards. Upon reaching London, Peter wished to maintain his poor charade of secrecy and took up residence in a small house at 21 Norfolk Street. There, as he and his retinue waited for the Thames to thaw, the Russians entertained themselves in typical fashion – drunken revelry. After making an impromptu visit to the incognito Tsar and being shocked and appalled by the cramped and dank environment, King William insisted they relocate to a large, elegant home in Deptford. While owner John Evelyn was pleased to fulfill this royal favor, it certainly was not received well by Admiral John Benbow, the current resident who was forced to vacate the premises. It was during this relocation that Peter dispatched a messenger with a note for his nephew in Bristol.

Life at Parker House had taken on a very different atmosphere with the loss of Thatcher and Caesar. After Beatrice and Yvgeny had gone, Parker House shed some of its staidness and conventionality, primarily because of the energetic spirit of its enterprising young masters. But now, as Abigail had to rely upon contracted security, Parker House felt less like a home and more like a business, and every day she missed her son even more. Bristol had settled in for its annual winter nap as the harbour grew thick with ice and commerce moved at a slower pace. The regulars could always be depended upon to frequent their favorite haunt, regardless of the weather, but as fewer ships were anchoring at the Bristol quays that quality of newness was absent.

Thomas Snelling, who had taken over the responsibilities of answering the door, came to the library to inform Abigail that a messenger had arrived from London. Her heart leapt with hope that word from Thatcher was finally arriving, and she ran to intercept the message. She was surprised that the bearer looked not like the typical London coachman or post-rider. Rather, this messenger was dressed in heavy furs and a sable hat, a style of dress she knew well.

"Good morning. I have been dispatched from London with a personal message for a Yvgeny Thatcherev Edwards with instructions to hand deliver it," the heavily accented Russian stated.

"Good morning as well to you, but I'm afraid Yvgeny Thatcherev Edwards is not here," she replied.

The Russian removed his hat and coat, handing them to Abigail as he planted himself on a seat in the entryway. "I will wait," he demanded.

Abigail smiled, familiar with the forwardness of Russians, a quality rude to many but endearing to her. "I'm afraid, my dear," she replied in her faultless Russian, "that you will be waiting a very long time, as Mr. Edwards is not in the country."

The Russian looked up at the petite, pretty woman, who slightly strained under the weight of the heavy coat and hat, and smiled at her. He stood, taking the cumbersome, damp outer garments from her. His face took on that easy, jovial nature so unique to these rough hewn Russians.

"You are her," he stated, half accusing and half in awe. "You are Abigail Edwards."

She studied the Russian for a second, trying to read his expression. "Yes, I am. I am she."

The big Russian looked as if he had just met someone he believed never existed, and his gruff exterior melted away as he took in the sight of the face that had swooned a Tsar. "My apologies for my rudeness, to treat you as some housekeeper. I did not expect to meet you. But

I'm very sad to hear Yvgeny Thatcherev Edwards is not here to receive my message."

"As am I. But perhaps you can give the message to me, and if I hear from him I will certainly pass it along."

The Russian pondered his predicament, remembering the very strict orders he was given to hand deliver this message to Yvgeny Thatcherev Edwards. When the Tsar gave an order, one did not question it or consider alternatives. Yet, this was she. This was Abigail Edwards. He thought for a moment more, then removed the parchment from his pocket, bearing the seal of Peter the Great, embossed with the message, in Russian, "I am a student, and I am here to learn." He handed it to Abigail, bowed and headed to the door, taking one last look behind to see the woman that could have made all the difference in the future of Russia – and a woman who could make great trouble for him.

Abigail held the letter in her hand. She did not quite know what to do with it, as it was not addressed to her but to her son. She had always respected his privacy, but staring at that royal seal was daunting. She walked to the kitchen where Nettie was busy preparing a stack of her meats between slices of bread and showed her the letter.

"And do ye think it might actually be from him?" Nettie probed.

"It's his seal. What shall I do?" Abigail asked.

Nettie answered her by taking the letter from her hand, breaking the seal with a knife and then handing it back to Abigail. "There, now it's just a letter."

Abigail slowly opened it and began reading. It had been quite some time since she'd seen that distinctive style of sweeping Cyrillic letters. Its contents were simple. It was an invitation for Thatcher to join his Uncle Peter in Deptford. She closed the letter, then opened it and read it again.

"Well?" Nettie questioned.

"Peter's in England. London, actually. And he's asking Thatcher to visit."

"So what are you goin' to do?"

"Think on it."

Abigail returned to the library and re-read the letter again. Apparently Thatcher must have made some sort of an impression, though he had never talked about any kind of intimate association with the Tsar of Russia, his father's brother. She pondered that for a moment, wondering what else Thatcher didn't say to her – what Yvgeny didn't say to her, and why they didn't tell her. She rolled these thoughts around in her mind for some time when her thoughts were interrupted by Nettie's appearance at the door, Abigail's coat and hat in hand. Abigail looked a bit confused. Nettie stood her up to put on the coat and hat and began scooting her toward the door, where she could now see Thomas carrying a large trunk down the stairs.

"Nettie?"

"Your carriage is waitin' and the driver's cold," Nettie replied matter-of-factly.

"Carriage?"

"What are ye goin' to do? Walk to London?"

Boris Schlenkov was quite confused and quite concerned. He had stood outside of Parker House, debating whether or not he should return and ask for the letter back. He had not been thinking quite logically when he handed a letter, specifically addressed to Yvgeny Thatcherev Edwards, to his mother instead. This was not going to please Peter. In fact, it was probably going to make Peter angry. So he paced for quite some time, trying to decide what he should do, when he saw a small African woman leave the house and walk toward the snow-covered center of town. He continued to debate with himself what he should do when, a short while later, a carriage arrived, parked in front of Parker House and the African women got out and returned to the home. He studied that for a moment, thinking that perhaps now he should go to the door and ask for the letter, but then a very large gentleman brought out a very large trunk and handed it up to the driver. Boris was a smart man, and he knew that someone was going somewhere. But as he thought about who that could be, he saw the small black woman escort the enchanting Abigail Edwards out the door by the arm and load her in the carriage. As it passed him, heading through town and onto the London Road, Boris Schlenkov realized that he may have to really do something about getting that letter ... and soon.

Boris Schlenkov was a cavalryman. As a member of Peter's Preobrazhensky Regiment, there were few things that Boris enjoyed more than a fast ride through fresh snow. And it took him absolutely no time whatsoever to catch up with the carriage bearing Abigail Edwards to London. The driver, on the other hand, knew winter was prime time for enterprising highwaymen, and the sight of a fast approaching rider coming to his rear forced him to put those carriage ponies into a very quick gallop. So down the London road they ran. Surprised to feel their sudden increase in speed, Abigail craned her neck out the window to see what was making the liveryman hurry. The unmistakable sight of that large Russian in his fur coat and sable hat giving chase prompted her to tell the driver to stop. Despite his protestations of highwaymen and land brigands and loud claims that he was not taking responsibility for anything that happened should she be raped or molested when he could perfectly well gallop his way to London, he brought the horses to a stop. Boris Schlenkov reached them in seconds and respectfully dismounted so as not to look down at the enchanting Abigail Edwards.

"Hello, Mistress Edwards. I'm sorry to chase you and give your driver a scare. But I think I must ask you to give me that letter back."

Abigail looked at him and smiled. Reaching into her bag, she retrieved the letter and handed it to Boris. He examined it, noting that the seal was broken, and began to look very worried. "I don't think I was supposed to let you read that," he replied, somewhat concerned.

"Alas, I have, but if you need it back, there it is," she replied cavalierly, amused at the concerned expression of the big Russian cavalryman.

"So you go to your son now, to give him the message?" Boris queried hopefully.

"No, my dear friend. I wish I could, but I don't know where he is. You see, he sailed for America a while back. So I thought I would deliver my apologies and regrets to Tsar Peter in person."

Boris began to look very nervous now. He looked at her, smiled and looked at the ground. He looked at the letter with the broken seal, then looked at her again. "No one is supposed to know Peter is in Russia. I don't think he wanted you to know he is in Russia. You're going to see Peter now?"

"Well, just as soon as we get this carriage back on the road to London, yes, that's the intention."

Boris looked at the letter and gave it back to Abigail. The damage was done, and he had some explaining to do. But first, he had to formally make the acquaintance of this famous and fabulous lady. There had been much talk on long, lonely nights about her, and as far as he knew he was the first outside of the Royal family who had actually met her. He took off his big heavy glove and his sable hat and extended his hand. "I am Boris Schlenkov, friend and loyal guardian to Tsar Peter of Russia, and it is my absolute pleasure to know you," he said, taking her hand and kissing it as the snow fell on his balding head there at the side of the London road.

"Boris Schlenkov, it is truly a pleasure to know you, and I'm sorry if I got you in trouble, for you seem like such a kind man. I would hate to think there would be any difficulty as a result of our having met."

He released her hand, replaced his glove and put back on his hat. He then mounted his horse. "It is a trouble worth having," he replied as he whipped the horse and sped down the London Road at breakneck speed, wondering how he was going to break this to Peter.

Life at Deptford was fashioned in Peter's likeness. Appointed in one-of-a-kind works of art and tapestries collected over a lifetime by its owner, Peter was astonished at how drafty this house was. These English and their love for windows – they may be fine in springtime but were simply impractical in the dead of winter. Their stock of firewood was exhausted in days, as the hearths were kept full and raging around the clock to accompany their endless partying. These English had gone to great lengths to clear the majority of their stands of trees, and Peter had dispatched his men with saws and axes to knock down the nearest ones they could find to restock the firewood. He began to look around the house for things that would serve in a pinch, should circumstances require.

He was in the midst of entertaining a few hundred of his newest friends, and, as had been the case for days, an odd assortment of high-born nobility and lowly dockworkers had coursed through this opulent mansion with spirits and food in hand, letting themselves and their victuals fall where they may. This owner apparently liked dogs, and Peter decided to put them to work, letting them into the house to feast on whatever they could find strewn about the floors. He was entertaining himself with a particularly high-strung hound when Boris Schlenkov located him at the far end of this rambling home.

"Ah! Boris, my friend. I hope you had a good trip to Bristol. Did you bring our guest as I was hoping?" Peter asked, throwing a rather large mutton leg as far as he could to see how quickly the dog could retrieve it.

"Well, um ... no, Tsar Peter, I did not bring him. He was not at home."

"Well, why didn't you go find him and bring him here?"

"He went to America. I did not know where to look."

Peter's face bore a look of great disappointment. "America? It seems everyone is going to America these days. Perhaps one day I'll go to America. I hear they make great ships. Well, that is a shame. Where's my letter?"

Boris looked at the ground and then he looked at his Tsar. Then he took his hat off his head. "I don't have it."

"You don't have it? What do you mean you don't have it?"

"I ... gave it to his mother," Boris answered, expecting the full wrath of Peter to be taken out on his balding head, perhaps with a leg of mutton.

"You gave it to his mother." Peter repeated as he took a bite of the mutton leg wrestled out of the drooling mouth of the bouncing dog. Peter's eyes began to widen, and Boris wondered if indeed his skull was about to be rapped with the greasy, spittle-soaked weapon in his Tsar's hand. "You gave it to his mother?" Peter began shouting. "What on earth possessed you to give it to his mother?"

"I don't know. She said she would take it, and at the moment that sounded fine."

"It sounded fine? Did it ever dawn on you that if I had wanted her to have the letter I would have addressed it to her?"

"It did. Later. When I stopped her on the London Road, I thought I should take it from her then. But she had already opened it, and I figured she should go ahead and keep it."

"On the London Road. You stopped her on the London Road? So she's on her way to London? Did she say why?"

"She said she wanted to deliver her regrets to you personally."

"So she's on the way here. Well. This is unexpected. And I really should teach you a lesson for not following orders," Peter stated a bit harshly, but then turned back to ask the million ruble question. "How did she look?"

Boris looked up, a little sheepish, a little ashamed for letting down his Tsar, but also smiling. "Like an English angel."

"You Russians do have a way with words, don't you?" Abigail Edwards stated from the doorway of the quite disheveled English manor.

Peter peered around Boris to see who was talking and his first thought was, *yes ... yes, she's an angel.*

"Tsar Peter Ivanovich of Russia. My, but you've grown into a handsome boy," Abigail Edwards stated proudly in Russian.

Peter leaned into Boris and very menacingly whispered to him, "You will pay for this ... mark my words! Get out!"

Boris bowed his head and turned around, passing Abigail and smiling. He whispered as he passed, "Your coachman made very good time."

"Good to see you, Boris," Abigail replied, patting his arm as he passed.

Peter stood there looking at Abigail and immediately flashed back to when he was eight and she was sixteen and how jealous he was of Fedor that he saw her first. While almost seventeen years had come and gone, she was still as beautiful ... no, more beautiful than she had been when he first saw her. He remembered how she used to talk to him, not as a child, not as a future Tsar, but as a young man with hopes and dreams. And he blushed.

Abigail closed the distance between them and put out her hand in greeting. "It's been a number of years, Tsar Peter, but allow me to introduce myself. I'm Abigail Edwards, and apparently you know my son. Would you like to explain that to me ... Uncle Peter?"

And so in the months to come, Abigail would learn more about the time spent by Yvgeny and her son in Russia. Peter told her about the genuine affection he felt for the teenaged boy, about how Romanov young Yvgeny Thatcherev Edwards really was. And perhaps most comforting, she finally heard his personal account of Fedor's short life after her departure and before his premature death. She was genuinely pleased to hear that Fedor had fallen in love and married some two years after she had been sent home, giving him a few short months of happiness until his illness finally took him.

Abigail had fully intended that when she reached London she would seek lodging with Sheila Brothers, one of the former ladies of Parker House who had married her way away from the brothel and into legitimate society. But as she spent those hours talking with Peter and catching up on the last seventeen years of Russia and the Romanovs and, in many ways, her own son's life, she never noticed when Peter signaled to Boris to remove her trunk, pay the coachman and carry her belongings upstairs. Somehow, amid all the cacophony and activity of Sayes Court, this rambling and once pristine estate, Peter and Abigail were able to find a quiet place to enjoy dinner and talk long into the night. She was having such a wonderful time, and Peter was truly enchanted, when she suddenly remembered the coachman and her belongings sitting out in the snow. She was about to rise when Peter placed his hand gently on her arm and said that all had been taken care of and that by now the driver was no doubt well sodden and warming his bones with a public house toddy. She at first insisted that of course she had no intention of imposing and that she had accommodations waiting, but Peter was more than willing to dispatch a rider with her regrets. She let the subject drop, at least for now. It was obvious to her that Peter and his company were used to a much more expressive form of conviviality. One by one his comrades would seek him out with a drink or a toast or some story he just absolutely had to share, but Peter would merely raise his hand to his friend and whisk him away with the tips of his fingers. While the party raged on late into the night at the other end of the house, Peter and Abigail sat by a massive roaring fire and talked about Russia and England and their mutual futures together, and in some ways perhaps England and Russia were being unofficially represented by the two people sitting in this much-too-drafty home before a much-too-big fire talking about things hoped for but not likely to be realized. She had not meant to dominate his evening, and, after her long chilly trip from Bristol, at her accustomed two a.m. she began to feel the exhaustion and the wine creep over her as she made her excuses for bed. Peter hunted down Boris to guide them to her room in this rambling estate, which he had yet to fully explore, and he was quite pleased with Boris' selection of the room adjacent to his. Of course, that meant evicting five of his closest associates, but most likely they would find quarters suitable under some table. He bid her good night and expressed his desire to continue their conversation further as she headed off to bed. Peter looked at Boris, half chiding for having put him in such circumstances, and then placed his big hands on the Russian's shoulders and kissed him on each cheek.

"You stay here and don't move unless someone is making too much noise, in which case you beat them into unconsciousness. Is this order clear?" Peter asked, slightly grimacing but very pleased with Boris.

"With my very life, Tsar Peter. With my very life."

Peter absolutely had to go downstairs and at least make an appearance before his guests. Boris, on the other hand, commandeered a comfortable British chair, its back to Abigail's door, with a firm commitment that his message would be correctly delivered.

And except for those occasions when privacy overstepped the need for security, whither Abigail went, so went Boris, a responsibility he was quite happy to shoulder. When she awoke that next morning with the light of day streaming through her window, she slowly crept to the door, opening it every so slightly, to see Boris' back. The sound of the latch aroused him from his sentinel – or snoring – as he was immediately to his feet to be at her beck and call.

"Good morning, Abigail Edwards." Boris smiled a big, broad smile.

"And good morning to you, Boris. Are you here to keep me locked in this room?" she questioned with a gentle smirk on her face and a twinkle in her eye.

"Of course not! Peter gave me strict instructions to make sure no one disturbed you, and I was not about to disobey him twice. I am certain you are famished. Do you wish food to be brought to you, or may I escort you to the dining room?" She gave a quick look to her nightgown, just a hint of which could be seen through the crack of the door. Boris noticed the peek of bedclothes and quickly corrected himself. "Of course, whenever it's best for you," Boris continued.

"And where is Tsar Peter?" she inquired.

"Out the door with the sun. He wants to see if there is any activity at the shipyard. He does not like the fact that the English let snow and ice keep them from building."

She looked out the window and could see a heavy snow falling, the type of weather in which no one should be out unless they must be.

These Russians and their love for snow, she thought, remembering how Yvgeny refused to stay in the house when near blizzard conditions would sock in all of Bristol. "Give me a few moments, Boris, and I would be happy for you to accompany me to breakfast."

She closed the door with a smile and could hear Boris' heavy footsteps running down the hall and the stairs. He was in full stride to the dining room to begin moving the bodies of the sodden and the soiled and attempting to find where the household staff was hiding so they could begin making the room suitable for human habitation. He was taking the less compliant, one in each hand, and moving them off to side rooms and stacking them, some side-by-side, some like cordwood. One particular couple less inclined to yield to his appeals for disengagement found themselves being carried under his arm like disobedient children and thrown on top of a pile of bodies. The household staff, who had been spending as much time as possible trying to avoid these barbarian Russians, began to put the dining room into order as Boris struggled to find the English words to describe his desire that English-type food be made.

"Food for English lady. Need now. You fix, make house ... room English." When it appeared that his command was being met, he ran back up the stairs to await Abigail Edwards. His face was still a little flush and his brow a bit wet with perspiration when Abigail made her appearance at the door. She placed her tiny arm in the crook of his massive one as he gently led her down the hall into the dining room.

"I hope you didn't have to go to any trouble for me," she whispered.

"For you, nothing is ever a trouble, Abigail Edwards," Boris replied, patting her tiny hand with his big paw.

Peter wanted to cave into his instincts to make this home more like a place that Abigail Edwards would find comfortable, but it was obvious to her that Peter lived a life more jovial and outlandish than Parker House. She made it clear to Peter that she was a guest at his pleasure and wished to see this aspect of him that had so obviously intrigued her son and Yvgeny Thatcherev. And while in London, she did take the time to show him some of those qualities of English culture that were so famous and heralded throughout Europe. She discovered that Peter had never before seen a play performed and, after much chiding, convinced him at least to attend one performance. She discovered that Peter in public was very different from Peter in private, as a shyness and nervousness struck him to an almost paralyzing level. And in a certain sense she could see why, for throughout the entire performance, the crowd's eyes were not on the stage and the performers but on Peter himself, and it was in this quality that she saw not the Romanov Ivan the Terrible but her own sweet Fedor.

The cast of the play was adamant to meet Peter the Incognito, and despite his protests to the contrary, he and Abigail made an appearance at the nearby hall for a reception. Abigail was quick to surmise that the beautiful leading lady Laetitia Cross was utterly fascinated with the young Tsar. As a woman who had made her living assuring her male guests were introduced and charmed by ladies of a functional form, Abigail found herself feeling something she wasn't quite familiar with, and as Miss Cross was introduced she made the point of moving forward from the background and possessively claiming Peter's arm. The young actress took in the beautiful but certainly, in her view, older woman staking her territory. She smiled, and Abigail replied in kind, holding her outstretched hand a little longer and firmer than perhaps Miss Cross had expected.

"Miss Cross, let me tell you how amazing your performance was. I should let you know, my son is a bit of a thespian himself, and I'm certain he would have been pleased with your acting, though he is a bit more critical than I and could offer suggestions to make you more prominent on stage," Abigail offered sweetly.

"Well, madam, I'm certain that you've seen quite a few excellent performances in your time as well," Laetitia responded, making a slight allusion to the age difference. "You say your son is a thespian. Would there be anything I've seen him in?"

"He has done limited engagements in Bristol and – correct me if I'm wrong, Peter – you've seen his performances in Moscow as well?" Abigail asked.

As mentioned earlier, Peter was always nervous in company, and this interesting exchange between these two English women was both fascinating and frightening to him. He hesitated for a moment, not knowing what to say, and then thought of that first night in Preobrazhenskoe when he had to pull Thatcher off his drum and two young women off him.

"I have only seen demonstrations of his musical talent, and I must say they were quite vigorous," he offered.

"Yes, he was a child prodigy of multiple talents. It's such a shame that he's not here as he's ventured off to America. But Peter and I would certainly love to have you for dinner, Miss Cross, and look forward to a visit from you soon," Abigail purred.

On the carriage ride home, Peter thought about the exchange and Abigail's somewhat possessive claim on his time. Never one for the demands so often set by women, one aspect that kept him far away from the Tsarina, he was surprised to find this behavior from Abigail to be most enchanting. She had held onto his arm all throughout the performance and the introductions, and now still, here was her arm in his. He tried to examine her face in his peripheral vision to gauge her expression. When this proved to be futile, he resumed his commanding air as Tsar and actually turned to look into her face, and she was smiling with great satisfaction. It was a smile that told him what was required of him at this very moment – he kissed her.

The winter snows fell on the long trip to Sayes Court. Ice crystals formed upon the glass of the opulent, unmarked carriage containing the Russian Tsar and the Bristol Madame. And while casual observers knew this to be the carriage of the Russian premier on his great embassy and they strained their necks to catch a view of the passing monarch through the window, they were disappointed that all they could see was fog. Boris Streshnev sat atop the carriage next to the driver, resplendent in his furs and invigorated by the fresh falling snow. He was pleased that his monarch was happy and, at the arrival at Sayes Court, most pleased that he was dismissed for the evening. He moved his chair to the foot of the stairs, his massive bulk an unmistakable barricade to anyone who may have a thought of venturing up to any of those rooms, for he was not there to insist upon silence. He was there to insist upon privacy.

Throughout February and into the spring, they settled into a lovely routine, as Peter would quietly rise just before dawn, putting on not the raiment of the Tsar of Russia but the simple clothes of an English workman. As dawn was beginning to lighten the London skyline, the Tsar of all Russia would be busy with saw or adz or standing high and precariously upon a scaffold with hammer and nail or a bucket of resin, taking pleasure in the construction of this yacht, a gift of King William. It might have seemed strange to some that a monarch would wish to take part in the building of a present for himself, but to Peter nothing gave him greater joy as he toiled away throughout the day, fascinated by the engineering of this most modern of English ships, built and designed specifically for his needs. While he toiled away in the shipyards at Wapping, Abigail would take the day to visit the many lovely sights of London, including calling upon old friends, acquaintances and clients of Parker House and availing herself of the finest shops in the city. And frequently she would receive dispatches sent from Bristol by Nettie, keeping her apprised of the business of Parker House. At night the house would erupt into a cacophony of merry making, though what once had been all night affairs grew shorter and shorter and more frequently absent the chief celebrant Peter, who would excuse himself the moment Abigail's expression revealed her desire to abandon the company of many for the attentions of one.

Peter was surprised one day on an early return from the shipyards to see Abigail at a large table, a variety of papers and ledgers spread before her as she perused them meticulously, so intently that she did not hear him enter. He stood for a moment looking over her shoulder, watching as she methodically worked the various columns like some scholarly translator of an ancient text..

"This looks very complicated," Peter mused earnestly. As one who had never taken his administrative roles in Russia seriously, he had never had to comprehend the unique form of mathematics involved in accounting and was quite surprised to see that Abigail, or any other woman for that matter, would have a mastery of this strange form of witchery.

She was somewhat startled when she heard Peter behind her, not expecting him for hours and thus feeling she could take some time to attend to the responsibilities of her estate. "Peter! Yes, I've been away from Bristol quite long. Nettie has done her level best to keep up with the accounts but, alas, she has a house to run as well, so she was kind enough to send me this so I may make heads of tails before I return to Bristol."

"But you are not considering going soon, are you?" Peter queried.

Abigail knew that eventually this conversation was going to have to occur. Both she and Peter were aware that soon he would be leaving London, and as much as she enjoyed being with him, the ice-free Thames and his urgency to take in so much more of England before his departure was a perfect excuse for her to resume the life she knew awaited her. "Peter, as much as I would love to spend an eternity with you, I have responsibilities, made more so by Thatcher's absence.

Nettie is now charged with the duties of four people, and it's time I return."

Peter was certain he could command her to stay, because after all he was the Tsar of Russia. But he knew she was right, and the longer she stayed the harder it would be for both of them to part until at last he may do something so foolish as to insist she return with him to Moscow. It was a thought he had entertained many times, as had she. But the same complications that existed in the times of Fedor were as present today. He lifted the beautiful Abigail Edwards to him, her tiny frame held lovingly in his arms, her beautiful face hovering a foot below his. This thought of her leaving was making the leader of the Jolly Company quite sad, and so, while the party raged below, he spent the evening making long, luxurious love to the woman who should rule Russia, for she had certainly ruled the hearts of two of its Tsars.

It was hard to tell who was saddest at the parting: Peter, Abigail ... or Boris. He had prided himself as chief among the revelers in the Jolly Company, yet, without a second thought, he had abandoned the tradition of endless debauchery to assume his loving service to their guest. When told of her departure, he accepted the sympathies of his brethren and the endless supply of wanton attendants for having to return to their brutal bosom. Being Russian, he had no difficulty in allowing his emotions to leak out, and as no one dared ascend those stairs when either Boris or his symbolic chair guarded entry, he spent that last night quite drunk, quite sad and plotting somehow to convince her to stay. But his most devious of plans were for naught, for in the morning he had to wipe away his steady stream of tears and accept the sympathetic embraces of the lovely Abigail Edwards, who told him he would always have a great and loyal friend awaiting him in Bristol, along with many young ladies for him to meet. He loaded the great chest on the awaiting carriage and stifled a whimper as he watched Abigail and Peter say good-bye.

"Should time allow me, my sweet Abigail, I will visit you in Bristol before I leave this country. I will sail my lovely new yacht into your harbour, and my Jolly Company will introduce your lovely ladies to Russian passion."

"They are already quite aware of the passion of Russian men, for they have grown up with two of them – the one who protected me all those years, and the one whom they protected. But, Peter Ivanovitch Romanov, as much as I would love to dream that your magnificent yacht will sail into Bristol Harbour, you will forgive me if I do not hold my breath."

"Long ago I said good-bye to your son, and told him that I would regret his never returning. But even though I now extend an invitation to you to come to Moscow, I know you'll never take it up, will you?" Peter asked.

She reached up to pull his chin down to hers and kissed him softly. Once again, she was abandoning a great love and a life of happiness, but at least this time she was given a chance to say good-bye, and she knew that this kiss was as much for Fedor as it was for Peter. She patted him on the arm and said, "Good-bye, Russia." And she walked with her confident air and magnificence to the carriage, planting a gentle kiss on Boris' cheek as he lifted her into it.

In her heart, she was saying good-bye to Russia, but in her womb she once again was taking it with her.

V

Half a world away, Thatcher Edwards was making a liar out of his mother. While she believed he and Caesar were at this moment most likely gallivanting around the wild New World of the American colonies, instead they were toiling away in the wilds of Madagascar trying to find a way home. These last few months on St. Mary's had been tense, but interestingly enough Thatcher had uncovered the potential for a great opportunity.

Captain Kidd and the last few men who had remained loyal to him had been abandoned by the mutiny of nearly their entire crew. Their prize ship, the *November*, lay sunk to her gunwales in the channel, and Captain Kidd had two leaky ships that could never make the journey back to America. But not all their crew had departed merely to go on the account with Culliford. Some, like their dear friend Darby, were so sick and tired from the deprivations of the sea that they were in desperate need of finding a way home.

Captain Shelley sailed out of New York aboard the *Nassau*, providing a unique and vital service to men who made their living on the account. His clientele was very select in that he served primarily pirates, and he had departed the New World loaded with merchandise of particular interest to this select breed of customer. In his hold he carried silver plated muskets, pistols, knives, gunpowder, plus an assortment of those simple things that a pirate could not easily find nor may rarely need, like soap. He also carried some items that every pirate lived for: rum and flouncy hats. Pirates possessed a unique skill beyond their bloodthirsty desire for other people's property, and that was their amazing ability at tailoring. Life aboard every sailing ship required endless hours of sewing, repairing the sheets and fashioning raw bolts of canvas into new sails. So much of what they tended to secure when taking the contents from a merchanter was endless yards of colorful fabric, and as pirates tended to be low-born men, civilized culture dictated the limitations to their dress so as to distinguish the common man from the gentry. Here in these waters of libertine freedom and self-expression, a man with a needle and several bolts of brilliant silk could make himself the lord and master of his rum-soaked dreams. These were the things that Captain Shelley and his financial backers understood, and with several casks of rum and a cardful of needles, he could send a pirate to fashionista heaven.

As the standoff between Culliford and Kidd was raging, Captain Shelley had made his way into St. Mary's harbor to discover a divided and contentious lot of men. He was impressed to see a small band of loyalists defending the beleaguered Kidd and less surprised to find that most of his crewmen had given in to their base instincts and were ready to go a-pirating. Then there was a small contingent who wanted nothing of this battle and just wanted to go home. Shelley was able to offer those homesick lads a way off the island ... for a price. Darby Mullins had laid low as Thatcher and Caesar ventured off onto the mainland. They had slipped away with nary a word, and Darby, still sick and worn down from the bloody flux, felt his spirits diminish as he feared he'd never see his friends again. But that morning when they waded across the channel, he felt a renewed sense of vigor. Still, his comrades worried how Darby had withered to a mere husk of a man, and when Captain Shelley offered passage home, Caesar and Thatcher began a long and convoluted argument with Darby to take this opportunity. They had discovered that there was more than his brothers and sisters and parents and trees waiting for him in Carolina. Only after their relationship had been sealed did Darby tell them of the wife and child he'd abandoned because of his craving for the sea. He knew it was time to go home, but with his health he wasn't sure he would make it. So at their insistence, he accepted berthing aboard the *Nassau*, paying a small portion of his take of silks and muslins as passage. Too weak to do more than lie in the shade, he was almost overcome when, as a parting gift, Thatcher and Caesar arrived with a cask of freshly killed, smoked and salted zebu to help keep him nourished, rather than pay the brigand's fee for food from Captain Shelley. He asked Caesar and Thatcher to do him one last favor, and that was to take what was left of his haul – those two large bundles of fabric and his small cache of silver – and bring it with them when they came to New York. Perhaps they could liquidate his stake, then find him amongst his trees in Carolina and provide him more money than he or his family would ever need.

So as Darby sailed away, Thatcher and Caesar and the few men remaining turned to the insurmountable task of making the *Adventure Galley* and *Quedagh Merchant* seaworthy so they could sail for home. Those months spent with Peter on Lake Pleschev had taught Thatcher a thing or two about shipwrighting, and as the carpenter and his mates had sailed off on the *Mocha*, Thatcher saw an opportunity to put his talents to good use. But he was shocked when Kidd announced to those assembled that, rather than trying to prepare the *Adventure Galley* for a return to New York, he was opting to strip her of parts, scuttle her and sail the *Quedagh Merchant* back to America. Thatcher was going to protest this scheme, convinced that with time he could make both ships seaworthy, but then he struck upon an idea.

The small crew began to offload everything they could from the *Adventure Galley* and moved her to a corner of the channel, preparing to put the match to her. Before doing so, they stripped off every bracket, corner brace and hinge to use in the repairs of the *Quedagh Merchant*. The most valuable commodity on that ship was her metal components, and every single one of them would be needed to make the *Quedagh* seaworthy. Thatcher took a position below the water line, ordered to hack away at her hull to begin the process of sinking her, but rather than take an ax to her ribs, he struck a few carefully placed blows that merely tore the planks from her seams, allowing the water to fill her hull but not to destroy its integrity.

As this process was going on, the crewmen were somewhat rattled by an ever-growing presence of Malagasy gathering on the mainland shore of Madagascar. They came first as groups of women and children who seemed never to take their eyes off Caesar. These few became many more, as bands of men and families took up a vigil along a sandy beach that had served as a launching point for tens of thousands of future slaves. Caesar tried to ignore them at first, but after the backbreaking labor of repairing the ship, they would come to him at night, wading across the channel, and speak to him in their ancient tongue to find out who he was and why he had returned to them. Stories of what he and Thatcher had done at that encampment of Betsimsakara slavers had spread throughout the forests and jungles of Madagascar, and his words to their leader had been in the distinctive dialect of the Antankarana. No man who had left these shores, to their knowledge, had ever returned. So who was he, and why was he here? Caesar had done what he had come to do and did not wish to make any more of it, but Thatcher saw another opportunity. As they were going nowhere anyway, why not see if these Malagasy would help them accomplish their mission?

The next morning, Kidd was surprised to see not only the dozen or so men who had stayed with him busy at work but also dozens of natives assisting in the task. He thought to organize his men to press these locals into work but was astonished to see that his sole African crewman, this Mr. Parcrick, was able to speak with these primitives and accomplish the goal without violent coercion. Mr. Evans, his capable Navigator's mate and apparently a gifted carpenter as well, seemed to take great pleasure in putting the *Quedagh* into service, and in just a few months the newly commissioned *Adventure Prize*, formerly the *Quedagh Merchant*, was ready to sail. As the cargo and supplies began to be loaded aboard, Kidd noticed that Parcrick and Evans had separated their take from the rest of the cargo, and he approached them to inquire.

"Captain Kidd, your *Adventure Prize* is ready to sail, but alas we are not going with you," Thatcher replied casually, as he and Caesar toted their two hundred pound loads farther up the beach.

"I don't understand, Mr. Evans. There's no reason to stay here, and there's no telling when another ship could arrive. Why would you want to stay on St. Mary's?" Kidd inquired.

"Well, as you can see, Mr. Parcrick has bonded with the locals, and we've decided to stay among them for a while to see what opportunities present themselves. These natives, they're so trusting. Perhaps there might be opportunities for slaving once we fully gain their confidence."

Kidd arched his brow. "I did not take you for a slaver, Mr. Evans. You always struck me as more of a free spirit."

"Thank you, Captain. I am a man of enterprise. And I see a great opportunity here at St. Mary's. So I bid you and your *Adventure Prize* well. And perhaps we'll see you again one day on the high seas."

Kidd was sorry to leave behind his two promising young navigators for this final leg, but he bid them good-bye and toasted them good health as he and his crew, with a few more recruits from St. Mary's, began their journey back to New York. No sooner had Kidd's sails disappeared from sight than the real work began. Caesar's Malagasy loyalists, now referring to him lovingly as Chasaa, began to appear from the woods bearing long stands of mast, recently stripped from the defunct *Adventure Galley*. Thatcher's meticulously conceived and carefully concealed plan was under way. While he'd spent his days toiling in the hot African sun, he had spent his nights trekking the four miles along the trail to the hilltop citadel of the English trader, Edward Welch, whose spies kept him abreast of the activities in the bay below. Like Shelley, Welch had crafted a unique form of enterprise, specifically catering to the pirates that called St. Mary's a refuge. He had come to St. Mary's many years before as one of the Brotherhood. But the ample food, generous women and uneducated pirates provided for a man of his intelligence and business acumen an unbelievable opportunity to profit from the risk taking of others. Pirates at sea lived only for one thing: to secure enough profit to blow every dime on rum and women. And Edward Welch was happy to provide plenty of both. He had nearly an exclusive lock on his enterprise for years, until the merchants of New York and London got wind of his unique weigh station off the African coast, giving rise to men like Captain Shelley. Welch's concept was simple: provide ready gold and silver for pirates anxious to unload their merchandise for pennies on the dollar, await legitimate merchants passing St. Mary's seeking good prices on quality wares, which he would sell for a profit or trade for pirate essentials, and then turn each of these into ample stocks of gold. He had taken the small structure built years earlier but long neglected and slowly being reclaimed by the jungle from which it emerged. But its unequalled vista of the waters below was incentive enough to begin the process of reconstructing and reinforcing the structure into the massive hilltop fortress, manned with cannon and well-paid English and native loyalists to protect him. And for a price he would even loan out his men for armed confrontation. Thatcher admired Welch's business moxie, but as a true man of commerce, he saw an opportunity for both Welch and himself to make a much higher return on their investment by cutting out the middle man. And when he approached

Welch about his plan, it was just too good an opportunity to turn down. He was especially enthusiastic when he saw the sway Caesar held over the native people.

The Malagasy who made their living from the bounty of the sea were easy recruits for the first part of Thatcher's scheme, and that was to re-attach those planks he had dislodged from the ribs of the *Adventure Galley*. Their capabilities to stay under water and hammer the planks back in place proved quick and expedient. Thatcher had fashioned pumps from pieces in Welch's stockpile and began a round-the-clock task of refloating the *Adventure Galley*. They used the waterlogged hull of the *November* as a platform to begin the task of careening and resealing the *Adventure Galley*, and it was with this close-up look at the hull that Thatcher could see why she was so leaky. In their rush to complete her, the workmen had not bothered to seal the inside of her planks. The sea worms had done a great amount of damage, and the sheet of glass that helped slow down the worms' progress was poorly made and lacked integrity. Thatcher solved this problem by commissioning the hundreds of willing Malagasy to begin cutting him new plank, which he laid as a double hull inside the ship. He covered those seams with another solid plank and caulked with the prolific tree gum that the Malagasy patiently tapped and boiled by the gallon. In no time, the *Adventure Galley* was ready to sail again, and Edward Welch opened up his fortress to have the hundreds of fabric bales, copper, silver, pewter, gold and china he had stockpiled over the years begin their four-mile journey down to the waiting ship.

The plan that Thatcher had come up with blended the piratical with mercantile aspects of the nautical trade that made his mission somewhat legitimate while letting others take the risk in the venture. Thatcher would immediately sail for Charles Towne, the growing seaport on the Carolina coast, where he would offload the merchandise at a reasonable price, but certainly not the low-end value typically received by the common pirate. If goods still remained, they would proceed up the coast until their merchandise was exhausted. As most men of the trade well knew who Edward Welch was, Thatcher devised a concept whereby Welch commissioned himself as the Governor of St. Mary's Island, citing this ship as the first of his fleet. While it may not hold up in court, it could provide him some measure of cover should he encounter their Brethren on the high seas. But whether or not the Royal Navy or the warships of Europe would acknowledge his sovereign claim was the reason he loaded aboard every cannon that Welch could part with. Unlike most merchant ships, who fled at the sight of an oncoming pirate, Thatcher instead would hail and welcome them, carrying those supplies so beloved by their Brethren of the Coast, to do a bit of mid-ocean trading and to query them for any products or merchandise they might be carrying in exchange for hard currency, at a reasonable discount of course. Among his array of odds and ends and supplies, Welch maintained a stock of most of the flags of Europe, a necessary precaution in their sailing of open waters. But there was one flag he was sorely lacking, and to this purpose Thatcher perused the odds and end of fabric and spent his time by firelight with his newly developed skill of needle and thread, and with it he fashioned the Royal Crest of Russia.

The final task before setting sail was arriving at a name for the flagship of St. Mary's Island. Caesar and Thatcher spent quite a bit of time looking at their lovely new ship and all her various qualities and began the debate.

"She is quite a thing of beauty, Caesar. Notice her elegance, the fine lines. Her uniqueness. The way she stands so proud in the water. When I see her I immediately think of one person – Abigail Edwards," Thatcher reasoned.

Caesar thought for a moment, studying her. "When I see her, I see a survivor. She was given up for lost, and yet here she is: strong, defiant, fearless, ready to take on any challenge. To me, she looks as if she would be the Nettie Edwards. Oh ... and my mother can kick your mother's arse."

Thatcher thought about Caesar's logic. Yes, he could see both qualities, and yes it was true that, while Nettie was a puny thing, she was feisty, and she could indeed kick Abigail's arse and ask for change. So, the mothers were out. Now they still needed a fitting name that bespoke of its very nature.

"You know, Thatcher, she was written off as dead. And yet, here she is, back to life. Does that not remind you of a story?" Caesar pondered.

Thatcher's face lit up as he caught the reference and her name became obvious: the *Phoenix*.

The two Englishmen and their company of Malagasy sailors set sail from St. Mary's Harbor in the full rich glory of a Southern Hemisphere autumn. At her helm, the captain and first mate of the *Phoenix* plotted their course south from St. Mary's, loaded with enough victuals and supplies to avoid having to make landfall at the Cape of Good Hope. The captain peered through his spyglass for any sight of sail and was pleased to see an empty, vast ocean before them. He studied his sheets and barked out a command to the crew to trim the topgallants and the spritsail and to bring the rudder three points to larboard. The loyal crew, though raw and new to the sea, took to their tasks with joy to hear these strange words transliterated into Malagasy. The Captain looked to his First Mate and Co-Navigator as they ran out the log to check the knots and smiled at how beautifully she sailed.

"She is a fine ship, Mr. Edwards," Caesar bellowed to his First Mate.

"A fine ship indeed, Captain Edwards," Thatcher replied as they took in the sinking sun to their west.

Chapter 5
Crests and Troughs
March 1699 – December 1701

I

It was not uncommon for ships of every nature, be they merchant, navy or pirate, to possess a broad contingent of landsmen. However, to have a crew's compliment made up of men whose only experience at sea was in dugout canoes without the complexities of sails and rigging would be to many a disaster waiting to happen. Thatcher and Caesar had to teach basic sailing to this crew, but unlike as was common with press gangs these new sailors were enthusiastic. To them they represented a proud, new legacy for the Malagasy people, sailing under a Malagasy captain. As word of the re-birth of this vessel began to reach the interior of Madagascar, men came in droves to see for themselves this man of whom a legend had quickly been born. On their heels came women and children to witness this chieftain who had been hauled away in chains but returned a free man. Many passed that encampment where the slavers had been slaughtered, and all beheld the sight of Panjaka, the spear that had entered his mouth and passed through his skull still holding his rotting body to the ground. It reminded the elders of a similar occurrence so many years ago when a young Antankarana warrior had suffered a similar fate. There had been stories of that warrior Najas, who counseled the old men of the tribes not to fall prey to the temptations of these Europeans, and he had paid for his resistance with his life. There had been tales that he had a son and wife, led off by the Betsimsakara slavers. Could this be the son returning to avenge his father and all those Malagasy who had suffered a similar fate?

Their curiosity drew them to that haven of Europeans, and there he was, just as the women and children had described him, his big, powerful body freshly scarred from a wound to his side. Such a man, they believed, must possess magic that made it impossible for these European bullets to kill him. They watched as he struggled with the European men to make a ship worthy of the sea, and when he and his white companion came to them to ask for help to rid them of these white devils, they were happy to comply. For months they toiled to bring timber and vine to be woven into rope and to provide whatever service they could to make this ship go away. As the repairs progressed, this Chasaa told them of another plan they had that would put them on an equal footing with these Europeans who had long profited from their misery. To a man they all said yes to his request to join him in travel across the broad water. Once the Europeans sailed away, the men raised the sunken ship and brought new wood to replace the burnt upon this mighty vessel, as they fashioned items of wood to replace those made of metal that had been stripped to repair the other ship. The women and boys fanned out throughout the forest to find meats and fruits to feed this hungry contingent of workers. They smoked dozens of zebu, hundreds of lemurs and thousands of fish to carry with them on their journey. And in those last days, as the ship was preparing to sail, for miles every piece of fruit that was approaching ripening was picked and loaded aboard in baskets and barrels. Likewise, hundreds of casks were made to be filled with water and placed in the hold, for this Chasaa and his friend T'atcha were going to sail long and far to avoid the Europeans where they perched at the point of the two broad waters.

Those first few days at sea were rough on all of the Malagasy, having never ventured beyond a few miles from shore in their small canoes. They had known these waters were wide, but they had never seen or imagined such vastness, where no land could be seen at all. And the waves, so big and endless, grew more ferocious as they sailed farther south to where the two oceans met. Caesar and Thatcher spent nearly all their time at the bow, calculating their speed and direction and constantly referring to the maps as they made every attempt to avoid contact with land or ship. To do this meant sailing a much more southerly course than was typical and making their westerly run much later and at a lower latitude than most seafarers would dare. But, even this far out at sea, there was no mistaking when they had reached that point where the Atlantic met the Indian. The waves grew more ferocious, the winds accelerated as the two great bodies and the skies around them clashed for dominance. Nature's battle took very little regard for what fell in between it, and at that moment, far from land, the *Phoenix* took a battering. The continuous presence of rain and fog made navigation at times nearly impossible. They could only trust their speed and the firm conviction of a southerly keel to hope that they had long passed the Cape as they made their western swing. This subtle shift in direction nearly tore the new masts and sails to shreds as the seas, their thirty foot swells washing constantly over the deck of the ship, threatened to send her to the bottom, forcing the sick Malagasy to constantly man the pumps to keep the ship afloat. For nearly a week, they fought against the battling winds on a course nature did not deem ships to travel. At long last, Caesar called for the command to swing north, and almost immediately the seas and winds acknowledged their inability to destroy this insignificant ship and gave up their siege. Miraculously, the seas reduced their height, the winds their chaos and the *Phoenix* once again emerged from certain death. While the crew continued pumping the thousands of gallons of seawater that had accumulated in the bottom of the ship, Thatcher could at last make his way to the nether of the holds to examine the damage done to her structure. To his pleasure, he noted that the only water that had entered the ship had come from the top, not the bottom. His double hull had accomplished its task, its integrity maintained, and unless they encountered something more ferocious than water and sky, the *Phoenix* was no worse for wear.

They had traveled nearly forty-five hundred miles over these long months to escape the oversight of any nation's fleet hugging the coast of Africa, and now they began their northerly run of nearly two thousand more miles to the Portuguese outpost of São Tomé. Their ample supply of meat, fruits and fresh water had served them well for most of the long journey. But as they began to approach the doldrums, where Kidd's innovation would be put to good use, these men began to feel the ravages of the dwindling food and water supply as they used all their energy on the sweeps. Since the barrels had begun to run low, the men would run out the spare lengths of sail during every rain that came their way, creating channels of fresh water to fill the empty containers while likewise providing a modicum of shade on deck from the unrelenting sun. As these men were seasoned hunters and fishermen, every moment of the day lines were cast over the sides and stern to attempt to hook a passing fish. The archers would take the guts and offal of their catches, placing them strategically on the tops and high points of the ship as offerings to passing seabirds, and any that ventured close enough to those tasty morsels of fish entrails would be quickly felled by these expert marksmen. The natural curative powers of citrus fruits were well known to the natives, though not yet fully understood by Europeans, and as well as the ample supply of fresh fruits the women had spent days pressing ripened pineapples, mangoes and limes to render their juice and pulp. These were placed in wooden casks and earthen pots, tucked away at the farthest reaches of the hold and sealed against the potential ravages of seawater to be uncapped when the fresh fruit ran out. And like the smoked meats, they carried a supply of dried fruits that would sustain them long after the fresh supplies were gone. And so with the wisdom of these ancient people and the skills of their captain and first mate, they survived these long months at sea. Now one more great effort was required to help them reach the virtual center of the earth, that point where zero latitude meets zero longitude, on a plantation island called São Tome.

This Portuguese stronghold off the western coast of Africa had not been a friendly trading ground for the English, but the Dutch had developed a good relationship with the planters who dominated this island by keeping them well-stocked in slaves from the mainland. This brief window of peace between Portugal and Holland's allies, Spain and England, had made doing business much easier, as in years past both Holland and Portugal were at war with each other via their proxy alliances. But both the Portuguese and the Dutch were much more pragmatic than their more strident allies, and business was business. As the *Phoenix* made its way toward the Port of São Tome, the Dutch flag flew prominently from her mainmast. Its nineteen-year-old first mate, now assuming the name DeBeers, was conversant enough in Dutch at least to make conversation with the Portuguese Master of the Port. Long before the *Phoenix* had crested the port's horizon, Caesar had sent out a few of his best rowers in one of their fast outriggers to survey the harbor for any sign of Dutch ships. They had decided that if any man-of-war were to be found in the port the Dutch flag would not be flying from their mast, but to their good fortune only two Portuguese merchant ships were spotted in the harbor, and thus the Dutch *Phoenix* made her way to port. There was the fear that some Dutchman would be serving in an official capacity there in the harbor, in which case Thatcher had his story prepared of being raised by his trader Uncle Johann in Bristol, thus accounting for his merely conversational command of the language. But to his good fortune, only Portuguese were to be seen. Thatcher climbed aboard the longboat with Caesar and a small band of Malagasy to make his introductions to the Harbormaster of São Tome. Joachim Portmão was an affable man of middle age who, as Thatcher had guessed, spoke barely passable Dutch himself.

"Mr. Portmão, my captain sends his humble greetings and his regrets that he cannot make this visit personally, but our ship's doctor has him confined to quarters with some form of tropical contagion," Thatcher offered as he presented a note from "Captain Van Reuten." The note stated simply that they were on a trading mission requesting to resupply their water, food and wood as they prepared for the return to Amsterdam.

Mr. Portmão appraised the young first mate and his African contingent, surprised to see so few Dutchmen making this call. "You have a very large African crew, it seems," Mr. Portmão commented.

"Well, actually, like the captain, most of the men are indisposed with the same tropical malady. I was fortunate because I was the officer of the watch the night they all went into town and apparently contracted the same disease."

Mr. Portmão studied the young man, and then it finally dawned on him what the young Mr. DeBeers was suggesting. "And you will, of course, assure those men stay aboard and not bring that disease to our small island, will you?"

"Of course, Mr. Portmão. We Dutch respect the health concerns of your beautiful island, and you can rest assured mine will be the only white face you see emerging from that ship."

And for the next week, an endless stream of Africans, led by Caesar, plied from the docks of São Tome to the *Phoenix*, standing a thousand yards off shore, to resupply much needed stores of food, water and wood. Thatcher was fortunate to find a few spare masts and stretches of canvas to make up for the tattered disrepair of his own complement. While in port, Thatcher maintained a convivial relationship with Mr. Portmão who shared a passion for coffee, which happened to grow quite amply on São Tome. Thatcher took a tour of a nearby plantation, where he learned the finer points of the cultivation of this magnificent and intoxicating bean. He was amazed to discover that it took a full ten years for one coffee tree to reach maturity and that it yielded but a pound of coffee per harvest for all that love and patience. He was so impressed with the operation and the fine product it yielded that he made a point to have a few dozen sacks loaded aboard the *Phoenix*. Likewise he had a chance to strike up conversations with the local merchants of this Portuguese outpost. He discovered that there indeed was some need for certain quantities of copper goods, and while he insisted that his masters were desperate for them in Amsterdam, having consulted with his captain he was able to part with a few dozen boxes at a much better price than he had expected. With a small chest of Portuguese gold and a final toast with Mr. Portmão, he once again offered his captain's most sincere apologies that he had been unable to convince the doctor to let him present personal thanks for the hospitality. Then he rowed back out to his ship just as the anchor chains were being hauled aboard, and the *Phoenix* made a course for the western tip of Africa.

Their timing could not have been more fortuitous, for as the *Phoenix* began to fix sheets for their northwest heading, one of the Malagasy screamed from the tops, "Sail!" pointing off to the port bow. The two Mr. Edwards grabbed their glasses to get a better fix on the approaching ship whose course was set to intercept theirs. They could make out the unmistakable standard of the Dutch, and as the ship grew closer they could see that behind her were at least three more sets of mast. Thatcher knew that his previous ruse would be a little harder to pull off, and another Dutch standard not reducing sail for a rendezvous with countrymen would be suspicious indeed, so he knew it was time to haul up another flag. But which one?

Captain Haupt of the *Rotterdam* turned his glass to the ship departing São Tome as soon as his watchman alerted him. His glass did not reach the ship fast enough to see which flag had just come down from the tops, but he could have sworn it was Dutch. Now, an interesting flag was being raised. It looked very similar to his own country's standard, but with its three colors slightly altered. The Netherlands standard ran from top to bottom red, white and blue, but the order on this flag was white, blue and red. Captain Haupt thought this to be quite curious, and he signaled his fleet of his desire to investigate.

As the Dutch fleet closed in, Captain Haupt gave a closer examination of this strange ship, its bizarre lower ports and that curious flag. Most importantly, he observed that this crew was virtually all African, except for the one fellow at the helm with the black hair and olive skin. Haupt took up his speaking trumpet and hallooed the ship. The fellow on the other deck answered back in what sounded German, and Haupt communicated as best he could to lower his sails and prepare to be boarded. Thatcher did as he was requested, and in a few moments Captain Haupt made his way across on his longboat. A small contingent of armed men accompanied the captain, who was led to the quarterdeck to meet what appeared to be a very youthful master.

"I am Captain Haupt of the Royal Dutch Navy. And who, sir, might you be?" Haupt asked in Dutch.

Thatcher listened for a moment as if trying to translate what the captain was saying. Then he smiled. "Captain Haupt. I am Captain

Thatcherev of the Russian Royal Navy, and it is a pleasure to meet an ally," Thatcher replied in a broken Dutch as he wrapped his arms in a massive embrace around the very stiff Dutch naval officer.

Haupt was quite aware that the Dutch had been working to help the Russians in building some semblance of a naval fleet. Their young Tsar Peter had developed quite the fascination for their ships. But this was certainly not a Dutch design. And as far as he knew, the only ships the Russians had were tiny boats and barges plying up and down their interior rivers. Such a ship as this seemed out of the realm of reality, but the young captain seemed quite enthused to see him as he was escorted down to the Captain's Quarters with the very large African man in tow. Thatcher cursed himself for not having secured a crate of Yvgeny's finest bread wine when he left Bristol, but as they had left with nothing more than the clothes on their backs, it was only one of many things he had to do without. He showed Captain Haupt the chair and took a place behind the opulent desk that Kidd had built for this ship. Kidd had so desperately wanted to take it and load it aboard the *Quedagh Merchant*, but, unlike desks of his past which rolled around and moved in high seas, this one had been built into the frame of the ship itself, and what an arrogant desk it was, with cup and plate indentations carved into the surface. Thatcher did the best he could to make his guest comfortable, offering him a glass of Madeira wine, which they were carrying for sale on behalf of Edward Welch. He ordered up a goat to be slaughtered, just purchased in São Tome, and invited his guest to dinner, but Captain Haupt was a man with little time and much suspicion. He would surmise quickly whether to wish this Russian a safe travel or to clap him and his crew in irons for transport back to Amsterdam.

"So, Captain Thatcherev it is, you say? I am certainly surprised to hear that Russia has sent out ships for commerce and exploration. I say this as I know of a number of captains who are contracted to carry goods to and from Russia through your port in ... oh, where is that?"

"Arkhangel'sk. Yes, our Tsar has so often thrilled to watch your ships come into port, and it was that inspiring view that motivated him to send me and a few others out on his first endeavors. Your fleet also sails into Kiev in the Ukraine, from which they transported me to Walvis Bay to pick up this beautiful craft, built to Tsar Peter's specifications."

Captain Haupt wrinkled his brow at the mention of the Dutch possession along the southwest coast of Africa. While he knew that ship repair was available there, this revelation of shipbuilding was news to him.

"And, Captain, why would your Tsar have a ship built in one our farthest outposts in Africa, when I'm sure there are many capable builders in Amsterdam or Rotterdam that could have done this more effectively?" Captain Haupt asked incredulously.

Thatcher smiled and beckoned for the Captain to follow him. They descended into the deepest bowels of the ship, a lantern in Thatcher's hand, until they reached the lowest point on the ship. Thatcher gestured. "Double hulls. Genus *Diospyros Celenica*. Ebony, a kind which, as I'm certain you know, is only available from your colony of Celebes. This ship does not leak, is resistant to cannon balls and your Dutch shipbuilders at Walvis Bay created it for our Tsar!"

The captain examined this bizarre feature on an equally bizarre ship. It was true that a double hull of this black hard wood was ingenious and something most likely to be created from the brilliant minds of Dutch shipbuilders. It gave him ideas of modifications he would like for his own ship at the next dry dock, but he still had a few questions that needed to be answered. "You, of course, have papers attesting to this fact, don't you, Captain Thatcherev?"

Once again, Thatcher smiled, leading the Captain back to the well-appointed cabin. Thatcher sat down at his desk, opening his drawers and rustling through papers, a look of confusion on his face as he could not seem to find the document the captain was requesting. This obviously disturbed Captain Haupt and began to confirm his suspicions, until Thatcher got a look on his face and walked over to the bookcase where, sticking out amongst the tomes was a folded document. He brought it to the Captain, those strange Cyrillic letters etched into that broken seal, and inside some very official proclamation signed at the bottom by Tsar Peter Ivanovich of Russia. The captain looked a bit perplexed.

"Unfortunately, Captain Thatcherev, I do not read Russian. But this is signed by your Tsar?"

"Yes, let me find the passage ... yes, here. 'Please extend all courtesies to our royal envoy, Captain Yvgeny Thatcherev, and please extend safe passage as he brings this ship of superior Dutch craftsmanship back to mother Russia.'" Thatcher read, showing precisely where the passage was that he was reading. Of course, the unique symbology of Cyrillic calligraphy was all Greek to Haupt.

All of this was highly unusual. But from what he had heard of this young Tsar, unusual was the order of the day. This captain could not be more than twenty or so, and yet would that be so strange for a twenty-seven year old Tsar? There was a light knock on the door, and Thatcher bid enter. Caesar offered his apologies for the intrusion and then began a short conversation with Thatcher in Russian, conveying a sense of seriousness, but just asking if they should really kill a goat. Thatcher gave the emphatic "Da!" and stressed that coffee likewise should be included, whether their guest stayed or not. Caesar once again begged his apologies and departed, which led to Captain Haupt's next concern.

"I'm curious as to why the Tsar did not equip you with some of our own sailors, or perhaps some of your own countrymen," Captain Haupt pressed.

Thatcher looked very seriously at him. "Have you visited our country, captain?"

"No, captain, I've never been to Russia. I've not yet had the pleasure."

"Well, then, you are not familiar with our Black Russians," Thatcher stated as seriously as he could. "Abyssians. Good sailors and great servants much treasured by the Tsar."

Captain Haupt had heard the term before but had not supposed that it actually referred to African looking gentlemen. Obviously, there must indeed be Black Russians. And he did not know how to inquire any further without possibly offending the Tsar of Russia.

Thatcher brightened, turning jovial. "Captain, I am certainly looking forward to discussing the sea with you and your own adventures here in Africa. Please promise you will stay to share my *zharenyi kozii* with me, a true delicacy for my country. We have only in the last few years mastered the art of domestication with them, and we believe that we have bred the gaminess out of the meat. I, being a young man, have only eaten the domesticated version, but the old men tell me that when it is wild, it is a taste not to be described."

Captain Haupt contemplated what strange manner of beast he was referring to and felt an odd quivering in his stomach. "Captain Thatcherev, I deeply appreciate the invitation, but alas I must make São Tomé before dark, so perhaps your next visit we can feast on your ... creature."

"Then can I at least offer you a hat made of its pelt?" Thatcher invited. "He's already been skinned, and one of my men could make a hat for you and you can let it dry in this bright African sun."

Captain Haupt stood and offered his hand. "Safe travels, Captain Thatcherev, and please be careful. There are pirates in these waters, and they are quite dangerous, specifically to someone so uneducated to their ways."

They walked out upon the deck, and the captain looked skyward at the flag hanging from the mast. He recalled one last question to pose. "Your flag is very unusual. It looks much like our own flag, but the colors are in the wrong order. It naturally made me curious to see the Dutch standard flying inappropriately."

Thatcher clasped his hand on Captain Haupt's shoulder, raising his free hand skyward to indicate the flag. "Dear captain, you must get used to that flag, for when our Tsar spent time amongst your ships and was awestruck by the majesty of your fleets, he knew that Russia would become a great sea power only by emulating the Dutch, the true masters of the sea. And he sat by a fire one night in a shipyard and with his own hands and sewed the new Russian flag in honor of Holland. Look carefully captain, for in the Russian flag is reflected the majesty of Holland herself."

This last statement by Thatcher, as Captain Haupt begged permission to leave the deck, mounted his longboat and returned to his own flagship, was the only truthful thing that Thatcher had spoken all day long. And he was pleased he could end this encounter with the Dutch Navy in pride and in truth.

The *Phoenix* weighed anchor, and the two captains saluted each other good-bye as they sailed off in opposite directions. Thatcher hoped that Captain Haupt would save his inevitable inquiries for when he returned to one of Holland's possessions rather than querying the Harbormaster of the recent visit of the *Phoenix*. Regardless, Thatcher and Caesar weren't taking any chances, so they plied on sail to speed their northwest passage to Cap Vert. From this African western promontory they would alter course to cross the Atlantic through an excess of Spanish and French merchant and war ships and finally the blockades of English that stood between them and Charles Towne. As they once again verified that no sail was giving chase, Caesar and Thatcher made one last pre-dusk calculation, then made their way to the galley to feast on whatever remained of that São Tome goat. As they walked shoulder to shoulder, Caesar smiled and leaned in to Thatcher. "Black Russian?" He veritably howled that big gregarious laugh, the first time he had laughed in many months, as the brothers Edwards prepared to retire for their feast.

The passage of the Atlantic took them across the most dangerous waters any lone ship could likely encounter. Thatcher had been busy in the Captain's cabin, meticulously forging documents and passports for any country and their nautical envoys whom they might meet. He wished not to press his luck, but that Russian flag had served his interest well, and as no one wished to offend the Tsar of Russia, with whom every nation was attempting to curry trade favor, Thatcher was confident that he could pretty well talk his way out of any situation should it be required. With his smatterings of Dutch, French, Spanish, Portuguese and German, plus the very unlikely circumstances of encountering nautical Poles or Latin mariners sailing in service to the Vatican, he felt fairly prepared for any circumstance he could encounter. But in preparation, in the event he could not talk himself out of a situation, he and Caesar spent many afternoons drilling the crew by running out the thirty guns that flanked the port and starboard, training them how to fire them with deadly accuracy. The Malagasy learned rudimentary musket and pistol firing and loading techniques, giving them ease and adeptness, and they practiced applying the ship's sail lines for moving about the *Phoenix* for the potential of boarding. These exercises gave the Malagasy a confidence in themselves and in each other that only fueled their passion for their captain.

They had been alone at sea for weeks when at last they encountered sails in the distance. Thatcher's eye was carefully trained on that ship to get some semblance of national identity, as Caesar prepared the crew for friendship or fight. The ship had obviously spotted them as well and began that meticulous dance that ships did on vast seas, first sailing very fast and very aggressively toward one another to verify seamanship and nationality. One could never trust the flag that any ship flew, for the Englishman at a distance could become a Frenchman up close. Thatcher trusted his instincts and kept his Russian flag firmly fixed to the topmast, and Caesar ordered the crews to stand by their guns.

The ship that approached them was a small one, a single mast ketch more appropriate for coastal trading than the wide waters of the unpredictable Atlantic. Thatcher watched as they lifted a Dutch flag, but as they grew closer he could tell they were not any close approximation of a Dutch merchant or navy crew. Their captain lifted his speaker trump to halloo the *Phoenix*.

"You're Dutch?" the captain of the tiny ketch inquired as Thatcher lifted his trumpet in response.

"No, we represent the Governor of St. Mary's," he replied.

The *Dagger*, under the command of Thaddeus Brownley, had recently gone on the account. Having stolen their tiny ship from a Portuguese fishing village and arming her with a mere two guns, she was no match for any ship of size, and Thatcher had to admire their grit for not running when they took in the impressive mass and girth of the *Phoenix*. This little crew of thirty men had filled their tiny hull with a fairly impressive array of china and crystal, which they had stolen one crate at a time from the docks and wharves all along the Portuguese and Spanish coast. Their methodology was simple: their tiny ship would hide in the nearest cove and wait until dark. Then the crew would take to their small boats, rowing in amongst the shadows of the harbor, and box by box they would load their little crafts until they were almost submerged, stealing back to their tiny ketch and making sail before the dawn. It was a very hard way to make a living, but Thatcher had to admire their determination. Their hope had been to scavenge enough to buy a few more guns and take on a slightly bigger ship, take her as a prize, transport their guns and whatever they held in their holds into their new ship and hope to continue the process of upgrade. Thatcher loved a start-up business. He welcomed the little crew of Scots, Irishmen, Englishmen and Welshmen – and one fellow from Poland whose presence they could not quite explain – and offered them a taste of rum, which they could scarcely afford and lacked the temerity to steal.

"I must say, Captain Edwards, only in my mind's eye could I have imagined such a fine cabin," Captain Brownley commented as he took in the books and custom-made furniture reflective of Kidd's taste and opulence.

"'Tis merely a place to store my things, Captain Brownley. I cannot take credit for its design, only its recommission. Sadly, her previous owner sent her to the bottom of St. Mary's Channel, but my Governor had the good sense to suggest we do our best to resurrect her. And thus, the *Phoenix* is alive today," Thatcher replied as he poured a generous ration of rum into a tankard and handed it to Captain

Brownley. It was the first rum the erstwhile pirate had had in months, and it nearly brought a tear to his eye as he fought the instinct to down it in total but instead savored this gift from the strange, young captain.

"We've yet to venture as far south as the Cape, Captain Edwards, for as you can see our little ship is quite unsuitable for such a passage. But given a little time and the right circumstances, perhaps I, too, shall have the good fortune of being able to recommission such a fine jewel."

"So what news do you have of the goings-on here along the coast of Europe, Captain Brownley?" Thatcher pressed.

"I wish I had much to share, Captain, but under the unique circumstances me and my crew find ourselves, we don't have much contact with our fellow seafarers. I was hoping perhaps you could apprise me of life on land, as it has been some months since we've set foot on a non-rolling surface."

Thatcher smiled, spreading out his hands in resignation. "Seems you and I find ourselves in very similar circumstances, Captain Brownley. Our little republic is not universally recognized, and so like you we minimize our contact with fellow mariners." Thatcher refilled Brownley's cup, indicating there was much more where that came from as he pressed the captain for more details about him and his brave little ship.

The brothers Edwards were intrigued by the merchandise-rich and cash-poor status of these low-rent pirates. The presence of the Malagasy, ever vigilant on their high ground with armed muskets, helped them maintain their upper hand and made Captain Brownley conducive to their business offer. They proposed to trade his merchandise, which they had examined earlier, for two cannon and two casks of rum. Brownley was overwhelmed by the notion that he could finally give these men something they wanted and needed to forward their enterprise. The gentlemen agreed, and two cannon were shipped over to the *Dagger* as her holds were emptied of the cargo they could scarcely hope to unload for a better price. The men of the *Dagger* watched as if an angel was descending as those two casks of rum were lowered onto their decks. Thatcher made a gift of a case of Madeira wine for Captain Brownley and wished his merry band well as the *Dagger* sailed away, a little higher in the water and ready to face whatever moderate sized ship they should encounter next. One case lifted from the hold of the *Dagger* was in itself not of great value materially, but it would prove to be one of the most significant pieces of cargo Thatcher and Caesar would ever handle as they proceeded on their course for Charles Towne.

Settled by wealthy merchants and landowners from Barbados, Charles Towne was barely twenty-nine years in existence, yet it was the most important seaport in Carolina. But its unique geography, which made it such an attractive place for commerce, also made it vulnerable to the ravages of nature, as Thatcher and Caesar discovered when they sailed the *Phoenix* into that tiny exposed harbor. Their timing was fortuitous, for late the previous year the town had suffered from a deadly wave of two devastating diseases. Smallpox wiped out nearly 300 of their citizens, and practically before the survivors had time to get the dead into the ground another 160 of them fell victim to yellow fever. These hardy Barbadians, now the pre-eminent of Charles Towne, went into the New Year with great hope, but their hopes were dashed when the ground beneath their feet began to rumble and shake, leveling a number of their shoddily constructed buildings. No sooner had the ground ceased to quake than the lanterns that had been shattered in the rubble took spark and set this young vital port town ablaze, burning one-third of the structures that counted as their downtown. This scene of devastation spread before them as the *Phoenix* dropped anchor in her deepwater harbor. Thatcher and Caesar and a few of their crew cautiously set out in their longboat to investigate the status of this seemingly devastated town. Hearing the words "pox" and "yellow fever" sent a shiver down their spines that nearly sent them swimming back to their boat. But a man who met them at the dock assured them that they had nothing to fear, as most of those who had contracted either malady had long been buried deep in their respective holy grounds.

Charles Towne had become a religious as well as trading enclave, boasting Huguenot and Baptist churches, Presbyterian and Congregationalist meeting houses and Quaker assemblies among their faithful. It seemed the only religious sect excluded thus far were Roman Catholics, but more for fear of their Papist loyalties than their religious practices. The resilient people of "Charleston," as the locals now dubbed their community, immediately went to work rebuilding the two most important types of structures in their devastated town: their churches and their taverns. For while the locals cleaved to those sacred institutions of religious freedom, Charleston was a port town serving sailors, and sailors preferred spirits from a bottle rather than in some subservient role within a sacred Trinity. Word had spread throughout all the Caribbean of Charleston's devastation, and fear that yet another Carolina settlement, as so many before it, was going by the wayside had slowed the number of ships visiting her harbor. As the citizens' sorely lacked the items essential to rebuild their lives, Charleston was the perfect marketplace for the very full holds of the *Phoenix*.

Scarcely a few thousand people, a majority of which were bonded African slaves, made up this reverent town. And for those slaves not charged with rebuilding, the remainder and vast bulk toiled away six days a week to bring in those first harvests of rice that would make Charleston an agricultural focal point in the years to come. In fact, when the local merchants approached Captain Edwards the Fair to consider a trade of merchandise for rice, which they assured him would sell handily in the northern ports, he consulted with Captain Edwards the Dark to gauge his feelings on the subject. Caesar stood and looked out from the quarterdeck of his ship, surveying all those fine English folks fanning themselves in the shade as their black property went about rebuilding their lives for them. While he could not see the rice fields, he was pretty sure that they, too, were being harvested, not by those brave white Barbadians and their religiously tolerant attitudes who thanked God every day for slavery, but by Guineamen and Bantu and, very likely, Malagasy, who had only the Sabbath to thank for even a semblance of a day of rest. And who would never have a dime to their name.

"To hell with these slavers. These black men are taking their gold," Caesar replied quietly, terminating the conversation.

Nearly three-quarters of the contents of that hold was exchanged for ten large chests of gold and silver, regretfully parted with by those poor Charlestonians. No amount of Christian appeal could sway these young Russian Orthodox to consider the value of their much labored for foodstuff, rather than settling for mere gold, something they reminded them one cannot take to heaven. Thatcher exchanged those crates of china and pewter, copper and silver utensils, thanking them for the reminder and likewise asking for their gratitude that he was liberating them from that earthly weight as well. And God bless them. As they were about to set sail with a small portion of cargo remaining and enough gold and silver to make any pirate cry like a baby, they were stopped at the docks by a Dr. Moore, who had been busy attending to the last few victims of God's wrath.

"Captain Edwards, I heard that you have brought so many worthwhile and necessary items for the people of Charleston, items that will help us deal with the grievous losses we have experienced and provide us a small amount of comfort from our grief. I must ask you, though, if by chance in your supplies you also had a quantity of physick?" Dr. Moore asked.

"Why, yes, Doctor, I do have one small chest of medicine, a small collection of sulfates and opiates. Did you wish to purchase that as well?" Thatcher inquired.

The doctor obviously felt the strain of having been unsuccessful to revitalize so many stricken, the fresh graves and rows of crosses a testament to his shortcomings. To him, his was a higher calling, as he reminded the survivors so often when he came to their doorsteps seeking collection for his failure. Alas, the poor doctor was penniless and hoped his rice futures would once again put him in the financial pink. He looked at Thatcher with earnestness, hoping to strike his humanity. "Sir, you walk away with our gold and our silver, leaving us with little more than flatware and crockery. There is no more that we can give you. Could you not make a small donation on behalf of this poor community of that chest of medicine? For surely, good sir, it will come back to you one day ten-fold."

Thatcher thought for a moment and then, looking at the earnestness of the doctor, felt a rare sense of pity, not for his need but for his horrible and pathetic performance. "And will you, good doctor, take my donation and give it to the most needy as well? I won't find out that you took these most rare and prized of my stocks and charged a robber's fee for them, will I?" Thatcher queried.

"On my word, as a good Christian, sir, I swear to you your donation will greatly enrich the people of Charleston."

Thatcher stared at him coldly and directed one of his men to go back to the ship and retrieve that chest of medicine. He brought it to Thatcher, and Thatcher handed it to the doctor. "I will take you at your word, Dr. Moore, for surely if I discover you profited off of my gift, I will come back and reclaim it."

Thatcher and Caesar and this Negro crew of freemen set sail, putting Charleston in their wake. The two never looked back at that city of dichotomies: the blood of Jesus, so sacred, but the blood of slaves of little value to them. As God was their witness, no matter how desperate they were, they would never again drop anchor in Charleston ... except of course to fulfill Thatcher's solemn promise.

The *Phoenix* set a northeast heading, hugging as close to the coast as the keel below them would allow. These long days and vast stretches of beach that made up the Carolina coast were broken up only by the occasional broad rivers that cut insistently through that bright white sand. As they came to the northeast head of Long Bay, they at last decided to attempt to navigate one of those rivers with a reputation as ominous as its name: Cape Fear. Traveling up its fairly deep channel, they could see the potential for development of its moist banks. It was here that Yvgeny Thatcherev had thought to try to create a new life with the members of Parker House. He had been attracted to the notion of making a go where others had failed. On its western bank, they could see the first attempts at establishing a permanent settlement at a place named in honor of Lord Brunswick. Yvgeny had visualized how he would construct long piers stretching out to the deepest points of the river and a small but ever growing community farming its warm dark soil with that most powerful of colonial commodities, tobacco. From their vantage point, they could see native tribes who came to the edge of the trees to investigate this strange sailing accompaniment of many dark-skinned men and only one white man.

Thatcher found himself surprised by the emotions he was feeling at the thought of what could have been had Yvgeny and Beatrice not fallen prey to the likes of Avery. If all had gone according to plan on these banks three years ago, that dock would have been constructed. A collection of fine homes would have been built to withstand the ravages of these volatile summer seas and the ferocious winds that accompanied them. Yes, there would have been the problem of the mosquitoes, but as he viewed the natives who seemed in ample numbers along these shores, it was obvious such pestilence was survivable. It was just a matter of tapping the local wisdom. When word spread of a few dozen English ladies having made a home of this unsettled land, it was well assured that many men would have found such a settlement much more attractive than the typical all-male primitive villages that dotted this coast. The ladies of Parker House would have had their pick of eligible bachelors with whom to build lives and families, and with husbands and children a real community could have grown here in New Moscow. Carolina had built a reputation of religious tolerance. What a test of that tolerance it would have been when those onion domes of an Orthodox Church had risen here upon the Cape Fear River. On many a night back in Bristol,

Thatcher and Caesar had sketched out designs based upon Thatcher's memory of Moscow. His recollection of the Church of the Annunciation, the smallest but most reverential of the Kremlin cathedrals, was to be his model, which they would christen as St. Peter's. While certainly an English colony, it was hoped that word would spread of a Russian-friendly town in Carolina, inspiring new trade opportunities with not only England but also its most treasured new ally. In the future, they would have to explore these waters to see how far they were navigable, but for now they had cargo to sell, and they began their southern journey back to the broad Atlantic, proceeding northeast along an impressive stretch of barrier islands labeled as the Outer Banks.

This long ribbon of sand could be at first glance thought of as the mainland, a sight no doubt considered by those hardy first settlers who at last discovered their true nature and sailed up one of its many channels to discover the broad flat waters that resided between these islands and the solid Carolina coast. They had made that first go on an island they named Roanoke, and, unlike so many typical settlements, this one had been made up not of bold trappers and hunters but of families. When its captain sailed back for England, he brought news of a child being born upon the island whose name, Virginia Dare, became a rallying point for the potential successes of this yet-explored New World. But that captain, who thought he would embark on the next set of trade winds, was delayed for almost three years, and when he finally returned with much needed supplies, he was horrified that not a soul could be found on all of Roanoke Island. When they investigated the settlement site, no clear sign of either struggle or organized abandonment was revealed. The only message left behind was one word carved into a tree: *Croatan*. This cryptic message offered much speculation back in London on the whereabouts of those settlers and that first American born child, ranging from massacre by local tribes to amalgamation and abandonment of their Englishness to live among the Indians. That failure prompted the next major attempt at establishing a permanent foothold in the Colonies, and as the *Phoenix* proceeded north, rounding Cape Henry and veering west into the Chesapeake Bay and the James River that fed her, they began to see the signs of that first success, the colony of Jamestown.

Jamestown had suffered any number of disasters since its founding in 1607, the most recent of which was a fire that burned down their capitol. Just weeks before the arrival of the *Phoenix* in July 1699, the Virginia capital had been moved to Middle Plantation, now renamed

Williamsburg in honor of the king. This famous settlement, a testament to English resolve, was being reduced in prominence to a much prettier and more modern city on a hill. The atmosphere at Jamestown was not of desperation, as in Charleston, but more of doom. It was hoped that the last of their cargo would find a ready market here as they had in Charleston, and with these final chests of gold the *Phoenix* would honor one more commitment in the Colonies and make its way with a light and agile ship back to St. Mary's. But to their dismay, unlike Charleston, whose wealth had been well-supplemented by its more open trading nature and less concern for such trifles as bills of lading and proofs of sale, these Virginians took a much different view of ships of dubious registry.

The Russian flag flying proudly from the mast was greeted with looks of suspicion from the Harbormaster, who inquired quite pointedly on both the cargo and the origin of the ship. Many had heard of the tales of Kidd and his strange ship that had departed New York three years earlier, and the latest news was that Kidd and his crew were now prisoners of New York Governor Lord Bellomont, with suggestions that they would be off to London soon to be tried for piracy. Those long days at sea and the virtual isolation at Charleston had not provided Thatcher with this morsel of news that would have made him reconsider his destinations. Thatcher feigned ignorance of this Captain Kidd the Harbormaster spoke of, as they were simple Russian merchants seeking new trading ports with their good friends the English. The Russian documents Thatcher presented were of little use to this high-minded Englishman, who instead insisted upon letters of introduction from bona fide British contacts before permitting these Russians opportunities for trade.

"You must understand, Captain Thatcherev, that these waters are full of the most un-Christian men who steal from hard-working merchants and attempt to sell their ill-gotten gain to respectable men. We therefore place high demands of merchants before risking the sullying of the good reputation of Jamestown, His Majesty's most honored port of call," Mr. Lee informed him with ever so slight of a sneer.

"Mr. Lee, I understand your concerns, and we did not think His Majesty's colonies would put such strictures on a nation she has sought so hard with which to establish trade. We could have sold everything to the good folks of Charles Towne, but thought it a good Russian education to visit England's most heralded colonial community. We were mistaken in our assumption," Thatcher replied with a sniff.

Any plans to offload their remaining cargo and to purchase necessary stores for the long trip back to St. Mary's would have to be considered at another port, for even if he could sell his cargo to these Virginians, he wished not to spend a dime in return. He remembered Yvgeny's warnings regarding these arrogant self-important people who seemed to place a premium on their greedy survivability and, like Kidd, tended to think themselves on par with the King whose very existence and prestige provided them their small measure of importance. Thatcher told his crew to remain aboard as he personally removed the mooring lines attached to the stanchions on the Jamestown docks. As he boarded his ship, he made the point of removing his boots, leaning them over the side of the bow and knocking them together in a symbolic gesture to shake them of this Virginian dust.

As the *Phoenix* made its way to the Chesapeake, Thatcher and Caesar once again made certain to continue facing forward so as not to take in the sight of these petty little people. It made him think of what potential may come when Charleston and Jamestown would one day face competition from a much more broad-minded people in the now unexploited area between them.

"Perhaps one day, Caesar, we can hope that a valley of humility will be found between these two mountains of conceit," Thatcher contemplated, as he considered the possibilities of those broad, still waters of the Carolina coast to his immediate south.

II

They proceeded north along the coast of Delaware and into Delaware Bay, up the highly navigable waters of the Delaware River to the Quaker port of Philadelphia. Now here were people Thatcher could deal with. Unlike these Anglicans, Huguenots and those Congregationalists in Massachusetts, Quakers were the type of people any smart Bristol merchant could appreciate. Many of the Quakers, who had heeded William Penn's call to join him in this new colony where their religious freedom and business principles were respected, had come from Bristol itself. Having suffered greatly at the hands of Oliver "Bloody" Cromwell, Quakers had been banished from much of England, and likewise cast from the presence of the good Puritans of

Boston for daring to teach their heretical beliefs. In waves they migrated to Pennsylvania. What made Philadelphia the thriving trade community it had become had much to do with the very reasons why Quakers were so reviled by all other faiths to begin with. Quakers lived a life reflective of their values and did not have to put their values on the back burner in order to do business. Their firm commitment to their mystical beliefs defied traditional categorization beyond Catholic, Orthodox or Protestant, making them reviled by all of them equally. But Yvgeny Thatcherev had absolutely loved to do business with Quakers. For one thing, he knew that once their word was given they would follow through, as to do otherwise would reflect poorly on the God within.

Sailing into Philadelphia Harbor in so many ways reminded Thatcher of sailing into Bristol. Not that it even enjoyed a speck of the opulence or prominence of that ancient seaport, but the cleanliness, orderliness and general friendliness of these people who made the City of Brotherly Love their home truly reflected that aspect of Thatcher's hometown. One distinctive difference in Philadelphia versus the other colonial ports was the lack of oddity and suspicion that was witnessed with respect to this all black crew and their one white officer. While it was true that some Quakers did own slaves, for the most part slavery was viewed as an abhorrent practice by most of the people of Philadelphia. Thus, for the first time in nearly a year, the entire crew of the *Phoenix* was able to place their feet on dry land – not that the Malagasy had much desire to go very far from the one vestige of Madagascar represented in their floating home. In fact, after a year at sea, the solid ground felt mighty unstable, as their sea legs made them wobble and distrust these wooden docks and stone paved streets, to the point that many of them returned to the ship very shortly after having stretched their legs.

Portmaster Francis Allen took in the strange ship making its way to his docks and its unusual Dutch-like flag with a bit of curiosity. He himself retrieved the stern line thrown down from one of the Africans and smiled, offering a warm "Welcome to Philadelphia." The Malagasy merely nodded, not understanding a word he said, and went to find Thatcher. Thatcher smiled and extended his hand, not bothering to offer the pretense of his Russian affectation.

"Good afternoon, sir. I am Captain Thatcherev of the *Phoenix*, and I must say yours is one quite pretty port," he offered honestly as he extended his hand to Mr. Allen.

"Captain Thatcherev. Unusual name. It's not British," Allen replied, sizing up the young captain.

"Russian, sir. My grandfather immigrated to England and settled in Bristol. It is from there I come with but a meager stock of cargo left and a hope the good people of Philadelphia can find use for them." He presented the manifest to the Portmaster, who studied the beautifully penned document.

"You've a nice supply of household goods, sir. And the origination is Bristol?" Allen inquired further.

"Well, the cargo, but certainly not all of its products. We've a vast array from throughout the kingdom and a few choice items from Spain and France whose origin I wish not to question," Thatcher smiled.

"Well, then, Mr. Thatcherev of Bristol, as I tried to say to your crewman, welcome to Philadelphia."

Their cargo was sold before the waning light of dusk. Thatcher took the kind offer of Mr. Allen to make a few brief introductions to potential merchants anxious to both buy and sell, as Thatcher had indicated he was returning to Bristol. Mr. Allen conducted Thatcher to the Meeting House where a number of Philadelphia's most pre-eminent had gathered to conduct church affairs. He was quite impressed with this assemblage of men who spoke candidly and frankly about commercial opportunities. He made excuses that he had contacts in New York from which he may be retrieving cargo to ferry back to Bristol as well, but certainly, should space allow, he would be most anxious to return to Philadelphia and fill up whatever hold space remained. As good Quakers, they could appreciate his previous commitments and welcomed the opportunity to discuss such possible transactions upon his return.

One of these gentlemen particularly impressed with Thatcher was William Fordham. Having established a very lucrative trading business with contacts in London, he was anxious to expand opportunities in England's second largest port and was quite taken with this well-spoken, literate young man with the easy smile and the charming personality. Quakers placed a high premium on education, and it was obvious that this young man was quite well read indeed, though obviously not boastful of which college he attended. This pleased the Quaker well as so often educated men felt the need to laud their letters, something from which Quakers tended to shy away.

"Edward Thatcherev, I am most anxious to catch up with all that is occurring in Bristol and would be so honored if thou would join me for dinner this evening," Mr. Fordham offered.

"While it would be my distinct pleasure, sir, alas I tend to take supper with the crew as this is one of those rare opportunities for us to share time in less demanding circumstances," Thatcher offered in kind decline.

"Certainly, thy crew would be understanding of one evening. Perhaps thou would likewise extend the invitation to thy first mate as well. I believe we have much business to discuss and would love to lay the groundwork as soon as possible, as I know thou sail for New York very soon," Mr. Fordham continued.

Thatcher was about to make one more excuse when Mr. Fordham brightened and gestured across the road. "Ah, there she is," he smiled, indicating a young lady approaching. "Please, let me introduce thee."

Thatcher turned to look in the direction Mr. Fordham indicated and felt his heart jump. Like her father, Melanie Fordham reflected the Quaker tendency toward plain clothing with a simple dress and bonnet to shield her hair although the faint trace of blonde curls could be seen peeking from beneath. There was no shielding that beautiful face and radiant smile that captured Thatcher in an instant. At sixteen years of age, Melanie's clothing did not betray the womanly shape beneath them. Since a child, Thatcher was used to women who went to great pains to emphasize every feminine curve and bulge to near exaggeration, yet here he was, taking in the sight of this petite shy girl, betraying no outward signs of overt femininity, and Thatcher's heart was in his throat. Perhaps it was the lovely blue eyes. But whatever it was, Thatcher, for the first time he could remember, was at a loss for words.

"Edward Thatcherev of Bristol, please allow me to introduce my only daughter and the light of my life, Melanie Fordham. Dear, Edward commands that very large boat thou seest there in the harbor, and I have invited him to dinner. Wouldst thou please explain to him why thy mother's goose is worth changing plans?" William Fordham begged.

Like Thatcher, Melanie was at a loss for words. She had to look away to avoid the penetrating dark eyes of the young, tall, dark-haired sea captain. She looked at the ground for a moment, and in a barely audible breath asked, "Wouldst thou?"

Thatcher, too, had to catch his breath and, finding what words he could, replied, "I wouldst."

He was in a dead run all the way back to the ship, where Caesar was overseeing preparations for offload of the cargo. The sight of Thatcher's anxiety and heavy breath at first alarmed him as he prepared to reach for his nearby sword. Thatcher avoided the gangplank and leapt over the gunwale, where Caesar deftly caught him so he would not crack his chin on the deck.

"Oh my God, dear Caesar. She is absolutely beautiful," Thatcher gushed between pants. "She has invited us to dinner – actually, her father did, and I know we're anxious to sail, but could we possibly, could we have dinner with this lovely young lady and her family, please?" Thatcher begged, betraying for the first time in a long time the teenager in him.

Caesar studied Thatcher, who was beside himself and flustered. He stared hard at his younger brother and then smiled, placing him in a headlock and rubbing his knuckles on his head. "Ah, T'atcha's in love," Caesar kidded and roared back, with a huge laugh at the pleasant silliness of his much-too-serious brother.

It was virtually impossible to distinguish Caesar from Thatcher in their matching uniforms in gold braids, except of course that Thatcher was giddy. They knocked upon the front door of the lovely and well-appointed home on Dock Street, where almost immediately Melanie Fordham appeared. She blushed when she saw Thatcher, and her eyes grew big at the sight of Caesar. She stood there for a moment holding the door and then her manners finally kicked in.

"Welcome, friends. Please, this way," she breathed.

Caesar leaned in to Thatcher and whispered, "She looks like your mother."

Melanie led them into the parlor. William Fordham stood for his guests, shaking Thatcher's hand first, then Caesar's, taking a moment to grasp the notion of a black first officer, and then indicated for both to take a seat. Melanie scooted off to retrieve refreshments, and whatever Mr. Fordham was saying fell upon deaf ears for Thatcher as he was counting the moments until she returned. For the time being, Caesar had to take on the uncharacteristic role of carrying on the conversation which, despite his disdain for it, he did so very well.

"I must say, thou art a curious sight, both thee and thy ship. The flag thou doest fly, 'tis neither British nor Dutch. Pray tell, what is it?" Mr. Fordham inquired.

"It is Russian, sir," Caesar replied as obviously Thatcher was oblivious. "We were contracted by the Tsar as his first merchant endeavor."

"'Tis strange as thou may know. We put no stock in flags; however we do require to know whom they represent," Mr. Fordham explained. "Doest thou encounter resistance from the more prominent flags at sea?"

"Our standard is an uncommon sight, Mr. Fordham," Caesar explained. "But one certain to be more common in the years to come. The Tsar has ambitious trade plans. "

"Please call me William, as we do not stand on ceremony. It would appear so, as thy Tsar made quite the impression in his recent travels through England." Whatever place Thatcher had been previously, he was now snapped to the present. The thought that Peter had been in England was shocking news to him. His expression of surprise no doubt was strange to Mr. Fordham, who smiled. "Yes, we realize he was supposedly traveling incognito, but such secrets are hard to keep, are they not?"

Thatcher cleared his throat and looked at Mr. Fordham. "Indeed, William, it was the Tsar's wish to go about unrecognized and had hoped his presence would not be noted," Thatcher offered weakly.

"But indeed, thy presence here in the Colonies is no doubt an extension of that mission, one would assume," Mr. Fordham offered.

Thatcher was about to answer when Melanie entered the room. She placed tea and sweet cakes on the table before them and once again retreated, offering a quiet "Dinner in five minutes, gentlemen."

"So, Edward, I must say our founder William Penn was quite impressed with the Tsar. He found it refreshing that a leader of Europe wished not only to acknowledge our beliefs but went to great lengths to express his hopes of bringing religious tolerance to his country as well," Mr. Fordham offered, impressed. "Is such tolerance a common thing in Russia?"

"Russia has been a country of one faith for over seven hundred years. My grandfather was an Orthodox priest before coming to

England and was representative of a small but growing body of clerics who enjoyed discovering the unique aspects of individual faith. Robert Thayler of your congregation in Bristol was one of my grandfather's dearest friends."

"Was, thou sayst. Is thy grandfather no longer with us?" Mr. Fordham asked sympathetically.

"We do not know, for he and my grandmother were lost en route to the Americas many years ago. We can only assume ..." Thatcher trailed off.

"Our sympathies and prayers for thee, Edward. To lose thy grandparents to the sea and choose it as a vocation must be trying. But God is with them," Mr. Fordham offered.

The moment grew somber but was gratefully brightened as Melanie entered to pronounce that the goose was cooked.

Thatcher had to admit that the prayer for dinner was unusual, as rather than the standard grace so common in many traditions, the Quakers offered their thanks in silence. While he should have been quietly thanking God for dinner, he peered through the crack in his lids to take in the beautiful and reverent face of Melanie Fordham across the table. It was a lovely dinner and quite the surprise when Mr. Fordham asked them to make themselves at home while he helped his wife do the dishes. As progressive as Yvgeny Thatcherev may have been, it would be impossible to imagine that old Russian removing his coat and rolling up his sleeves to scrape burnt bird carcass from the bottom of a pan. Thatcher and Caesar retired to the front porch with their pipes as smoking was against the tenements of the Quaker faith, though a vigorously traded commodity in Pennsylvania.

"What do you think of these people, Thatcher?" Caesar asked as he exhaled a delightful yellow ring from his mouth.

"Like my grandfather, I always liked Quakers, for there is no pretense or deception. They do not preach, they do not proselytize, and they do not attempt to convert. And, well, she is quite lovely."

As if on cue, Melanie appeared at the door. "My apologies for the intrusion. Edward, my father told me about thy grandparents, and I wish thee to know I shall have them in my prayers," she offered. "I wished only to say that, and bid thee good night, and trust thou have a safe journey back to England." She looked up and gave him a long glance with her beautiful pale eyes.

"Melanie, thank you, but I did not have the chance to tell your father that we may be some time in Philadelphia, as we are not expected in New York just yet," Thatcher explained, feeling Caesar's eyes bore into the back of his head.

Melanie brightened and then smiled sweetly. "Well, then, Edward, this is not good-bye but merely good night."

And as the door closed with her small frame silhouetted in the glass, Caesar demanded quietly, "So, we don't make sail tomorrow for St. Mary's."

"Yes, we need to discuss that, don't we?" Thatcher replied somewhat sheepishly, but not feeling the least bit bad about his unilateral decision.

When Caesar broke the news to the Malagasy crew, it was received with stunned silence. They seemed neither angry nor overjoyed at the prospect of delaying their trip, but as Caesar was informing them, not fully explaining that the reason was because Thatcher was struck with puppy love, he offered to find them suitable quarters on land, but to a man each preferred to stay on the boat. The sights, sounds and smells of the busy city were very discomfiting to these men of Madagascar, who were surrounded by white men and anxious to return to something more familiar. But if Caesar required them to stay, then they would make a bit of Madagascar right here on this boat. And thus did Caesar order up a number of cows that the crew joyously went about roasting right on deck. The merchants who often watched their fruit stocks rot and die in their cases were more than pleased as a happy and steady customer base was found on that strange ship at the end of the dock. Meanwhile, Caesar and Thatcher found a home to rent a block away from the Fordhams so they could discuss business with the men of Philadelphia and Thatcher could find every excuse to make his way to the Fordham house. When it was obvious why Thatcher was omnipresent in his household, Mr. Fordham suggested they take a stroll and enjoy the evening air of Philadelphia.

"I wish not to presume, Edward, but it has grown quite obvious that thou hast developed a measure of affection for my daughter," he began quite honestly and bluntly.

Thatcher gave it a second of thought. "William, to make any feeble attempt at offering an alternative observation would be both dishonest and futile."

"Thou must know, Edward, that my daughter is very committed to our faith," Mr. Fordham offered.

"Which leads me to the question: how does one begin the process of entering a Quaker congregation?"

Mr. Fordham smiled, placing an arm around Thatcher's shoulder, continuing their walk and alerting him to the mysteries of the Quaker faith.

While strange and unique, Thatcher genuinely found the experience of meeting with the Quakers pleasant, as its lack of structure, authority, dictation and austerity suited his taste for free thinking. And for the next few months, as the Malagasy crew patiently awaited whatever was going to occur, Yvgeny Thatcherev Edwards became a Quaker. His conversations with Mr. Fordham grew more frequent, and at times he was afforded unescorted conversations with Melanie Fordham. The two typically sat on the porch, talking about life and faith, though of course never engaging in any physical contact whatsoever. While it was true that Thatcher was dying to see if his imagining of her shape beneath that simple, plain dress was as awe-inspiring as he thought, her gentle sweet conversation, her kindness, her sweetness, and yes, the many qualities that reminded him of his mother, intoxicated him and drew him closer and closer to her.

As their discussions began to grow more intimate, Thatcher and Melanie agreed where their relationship was heading, and at the next meeting, after a few testimonies, both stood to their feet. This was the first time Thatcher would be addressing the congregation, and while priding himself on his performance skills, he had to admit his absolute terror at that moment.

"Melanie Fordham has agreed to be my wife, and we pray for the guidance and blessings of the assembled," Thatcher stated. He was about to sit down, feeling it had been completed, but noticed Melanie still standing so he stood beside her.

"Edward Thatcherev blew into our city on a chance breeze that should have quickly carried him off to the next port, and yet his sails remain slack and thus the winds blew him to our congregation. When we met upon that street, it was then I felt that same wind blow, and it was carrying me to him as if the breath of God itself. He has come among us and become a part of our body, and we ask that God's breath blow over all of us now."

As both stood there, the room remained quiet and at last Thatcher had the opportunity to understand where this sect's strange name came from as from a distance part of the room their bodies began to shiver until all within the room as a body began to quake. Thatcher had no idea what to do at that moment, but as he stood there, Melanie Fordham's hand reached to his and he could feel it trembling, as was his.

As the room slowly came once again to stillness, a man stood up. "As Edward and Melanie have declared their love for one another, I call for a meeting of the Clearness Committee so we may assess that they have prepared themselves for marriage." One by one, a group of men and women stood, and the whirlwind process that was the Clearness Committee began. As well as proffering extensive counseling, the committee immediately pushed to find which date they wished to choose. While not an organized body in some elements, on this subject this committee was pure details. When probed for when they would choose to marry, both suggested immediately, and as the will of God is a testimony in the light of young lovers' eyes, all speed was applied to make sure that arrangements were made. And that time was the very next meeting.

Thatcher remembered the elaborate ceremony that had been created for Yvgeny and Beatrice, so he was a bit surprised at the Quakers' very casual approach to this holy nuptial. The two were conducted to the front of the meeting room and took seats. As was the tradition, the moment they were seated the meeting began and silence ensued. Melanie's hand entered Thatcher's, and he could feel her strength lift him to his feet, where first she began.

"Edward Thatcherev, I promise to love thee and to cherish thee from now until all eternity, no matter where the seas may carry thee and God's wind may blow thee. I shall, now and forevermore, be at thy side," she stated, looking at him with absolute love and earnestness. They had never discussed beyond today where their lives would carry them. While he was sure that he would figure that out eventually, it was obvious that she already knew that very soon he would return to the sea. Yet despite what may be a temporal thing in her life, she felt prepared to make a lifelong commitment to him in spite of it.

"Melanie Fordham, I do not know what spirit guided me to this port, but it was a spirit that told me I would find home. I had come here for the sake of commerce and have instead found the love of my life. Winds will carry me to the four corners of the planet, but every corner will always show your face to me and carry me back to you," Thatcher replied, feeling her hand squeeze his.

"And now before this assembly, we are married before God," Melanie stated, and Thatcher repeated, "And now before this assembly, we are married before God."

William Fordham brought forth the marriage certificate which both signed and took their seats. It was a surprise to Thatcher in this short time that he had been among the assembled how many people stood up to say that this couple was chosen by God to meet and that they had been blessed by the chance appearance of the *Phoenix*. And at last someone rose to shake Thatcher's hand and with his other hand took the license, turned it over and signed it, as was the case with every single person in the assembly as they witnessed as a body the marriage of these two young people. When all had signed the document, William put an arm around Thatcher's shoulders and, along with his daughter, led them out of the front of the meeting house where a carriage awaited.

"It is time thee begin thy marriage," he said. The assembled, including Caesar who had witnessed the ceremony from the back of the hall, crowded out the door and with smiles and waves sent Edward and Melanie Thatcherev with absolute speed toward the house that Thatcher and Caesar shared.

The carriage had no sooner cleared the front of the meeting house than Melanie Fordham Thatcherev threw her body on top of her husband and kissed him for the very first time. Thatcher had expected that first kiss would be something gentle that carried them away to a place of bliss. But Melanie was having none of that. Since the moment she met him, she wanted him, and in her mind's eye she could not wait to see what this handsome dark-haired man had under that dark clothing. And she certainly did not want to have to wait to find out, for as her mouth met his, her tongue forcing his lips to part, her body began to slide against his. Not since he was ten years of age and that German bar wench from the German Suburb in Moscow had pulled him under a table and nearly torn the buttons off his shirt had he been so intimidated by a woman in his life. He had the good fortune of having had sex with incredibly passionate and incredibly talented women, but he could not remember a time when he had been with one with such groping hands.

The carriage driver had the good graces to keep his head forward, though Thatcher could hear the little chortle he was giving, because as everyone knew nothing was naughtier than a freshly married Quaker girl. Thatcher didn't even have time to tip the driver before Melanie was dragging him by his pants to the front door, and he barely got it closed before she began tearing the buttons off his tunic. As soon as she had wrestled his coat off him and torn off the buttons of his shirt, she finally took a moment to stop and appraise the first half of her imaginings.

"Better than I had hoped for, Edward Thatcherev," as her mouth immediately went to his chest, her tongue vigorously lashing at his nipples and down his well-muscled torso. As he tried to remove his boots, Melanie grabbed hold of his trousers, tearing at their buttons and hauling his breeches down around his ankles. And there was beauty in the simplicity of that plain dress for she lifted it over her head, revealing not the layers of petticoats and undergarments that were the hallmark of most women, for there in less than a second Melanie Fordham stood absolutely naked, not having to be bothered with all those trappings of fancy dress. Thatcher had only a moment to survey that magnificent little body with the light blonde hairs beginning from her navel and traveling down to her knee. As a young woman, she possessed a young woman's nest, and her apple-sized breasts were now framed with the long, luxurious blonde locks of her hair, finally free from the pin and bonnet that had restricted them for these months, now showing ringlets that curled from her face to her waist. The magnificent sight left no question to Melanie Fordham how pleased Thatcher was to see it, and she smiled a devilish smile as he lay sprawled across the staircase, his breeches trapped immobile around his ankles as Melanie Fordham reached down with one tiny hand, placing it around his long, hard, thick, seasoned shaft and guided it very slowly into her, biting her lip and letting out the slightest little cry as her husband's hard penis pierced her maidenhead. As it slid so slowly and deep inside her, her hands found his chest, her fingers and thumbs grasping his hard nipples as she arched her back and said, "I will love thee all my life, Thatcher Edwards," as she slowly and rhythmically began sliding up and down this wondrous gift from God. It took them hours to reach the bedroom, with many stops along that flight of stairs and the hallway that led to their boudoir. And when at last he could finally take command of the situation and get his goddamned pants off, she absolutely insisted he leave the boots on.

Caesar enjoyed spending some time with Thatcher's new friends, all such a polite and kind lot. When at last the congregants began to depart, Caesar made his way to the *Phoenix* where the Malagasy crew was quite inebriated from a long day of drinking. Seeing Caesar made their spirits rise more as their chieftain showed such great joy at the wedding of his brother. He recounted in detail this strange ceremony of the Quakers, and the crew laughed and staged their own version of the events, to his great amusement, as the Malagasy people are known for their great sense of humor.

Melanie and Thatcher spent most of the next week cooped up in their house, and Caesar was happy to string his hammock on the deck of the *Phoenix*. While there was a perfectly good Captain's Cabin going to waste, he was pleased to be among his people, who sang him to sleep with the songs of their far-off land. They spent the time waiting repairing the sails and riggings like the master sailors they had become. As they had been taught on the island of St. Mary's, they carried the ship to a place to careen the hull and prepare the *Phoenix* for her long voyage home. Dozens of good Quaker cows had been slaughtered and smoked and stored below deck, and the fruit merchants worked overtime to locate every last delectable morsel to load aboard. The night before sailing, Thatcher came to the ship at the darkest of the moon and took Caesar to the Captain's Cabin.

"I have made a decision, and I hope you understand it," Thatcher stated. A great feeling of concern swept over Caesar as he considered the possibility that the *Phoenix* may make sail with only one captain. "I've decided that I want to offload my shares to leave here with Melanie. I figure if I carry them with me, I'll just be tempted to waste them on women and rum. So with your blessing, my friend, I would like to count out my portion and have your help taking them to her."

"Is this what you want to do or think you should do, Thatch?" Caesar asked.

"Both, my brother. Both."

They spent the next few hours making a detailed count of every pence and farthing, subtracted them from the ledger and then swiftly and silently made their way to Melanie's father's house. They separated the portions into ten distinctive caches and carefully logged where each portion was hidden, all but one portion which Thatcher handed to Melanie along with a map.

"It is in your hands now, my love, and a promise to you that one day I will return, for I leave you all my earthly possessions as merely a deposit on the bank of love I have for you."

Melanie didn't realize it, but the treasure she secured was not just that of her beloved but that of Caesar as well. Not until much later, when she at last forced herself to seek out and account for it would she realize that, at sixteen, she was the wealthiest person in all of Philadelphia.

In those grey hours just before dawn, she returned with them to the *Phoenix* and made long passionate love one last time to her husband on that magnificent desk. The meticulously crafted and unusual railing that extended around its edge made the most wonderful handholds, and the only thing that could have made it better would be if they were riding upon a wicked tide. But if nothing else, what other woman could ever claim to have spent a night making love to the man of her dreams while being serenaded by a boatload of Malagasy sailors?

The waning days of autumn in 1699 greeted the *Phoenix* as she began her departure down the Delaware River on her last mission in the colonies before returning to St. Mary's Island. Thatcher was moved to see so many of the men and women from the meeting hall there to say good-bye, most importantly his lovely Melanie. They stood upon the docks and took a moment of privacy before Thatcher loaded aboard the crowded ship.

"I need to ask one more favor of you," Thatcher asked of Melanie. He drew a letter from his pocket and handed it to her. She looked at it and saw it was addressed to Abigail Edwards of Bristol. "Within a few days of my departure, through a discreet contact, if you would have this put aboard a ship en route to England, it would make me most happy, for I wish my mother to hear the news of her wonderful daughter-in-law. She will love you as I do, of this I am certain."

The Quaker girl in her for a moment relinquished her discretion and she wrapped her arms around her tall, handsome husband and kissed him with a desperation that may have to span the years. "Do not forget me, Thatcher Edwards," she whispered.

As he was about to depart, he heard the sounds of a young hawker of the local broadsheet heralding in print the latest news. Such a strange concept to Thatcher, as rather than relying upon the rumors from passing ships, someone actually bothered to write it down. He grabbed one of these unique oddities and loaded aboard the *Phoenix* as she began to warp away from Philadelphia Dock. Once she was positioned in the channel of the Delaware River and its eventual end in Delaware Bay, he removed the sheet that he had placed in his pocket to consult the news of the day. His heart sunk when he saw a small article and sought out Caesar to show him as well. There in the bottom left hand corner was a small notification that Captain Shelley and all the persons aboard the *Nassau* had been arrested for piracy in New York and were awaiting transport to England. This small bit of information, no doubt a moment of celebration to many a merchantman, was a sad moment for Thatcher and Caesar, as among those listed was their friend David "Darby" Mullins. Their desire to remove him from harm's way on the first available ship not linked directly to piracy had very likely sentenced their friend to death. Had they instead held him back with them in St. Mary's and brought him aboard this crew, Darby Mullins would be home by now. But it was his own wisdom and fear that prompted him to transfer his wealth of cloth and silks to his friends' custody, a wise business move as their sale had netted Darby nearly £500, more money than his family could ever dream of earning in all their lifetimes, and much more than Darby would have kept after the pack of wolves descended on them when they reached New York, for all that cargo put in the trust of Captain Shelley had been seized by Lord Bellomont, the Governor of New York.

The *Phoenix* made good time in their southern course to Carolina, but once they reached those sandy barrier islands they found difficulty in finding a passage to the waters on the west side. At last, they encountered a navigable channel between two islands with lush vegetation. To the port, one island could be seen dotted with large trees, while to the other at starboard was an island possessing strange trees that seems to have assumed the shape of the ever-present ocean breezes. This entrance showed promise, and over the next few days Thatcher and Caesar manned a near continuous presence with the sounding board on the bow. What made this both tolerable and at times entertaining was the constant presence of several strange and lively fish that darted and raced in and out of this channel. The Malagasy were apt to want to take advantage of such easy fresh meat and began to fix their spears and muskets to waylay the fearless prey, but Thatcher and Caesar brought an end to their easy hunt as they were still quite set on freshly smoked meats in the hold. Besides, the fish were entertaining and quite amusing, with their humorous faces that seemed to laugh, their long silver bodies that moved agilely through and across the water and their strong prominent tails on which they possessed the most peculiar ability to balance and virtually dance backwards across the water. But one thing that Thatcher noticed was not only their agility but their tendency to very carefully ply the deepest part of the channel, a necessity as they would race to the bottom and spring to the surface nearly as high as the deck of the ship. Thatcher struck upon an idea and took up a watch at his bow to see where they moved and then yelled to Caesar course corrections in response. As they made their way into that broad, still sound and began tracking northward, he told the crew to mind the sails and winds and put the sounding log aside as he let these strange fish called dolphin guide them.

Finally they were in the broad, generally shallow sound, and in short order they came to the island so linked with fear and folly that had served as England's first settlement. What had been thought would be a teeming metropolis by this time was now still and quiet, occupied only by those stealthy, observing Indians, who neither molested nor inquired upon the large ship sailing past them. As they proceeded north, this broad body of water began to narrow, funneling to its closest points as they passed by Roanoke Island. They kept their bearings, affixing their position on the mainland to port, and followed it as it once again opened up into another broad bay of water, which their maps indicated was the Albemarle. This east-west expanse of water made sailing easy as those heavy winds were now to their back, pushing the massive *Phoenix* easily through the sound's middlemost section where the depth of the water was obvious with the change of color. As land could be seen to its west and off the bow, Thatcher had the crew drop anchor and the longboats run out. While the Chowan River, which traveled from the north into the Sound, was itself a broad river, Thatcher and Caesar decided that this next part of their journey would be in a fashion similar to what Darby used to travel, and the Malagasy took a special joy in once again taking to oar to pull them north against the mild current. Signs of civilization could be noted along the riverbanks, as great broad stands of pine were meticulously and regularly carved away to reveal land freshly turned following harvest. Thatcher held in his hand a small handwritten map, penned by Darby's weak and unskilled hand, indicating key landmarks that would carry them to Mullins' land.

It was getting close to dark as they reached the last of those geographical markings indicated on the paper, and they rowed to the eastern bank. The distinctive scent of cooking fires carried on the breeze as the two longboats found a set of dories tied to a strong, compact pier. Thatcher exited the boat first and stood upon the dock, knowing that, though there was no movement, eyes were upon him.

"Halloo the settlement!" Thatcher called out. He could now see a few well made but small cabins sitting at the edge of a clearing, all light extinguished except for the cooking fires in the gathering twilight as he waited in silence for a response. Knowing how the sight of strangers could be a point of caution to these rural dwelling settlers, he tried once more. "Good evening, Mullins family. My name is Thatcher Edwards, and I bring news and tidings from Darby, my shipmate and friend."

"Ye bring word of my boy?" a voice with a strong Irish brogue whispered to his left, mere inches away.

"Aye. You are William Mullins, sir, and though I see you not I take pride in making your acquaintance. Your son has told me many stories of you and when these woods were virgin and you pierced her maidenhead," Thatcher offered into the darkness.

William Mullins stepped from the deepening shadows of yet uncut wood, a musket at the ready in his hand as he surveyed the young man who entered his property without invitation. "So ye've word of my boy, have ye? We'd long given him up for dead."

"No, sir, he's quite alive, though the last time I saw him quite ill, which is why we parted company so he could come home to his family and trees in Carolina. I had hoped to see him here when I arrived so I could off-load his baggage as he had asked me to do. But it appears I've beat him home and thus I must entrust this small cargo to your care, if you'll permit me, sir."

William Mullins nodded as Thatcher stepped to the edge of the dock. Caesar stood in the boat and handed up a compact chest. Thatcher set it before him, making sure the last rays of sunlight could shine upon its contents as he retrieved a key he wore around his neck, placed it in the lock and opened the chest for William Mullins to inspect. He stepped away a few paces, allowing the old Irishman to have a clear view of him and the chest, and the sight that beheld this old penniless woodsman made his Irish eyes smile in disbelief, for twinkling there in the last shafts of daylight was a chest full of Spanish pieces of eight.

"So Darby did make something o' his life?" William offered as he studied this pot of gold in amazement. It took some time for Thatcher to convince this elder of the Mullins clan that everything within that chest now belonged to them. The sight of the gold-filled container brought the Mullins boys from their places within the shadows, still training their muskets, the single most valuable of their possessions to date, upon this strange collection of Africans and one Englishman. Two Malagasy were brought up to carry the chest to the edge of the clearing, where those well-built log cabins stood, and placed it by the fire, joining their comrades who stood in a knot at the edge of the blaze. Mary Mullins led a collection of women and a sea of small children out from their places inside the cabins, where each in turn looked inside the chest and ran their fingers through the gold coins in disbelief.

"Your son has been at sea for many years, and his only thought all that time was to one day be able to return home to his family with the means to make their life a little less difficult. It was his hope that this would help," Thatcher continued.

"I must say, Mr. Edwards, that I'm havin' a difficult time buyin' yer words, for no man has ever left these woods and come back with chests of gold. Why would Darby?" William Mullins inquired.

"Mr. Mullins, Darby and I set sail from New York a number of years ago with a great captain charged to hunt pirates. We were moderately successful, and this is Darby's share of the proceeds," Thatcher explained.

"So where's my boy now?" William asked.

"Yes, where is my husband?" Theresa Mullins, a small, tired woman asked.

"Mrs. Mullins, it is a pleasure to finally meet you. Please know that Darby left only with the hope that he could better provide for you and his son and his family. But perhaps, if you'll permit, I could sit down and give you all the details," Thatcher offered.

"Bring extra plates, Mary. Our guests look hungry," William Mullins called, gesturing to all to be seated as Thatcher began to tell the tale.

It was good to hear these people laugh as Thatcher explained the more humorous aspects of life at sea. They were amused to find that Darby had gotten good use in his profession and love for topping trees. Since he had departed them some ten years back, there had been great sadness, as he left his wife with a newborn babe, explaining only that the sea was calling him, and he'd return when at last she grew silent. They explained how their youngest boy had always been a restless one and that though he aptly handled ax and saw, to him it was merely a means to an end and not a passion. For they, despite their years of toil, were merely tenants on another lord's land, no different than back in Ireland. And while they had eked out a living on these borrowed acres and the ample game in her woods, the best they could show for their efforts was this small measure of freedom. That troubled Darby as he felt that men who worked so hard to make something of the land should have some claim to it, and he swore that if he could not own something he wasn't going to make it great for someone else who did. So he took to the sea, and not a word had been heard from him in all these years. One person most moved by the stories of Darby was young David Junior. His father had been seldom spoken of all of his life, partially out of regret and partially out of anger. Theresa had nowhere to go once her husband had abandoned her and their child, and the Mullins took their name with pride and all who held it, so she became as much a sister to these strapping woodsmen and their wives as if she were born to it. But this news of her husband was both exciting and depressing at the same time, as she contemplated her ill husband, rotting away in that New York jail.

"And there's nothin' to be done for him?" Theresa inquired.

"That is what Caesar and I discussed for nearly this entire trip. You see, Mrs. Mullins, should either of us darken New York's door, it is likely we, too, would be clapped in irons, as alas we established some repute in that town," Thatcher explained.

"But no such threat hangs over us," Patrick Mullins, the eldest son, replied. "It seems to me if Darby earned this money, then Darby should be able to achieve freedom from it as well. And so, I resolve that me, Michael, Seamus and Theresa take some of this to New York to see if we can buy his freedom."

"Ye're needed here, Patrick," William stated. "Ye're strongest of us, and ye need to stay. But I'll take yer place, and we'll venture north tomorrow, perhaps hailin' a ship that way and see what we can do for Darby. Mr. Edwards, I know not whether ye men are guilty or not, but 'tis an honorable thing ye did, bringin' this to us, and it's family that needs to do for our own now. We're not folks who took anythin' that didn't belong to us, and if it turns out my boy be guilty as charged, then we'll do the honorable thing and give this back to the people it belongs to."

Thatcher reasoned, how could he argue with morality? Lesser men would justify every reason to keep this money, which he could attest was not ill gotten. But William Mullins had his suspicions and would not cave for a pile of gold.

At first light, William Mullins, his sons and daughter-in-law began their long trip down the Chowan River, bidding adieu and thanks to Thatcher and Caesar.

"If it would be all right with you, sir, perhaps we'll wait a spell here with your family to see if word arrives as to Darby's disposition. Besides, it seems you'll be a few hands short, and we would consider it an honor to remain in your company."

"Ye've done all ye need to, Mr. Edwards. But stay if ye wish, and welcome."

And so, Thatcher and Caesar and the Malagasy crew made their way back to their ship, plotting the most logical navigation they could, and brought the *Phoenix* into a quiet cove shielded by a copse of trees just a few miles short of Mullins' land. Throughout the winter, the Malagasy hunted in the woods along the Chowan River, both to recreate a sense of home life and to share in the bounty of the Mullins' hearth. Their traversing of these broad stands of tall trees brought them into proximity of the native tribes that peopled them, finding a reception much warmer than was often rendered for the whites who encroached upon them. Thatcher and Caesar took to the task of felling trees, venturing out with the Mullins clan to clear new ground before the next spring planting, for more tobacco land was always needed, and with the onset of winter those trees would be burned by the acre to keep the family warm. This unexpected visit from these strange men from Africa and these two brothers from England impacted the Mullins in ways they could not appreciate at first, but as those Malagasy brought in first dozens, then hundreds of the ample deer that filled those woods and dried those thousands of pounds of meat, a new revenue stream was created for the Mullins, as freshly smoked venison was shipped down the Chowan River where it meets Salmon Creek to Batt's trading post for hard cash and those rarest of luxuries like overpriced muslin. And Thatcher's love for the tops which he discovered when he first looked out across thousands of miles of trackless sea was re-kindled as little Darby Mullins showed him the strenuous trick that would get him to the tops of trees. And from their tops, he looked east to see the Chowan River as it spilled into the sea-like vista that was the Albemarle.

February's chill found the Mullins still busy at their task of clearing trees to meet their springtime planting deadline, and Thatcher was growing expert at topping trees along with his constant companion little Darby. And it was Darby Junior who caught the first sight of the dories making their way up the Chowan River. Thatcher and Darby quickly shimmied down their giant pines, calling out their sighting as they dropped. Travis Mullins jumped in his dory and rowed with all fury upstream to notify the women and children of the family's return, and together they joined as one to await news of their travel. As the boats rounded the river's bend, they strained to see if Darby was among their number, and to everyone's sadness he wasn't. The dories touched the beach and the weary travelers came to shore as William Mullins gave the news. Before they could reach New York, Darby and his companions had been loaded aboard a British man-of-war in chains and sailed to face their fate in London. There was no more that Thatcher or Caesar or those hundred Malagasy could do to help this family through the long months and possibly years of waiting, and so before spring could come to Carolina, and before those ill-fated winds and seas could make their southern journey a lethal one, they boarded the freshly restocked *Phoenix*, bid the Mullins family joy and best of luck, and set sail down the Chowan, through the Albemarle and Pamlico and finally back to the open sea.

III

To write a letter in the colonies and to put faith that it would reach anywhere in Europe in any kind of timely manner or, more often than not, at all, was an acknowledgement itself of Providence. Throughout much of Europe, most kingdoms had established fairly reliable methods of communication, rapidly sped by dedicated horsemen utilizing the system of roads, trails and ferries to make most points joinable. The same could not be said for communications from these kingdoms to their colonies or from the colonists to their home nations. Considering the distance, the weather and all forms of natural and man-made interruptions that came between the writer's pen and the reader's eye, it was a small miracle that letters ever reached their intended destination.

On that crisp morning in November 1699, when Thatcher handed his letter to Melanie, he did so with hope but no expectation of its ever reaching its final destination. But Melanie was intent that she would perform this task for her husband to her utmost capability, so she secreted the letter until a nautical friend made port in Philadelphia. Captain Farrow of the *Cumulus* arrived on the 15th of November. An old friend of the family, he stopped by the Fordham house for dinner, stating he was in port only for a day or so. Afterwards, Melanie queried where he was heading next, and he mentioned that after a brief stop in Barbados he intended to push on to Bristol. She could not believe her stroke of luck that a letter intended for her beloved's mother could almost directly reach her, and so she handed him the letter, asking if he be so kind to please deliver this upon his arrival in Bristol, to which he most happily agreed. No sooner was his cargo offloaded and his oncoming freight secured in the hold, he weighed anchor and set sail in fair, clear conditions for Barbados. It was November and the storm season should have been nearly over, but halfway between Delaware Bay and Barbados, a nor'easter came up, battering his ship and crew for two solid days in thirty foot seas. His cargo had appeared secure when they set out, but in the movement and shifting from those lethal waves, part of it came loose, ramming a hole below the waterline. The volume of water she was taking on became obvious, and for the next three and a half days his crew violently pumped every ounce of seawater they could to keep the *Cumulus* afloat.

Upon reaching Barbados, he was able to assess the damage and realized he would be holed up on this Atlantic island for a number of weeks if not months. In Bridgetown's port, preparing to make sail, was an old comrade, Captain Louis Bennett of the *Bulldog*, who was preparing to set sail for Charleston. Of course, he had every intention of making his way to London with large quantities of Carolina rice after depositing his cargo of slaves. He was happy to take aboard that small packet of letters and correspondences intended for the motherland, and off to Charleston he sailed. Upon reaching Charleston Harbor, he received an urgent communiqué from the ship's owners in Boston, indicating that the price for the cargo would fetch much higher in New York than London, so please post-haste divert his course to New York instead. As there were no ships in the harbor to pass off the bundle he received from Captain Farrow, Bennett proceeded to New York with his trusted paper cargo. As he was sailing along the Carolina coast just short of the Chesapeake, he encountered a group of people aboard small rowboats seeking passage to New

York. As they were willing to pay in pieces of eight, he was happy to accommodate. He had his crew lift their boat aboard the *Bulldog* and on they proceeded to New York. His happy buyers were likewise more than pleased to pass along those letters on the first ship sailing for England as those buyers were anxious for him to return to Charleston with stocks of house wares. And so for the rest of December, those packets sat until Captain Russell of the *Russell*, bound for Boston and then to Southampton, was obliged to take the parcel with him. And so, after offloading dry goods in Boston and taking on five hundred barrels of whale oil, the *Russell* began its nonstop cruise to the southern shore of England. A coastal trader boat en route to Swansea carried that little bundle of parcels within a hundred miles of Bristol, where it sat for nearly two months on the desk of the ship's owner who had gone to London for holiday.

Upon his return, he discovered that little packet with a variety of parcels for all of southwestern England. But the one that most intrigued him was that which was addressed to the mistress of Parker House. It had been some time since he had paid a visit to the fair ladies of Bristol, so with ready excuse in hand and a desire to shed himself of a dozen stone in the person of his fat, psychopathic midget of a wife, Mr. Earl Tompkins told his spouse that he needed time and spiritual guidance from his brother, the Right Reverend Hubert Tompkins of Bristol Cathedral. Things at Parker House had changed much since the strange disappearance of those two young men who took over the management of the place from their grandfather. Seemed all had gotten a bug for America, and now the dear ladies were charged with having to do men's work and hold together that wonderful place named after dear Mr. Parker, a nice fellow, whose first name he could not remember. And all that drive to Bristol, he searched his memory trying to recall Mr. Parker's name.

The ferry running between Newport and Bristol was out of service again, forcing him to take the long way around Bristol Bay and arriving at Parker House at the very latest of hours. Hubert was going to have quite a fit when he answered the door at the Rectory at two a.m. or so, and no doubt with one of his lengthy lectures regarding adultery and alcohol. He knocked on the door and Anthony DeWayne, the large, impersonal fellow who was responsible for guarding the door, showed him to the parlor where that very personable African lady was busy serving coffee, cigars and her delightful little bread and meat treats. He was famished, so he happily dove into a small stack of them as Sharon Campbell, that most lovely, tall redheaded angel from the Scottish

Highlands, treated his return as if her long-lost lover had once again been found. Still hungry, he took two of the sandwiches and a cup of coffee with him to Sharon's room where she fed him his treats as if he was Nero being fed grapes by a slave. And how she made him feel, as if he were Caesar. He was quite full and sated as Sharon led him down the stairs to hand him off to the loving care of Mr. DeWayne, who escorted him to the library where Abigail Edwards sat, wrapped in a number of shawls, looking quite haggard and tired. He remembered her when she was such a beautiful young woman, and yet some sort of illness must have taken its toll on her. She looked up as Anthony made his announcement, and Abigail showed Earl to a chair.

"Mr. Tompkins," she began, her voice weak. "It has been some time since we've seen you. Tell me, how is your dear brother? I seldom encounter him these days."

"Well, ma'am, as you know he has been desperately seeking higher office to minimal effect. But he accepts his station in service to God with as much humility as he can muster." This was followed by smiles from both Earl and Abigail, as humility and Hubert Tompkins had not made each other's acquaintance in many years.

"You must come from Swansea more often. I cannot tell you how many times Sharon simply seems to pine for you when you are gone for so long." Abigail looked at him most seriously as she pushed a small piece of paper to the edge of her desk.

Earl surveyed this accounting for Sharon's pining and then reached into his jacket pocket for his billfold. He was irritated to feel something else which he was about to transfer to the other pocket when it dawned on him the initial reason he had come to Parker House.

"Mistress Edwards, I so apologize. I was so tired from my travels I failed to remember that this letter came for you at my office some time during my winter in London." He handed her the note. And the distinctive handwriting made the very poised Abigail Edwards lose her composure as she burst into tears. Earl Tompkins was quite confused by this uncommon demonstration of emotion from Mistress Edwards and realized that perhaps this strange malady that had ravaged her had somehow forced her to take leave of her dignity. He reached into his pocket, retrieving his billfold, hoping to complete his business and depart the presence of yet another overwrought, psychopathic woman, when she pushed his hand away and through her tears she breathed, "Mr. Tompkins, Sharon and I have missed you so, and we wish to say thank you for coming. Your money is no good here tonight. Please tell your brother I send my most heartfelt greetings."

"Yes, well ..." Earl Tompkins let whatever he had to say go, as he was sad to witness that before his very eyes Abigail Edwards had gone completely mad and lost her head for business. As he was being led to the door by Anthony DeWayne, Earl almost had a mild seizure when that tiny woman's voice screamed at the top of her lungs, "Nettie, get in here!"

The black woman sped by him as Anthony DeWayne took him to the door. He looked at the young guard and offered a bit of sympathy. "It's a challenge, I must tell you, to put up with my wife. I can only imagine what it must be like to be in a house full of crazy women."

Anthony shrugged his shoulders. "I don't give it a thought, guv. I just work here," as he shut the door on Earl Tompkins, placed his broad back against the double doors, crossed his arms and counted the minutes until he could go home.

Abigail was virtually hysterical at having finally received word from her long-lost, beloved son. Nettie, on the other hand, was panic-stricken when she first heard Abigail screaming, remembering the last time she had been this way, until at last she had become this shell of herself, that was until this very moment.

"God has answered our prayers, Nettie. Thatcher and Caesar are alive," She cried as she handed the letter to Nettie. She began to open the letter, but Abigail insisted, "Please call the girls and read it aloud."

"Abigail! Some of the girls still have guests. This can wait for later," Nettie reasoned.

"And do you want to be the one who explains to the girl who missed out on hearing about someone she truly loves while she's faking interest in someone else? Go knock on the doors and bring the girls here. Please!"

Abigail's shouts moments earlier had done part of the work, as the women of Parker House had already begun streaming downstairs to investigate. These last few years had been a very emotional experience for all of them, beginning with the loss and disappearance of Beatrice and Yvgeny, the killing of Terrance Higgins and the subsequent flight of Thatcher and Caesar, followed by a brief period of incredible high hope and new life to the very pits of despair when they thought they were going to lose Abigail. This family of women felt the beating of each other's hearts, no matter how loud may beat any other racing heart in proximity. Nettie made her way down the hallways, knocking on each of the doors and telling the girls to go to the library immediately. After making her way back down the last row, she hurried down the stairs, physically moved Anthony DeWayne to the foot of the stairs, pointing her little finger in his very big face and cautioned, "No one goes in or out of this house without paying!" as she returned to the library, which was abuzz with energy, excitement and a bit of fear. Nettie closed the library doors behind her and stepped to Abigail, who was both laughing and crying into her hands. Nettie picked up the letter, shushing the women, and began to read.

"My dearest Mother." At those words, the women began to scream with joy, for they knew that Thatcher was alive, and with Thatcher being alive, it was easy to assume, so was Caesar.

> *Forgive my poor hand as the light is dim, but I wish to dispatch this note to you before my boat makes the next tide. I wish to tell you your sons are well and that we think of our mothers and our treasured ladies every day. Ours has been a long and circuitous journey, carrying us to points on the globe you could scarcely imagine and at this time I do not have the capability to detail. Just know that we are well and hope one day to find our way back to Bristol to you and to all those women who carry a piece of our hearts and sustain us through the most trying of times.*

> *I had hoped to make such an announcement under more appropriate circumstances. However, as time and distance preclude my capability to do so, I wish to let you know that I have met the most amazing young woman I could ever have imagined. She is a merchant's daughter here in Philadelphia in the Pennsylvania Colony, and I took her as my beloved wife. Her name is Melanie, and she is almost as beautiful as you, Mother. I can say that she embodies so many of the qualities of you that have made me into the man that I am today, and most wonderful and endearing of all, she has your eyes.*

> *When time permits, we will make sail for Bristol so she can meet my mother, my Nettie and all those wonderful women of the House, about whom she has heard so much. I know you will like her, Mother, for though her ways are different than ours, she shares something with us that few we know possess – sincerity.*

> *I must go now as my beloved is about to stir, and I must alas bid her good-bye as our ship makes sail for more distant ports. Know that*

your love spans these many miles, and we carry you, each of you, with us
wherever we may go. And may Providence and the winds carry us home
to you soon. Yours &c., Thatcher.

At the bottom of the note, scrawled in a simple hand, were just a
few words:

If he loves me even half as much as he loves you, I am the luckiest
woman in the world. – Melanie Edwards.

The women of the house were silent but tears fell like a Bristol rain
as at last a moment of joy had come to a very sad Parker House. And
while each silently bore just the smallest measure of jealousy that
Thatcher had finally found one that made him truly complete, it was a
momentous occasion, and they knew she must be an amazing woman,
for they had raised him right.

Nettie gave the ladies a few moments to hug and celebrate, then she
immediately shooed them out of the library, reminding them there was
still business to conduct and to do so in tribute to Thatcher and
Caesar. Nettie returned to the library and found Abigail completely
wiped out from the overwhelming moments of emotion. She closed
the ledgers, locked the drawers and gently lifted Abigail to her feet,
taking her upstairs to undress her and put her to bed. She lay next to
her and stroked her hair and reminded her that this was the news that
she had feared would never come. After she rested they would discuss
it more. As soon as Abigail was asleep, Nettie quietly left the room,
returned to the library where Mr. Dinkins sat quietly and patiently
waiting. Nettie sat at the desk, opened the ledger and asked him how
pleasant his evening had been.

After the last customer had gone home and Nettie had attended to
the distribution of clean sheets and retrieved the soiled, stacking them
in the kitchen, she made her way to her room, sank to her knees and
silently wept and thanked God for having answered at least one of her
prayers to the affirmative. And then she gave a word of thanks to the
ancestors for having protected their child Chasaa.

Answered prayers had been few and far between these last few
years, and as ridiculous as it may seem Nettie could not help but sense
that somehow, those many years ago when she brought violence to
Parker House, she had unleashed an evil spirit that lurked in the
darkest corners and shadows, intent on bringing misery and pain to
everyone she loved so dearly. Abigail's whirlwind trip to London to see
Peter was something that Nettie knew had to be. Since those first days

when Abigail had rescued her and her son from the clutches of slavery, an inextricable bond had formed between them that words were incapable of describing. Perhaps it was those long weeks when Abigail spent night and day working to save the lives of her and her child, when she poured so much of her heart and soul and passion into making these lives the most valuable ever. Nettie never talked about Malagasy things and ways with Abigail, as it was difficult to translate into these rough and unimaginative English words. But Nettie had a sense of things about her that had been with her since she was a child. When she looked at people, she didn't just see the person, she saw something else – colors and shapes that told her their natures. The darkness of those men who abducted her and her child, who assaulted and molested her during those long months on that passage, put forth a pure, pale black that she had believed no light would ever penetrate again.

But that day, in the slave sheds, when she had called to her ancestors to spare her and her child a life of slavery and to take both of them, a voice told her to look up and see their answer to her plea. And there, in that filthy, noisy, chaotic environment, was cast before her the most brilliant and beautiful light that seemed to diminish every aspect of darkness that had enveloped her and, she believed, claimed her soul. A young girl, not even a woman, reached through the pen beyond the filth, touching her and telling her everything would be fine. When she awoke, she and her child lay here in this bed, and that young girl and her brilliant light illuminated the room and said simply, "See?" And she did see. She saw clearly that every bit of pain and suffering she and her child had endured had been necessary to lead her to her soul mate. And it was only the strength of that soul, that sharing of her inner light, that brought this woman and her child back from the brink of death. It took her quite some time to understand this whole English concept of "freedom," so different than the freedom of her people. When at last it translated to mean that she was no longer obligated or bonded or property of this child who had purchased her freedom, she could not explain that there was no amount of freedom that could release her from her bond to this girl. She knew that for the rest of her life she was committed to this child, for her gentleness needed the complement of Nettie's ferocity.

She was at a loss those long months when Abigail had sailed off to that faraway country and only became truly whole again when she returned, bringing her a new responsibility to care for, and that child she bore possessed a rare quality of both light and darkness. While there was a sweetness of his spirit and a kindness to his mannerisms, she could see from the beginning the darkness that resided in the shadows of that light. As he grew and took on the ways and airs of their beloved Yvgeny, his honesty, his compassion, but likewise his ferocity, she believed that perhaps that darkness that she had brought into this home would not touch him as she had feared. But when he, too, ventured off to that faraway place where he had been created, he had brought back with him a greater amplification of that darkness. Losing Yvgeny and Beatrice only made the darkness more palpable, and his attraction to the violent ways also touched the darkness in Caesar, and she could feel the light of both of these boys slipping away. For Thatcher was merely the source; Caesar was the amplification. The manifestation of that violence, taking first the life of that man in the warehouse and then the man upstairs in his mother's bedroom, showed that the darkness was where Thatcher preferred to reside and, likewise, where Caesar would dwell.

Their sons' absence did not take away the darkness or allow Abigail's light to shine, for that brilliance had begun to dim as Thatcher's darkness began to grow. And when Russia called, despite Nettie's belief that no good would come of it, she knew that, good or evil, there was no stopping fate. So she surrendered to it and hoped that Abigail could confront it head on. Perhaps this opportunity to face the past would give her a chance to let that light shine again, and when she returned it veritably beamed. Even before Abigail knew why her light shone so brightly, Nettie knew. Before that first bout of morning sickness signaled the obvious, Nettie could feel that presence, and it finally dawned on her what made Abigail shine – when she was giving life to darkness.

When Abigail realized that she was pregnant, her first response was to laugh. Having grown up in a home where giving up oneself was done frequently, daily, here she was a woman, now in her mid-thirties, having only given herself to two men, both brothers, both kings, and from each she had conceived a child. She had already decided that if there was any way, Peter would never know, for this was not about the Romanovs or Russia. This was about her child, the child she was intended to carry. And her pregnancy was picture perfect in every way. Rather than draining her and making her feel sickly or burdened, she felt lighter than air, and the women of Parker House were delighted to have one more chance to bring up a child with the unique flood of love they, who would likely never bear children of their own, could give. The debate was whether this one would be a girl and how girly they could make her. But of course, many secretly wished deeply for yet another boy to help fill the absence of that child they loved so much.

Bristol's winter came early and deep, and the snow and chill that permeated throughout the region kept Parker House relatively quiet. The women, now quite adept at their seamstress skills, brought to life by that distant dream of a new life in America, now took on a wholly new purpose as endless bolts of material were delivered to Parker House and every piece of fabric in the warehouse below had been carefully scrutinized and picked over. The house overflowed with new clothing, perfect for the coming child, no matter what sex it may be.

It was deathly silent in that early morning, when Abigail woke with a scream. The baby was expected any time, and hearing the sounds of impending labor, each woman performed her carefully rehearsed role, both to assist and to stay out of the way. As Louise went to the stove to begin heating water, Nettie climbed the private staircase that spiraled from the kitchen to the family quarters carrying a lantern, the first of many that would illuminate the room in the coming hours, Nettie opened the door to Abigail's room and allowed the incandescence of the oil lamp to fill the room. She knew what Abigail needed to hear for reassurance, but she was not prepared for the sight she saw, for rather than the expected straw-colored water, the bed was covered in dark, black blood. Abigail lay there with her hands and arms covered in her issue, and between her legs Nettie could see the cresting of a dark black head, its skin as dark as the hair upon it. It took her a moment to gain her composure, and then she turned to Allison Simms and told her, "Just you, and I need you strong." The two women closed the door, allowing only that one lantern to provide basic illumination. Allison laid Abigail back upon a mass of extra pillows stored in the room for this occasion, and then she raised a fresh sheet, which she stretched in front of Abigail. Nettie came around for just a second, placing her hands on Abigail's cheeks, and said, just as she had said to Allison, "I need you strong." Abigail studied those strong black eyes, knowing that this was not good. Nettie returned behind the sheet, and Allison bit her lip, doing everything she could not to cry. She tried so hard to be a source of comfort for Abigail, but she knew that she was failing, and Abigail turned to her, placed a hand upon Allison's head and said, "We'll be all right," as the wave of pain began to grip her abdomen, and behind the sheet Nettie said, "One strong push." The intense and ferocious pain that overcame Abigail as she delivered that long dead child spared her the moments to follow as she lost consciousness.

Nettie cut the umbilical cord, wrapped the child very lovingly and carefully into a small blanket made for the occasion and, before covering the face, gave it one small kiss to say hello and good-bye to the world it would never know. Tears were streaming down Allison's face, still holding the sheet to bar Abigail's unseen view of the grisly scene, as Nettie passed through the knot of women standing at the door. She gave only one comment in passing: "Get those sheets off the bed, and I'll be back momentarily." She carried the child down the stairs and into the basement to a small crate that sat in the corner. She would attend to this later, but right now she needed to get back to those women and help them deal with all the things they were feeling.

Abigail had no idea how long she had been out, but long enough for the women to strip the sheets, clean her, lift her up, remove the blood soaked mattress and replace it with one from an adjacent room. Sitting at her side was Nettie, with a look of sincere love and compassion. She didn't need to ask what happened, but she needed one question answered, a question Nettie already knew.

"It was a boy."

IV

The trip south through the Atlantic was exceedingly treacherous for a lone ship with an unfamiliar flag, as tensions began to reach a fever point between England in their short-term alliance with Spain. In 1697, after years of never-ending conflict between France and England over the recognition of the Protestant William I, formerly known as William of Orange of Holland, as King of England – a minor point of contention with France as for nine years they had chosen to recognize the Catholic James II – a treaty was signed at the Hague with France formally acknowledging William and thus bringing an end to their conflict. With this also came peace with Spain, now under the sphere of influence of King Louis XIV of France, whose armies dominated all of Europe.

It was with this reality that Thatcher and Caesar realized that flying a flag as a flotilla of one did not give them the safety of numbers, and so the Russian flag came down as they sailed off the coast of Africa, and the Union Jack was hoisted as they rounded the Cape of Good

Hope. Pressing a ship and crew this hard and this far was an act of insanity, and in some cases suicide, as men and ships, no matter how seasoned and salty they may be, needed land every now and again. But the fear of falling prey to the same false promises of safe passage that had led to Kidd's doom, a promise that had led to the imprisonment of their friend Darby Mullins, motivated them to take the chance and push on to Madagascar. They followed the reverse of their course to America, heading south, far from the southwest coast of Africa, dipping way below the Cape and turning due east along the 20th parallel. Once again, the insane and conflicting winds where the two great oceans converged threatened to tear the ship apart, but for a week they maintained that course with a steady resolve. After seven days, they altered their course for due north with steady winds and manageable waves, and despite the vast emptiness of the Indian Ocean, they spied the Madagascar coast on the 1st of November. The Malagasy, near starving and desperate for a touch of home, disembarked the moment the ship made ground and disappeared without a word into the wilds of their homeland. Thatcher knew he had asked much of these men over the last few years, and they had never denied any request. They had put to sea without any modern nautical skills, been subjected to the punishment of those vast intractable oceans, had been thrown into the wilds of America and the alien realms of the colonial cities, and they were no doubt tired and ready to call it quits. Thatcher was certain that he had lost his crew to the unspoken lure of homesickness satisfied, but Caesar smiled at him and said, "Trust them. They are home, and they feel familiar ground under their feet. They crave the taste of zebu, but they know the mission is not over. They'll be back."

Unlike Europeans, the promise of gold held little weight with these Malagasy, for their loyalties were not to the contents of the chest but to their Captain of this ship, and within a week the crew began to make their way back from the jungles to their ship and captain. Within two weeks, the entire complement was well fed and ready to complete the few short days of sailing to St. Mary's so they could honor their word to Chasaa. The worn and tired *Phoenix* traveled up the eastern coast of Madagascar and made short work of returning to its homeport.

From his rampart at the highest point of St. Mary's, Edward Welch had a command of the surrounding seas that gave him ample time to prepare for any contingency. Countless times he had questioned his sanity to outfit a ship with all his treasure and most of his cannon to a novice crew made up of an enthusiastic teenager, his slightly older black companion and a cult of worshipful Malagasy. He had plenty of reserves of gold and silver to sustain him, to rebuild his stock of pirate goods at amazingly low prices, and the loss of this ship to piracy, greed or the Royal Navy would hurt but not destroy him. He hoped his threat that failure to return would not only launch a slaving mission against Madagascar that would put all others before it to shame, but would also see every village in the area burned to the ground and what could not be sold would be put to the sword, would motivate them to fulfill their contract. He hoped this would be sufficient insurance, but men and gold quickly discovered that conscience can stand between them and is always the first casualty of this *ménage a trois*. So it was to his pleasant surprise when his spyglass oriented south, and he saw approaching the battered and bruised and unmistakable hull of the former *Adventure Galley*, now dubbed the indomitable *Phoenix*. He sent his men to meet the ship when it dropped anchor in St. Mary's channel.

Thatcher and Caesar were certain Welch had seen them arriving and were prepared for the honor guard that met them. As the anchors were being lowered, so were the longboats, and from the shore these men could see the twelve large chests being lowered into them. Not wishing to signal any hostile intent, the Malagasy crewmen lowered their weapons and allowed the ship to be boarded to assure that every chest had been removed from the hold and the Captain's Cabin and any other place where a coin could be hidden. Satisfied, Thatcher and Caesar led a contingent of their crewmen, under the watchful eye of Welch's men, as they toted those heavy chests up the narrow, four-mile path to the "Little King's" fortress. Not wishing to appear excited, Welch busied himself with a sumptuous meal served up by his many Malagasy wives and casually waved the contingency into his well fortified home.

"Well, gentlemen, it's been nearly two years. I'd given you up for dead, or soon to be dead," Welch offered, waving them into chairs across from him. Caesar motioned to his crewmen who carried the twelve large burdensome chests to bring them in and set them down next to Mr. Welch. Welch tried not to appear too impressed by the sight, and he continued to eat his meal, offering his two guests wine and food. Thatcher and Caesar declined, but responded by placing the ledger book and twelve keys on the table in front of Welch.

"You will find here, sir," Thatcher indicated as he began turning the pages, "an inventory of every item you entrusted to us, including your estimated value based on your understanding of the market. You will note here, where we made a trade for two cannon, adding these items to our cargo. This, sir, is what we sold the bulk of our merchandise for to the merchants of Charleston. And then finally, sir, the disposition of the remainder of our product in Philadelphia. You will note, sir, here, your estimation, and you will note here, sir, the reality of our success."

Welch casually perused the numbers and tried not to let his eyes bulge too significantly, as he noted the difference between his estimation and the final actual sale and the appreciable gain these two young men had made. The return on his investment anticipated at two-to-one. In reality, it was ten-to-one.

"And finally, sir, you will note here that the following amounts, the agreed to shares for Mr. Parcrick and myself, have been deducted from the total amount – minus expenses which I must tell you, sir, we kept to a minimum – these final totals indicate the crew's shares and at last your remainder as owner of this ship and financier of this venture." Thatcher at last pushed the twelve keys forward to Mr. Welch and smiled as he said, "I hope you find it to your satisfaction, sir."

Welch studied the numbers for a second, and his eyes kept turning to those keys that were covering part of the numbers. Then he leaned back in his chair, smiled at his two companions and then asked, "So, how soon until you'll be ready to sail again?"

The Malagasy crewmen sat quietly and patiently along the gunwales of the now-battered *Phoenix*. Darkness had fallen, and yet they waited patiently, ever confident in their chieftain. Up the trail on which they had departed so many hours before, the first signs of torchlight could be seen as it snaked its way down those precarious heights until at last they could see their captain, Thatcher and their fellow Malagasy toting back four large chests. That evening, six zebu were slaughtered and the men drank their first sips of their native alcohol, toasting their captains and marveling that they had kept their word. In truth, the money meant little to them, for these men held no stock in these heavy coins that did not taste good. But what it showed them was that indeed there were honorable men in this world, and though they had no love for the sea they would follow these men anywhere.

The plan was to rest and relax for a few short weeks after the long and arduous journey, and then it would be back to work, careening the hull to scrape off a year of accumulation. They would dip into the ample supplies of Welch's sails and rigging and once again empty the stores of Welch's bargain warehouse, then seek out other ports where that entrepreneurial spirit was still a valued commodity. Of course, while not specifically discussed, Thatcher's goal was to make the next run a straight one to Philadelphia and back to Melanie.

Thatcher and Caesar had been at sea much too long this last cruise, and while their passions to prepare for sail seemed all consuming at first, the faithful work of the Malagasy crew provided them for more idle time than either would have imagined. As the crew refused to let their captains shoulder the bulk of the work, they had to contend with the constant parade of crewmen introducing sisters and daughters who wished to see for themselves this great Malagasy warrior and his European companion. The kindness bestowed upon them by these ladies may have begun with endless supplies of zebu and lemur and betsabetsa, an amazing potent concoction brewed from sugar cane and not dissimilar from rum, but in his cups Thatcher could not help but notice those beautiful dark-skinned women, with their long pendular breasts ever on display. And while Malagasy were certainly not shy about the concept of frequent and public copulation, there was a requirement that such entanglements required a marriage commitment, if only temporarily. Thatcher kidded Caesar, who quickly took one, then two, then three wives. But when he surveyed that lovely chocolate-skinned beauty that his carpenter kept insisting make his repeated introduction, he began to realize that marriage, in its true sense, was more about the deeper aspects of a relationship, beyond the skin and the flesh and the fleeting lust that any man may encounter. And while he may have initially attempted to shrug off the temptations and talk at length to Sataa about his lovely wife Melanie, he realized that this did not seem to bother her in the least and that it was good that T'atcha had such a wonderful wife so far away in Philadelphia – and that Sataa was certain she would not want him to pine and agonize without a suitable shoulder to lean on. And so, one night after one too many of those potent punches, he took Sataa as his wife. A week later, he added Banaa, her sister, and a cousin, Pelaa, and finally a friend whose name was difficult to pronounce so he just called her Madge. His four lovely wives, who made certain that his stomach was always full and his scrotum was always empty, made his pining for Melanie more tolerable, and there were entire days when he found he could barely remember her name. Caesar, on the other hand, never gave it a thought, as it was his understanding that any good chieftain with less than a half dozen wives was really not demonstrating that warrior prowess. He rounded it off to seven, figuring that if God could make the world in six he could make his rounds on these women in a week – and it would be good. These lovely teenaged girls, with their mocha skin and enchanting dark eyes, made them very tired in the morning and more prone to take up comfort from the heat of the day in the ample shade and the loving attention of their brides. So perhaps work didn't progress as quickly as it could have.

But as much as the damp heat of the tropical environment and these tropical women were intoxicating and a natural harbinger of idleness, it was time at last to begin the process of weighing anchor and beginning the long and arduous journey back to the colonies. And in truth, it had been difficult for Thatcher to surrender to such tantalizing slothfulness. Having been raised as a man of industry and productivity, he could only imagine what Yvgeny would think if he had seen his grandson being so unambitious. So on the 1st of April, Thatcher and Caesar accepted Edward Welch's invitation to one last dinner in his fortress before they made sail. Welch was surprised to see the few dozen Malagasy that accompanied these men and their wives to his fortress.

"We thank you, Edward Welch, for your kind invitation, but our men have come to us to secure one last provision before we depart," Thatcher stated as a small chest of gold was brought forth. "My crew wants to make certain that their families are provided for during our next long absence, and if I remember correctly you've still a number of cases of muskets and casks of powder and ball in your inventory. I wish to make a purchase of all you have to sell."

Edward Welch had long expected this, but he had his qualms providing so many arms for these natives who peopled the land across from his island. "You must understand, gentlemen, my reservations of making such a sale," he mentioned as he surveyed this hardened crew.

"You may take my word, Edward Welch, that my men ... my tribe will never bring one moment of concern to you, so long as you are of no concern to them. On this you have my assurance," Caesar stated emphatically. "Yours has been an uneasy alliance with these people, for they know the part you have played in so many of them being no longer with us. But they understand that Europeans think only of business and not the lives it affects. I tell you now, they understand this and realize it is in their best interest that you remain secure so that their husbands and sons remain secure. Edward Welch, what you have across the river will not be a threat. It will be in your times of need a private army."

Welch considered this and realized that what this young African said spoke for them all, for to them he was not some mere man but a great warrior to whom their fealty was assured. He took the key to his well-secured armory and turned the lock, lighting a lamp and gesturing. "Whatever you think is fair, gentlemen."

At first light, the entire complement of the *Phoenix* was decked out in their sailing finest. On their last trip they left as primitive warriors. This time, they left as professional sailors. The brides gathered in a sad and solemn lot as their tears flowed, watching their husbands make sail. Under their traditions, the moment their sails were out of sight their marriage contract was annulled. But the half-dozen children who would make their appearances over the next number of months would be a permanent reminder of the husbands that left them behind.

One word of news that had reached them as they made their way toward the Cape was that the tensions between Protestant England and its Catholic allies had been strained to the breaking point and that, while no formal war had yet been declared, English and Dutch ships viewed the flags of Spain and France as hostile. And so, this time around the Cape the Union Jack remained permanently affixed and, rather than the arduous journey of the past two sailings, this time they would make the Cape like Englishmen. In their cabin, locked carefully away, was one sign that Thatcher had not been completely idle these long months, for carefully scribed were his bills of lading for his customers in Philadelphia. While not actually penned by them, he was certain that this cargo, "purchased" from the East India Company in Bombay at the behest of their colonial customers, provided Thatcher and Caesar with ample cover to allow them to make port of call. As the King had issued blanket Pardons to dozens of their most hardened pirates, and as their greatest fear, Captain Kidd, was now awaiting trial in Newgate Prison in London, and as Captain Avery wandered the streets of Dublin a free man, despite his horrid depredations, they felt a new confidence that they need not hide at sea but rather in plain sight. They made port at Cape Town to provision with stocks of fresh meat and fruits and ample supplies of water and wood. Their documents, carefully scrutinized by the Dutch Royal Navy officers that garrisoned the port, passed muster without the slightest reproach. In less than a week, the *Phoenix* began that torturous but comparatively short rounding of the Cape. They had fallen in line with a number of merchants, under the protection of a contingent of British Royal Navy warships, giving Thatcher and Caesar the oddest feeling of respectability. While their strange ship drew a number of curious stares from the captains of their escort, as Thatcher explained one evening over dinner, "She was designed in Goa for the Portuguese merchants that carried trade on behalf of the Mogul. But alas, her dealings with less reputable types led to a seizure and sale by the East India Company to our owners, who of course saw a perfect opportunity, though desperately lacking respectable men to sail her. Thus, our only option was to crew her with seasoned Lascars and these few poor wretches we picked up in Cape Town. While she may not feel like a wholly English ship, to hear the English tongue being spoken at least gives me a feeling that I'm in service to my motherland."

"And it is on that note, Captain Drummond, that we must appeal to you for some of those hands on your crew," stated Captain Cooper Wade of the HMS *Greenwich*, a 54-gun fourth rate ship of the line. "So many able bodied seamen made sail to England, and thus my crew is short. As much as I hate to do this to you, I'll need no less than twelve of your men."

Thatcher thought of his complement and those ten men he had brought aboard his crew to give him English cover. "Captain, I, too, am undermanned, and the best that I can part with would be eight, at most," Thatcher replied most earnestly.

"Let's split the difference with ten and call that fair, shall we?" Captain Wade offered in compromise.

Thatcher shook his head in acceptance as he raised his glass to the Captain. "You drive a hard bargain, sir, but who am I to say no to England?"

The drunken sots Thatcher had recruited from the taverns and constable of Cape Town was at first a gesture of sympathy for these land-trapped men who had been cast off some of the worst pirate ships in Africa. But his generosity was now being rewarded, as none of his men, his true crew, would suffer at the hands of the English Navy. And at dawn, when the Navy longboats rowed out to the *Phoenix* and Thatcher endured the curses being hurled at him for allowing them to be pressed when there were so many Africans he could have given up, he simply shrugged his shoulders and offered in parting, "May your service to your King be as appreciated by him as it is by me."

With the Navy now off their backs, Thatcher and Caesar settled in for what they expected to be a very leisurely cruise. However, as the ship neared the northernmost point of its northwest African passage, one of the Malagasy in the tops spotted sails to their north. The eight merchant ships and their two Royal Navy escorts would not have been concerned for one or two sails off their starboard bow, but as the horizon expanded before them they ascertained that nearly twenty dotted the horizon. And as those ships grew closer, they could see the unmistakable crest of the Spanish sovereign.

While not in a formal state of war, their numerical disadvantage prompted Captain Wade to consider giving these Spanish a wide berth. And as their presence grew larger off their starboard bow, they could now see that their two Royal Navy ships, the *Greenwich* and the fourth rate *Defiance* with only 64 guns, were no match for the six Spanish brigs-of-war, and they poured on full sheets to expand the distance. The English convoy grabbed their wind and tacked a west-northwesterly course to carry them away from the African coast and into the open Atlantic. Once they reached the western tip of Africa they would sail due north toward England and, after escorting their convoy of merchant ships to the mouth of the Thames, with any luck find the other four ships they were ordered to link up with as part of a squadron under Vice-Admiral John Benbow sailing for West Indies. With the wind to their back, they had the advantage. The Spanish fleet saw them, altering their course to a west-southwest heading intent to intercept the English. But in these waters of unpredictable wind, advantage could change at the drop of a hat, and the steady northern wind that had first pushed them along now began to slacken and turn to the benefit of the Spanish. This put the *Phoenix* in a precarious position. They had an ace in the hold, but to make visible that leverage would not only make them a target of the Spanish but the English as well, for as far as anyone knew only one ship in the last few generations possessed the power of oars.

As the Royal Navy escort moved to provide a line of defense between their merchants and the Spanish, Caesar pressed his crew to lay on as much sail as was possible, as Thatcher attempted to make minor adjustments for the crew at the keel. When all hope seemed lost and the interception by the Spanish inevitable, the distinctive sound of ripple began to be heard in the sheets, and Thatcher could feel a gathering breeze in his curls as at last the *Phoenix* received the breath she needed. It was a begrudging seven knots, but enough to give them the advantage over the Spanish man-of-war that was focusing on their big, odd ship. Caesar ordered the lines drawn taut as every ounce of wind was wrung to keep those sheets unfurled, and the chase continued into the night, as a lone brig piled on her sail to give chase. Caesar ordered half the crew down into the hold and told them to stand by the sweeps as the darkness began to gather. In the last remnants of light, Caesar and Thatcher fixed their course, and before night could demand it every light on the ship was doused, for now this dark-hulled ship with only her sheets to betray her virtually disappeared as the dark of the moon provided them one more amount of cover. On command, the ports were opened as a unit and out came the sweeps, where every man not needed on a line or sail, including Thatcher and Caesar, took to the oars and began pulling the *Phoenix* as if she were a coastal canoe. This little advantage of backbreaking labor added two knots to their speed, and, over the course of twelve hours, gave them twenty-four miles more distance than sail could ever give them. And as first light began to break and the watches in the mast swept the seas for signs of their pursuer, they were greeted with the pleasant relief that far over the horizon the Spanish man-of-war had lost her prey and the *Phoenix* her warship escort.

They pulled in the crew for congratulatory toasts of rum and to beat the men to breakfast. Their sheets remained full, and they felt as if they had proven the capabilities of the *Phoenix* as they began to contemplate correcting their course for a more northerly swing. But just as they were preparing to tilt their tiller a few points, a watch in the tops signaled the return of that press of Spanish sail. The option of sweeps was not theirs for many hours to come, so every man did his best to get whatever he could out of his section of sheet, but it just didn't seem to matter. The Spanish captain had the advantage of the wind as his ship continued to close the distance between them. These games of cat and mouse were common in the broad seas, but the persistence of the Spanish man-of-war seemed out of character, abandoning his station to protect his merchant fleet. Caesar ordered they scan the seas for any sign of the *Greenwich* or *Defiance*, but each check netted the same negative result. Meanwhile, Thatcher had his eyes fixed firmly on that Spanish man-of-war, and her inevitable interception was going to happen long before the cover of night. He looked up at that Union Jack, fluttering persistently in the breeze. Only a day before, that flag had been his security blanket. Now it could very well be a pillow smothering his face. There was no way they could outrun her, so Thatcher and Caesar met upon the quarterdeck to devise a different course.

Captain Jimenez had been intrigued by that ship since the moment her saw her. Having sailed for Spain these last forty years, he knew a galley when he saw one. That unmistakable hull and her low-slung ports were not designed for cannon and cargo. It was designed for sweeps, and, like the British captain who escorted her had suspected, he knew this ship fit the description of one that supposedly no longer existed. While not necessarily intending hostilities, his curiosity got the best of him, and as the remainder of the Spanish fleet continued their southerly course after running within cannon shot distance of the nervous English Navy, he was intent on investigating before he returned to Cadiz. And there she was. As he expected, she was still running. At first light, he had told his watches to keep a firm fix off the port bow, and, almost to the minute calculated, he caught her.

He studied that broad bow, streaming a solid west-northwest, and he almost began to believe that his eyes deceived him when he saw her sheets begin to slacken and then reposition, as her bow turned directly to him. She remained dead in the water for only seconds, then amazingly she was on a head-to-head course with him. *Well,* he said to himself. *It seems our English friend wants to test my nerve and resolve. Who am I to let him down?* He calculated the distance and figured he had time to drum his men to midday meal, and they began to descend from the tops to take their hard tack rations, washed down by good Spanish wine. He took his plate up to the bow to study the ship, and it took him a moment to realize that what his eyes were seeing was precisely what he suspected. He put down his plate, picked up his spyglass and confirmed that her ports had been opened and her sweeps deployed. It was an amazing sight, remembering how much he had thrilled as a boy to see the ancient galleys in their waning days. It was almost as if their captain was giving him a pleasant little remembrance of a bygone era, and he adjusted his course so that both ships' starboard sides would pass one another. He fully planned on toasting that captain as she passed.

Some of the older sailors returned to the riggings to watch this display of their nautical past. But the captain began to note another sign at those ports, and as a cannon shot's distance closed between them, those sweeps were pulled inside. It was at that moment it dawned on him what this English captain was up to. Urgently he ordered his men out of the riggings and into the hold and called for his gunner's mate to prepare for an attack. His crew was well-polished and disciplined, and he took pride in keeping his gun crews ever prepared, but no captain of a ship of warfare kept his guns at the ready, for sea moisture quickly crept into the powder, making it ineffective. His gunner's mate was screaming to the powder boys to begin passing up powder and shot as the gun crews on the starboard side made their cannon ready, preparing the tackle and the primers.

They were less than two ship lengths apart when once again this English captain did something most curious as he dropped the starboard bow anchor. Jimenez watched as the long chain and line ran out, the other ship closing on him. When they were within one ship's length, he screamed to his gunner to quicken the pace as the Englishman ran out his starboard side guns. Those black barrels were polished to a gloss, poking through their portholes. He could now see the captain of the ship standing at the starboard bow beside a tall African. The young man raised a glass to toast the Spanish captain as their ships drew alongside and a deafening broadside sailed in, the Spanish ship rising in the swell while the English ship dipped. Sixteen cannonballs slammed into the *Portillo's* hull just below the waterline. But what happened next Captain Jimenez could never have fathomed. As the smoke and deafening blasts rang in his ears, he heard the distinctive command of an English voice yell, "Brace!" That strange sight he had witnessed just moments before those cannon crashed against him had just proven its purpose as the starboard bow anchor found purchase on a rocky seabed. The huge galley slowly began to swing on its axis, dipping the bow and lurching her cargo, but driving the stern of that ship to the place the prow should be. And as that ship swung, Jimenez could see the row of cannon peeking out the port side, crossed himself and asked Mother Mary for help as those cannons blasted into the rear of his starboard and raked his stern. The captain looked up at his sails, still perfectly intact, a steady breeze carrying him forward. But down below his decks, as his gun crews screamed in agony from the blistering wither of two broadsides, his carpenters engaged in a desperate race to try to plug those twenty-odd holes, where the sea was pouring into his starboard side and stern. His last sight was the English captain taking a woodsman's ax and cutting that bow anchor as the treacherous galley began to tack north.

Thatcher could see in his spyglass that the *Portillo* began to list to starboard, obviously taking on a lot of water. But he had his own issues to attend to, as this little maneuver sent his starboard guns, freshly discharged, flying through the gundeck and ripping his cargo free below. As far as he knew, no one had ever attempted this stunt, or at least lived to tell the tale. But to him it was a simple case of mathematics. Caesar had been running soundings of the bottom for the hour or so as they closed in on the Spanish man-of-war, and they had a fairly consistent draft of fifty leagues and rocky bottom. They calculated the time it would take for the anchor to drop and roughly how long it would have to drag before it would find something solid to grab. Caesar sent whatever available crew he could to the hold to begin lashing down their cargo as tightly as possible and securing whatever may be loose in the ship that could serve as a projectile. They warned the men of what they were attempting, and if it worked how disconcerting it could be for them all, Thatcher and Caesar included. But if it didn't work, the least they could do was pop off their starboard guns, cut the line and run as quickly as possible before the Spaniard had a chance to give chase. They never expected that the first broadside would hit just as they rode opposite ends of a swell and that her guns would tilt to hit the *Portillo* at her most vulnerable second when she was most high in the water. When the anchor grabbed, no one was sure exactly what would happen, but when the stern began to make her turn and the *Phoenix's* guns seemed perfectly trained, they got off that second broadside and shattered a corner of the *Portillo*. Now her beautiful furl of sail was speeding her demise as those six knots of travel dragged her through the ocean like a sieve. Thatcher watched as her bow slowly lifted skyward, and before her crews could release the longboats, her stern began to sink beneath the waves. And that bow, so beautiful and so elegant, glided along behind her.

The thought of sinking a Spanish man-of-war for no good reason other than her opting to give them chase was an unsettling feeling for the crew of the *Phoenix*. And what had been an academic exercise in mathematical principles and a chance to test the capabilities of her guns had never struck the young captains that this was to be their first kill on the open sea. There was an instinct to want to turn back and find survivors, yet at the same time they had inadvertently created an unprovoked act of war between England and Spain, and to do the most humane thing, to attempt to rescue her crew, would likewise drag the King under whose flag they flew to the very brink of war. While they could not satisfy themselves with the knowledge that the captain of the *Portillo* would have done to them the same thing under the circumstances, they could rationalize that to do anything other than proceed north post-haste in hopes of intercepting the British convoy could at least give them cover when the *Portillo* was finally discovered missing. So they plied on all sail, making seven knots on what they thought would be an interception course. What they could not know was that the English flotilla had themselves proceeded westerly and no interception would be made. And they could not know that in these high days of summer the hot air of Africa was being pushed offshore by persistent western breezes, and those air masses were mixing with the warm water off the equatorial coast. The ensuing turbulence was generating a storm system that in days would be on a collision course with the *Phoenix*.

The squall lines were noted just as the sun was setting, and Thatcher and Caesar made ready for what they thought would be just another bout of windy, rainy days. Despite the pounding they had taken rounding the Cape, they were not prepared for what they were about to face as those ferocious winds began pushing to their starboard. The seas began to kick up the waves to towering proportions. They poured on as much sheet as they dared for fear these powerful winds and those gusts contained inside of her would tear the mast from the deck if given too much sail. Rather than trying to fight the wind, they made a course due west, hoping to use these massive breezes to push them away from the storm. For two days, the *Phoenix* cut the high swells like a knife at speeds the crewmen would never have imagined. Their western course saved both them and their ship, and as the winds and rains began to move off in a north-northwesterly direction and the skies began to reveal once again that miraculous blue, Thatcher and Caesar did their best to calculate where their ship had been tossed. The Malagasy had valiantly remained at their places on deck and in the holds manning the pumps, for the very sea herself seemed to want to claim every square inch of the hold with every wave that passed over her deck. They began to sight traces of land, though not the large broad masses of the continent for which they had been aiming. Instead, the persistent western winds and the small lush islands told them that had most certainly blown into the Caribbean. How far was difficult to tell, but the first small coastal boat they spotted was captained by a man who spoke English, telling them they were at least within the colonial waters of their home country. They hallooed the man to ask him from where he was sailing, and he replied, "Port Howe." They retrieved their charts and surveyed this long, narrow island along which they were sailing and determined that it had to be none other than Cat Island, which told them that by proceeding northwest to the northernmost point of the next island, following it around and correcting their course to southwest, within a day they would find themselves at New Providence.

It was July 6th, nearly four years to the day when Thatcher and Caesar had made port in New York under names they once again had assumed. There was too much baggage associated with the names Evans and Parcrick, for those names now sat on manifests that were no doubt in the hands of the Admiralty Courts. Their battered sails and masts gave every bit of service they could muster as they sailed into the broad port of New Providence, where Edward Drummond and Johann DeBeers began to go about the task of finding a shipwright with ample stores to put their ship to right. New Providence was a wild and teeming port that, despite her important placement on the edge of colonial England, enjoyed a unique status as a port without law. For generations, since Henry Morgan had settled into these islands after his conquest of Panama and the Spanish Main, they had become home to a breed of men who knew that the honor to be found among thieves was the only one to be trusted. While few Europeans dared set foot on these wild islands, these men had come looking for adventure and riches and instead found only each other. While to the outside world they may have been little more than lowlifes and the dregs of society, they had formed a cohesive community and family rooted in traditions of alcohol, women and quick but deadly money. These common bonds formed the basis of this society, where men often survived on nothing more than their capabilities to catch wild cows and prepare them over open pits, a method that the local natives had dubbed *boucan*. Their expertise in this common practice gave rise to their name, boucaniers, later anglicized to the term buccaneers. These buccaneers understood the hardship and the short life expectancy of such a hand-to-mouth existence, but it forged the bonds that gave birth to the Brotherhood of the Coast. On New Providence, with its absence of European law, came a new form of society, one based upon the honor-bound traditions these brigands had developed, whereby no man commands by title or birthright but at the will of those he leads. And despite the libertine nature where all things were permitted, there was a relative measure of peace and civility for those who knew best to mind their own business and to leave others to do likewise. And for a price, a man could find anything he needed or desired, no matter how much it was looked down upon by proper society. Yet unlike the civilized world, where men could not be trusted at their word, here a man's word was all he had. Without the ability to take a man at his word, it went beyond mere being distrusted. It could mean the very end of one's life.

Such simple standards would bring great fear to many men, specifically because their word meant nothing. But to people like Caesar and Thatcher, it was the perfect environment in which to regroup while making their ship once again sailable and for the Malagasy crewmen to walk streets free of fear of the slaver's lash. Throughout the remainder of the summer and into the fall, as the crew of the *Phoenix* went about preparing their ship to sail, they enjoyed the opportunity to spend their ample wealth, which had no real value to them in Madagascar except, of course, to buy overpriced goods from Edward Welch. Here these African men could imbibe in the Caribbean version of rum so favored by the men who came to St. Mary's, and they had developed an appreciation for that sweet, burning elixir very similar to their own betsabetsa. While there were many of their kindred sisters who offered up their wares for that gold in their pockets, there, too, was the opportunity to sample the goods of women with smatterings of European ancestry. Unlike the rules of Madagascar, no promises or pretenses of marriage were the least bit necessary.

While anything could be had for a price in New Providence, Thatcher and Caesar discovered that indeed those prices could be very high, and while they had set out with a small cache of gold for expenses, they soon discovered that the New Providence exchange rate quickly depleted their resources. In order to meet their needs to outfit the *Phoenix*, they changed their plans of offloading their merchandise in Philadelphia and instead began working the local tradesmen and merchant ships to seek buyers for their wares. But unlike the men of Charleston and Philadelphia, these merchants were much more savvy to the likely origins of those proffered goods, and Thatcher and Caesar, despite their best negotiation skills, found themselves parting with their merchandise for far below what they had anticipated. Likewise, these idle months, with all of New Providence's temptations, found them spending much more of that money on non-essentials. And as November rolled into December, they found themselves with a ship ready to sail but little money to supply her. This would not reflect well upon their business relationship with Edward Welch, and thus they decided that they must quickly discover a way to recoup those losses so, at minimum, they could honor their financial commitment to their business partner.

To these men who peopled New Providence, the answer was as simple as the ship they had so lovingly put back together. To their west and south lay Spain, and while the pickings may not be what they were in the great days of the Spanish Main, a man need only to greatly desire it, apply cutlass and musket to that desire and whatever he found was his for the taking. But Thatcher's view on piracy was still tinged with the loss of his grandparents, and while he may have been in the midst of the Brotherhood, enjoying the conviviality of their society, his desperation wasn't quite that strong just yet. But other opportunities were just on the horizon, as word from the colonies and Europe streamed in on every ship that the truce with France and Spain would soon be coming to an end.

It began in the French controlled colonies of Canada. The unresolved borders between the English American colonies and the French territories known as Acadia had been in dispute for years, and as more Englishmen streamed into the Massachusetts Colony, their numbers began to spread farther north, both into the woods that reached to the very edge of the St. Lawrence River and along the coast where Boston shipbuilders were ever churning out more boats to ply the ample fishing waters along that northern shore. More frequently disputes occurred upon the waters between French and English fishermen, often leading to bloody conclusions. This dispute between France and England was only amplified by events on the Continent, as the much feared demise of Carlos II, quite suddenly and without an heir, led to Louis' installing his grandson upon the Spanish throne. Despite their best efforts to find a suitable compromise, those efforts had now come to an end, and two wars – one in America and one in Europe – were about to engulf the English, the French and all those nations who chose to align with them. For many, this was the worst case scenario. But for the Brotherhood of the Coast, and for those like Thatcher and Caesar who were seeking out legitimate opportunities to put their ferocity to profitable use, it was a dream come true.

Chapter 6

In Service to Queen Anne
January 1702 – June 1703

I

Gods and kings would never have been possible if men had not been imaginative enough to invent monsters and devils. Since the dawn of civilization, when groups of people first bound together, it was done so typically as a means of providing mutual protection against the natural world. When they began to cooperate, to stop viewing each other as the competition and to use their superior brains to offset their puny bodies, they discovered their capability to elevate themselves in nature's pecking order. While humans may have found their ability to rest a little easier knowing that someone else was keeping an eye open for lurking predators, it became obvious to those who could provide a greater sense of protection that they could obtain positions of leadership and then, with time and manipulation, dominance over their communities. Such power was only achievable when a leader was able to convey a sense that life was better as a group, versus as individuals. To do so required creating something greater than themselves and convincing the masses that they spoke with exclusive authority on behalf of that greater thing, whatever it may be. But this trade-off of fealty was met with demands for better lives and better existences, which required leaders to constantly guide their people in new directions, ever expanding the circle of that community until eventually running up against the boundaries of another community, with a leader making the same promises. Killing one another became an important, albeit distasteful, aspect of humanity's rise to its dominant position in the food chain, for when men were merely scavengers they competed on a one-to-one basis for those minimal resources left over by more dominant predators.

But killing each other was such a human inevitability, for unlike the lower species which only kill their own kind defensively or out of the deepest starvation, humans developed the capability of killing one another for no other purpose than subtle differences. Those distinctions could range from the color of their skin to the choice of their deity, or simply because the presence of the other becomes intolerable. It was during these killing sprees, as tribes became communities, communities became territories, and at last territories became countries with imperial designs, an end to the killing could be periodically mustered. As boundaries were drawn, agreements made and alliances forged, leaders could then focus their time and attention on educating and instilling a sense of loyalty to themselves. During these periods of relative calm, such aspects as nationalism and dogma were instilled into entire generations so, when war inevitably returned, the subjects, these faithful, could be counted upon to rise up on behalf of their leader, who, as they had been so carefully trained to believe, represented all the aspects and embodied all the qualities of their nation or religion. And for the thousands of years of all the great national and religious empires, these kings and patriarchs, and later presidents and prime ministers, could always trump out that loyalty card, that pledge of fealty and allegiance to a flag or religious tome, to rally the people to the goals of their administration, under whatever pretext they deemed.

Of course, the most heartfelt loyalty to a land or a deity could not always guarantee the success of a military venture, particularly when faced with an equally strident foe of superior numbers or greater loyalty. While armed objectives could usually be accomplished with standing armies or the rallying of tribal clans, often kingdoms and holy empires were required to contract groups of professionals whose only loyalty was to the size of purse being offered. As far back as the ancient Greeks, groups of professional warriors began to find more value in their martial skills that could be brokered abroad, rather than returning to their homeland fields and trades to await the next great calling from their leaders. And so rather than splitting their time between lands and arms, they began to offer their services to neighboring kingdoms and distant powers desperately in need of skilled military experts.

The seas were likewise a battlefield, where typically ships waged wars of a mercantile nature, and for the early periods of European nautical history most ships were built specifically for the purpose of transporting cargo. But as the seas became more competitive and ships such lucrative targets to competing nations, it became necessary to likewise employ professional sailors with the capabilities and ferocity to protect merchant ships while putting competing flags to the bottom of the sea. In 1243, Henry III, King of England, became the first monarch to formally acknowledge this lucrative trade as a means of protecting his growing merchant fleet. He issued the very first Letter of Marque and Reprise to specifically "annoy our enemies at sea or by land so that they shall not share with us half of all their gain." And throughout the decades, though empires all sent to sea warships flying their nation's flags, there never seemed to be enough men and ships loyal to God and Country to effectively serve those commercial agendas of the great kings of Europe.

In the latter days of the 17th century, a general impasse had been reached in the Caribbean. Most of the nations with naval might had fairly well sorted out their claims to those islands and seaside colonies. As new tensions began to develop in Europe, so too, were they manifesting amongst the colonials who occupied these far flung sovereignties. Europe's great armies and navies had stretched themselves to the limit and could barely defend their claims abroad. England's King William reluctantly reached out to that particular breed of sailor whose loyalty was not to him but to the plunder to be gained from destroying his enemies. Thus, the call went out to all ship owners and their captains that England needed her private vessels of war to answer her call post-haste.

It could not have come at a better time as Thatcher and Caesar had reached the end of their gold and silver reserves in refitting the *Phoenix* and indulging their idle fancies. Here was the prime opportunity to put the crew back to work in hope of earning back Edward Welch's investment. Sitting in New Providence harbor was a like-new man-of-war, still rich with her forty cannons but poor in stocks and provisions. Caesar and Thatcher went about making her ready the only way they knew they could. Caesar polled his land loving Malagasy for any amount of money still left over from their personal shares from the last venture, while Thatcher sought out Ellis Lightfoot, the Governor of the Bahamas, in an effort to obtain a privateering Letter of Marque. There was one obvious problem: at twenty-one years of age, Thatcher Edwards was much too young to command a ship – on paper anyway – and the other captain had the misfortune not only of being young but also of African descent. That such a crew could achieve one of those heralded Letters of Marque was an outside chance at best, so Thatcher did what he did best when he met with Governor Lightfoot. He told him a story.

"I appreciate your time today, Governor Lightfoot," Thatcher began, as he was shown to the Governor's office in his royal mansion overlooking the beautiful harbor of Nassau and its ugly collection of buildings below.

The Governor appraised this cocky youth, whom he had been told was there to seek a Letter of Marque, and he could not help but be amused that such a young man could think himself seasoned enough to obtain such a commission. While his time was short, he was amused by his earnestness. "Young man, I'm very busy, you know. While our King is issuing a limited number of Letters of Marque, it is obvious that we do so only to those who actually have a fighting chance of being effective. While England appreciates your enthusiasm, we simply cannot entertain the notion of providing a privateer's license to a mere youth. Besides, young man, where would you get the ship? Steal one?"

Thatcher walked to the balcony of the Governor's office and looked out to sea, and from his pocket he removed a spyglass and found his beloved *Phoenix.* "She's right there, sir," Thatcher indicated, pointing out his vessel standing at the mouth of New Providence Harbor. "She's the *Phoenix,* of late from the Red Sea station, where she was charged with protecting ships of the Great Mogul under contract with the East India Trading Company. Your chandlers and shipwrights can no doubt attest to the amount of money we spent in refitting her these last few months in your harbor, as she was quite battered from her actions in the Red Sea and her crossing of the Atlantic. You will see here, sir," he said retrieving a document from his jacket pocket, "From Mr. Thomas Penning of the East India Trading Company Post in Callicut on the Malabar Coast. Please note his letter of recommendation on the behalf of the *Phoenix* and her crew, and specifically on the merits of her captain." He handed the document to the Governor.

Lightfoot examined it carefully as he noted the seal of the East India Trading Company, which had been broken, but all aspects of the documentation looked authentic. He noticed the commendations of the captain, and they seemed both in order and impressive. "Well, that is all well and good, son, but again, while you may have a ship, you don't have a captain," the Governor replied.

"Ah, not yet, Governor, but I have received this from the Captain of the *Yorkminster,* which made port yesterday, as you see there in the harbor," he said, producing yet another document from his pocket and handing it to the Governor who likewise reviewed the paper and then looked up.

"This is most impressive, young man," the Governor said. "I'm pleased to hear your captain is en route. As soon as your Captain Drummond makes it to port, I welcome the opportunity to meet with him and discuss the potential of your privateering commission. As for now, young sir, all I can say is continue to enjoy your stay in New Providence."

Thatcher departed the Governor's mansion, having fully expected this outcome. He hurried back to Caesar to discuss the meeting with the Governor and to find out how much he was able to pull together from the Malagasy. The total was far from impressive and more than a little surprising for the typically thrifty Malagasy, but with this amount of money he figured he could resupply with enough staple goods to keep them at sea for six weeks with just a little money to spare. And with this extra money, they went captain shopping.

The dirt pathway that served as the principle "avenue" for New Providence was primarily lined with taverns and tap houses filled with that odd assortment of men that made up the Brotherhood of the Coast. Caesar and Thatcher prowled the establishments looking for one run-down old salt who might clean up well and be willing to pose as Captain Drummond. To make the task a bit more difficult, this candidate had to be able to write as well. It took them the better part of the day, but they found a few likely candidates, culled from a very specific and heralded breed of men: a falling down drunk with virtually no long-term memory and no particular reputation in New Providence.

Eventually three candidates were found and brought out to the *Phoenix* to begin the painful process of detoxification. Thatcher had written a very carefully thought-out script for them to remember, about forty-odd lines which would serve to answer any question the Governor may wish to ask. Each of them was working for the most valued of prize this type of men could wish for. For their time and trouble, each would be given twenty gold sovereigns, plenty to keep him quite drunk for weeks to come. The winner would get an additional fifty gold sovereigns and his own keg of rum, with a bonus of a cask of Madeira wine and his choice of New Providence's finest ladies to share it with. But this bonus came only if they walked out with the signed Letter of Marque from Governor Lightfoot.

The three were of a suitable age, all in their fifties or sixties or that indeterminate age that testified to a life at sea. Gene Downs had sailed out of the Caribbean for the last thirty years on a number of ships of no respect and had only one thing going for him – he lived to tell the tale. Tim Robispeu was a Frenchman who took to the sea in his teens and fell in with the Brotherhood of the Coast. He had served so long with Englishmen that he lost any hint of a French air or accent and had developed that odd patois unique to professional sailors. And finally, there was Morgan Thurmond. A sad story, Morgan, as he had worked legitimate merchant trade, working his way up to First Mate with great promise. But in 1693, with his first command of a merchant ship, the *Good Fellow,* he had sailed his ship from Charlotte Amalie on St. Thomas to Port Royal, Jamaica, loaded with molasses. He had gone ashore to celebrate his new command when the Port Royal earthquake struck, wiping out most of that nefarious and wild town, killing many of his crew and sending the *Good Fellow* to the bottom of Port Royal Harbor, still attached to the dock he had left it tied to. Having to write that letter to his owners, having to explain how a ship tied to a wood dock sank from a land-based earthquake, was difficult and frankly quite hard for him to believe as well. But the *Good Fellow* sat at the bottom of Port Royal Harbor just the same, and the owners began to circulate the rumor that Captain Thurmond had pirated their ship and cargo and was trying to use the excuse of an earthquake to cover his foul deed. This misadventure brought him here to New Providence, where for the last seven years he had spent his time reflecting in a bottle.

None of these men had any desire to return to the sea, but of all of them, Thurmond needed to demonstrate that he was a good captain, and after the crew voted, Captain Morgan Thurmond became Captain Edward Drummond. Thatcher had taken the few sovereigns left to find good material to make this down-and-out drunk look like a respectable sea captain, and having found just the right fabrics for his blouse and trousers, plus a decent pair of boots, Thatcher sat through the night sewing to make his actor look his part. Thatcher also had to take time to coach this captain's shaky hand to achieve a level of penmanship with a signature closely resembling the one he had penned for the ruse letter he had written for the Governor.

Just before the *Windward* made port at New Providence, a longboat from the *Phoenix* rowed out to the ship bearing a bundle of tobacco and a cask of Madeira wine for the captain, complements of the crew of the *Phoenix*. Captain Edward Drummond climbed aboard the *Windward,* taking his gifts to the captain, Robert Miller, who was a bit put off by this strange and unexpected visit. But after a long cruise from London, this fresh Virginia tobacco and Madeira wine would be nice repast to celebrate a successful cruise, as Captain Drummond told him of the *Phoenix* and how she was about to be heading off on a privateering mission. It seemed that Captain Drummond and Robert Miller knew someone in common – Captain Woodes Rogers, Sr., of Bristol, one of the partners in the *Windward*. Both had likewise in years past had many business dealings with an old Russian in Bristol, Yvgeny Thatcherev. Captain Drummond wished to have Captain Miller give his best to Captain Rogers when he returned to England and let him know he looked forward to dealing with him again soon. As the *Windward* reached port, Captain Drummond shook Captain Miller's hand and told him he hoped to see him again before the *Phoenix* sailed, but alas he had to meet with the Governor and would give Lightfoot Captain Miller's compliments as well. As soon as the gangplank had been lowered, Captain Drummond exited the *Windward* with a flourish, finding his young First Mate awaiting him at the dock. Mr. Edwards conducted him to the Governor's Mansion, where Captain Drummond penned a short note announcing his arrival.

As luck would have it, the Governor had been taking tea on his verandah overlooking the harbor and noticed the arrival of the *Windward*, and he had watched these two fellows make their way up the path to his mansion. As they drew closer, he recognized the younger from the week past and the apparent arrival of his captain. He awaited their announcement and had them brought in.

"Governor Lightfoot," Thatcher Edwards began, "It is my distinct pleasure to introduce the distinguished captain of the *Phoenix*, Edward Drummond. Captain Drummond, his Excellency Ellis Lightfoot, Governor of the Bahamas."

"They're saying great things about you in London, Governor," Captain Drummond offered as he heartily shook the Governor's hand.

"Are they, Captain Drummond?" Governor Lightfoot asked. He then turned to Thatcher and offered most kindly, "Mr. Edwards, I would like a moment, if I may, with your captain."

Thatcher bowed respectfully. "Why, of course, Governor. The Captain and I will catch up later. Sir, do you wish me to wait for you here?"

"No, that's fine, boy. Head on out to the ship, and I'll be along shortly," Captain Drummond said.

"Aye, aye, Captain," Thatcher responded. Turning to their host, he offered a quick bow. "Governor," and Thatcher dismissed himself.

"And so you come from London?" the Governor continued.

"Yes, sir, six weeks of beautiful wind and water aboard the *Windward*. I must say it's sometimes hard to travel as a passenger, but

Captain Miller and I enjoy a fondness for good Virginia tobacco and Madeira wine, so it made the passage and lack of command easier. But it's good to be back, sir, aboard my lovely *Phoenix* I saw moored at the mouth of the harbor."

"So, Captain, tell me about your experiences in the Red Sea,"

"Must say, Governor, the most boring duty of my life. It was my understanding the Red Sea was crawling with pirates, except for a few exchanges of questionable ships who seemed more inclined to flee than to fight or do harm to my convoys once they saw that warship and British flag. Overall, sir, a quite dull station indeed."

"Well, this letter of recommendation from Mr. Penning out of Goa ..." Lightfoot rused.

"Callicut, sir. Goa, as you know, is under the control of the Portuguese. We have a small trading station there, but Mr. Penning is much too important to be in such a miniscule post as Goa."

"Callicut, that's right. Well, then Captain, how familiar are you with our waters in the Caribbean?"

"Spent quite a bit of time here in the late 80s and early 90s with the merchant fleets, primarily running the routes between St. Kitt's, Port Royal and Bridgetown," Drummond replied. "But most of my time was concentrated running the coastal trade for the colonies out of Boston aboard the *Argus*."

"So you're familiar with the northern waters, then?"

"Spent a fair time running trade up beyond the mouth of the St. Lawrence, which I must say was chancy work with an English or Dutch flag."

"Oh, so you've flown under other flags, have you Captain?"

"Governor, while I am an English mariner, not everyone sees our Union Jack as a source of saluting. So as all good men of the sea, I have the wisdom to fly whatever flag must be necessary to get me from one customer to another."

The governor listened to the captain as he watched Thatcher disappearing down the trail leading back to the harbor. "Captain, you of course realize that I'll have no choice but to check to confirm your references," the Governor stated.

"Guv, you may do as you wish and feel necessary, but right now France isn't waiting to consult with references before issuing Letters of Marque to their privateers. So me and my ship will happily sit in that harbor as long as necessary until you feel satisfied about our credentials. But meanwhile, British merchant ships and fishermen are getting blown to hell in those waters off the coast of Massachusetts. So I'll wait if I must, guv. I'll leave my calling card and spend the valuable time with my crew."

"As for your crew ... I am concerned. It appears your young first mate is the only Englishman aboard and the rest are Africans. Do you not find that strange?"

"No, sir, I find it a rare opportunity to have a crew so loyal. Yes, I can flesh out my complement with plenty of out-of-work seamen, spending their time and money here in New Providence ... excuse me, my Lord, Nassau. Those of us from the old days of the region tend to remember her before the re-dubbing of our port in honor of our great King William, Duke of Nassau."

"Yes, there is this tendency to give a slight malign to the great honorific we've given to our island on behalf of our King, for I note you say New Providence without likely referring to Charles Towne," Governor Lightfoot offered.

"Governor, in this region there have been a lot of Charles Townes, and it's hard to keep them straight sometimes. We old-timers prefer New Providence because we know of which town we speak. But in answer to the question, sir, why the all-African crew – well, it's simple. I trust them. Except for this last year, I know what each of them has been up to and I know each of their families back in Madagascar. Crossing me means death to each of their kin. Can't say the same for these fine English seamen, many of whom would sell their mother for a pint of rum, providing, of course, they have a mother."

"And speaking of which, Captain ... after your long sail, I'm sure you're parched. Please, sit, and let me offer you a glass or two of my finest rum," the Governor offered, calling for his aide-de-camp to bring a decanter and a glass.

None of this was necessary, this inquiry into the *Phoenix* or its captain. As Governor and Suzerain of the Bahamas, Lightfoot could without pause decide to give his Letter of Marque to any man he chose, provided he promise to abide by the terms of the Letter. His Harbormaster made certain to copy every manifest of every ship arriving and departing, plus the nature of all business being transacted. In every tavern and on every dock, Governor Lightfoot had men on his payroll who kept him informed of all he needed to know. And what he knew of that young man and his ship, the *Phoenix*, plus this fellow whom he had recruited to play his captain, testified to the young man's intelligence and organizational skills.

As the rum arrived in a beautiful crystal decanter, Governor Lightfoot filled a crystal glass to the very rim. "Our very finest local rum, Captain. Please, try it and tell me what you think."

Thurmond eyed the glass, an expensive dark brown rum usually reserved for export to the finest houses of London and most assuredly typically out of the price range of a broken down old drunk like him. This past week of sobriety had been at times challenging, but the assurance of the payment at the end for one little letter from the Governor had made it well worth the painful drying-out period. Thatcher had warned him that the Governor might proffer spirits and that Thurmond's failure to handle such a situation carefully might result in a deal-breaker all around. Sobriety was the recommended course, but a chance to sample that wonderful exotic spirit, rare to his common palate, was just too much to refuse. And as he took a deep sip, closing his eyes and enjoying its smooth body and fragrant sweetness, he leaned back to answer the question now posed by the Governor.

"And while you're at it, why don't you tell me more about this boy?"

Thatcher made his way back to the ship, knowing full well that Governor Lightfoot was watching him for as long as he was in sight. For now it was out of his hands and up to Thurmond. As he sat on the gunwale, waiting for the longboat to arrive with Captain Drummond, he could only hope that the old sea dog had enough liar still left in him to hold up against the inquisition of the Governor. The men were roasting freshly killed wild boars that they had spent the afternoon hunting in the traditional method, and the sun had long set when at last Thatcher could see the longboat wag its lantern, indicating its return. It was obvious in how difficult it was for Thurmond to negotiate the rope ladder climbing the side of the ship that he had caved in to the one temptation Thatcher knew would be most difficult for him to avoid. Thatcher helped Thurmond onto the ship, where he stood uneasily with the rocking motion of the deck, and helped him find a seat on a nearby crate. He grabbed one next to him, pulling it close to Thurmond to read his face in the waning light.

"So how did you handle his inquiries?" Thatcher began.

"His questions were pretty much as expected," Thurmond slurred. "Tried to trip me up with a few questions about the Red Sea, but if your information was correct I should have handled them pretty well. He did want to know quite a bit about you and this crew."

"And was this before or after the rum?" Thatcher led.

"All during, my boy, all during. But there's a beauty of being an old drunk, 'cause it's actually easier to remember a well-concocted story when you've got a little bit of the taste to deaden the nerves," Thurmond responded.

"So you think he bought the story?" Thatcher probed.

"In all honesty, boy, not for a second," Thurmond responded, a look of resignation on his face. Thatcher sat quietly, contemplating the failure of his ruse. He was sure that Thurmond had given his all, but no matter how gifted he may have thought he was with drink, his experience with drunks was that they seldom possessed the prowess they boasted when under the sway of Dionysus. He was trying to give thought for his next plan when he saw the paper being waved under his nose by Thurmond. Thatcher looked down at the folded parchment and over to Thurmond who was grinning, most self-satisfied. Thatcher took it and asked expectantly of Thurmond, "Is this it?"

"One Letter of Marque, Captain Drummond. Now, where's my wine and whore?"

The deck of the *Phoenix* that night was the party of New Providence. With roasted pig and endless casks of rum, the men of the *Phoenix* had scored a prize of immeasurable value. And Thatcher himself rowed ashore to retrieve the lovely Shirley Darvis, a beautiful Creole woman with honey skin and light brown hair and charms that would wake the dead. That night Captain Thurmond had exclusive rights to the Captain's Quarters, for this night he was their captain and would enjoy every privilege and pleasure afforded the rank. In the morning, as Thatcher rowed her back to town, he breathed in that glorious scent of a night well spent and the very self-satisfied smile of Shirley Darvis, who in his mind was worth every farthing he spent.

When Thurmond finally poked his head out onto the weather deck, the sun high in the sky, he found Thatcher and Caesar making the ship ready to sail. They smiled at Thurmond, who was shielding his eyes from the light, and came over once again to congratulate him on a job well done and a prize well earned as they indicated the casks of Madeira and the fifty gold guineas.

"Now, dear Captain Thurmond, you need only indicate where we deposit you, and we'll certainly look you up when we return," Thatcher offered.

"About the deal, son … I must say that I never thought I'd return to sea, but this little venture of yours has me intrigued. What say you keep the guineas, give me my fair share of the daily rations of grog and rum, and let me come in for a crewman's cut of the take?" Thurmond proposed.

"You know the complications of this, Mr. Thurmond. You've been a captain, and you've been very long in New Providence under the rules of the Brotherhood of the Coast. As much as we would enjoy your company, we fear the influence it could have on the crew," Thatcher explained.

"I understand your concerns, young man, but unlike so many of my Brethren I've sailed only the pewter seas these last years. And I'm not asking for the captaincy or an adherence to the Brotherhood Code, only a chance to get back where I belong," Thurmond argued.

Thatcher and Caesar took a moment to discuss Thurmond's plea. There was a rationale in his argument, and though they didn't necessarily need Thurmond, his experience in these waters could be invaluable in other ways. Besides, he played this Drummond so well that perhaps there could be use for that in the future as well.

"All right, Mr. Thurmond. It's a fair offer you make," Thatcher replied. "But realize, this is not the hotbed of democracy you are so accustomed to. This is a very disciplined crew, so if you can accept the authority of this young Englishman and African absolutely, then perhaps we can make this work for all of us."

Thurmond was excited that at last he would be returning to the sea with a measure of honor, and he would indeed prove valuable in the future. He begged only for a chance to return briefly to town to retrieve his few meager belongings and would be back before the first turn of the capstan. Thatcher chided him not to make too many stops along the way and certainly not to breathe a word to his fellow men of New Providence, word of which he gave upon his honor, and he grabbed a boat back to port. He planned to make only two stops, the first to his ramshackle room over the Bloody Goat Tavern to retrieve his change of clothes and few personal items he kept hidden. The second was the home at the end of the long winding path leading to the top of the promenade overlooking New Providence. He was quickly shown in to meet with the man of the house.

"We sail as soon as the tide rises, Governor," Thurmond reported.

The Governor was staring idly out the window toward the harbor. Moments before he had let out through another door the owner of the Bloody Goat who had reported Thurmond's return to his room. "And what did he say when you told him I didn't believe a word he said?" the Governor asked out of sheer curiosity.

"That he had to come up with another plan. One that you might believe," Thurmond replied with a snicker as he helped himself to a glass of rum.

"Do you think he'll abide by my terms?"

"I think he's anxious to prove his merit, and if logic dictates I'm sure he will be quick to agree."

"When you've reached a point well away from here, give him this," the Governor demanded, handing yet another letter to Thurmond. "If he chooses not to agree, have him be so kind as to deposit you in Jamaica and grab the first packet back here."

"And if he chooses not to agree either to your terms or depositing me in Jamaica and I find myself swimming, what then?"

Lightfoot shot him a nonchalant eye, bored with the interrogation and unconcerned that Drummond knew it. "Well, then, I guess when we recover your shark-gnawed body we'll have our answer, won't we?"

II

On June 20, 1701, just before the afternoon tide rolled in, all hands were on the capstans raising their anchors, including the replacement one on the starboard bow. The *Phoenix* began sailing northward out of New Providence Harbor, catching a strong breeze that would carry her beyond the Bahamas chain and into the Gulf Stream, which Thatcher intended to follow to its northernmost point off the coast of Acadia. As the night watch settled in and before Mr. Thurmond took his place upon the bow watch for his hourly measurements of speed and depth and to read the ample stars for his northern fix, he ducked into the Captain's Quarters where Thatcher and Caesar were pouring over charts and feasting on leftover pig from the previous day.

"Mr. Thurmond, how are our readings?" Thatcher inquired as he entered the cabin.

"Strong and steady nor'easter wind, sir, good tides. I'll be running the log out momentarily to fix her speed and heading, but I needed to speak with you for a moment, if I may," Thurmond replied, taking the seat he was offered.

"Of course, Mr. Thurmond. What concerns you this fine evening?" Thatcher asked.

"Well, Captain Edwards," he began, but was cut off by Thatcher.

"Actually, that would just be Mr. Edwards. Captain Edwards will be who you wish to address now," Thatcher replied, indicating Caesar.

"Would this have anything to do with your visit with the Governor today, Mr. Thurmond?" Caesar asked, then explained, "My men, they're very distrustful and wished to make sure you arrived safely back on board."

"Yes, Captain, I did return to the Governor's mansion today, as it was his term of granting your Marque that I personally report your receipt," Thurmond replied.

"And what was the Governor's feeling of your report?" Caesar inquired, as Thatcher took a seat on the windowsill facing out on the stern.

"He's pleased that his disbelief only prompted more creative thinking," Thurmond replied as Thatcher snickered to himself. "And he wished for me to deliver this letter to Mr. Edwards."

"I think he wished you to deliver it to the Captain of this vessel, for you must understand, Mr. Thurmond, that while I may be the actor, Caesar is as much responsible for directing these little plays as I," Thatcher replied, indicating that the letter should be handed to Caesar.

Drummond handed the letter to Captain Edwards, who read carefully through the multiple pages. He then handed it to Thatcher, who began reading as meticulously.

"Well, it seems as if our Governor operates very differently than do most of his contemporaries," Caesar offered when Thatcher was through.

"So if I'm to read this correctly, only the following French ships may be targeted, and all Spanish ships we encounter are to be greeted with the Governor's flag and then ignored?" Thatcher questioned.

"While there's no formal hostility at present with Spain, and as many French ships serve Bahamas' interests as much as Spain's, he felt that these slight requests would not be too much to ask in exchange for carte blanche otherwise. And by that, sir, he means carte blanche. He's not too concerned about other flags, provided of course their colors don't bleed on him."

"This rendezvous he speaks of – he is assured that his standard will protect this ship from Spanish guns so close to their shore?" Caesar inquired.

"Gentlemen, I think I don't speak out of turn when I say yours isn't the first such request he's made. The Spanish are naturally jumpy when it comes to English ships and their proximity to Spanish vessels. Even now, there is concern as one of their ships in convoy to Cadiz mysteriously went missing when they encountered a northbound English convoy. Her seasoned captain and crew fell prey to something, and they're hoping it was weather. For no one in New Providence or any ship that sailed into her these last few months have reported any sign of her. And that is truly odd indeed."

Caesar and Thatcher looked at each other for a moment without saying a word. They had spent too much of their lives together to have to always verbalize their most important of conversations. After a moment of silence, Caesar turned to his crewman. "Well, then, Mr. Thurmond, it seems we need to make a new course," Caesar stated as the three made their way to the main deck to make corrections.

The Spanish ships which comprised La Costa Guardia tended to view any English vessel as yet another invasion fleet waiting to steal their Spanish gold, which they had rightfully stolen from the Indians. And how dare the English think they have a claim to it. Thatcher and Caesar had to admit they were slightly uneasy about hanging so close to La Florida, but the letter assured that if they followed protocol as detailed, their passage would be assured. It was less than a few hours' sailing when they encountered their first chance to prove the viability of this protocol. As the letter had directed, the *Phoenix* slacked her sheets and fired two shots from her bow chasers. The Spanish La Guardia Costa continued to press full sail as her captain spied that English flag flapping so prominently from her topmast. When they were about a league apart, the Spanish ship fired her bow chasers and immediately the *Phoenix* fired one stern gun, hoisted the Governor's flag and dropped anchor.

Captain Morelos noted the response to the protocols and likewise slacked his sheets and had his anchors dropped until the two ships were only a few hundred feet away from one another, their iron reaching for the bottom on this coral coast as both captains took to their longboats. Captain Morelos brought along with him his First Mate and Quartermaster, and Thatcher, Caesar and Thurmond made up the complement that joined their Spanish counterparts halfway between the ships. As the two longboats came astride one another, Captain Morelos studied these three men, two English, one African, and surmised who their captain might be, addressing the older one as he stated, "I am Captain Morelos of La Florida Guardia Costa ship *Esperanza*."

"And I am Captain Drummond," Thurmond replied, repeating the tip of the hat from the Spanish captain.

"May I ask what brings such a large warship to sovereign Spanish waters?" Captain Morelos inquired.

"Governor Lightfoot asked us to pay compliments to your governor in light of the recent unpleasantness between our country and your ally," Thurmond replied. "And we ask that you, Captain Morelos, and the *Esperanza*, serve as our escort to St. Augustine."

"Our governors do seem to have a respectable working relationship, and yes, the *Esperanza* will consider it our duty to convey you to Santo Augustine. Captain, you will maintain a position of no more than one-half league to my leeward bow at all times. And please, be so kind as to secure your ports while traveling in our waters as we will provide whatever security you need."

The two contingents of officers returned to their ships and continued their northern course along the coast of La Florida for their three-day journey to St. Augustine. While portions of this unique arrangement between the governors of La Florida and the Bahamas were beginning to unravel for the crew of the *Phoenix*, they could not understand the depth of relationship that existed in this unique triune with the Bahamas, La Florida and Cuba. All three governors maintained an extraordinary and similar relationship to their kings. Joseph de Zuniga y Cerda was the present governor of the colony of La Florida, whose capital at St. Augustine was fortified by the Castillo, a massive fortress that reinforced Spain's power in this area of the globe. Along with Governor Diego of Cuba, Zuniga and Lightfoot had forged an unofficial alliance, whereby each would respect the trade and commerce vital to their colonies, which at times required casting a blind eye to the less reputable aspects of some of that mercantile trade. While the Spanish and the English begrudgingly accepted the necessity of privateering, there were times when being very liberal in the application to certain aspects of a Letter of Marque, while likewise holding a firm rein to other terms of the agreement, could serve each of these governors in extraordinary and profitable ways. When war between England and France loomed – and by virtue of Spain's alliance with France these governors found themselves at odds - it was their hope that this successful relationship which the three governors had established would supercede these uncomfortable disagreements between William of England and Louis of France. True to the alliance, Governor Lightfoot agreed to counsel those English privateers chartered by the Bahamas of the delicate nature of their arrangement. And thus, the *Phoenix* found herself sailing past the massive stone citadel and into the well fortified St. Augustine port.

One of the first things that Caesar noted as he disembarked from the *Phoenix* was the omnipresence of so many black and mixed-race soldiers that made up the security detail of the Castillo No doubt, too, the Malagasy crew received wide-eyed attention, as black Hispanics in service to Spain took in the sight of black Africans sailing under the English flag. Thurmond, Thatcher and Caesar were conducted to the Governor's mansion, where Don Zuniga welcomed them into his palatial office with its magnificent view of the fortifications of the citadel, the star-shaped work of architectural wonder that truly demonstrated to them how unprepared England's colonial towns were should Spain or anyone else choose to assault or siege them. The Colonial Governor was a gracious host, welcoming these masters of the *Phoenix* to his humble but impressive town, the oldest European town in all the Americas. It was obvious he took great pride in what

Spain had accomplished, as he talked at length of the struggle to build and maintain Spain's longest permanent settlement in the New World.

"... which is why I am so honored my good friend Governor Lightfoot asked that you make this call to me. As Englishmen, you know how temporal alliances and enemies can be and how difficult it can be one day to face a foe and then the next day to view him as a friend. While we are not the ones charged with making these decisions, it is a fact of life and we must live with them. Governor Diego of Cuba and I are charged with a task of maintaining these important but distant colonies and to create a semblance of perpetuity and consistency that perhaps may lack back on the Continent. It is for this reason that we understand England's need to contract privateers to face her foes on the seas. But gentlemen, the seas are vast, and a foe is merely a matter of perspective."

"Governor Zuniga, Governor Lightfoot has made it clear to us that he is sensitive to the need to maintain trade continuity with his neighbors. We are not politicians. We are merely armed merchants in service to good business," Thurmond spoke on behalf of his compatriots. "Our only question is, who is not our enemy... at least from your perspective?"

"Ah, Captain Drummond, I am pleased you understand the nuance. We ask only that you realize Spain must honor its commitments to seek out those ships which pose a threat to our ally France, but again, this is a matter of perspective. While one may fly an English flag out of patriotism or commercial necessity, it does not mean that Englishman is necessarily a threat to France or Spain, does it?" Governor Zuniga reasoned. "And one can tell a friend or foe even across a vast distance with mere recognition codes, such as you followed here to meet with my captain on the *Esperanza*. And after your making Captain Morelos' acquaintance, did you feel threatened or in any way in the presence of a foe?"

"Most certainly not, your Excellency. Once we recognized we were in the presence of a friend, we were quite pleased with the lovely journey up your beautiful coast. So am I to gather, Governor, that, should I encounter any ship upon the seas that provides this same hail of friendship, I should merely salute and allow her to pass?"

"Precisely, Captain Drummond," Governor Zuniga smiled.

"And if such signals of friendship are not offered, one can assume the ship is hostile, regardless of the flag they fly?" Thatcher further inquired.

Governor Zuniga paced the room, his hands behind his back. "I cannot tell you who is your foe, Captain Drummond. I can merely suggest to you who is your friend. Naturally, you have to determine for yourself who your enemy may be."

The three men enjoyed a sumptuous dinner as guests of the governor and a wonderful night's rest in his palatial estate, and in the morning they were conducted back to their ship where their escort, the *Esperanza*, awaited. The *Phoenix* maintained her position as she had on the trip up the coast. And when at last La Florida was far from their horizon, the *Esperanza* fired her bow chasers, dipped her sails and began a hard turn to stern, returning back to her station off La Florida. Captain Drummond now resumed his role as Mr. Thurmond and took his place upon the bow, running the log and weight for speed and soundings as Captain and Mr. Edwards took the noonday readings of latitude and made a north-northwest heading across a wide expanse of the Atlantic Ocean, their destination firmly fixed toward the easternmost reaches of Acadia.

Their plan was a simple one. At present, France was harassing English colonies, and her ships that preyed on English merchants or fisherman were fair game – provided they did not give the recognition symbol to provide undocumented passport across this negligible water. On July 1, just west of the Bermuda coast, they spotted a sail in the distance, and the lookout kept a sharp eye and finger pointed for Caesar and Thatcher to train their spyglasses. She was a pretty ship and French without doubt. Her three masts and tapered body showed the sleekness of a schooner with a bulk of a brig, and she was riding heavy on the water. Caesar called a course correction to his Malagasy crew, and they began immediately trimming sail to obtain a course of intersection. This very obvious act caught the attention of the French captain, who likewise changed his course to run head on toward the *Phoenix*. Within a league, Thatcher ordered two shots from the bow chasers, but Caesar was hesitant to slack the sails until he received the response in kind. In seconds, which felt like hours, the *Foucault* responded with her bow chasers and began to slack her sails as the *Phoenix* responded with a shot from her stern and repeated the act in kind. Once again, as the ships dropped anchor two lengths apart, matching longboats met each other in the chasm, where Captain Briart and his mate and quartermaster gave a hearty greeting to Thurmond, Thatcher and Caesar.

"Salut, *Messieurs!* I am Captain Briart of the *Foucault*, and I see from your hail you must be of New Providence, *non?*" Briart began, avoiding the pretenses.

"And I am Captain Drummond of the *Phoenix*," Thurmond offered in response. "And your geography would be accurate. So may I inquire your heading and your mission? Or is that too much information for those of us under the arrangement?"

Briart liked this Englishman right away, for he so often hated the word dances that wasted time and energy when bluntness was much more effective and timesaving. "Very simple, Captain, I am nothing more than a humble merchant seaman, carrying goods from Acadia to our customers in the Caribbean."

"So we are to assume yours is simply a mission of commerce and in no way a threat to English merchants or our fishing fleet," Thurmond probed.

"Why, certainly not, Captain. These tensions are bad for business, and I am merely attempting to make my owners a small profit in honest commerce," Briart explained, a mild look of surprise upon the captain's suggestion. "And you, sir, if I may ask, what is your mission?"

"We're hunting French who pose a risk to our commerce," Thatcher offered, smiling at the French captain, who returned the pleasantry, appreciative of the young man's candor.

"Well, *Messieurs,* certainly by now you know friend from foe, so I will trust you to discern wisely. Now, if you will pardon me, I have customers anxiously awaiting my humble cargo."

The two groups bid a polite adieu and returned to their initial headings, but as the *Focault* began to sail out of visibility, the watch once again sounded multiple sails off the starboard bow. They were farther afield, but their formation suggested a military convoy, and there was no mistaking they were French and not a merchant ship among them. Outgunned and not desiring a scrap with this many ships at one time, the *Phoenix* tacked to port, giving a wide berth to the flotilla. But as the sails drifted farther to their stern, Thatcher's curiosity got the best of him, and he consulted Caesar. They agreed when the convoy was clearly out of sight they would follow to their rear and investigate their course a little more carefully. Their course carried them past the western coast of Bermuda and swung wide to the east of the Bahamas but continued sailing south along the Windward Island chain, where the six ships began to sail on Antigua. On July 6, the lookout saw sails heading straight to port, and as the ship came into view they could once again see their friend the *Foucault*. This time, however, neither ship offered the pleasantry of the bow guns but sailed a-port one another, slackening their sails as their guns ran out. The two ships slowly glided along each other's port rail, as Captain Briart and Thatcher Edwards took up speaking trumpets and began walking the length of their ships to communicate.

"Messieurs, I am surprised to see you have changed your course. Has your mission changed?" Briart offered innocently.

"Captain Briart, when you were a single vessel on a mission of commerce, our mission was clear. You, however, forgot to mention your five companions sailing in English waters," Thatcher responded as the two ships and their guns drew abreast of one another, as the two captains walked and talked along their lengths.

The gun crews gazed across the water at each other, the French faces staring curiously at the sober-faced Malagasy, who held their quick matches at the ready but showed no signs of uneasiness. In the middle of those sixteen portside guns of the *Phoenix*, out of view of the French gun crews, stood Caesar, quietly and patiently awaiting word from Thatcher on top. It would be a simple command: three raps of his foot, and the French would feel a broadside without remorse.

Briart smiled and shrugged. "Well, I am a man of commerce, but of course that comes in many forms. Perhaps I should have added that my client at present is King Louis and his grandson Philip of Anjou, the sovereign of Spain. As I said, I am merely a merchant, and these ships are my cargo."

"This is true, Captain Briart. In a certain way, we are all merely merchants," Thatcher stated as he stood at his port stern, watching Briart take a similar pose and size up the two cannon pointing out the stern windows of the *Phoenix*. "Let me introduce you to my cargo."

Thatcher smiled, saluted Captain Briart and gave a quiet yet distinct "Fire."

Both twenty-pound guns discharged their load of grapeshot, chain and silverware at the port stern of the *Foucault*, cutting her rigging and her captain to pieces. Thatcher moved close to his men controlling the whipstaff, the long pole hooked directly to the rudder, and yelled, "Hard to port!" The crew moved the heavy rod as far and as quick as they could to bring the *Phoenix's* port gun deck to the stern of the *Foucault*, now a site of chaos as the men on the port and stern had been raked by the shrapnel from the guns. The damage to her sails and rigging was merely superficial as the *Foucault* continued to steam away from the turning *Phoenix* and would soon be out of range. But as each gun came into view of the stern, Caesar ordered each gun fired one at a time until a steady cadence of balls slammed into the retreating *Foucault*, shattering her windows and scoring hits on her hull, the final shots striking at her tiller. Thatcher was using the confusion on board the *Foucault* to right his ship and give chase. With her captain now dead on her decks and crew scrambling to ply sail to the undamaged rigging and masts, the *Foucault* suffered from a lack of maneuvering as those last few shots had blown away the whipstaff from the tiller, meaning they had only their sails and the skills of their First Mate to take her out of harm's way. The French sailors hoped that the concussion of fire had carried across the waters to the other five ships. However, they had continued their southern course as the *Foucault* had peeled off, heading north to intercept the *Phoenix*.

Mr. Thurmond was demonstrating his talents at seamanship as he took charge of the sail crew, plying full sheet to take advantage of their unscathed sail and rigging. The sight of that full crest of sail should have been intimidating enough for the *Foucault*, but when her desperate crew looked behind them they saw a sight few would ever expect to behold. All the *Phoenix's* ports were opened and out came those long sweeps, which began methodically slapping at the water, giving her that extra one or two knots to chase down the crippled ship. The small bow chasers of the *Phoenix* did little more than harass the crew at the *Foucault's* stern, who were desperately trying to run out guns, but the continuous fire of grapeshot made the task of fixing those guns even more complicated and dangerous and inspired men to press their faces close to the deck rather than to place their heads in that deadly zone of fire. Thatcher directed the *Phoenix* to come to starboard of the *Foucault* where, the first moment he could apply a gun to her hull, Caesar began ordering fire. As each oar was pulled into its port, seconds later the gun took its place. Yet on the port side the oars continued to push, driving the nose of the *Phoenix* ever closer to the *Foucault*, nudging her bow into the hull of the French ship. As the port guns continued to blister the boards, those usually harmless bow chasers poured deadly fire into the sails, rigging and crew that populated the weather deck, now a hell of flying splinters and shrapnel. Thatcher stood between the bow guns, a boarding ax in hand as his Malagasy crewmen began to pour toward him to follow his lead. As the bow of the *Phoenix* slammed mercilessly into the starboard hull of the *Foucault*, Thatcher held the wood frames of the bow chasers to steady himself and brace for the jolt. The moment the two ships came to rest, Thatcher leaped onto the *Foucault*, swinging his boarding ax, in truth a simple woodcutter's tool, with deadly efficiency to anyone still standing on her deck. The Malagasy came across like a tidal wave, hacking and slashing at everything that moved. Caesar joined the fray, a saber in one hand, a dagger in the other, as he led the men into the dark, dank hold of the *Foucault*. The paralyzed French crew was in no mood to fight after such a blistering, brutal assault on their ship, and for those still standing surrender came quickly and easily as the African warriors seized control of the *Phoenix's* first prize.

The first order of business for the remaining French crew was to begin the gruesome task of dumping their dead comrades overboard. Those men experienced with sail and rigging now turned to making the *Foucault* ready to sail as quickly as possible. Matasaa, the *Phoenix's* gifted carpenter who had learned about ships on the shores of St. Mary's, now took to the task of repairing the shattered rudder, as his crew of assistants dangled him over the stern, handing down to him sections of wood, rope and tar to serve as a jury-rigged patch between the scarred rudder and the whipstaff. He was lowered down to a longboat where three of his experienced divers, men who had survived harvesting pearls off the coast of Madagascar, went about the task of tying pieces of wood around the shattered rudder. Malagasy in the tops of both the *Foucault* and the *Phoenix* kept their eyes peeled on the horizon for any sign of sail, as the crews sped to make the shattered *Foucault* seaworthy. An inspection of the hull revealed that damage below the waterline was minimal, and Matasaa's crew was able to quickly patch the damaged sections while the French crew was put to work on the pumps. As soon as they could press enough sail and operate the rudder, Caesar took command of their new prize as both ships began beating a hasty path to the north-northwest, making the decision to sail for Boston before continuing on to Acadia.

The people of Boston were grateful to see English flags flying over those ships, a beacon of interest to the people of the region, who flocked to the docks to watch the hastily repaired *Foucault* undergo more permanent repairs in record time, as it was now to be charged with an important duty in protecting the citizens of Massachusetts against the depravities of their Acadian neighbors. Farther up the coast, the citizens of Acadia were preparing for what they were certain would be a brutal war over the years to come. The Acadians, while of French derivation, had over the years developed a unique culture that separated them from both the settlers of New France to their west and New England to their south. While in every sense of the word French citizens, they had often felt as if their presence on these far-flung maritime provinces was of little value or importance to France, as they served only as a buffer between New England and the much more prosperous and populated New France further up the St. Lawrence River. Numbering little more than two thousand people, the Acadians had suffered raids and assaults from the English since their founding in 1608. Little did the Acadian people know, one of their first commissions, the largest ship of Acadia, the *Foucault*, had now been drafted into service, not as a privateer defender of her homeland, but as a warship for France against the English colonies of the Caribbean.

Gerard Mercier had set out in a small boat from Pobomcoup that chilly December morning in 1701 in hopes of landing a bit of extra whitefish, not only to feed his family but to trade in Port-Royal, Acadia's largest town. He laid out a long leader of gig lines and slowly rowed his pirogue not far off Cap-Sable in that pre-dawn mist when he first caught sight of sails. His small boat was insignificant and virtually invisible in these conditions, but he immediately recognized that trim bow and stern as none other than the *Foucault*. She had been at sea for some six months now and was at last returning, hopefully with riches from the Caribbean. Perhaps, he reasoned, she would turn to Port-Royal and be in need of fresh fish, now tugging at his lines. As he began reeling in the stringer of gigs, he noticed a second ship not far off her stern. This was a strange ship, one like he had never seen. But neither was turning to Port-Royal, instead continuing their course along the southern coast of Acadia. It struck him as strange that this Port-Royal ship and her companion were not heading to her homeport, where Captain Briart would be greeted as a hero. Instead, they continued to move away, disappearing into the fog on their way to Isle Royale. He would tell his wife Nancy about seeing the *Foucault* as they enjoyed these few fish on his stringer tonight. But their isolated outpost was far away from Port-Royal, and unless Gerard Mercier had a specific reason to go there, he would seldom travel to that big city and its hundreds of people, preferring the company of his wife, four boys, two girls, their four arpents, eight cattle, five sheep, three hogs and one gun, his entire net value according to the most recent census.

It never ceased to amaze him how France cared enough to pry every year for a tally of his few meager possessions, and yet what did they do with the information? In his tiny outpost at the edge of Acadia, he was accounted for but certainly of no account.

That fog may have been of no consequence to Gerard, but it had perhaps saved his life as the *Foucault*, now renamed the *Protocol*, and the *Phoenix* were en route to the ship-rich waters on the east side of Acadia. Their hope was that, with winter weather approaching, they would have the element of surprise as they headed northwest to the superhighway of North America, the St. Lawrence River. The Acadian crew that survived had no real love or affection for the arrogant sophisticates of New France and were happy to serve as pilots into the St. Lawrence, where perhaps they could earn a little gold to provide for their families back in Acadia. And now as they were guiding the *Phoenix* in to the mouth of the St. Lawrence, they were at last pleased to fight on their own grounds, even if it was against their own countrymen.

Thatcher, Thurmond and half of the Malagasy, along with half of the remaining French crew, kept command of the *Phoenix* as Caesar and the other half of the Malagasy and French took the helm of the *Protocol*. They poised themselves off the island of Île d'Anticosti at the mouth of the Gulf of St. Lawrence. This large wooded island was very sparsely populated and, as the last point of land before the open North Atlantic, both ships were able to take positions facing the passageways on either side and strike merchant ships making their run out of the St. Lawrence River. Their goal was simple: attack any merchant ship departing the St. Lawrence, overwhelm them with their obvious force of fire, remove their cargo typically laden with rich furs destined for Paris, and then sink the ships in the deep waters off the coast of Île d'Anticosti. Those crewmembers wishing to join their party would be offered full shares once both ships were filled. Those men not wishing to join were given a chance to spend their winter on this barren isolated island.

The *Phoenix* and the *Protocol* made a vicious hunting team. Throughout December and January, they took six ships with minimal loss of life to their crews. While there was a temptation to keep the ships and sail them back to Boston as prizes, in truth this made it more complicated and required trusting these Frenchmen much more than they were willing to go. The captains and supercargoes of these ships made more than small protests when their cargoes were looted and repacked aboard the two raiders, and the Malagasy crew took such great relish in driving very large holes below the water line just before they put a generous coat of whale oil, courtesy of the merchants of Boston, along the entire length of the decks and set the things ablaze. The weather was quite atrocious for these men of Africa, and these beaver, fox, bear, mink and wolf pelts made quite attractive and warm new clothing for men who had spent most of their life virtually naked. Being seasoned sailmasters, their deftness with needle and thread allowed them to get creative with mixing and matching of furs, and on those long, cold days awaiting the appearance of a merchant ship, it was not uncommon for fiddlers to strike up a tune as the Malagasy strode down the main deck with their most fashionable English-type walks. And having met Frenchmen and their effete self-important airs gave the Malagasy a whole new level of mockery to achieve as they modeled their fur creations.

Governor Vaudreuil of New France had been very busy issuing Letters of Marque to privateers wishing to take on the English, and it would be months before he received word that a half dozen of the ships sailing from his colony had been captured and plundered by the English. Captain Blanchard of the *Debordieux* along with a small contingent of his men had made the hundred-mile trek across the frozen Île d'Anticosti to Port-Menier, where they were able to convince a captain of a trading vessel who had already secured for the winter to sail the nearly four hundred miles to Quebec to bring word of these roguish Englishmen and their depredations against his ships. The Governor could scarcely believe their wild tales of strange African men dressed in furs and the English and Acadian sailors who took such great pleasure in their ridicule of all things French. It was his hope that his most valued privateers, the seasoned Captains Pierre Maissonnat or Jean Baptiste, would likewise get word of these brigands and dispatch them before they could do any more damage. And were it not for the absolute success of the *Phoenix* and the *Protocol*, it is likely they would have. But, in early February 1702, their ships laden with exotic furs, this little flotilla made its way back to Boston where the proper ladies and gentlemen of this rough and tumble seaside town would end their winter in the finest of New France apparel.

III

The bitter nor'easters that blew down from the easternmost reaches of New France carried their cruelty south along the eastern coast of

Acadia and swung down to the northern English colony of Massachusetts. Gerard Mercier knew that all the clothing he possessed could not entirely stave off this bitter cold. After all the years fishing in these icy waters, working in such extreme conditions, frostbite had taken the tips off three fingers, making it nearly impossible to grip his lines to pull into his boat while wearing heavy gloves. But this was a reality with small Acadian fishermen. The early darkness of February so far north limited the number of hours per day he could attempt to make productive use of fishing time, and as the shadows of the winter's eve began to gather around him, he took one last haul on his gigs, pulling a few sizeable whitefish certainly suitable for dinner but not for sale in Port-Royal. The snow that now covered the ground and the grey skies above him washed everything out into a near monochrome, so it was no surprise that he heard voices approaching before he spied that sweep of sail. Though not far off the coast, he had ventured out to deeper water, putting him in direct path of ships plying their trade along the southern coast.

What he believed to be the *Foucault* was bearing down straight on top of him, and her closeness to shore made rowing that direction a guaranteed suicide mission, so instead he rowed to her port into deeper water to allow the ship to pass. He hoped to catch a sight of Captain Briart or perhaps René Bernard, his friend from Beaubassin, who had signed aboard with the captain when she had shipped out last summer, so he stood off about thirty feet from her port, close enough to offer a salute to his old comrades. The wind in her sails only made the air around her that much chillier, and he pulled those layers closer to him as he scanned the rail of the ship, hoping to catch sight of a familiar face. What he saw was far from familiar, as instead of hearty Frenchmen his eyes met those of black men in heavy furs, staring down at him and all his vulnerability. As far as he knew, there were no black men in Acadia, and their expressions gave him the feeling that they were not enthused to see a proud citizen of this rugged country. He was most disconcerted by a very large fellow whose hands gripped the rail and stared at him and his tiny boat, but from whom the others seemed to await some command with respect to Gerard's presence. His boat began to jostle from the wake of the passing brig, and at last he saw her stern and considered himself free to go. He did not notice her traveling companion whose bow he saw only after its heaviness began to crush his boat beneath its keel.

It was not uncommon to encounter any array of floating hazards in these waters teeming with downed trees and a variety of flotsam, much of it made by Thatcher and his men aboard the *Phoenix*, and so the heavy crunch at his bow while at first unsettling was not totally surprising. Unaware that, instead of sending another log under his keel and posing a threat to his rudder, the *Phoenix* had just swallowed a fisherman's boat it had no intention of consuming. Thatcher could not know that Gerard Mercier, humble fisherman, who plied his meager living from the same waters in which his ship had just sailed, would not be returning home that evening with the small stringer of whitefish his family had been anxiously awaiting. In a few days, scattered bits of wreckage from his dory would wash against the shore of Acadia, and perhaps one of those rare neighbors of the region would notice it and be able to explain to Nancy and their six children why Gerard never appeared for dinner.

The nor'easters sped the small flotilla laden with furs as they proceeded along the treacherous coast and across the line that demarked France from England. At that same time they were making this crossing, Captain Maissonnat was sailing into Montreal Harbor aboard the *Charlemagne*. She was heavily laden with the cargoes of English and Dutch ships he had encountered on his long Atlantic crossing. Not an entirely cruel man, Maissonnat would be satisfied with stripping his prey of their goods, placing the crew in whatever small craft they happened to be carrying – though often there weren't enough boats for the entire crew, and their captains would make a sacrifice of the able-bodied seamen in an effort to protect the officers – and then Maissonnat would unceremoniously sink the ship where he found her. Sailing into Montreal he knew would make him a fairly wealthy man and provide a tidy profit for the backers in Calais who had financed his little expedition. He was surprised to see Governor Vaudreuil bustling along the chilly, ice-covered docks at Montreal to greet his boat. The expression on the Governor's face was one of distress.

"They must be stopped, Maissonnat!" he shouted from the dock as the captain came to the port bow to take the greeting from the Governor. "I have lost six ships in the last three months, and I cannot afford to have pirates operating off my coast. You must do something about it immediately!"

Maissonnat saluted his governor as calmly and officially as he could, despite the fact that he was raving like a lunatic in front of the crew and the men working the docks. "Your highness," Maissonnat replied. "You know, of course, as soon as I made port I would report to you.

You did not have to come here to see me. Perhaps you can enlighten me as to what has you so distressed. Why don't we get out of this cold and let the men go about unloading, and then we can formulate a solution to your panic?"

"There is no time, Maissonnat. I want you to make sail immediately and hunt down those two English ships that have been camped out for weeks off the Île d'Anticosti," the Governor insisted.

"It is a big island, Governor, and I am short on provisions and heavy on cargo. It would probably be best to let my crew offload and reprovision, and we can sail on the very next tide," Maissonnat reasoned.

"Pointe de l'Est, Maissonnat. That is where they are. It is only a few days away. Get them out of my waters, and then you can reprovision," the Governor stated finally.

Maissonnat had been at sea for months and, like his crew, away from his women and their warmth for much too long. He had expected to be congratulated for making a dent in English and Dutch shipping, but rather than congratulations, he was being chastised like a bad child. However, his Governor was his highest authority and, much to the dismay of his men, he ordered the lines retrieved and began the long journey back up the St. Lawrence River. Five days of hard sailing brought him to Pointe de l'Est where he ranged the waters to the north and south, keeping his forty guns at the ready. It was obvious to him that if these English ships were here, by now his constant sailing around these waters would have attracted them, and his temptation was to call his mission a partial success and return to Montreal. But he knew how inconsolable Vaudreuil could be, so he continued his course to Acadia's southernmost point without the hint of sail, English or French, to be seen. Once again, he could take small victory in proclaiming the ships cleared from French waters, but he had to make at least one more attempt. So he changed his course once again, heading northeast to Port-Royal, the capital of Acadia.

Inquiries of the officials at the port proved fruitless, but as Maissonnat was returning to his ship, he queried a fisherman now making his way into the spartan post. Gerard Mercier had managed to swim across that wide body of open Atlantic, half frozen but resolved to make it home. His strong will to survive prodded him on across the frozen Acadian frontier until he reached a nearby native village, where he found warmth and food and a chance to dry his clothes. The next morning he made the one-day trek to his home at Pobomcoup. While his wife was discouraged about the notion of his returning to the sea anytime soon, he desperately needed a boat and knew where he could find one. A local trader was passing and responded to his hail and request for a ride to Beaubassin, where his old friend René Bernard had a boat sitting unused, as he had signed aboard with Captain Briart.

"... which was quite unusual, Captain, for I saw the *Foucault* head off to the north before winter with a strange companion ship, and saw them return just a few weeks back. When I saw the *Foucault*, I thought I would see my old friend René, but it was quite strange, for the crew did not look French. They were dark-skinned, but not like our Indians. Very dark, like the bear pelts they wore. The *Foucault's* companion ran me down and nearly drowned me and destroyed my boat."

"The *Foucault?*" Captain Maissonnat questioned. "You're certain it was the *Foucault?* She should not be in these waters at all, but instead in the Caribe."

Gerard could only shrug. "I cannot answer that question. The only question I want answered is, who's going to pay for my boat?"

"And you say they were sailing south?"

"*Oui, Capitan.* I was at Cap-Sable, and when I made my way to shore the ships were continuing south toward the English colonies."

The Captain walked Gerard Mercier to his ship and had crewmembers still aboard load a cache of English china and a stock of their salted provisions into Gerard Mercier's, or rather René Bernard's, boat. These small parting gifts were a huge boost to Gerard's meager list of possessions. He would let Nancy have a chance to dine on something other than their tin plates, if she didn't insist that he sell them. And this half-barrel of salted meat would feed his family for a few more weeks to await the birth of spring. He began rowing the borrowed boat back to Pobomcoup, to be passed hours later by the *Charlemagne* under a full press of sail heading south.

The arrival of the *Phoenix* and the *Protocol* back at Boston Harbor was greeted with great celebration, as the tales of those half-dozen French ships finding their way to the bottom of the Atlantic brought great joy to these pious Puritans. Of course, many were disappointed to hear that their Papist crews had been released on shore rather than be put to the sword. But at least there was some small measure that these heretics were paying a price for the devastation English settlers had suffered over these last years at the hands of the French and their Indian consorts. As expected, these bales and bales of pelts were quite the rage amongst the good people of Boston who, though priding themselves on their austerity, could give good reason and logic for the need of mink and fox to fight off the winter cold, no doubt liberated by the will of God from these Papist French.

As the crew was hoping to warm their bones at one of the many fine Boston public houses, Thatcher and Caesar caught wind that an infamous French privateer had been recently spotted off the coast of Massachusetts. Captain Baptiste aboard the *LaSalle* had been preying on English fishing vessels for months. What made this particularly brutal was that there was virtually no commercial value to a privateer to concentrate on such small vessels. Thus, logically, he was little more than a vicious murderer to them. This quarry was personal to the Governing Council of Massachusetts, the chartered body who had taken over affairs in the colony since William Stoughton, the acting governor and noted Salem Witch Trial judge, had stepped down to accept duty in England. They had posted a bounty for Baptiste's capture and return to Boston where the good citizens had very personal plans for him. Being in the good graces of the people of Boston was important to Thatcher and Caesar, and the two hundred pound bounty was worth investing a cannonball or two into the *LaSalle*. The condition, however, was that Baptiste had to be brought back alive. So after a few days rest and relaxation, the fur-bedecked Malagasy, their French expatriates and their captains set sail on March 2, 1702, heading north along the coast of Massachusetts.

Captain Baptiste was in many ways the polar opposite of Captain Maissonnat. To Maissonnat, his commission was an opportunity to give French mercantilism a leg up over their English competitors. Every cargo that did not make its intended port put a hurt on the commercial surety of Britain and strengthened the values of French merchandise. But he was a pragmatic man, for today it was the British and the Dutch – tomorrow it could be Spain and Portugal. Either way, business was business, and he would plunder whatever his Marque allowed him to. Baptiste, on the other hand, was a pure patriot. His French pride compelled him to put a crusader's zeal behind his hunt for the English interlopers who so greatly desired possessing all of the Americas for themselves. It was his firm conviction that, by targeting these small fishing fleets, a message would be sent to settlers that this part of the Americas belonged to France, and they should perhaps consider finding more English climes to habituate.

Thus, as his warship was pounding cannonball after cannonball into the defenseless Boston fishing vessel that had most recently crossed his path, the sight of the two approaching warships flying English colors was a chance for him to prove he was happy to take on someone his own size. He broke off and tacked the *LaSalle* to the south, ordering his gun crews on port and starboard to prepare for full salvos. Thatcher and Caesar aboard their respective ships had to appreciate Baptiste's moxie for choosing to charge headlong into them, as it was obvious he was not going to break and run. They surmised his intent was to run up the middle and fire broadsides into their ships, so the two closed nearly port to starboard with one another as the crews made ready to greet the French privateer. Baptiste viewed this closing of ranks as a fear for his ferocity and determination and was about to choose which ship he would instead rake first. When a little over two leagues separated them, he was surprised to see them move apart, providing him ample room to make his run between them, and Baptiste thrilled that they were teasing him to run their gauntlet. He resumed his heading, pointing his ship directly between the two attackers and attacked with a full press of sail, the nor'easters to his back, pushing him forcefully at the *Phoenix* and the *Protocol*. He wished to see the faces of these two captains who dared to tempt him to such a bold move, and his spyglass first encountered a young, dark-haired Englishman giving a broad smile in obvious respect of the brave Baptiste. In his hand he held a goblet raised in toast to his courageous foe. Baptiste then panned his glass to the other quarterdeck, where a very large, sober African man stared at him with his arms crossed, unmoving and unamused.

The *LaSalle* had the wind and great speed, and her gun ports were ready when Baptiste noticed something strange in his path. His glass scanned the water between the two boats as their bow chasers began to bark at one another. He commanded his crew at the whipstaff to go hard to port, but his speed made it impossible to veer his course, as now those guns for which he would run his gauntlet ran out, fully prepared to match cannonball for cannonball. But that was the least of his concerns. As he braced for impact, that heavy length of anchor chain stretched between the *Phoenix* and the *Protocol* made contact, first with his bow, tearing at the wood and violently shaking his ship, then up over the deck, sliding along and tearing at the gunwales. The bow chasers careened backwards along the deck, his crew being torn to shards by the heavy metal that pummeled and ripped at them. The heavy chain tore at everything in its path, ripping first at the mast, tangling in the rigging and heading straight for everyone on deck, including its captain standing on the quarterdeck. Baptiste had only a second to react as he dove for the hatch leading into the ladderwell below, diving headlong into other sailors attempting to do exactly the same thing to avoid being ripped to pieces by those tons of saw-like chain. To make matters worse, as his gun crews were trying to recover from the brutal concussion of that chain when it initially impacted with the *LaSalle*, the crews of the other two ships were quite prepared for them. Their guns began to discharge with brutal ferocity into his port and starboard sides. The horrific cacophony of cannon and chain tearing his ship to pieces was a sound Baptiste had never expected to hear. As the chain reached his elevated quarterdeck, the two ships swung in against the sides of his crippled craft, as Malagasy and disgruntled Frenchmen poured onto his deck and put pistol and cutlass to anyone who resisted.

Baptiste covered his head, awaiting the inevitable, knowing that at any moment his captain's braid would betray his position. But instead of feeling the stab of a blade, he was surprised when two pairs of large, dark hands grabbed him and lifted him to the deck. In his shock and horror, he looked into the face of that sober, serious African who, moments ago, had won the stare-down contest. Hoisting him by the nape of his collar, Caesar carried Captain Baptiste to the waiting Thatcher, who still sported that same warm and winning smile. Thatcher was now standing on the deck of the *LaSalle*, still holding that goblet out in tribute to Baptiste.

"Captain Baptiste, how very good to meet you. I could not bring myself to drink this glass of fine French wine, recently liberated from one of your ships, for I thought of you and how such a wonderful taste shan't cross your lips ever again. So, Captain, please, with my compliments," Thatcher said as he proffered the goblet to Captain Baptiste.

Baptiste sized up his young foe, who was obviously taking great pleasure in his humiliation. Baptiste took the goblet and poured it out upon his wounded deck, its brilliant red joining the streams of like-hued blood from his defeated compatriots. "While the wine may be French, the sommelier is English, and your touch has soured its vintage," Baptiste spat in an arrogant huff.

"Well, Captain Baptiste, I think you'll come to regret not having taken my kindness, for the good people of Boston have plans for you reminiscent of your namesake. So perhaps if you would not take my wine, you'll be more grateful when I personally deliver the silver platter for your head," Thatcher offered.

The Malagasy crew made short work of removing anything of value from the badly crippled *LaSalle*. As had become symbolic from the people of Boston, a generous dose of whale oil was slathered over the surface of the dying ship, and before the waves could claim her, those crewmen who were hacked to pieces on her deck received a fitting Viking funeral.

The flames and smoke reached high against that flat and featureless sea, visible for miles, like a moth to a flame for Captain Pierre Maissonnat. While the dark cloud obscured the identity of the victim, the two ships that flanked her were unmistakable. The ship to starboard could be none other than the *Foucault*, which meant that the other must be her fellow English predator. Obviously, the two had just successfully taken down yet another defenseless French ship plying the merchant trade, most likely to the Caribbean colonies of Spain and France. Perhaps, he reasoned, it was time they took on someone their own size.

The smoke obscured the sight of the *Charlemagne* for quite some time, allowing her to run close to the *Phoenix* and the *Protocol*. Their crews were busy securing their prisoners in the hold and not suspecting another French privateer so far south. Privateers were the same, regardless of the flag they flew, in that they liked their space, for the more ships in consort meant smaller shares of the take. The general rule of privateering was that if more than one ship was taking a prize, those within a cannon's hearing who responded got to share in the spoils. The arrangement with Thatcher and Caesar was unique only in that they had every intention of splitting anything they found, regardless of how many ships were in their squadron. So when the watch in the tops cried "Sail!" they had to admit they were caught unawares.

The two captains raced to their bows and both quickly surmised that, indeed, it was another French ship, and like the *LaSalle* she had a full press of sail. There was no possibility of pulling this ruse twice, though it would be kept for future reference, so both arrived at a different plan as the *Protocol* tacked hard to port and the *Phoenix* tacked hard to starboard, providing a wide berth and a choice of targets for the oncoming French man-of-war. To Maissonnat, this tactic only confirmed his initial assessment that these two English captains were not prepared to face a French man-of-war. How they had achieved a victory over the *Foucault* was beyond his reckoning, but he knew without doubt that, given the choice, he was chasing down the captain of the ship that had taken her. He tacked to port, setting an intercept course for the *Phoenix*. With the wind to his back he had the advantage as he watched the *Phoenix* clumsily work her sails and attempt to reverse her course for the English mainland. He was in pure awe at how obviously bad the seamanship of this captain was, as he watched her sails rise and fall in the most amateur of fashion. His seasoned crew could read the wind almost as well as he, and his bow now faced the stern of the fleeing *Phoenix*, who at last had found a measure of wind to propel her, though certainly not of the quality of the *Charlemagne*. He scanned the seas for her companion, now also in full retreat and heading for the Massachusetts shore. He had closed within three leagues of her as darkness began to fall, and her view became obscured in this moonless night. He adjusted his course, tacking slightly to starboard, figuring she'd begin a run for the Massachusetts coastline herself in the dark of night. As the glass turned and eight bells sounded, indicating midnight, he directed his officer of the watch to wake him at four so they could resume their hunt for this fleeing predator.

He was on the deck before the first rays of dawn were to grace the horizon, and his glass scanned the pre-light sea for signs of sail. The sun began to rise to his east, glimmering the water off his port bow with its beautiful late winter luminescence. He squinted against the sunrise as he began a three hundred sixty degree sweep of the seas around him. As his glass came to his stern, he could at last see a press of sail. It took him a second to make out that distinctive shape of the *Foucault*, now behind him. Apparently in the night, she had decided to give chase as he sought out his quarry ... but where was she? His musings were answered in seconds as shots rang out to his port. He swung his glass into the sun where he could at last make out the shape of the *Phoenix*, its sails now expertly grasping the breeze, running at a course diagonal to his bow. He adjusted his course a few points to port, presenting a smaller target for the *Phoenix* who was now racing to catch him with her starboard guns. Her second round of bow chaser shots slammed pointlessly into the water between them, but his view to his rear showed the *Foucault* closing the distance, maintaining her course directly as she had been sailing when she was chasing the *Charlemagne's* stern. The *Phoenix* now adjusted her course again, this time bringing her bow in a direct collision course with the *Charlemagne*, and to Captain Maissonnat it seemed she wished not to use guns but her bow as her chief weapon. Maissonnat was willing to allow these ships to play floating battering rams if that was what this captain chose, but he ran out his guns and, when his ship was within cannon shot, began delivering a blistering fire against the hull of the *Phoenix*. At this distance, though, his balls merely bounced off her hull, but his message to her captain was *the next round goes through your ports.*

He fully expected the captain would yank her hard to port, increasing the distance between their two opposing hulls, but instead he adjusted his course once again to starboard, now pointing the nose of the *Phoenix* directly at the center of his hull. As soon as she was pointed at his deck, he noticed that, in addition to her two standard bow chasers, the *Phoenix* had rolled up two forty-pound guns. Between them stood a young man in his twenties, a broad smile on his face, and a slow match in each hand. He touched the matches to those two outsized cannons pointed directly at Maissonnat's mainmast and fired. These big guns, designed to launch big balls, were instead loaded with every piece of scrap metal and section of chain that would fit inside her muzzle. And as that hurling mass of shrapnel began tearing at his mainmast and ripping into the flesh of everyone underneath it, the two small bow chasers repeated the process as the *Phoenix* continued her crash course for the *Charlemagne*. Captain Maissonnat lifted himself from the deck and prepared for the inevitable ramming, but just before the two ships collided, he could see that young man standing at the bow holding in his hand two small cannonballs. Most ominous of all was what he wore on his hat – those two sections of slow match now dangling from his tricorner like smoking snakes, as he touched the cannonballs to the matches. Instantly they began smoking, and just before the two ships impacted Thatcher hurled both of those balls directly toward Maissonnat.

Whether the collision happened first or the explosion he wasn't sure, but as he discovered later those projectiles had been meticulously hollowed, stuffed with gunpowder and a slow match inserted in the ends, and the ringing in his ears and the blood that dribbled from them was from the concussion of two hand grenades exploding at the base of his quarterdeck. While his sails and mast were riddled and his deck now a mass of splintered wood, the collision had done little more than slow his ship. But it was slow enough to allow the *Protocol* to come to his stern and deliver an equally devastating blast, tearing at the remainder of his mast and sheets and sending his men for cover. Her bow slammed into his starboard, pinning the *Charlemagne* between her two predators, the crews of which were now pouring over her gunwales. And as Gerald Mercier had told him, indeed these fellows had skin as black as coal. Now they took command of his ship, as their captains took him to the hold to remake the acquaintance of Captain Baptiste.

On March 9, the contents of the *Charlemagne* were at last emptied of their cargo, as Captain Maissonnat so wished he could have done back in Montreal. While his ship was still seaworthy, these captains had no interest in this prize for now, and as his ship's contents were lowered into the holds of the victors, up came the barrels of whale oil. He did not get to witness his ship being torched, but that unmistakable smell of burning oil and wood wafted on the steady breeze, snaking into the fetid, stifling confines of the hold as their captors began their return trip to Boston. Maissonnat and Baptiste were chained together in the same cramped space, now bulging with English merchandise, a cache certain to have been greatly appreciated by the upright and dignified French citizens of New France. Now only a small portion of his take would be enjoyed in some small measure by a humble fisherman and his family in Acadia.

As the English privateers made their way to Boston, at that moment across the sea King William had died and his sister-in-law Anne succeeded him on the throne. It had long been feared that Anne held Catholic sympathies, and there was trepidation that William's plan of taking England effectively to war on the Continent and to the gates of Versailles would die with him. But what surprised everyone, most especially Louis of France, was that Anne would not only proceed with William's ambitions but launch a contest of ideologies as well, spanning the lands and seas of two continents, that would forever change the face and tilt the power of monarchial Europe. She had every intention of reestablishing England's prestige by putting Louis and France in their place, and Anne's declaration of war was a throwing down of the gauntlet, challenging the Sun King to, in essence, bring it on. At the same time, the Crown chose this time of transition as the perfect opportunity to take a stronger hand over its far-flung colonies, kicking into overdrive a plan to centralize the power of England and its uniting kingdom firmly around the throne. This power play touched off a fight with the Lords Proprietors, the eight powerful Lords of Parliament who held sway over a vast number of England's colonies, a political battle that would rival the physical one with France and Spain. For to the Throne, her enemies and challengers abroad were not nearly as dangerous as those to be found in Scotland,

Ireland, Wales and Parliament. This was to be her hallmark, an absolute seizure of power.

This was to be Queen Anne's War.

IV

The *Phoenix* and the *Protocol* took up station in those dangerous waters between the English and French colonies. They had been a bit daunted by the need to follow the protocols set forth by Governors Lightfoot and Zuniga, as it appeared that every French merchant ship they encountered seemed to know the same code that precluded their ability to make use of these well-gunned, deep-hulled ships. And Mr. Thurmond, who had of late enjoyed only the ceremony of his post when in Boston, found himself an object of scorn by Thatcher and Caesar every time another French ship was allowed to pass. In title and in deed, the *Phoenix* belonged to Captain Drummond, and as its titular commander Thatcher was required to live up to the terms of the agreement lest he, too, be branded a pirate. But one night, deep in their cups, a thought crossed Caesar's mind that for some reason had failed to register these last few weeks. That Letter of Marque was only applicable to the *Phoenix*. The *Protocol* didn't exist. And so perhaps there was a way to make this process a better and more profitable compromise for all involved.

The *Calais* was making her run from Quebec to Havana, carrying a cargo of finished silver products meticulously crafted by the smiths of New France. The forward watch sounded the alarms of sail on the horizon, and Captain LaForte took to his glass, hoping to see French colors. To his great dismay, he saw only the Union Jack and began going about preparations for this strange but necessary mid-sea procedure to assure his safe passage. Thatcher, Thurmond and Jean-Marie LeBat, one of Briart's former crewmen now serving as a navigator of the *Phoenix*, took to the longboats and met LaForte in the usual manner.

"Well, captain, I must say I hope to one day have a chance to personally inspect such fine silver goods," Thatcher offered kindly to LaForte.

"Perhaps when all of these unpleasantries are behind us, you can come to New France and see the impressive work of our craftsmen," LaForte offered with a flourish.

As they spoke, he could hear his forward watch proclaiming sails off the starboard bow, and LaForte craned his neck to see what was causing the ruckus. He was familiar with the *Foucault* and had heard she had fallen into English hands and had been serving in companionship with a rogue English ship of strange and odd proportions ... like this one. He turned to Thurmond, now serving in his capacity as Captain Drummond, with a puzzled expression.

"It was you who have been plundering our ships off of Île d'Anticosti!" LaForte claimed in outrage, nearly spewing with venom and disgust.

"My agreement is only for ships following the protocol," Thurmond explained. "I do not think those ships destined for France had made the acquaintance of our three gentlemen in the Caribbean. Thus, they were fair game."

"But are you now relinquishing your agreement with me as well?" LaForte demanded.

"No, captain. I am fulfilling my agreement. However, the captain of that ship is under no such bond, and I suggest whatever arguments you have you take up with him," Thurmond replied.

LaForte could be heard screaming a stream of epithets in French as his longboat began making its harried sweeps back to the awaiting *Calais*, but he knew he had little time to prepare to flee or fight with his few guns. The best he could do was climb aboard his quarterdeck and strike a defiant pose as the *Protocol* reduced sail, her bow chasers pointed squarely at his ship. LaForte was quite disturbed by the sight of the captain standing at the bow, with only yards between them and the *Phoenix* now standing off a mere cannon length away. He took up his speaking trumpet and hallooed the African in French.

"I am Captain LaForte of King Louis the Fourteenth's Imperial merchant fleet, and I protest your harassment of me in free and fair trading with my allies," he spoke.

Caesar placed his hands upon his bow chasers, stared across at the captain and replied in perfect French, "And I am Captain Chasaa who sails on my own accord with a very armed ship, formerly in service to King Louis of France, and I demand to see your manifest so we may discuss appropriate passage fees."

Captain LaForte seemed surprised to hear this African respond in his native tongue but reasoned, certainly, he must have been a former slave in one of France's colonies. He had to admit it was bad enough to encounter a pirate, but one who had been a mere field hand and now dared to question his betters? He was about to challenge Caesar on these fine points of class distinction until he noticed that this insolent slave was now holding a slow match in his hand and poising it above the touch-hole of the cannon his big arm wrapped around.

Caesar smiled. "Now, Captain, we can do this one of two ways. You can get in your little boat and bring your manifest to me, or I can come take it. Which would you prefer?"

The captain stood his ground, his arms crossed in defiance, a symbol of unmoving pride. Caesar smiled to himself, undoing a line hanging down from his sails, removed his pistol and swung across on the rope to the deck of the *Calais*. The French crew stood, quiet and motionless, as the very large black man touched down lightly on their deck. They stared across at the *Protocol* with its odd mixture of black and white faces who, along with the crew of the *Phoenix*, were cheering their captain. Caesar walked up to one of the French crewmen and handed him the rope.

"I'll need this later, if you would be so kind."

He walked to the captain and, with a humble bow and a sweep of his hand, indicated for him to lead the way to his cabin. LaForte studied Caesar's genteel manners and the cocked pistol in his other hand and led the way to the Captain's Quarters.

It was quiet now on all three decks as Caesar and LaForte conferred in privacy. LaForte was adamant that he carried no gold or silver and only merchandise and that, as he could see, it would be impossible for him to offer anything other than his wares. Caesar perused the ledger sheets and let his finger fall upon a line. He then indicated the amount to the captain and asked quietly, "And what about this?"

In Caesar's estimation, the ready amount of Spanish doubloons would be more than a fair "passport fee" in light of the fact that it was approximately ten percent of the value of the cargo. LaForte protested, claiming he did not have access to it.

"Captain LaForte, there are two ways we can do this. You can either lay your hands upon those coins," Caesar stated as he removed the curved blade he had purchased off the coast of east Africa, "or I'll cut off your hands and find them myself. And your choice will be, sir?"

LaForte studied the long, curved blade. He instinctively removed his hands from the desktop as he contemplated the question. He pushed back his chair and stood up, walking to a nondescript cabinet where he placed a key, removed a small lockbox and opened it. Caesar began counting the doubloons, verifying it against the amount in the ledger, and left a small stack of gold on the desk for the captain. He took the key from LaForte, putting the chest under his arm, and stated calmly, "As I said, Mr. LaForte, we are only seeking ten percent."

In a few moments, LaForte led Caesar back to the main deck where the French crewman was still holding the rope. The heavy chest was tucked under Caesar's arm, looking very precarious and loosely held as he swung back onto the *Protocol*. Upon returning to the ship, he once again turned to Captain LaForte, bowing at his waist and waving his hand with a flourish.

"Safe travels, my dear friend. Be careful out there. There are Englishmen who want to send you to the bottom of the sea, but know you have friends in Massachusetts."

LaForte commanded his men to weigh anchor and make sail as quickly as they could, sailing much further to the east of the American coast than he had originally intended. He would make certain Governor Diego heard about this when he reached Havana. But he could not know that this small passage fee was only one-way.

Throughout April and May, the *Phoenix* and the *Protocol* took pride in the fact that they were able to provide this protection service to the many friends of Lightfoot, Diego and Zuniga. While it may meet with some protest upon their return to New Providence, quite frankly such easy sources of income and civil exchanges between French and English would soon be coming to a crashing halt, as news of William's death reached Boston. There was much speculation as to whether Queen Anne would forward William's plan for war, but there was no doubt that Louis was making overtures that soon he would be declaring war if she did not. In such a situation, the three governors may find themselves unable to fulfill the terms of their agreement, and this quiet protocol would in time be one more civil gesture sunk in the shark-infested waters of the Caribbean.

Joseph Dudley was a faithful crony to Queen Anne, and in her quest to reign in the Colonies one of her first acts as queen was to appoint him governor of Massachusetts. When he arrived with little fanfare but much command, Dudley presented his documents to the

Massachusetts Council. The Clerk meticulously took down the minutes of the meeting and the routine exchange of pleasantries, welcoming the Governor and such. As at last Dudley began to speak of the less routine aspects of his presentation, the Clerk began to listen very carefully, making certain that he captured every word quite clearly.

"On behalf of Her Majesty Queen Anne, I, Governor Joseph Dudley, do hereby announce that England and Holland are now at a state of war with France and Spain. Heretofore, all orders and command of this Colony fall under the direct auspice of Her Majesty with me as her representative. I hereby command that all able-bodied men be mustered for service in Her Majesty's war against the French upon our borders and that all lands between the Atlantic and St. Lawrence River are hereby proclaimed as sovereign English soil under my auspices. As of this day, I suspend this Governors Council and assume full authority on behalf of Her Majesty and her united kingdom. God save the Queen."

These last few words of this presentation were to forever change the power and scope of Puritan power in Massachusetts. Having enjoyed autonomy since the arrival of the *Mayflower*, England had now at last arrived in Massachusetts. And a new sheriff was in town in the embodiment of Joseph Dudley.

Word that England was now at war with France spread quickly throughout Boston and the surrounding countryside. By the next dawn, all these long-suffering Puritans were thoroughly informed that their primacy was over. They had come to the colonies to escape the long arm of England and her natural interfering. They had endured the persecution of the Catholics and then the Church of England and had taken hope in Cromwell's purging of infidels and the Protestant William's ascension to the throne, with little impact on their daily colonial lives. But this Anne was now putting them all on notice that their days of freedom and self-determination were rapidly coming to an end, and they debated amongst themselves by their hearths and in their churches, trying to decide where they could flee to escape the Church of England. But while Governor Dudley was delivering this speech to the Puritans, so, too, were other governors and royal envoys fanning out to the far reaches of the Empire to pass along the same message.

To the crews of the *Phoenix* and the *Protocol*, this was welcome news, for in their minds, all bets and prior commitments were off. For the last few months they had watched way too many French ships pass unmolested under their guns, and their recent foray into protection services had kept them in silver and gold enough to put a little weight in the reserves with the intention, of course, of paying back Edward Welch once they finally returned to St. Mary's. Life in Boston for Thatcher and Caesar was everything young men could hope for. Now heroes for having dispatched the pirates Maissonnat and Baptiste, the citizens of Boston made certain that their young heroes received the royal treatment. Many of the days spent in the colony found Thatcher and Caesar at the Boston gaol, conversing with the French captains. While they were enemies, they were kindred spirits, and as Governor Dudley was, no doubt, going to approve the Council's request to proceed with trial and try them as pirates, there was no reason they could not enjoy a few last days of conviviality. Of course, Baptiste maintained his composure of French defiance and became an object of great sport to Thatcher and Caesar's harassment, while Maissonnat seemed to appreciate these gestures of professional courtesy being extended by his captors. But the biggest surprise to all of them came when Governor Dudley denied the Governing Council's petition to try these two Frenchmen for the depredations suffered by the colonists. Unlike the good old days, when men like Judge Stoughton could apply that strange mixture of folklore and religion to determine the level of witchery and the fitting punishment of burning at the stake, English law was the order of the day. And now, rather than being mere pirates, unlawful combats if you will, Maissonnat and Baptiste were prisoners of war.

V

Despite its Puritan nature and history, Thatcher had to admit he liked Boston. While the Puritans made broad show and overt display of their abiding faith, as he had discovered with religious zealots all throughout his twenty-three years, they were, first and foremost, businessmen. Boston had long been a port of call for the Brethren of the Coast who ventured farther north than the typical Caribbean or mid-Atlantic trade. Because of their revulsion for all things not Puritan, specifically Catholics, they considered it God's calling that they snatch up as many Papist designed goods and arts as they could get their hands on, almost as a means of displaying their conquest of the devil through the presentation of his fabulous flatware. Because of their relationship with the community, having hauled in their two most reviled predators, Thatcher, Caesar and Thurmond, along with their savage and "reformed" French Catholic crews, they were treated as local celebrities and found life among these priggish and austere "saints," as they liked to dub themselves, quite amusing, particularly their daughters. Thatcher was coming to discover something about religion and the sacred vortex. The more religious a woman proclaimed to be, the more dirty and experimental she was likely to make of her holy temple. He had known this aspect since he was a young boy, growing up in a house of professional nymphs, who seemed to cater to a particularly religious and pious customer base. What made them, and in turn the masters and mistresses of Parker House, so wealthy was their willingness to perform the most unspeakable acts that their good sainted wives would never perform. The ladies of the house used to joke that the reason why their men were so anxious to partake of these odd, nay evil, nay wonderful carnal activities, was because they weren't the ones who initially got to enjoy them with their sainted brides. While it may be an unfair sample, to a woman, the ladies of Parker House were adamantly convinced that no woman ever went into marriage a virgin. What made the difference between a poor marriage and a great marriage, where such services as provided by Parker House were unnecessary, was whether or not the husband had the first bite of that fruit. Thatcher was told repeatedly that if he truly wanted free and great sex to not to waste his time on the overt girls but to go after the religious ones, for the more their ministers extolled against the wages of sin, the more they wanted it.

Thatcher's sex life had been one of great accommodation, first by witnessing the practical realities of its commercial side in Parker house, then being steeped into it by those lovely European women who provided endless and ample servicing to Peter and his beloved Boy Brigade. The experience came there, and the clarity of its ample and willing supply at Parker House made him a very fortunate fellow indeed, as he had never had to experience the awkwardness associated with the courtship and pursuit involved in most young men's early sexual experience … From there to New York, where his reputation once again allowed him to freely sample of the limitless tray of goods, and then off to Africa and the Red Sea where accommodation of a sailor's sexual desires was part and parcel of the nautical trade. Thus the experience in Philadelphia, where his heart took the lead over his loins and allowed him to participate in that delicate dance of courtship and pursuit with one of those rare young ladies who was actually saving it for the marriage bed. And as he had discovered over that month, the insatiable desires of this most holy of young Quaker girls taught him how wonderful it was to unleash the demon hiding under that angel's exterior ... From there to St. Mary's and those lovely brides who served not only their husband but also the best friend of a god ... And off to New Providence, where finally he had a chance to experience just what it meant to be a good customer. Thatcher had a few advantages in New Providence that most of the unwashed masses lacked. First, having been raised in a brothel he knew what it was that prostitutes loved even more than gold, and that was to be treated as if she were gold. He was young, handsome, incredibly charming, educated and possessed that most unique of quirks instilled in him from childhood in Parker House ... he bathed. This made being around him a rare opportunity for these women of minimal means and breeding with a man who actually demonstrated manners. And he was never a disappointment, for while he came in with gold, he often departed with it still in his pocket, leaving a happy and freshly bathed lady asking when he would return.

Since childhood, Thatcher had loved the water, and, while he could not actually remember it, he was certain it must have started with the baptismal font, only reinforced by Beatrice and Abigail's fastidiousness and Yvgeny's love for a nice dip in the Harbour. He was only a boy of two or three when, against the protest of Beatrice and Abigail, Yvgeny took his young grandson down to the Harbour at the first full freeze, carrying with him a woodsman's ax as he chopped out a rectangular hole in the ice, stripped himself and his grandson down to their bare skin and took their first of many polar plunges. This ritual had been one practiced by Yvgeny and countless generations of men from Pskov and had now been passed on to his grandson. While Caesar was happy to join him for a nice springtime swim, he told the two Russians they were insane and would never join them in their winter water game, though he would hold their clothing and laugh at them when their shriveled bodies emerged from the water. Thatcher and Caesar's first experience with filth and grime was their crossing from Bristol to America, where the obnoxious smell of their fellow seamen and their cramped quarters nearly knocked them over within a few days of sailing. However, any time the *Regent* slacked her sails to a one or two knot crawl or dropped her anchor, it could well be assured that Thatcher and Caesar were over the bow rail, taking advantage of however many moments of water they could have, if even nothing more than the length of the moving ship. It was no better with Kidd, who despite his wealth and austerity practiced the same primitive bathing habits as his common men below, and he, too, found this whole practice of naked bodily immersion to be truly reprehensible.

When Caesar and Thatcher sailed from St. Mary's, however, the *Phoenix* was not only decked out with double hulls and Madagascar hardwoods, but in her Captain's Cabin she contained the most prized possession of all: a bathing tub. While not so arrogant as to demand fresh water be hauled into her, they were adamant that the cook heat up ample amounts of salt water for those moments when a luxurious soak was just what the captain ordered. And to the Malagasy, as strange as the ritual may have been, if Caesar did it they did it, and at times it was most difficult to determine which line was more crowded – the one handing out grog or the one for a five-minute soak in the tub. Add to that a cup of coffee and a pipe, and a man could discover exactly what it meant to be in heaven. It was an odd sight to witness when the two captains were to be found bare-ass naked, wrestling for the rights to the first soaking while the other had to stand by holding his coffee and pipe.

This curiosity extended right into Boston, where word that those two ships contained not only strange Africans but also an object specifically designed for the purpose of naked immersion. This was particularly of intrigue to the young women, who were so raptly fascinated with these strange young men from England. Often would be the time when Thatcher and Caesar would be enjoying the company of a grateful Boston merchant when a young lady, more often than not a daughter and in a few instances wife, would guide their conversation around to this curious rumor they had heard. Of course, Thatcher and Caesar would not only confirm such a rumor, but also when their fathers or husbands were out of earshot offer to give them a tour of the ship and show them that strange item. While this was often met with a blush or a titter or perhaps even flight by their inquisitor, it was always amazing how many times they would be taken up on their offer. It was for these reasons and many others that Boston was becoming a quite comfortable place.

But there were the nagging aspects that began even before the arrival of Governor Dudley. One particularly bothersome annoyance was embodied in a man who never ceased to sermonize. So prone was he to lecture endlessly that his zealotry extended far beyond the Sunday pulpit and into the six other days of the week with whomever he encountered. This proud native son of Boston had become the spiritual cornerstone of the colony and, like so many zealots, saw both the good and the evil in these itinerant men who had taken up residence in his port and off his shore. On one of their early extended stays, the minister made the point of introducing himself and inviting Thatcher ... oh, and yes, Caesar ... for dinner at his home.

Cotton Mather's reputation extended far beyond the colonies, and his name was synonomous wth every self-righteous, pompous, arrogant, self-absorbed man of God. Mather was the worst kind of religious fanatic in that he actually believed England and he had been ordained by God to make the world in their image. In a nation overflowing with pomposity, it was very difficult to rise to a level of arrogance that actually offended the Church of England, and Richard Mather, Cotton's grandfather, had accomplished that goal in spades as a very young man, finding himself exiled to Massachusetts. Increase Mather, like his father, elevated that pomposity to a new level and inspired in his son Cotton the belief that the Mathers were singularly blessed with God's great wisdom. Cotton had a chance to demonstrate that during the Salem Witch Trials, where God spoke to him and told him that, indeed, these eighteen seemingly innocent women were in fact witches, and being burned at the stake would purify their souls to the blessing of God. Like his Spanish competitors in the Roman Catholic faith, Cotton Mather's goal was not only to turn all of these varied religious exiles toward his brand of Christianity but also every Indian. The difference between Cotton Mather and the Roman Catholic Church, however, was that Cotton Mather had no intention of modifying his faith to accommodate the spiritual and religious practices and symbology of these savages in the Americas. In his view, it was the duty of all English colonists immediately to Christianize these Indians in the ways of the true faith and, the moment they resisted, to send them to hell. One most notable and indeed most infamous of Cotton Mather's actions was to celebrate the fiftieth anniversary of the 1636 Pequot Indian Massacre, where six hundred so-called savages were slaughtered on Block Island and on the Massachusetts mainland in a single day. Three hundred of them had been invited for a dinner at a Massachusetts church, and once every man, woman and child were inside, the doors and windows were sealed, and the church was put to the torch. This most infamous of deeds by the early settlers of Massachusetts was, in Cotton Mather's mind, cause for commemoration and festive celebration, for these ungodly natives had met their rightful end. And thus he made it his personal campaign to make this commemoration an annual event which he dubbed Thanksgiving.

Thatcher prided himself on being able to meld his personality to accommodate even the most difficult of human beings. Since birth, he had been taught how to be a chameleon and to find in each person some common ground by which the two could have a civil rapport. Until Cotton Mather, he had never proclaimed a failure in this respect. But Cotton Mather made one not want to find common ground. As Thatcher and Caesar sat through that way too long dinner with way too many prayers and way too many intonations to God, King and England, Mather's' true Holy Trinity, the two had hoped they could find an opportunity to slip out as early as possible and chalk this night up as one not to be replicated. But to their frustration, Cotton Mather had them placed next to him, where for the six hours of the meal he went on and on and on about his vision for Massachusetts, England and the rest of the world. Thatcher could no doubt imagine that Cotton Mather would be in the vanguard of this movement with a crown as big as William's itself firmly resting on his head.

"You young men were called by God to come to Boston," Mather said through a mouthful of potatoes. "You may not know it now, but I have been praying for young men such as you to take up the mantle of this new crusade. And God answered my prayers, and you will soon discover he has answered yours. For while some may question your ferocity, I see the sword of St. George firmly grasped in your hands as you stand proudly upon your bow to vanquish these Papist dragons."

"Well, actually, Reverend, we stand on our quarterdeck, and I don't know if you've ever held a sword for very long, but days at sea in that position would be quite painful," Thatcher quipped.

"Of course I speak metaphorically. All great men of God speak metaphorically, as our Lord Jesus Christ Himself did. What I am saying, gentlemen, is that I have been praying that William, our beloved King and sacred Christian knight, will take up arms against his Papist foes and at last vanquish these infidels, not only from England but from the face of the earth itself." He leaned in to the two young men so they could hear his every word and smell his fetid breath. They tried hard not to stare at the generous piece of meat that hung from his blackened top teeth, with every word dancing and shimmering like a belly dancer upon a Great Mogul ship.

"What I'm talking about gentlemen is a Holy War." He held that pose, staring at the men so they could gather the gravity of his words. And that dancing piece of gristle.

Thatcher paused, letting the words sink in, closing off his nasal cavities to shut out the rancid stench of the Right Reverend's breath, which he swore smelled like those bits of flesh that somehow went missing on the ship after a right deadly scrum and stunk up the crew's quarters so bad that every man was on hands and knees searching every crack and crevice of the deck for that foul, rotting piece of matter. When an appropriate amount of dramatic pause had been allowed, Thatcher responded with the only question he could under such serious and grave circumstances.

"So how is the venison, Reverend?"

Caesar had been in mid-sip from his glass when he began coughing and choking, sending a little stream of apple cider out of both nostrils. The sight of the fearsome African captain nearly choking on his unfermented cider drew the attention to him and briefly softened the atmosphere just long enough for Cotton Mather to reach for a couple of dozen more metaphors about saints and crusades and holy wars to fill the next hour. Thatcher and Caesar tried to find a moment when Mather was particularly foaming at a gathering of rapt devotees to attempt to slip away, but his rabidity was stanched just long enough to see the two captains leaving, motivating him to clear a path of loyal worshippers to catch these two before they could hit the door.

"Gentlemen! I wanted to thank you for honoring us with your presence. I should let you know, the Governor's Council doesn't quite know this yet, but many of us have worked hard to convince our beloved Majesty to send us a Governor worthy of our noble mission here in Massachusetts. I know that you are presently under a Letter of Marque with another governor, but I am certain that this governor will have the same power, and I am going to encourage him to issue Letters of Marque to you. God has a role for you that cannot be trusted under the terms of some vile, worldly charter but requires a commission of Holy Writ. I hope you will allow me to personally recommend you as the emissaries of our Holy Commonwealth. I just have one question: your ships' names. I was thinking something along the lines more appropriate for such an endeavor. What are your thoughts of Archangels Michael and Gabriel?"

This idea was no doubt one of great joy and self-satisfaction to Cotton Mather, as the very thought of these two ships sailing with such ecclesiastical names sent his eyes heavenward. He scarcely noticed as Thatcher and Caesar quietly bid their adieus and walked away, as now Cotton Mather had one more great metaphor to make for the assembled masses, waiting with baited breath for the next round of vile spewing.

Thatcher and Caesar merely shook their heads and walked away silently, absorbing everything that they had endured these tedious hours they knew they would never get back. But fortunately, a block away, two of Cotton's particularly attractive young parishioners were waiting just where they said they would be as the two captains fell in rank behind the two teenaged girls. While it had been a pressing thought throughout this entire evangelical orgy of an evening, now more than ever somebody needed a bath.

On their last day in port, Caesar and Thatcher did the other thing - other than deflowering young Puritan girls - that gave them most pleasure while in Boston. They stopped by the jail to say good-bye to Maissonnat and Baptiste. During these months in the Boston gaol, that strange contradiction continued to exist between the two inmates, as Maissonnat maintained his air of dignity while Baptiste began to descend into the bedraggled presence of his namesake. Caesar and Thatcher had one final mission to accomplish before they bid adieu to their French competitors.

"Well, so here you two will be sitting until Louis finally decides to part with a British privateer. What a way to sit out the war, gentlemen," Thatcher stated, shaking Maissonnat's hand as Baptiste hissed from his little corner wyvern.

"Have your little laugh now, English pig-dogs. But when France defeats your puny country, we'll see who scoffs at whom," Baptiste sputtered as he hurled a little spit in Thatcher's direction.

Maissonnat merely shook his head, doing all he could to ignore his compatriot. "I am sure we will see you again soon, gentlemen. For you're right, we are all too valuable to sit out wars in jails. But the next time I see you, I'll begin firing the moment I see your sails." From behind his back, Caesar presented Maissonnat with a bottle of French claret. Maissonnat brightened at the sight of that fine wine from home. "You are too kind. I will save it for a special occasion," Maissonnat gushed. But he was a little surprised when Caesar produced his saber and docked off the end, offering Maissonnat the first drink.

"Do not worry, Maissonnat. There will be a case waiting for you upon your release. Enjoy this while you have it, as we drink a toast to your future freedom," Caesar replied as he took up the bottle, took a long pull and passed it to Thatcher who gave a sidelong glance at Baptiste, still muttering and cursing in his corner.

"You need not worry, Baptiste. I offered you your glass of wine and you refused it, and I'm certainly not going to offer one now. But I do have a parting gift for you as well, a little something for you to remember me by," Thatcher said as he walked to the edge of the cell. From behind his back, he produced that symbolic gift, which he held out through the bars hoping that Baptiste would accept it in the spirit of brotherhood and generosity with which it was being offered. Baptiste's rudeness intact to the last moment, Thatcher shrugged and sailed his gift to come to rest at the Frenchman's feet. Thatcher took one final pull from the bottle and passed it back to Maissonnat to enjoy the last few swallows of his wine as Baptiste contemplated his reflection in that silver platter.

Governor Dudley was waiting at the docks as Thatcher and Caesar made their way to their boats. Surrounding him were his escort of marines who stood by him as if it were an honor guard, not quite barring access to the *Phoenix* and *Protocol* but certainly sending a message that boarding now was turning their backs on their Queen.

"I must say, gentlemen, that I am quite disappointed that you have chosen to continue your present contract rather than the one I proffer," Dudley intoned with sobriety.

"Governor, as much as we appreciate the offer and having had this chance to serve the citizens of Massachusetts, we are confident that they are now in your capable hands so we can continue our mission on behalf of our governor," Thatcher offered as sincerely as he could.

"I should tell you, gentlemen, that there is no telling how long your Letter of Marque will be in effect, as France and Spain have made the Caribbean one of their major objectives, as well as Massachusetts. The difference, of course, is that Spain is well armed, and there is no telling how much naval protection Britain will be able to provide for these outposts. I hope you will consider this as you sail back to Nassau."

"When Nassau no longer exists, then we will seek a new employer. Until then, Governor, we must honor our agreements," Caesar replied. "Besides, our Captain Drummond is insistent we return to protect his home, so we must honor our captain."

Thurmond was busy at the helm of the *Phoenix*, preparing to sail. While this pretense was no longer necessary, as everyone knew who really commanded these ships, they maintained the charade with one simple goal in mind ... plausible deniability. Caesar and Thatcher bid adieu to the Governor and mounted their respective quarterdecks, waving good-bye to those fine folks of Boston and the small knot of those dirty little girls now washed as white as snow.

While prizes were always a hope and a prayer, their goal was not the pretense they had given, for while they made a southwest course leaving Boston Harbor, as soon as their sails were over the horizon they corrected their course for due south. There was a long war to come, and Thatcher and Caesar planned to be in there for their punches. But right now they had an agreement to honor, and so they began their months-long course crossing the hurricane-prone Atlantic, put their backs to the sweeps through the doldrums and sailed south with their Letters of Marque in hand, one legitimate, one forged. There was always the outside possibility that, somewhere in these wide waters proclaimed by all the warring parties, a Spanish or French ship would be encountered. Thatcher and Caesar had proven their mettle under fire and were ready for any task to face them. Almost with disappointment, their cruise was uneventful and the Dutch outpost of Cape Town a welcome sight as they made port to restock, then it was on for their last long haul to St. Mary's.

The island was ghostly quiet. The wrecked hulls of the *November* and some other craft were visible, with their scorched ribs poking up through the water. They had fully expected a contingent of Edward Welch's men to be awaiting them when they arrived, but surprisingly not a soul was to be seen. Keeping half their men in the boats and half accompanying them on the four-mile hike to Welch's castle, they were once again disquieted by the eerie silence and seeming abandonment of the citadel. Slowly they made their way through the gates and courtyard, pushing open the door to the estate. Not a single sign of recent life could be seen as, room by room, they examined Welch's palace to find the place completely empty and deserted. They hiked back to the boats, not dropping their guard one bit until at last they reached the channel. Thurmond was waiting for them on the beach.

"Shortly after you left, this gentleman came out from the woods on the other side of the channel." Thurmond gestured to a withered old Malagasy.

Thatcher and Caesar walked to him, and the old man had a look of fear and surprise to see Chasaa had once again returned. He fell to his knees, his hands over his head in reverence and grief, as Caesar lowered himself to his knees to take up the face of the old man.

"Sagaa, dear old fellow. I am glad to see you are well, but where is everybody?" Caesar asked quietly.

"They are all gone, Chasaa, all of them. I am the only one left because I was the only one gone," Sagaa replied through sobs.

"I need you to tell me what happened," Caesar asked.

"It was not long after you left that many ships arrived, and Edward Welch was here to greet them. He sent word throughout the area that you had sent a great gift to your people and that all were asked to come to hear your words. And they did, everyone but me. For as much as I wanted to hear them, I had to see my wife before she died. I was gone many days, but when I came back everyone was gone except for those who resisted. I found one young boy who had suffered many wounds and was near death, and he told me that Edward Welch gathered all the people here on this beach and then from out of those ships came many men with guns. Those who fled or resisted were killed. The rest were chained together and made slaves. And their first act of slavery was to take everything from Edward Welch's home and pack it into the same cargo holds they were to be packed into. And then they left. A few managed to escape and disappear deep into the forest and jungles and back to our caves where our ancestors are buried. Many of them cursed you that you had sold your people into slavery, but I knew you did not. I knew you would come back, and I could tell you what happened, tell you what that faithful young boy told me before he died. I told him I would wait for you, and he asked me to tell something to you when you returned." Sagaa rose to his feet and, lifting his chin as proudly as he could, he repeated the words of the dying young boy. "We are Antankarana Malagasy, and we will never be slaves."

Caesar looked at his men, who had come close to listen to Sagaa's words. They understood how he felt, and they were resolved to accomplish the mission they knew was certainly to come. "I want to leave you with a choice, Sagaa," Caesar offered. "To join me and hunt down Edward Welch, or to stay here and tell my people the truth. Neither choice is safe, but either choice is yours."

Sagaa looked up into the eyes of his chieftain. "I would follow you to the ends of the earth, Chasaa, but our people, those who remain, need to know that you have returned and you will avenge them. I will tell them, and I will tell them to await your return."

"I make you this promise, Sagaa. I will return, and it will be with Edward Welch's head and as many of my people as I can I will bring home."

Sagaa embraced his leader and kissed his hand and then crossed the channel to the Madagascar mainland. He turned one last time before entering into the trees to survey his chieftain and then in seconds disappeared.

Caesar turned to his crew, his Malagasy. "Antankarana, we have once again been betrayed, and I have made a promise to find our betrayer, but I believe our people need you, for amongst the caves of our ancestors hide those of our people who escaped this betrayal. I know you share with me this anger and fury for vengeance, but we must preserve our tribe and I want to give you that chance to find our people."

Matasaa, the carpenter and leader of the Malagasy crew, stood upon the bow of the *Protocol*. "We always knew this time could come, Chasaa, and we made every provision to protect our people. But you are our chieftain, and where you go we go. Our people need not for us to find them, they will find us, in this life or the next, in this world or in the one to where they were taken. The Antankarana live on in you, and it is with you we must be. If you command us to stay, we will disobey you, for we cannot abandon our king."

The fealty to Caesar had never been spoken. It had only been expressed through their every action and every moment of loyalty, no matter what the circumstance. But Caesar was taken aback by their declaration of him as their sovereign. And while the words held such a tremendous and burdensome impact, the sight of these hundred Malagasy, now prostrate before him, gave him a sense of awe and dread. And in his humility he bowed his head in acknowledgement, for heavy is the head that wears the crown.

Through the rest of 1702, the crew busied themselves with resupplying their stocks of zebu and lemur and once again scoured the forest for every piece of fruit they could find. Unlike the last time, where they lingered to enjoy family, friends and home, this time they worked with a speed and desperation that was endured by each of them in silence. In January of 1703, the two ships made sail. This resolved crew would hunt Edward Welch to the ends of the earth and destroy anything that came in their path. They would spend the rest of their days searching for their people, whether in the Caribbean, New

Spain, New France, New England or Old Europe. When they found them, they would bring them into their company with the intent of one day returning home.

They rounded the Cape of Good Hope after resupplying and inquiring on the whereabouts of Edward Welch. To no one's surprise, particularly Thatcher's and Caesar's, Edward Welch had gone to great lengths to mask his destination. It seemed that every person they talked to in port gave a different answer. They put together their target list from all the leads, for amongst them one must surely be true, and they would work them systematically, beginning with Antigua and Montserrat, then Jamaica, New Providence, then Bridgetown and Charleston. If they still had no success, then it was on to Williamsburg and Philadelphia and New York and Boston. And at last if it required them to sail up the Thames and into the very mouth of hell itself, they would find Edward Welch, and his head would hang from their bowsprit.

As they plotted their course for the Caribbean, Thurmond joined Caesar and Thatcher for dinner. As they were into a few bottles of Madeira wine, Thurmond at last brought up what had been on his mind for months. "You know I can't return to New Providence, don't you?" Thurmond questioned.

"I don't think you have anything to fear from Lightfoot, do you?" Thatcher inquired.

"No, it's not Lightfoot I fear. It's the person I'll rediscover when I set foot on that desperate shore. For these last few years, I have played a captain, if on paper only. But you two have never attempted to assert your rightful dominance over me. You have always made me a part of this crew, even though I dragged you into something that should have had me marooned. And yet, through it all, you've given me a chance to fill the command lost to me in Port Royal. I lost more than my command in Jamaica. I lost myself. This ship has been an inspiration from its rebirth to its journeys to this surprising and amazing crew. The *Phoenix* fits not only the ship but also the people aboard her, and it has brought me back to life. And now, I want to return to where I died. But when I set foot on Jamaica, it will not be Morgan Thurmond. It will be as Edward Drummond, for Morgan Thurmond died in 1693, and Edward Drummond came to life in his place. I think we need a base of operation, free of the atmosphere of New Providence, for one day these wars will end and whoever owns New Providence will reshape it in their image. I think we need to be prepared for that day when our capers and enterprises have no choice but to come to an end."

Thatcher and Caesar thought about this for a moment. What Thurmond was proposing was an interesting concept, for they still carried the gold they had promised to Edward Welch and many more thousands of pounds that needed investing, someplace other than the taverns of New Providence.

"So what you're suggesting is we begin preparing for the end now so that when the easy money ends the hard currency will have already done a lot of the work for us," Caesar reasoned.

"I believe I have your trust, as obviously you have mine. But I think there are legitimate opportunities that could go quite far with ready specie and a little imagination. We are three men living under false identities, identities that could consume us. Let's instead consume the identities and the opportunities they can present when good men of commerce and reputation find unlimited sources of investment in the holds of Spanish and French ships, or whatever other flag we may deem in the future to be our bank."

That night in the Captain's Cabin of the *Phoenix*, the men drew up the papers modeled after the fashion of the powers given to the great companies as Hudson and East India and West India. Rather than men taking the brunt for business failures and downturns or being held personally responsible for the negative outcomes in their quest for profit, this new creature would now be the living breathing faceless entity that took all the credit and none of the blame and would shield her owners from the all-seeing eye of the world's monarchs. For Thatcher Edwards and Caesar Edwards were simple men of the sea, fighting their Queen's enemies for the hope of a small profit. But those profits would move onshore and weave their way back into the Colonies and England and the rest of Europe in the guise of the Drummond Corporation.

The sloop *Dominion*, a small one-masted vessel, sailed into the once-devastated wasteland that was Port Royal. Only days before, she had been intercepted by two hulking men-of-war, who offered their owner much more than she was worth and a free ride to anywhere but Jamaica. Aboard her was a crew of eight Malagasy, who accepted the role as "slaves" to their "master" Edward Drummond. The tiny boat had a small cargo of Spanish silver jewelry and cutlery, items that would be well prized on Jamaica. The ship also contained an undisclosed cargo of eight chests of silver and gold that would be carefully guarded and protected by the Malagasy on behalf of their crew and king. Captain Drummond was a fiftyish year old man with a finely trimmed wisp of silver at his chin, and in a few days he would begin to go about erecting the first of many structures to make up the holdings of the Drummond Corporation.

As he negotiated through those troubled, tangled waters of Port Royal, the *Phoenix* and the *Protocol* were making their way under the shadow of Boggy Peak, a thirteen-hundred-foot craggy promontory on the southwest corner of Antigua, a resupply outpost of the Lesser Antilles. Few large ships attempted to negotiate these waters for the ring of shoals and large coral reefs, but Thurmond had drawn a very good navigation map based on his many previous trips to this island. Despite the treachery of the passage, they were able to creep through the reef and into a sheltered cove big enough to hide these two men-of-war. The adjacent island of Barbuda, a good day's row away, was inhabited only by the native Carib Indians. Europeans had yet to brave attempting settlement of Barbuda, making it the perfect likely new home for the likes of an Edward Welch. A place like Barbuda would remind him very much of St. Mary's and allow him to attempt to create a new empire before England had a chance to establish a solid footing. The islands of Antigua and Barbuda were only the first stops of many more to come as the crews began following up their leads in their ongoing search for Edward Welch. Of course if they found him they would not be repeating their last performance by handing him chests full of gold plucked from the pockets of colonial merchants.

The only thing they would be handing him would be his head.

Chapter 7

Captain Drummond and the Admiral's Daughter
July 1703 – June 1704

I

Vice-Admiral William Whetstone of the British Navy had taken a long, tortuous route to at last achieving the station his name should have brought him. Having commanded the *Mary* of Bristol and achieved membership in the vaunted Bristol Corporation, he had become well acquainted with these waters, particularly Virginia and Barbados where he had established a lucrative trade in English serge. War found William continuing the family legacy in naval service, first captaining a supply ship to Ireland and a eventually a number of commands aboard His Majesty's Warships *Portsmouth, Norfolk, York,* and a three year station off Acadia aboard the *Dreadnought.* It was during this post that his wife had passed away, yet he remained vigilantly on station for ten more months, missing his wife's interment in the churchyard of St. Nicholas Church in Bristol. As Captain of the *Yarmouth*, he had received his promotion to commodore and was transferred back to the *York* where he was given orders to take up a post in Jamaica under Admiral Benbow. His flagship *York* was a boondoggle and, after repeated trips back to Plymouth for repairs, he transferred his flag to the *Canterbury* where Benbow promoted him to Vice-Admiral upon arriving at Port Royal. Given six ships to pursue French Admiral Jean du Casse, he sailed west to Hispaniola while Benbow sailed north to Cartagena and into the fateful duel with his nemesis. Benbow ordered Whetstone to convene a courts-martial for cowardice and disobedience against the six captains who had shirked under Benbow's command. Benbow died of his injuries sustained in the battle before he could see his captains convicted. Benbow's death propelled Whetstone into overall command of the Jamaican station and, along with battling the French, he made it his personal mission to quell the breakdown in discipline that had developed in the Caribbean fleet.

As was the case with most professional sailors, his life had been spent so much at sea that his children were virtual strangers to him every time he returned, most especially his precocious daughter Sarah. She had just turned twelve when he accepted his flag and, unlike his other children, was young enough that he could have a real influence in her life. But his daughter suffered from two great maladies: heart stopping beauty and unmitigated charm. It was obvious to him that he would have a real challenge on his hands as the father of an irresistibly attractive daughter. At least, he reasoned, he would be able to keep an eye on her in her formative years. After her mother's death she was ever in his company at all his official functions and dinners amongst England's luminaries. Despite his intent to be a force of discipline and structure, in truth she was the light of his life, and he was putty in her hands. The sheer weight of his rank made her that much more attractive to the young Naval officers who came a-courting as she reached her teen years. To Whetstone's way of thinking, the sheer magnitude of his station could frighten away the most weakened of heart and assure that only the strongest would curry his and his daughter's favor.

That inevitability came in the person of a young man whose father was well connected through his shipping empire and a vaunted member of the Bristol Corporation. Though a few years her senior, he had watched Sarah grow up from afar as he spent so much time at sea captaining one of his father's many merchant ships. He had finally caught Sarah's eye at one of his father's dinner parties celebrating the expansion of his merchant empire. This suitor's light hair and eyes, bold swagger and his recent commission into the British Navy had turned her head like no other, and it was her full intent that when she reached the age of majority and consent she would be betrothed to him. But his career put him on the same course that was the lot of all professional seamen, and he was adamant that, until he made his mark in the Navy, she would have to delay any plans of betrothal. As much as he loved her, he had a career to think about. As he bid good-bye to her at Redcliffe Quay, off to fight Queen Anne's enemies, her heart sank. Her only consolation was her father, and he, too, had received orders that would carry him off to the Caribbean. What power she could not wield over her intended betrothed she could wield over her father, and despite his protests, sixteen-year-old Sarah Whetstone joined her father aboard the *Canterbury* as it sailed for Jamaica. In this remote backwater of the British Empire, poised only a few hundred miles from the might of the Spanish Navy, which used Havana as their chief port in their ramp-up for war with England, fears for her safety were of chief concern to the Admiral. But this would be his port, where he would build up a mighty Navy to protect England's Caribbean colonies and begin taking Spanish and French islands for the British Empire. And so, other than in England itself, she was likely as safe as she could be. Plus, he reasoned, her presence would send a message to the Jamaican colonists that Britain had not abandoned them, for if they had, would they allow the Admiral's daughter to be here?

While Sarah was the toast of Jamaican gentry, the seamen and merchants of Kingston likewise were a-titter about the beautiful, statuesque teenaged daughter of Britain's might in the Caribbean. While it had been the Admiral's hope to restrict Sarah's movements to those places where she would be among her kind, there was no stopping his precocious, brazen daughter, who insisted that her place was as much among the people of Kingston as it was among the mansions of the plantation class. On any given day, Sarah could be seen strolling through the muddy streets of Kingston, a small contingent of adoring marines a respectable distance behind her, as she made her rounds to the shops and homes of the Jamaican merchants. It was only through happenstance that Captain Drummond made her acquaintance, and he could understand why the streets and docks of Kingston were filled with the lustful and lovelorn.

"Miss Whetstone," Daniel Hunter, a dry-goods merchant, intoned as she bounced into his small Queen Street store. "May I introduce you to Captain Drummond?"

Sarah wheeled around to make the acquaintance of the old, dapper man standing a few feet away. She was used to introductions to total strangers, as her position could be lucrative under the right circumstances to the right person. She smiled her radiant smile and offered her hand.

"Captain Drummond. Are you under my father's command?" she cooed as she shook his big, rough paw.

"No, ma'am, I'm merely a retired sea captain who's come on shore to try my hand as a proper man of business," Drummond replied as he took in the loveliness of Sarah Whetstone.

"Miss Whetstone, this is the fellow I was telling you about. Captain Drummond is terribly resourceful and able to fulfill special orders. You had mentioned an interest in bolts of silk?"

Sarah's eyes brightened. "Why, yes, Captain. While I certainly miss my dressmaker in London, I have found a most charming woman here in town, capable with a needle but short on appropriate material. I believe that with the right bolts of cloth, she could do wonders. Would that be in your purview, Captain?"

Captain Drummond studied the young woman and imagined what it must be like to watch her undergo a fitting. "Silks may be difficult under these circumstances, but certainly not impossible. Is there is a specific color you have in mind ...?"

Captain Drummond was the envy of all Jamaica as he escorted Sarah Whetstone up the hill to the Vice-Admiralty palace where she chattered away about colors that would certainly bring a glow to her cheeks. He knew not where he would get them, but he knew whom he had to contact to have that order fulfilled. And if filling the small request of this lovely sixteen-year-old girl could put him in good stead with the Vice-Admiral, why, that would be worth whatever trouble or expense he encountered.

In a quiet, sheltered Antigua cove, the *Phoenix* and the *Protocol* took turns being hauled onto shore and careened to prepare for the opportunities that lay within these waters. It was obvious that the dynamic had changed since they last departed the Caribbean, as now the seas were crawling with British Royal Navy ships. Likewise, the Dutch had supplemented their merchant fleet with a number of three masted men-of-war to protect their holdings in the Netherland Antilles. France and Spain were doing their level best to muster a large naval fleet both to harass the British and Dutch and to attempt to reclaim some of the island possessions lost to them in the previous years of conflict.

The Malagasy had done a yeoman's task in developing a relationship with the Barbudian Indians. While there were a few brave Englishmen who had set up temporary camps on Barbuda and initiated trading relationships, the island was still free of an omnipresent force of English influence, officially or unofficially. The Malagasy used their relationship with the Caribes to gain unprecedented access to the island, searching every square inch for any sign of Edward Welch. Though they uncovered no intelligence of his whereabouts, Caesar and Thatcher were pleased that the Malagasy had made important new contacts that could serve their interest in the future. As the *Phoenix* and the *Protocol* were at last refitted and as Thatcher and Caesar had taken this time to map Antigua's waters in greater detail, they began to get a sense of their very private neighbors, who likewise sought the shelter of Antigua to practice their own form of trade. For the most part, they were older Brethren of the Coast who had somehow survived colonialization and England's various attempts at ridding the Caribbean of pirates. Most still followed the old traditions of the boucaniers, capturing wild cattle and game and living off the smoked meat that would feed them and sometimes fetch trading opportunities for the citizens that made up the frontier outpost at St. Johns. Periodically they would wheel out their small ketches with the hopes of catching an unprotected merchant to roust for whatever gold they may carry, not bothering with the cargo as they had neither the space nor inclination to deal with merchandise. But their normally shy and reserved nature, specifically of outsiders and Englishmen, began to melt away as bit by bit Thatcher and Caesar entreated them with that most valuable commodity beyond gold: rum. From these old and wizened brigands, they were able to ferret out valuable information and intelligence that would help them with their developing plans of capitalizing from the disorganized grey market of the Caribbean. As their familiarity with these waters became more ingrained, they learned the tricks of navigating the coral choked and shoal infested channels, and while these coves provided them cover, understanding those hidden passages gave them the ability to hit and run in ways most large vessels could not manage.

One of the most effective tactics they had developed was to post lookouts on Boggy Peak, which provided them with virtually hundreds of miles of visibility in all directions. When a contingent of Spanish or French ships were spotted, the lookout would signal to a chain of relays who would convey the message by a rudimentary form of semaphore to indicate numbers, speed and approximate distance. The *Phoenix* and *Protocol* stayed at a level of readiness, using trees and rocks for anchorage and keeping their sails ever at the ready. Part of the uniqueness of their approach was a feature endemic in the *Phoenix*, with its broad rows of sweeps. While half of the crew would man oars in the *Phoenix*, another group of crewmen would be aboard the longboats with either Thatcher or Caesar in the lead boat, taking constant soundings and making adjustments to guide their boats through these precarious waters. As long as they could maintain sight of their landborne signalmen, they would continue to adjust their course planning until the last rays of light eliminated that possibility, and then they would launch at the best estimate of an intercept course. By night, the crewmen would stay on the sweeps, providing that extra one or two knots to give them the advantage over their prey, the *Protocol* trailing behind as best it could. With the rise of dawn, they would return to their positions in the sails to coax out every inch of cloth they could to catch the end of that train of ships. If planning was correct, they would catch sight of those ships within a day, reaching them with the waning hours of sunset. Then in the dark of night, sometimes with virtually no moon, the *Phoenix* would come along the trailing ship and send their crews to the longboats. These Malagasy warriors possessed a stealth that few others of their kind could boast as they would silently and quickly take the oars, rowing first behind and then alongside their quarry, using grappling and baling hooks to make their way up the sides of the boat. In these late hours, the night watches would be groggy from the late hour combined with illicit sips of rum, making the process of dispatching the man on the stern that much easier. Once the Malagasy were aboard, they would fix those grappling hooks into the gunwales of the ship, signaling with a tug as the crew on the *Phoenix* began to haul in the capstans. The subtle drag on their quarry's stern was virtually imperceptible, but gave the pursuers the opportunity to furl their sails, removing those reflective yards of white and making them virtually invisible behind their captive.

Before the officer of the watch of the target vessel was aware of what was happening to them, the crew of the *Phoenix* were making their way across those taut lines after lowering their anchors as silently as they could, creating a brake that would grind that unsuspecting ship to a virtual halt. The sleeping crewmen would be neutralized, sometimes violently, often times complicitly. With the predators now firmly affixed to her stern, the captive crew was pressed into service to begin unloading every bit of their cargo, which was passed abaft onto the decks of the *Phoenix*. This process would continue until just before dawn and the last of cargo was offloaded.

Before departing Thatcher and Caesar would take the vanquished captain aside to make him an offer he couldn't refuse. Every captain of every merchant vessel always hid a stash of gold to purchase supplies and stores, and ferreting out that hidden treasure could sometimes take days. So the option presented to the captain was straightforward: reveal the hiding place without resistance, or a copious portion of the gunpowder maintained on board the *Phoenix* would be loaded into his hold and blown, and he and his ship would be left to contemplate their hidden wealth at the bottom of the Caribbean. A sea captain was a vain creature, and while he may be able to live with the removal of his cargo, the notion of having to make his way back to port on a piece of flotsam, or as the guest of a rescuing ship, was a fate worse than death to many of them. The wiser choice allowed them to at least keep a shred of dignity and more often than not prompted them to reveal their hidden cache.

Before cutting the lines that held them, the Malagasy crew would busy themselves by stripping the sails from the captive ship's rigging, making a game of tying them into a big knot and setting them afloat in empty barrels before bidding adieu to the waylaid ship. Before that crew could make their way over the sides and into the boats, then paddle to those floating barrels and begin unraveling the Gordian knots left for them, the *Phoenix* would be long gone over the horizon to rendezvous with the *Protocol*, if she hadn't caught up already. And after those hours and sometimes days when at last their escort arrived to find the crew making attempting to make the ship sailable again, the captain would always have to explain how in the dead of night he was captured, drained and cast aside, no better than a zebu endures a vampire bat.

When their holds were full, the *Phoenix* and *Protocol* would make their way to the southeast tip of Jamaica. This remote jungle-choked and cove-pocked end of the island provided ample cover for retreat, their holds laden with merchandise. A few of their Malagasy crewmen would take a boat, rowing the few dozen miles to just outside Port Royal, where they would report to the Drummond Corporation offices. There they would notify Captain Drummond of their arrival then carry back any dispatches for Thatcher and Caesar.

On this latest venture, having taken a particularly fat Spanish merchanter en route to Havana off the northern coast of Puerto Rico, the *Phoenix* and the *Protocol* had to negotiate the very dangerous and tricky waters between the coasts of Puerto Rico and Hispañola, an area typically crawling with Spanish gunboats. They were given chase as they rounded the northwest port town of Aguadilla and had to run due south for nearly two days to escape their pursuer, making a circuitous route northwest to Kingston. While they could have easily faced their pursuer and stood an excellent chance of blasting her to the bottom, they realized that they were gaining a certain reputation as the "ghost fleet" of the Caribbean. Their hit-and-run tactics did minimal damage, except to cargo and ego, and left their adversaries with yet another ship to refill and send to them again. They knew that in Spanish and French colonies, word of these curious *vampiro* was creating a profound sense of both fear and curiosity. Being a superstitious lot, these specter-like strikes were playing on the natural fears seamen of the unknown far more effectively than would the standard, less sophisticated blast, steal and sink technique of the pedestrian privateer or pirate and prompted less vigorous chases by would be pursuers like these which were steadily disappearing in their wake. Having shaken their stalker, they at last made their run to their favorite cove just outside of Port Royal and dispatched their messengers with the usual aplomb. The ships' crews lounged in the balmy tropical heat, awaiting the return of the couriers, and they were surprised when the envoys made their return appearance in less than a day. As was typical, Edward Drummond sent his dispatch to update them as to affairs on which he would extrapolate in greater detail when he saw them, but Thatcher noticed a curious little post-script at the end of this note: *Please tell me you have bolts of silk in red and in green.*

When Captain Drummond arrived in the *Dominion*, he greeted his two captains with great joy and caught them up on the news of the day. It seemed as if they had guessed correctly – word of this phantom fleet of mostly Africans was beginning to circulate throughout the Caribbean. Captain Drummond had entertained a Dutch merchant from Bonaire who had heard from contacts in New Andalusia about a mysterious ship that appeared out of nowhere in the dead of night and had picked ships clean without waking a single crewman. Seamen being a superstitious lot, there were suggestions that these were the ghosts of pirates who had died and gone to hell and were sailing under the commission of Satan himself. One fellow even swore he saw cloven hooves on the crewmen and claimed that the very distinct scent of brimstone permeated the ship for days afterward. Because they were in legion with hell, they could not show themselves by daylight, and the ships mysteriously disappeared with the first rays of dawn. Thatcher and Caesar rolled with genuine mirth that they had gone from being mere pirates to spawns of Satan. Ironically, they mused, the legion of hell must deplore violence more than the typical living and breathing sea raider, considering the minimal loss of life associated with their own captures. As they enjoyed their cups and their growing legend, Thatcher handed the manifest to Drummond so he could peruse for himself the merchandise he would have to unload.

"Oh, and, as you can see, Captain Drummond, you will note we have a fine array of silks in a rainbow of colors. This should, I'm certain, make your lady friend quite pleased," Thatcher teased.

"My dear boy, please understand that my urgency is not from a mere sense of latter-day affection, for the customer in question is quite connected and could be most helpful in our commercial enterprises.

Besides, dear boy," the Captain blushed, "no matter how beautiful, radiant and ravishing the lovely Sarah Whetstone may be, alas, she is merely a child of sixteen."

"Whetstone?" Thatcher queried. "As in Admiral Whetstone?"

"Yes, indeed, lads. The charming young daughter of the Commodore of her Majesty's Royal Navy."

"Do you think that doing business with a daughter of the Royal Navy is a smart thing, Drummond?" Caesar pressed.

"As we strive to strike an air of legitimacy, who better to make that entre for us than the most respected young woman of the island?" Drummond replied, a broad smile on his face. "Besides, even I must confess that the charms of Sarah Whetstone are difficult to ignore, no matter how risky."

Thatcher nodded his head in agreement. Back in Bristol, he was well familiar with the comely mother of this young woman though, like most smart mothers, she had been ever vigilant to keep her daughter away from the son of the infamous brothel owner. As she could not have been more than ten or eleven when he left Bristol, he could not recall the younger but the womanly shape of the mother was well remembered. The fact that Drummond had scored such an important contact was underscored by his intriguing description of the person in question. Thatcher had been at sea a number of months, and while he and Caesar had made their share of trips into St. Johns to blow off steam and pursue carnal pleasures, he hated to admit that the quality of the merchandise had most certainly been wanting, and the idea of breaking the routine and perhaps an innocent nymph's hymen was quite motivating to him. "As usual, Drummond, you make perfect sense. So it only makes more sense that you have a chance to introduce her to your nephew, do you not agree?"

"Thatch ..." Caesar warned, raising an eyebrow.

"It would only be proper. Besides, what harm could a little flirtation cause?"

"I can't leave these ships by themselves, Thatcher," Caesar pressed.

"And you need not be my nursemaid, dear brother. Captain Drummond will keep a good eye on me and make certain I remain on my best behavior ... won't you, Uncle?"

The gleam in Thatcher's eye was both dangerous and infectious as a crooked and mischievous smile crossed his face. Caesar had to remind himself that Thatcher was only twenty-three, and no matter how irrational such a venture may be, at times the boy still had to be a boy.

"One week," Caesar insisted, "and then I come looking for you."

"One week?" Thatcher queried as if time really mattered in this place where time stood still.

"We are not having a repeat of Philadelphia," Caesar warned.

As the sloop caught its wind and sailed free of the sheltered cove in which the *Phoenix* and *Protocol* virtually disappeared, Captain Drummond set his westward course for the short sail to Port Royal. Beside him, Thatcher was quiet in his thoughts, that roguish smile still fixed firmly on his face as his mind turned to the adventures that faced him over the next seven days.

"So, Thatcher," Captain Drummond asked as they neared the dock built for the *Dominion*. "What happened in Philadelphia?"

II

Since returning to Jamaica, Captain Drummond still could not help but feel a sense of unease as he made his way through this tragic body of water, still known as Port Royal. As he picked his way through the shoals and submerged wreckage to the deep and navigable channel, he could still imagine the landmarks, those homes and warehouses and taverns, that vital city built with the gold-laden sailor in mind, now nothing more than a graveyard under the still water that led to newly constructed docks now serving merely as a port of entry to the thriving town of Kingston. Before that tragic day in 1693, Kingston had been simply a small village on the outskirts of the raucous Port Royal. After the earthquake, those survivors who chose not to put this horrible memory behind them and move on to safer colonies had relocated up the hill and turned this sleepy village into the thriving capital of this indomitable Jamaica.

Captain Drummond put the crew to work offloading the merchandise and turned to retrieve the bolts of silk he had requested, only to see them cradled in Thatcher's arms. He was standing on the dock, anxiously awaiting the much slower Captain Drummond to get a move on.

"We mustn't keep the Admiral's daughter waiting, must we?" Thatcher insisted as he motioned for Drummond to lead the way.

The steep trip up the path to the Admiralty mansion left Captain Drummond winded as Thatcher's long legs pushed the pace ever quicker. From her window, Sarah Whetstone had seen the sloop *Dominion* arrive and was anxious to see if Captain Drummond had really come through so quickly with her request. She noticed that with him was a tall, dark-haired stranger, unusual for Captain Drummond considering his all-African crew. She could see the young man carrying in his arms two wrapped packages of a size and shape that would indicate bolts of fabric, and she began to feel a little thrill and girlish giddiness at the thought. As the captain and his companion drew closer, she could see that he was quite a bit younger and very handsome, with black clothing and long black hair. As they approached the door, she bolted down the stairs to answer before the servants could.

Having scanned the seas for years for the most minute signs of sail, Thatcher's trained eye quickly caught the sight of the lovely young girl at the window watching their arrival. While she peered out through curtains, it was impossible to hide her loveliness. Seeing as they were being observed, he attempted to slow his pace and allow Captain Drummond to catch his breath and muster a measure of dignity. Thatcher stopped just short of the door, checking Drummond's appearance and likewise encouraging him to check his own. His tongue reflectively ran to his teeth to assure that no vile piece of meat hung from them as they stepped to the set of double doors. Captain Drummond knocked, and it was flung open almost instantly by Sarah Whetstone.

It didn't happen often for Thatcher, but when it did it was obvious and almost excruciating. There she stood at the door, that beautiful, faultless skin framed in dark curls, wearing a cream colored dress with her tiny frame cinched at the waist, sending her lovely grapefruit-sized breasts into two mirroring arches peeking over the lace-trimmed neckline in the most playful and inviting display. There was no mistaking this as Sarah Whetstone, for she had blossomed into the spitting image of her mother. This man, who prided himself for his command of many languages, was incapable of giving anything more than an audible gasp.

Sarah studied the tall, handsome, sun-kissed young man who towered above her, his eyes firmly fixed on her carefully sculpted décolletage. The sight of Captain Drummond, visibly embarrassed by the obvious enrapture of his young companion, provided a moment of painfully uncomfortable silence as he reached for the right words to say. But as he reached for them, Sarah brought them home in her most direct fashion.

"Captain Drummond, you've been a love and brought me my silks! Now, who is this handsome young fellow you've brought me as well?" she purred.

It was the most English of tendencies for families to make great strides to preserve their ancestral names, and now again, far from England, she was being reminded of that as Captain Drummond made the introduction.

"So, you are Edward Drummond as well?" she offered as the silent, staring young man sat in the chair across from her. "So, Edward Drummond, tell me all about yourself and what brought you to Jamaica." Sarah leaned forward on the edge of the couch, placing her hands upon her knees as she waited with baited breath for this mute young giant to speak.

"Um ... well, I'm ... I'm ... here to learn the family business," he stammered, as Sarah Whetstone playfully manipulated that prominent neckline, mesmerizing the dumbstruck lothario.

"And so you are from where?" she inquired.

"Bristol," he replied, forgetting his need for deception and discretion, one that would not only cover his tracks but possibly spare him a bit of heartbreak. For when she heard Bristol, Sarah Whetstone smiled.

"Bristol, you say?" she stated joyfully at the mere mention of the word. "What a small world, Edward Drummond. I'm from Bristol as well. And yet, I don't believe I made your acquaintance there. But, perhaps you may know my fiancé. He, too, is from Bristol. Certainly you've met him – Woodes Rogers?"

The very mention of Woodes Rogers' name drove a dagger into his heart that momentarily disengaged his stare from those lovely pert breasts, and he once again discovered that breathtaking face, now beaming with utter happiness. Her violet eyes virtually radiated with warmth and affection at the hope of obtaining a common ground with this handsome stranger. What she saw instead was the color draining from his face.

"Woodes Rogers, you say?" Thatcher replied pathetically. "Your fiancé? You're engaged to Woodes Rogers?"

"You do know him, then! Well, perhaps engagement is not the correct word. For he refuses to finalize arrangements for our nuptials until he makes captain. But I'm confident," she said, leaning forward conspiratorially, "that such a commission will come soon, what with this war and all."

If she noticed his pain and suffering, it certainly wasn't obvious, for Thatcher was now in utter misery at the thought that this lovely, vivacious young woman would wish to engage herself to that uptight, self-righteous prig. The very thought that that simpering fool would one day bed this beauty, if, God forbid, he hadn't already, was more pain and suffering than Thatcher could bear. This sudden overwhelming skin-crawling disdain made him crave nothing more than his ship and Caesar's unsympathetic mockery. He stood as if to go when her hands came across the small gap between them and landed on his thighs, pushing him back into the chair. Captain Drummond sat silently watching this tragic yet intriguing event unfold before his eyes, feeling so immensely uncomfortable and yet, reminiscent of a cockfight, unable to turn away from the horrific gore. Sarah's eyes now fixed on Thatcher's, and his motions ceased as he acquiesced to the demands of her delicate hands.

"Oh, certainly, you're not going so quickly? I'm intrigued to learn more about you, young Edward Drummond. So tell me," she insisted, her mouth now shaped into a wicked little grin. "What did you do to occupy your time in Bristol?"

"An apprenticeship, Miss Whetstone," Captain Drummond interjected, knowing the revelation of Bristol had been an unintended faux pas of his young partner. "Actually, the Drummonds of Bristol are distant relatives, but they, too, are in shipping, and when our Southampton branch decided to put forth this venture in Jamaica, my brother, Edward's father, arranged for him to apprentice with one of our cousins. Naturally, we're all aware of the Rogers family. In fact, Edward, if I remember correctly, you attempted to sign aboard one of his crews, did you not?"

Thatcher realized that Drummond was trying to cover for his mistake and hoped to tag onto that line of monologue to further amplify the story and distance himself from any intimacy to Woodes

Rogers, Jr. He searched his mind and the best that he could come up with was a weak pathetic, "Yes."

"So I take it, then, your attempts weren't fruitful?" she further inquired.

"Um ... no," Thatcher stammered.

"Well, my understanding was he was outfitting his ships for naval service. I'm surprised that he would turn down someone willing to sail with him against the French," she puzzled.

This turn of events in this inquisition did nothing to resurrect Thatcher from his obvious dying as now it was giving the impression that he was unfit to serve Her Majesty's fleet. In his attempts to aid the boy, Drummond was only making him look worse, and if he could not find himself quickly his tiny ship was tossed.

"Actually, a better opportunity came up that would help my family forward their business endeavors and allow me to serve her Majesty on this front," Thatcher mustered.

"So it wasn't that you were unfit, just not motivated to serve in the Navy then?" Sarah inquired further.

"Her Majesty's Navy is an honorable profession for those who seek that career. As a child of an Admiral, you certainly understand how such an arrangement, though rewarding personally and patriotically, can limit one's capability to serve familial interests," Thatcher reasoned, finding the strength in himself to strike a chord with this inquisitive teenaged girl. As he found his voice, he once again turned his attention to her wares.

"Yes, Mr. Drummond, you are correct, Naval service can be hard on a man with a family. And do you have a wife and children as well that would lead you to make such a career choice for yourself?"

"I do have family to whom I'm very close, but a wife and children aren't my motivations at this moment."

"That I do understand, Mr. Drummond. My dear Woodes said exactly the same thing as he sailed off into the waters of our enemies for God knows how long. But you mentioned similar opportunities without a naval commitment. Am I to understand that you're a privateer?"

"Actually, ma'am, that would be me," Captain Drummond replied. "But as I can extend my Letter of Marque to my choice of captain, I have designated it to my nephew while I pursue more land-borne interests."

Sarah took all that in for a moment, and then it dawned on her as she reached onto the couch next to her and took up the bolts of silk. "So am I to surmise, then, that this is privateer booty? Taken by you, young Edward?"

Thatcher's confidence began to return to its rightful place. "Yes, Miss Whetstone, you may safely surmise that."

This turn of events was quite intriguing to Sarah as now she discovered that the handsome young man across from her was very much like her dear Woodes, only smarter. For while Woodes may hunt down the enemy, destroy its warships and plunder the riches of its merchants, his efforts were for the Queen and all his takings belonged to Her. Whereas Edward here, with his uncle's Letter of Marque, got to keep what he found and decide what was fair for the Queen, upon proper accounting of course.

"You know, I would be so fascinated to hear about your adventures at sea, Edward," she breathed as her eyes once again studied Thatcher carefully. Captain Drummond took this as his cue.

"Well, if you'll excuse me, I alas am quite late for an appointment. Perhaps you'll allow me to take my leave while Edward tells a tale or two," Captain Drummond stated as he stood to leave. Neither Sarah nor Thatcher bothered to rise or offer resistance.

"Very well, Captain. Please don't let us keep you from your next engagement, and thank you so much for my silks," Sarah replied, looking in his direction with gratitude. Whether that look was for the silks or the taking of his leave was debatable, but he bowed his head toward the lady then cocked it toward Thatcher and replied, as humbly as he could, "Don't thank me, thank him."

Without missing a beat, she smiled at the Captain and said, "Indeed I shall."

Captain Drummond allowed a little spring in his step as he traveled down the path and back to his office. He kicked up his feet onto his desk, placing his arms behind his head, and smiled as his imagination allowed him to live vicariously through his young namesake.

Thatcher's life had often demanded a measure of discretion. All his years at Parker House had required that the men who patronized were given a measure of pretense for their visits with Yvgeny and Thatcher. While all knew why they were there, there was the illusion that this was mere friendly chatter and then a discreet departure to the upper rooms. But that lifelong discretion had been slowly melting away over the last few years, what with his bawdy exploits in New York and his polygamist audacity on St. Mary's. He had regained a measure of politic in his courtship with Melanie, but that discretion quickly melted away the moment she became Mrs. Thatcherev and her passionate exploits quickly shattered that reserved Quaker veneer. Still, he had tried to have the good sense to reclaim even a measure of that circumspect when in the company of those good men and women of Philadelphia.

As the noon bell sounded in the Admiralty mansion, Thatcher had to surmise to himself whether the Vice-Admiral maintained his Naval rigidity to schedule and would be walking through his door in mere moments to see a young stranger fornicating with his daughter on his couch. This drafty Caribbean home with its multitude of windows opened wide to capture the breezes certainly provided no measure of barrier as the spirited Sarah Whetstone demonstrated her audible pleasure at the vigorous thrustings of Edward Drummond. He prided himself on being able to put his full attention toward the young lady or ladies with whom he was carnally entwined, but the thoughts of the whereabouts of the servants of this magnificent home, combined with his attempts to listen for the Admiral's footfalls on the walk below, were distracting irritations. Yet Sarah seemed oblivious to these minor concerns as her fingers dug into his hindquarters, insisting he pump faster and, yes, it would seem, deeper. From his vantage point he could see not only the gorgeous face of the half-clad woman below him but also the top of an Admiral's hat slowly growing larger and more prominent as it made its way up the steep walk.

His eyes turned back down to hers, indicating an item of concern, but through her pants and lustful pleas she demanded, "Don't you dare stop!" Thatcher now had other thoughts to consider, relying upon his naval skills of distance and speed calculations to determine that in about twenty-five seconds the Admiral would be walking through the door, and if they were able to disengage now he would be able to pull up his trousers and disappear out the French doors which spilled out on to the broad lawn behind the house. But her possessive grip on his arse and her vigorous bucking and painful biting of his hand, which he was attempting to put over her mouth, began to make the seconds wind down, and he figured he now had about five seconds to disengage and run with breeches in hand. But as the chronometer in his head counted down to four, three, two, one ... the door did not open, and he began his minus count backwards from what should have been a collision course. Once again, she was trying to speak, but his hand covering her mouth to stifle her moans was making that impossible, so she raked his hindquarters with her nails in an effort to get him to remove his hand while still insisting he keep up his manly ministrations.

"He always takes his noon meal on the green," she informed him as she bit her lip and commanded, "Faster!"

Admiral Whetstone was enjoying a heady tankard of draught beer following his midday feast as he reviewed the notes for his upcoming survey of English fortifications. He was somewhat disappointed that Sarah had not joined him, but he knew how she was with her endless rounds of visits and engagements that she so graciously committed to on his behalf. He was very pleased to hear her voice, and he turned to see her coming onto the green from the front of the house, a young man in tow toting two parcels for her.

"Hello, Father. I am sorry I'm late, but I was so excited at the arrival of some parcels Captain Drummond – the commander of that small trading sloop the *Dominion* – had arranged for me to receive. When I got his message, I virtually flew down the walk to retrieve them, and this young man was kind enough to bring them back here for me," she explained as she embraced her father's shoulders, kissing him on top of his forehead.

"Darling, you need not go to the trouble of retrieving such things yourself. That's what we have servants for," he admonished her fondly.

As she sat beside him in her chair, she motioned for her guest to approach. "Father, you know me, I get so excited about these things. I just have to dive in myself. It did leave me with a dilemma of how to carry those heavy parcels here. But this young man, Edward Drummond, the Captain's nephew, was such a dear. Edward, I would like to introduce you to my father, Vice-Admiral William Whetstone. Father, Edward Drummond."

Admiral Whetstone, while quite accustomed to but never pleased with the constant male attention given to his daughter, sized up the tall, good looking young man with the weathered skin. His dark complexion betrayed a man who had spent some time exposed to the ocean skies.

"Mr. Drummond, thank you for your kindness. My daughter can be quite passionate and headstrong when she wants something and sometimes does not have the good graces to wait patiently for what she wishes for to come to her. We appreciate your kindness," the Vice-Admiral stated as he turned away from this latest of his daughter's gentlemen callers.

"It's my pleasure, Admiral Whetstone," Thatcher replied. "She seemed quite helpless, attempting to handle such a precarious load in those tiny hands, and I was happy to give what I could in assistance."

"Father, young Edward has just sailed in to learn more about his uncle's enterprises, and I was hoping as a way of showing my appreciation ... well, I invited him to dinner."

"Dear, as you know we're entertaining the captains of the fleet this evening. Under the circumstances ..." Whetstone's voice trailed off.

"Oh, pooh. There will be no call for me to be there as you'll be so busy talking navy things, I'll just get underfoot and be left to dine by myself. Perhaps Mr. Drummond could join me here on the lawn and leave you busy important men to your busy important things," she reasoned, her big eyes and innocent face being worked to great effect on her father.

"That would not be appropriate, dear, without a chaperone," he replied, kindly but dismissively.

"Well, I certainly intend to invite his uncle as well. You've met him, haven't you?"

"Yes, I've encountered Captain Drummond on a few occasions." Arguing with his daughter was pointless, for while he may have been commander of the seas and of the men who sailed it, in his home he was a mere midshipman under the direction of the insistent and delightful Sarah Whetstone. He sighed, slumping his shoulders in resignation. "Under those circumstances, I may consider that acceptable. However, my men will be very disappointed you won't be joining us."

She wrapped her arms around her father's neck, an inappropriate gesture for a man of his station, hugged him tightly and sweetly, and once again gave him a little kiss to his forehead. "Oh, Father, they'll scarcely know I'm gone," she said. She turned to Thatcher. "Eight o'clock then?'"

Thatcher tipped his hat in acknowledgement and bid adieu to the Admiral's back. "Pleasure, sir, and thank you for the invitation." He was about to engage Sarah further, but she was now sitting on the arm of her father's chair, her arm around his shoulder as he was untying the length of canvas wrapped around those bolts of silk, and as he walked away he could hear her high sweet, voice titter. Thatcher shook his head as he mulled over these last few hours and the amazing power of this sixteen-year-old nymph, and he thought of her comments to her father as she made excuses to miss this dinner with his captains. *Scarcely know you're gone, indeed.*

When he told Captain Drummond of their dinner plans, the old man smiled as he knew the dangerous waters they were wading into. This dinner she was bypassing was a critical one. Though not an official occasion, demanding her hostessing, all the captains of the Royal Fleet had been making their way into Port Royal for the last few days in preparation for this evening's engagement. And while there would not be dancing and song, where the ladies of Port Royal would turn out in their fineries, it was one of the most important events the captains would attend in some time. For Admiral Whetstone was here for one specific purpose, and that was to put his fleet in ship-shape. Since the conclusion of the previous unpleasantries with France, the Royal Navy had struggled with poor command and control of her Caribbean waters, owing as much to the class of officer as to the difficulty of recruiting sailors.

When they arrived at the appointed time, they were greeted by the lovely Sarah Whetstone, whose seamstress had miraculously fashioned that bolt of red silk into a lovely gown. When Sarah had summoned her with the impossible demand, the dress-maker turned to every woman she knew on the island who could handle a needle and thread to join her in her cramped shop to take those measurements she had retrieved only an hour before and transform that raw silk bolt into a work of art, complete with gem trimmings and appliqués. This small legion followed her up to the Admiralty, where they fitted that gown to utter perfection in record time so Sarah Whetstone could give those captains preparing to sail into harm's way a good memory and a reason to return to Jamaica. She made the point of introducing Captain and Mr. Drummond to all the assembled Naval captains, who were surprised to see civilians horning in on their private affair. But, as

Sarah explained, "I'll do little more than get underfoot and distract you from your responsibilities at hand, so consider it a blessing," as half the servant staff now attended to the three who would dine on the verandah and the other half attended to the fifteen naval officers in the dining room.

While Admiral Whetstone held court with his officers, Sarah Whetstone was the Queen of the green, engaging her guests in humorous banter and flirtation, sending titters and giggles resounding through that empty space between her small party and that grave collection of officers a few dozen feet away. During one of her many brief flights from her company to make a short appearance with the officers, she left open the door between the officers and the privateers. Thatcher could not resist taking this opportunity to listen to the Admiral present his best intelligence on the presence of the Spanish and French ships plying the Caribbean and England's plan for their defeat.

"Captain Coddrington has done bang-up work in pushing the French toward their southern possessions. He has done with a few men what our Navy can't do, and by God, gentlemen, that is an embarrassment – that a few ragtag planters under the guidance of a colonial governor can give defeat and harm to the French while we tuck our tail and retreat. Look what happened with Carolina and their foray against St. Augustine. Some may argue it was a fool's venture, but they sent those Spanish into their citadel where they hid for a month, and it was only the replacement of one Havana governor with another who had more gumption that the Spanish received any relief. I am telling you, gentlemen," the Admiral demanded, "we must push Spain and France out of our waters. We have good intelligence that a gentleman's agreement existed between our governor in the Bahamas and the governors of Cuba and La Florida allowing open trade despite our war. This sort of behavior will not be tolerated. But the despicable actions of the captains under Admiral Benbow and the successes from these 'phantom' privateers is making us look like rank amateurs. And this will not stand. Here is my command, gentlemen. We're going after the French and the Spanish. We will not have a repeat of what happened to Admiral Benbow. And the first of you who does not adhere to my command immediately will be met on his quarterdeck and personally hanged by me at sea. I want this perfectly understood."

Thatcher listened to the Admiral threaten his captains with the death penalty and knew that, despite his best efforts to motivate and frighten his men into complicity, there would be those who would be inclined to risk the rope to mask their cowardice. What he needed to do now was to see where they planned to go in pursuit of the French and Spanish. If he knew where England was, he could surmise where their enemies would run, and that would be an opportunity for his ghost fleet. He was caught up in his thoughts when Sarah Whetstone slipped behind him in those darkened shadows where he eavesdropped on this conference.

"I knew you couldn't resist this opportunity," she whispered in his ear.

"And is that why you had us come here and entertain you this evening?" Thatcher replied as he felt her hands trailing down the front of his trousers.

"Well, I certainly knew that a man like you would use any advantage he can gain. And more for you means more presents for me," she replied as her body circled around to face him, her hands rubbing and gripping at the front of his pants. "But also, I was desperate for entertainment this evening, and Mr. Drummond, I think you can provide precisely the type of diversion I need."

The porcelain skin of her pert breasts could still be seen in this dim light as she pressed her body to his. He marveled at the sound of that flame-red silk as it slid down the rough material of his tunic. As Sarah slipped to her knees and extricated his swollen penis from its constricting prison, Thatcher leaned against the wall, keeping his hands on her head and his ears on the Vice Admiral's words. As he enjoyed her vigorous oral manipulations, his head turned to look out onto the verandah where he saw Captain Drummond sitting with a glass in his hand and a smile on his face, toasting his young protégé.

In the morning, the fleet took sail as the dozen-odd ships under the command of Vice Admiral Whetstone sailed south out of Port Royal Harbour to make a course due west toward the Spanish Main. The dutiful daughter, Sarah Whetstone stood on the balcony outside her room in her father's favorite gown. From the quarterdeck of the *Canterbury*, he trained his spyglass on her as she waved her handkerchief and blew kisses to him. He remembered when she was just a little girl and he would set sail, and she would join her mother on the docks to repeat that same sweet gesture as he sailed off in service to His Majesty. And though she was growing to be a beautiful woman, in some ways she was still that little girl that warmed her father's heart.

It was good, however, that his spyglass and the blind love of a father could not take in the entire scope of that balcony to see Thatcher, who had climbed out of her bed and skulked over to where she was waving and was now making a feast of her fine, firm derrière.

As soon as the *Canterbury* was clear of Port Royal, Sarah turned and ran inside her bedroom, where her young Captain Drummond now lay sprawled naked on her bed. She didn't bother closing the door as she began tearing off that sweet and innocent white gown, the only stitch of clothing she was wearing that day. When she was in her full naked glory, she stood back from the bed and let dear Edward fully appraise her in this glorious light. And thus his "apprenticeship week" with his dear uncle, alas, proved less than instructive, for other than those times when Sarah wished to walk to the garden to be ravaged or to take a stroll along the beach to ravage him, they had little cause to leave this lovely mansion, where the servants got into the habit of leaving their food on silver trays outside the bedroom. Almost immediately the young master instructed them in the art of preparing coffee, enticing his new obsession to likewise crave this favorite addiction, and the two made constant demands for fresh urns of the hot beverage.

It was under such conditions that Thatcher began to lose track of time, and he had to admit he was somewhat perturbed when the servant knocking at the door announced that Captain Drummond was downstairs to see him. Despite Sarah's protest, Thatcher disengaged and poured himself back into his trousers to receive his "uncle." Captain Drummond still had that very amused smile on his face as he handed him a note.

"This was just delivered to me. I was told it was urgent," Captain Drummond chuckled as Thatcher noted the distinctive sweeping style of Caesar's hand. He opened it and could not stifle a short burst of nervous laughter as the note, in typical Caesar style, got to the point.

Day six, Thatcher. I arrive on tomorrow morning's tide if you are not here.

He folded the note, stuck it into his pocket and told the Captain, "Stick around, will you? Tell the servants to get you some coffee. They're experts at it now," he insisted as he ran back up the stairs. He then ran back down and added, "Tell them we'll be needing another pot shortly as well."

"I just don't understand, Edward," she whined as he explained his need to depart. "I know you told your brother you would be gone for a week, but certainly he'll understand if you need to delay a day or two."

"Well, actually, no he will not," he replied, staring up from between her legs, a cup and saucer resting on her flat little belly. "We have an agreement that we shall always live up to our word, and unless it's death or imprisonment, we must fulfill our obligations to one another, and I promised him one week. That week is up tomorrow."

"And if you don't show?"

"He'll come here."

"And what's so bad about that? I would love to meet your brother," she cooed.

"It won't be a matter of meeting him when he slings me over his shoulder, throws me in the boat and prohibits me from ever coming into Port Royal again."

"Certainly he's not that threatening and intimidating," she challenged. "I think you can hold your own just fine."

"It's not a matter of threats or intimidation. It's a matter of embarrassment, and he will work overtime to embarrass me just to make the point."

She removed the saucer and cup from her flat, stiff belly and pulled him up to her so his large body was laying on hers. She wrapped her arms around him and began kissing his face and neck as her legs encircled his waist, whispering, "But I'm not through with you yet. I'll say when it's time to go."

She made an amazing argument all that evening long, even going so far as to walking down to the sitting room where Captain Drummond was sharing a pot of coffee with the servants as they were passing around his pipe. Wearing only Thatcher's shirt, she plopped down in a chair opposite Captain Drummond and made one final appeal. The coffee's effect was certainly being felt by all in the room as the servants tried to remind themselves of their place and not to study the long, shapely bare legs of the mistress of the house."

"There is just no reasoning with him, Captain. Try as I may, my arguments are falling flat, and I don't want to lose this time with him, nor should I have to. Do you not agree?" she said with all the insistence that a pampered and privileged sixteen-year-old could make.

Captain Drummond adjusted the way he was sitting, crossing his legs and repositioning his saucer and cup, and smiled at this horrible dilemma dear Thatcher had put himself into. "Ah, sweet Sarah. Were it my decision to make I would grant him a reprieve, but his brother will not stand for it, and there is nothing he can do short of running into those mountains to escape his obligation. So if you have some sort of suggestion I could ponder, I'll be happy to consider it." He sipped his coffee, appraising the beautiful young girl with that shirt being held together by one tiny clasp at the waist.

Caesar was readying the dinghy, preparing to sail to Port Royal and retrieve the tardy Thatcher, when off in the distance he saw Captain Drummond's sloop. He was absolutely pleased that he did not have to go through with his plan, which would have certainly humiliated Thatcher and, depending upon his mental state, brought great bodily injury to both of them. He watched that lovely small vessel slice through the waves with Thatcher standing on the bow. When they came in sight of one another, Thatcher waved, a large smile on his face, and Caesar returned the greeting and expression. The sloop slid elegantly alongside the *Protocol* as Caesar reached his hand down to pull Thatcher aboard, the two embracing as loving brothers.

"You had me nervous there for a while," Caesar stated, wagging his finger in Thatcher's face. "It is good you came to your senses." Caesar was beaming in pride to see this display of maturity, when he spotted a movement from the small cabin of the *Dominion*. Caesar and Sarah gave each other the same strange look as Thatcher reached down his hand to bring her aboard. Thatcher sheepishly wrapped an arm around Sarah then faced Caesar with a look of both pride and nervousness.

"Sarah Whetstone, I am very pleased to introduce Simon Drummond," he stated with pride.

Caesar and Sarah studied each other with looks of horror and disbelief. Sarah finally broke her stare contest with Caesar and turned to Thatcher.

"This is your brother?" she asked innocently.

"Have you lost your mind, brother?" Caesar demanded.

"I'm going to head back to Port Royal and let you all sort this out," Captain Drummond called up, a very amused look on his face. "Send for me if you need me before the end of the week." He and the crew of the *Dominion* could be heard laughing their heads off until they were out of earshot. The rest of the Malagasy crew watched in silent horror and amusement as they knew these next few days were certainly going to be a break from the routine.

"She's got to go back, Thatcher," Caesar demanded as he paced back and forth in the cabin of the *Protocol*. "Have you completely lost your mind?"

"It will only be for a few days, Caesar," Thatcher reasoned as he pulled out a bottle of fine Jamaican rum and sat it between them. "I mean, what harm can it do? Her father's at sea for God knows how long. A few more days of idle amusement and all will be fine. I'll send her back with Drummond. It'll be a fantastic memory, and we'll be gone."

"Have you completely lost your mind?" Caesar repeated. "You above anyone else know what it is like to have a woman on board ship. Forget your lack of focus. Think about the crew. Think about who she is. Think about where she's from."

"Oh, Caesar. The crew can head into Port Royal anytime they choose to settle their discontent. It is my understanding that they've been venturing off into the mountains where there is an ample supply of young women who seem to take great pleasure in their sea tales. And as for you, my dear brother, you've been cooped up on this ship much too long. I say go break a headboard or two, and I'll watch the ships and prepare for sail."

"Have you completely lost your mind? You're not going to get a damn thing done around here and that's fine. We're used to your idle diversions. We love you for it. But you don't need to be making yourself miserable and heartsick over something you know you can't have. Particularly ... her!"

"You're misreading the whole thing, Caesar. I mean, look at her! I'm telling you, my dear brother, I just can't get enough of that ..." Thatcher admitted, putting his fingers in the shape of a triangle. "And most intriguing, she's engaged to Woodes Rogers! Now come on, please allow me this one small pleasure. If not for me, for Bristol!"

Caesar sat quietly for a moment and then began to chuckle to himself. "Okay, now that I can appreciate. But here's the deal, and I'm holding you to this. You have your playtime. Keep it on your ship, in your cabin, and when it's time for her to go, no protest. Deal?"

Thatcher ran around the desk and hugged Caesar, grabbing him by the waist and lifting him up. "This is why I love you so much! You understand me."

Caesar didn't like it when Thatcher lifted him up, and he swung around his back, grabbed his legs and pulled them out from underneath him, sending Thatcher crashing heavily to the ground with Caesar landing on him. And like kids, they began wrestling in the cabin of the *Protocol*, knocking over the desk, much of the cabinetry and breaking the rum bottle in the process. They failed to notice when the door opened and Sarah Whetstone was standing there, watching these two grown men fighting like little boys.

"Now there's something a girl doesn't see often enough. Two grown men gallivanting like bear cubs?" she commented, taking in the sight of the two men, their shirts ripped from the roughhousing and both sweating in the tropical Jamaican heat. For a moment, a story of Bristol past crossed her mind. It was about two boys, one English, one African, calling themselves brothers. She mused for a moment and Caesar noted her curious thoughtfulness.

Thatcher stood up, putting a hand down to Caesar and lifting him. As he came to a standing position, Caesar pressed his mouth to Thatcher's ear and whispered, "Keep her on your ship, brother."

The next few days passed uneventfully, save Thatcher and Sarah's endless need to copulate as her constant whines, cries and cursings announced. It was quite distracting for the crew, but Sarah seemed to relish the attention it brought her, and Thatcher was oblivious to anything but her. Caesar had learned to tune it out and went about the business of preparing the ships for sailing as the sloop repeatedly returned from and to Port Royal for supplies and provisions. Many of the Malagasy amused themselves with visits to the mountains, both to seek out carnal companionship and to hunt the prolific game available on the island. The smell of cooked flesh was omnipresent nearly around the clock, and a healthy stock of pigs was reportedly en route to be carried live on board.

It had been many long and torturous days in the sun, and Caesar was enjoying the relative quiet, noticing the silence from the adjacent *Phoenix* as he settled into his tub for a long leisurely soak. He let his mind wander back to Madagascar, wondering whatever became of his wives, those beautiful women with their long, pendular breasts and glorious dispositions, and hoped that one day he could find them and show them how much he missed them. It was in this idle reminiscing, with his eyes closed and his head leaning back in the tub, that he noticed a draft coming from his cabin door.

He opened his eyes to see Sarah Whetstone standing there in little more than a simple cotton gown, and the light coming from the passageway shone through that thin material, showing those outrageous curves that need not be emphasized by whalebone.

"I'm sorry to interrupt, but may we have a word?" Sarah inquired as she stood there in the doorway, fully aware of Caesar's appraising survey of her femininity.

"I think you're on the wrong ship," Caesar replied, his face turning to the normal sober expression for which he was famous.

"I think the poor boy is exhausted, and as I could not rest for the thought of your disdain for me, I felt it important to come here to discuss this matter, if we may," she continued as she slowly crossed the floor toward the tub.

Caesar wasn't surprised by her brazenness. He knew Sarah's type well. Growing up in Bristol, he may have been an Edwards to the household, but he was a big African man to everyone else. Many, particularly the gentrified class, went out of their way to avoid him, giving him a wide berth out of fear and general disdain for his ancestry. But then, there were those particularly pretty young women who, despite the protests of their mothers as they would catch them in their long, curious glances at Caesar, every now and then had to give in to their curiosity. And whether it was down at the docks or in the markets, there were those few who were brazen enough to place their tiny, pale bodies in close proximity with this very large black man and with their defiant little attitudes challenge him to scare them. Sometimes it was nothing more than a little girl sating her curiosity of something strange and unusual, but then there were those times when a pretty teenaged thing would approach him with her brazen talk, to be met by his menacing smile and an invitation to discover the truth for herself. He often wondered how many chocolate covered babies were being raised in London right now or had their Royal lineages cut short under the knife of the discreet midwives who specialized not only in the bringing but taking of life. Sarah Whetstone was one of those little girls.

Sarah studied his face as he appraised her with a look of amusement and disdain. She knew her effect on men and seldom was there one whom she could not soften - or harden as the situation may require. But this one was an enigma. It was obvious her Edward loved him and respected him in ways she could not understand. He had finally explained how Caesar was adopted when he was a small boy and raised by these very progressive Drummonds as if he were their son. He was obviously a very commanding man and no doubt quite intelligent. Yet he possessed an impenetrable shell and disdain for her that just didn't make sense.

"It has puzzled me why you despise me so," she stated bluntly as she sat upon the edge of that small tub, big enough only for Caesar to sit in with legs crossed. She could see his knees breaking the surface of the water. Caesar made no effort to shield her from her source of curiosity, and he felt her eyes traveled down his knees and thighs into the crystal clear water, the copper bottom reflecting all available light in the room.

"It's not that I despise you. It's just that I know you," he replied, now gaining that cocky smile that made one either loathe him or love him.

"You say you know me. How can that be when we've never even had a conversation?"

"I should say, I've known your kind, more times than I can count."

She studied that deeply muscled chest and shoulders and those powerful arms resting on the edge of the tub. His chiseled stomach was cut not only with knots of muscles but with what appeared to be numerous injuries, some old, some new. His body was hairless, including that prominent skull which he meticulously shaved every day, giving it a sheen from the lamplight in his cabin. The dark skin only emphasized the muscles and power in his body.

"I must say I've never had this kind of conversation with an African before, though I have known girls who have. So I am not surprised to hear that you may think you know who and what I am, but I say you should not judge a book by its cover, or your past experiences with present." She could not help but look down in that water, where that prominent dark object that had been lying upon the bottom had over these last few moments raised itself closer to the surface. She very openly admired the sight of that long, massive appendage that, as she gazed, seemed to be looking back, not blinking from this staring contest. "I can confess that since I've heard the tales, I have been ever so curious to know if the rumors were true."

"And? What of the rumors? Are they true?"

She sighed and nodded. "Yes, apparently so, only I would guess greatly underestimated."

"Well, now you know, and so your curiosity has been satisfied, has it not?"

Her eyes now escaped the gaze of the cobra and looked into Caesar's dark penetrating stare and confessed, "Alas, I think not."

She was now in a staring contest with an even more intimidating opponent, and she was adamant that she would not blink. Neither did he as she lifted that thin cotton gown over her head, grasped the edge of the tub and lowered herself into the water. It was in no way to diminish the power and prowess of her most recent playmate, but unlike those times with him when all she wanted was for him to make every attempt to saw her in half, in this circumstance all she desired was to slowly luxuriate and soak in every delicious second of this mind and body expanding experience. Caesar never moved a muscle – well, only one – as he sat back and enjoyed Miss Sarah's ride through Africa. Her limbs found a firm footing around his back as she gripped the edge of the tub and arched her back, her long curls cascading behind. What surprised him, considering the audible performance he had been an involuntary audience to these last few days, was how quiet she was, as she took in deep breaths and bit her bottom lip, slowly sliding up and down his proud Malagasy spear.

Thatcher awoke, still naked and smelling of that wonderful youthful fragrance so distinctive to Sarah Whetstone. It made him smile, for "Whetstone" seemed so appropriate for her. Smelling his thin moustache, in emulation to Uncle Peter, he realized that he was much too dry for his preference. He called out her name, thinking perhaps she had made her way to the cathole at the head of the ship, and in this moonlight what a wonderful chair it would make. But she was not there, and he could see the small dinghy that had been tied to his boat was now attached to the *Protocol*. Being the seasoned sailor that he was, he lowered himself onto the rope and shimmied over the line that was attached to his sister ship, quietly making his way down the long dark hall where a number of the crew were slumbering. It had been his hope that Sarah and Caesar could get acquainted, for he knew that when Caesar got to know her he would have as much affection for her as did Thatcher, and he hoped that, in these quiet hours the night before she was to return to Kingston, he would find that at last they would have broken the ice. He listened for a second at Caesar's door, not wishing to interrupt a rapt conversation, but all he heard was the jostling of the tub and the very quiet, deep breaths of Sarah Whetstone. He thought for a moment what he was likely to see, but he and his brother had shared everything in life, so it would not surprise him if again they found a common ground.

He opened the door to see Caesar leaning back in the tub and saw the shapely naked back and long dark tresses of Sarah as she moved slowly in the water. Caesar was the first to notice Thatcher standing at the door. He studied Thatcher's face, whose expression was more one of curiosity and resignation than of anger. Sarah opened her eyes to see Caesar staring at the door, and Thatcher watched as she turned to look at him. She, too, was reading his expression. She extended her hand out to him and said simply, "Come here."

Captain Drummond tried to read the tension that obviously existed when his sloop made its way against the side of the *Protocol*. As the crew offloaded the last few items they would need to prepare for the long cruise to come, including thirty very loud and protesting pigs, he was struck by the sight of the three starring attractions sitting, talking quietly on the steps leading to the quarterdeck. He maintained his post on the sloop, guiding the offloading, and tried to surmise what had occurred these last few days, chock full of stories from the crew as they made their way back and forth between the boats and Port Royal. When the last item had been offloaded, he signaled to them that he was ready to shove off. Thatcher and Caesar trailed behind Sarah Whetstone, who bore an expression of both satisfaction and sadness. She hugged Caesar and kissed him on his cheek, then hugged Thatcher and kissed him on the lips, and both men gently lowered her to the deck of the *Dominion*.

"I will see you two in a few months. Take care, for the seas are crawling with warships of every flag," cautioned Captain Drummond. "I know your capabilities, and I also know your swagger. Think profit, not point making." He shook each of their hands and showed Sarah to the cabin.

Thatcher and Caesar sat down upon the starboard capstan of the *Protocol* and watched in silence as the *Dominion* slowly disappeared from view. When at last there was no more to see, Thatcher broke the silence.

"I cannot say I was surprised, nor can I say I was distressed that you had found a way to let Sarah in," Thatcher commented.

"These things are always inevitable, Thatcher. We may sail under different flags and different names, but we are still those two boys from Bristol. Circumstances may influence us, but they never change us from who we are."

"Do you think this was just a fleeting moment, or do you think that when we return there will be opportunities to pick up where we left off?" Thatcher queried.

"Only if we want them to, Thatch. Only if we want them to."

III

The choice of Jamaica as Drummond Corporation's base of operations had been one of many possibilities. In their unique form of trade, there were a number of locations they could have chosen as their headquarters, one being as good as another and each affording good opportunities by virtue of that community's moral and mercantile composition. Curaçao had been discussed, as the bawdy nature and free trade zone atmosphere of the port made it ideal for gleaning news and scuttlebutt of the goings-on of the flags of all nations. Of course had they known that Edward Welch, now passing himself off as Edvart DeVyck, had set up shop on Curaçao, perhaps that small measure of St. Mary's business could have been settled long ago. But Curaçao was the place one went to disappear, and for the right amount of money you never came and you never went, and this was exactly the way Welch liked it. Having grown a van dyke and adopted the clothing habits of the Dutch, he was difficult to distinguish on the streets, and the time or two that Thatcher and Caesar had wandered those wild boulevards when visiting the port in their travels, they had passed by Edward Welch without noticing him.

The trip to Madagascar nearly two years before had been undertaken with much reservation by the captains and crews of the *Phoenix* and *Protocol*. At last war had been declared, and Anne's proclamation meant open season on any ship of Spanish or French registry. Privateering had been a last-ditch effort to make good on their promise to Edward Welch, and it had paid off in spades. But Welch had read the tea leaves in the changing tides on Africa's east coast as fewer and fewer ships made their way to St. Mary's, and new opportunities were burgeoning in the Caribbean. He had made a fortune from these young, ambitious brigands and now considered the ship and the second load of merchandise a gift to them. When he had received word that a contingent of Dutch slavers was in Cape Town, he knew this could possibly be his last opportunity to make a big score, so he sent word to the small fleet of his offer – access to hundreds of slaves for a third of the profits and passage for him and his cargo to wherever they sailed. He discovered their destination was Curaçao in the Netherland Antilles, one of three Dutch islands now prospering off the coast of New Andalusia and already teeming with the rich mercantile traditions of the Dutch. While he was skeptical that Thatcher and Caesar would return to St. Mary's, feeling they had gotten caught up in the gold rush of privateering in the Caribbean or Europe, he knew that were they to discover he had sold their Malagasy clansmen, there could very well be hard feelings, so he made the point of spreading false leads, giving them many places to search other than Curaçao. He would hope, of course, they would see it as a fair trade-off, whatever wealth they could glean from this last cargo and the ship to do with as they pleased. He did not take into consideration how personally they would take this change of plans. All that he could hope for was that they would see this new opportunity before them and take it as a lesson learned.

But Jamaica had been chosen, at least in part for Morgan Thurmond's need to overcome that personal stigma of the fateful earthquake, and certainly he had done that. And then bad luck struck this idyllic island again when Kingston ignited in May of 1704. The all-wood construction, combined with the persistent offshore breezes, spared the citizens of Kingston nothing, as one by one the flames leaped from building to building, burning everything an ember could ignite. The town was shattered and about to spiral downward financially once again, as the Crown was too committed to its war and too enamored with its American colonies to give much concern to Jamaica's demands for relief.

As much bad luck as Jamaica had, the Drummond Corporation could only proclaim an equal measure of good luck. Just days before, their warehouse had been crammed to the rafters with merchandise, awaiting the arrival of ships. Captain Drummond had arranged a number of buyers, but as long as it sat in his keep it was his responsibility. As he began to make inquiries of potential new buyers, he was pleased to see a number of ships from Boston arrive in convoy into Port Royal. He had just conducted his transactions and had the cargo loaded aboard those ships sitting in the harbor when the flames began to make their claim on the buildings of Kingston. He quickly had his crew move all their chests of gold and silver aboard the *Dominion*, then they sat on the deck and watched the flames grow closer to Drummond Corporation until they at last consumed the building.

This was the sad news Captain Drummond had to report to his partners, riding high from their successes and now faced with vexing choices in the weeks to come. As the *Phoenix* and *Protocol* sat securely in their secret cove, Captain Drummond went into detail about the fire that had devastated Kingston. With their holds full from their last round of privateering, much thought had to be given as to the disposition of cargo with no warehouse in which to store it. Drummond was confident that he could survey the spoils of their recent victories and find Port Royal customers desirous of replenishing similar items lost in the fires, though the remainder may warrant running the Hispañola gauntlet to New Providence. Despite these issues, Thatcher's greatest concern now moved to the scintillating Sarah Whetstone. Captain Drummond informed him that no harm had come to her or the rest of the mansions at the top of the hill.

"But I can tell you, Thatcher, that much has changed for her and her opinion of the island."

"You know, Caesar, really, we do have a civic responsibility to the fine folks of Kingston to assess the damage and see if there's anything that we can do to aid her in this time of trial," Thatcher reasoned as he studied Caesar's skeptical expression.

"And so, what good and great things do you think we can do for Jamaica that would require our doing anything more than working through our business partner who has established himself in this town?" Caesar inquired.

"Well that, dear brother, we cannot know until we see the extent of the damage. I say, let's you, me and the Captain head now into Port Royal, where we can make our assessments in each of our areas of expertise."

"So now we're civic planners, are we Thatcher? And I'm guessing you'll be doing your surveys from Sarah Whetstone's balcony, am I correct?"

"Well, different perspectives, and all ... it does have a commanding view of the town, after all. And I figure that Sarah would be quite understanding and allow me to make those surveys at my leisure."

Caesar shook his head and realized there was no reasoning with Thatcher. In truth, he had not yet been to Port Royal, leaving business to Captain Drummond, pleasure to Thatcher and the work to the Malagasy. He had instead enjoyed his peace and quiet when he could get it here in the cove. But as circumstances dictated that they might abandon Jamaica for a less tragic environ, now would be the time, if any, to visit the town, as his Malagasy crewmen had long been telling him that there was much for him to see there. Those previous pronouncements may prove moot now in light of the fire's devastation, but as he announced to the crew that he would be heading into Kingston, Matasaa stepped forward and asked to accompany him.

"I have come to know this island well, Chasaa, and there are things I would like to show you," Matasaa explained.

Caesar shrugged his shoulders and indicated for his first mate to join them. After they had transferred their silver and gold onto the *Phoenix*, the *Dominion* began the trip back to its homeport.

The English had been entrenched on the lowlands of Jamaica for sixty years. And for all that time, they had been engaged in warfare with the inhabitants of the mountains, initially the African slaves left behind by their Spanish predecessors. Originally dubbed the *Cimarrones,* a Spanish word used to identify livestock that had gone wild, in typical British fashion the word was anglicized to Maroons, and this slur eventually became an appellation of pride. These Maroons of the Blue Mountains were not simply seeking out an idyllic life, free of European mastery. They were intent on claiming Jamaica's interior for their own, and as Englishmen attempted to penetrate the deep inner lands, they were met with bloody resistance. As stories of successful Maroon raids against the settlements began to circulate among the slaves who had been hauled to Jamaica as England's labor force, a new wave of emboldened bonded Africans took to the hills as well, joining the Maroons in their assaults against the British. Even now, there was speculation that this great fire in Kingston was no mere accident, and if the rumors were true it would the Maroons' greatest success against the British to date, for now it brought the battle to England's colonial home court.

These were the rumors whispered quietly among the blacks that continued to work and live in Kingston. These were also the opinions of the Malagasy, who spent much time amongst the Africans in both Kingston and in the higher elevations. Caesar had heard the talk as well, for on those idle nights since they had first arrived in Jamaica and when they were out to sea, the Malagasy would tell the stories of their contacts with the Maroons and their surprise that the Malagasy did not serve England as much as they served their Antankarana chieftain. While the Maroons would take pleasure in telling the stories of their war heroes, the Malagasy could match their stories with tales of their chieftain's bloody legacy. It was difficult for the Maroons to understand that though Caesar was an Englishman in everything but birth and pigmentation, he likewise sailed, not in subjugation to a King, but out of loyalty to his English brother. As difficult as it was to understand Caesar, the Malagasy attempts to explain Thatcher was even more confusing. But the bottom line delivered to the Maroons: though the British Jack flew over their ships, their decks were commanded by princes of other nations who saw the British standard as merely an accommodation of commerce.

Upon reaching Port Royal, Thatcher explained his plan to take up the high ground survey from the Admiralty mansion and for Drummond and Caesar to proceed with their evaluations from the low ground.

"And let's take our time on this, gentlemen. For there's no reason to be hasty in our assessments, nor to jump to conclusions with first impressions. I say, take your time, as I shall take mine. Drink in what we see here at Kingston so we can know of it encyclopedically."

Leaving the time of rallying intentionally ambiguous, Thatcher was at a dead sprint up the path leading to Sarah's abode.

Captain Drummond began his tour with the blackened devastation that had been the Drummond Corporation headquarters and warehouse. He could not help but feel the irony, having lost a ship in Port Royal and then choosing what he thought would be a safe location in Kingston to build their new facility. Now it was nothing more than a burnt-out ruin. Already, so many of the merchants who had built successful enterprises in Kingston were making their way to other ports, while a brave few, many of them survivors of the Port Royal earthquake, began to formulate their plans to rebuild yet again. These men engaged Captain Drummond in conversation, in hope of convincing him to give Jamaica one more go for, as they reasoned, what more could happen to them?

Caesar and Matasaa left them to their conversations and began to walk down the long, charred row that was the main street of Kingston. A mere ten years old and beginning to take shape as a thriving

Caribbean city, it was now, for the most part, a jumbled mass of burnt timber and ash piles. As they reached the end of road, they were surprised to see one small collection of buildings that were virtually untouched by the fires that had devastated the rest of town. Caesar would have fully expected to see this most fortunate of survivors now teeming with the grateful residents who had been spared the ravages of their neighbors. But despite the habitable condition, its abandonment was obvious. Caesar was intrigued by the peculiarity as he picked his way across the carefully laid out walk of stones that had been flattened and meticulously placed leading up to the simple but well-built main structure.

The white paint was beginning to peel and flake, Caesar noted, holding in his palm a handful of flaky whitewash that had rubbed off when he touched the post supporting the overhang of the porch. He looked inside the window of the simple three-room structure, noting its absence of furniture. The wood floors, save a layer of recent ash that had permeated the air of Kingston, betrayed the hints of a high polish. Someone had been taking care of the inside of this empty house. His eyes scanned the room and his studied gaze came to a rest on the mantle. While every stitch of furniture may have been picked from this home, one item still remained, and his eyes focused through the hazy gloom to take in the sight of a simple drawing of a young woman, black as he, with her head wrapped in a scarf. Her long neck and penetrating stare were set off by an aquiline nose, with full lips and nostrils. He studied those eyes, so deep and penetrating, looking not at the artist but captured as if she were in deep thought, someplace else. Below the drawing, resting upon the mantelpiece, was one recent sign of life ... a white flower, still fresh and in full bloom sitting in a small glass vase. He surveyed the area around the mantel, looking for a trail of footprints across that layer of ash but was amused to see no such evidence. Obviously, someone had recently been in the house but had moved with a stealth and a subtlety so refined he had not disturbed the ash beneath his feet. Caesar smiled to himself at the display of both devotion and mysticism as he took one last look at the picture.

Matasaa had fallen back when they reached the property of this spared home, and he had remained at the edge of the walkway awaiting Caesar's return. These Malagasy read the supernatural into any odd occurrence, and while Caesar could not deny his own spiritual roots and traditions, he tended to chalk such situations up to little more than what they were – freak coincidences and damned luck, good or bad. But Caesar could see that Matasaa was a bit on edge and staring off at the far corner of the property, fading into a deep stand of woods that swept up a hillside and continuing on into the high climes of the Blue Mountains. Caesar looked to where Matasaa's gaze was fixed and allowed his eyes to adjust against the brilliance of the Caribbean sun. At last he made out the shape of a small group of men gathered at the edge of the property and studying him. Such blatant inspection may have intimidated many, but Caesar was not easily ruffled. He did not feel hostility but rather a need to demonstrate no intent of either malice or intrusion. He walked across the carefully cleared lawn and stood before the men, none of whom moved a muscle or facial expression.

"My apologies if I have intruded on your property," Caesar offered. "But one must yield to one's curiosity, and that untouched home is most curious indeed."

The group of men studied Caesar in silence. Their leader then looked toward Matasaa, giving him a single nod as the group turned and before Caesar's eyes, within steps, were lost to the shadows and trees. As he observed these men traveling across that short distance of deadfall and tangles, he noticed how silently they moved in those few steps before their disapparition. Just as silently, Matasaa had made his way across that broad lawn and was at Caesar's side, staring in the direction of where the men had just vanished.

"They want to meet you," Matasaa stated as his eyes picked out the invisible trail he was expected to follow.

"They had a perfect opportunity right now," Caesar replied, a slight chuckle in his voice.

"On their ground and in their time," Matasaa answered. He looked back at the house and then to Caesar. "This is not their ground, and this is not their time. But they have extended the invitation, and it's up to you to decide if you wish to accept it."

Caesar studied Matasaa and his deadly stoicism. His trip to Kingston was one of mere curiosity, to see the devastation and to assess for himself their best business options. But as Drummond was engaged with the merchants of Kingston who were attempting to sell him on the colony's future, and as Thatcher would be engaged trying to hold on to the present, Caesar knew that time was really not a concern, and his absence would scarcely be missed anytime soon. But he still had to ask the question.

"Any idea how long or how far we must go for this meeting?"

Matasaa looked at Caesar and at last gave that rare smile. "However far and however long it takes."

With little more than the clothes on his back and the omnipresent curved blade at his side, Caesar's silk shirt and pants and heavy boots were not his first choice for trekking clothing. With no food or water or firearm for protection or forage, he was putting himself in the trust of his Malagasy, which had always been unflinching, and the good graces of these storied warriors who owned every bit of this island beyond this patch of lawn. For no good reason to the observation of either Matasaa or anybody else who may have been watching, Caesar reared back his head and gave a bellowing and hearty laugh as he slapped his companion upon his back, sweeping his hand before him, and commanded, "Lead on."

Not every African who came to Jamaica did so in the hold of a slave ship. As England expanded her empire onto the continent of Africa, it attempted to infuse its new and loyal subjects into the vastness of their empire, providing them opportunities and introductions into their vast colonial holdings. To an educated or intelligent ruler, England had always been a master salesman. While they may have been overwhelmed by the hostility and resistance they encountered from an indigenous population, the British always had a knack for finding those select few in any country who were anxious to be sold on England. The British demonstrated their power with every invasion. To the masses, who watched St. George's Cross flag rise over their once sovereign lands, England was an interloper and a pariah destined to destroy everything unique and ancient about that culture in their quest to anglicize the populace. This would have been an impossible task were it not for those few who were sold on the idea that the benefits of English power far outweighed the compromises to their sovereignty, history and culture. Theirs was not usually a malicious intent, for they saw in England the capability to elevate their people above their enemies and regional adversaries. This small price of an English flag was to them a necessary evil for the progress of their people. And for those compliant few, England rewarded them handsomely with titles and tools and trappings and, most important of all, power. For nations who possessed mineral wealth, these local leaders could feign fealty while at the same time being allowed to shape their countries as they wished, with the blessings of England. These privileges would not be bestowed to them alone, for their children and most privileged loyal supporters could now benefit from the very best that England had to offer. From England, they would learn western business and western language and receive western education. These newly-anglicized subjects would eventually return to their homelands to apply their newfound knowledge in the hopes of forwarding the objectives of their sovereign, but in the process they would lose their national and cultural identity.

At times, this exposure to all things English would backfire with those who should have felt privileged enough to be anglicized. Rather than fueling their desire to be more British, it would touch off in some a desire to destroy all things British. For in this great realm of knowledge and power many saw, instead of greatness, the manifestation of evil itself, and with their knowledge, combined with the will of the people, rather than becoming England's greatest allies they would instead become its most deadly enemies.

Such was the case, here in these mountains, where one, who had benefited from all of England's gifts to a subjugated country, began not to reap the harvest of colonization but to sow the seeds of an organized movement against the Empire. The Gold Coast's rulers had willingly surrendered her lands and people in the name of progress, but rather than the gratitude England had expected for the privileges bestowed upon the compliant, they had touched off the warrior spirit of resistance, not only to bite the hand that fed it but to consume its heart as well. Here, far from the lands given up to England, was one who was using these mountains as a staging ground to touch off an empire-wide campaign to topple the Throne and begin the process of de-anglicizing the world.

When Nanani prayed, she did so only in the Ashanti tongue, for her ancestors knew no other language. On this morning, as she gave reverence to the spirits that followed her, so far from home, she could feel their presence. She always felt them most strongly in these moments just before dawn, when the animals of the forest grew silent as the night predators retired and the day hunters had yet to begin their foraging. In her hut at the top of the mountain, she could look down upon her people and pray for them every morning, confident and assured that the blessings she felt from her ancestors would radiate out to all of them as they rose to begin another day of freedom. Before word could reach her of the arrival of the stranger and before the first blast of the abeng, a cowhorn, to proclaim the presence of strangers in their midst, she knew at last the day had come. It had been so long ago when she first sensed him. It had been minor, yet troubling, for it had been the remnants of a residual spirit caught at a moment of chaos and confusion. The intuition was that this was a wanderer and a traveler, taking to the sea not for adventure but out of a sense of mission.

She remembered that day as if it were only yesterday, when the large English ship and its English crew prepared to take her and her party aboard for their long cruise from Accra, the established English trading center on the Gold Coast of the Ashanti kingdom. In her life, she had never thought she would leave the banks of the mighty lake that spread out from her village of Yeji. The two great rivers that fed this lake flowed from the north and west, and oftentimes as a girl her father would take her on the journey to where those two magnificent rivers met, filling this huge, long lake. It was at this confluence that their magic was strongest and where her father, also an Obeah, would sit and meditate and let the sounds of the waters flow through his ears where he could pick up just the faintest of ancient echoes from the spirits of the land, and in their final moments of madness, they spilled into the calm of the lake, finally putting these troubled waters and the voices they carried to rest.

"You must always listen to the waters, Belani," her father would tell her. "For in the chaos, you will hear clarity if you will only listen beyond the noise."

The noises of their homeland had been great, for now even in their isolated village along the great lake, the English were coming. It had been her grandfather who had first predicted to the great chief that across the waters men would come, bringing all their wisdom and with it all their pain. Her family had a long legacy as Obeahs to the kings, but this responsibility brought with it the necessity for truth, no matter how unwelcome it may be. When asked what the king should do when these men came from across the waters, her grandfather could only shrug and answer the question with a question: "What can you do?" The prediction that came true in the youthful days of her grandfather was a reality she had lived with all of her life. With the English came all of their wonderful innovations and mechanical mysteries. At last her people could hunt with greater accuracy, as guns made the job less dependent upon the speed of an arrow to fell game. Their strange adornments were to every child, even herself, objects of fascination and curiosity that even she had difficulty resisting. The English seemed to give freely of all they had in those early days, asking for nothing more than the right to build their strange stone structures and to bring their large boats into the broad harbors where they could use their guns to hunt game, to fill their barrels with water and to collect wood for their cookfires and camps. As the relationship matured, these new friends invited the sons of the King to visit their land and to learn their language and customs with the hope that they would be able to come back home and educate their people in the ways of the English. When they returned, their clothing and mannerisms reflected their time among the English and, with it, that thinking that questioned the wisdom of the village ways. They talked of strange concepts like commerce and politics and a strange single god who took the place of all the spirits. Their people, now with guns and laws and structure, were capable of buying things they never knew they needed and selling things they never knew had value.

In their land, it had always been accepted that, when tribes go to war, the losers thanked the victors with their submission of labor. With this came the burden of caring for and providing the essentials for these servants to assure cohesion of these tribes and faithfulness to their victors. But these English, with their different customs, convinced them that conquering a tribe did not obligate one to care for them, but instead made them a commodity with which the tribe could buy more things they did not know they needed. Her father now took the role as chief counsel to the king, who sought his wisdom in these concepts. Her father could only reply, "Because a body is absent, can you not still hear his voice? And if you hear his voice, are you not still obligated to answer his questions? And would not his questions be, what of my family?" The king did not wish to dwell on this subject, for he did not wish to hear the voices of those taken from their families. But he did hear the voices of the English, who said that by ridding himself of the defeated he need never fear that they would question his authority again, and their absence would make their voices disappear. The king was convinced that these things he did not know he needed had truly become essential, and in order to purchase them he needed worthwhile commodities. And so he yielded to the English wisdom and sold his enemies, who were now loaded aboard those strange ships after passing through those strange stone structures and forever disappeared.

But Belani could hear their voices, even though the king pretended he couldn't. She heard them in her dreams, and she told her dreams to her father. Their voices, she said, could be heard through water, just like her father had told her, and she had learned that she need not travel to the confluence of those two great rivers to listen to their voices, for she could hear them lapping on each wave that touched the shore of their village. Her father had great influence on the king, and she asked that before they sold these people to the English she have a chance to go to the waters to listen for their opinions on this matter. The king did not want to hear about voices of people he could no longer see, and he grew concerned, as the voices of those he could see began to declare their rights to be heard. He did not wish to hear these rationales, for certainly they could serve the English as well as they could serve him. And so instead, Belani began to speak for them. The king could not refuse the counsel of his Obeah, and following the death of her father, Belani took this position. What she told the king troubled him greatly, for she spoke of a truth he could not bear. She told him that it was not in his best interest but in England's best interest that his vanquished enemies disappear to faraway lands, for the fewer of his people that were here, the fewer the English would have to deal with when at last they coveted and took all of the lands for themselves.

"Could you not, if any other enemy threatened you, depend upon your vanquished subjects to rise in your defense?" she questioned. "Would they not consider their fortunes better with you than with one who hated you?"

Of course her arguments were dismissed by the well-educated sons and minions who had ventured off to England to see and be part of all of its majesty. To them, the English would be their greatest protectors and would bring with them all of the wonders that made them great. Her warnings of an England one day rising against them was unfathomable, considering all the English had given them in exchange for little more than hunting, portage and their vanquished enemy. Belani asked the king if he would then grant her the wish to determine which of these people selected for sale possessed a sense of Obeah. If she found any who indeed were magical, could she have them as her servants instead? The king saw a logic in her request and, knowing that few possessed the powers of Obeah, he did not fear that this would make any significant difference in satisfying the English requests. But Belani saw magic in everything and everyone. At first it was a few, and then dozens who possessed this magic, and he had promised she could keep them. His advisors began to sow seeds of discontent, telling him that she was using her magic to confound the king and that such magic was dangerous to his future. For what if it was true that all these people were magical and now all held fealty to Belani? Whose orders would they follow? Hers or the king's? He had to give great pause to this notion and realized that by fulfilling his promise to Belani he could not keep his promises to the English. And so, he took Belani aside to discuss his wish for her.

"You have assembled around you people you claim to be Obeah, but you did not clarify if their magic is good or bad. And I fear that what good magic you may possess may be amplified by the bad magic that could be found amongst your people. Therefore, I have decided you need to take your magic elsewhere."

Belani could not refuse the wish of her king. He told her that the English had granted his request to carry her people to someplace where they could practice their magic far away from him and his kingdom. The large English boat that would carry them made port at Accra, and the young fair-haired captain was instructed that no harm was to befall this woman and her people and that he must carry them as far as he could from the kingdom to the place where her magic could do the king no harm.

It was the summer of 1697, and Woodes Rogers was given responsibility of traveling from Bristol down the African coast to Accra. The *Regent* had made its run from New York, bringing cargo to London and carrying manufactured goods back to Bristol with the intention of returning to New York. This request by the West India Trading Company to travel to Africa to retrieve human cargo was at first quite shocking to Woodes, as the Rogers family did not practice the slave trade. But his father reassured him that this was not typical human cargo but rather honored guests of the King of the Gold Coast, relocating religious dissidents to one of England's Caribbean colonies. He was pleased to see his cargo was not chained, though they still had to occupy his holds for lack of suitable accommodations. He was able to arrange quarters for this young African girl who was apparently their spiritual leader. As he escorted her to her quarters, he noticed her strange behavior as she walked through the crew's quarters, stopping briefly at one spot along the leeward hull and closing her eyes. He had no concept of her religious philosophies and could not know she was drinking in an energy, an energy that would draw her to this spot many times throughout the passage. Here she would sit for hours on end against the hull, listening to the waves lapping against its exterior and the waves crashing against its sides, quietly listening to a voice in the water.

Now, as she awaited the arrival of their visitor, hearing the abeng announcing the approach of guests, she sat next to the stream that ran beside her hut. She always felt most comfortable when near the chaos of water, for in it she could most clearly hear the voices of the forests and the mountains. And as they had been saying for days, this was a voice she must listen to, for it could mean great things for her people.

She had found the small plot of land and simple structures provided for her in Kingston to be too stifling and too English. As promised, she and her people were left alone and allowed to bring their traditional weapons to hunt game in the hills beyond Kingston. It was here she encountered these Maroons, who had long since made a home of the mountains that dominated the vista behind her. They had begun by suggesting to her and her people that they need not be slaves to the English but could find refuge amongst the Maroons. They were surprised to find that she was not a slave and that these people belonged to her. She discovered that many of them spoke Ashanti dialects, indicating that perhaps previous generations of her people had been taken here in captivity and had at last found the freedom they did not find under their kings. What she found among them and their words were those voices she had heard upon the waters that crashed upon the shore at Accra and that, despite her king's attempts to shut them out, he had in truth heard their words and sent her to them. It did not take long for Belani to realize that at last she had come home to the Africa she had lost, and, for these people, they had at last found the person they had so desperately been seeking. Their Obeah. Nanani. This young woman would be their first mother and spiritual leader, for while they had successfully thwarted recapture, they had not accomplished their ultimate goal: the defeat of these English. And with Nanani they could at last tip the scales and create Africa here.

She could feel the energy drawing nearer, and she watched as that large African man ascended the narrow trail leading to the camp below. It was important for her to see if he truly had the magic she believed, so she sat quietly, masked by the trees and rocks beneath her.

Caesar felt slightly winded from the long climb into the heights of these Blue Mountains and was surprised when his Maroon guides gestured for him to stand here and wait. He looked around the encampment, a collection of thatched huts built into the brush and growth. From a few feet away, one could not percieve the signs of an encampment, and only here in the center of the camp could you at last see these dwellings amidst the camouflage. The huts bore no sign of life, and as he studied them he felt as if he were being watched. The long climb had left him parched, so he bent to the stream for a handful of water. In this stillness, he could make out the faint trace of voices, far off and unclear, but certainly present. His eyes traveled up the stream, drawn by the curious melody of the water passing over the rocks. At last his gaze fell upon a tiny woman, sitting on a rock next to the stream some hundred feet above him. On her face, the one he had studied a few days earlier in the cabin below, she wore a welcome smile as she began to descend the slippery rocks in the midst of the stream. She possessed a strong and confident stride, picking her way down those moss-covered rocks as if strolling the streets of Bristol, until at last she stood midstream before him. Her eyes studied his face and again she smiled broadly.

"So tell me, Chasaa, what do the voices in the water have to say?"

IV

Sarah Whetstone greeted Thatcher's unannounced appearance at the Vice-Admiralty house with both relief and mild chastisement. As she had watched the fires rage below her, wondering if those flames would at last rise up this green and rocky hill, her thoughts kept wandering to rescue, for certainly if anyone was a damsel in distress, Sarah Whetstone could fit the model when the circumstances required. With her father still at sea when the conflagration began to spread throughout the town, its citizens unable to do anything about it, Sarah began to imagine the very worst – that if the black billowing clouds of smoke did not fill her lungs and choke her to oblivion, then those flames would claim her oxygen-starved body and burn it beyond recognition. The servants had at last convinced her to abandon her balcony, where she made quite a pretty picture in her silks and ribbons watching her town burn, and take the less picturesque but certainly much safer shelter of the basement below. But appeals to her safety and the sanity of escaping the direct path of the smoke was no easy task for the help, as she would only surrender her vigilant post on the balcony if they first promised to pack away her dresses and carry them to the basement. When the last of her muslin petticoats and those lovely new shoes were at last in a place of safety, she surrendered to the will of the servants, taking one last look at Kingston, dabbing the tears from her eyes, and retreated to the security of the bunker. For even if the flames did reach the Vice-Admiralty house, here in this stone shelter they would have a measure of safety, and as last resort retreat down the passageway through the cold storage room and to the service door that exited beyond the broad green. She had little comfort in those days of waiting in the well-stocked pantry, still hanging with smoked meat and amply supplied with fruits and vegetables and casks of water and wine. But the true saving grace of this subterranean shelter was the new bag of coffee she sat upon and which she insisted her servants roast, boil and serve to keep her mind active in case of the need for sudden flight.

It was while she sat there waiting in the dimness of the basement, expecting imminent death, that she realized just how alone she really was ... well, her and the dozen servants who were attending to her every need and constantly reassuring her that everything would be fine. But even with all this company, she could not help but be alone, for they could not understand not only how tragic this fire was to the Jamaican colony but also how utterly tragic it would be if she fell victim to it. How would England take this loss of one of her fair children? Would not her smoky disappearance be akin to the disappearance of that infant Virginia Dare, so eloquently spoken of by Sir Walter Raleigh in his tales of the Lost Colony? And how would her father explain to her siblings that the family's fair flower, who had ventured off with the assurance of the security of the Royal Navy itself, had fallen prey to the wild ravages of untamed nature? And what about Woodes? By candlelight in this dank, dark hole, this well-provisioned prison, she read over and over again his most recent words to her – that he had received his commission, had obtained his captaincy and was at last prepared to marry his distant angel. How could Woodes bear the exile into which he had forced his lovely Sarah, only now, upon achieving his career ambitions, to lose the most important ambition in his life – her hand? How could he live with himself? And, God forbid, would he marry someone else?

These thoughts only led to greater sadness and a feeling of imminent doom, yet strangely it also made her incredibly conscious of the pernicious aching in her loins. And when these thoughts came, it angered her that the face she conjured was not that of her brave sea captain, pining away for his treasured Portia, but instead that dark-haired, dark-eyed privateer who had not bedded her in weeks and who was probably, right now, submitting to the alcohol fueled temptations of some Nassau mulatto prostitute rather than here, right now, comforting and screwing her? This image made her even more angry ... and more randy at that. She imagined that filthy whore looked much like young Cassie, her dressing servant, now curled asleep only feet away, with her cocoa skin and long black hair. Cassie's family had been in service to the Greenes, planters a few miles from Kingston, who had entertained Sarah on numerous occasions. Sarah had insisted she must have this lovely servant girl for her own. The other servants of the Admiralty were quite nice and very attending, but they had one failing. They were old. Cassie, on the other hand, was thirteen, beautiful, and possessed the best qualities of her mother and the gorgeous features of George Greene, the plantation owner, who freely frequented the many pretty women of his vast, albeit fruitless, holding. It took much convincing on her part for George Greene to part with his lovely and nubile lust-child. But at last he had succumbed to the charms and arguments of Sarah Whetstone, as she promised that whatever service Cassie would render, George Greene could be assured, would not be missed. This Sarah could guarantee.

What made Cassie such a perfect choice was not only her age but also her body type, for on those days when Sarah did not feel like standing for a fitting, Cassie had always been a perfect stand-in. And how lovely she looked when Sarah played dress-up with her. Despite her common breeding, Cassie possessed the inherent talents to effectively mimic the carriage and grace of her betters, which set Sarah's heart a-flutter, for Sarah could pretend she was a peer when the moment occasioned. And yet as elegant as Cassie looked in her dresses and fineries, here, curled up just inches from Sarah's pretty feet, her long, lovely dark strands within reach of Sarah's toes, Sarah had to confess that when Cassie looked common she most certainly looked best. In this dim light, it was amazing how familiar those dark curls looked, for though she had seen them a thousand times before, now they didn't look like those affixed to the enchanting mulatto girl, who served her hand and foot. They looked more like the dark locks of that handsome young sailor who served her in every other way. And she wondered. The evening was still and quiet, the servants retreated to the shadows of this vast cellar, and Cassie was so close.

Sarah's toes in her hair did not immediately strike Cassie as unusual. As Sarah was not usually a fitful sleeper, Cassie was certain Sarah just could not get comfortable, and her long black tresses were getting in the way. But it was when she noticed Sarah's toes curling themselves around her locks that Cassie's eyes came open. Sarah had been amazingly good to her, despite her constant demands and insistence that Cassie keep her company until all hours of the night, as coffee had kept her mind racing and her mouth moving. But there were those times when she noticed Sarah appraising her in ways that reminded her of her former master and his sons. She took this to be an English thing that they were unconscious of, this rude casting of the eye up and down her length, pausing at her most prominent and private of parts. She had learned to ignore the looks and appreciate how much better this job was than scrubbing floors for the temperamental Mrs. Greene or, even worse, chasing cattle through the hills, as was the lot of many of those with skin color such as hers. But Cassie lay there quietly as Sarah's toes played with her hair and was about to go back to sleep when she heard her mistress whisper.

"Cassie," Sarah breathed. "I do hope I have not woken you."

Cassie thought to lay there quietly, living up to Sarah's whispered hope, but due to the fact that her words were being spoken and she could hear them, she knew she had a service to perform for her mistress. She lifted her head from the palette and turned to address her mistress's needs and was somewhat surprised to find Sarah, now absent of bloomers and petticoats, her silk gown pulled up at the waist with her fingers now lost in that fine stand of lawn betwixt her thighs. Cassie took a moment to drink in the image, feeling perhaps she should avert her gaze to allow her lady a moment of privacy, but Sarah's toes were still curled in her locks, her finger triumphantly poised in an arch, beckoning her to come forth. Sarah bent her knees as she reclined, giving Cassie no choice but to be guided by those possessive appendages. Cassie was not certain precisely what it was she was expected to do as her face grew ever closer to that dew covered garden, but Sarah's hands, now on her chin, brought her insistently to its intended destination. She was further coaxed by Sarah's demand to kiss it.

In one of their many nighttime conversations, Cassie had been instructed to the strange nuances of these Europeans' obsession with oral conjoining. Sarah described how each kingdom had its customs appropriate to the breeding and culture of the monarchs. Being an English girl, she fully expected that Sarah intended an English kiss, but as her lips pressed against Sarah's swollen nexus and her mistress's hands wrapped inside that long luxurious black mane, Sarah lifted Cassie's chin again so their eyes met and gave her final instruction so Cassie could be totally clear of the intention. "Like the French, Cassie, like the French."

And thus was Sarah able to amuse herself and achieve a modicum of secure feelings to sustain her through those long, lonely days when neither of her captains had yet come to her rescue. Of course, once the smoke had cleared and she could safely return to her quarters, and when Cassie had unpacked the last of her dresses and petticoats, she was able to more effectively school her young servant girl in a more appropriate venue. And in this tragic yet more luxurious clime, with Cassie happily attending her mistress's every need, every now and again she would remember one more item left in the basement, and Cassie would dutifully follow her mistress to that cozy little coffee bag where the lost item would magically be found.

It was important that Thatcher know how barely poised on survival Sarah Whetstone had been. She relayed to him what desperate steps she had had to take in order to find even the smallest measure of comfort, to which Thatcher should feel a dent to his manhood that she had been capable of finding even a modicum of consolation between the legs of a young mulatto girl. Thatcher did not know how to respond to this assault to his manhood, only to insist that at the very minimum he owed both an apology and a thanks to Cassie, and he insisted that it be delivered in person by him in Sarah's bedroom. Should she ever find herself in such a circumstance again, he reasoned, the least he could do was to provide options to both mistress and servant that would make such meager survival more tolerable, and it was his obligation, of course, to make certain that both were properly trained. He may have been stretching the metaphor a bit when comparing it to his shipboard drills of having the crews run out the guns and boats to prepare for battle or ditch, but neither was willing to call him on his tortured analogy and let him conduct them in repeated safety drills and battle stations for their own good.

Thatcher did his best to demonstrate his sorrow for Sarah's distress for days to come, but on one particular evening, when he bothered to pose the question of what her plans were as the town struggled to come back to life, she confessed to him that, though she was confident Kingston would rebound, it would be doing so without her. She climbed up on his chest to explain that, as Captain Drummond had hinted, her time in Kingston was drawing to a close.

"I have received many letters from home these last months, telling me that it's time for me to return to Bristol and to give up this girlish escapade of gallivanting in the Caribbean," Sarah explained. "And there's the issue of Admiral Graydon."

"Admiral Graydon?" Thatcher queried.

"It appears that father is being replaced. I can only imagine that this could lead to eviction to less suitable quarters, and I can scarcely be expected to move to one of the small hovels her up here."

Thatcher's eyebrows arched. Word of a new commander had not yet been related to him and this could be valuable intelligence for their enterprise. But certainly he could talk Sarah into staying even if it meant occupying a somewhat smaller mansion. The thought of her leaving so soon was an unexpected blow to his short term plans and, though he did not ask, he sensed the real reason for her going home

Rather than seeing Thatcher's sadness or feeling his disappointment, her face brightened as she announced, "It appears that Woodes has demonstrated his naval prowess, exemplified himself before his commanders and received his captaincy. His most recent note to me said that at last he is able to live up to his promise to me, and upon my return to Bristol he shall make me Mrs. Rogers."

Thatcher had known this moment would come one day. As much as he had hoped that all the other advantages he offered would sway her, no amount of prowess or sexual demonstration was as titillating a fetish or as strong an aphrodisiac as the fantasy of a British naval officer husband. Sarah could read the disappointment in his face, and with the sweet butterfly kisses on his belly tried to let him know that this in no way diminished her feelings for him nor the ecstasy she found when he was tearing her in half from the inside out. But these were temporary things, she reasoned, joys of youth that were quickly smothered with the realities of adult life and responsibility.

"But fear not, my beloved, for until I leave Kingston for good, I am yours wholly and wantonly," she purred, as her words now yielded for a more appropriate application of her lips. As Thatcher leaned back against the pillow, attempting to face this crushing reality, he could at least enjoy this one great advantage over his rival and know that on that long journey back to Bristol, while she may be practicing her signature as Mrs. Rogers, her hands would be signing his name on other parts of her body. He fantasized that when Woodes saw her exit the boat at Bristol Quay, he would be receiving a woman who had spent a long journey thinking not of her betrothed but of the one she left behind, and he relished this point as she climbed on top of him and began to lower herself onto him.

"I shall make certain, my love, that moments before you board that boat for home the last thing you shall feel and smell and touch and taste will be me to sustain you on that long journey," he boasted as she quickly increased the tempo to the demands of her satisfaction.

But as she continued to use him like the ample supply of fall zucchini in the basement, she looked into his eyes, smiled her perfect smile and announced, "Well, as long as possible, Edward. But until the last moment? Hmm. I'm not sure how much Woodes would appreciate the notion of your being in my bed when he comes to call for me."

Thatcher's focus now fixed on her sadistic pronouncement, as this stab to his soul was an obviously delicious morsel on her lip. She bore down with even more ferocity.

"Are you telling me that Woodes Rogers is coming here to retrieve you?" Thatcher replied as her long hair whipped across his face in teasing mockery. She lifted her head as she drove herself down onto his absolute length, clenching that vise-like, quivering muscle onto him as her nails dug deep into his chest. Her face bore a dark and sinister grin as she arched her back and held him as if he were an appendage of her own body. As her stomach began to quiver and her breath began to shake, she was able to issue one last crushing statement.

"Who else would I trust with my body but my captain?"

Captain Drummond was among the gathering of luminaries who had put aside their attempts to rebuild their lives to welcome the small but impressive collection of Her Majesty's warships now moored in Port Royal. Governor Handasyde was proud to welcome Vice-Admiral John Graydon who sailed in accompaniment with the brave and illustrious Captain Woodes Rogers, Jr. All of the Caribbean had been heralded of the tales of Captain Rogers' bravery in his battles against Queen Anne's enemies, and it reminded Governor Handasyde of similar tales linked to the bravery of the senior Captain Rogers, a man whom he was proud to count among his closest friends.

"We apologize, Captain Rogers, that we were not able to turn out our town for a more auspicious welcome worthy of your daring and devotion to England," Handasyde gushed. "Know that our fair town does not at this moment make an admirable first impression, but the spirit of the people and Kingston's greatness is not reflected in its buildings alone. We are saddened to lose our beloved Sarah, the First Daughter of Jamaica, but know that as you ferry her home to England, you take not only her but also our hearts with you." Of course, Governor Handasyde made an important showing of welcoming Woodes Rogers, for as he was the future son-in-law of Admiral

Whetstone, Handasyde hoped that the Vice-Admiral would continue his support of this devastated island which had embraced his child and would pass on much needed complimentary words to assure the recovery of Kingston. While Port Royal may have the harbor that served the needs of the fleet, the lack of amenities for the foreseeable future made Kingston an unattractive port of call or base for the Vice-Admiralty, a point made by Vice-Admiral Graydon as he surveyed the fire wrecked capital.

Woodes accepted the gracious greeting from the desperate governor, understanding the gravity of his circumstances. "Thank you, Governor, for your kindness. You could not know this, but your predecessor, Sir William Beeston, whom I had the honor of meeting on my first trip to Jamaica, was in the same uncomfortable predicament, as Port Royal stood shattered around him, just as Kingston stands shattered around you now. But know this, Governor: Jamaica possesses that one true English quality, the indomitable spirit. And she, sir, shall rise again from the ashes."

"Like a phoenix, sir," Captain Drummond added from the crowd.

Woodes Rogers smiled, thinking of the obvious reference and nodding his head in agreement. "Precisely so, sir, like a phoenix. Should I have the power to do so, I would recommend that, when you rebuild this town, you should christen her not Kingston but Phoenix," Woodes proclaimed, obviously impressed with his noble suggestion. Of course all the assembled agreed, applauding furiously and dabbing at their eyes, that his magnificence and brilliance were astounding and that they, too, would push for such an appropriate appellation. The assemblage escorted Captain Rogers to the Vice-Admiralty house, where the lovely Sarah Whetstone awaited him on the balcony, dressed in her finest red silk. The tears of joy that spilled that day for this great reunion were to be recounted for weeks to come as a source of hope and inspiration to the devastated people of Kingston. Or was that to be Phoenix?

Thatcher had hoped to find Caesar when at last his services were no longer required by the lovely Sarah Whetstone, for all he hoped to do was to return to his ship to the jeers and abuse of his dear brother. Caesar's mockery was precisely what he needed right now to pull him from the doldrums and remind him why silly girls would forever be his downfall. To his disappointment, Caesar was nowhere to be found in Kingston, so he returned to the ships hoping to find him there. But the crew said that he and Matasaa had not been seen since the party left for

Port Royal. This wouldn't normally have concerned him, but Thatcher's need for Caesar and his expectation for him always to be there only added to his vexation, and despite his hatred to do so he took to the dory and set out for Port Royal. He knew what he was likely to see when he got there and hoped to avoid catching a glimpse of Sarah Whetstone as she began her process of transforming into Sarah Rogers, and certainly the last person in the world he wanted to see was Woodes Rogers himself.

But fate would not allow him to avoid the inevitable, for as his small boat came close to Port Royal, he could see the flotilla of naval vessels beginning to work its way through the channel, and at the head of the convoy stood Woodes Rogers on the quarterdeck, every measure of the arrogant, self-important captain his father was. Beside him, beaming with the pride of a future bride, was Sarah, dutifully attended by the enchanting Cassie who would begin a new life as the personal attendant to Sarah Rogers in a grand Bristol home. Thatcher hung back from the harbor long enough to let the ships pass, hoping not to be noticed by the departing fleet. Woodes Rogers looked in his general direction but seemed not to see the man that used to be his dearest friend now bobbing in the wake of his great ship. But Sarah did. And for one brief moment, her eyes met his and told him that at last she had found what she had been looking for. As painful as it was, he knew it was time to move on, figuratively and emotionally as well as physically, as he rowed across those ripples of passing ships into Port Royal. Sitting on the dock, as if expecting him to arrive any moment, were Captain Drummond, Caesar and Matasaa, grinning at Thatcher, struck by the irony of the sight of their great captain in this tiny boat, framed against the majesty of the departing Royal Navy ships.

"Yes, there he is, lads, the infamous Captain Edwards, commander of the most feared privateer fleet in the Caribbean," Caesar mocked as Thatcher rowed up to the dock.

"If you think I looked forward to coming and looking for you, you are sadly mistaken. But you know, we have responsibilities, and I needn't have to remind you that idling about in Port Royal is not making any of us any wealthier," Thatcher chastised.

"I should let you know, Thatcher, and you may not realize this, but you are a great inspiration to the great Captain Woodes Rogers," Drummond informed him.

Thatcher looked confused as he studied the smiling Captain. "I am an inspiration to Woodes Rogers."

"Why, certainly. He was so moved by the struggle to rebuild Kingston, he suggested they rename it Phoenix," the Captain replied as he, Caesar and Matasaa roared in laughter at the delicious irony of Woodes Rogers' words to the citizens of Kingston. When their mirth had subsided, Captain Drummond continued, "But be it Kingston or Phoenix or Alexandria, for that matter, I think we're in general agreement, gentlemen, that it's time we pull up stakes for a new port. For in the short term, Jamaica promises nothing for us."

Caesar pondered that for a moment and then replied, "In the short term, Captain, you may be correct. This phase of the Drummond Corporation has reached its end on Jamaica. But something tells me our long-term future may depend on this island."

"Are you suggesting we should stick it out, Caesar?" Thatcher queried, surprised that Caesar, who had never been a fan of Jamaica in the first place, had somehow warmed to the island in the shadow of the fire that had devastated it.

"We can joke all we wish about Woodes' suggesting this place be named Phoenix, but I must admit I do see it one day rising from the ashes. When it comes to its rebirth, it may not look anything like it was when it was consumed. For Jamaica will rise, not as an English island, but an African one. And that is something Woodes Rogers could never have foreseen in his prognostication."

Captain Drummond had business to attend to, for while Captain Rogers and his fetching bride-to-be were furling sails for Bristol, Admiral Whetstone and Admiral Graydon were assembling the fleet for one more run north to bring hell to the French off Acadia. This would open up more opportunities in local waters for the "ghost fleet" without having to compete with the British Royal Navy for prizes. But before departing he turned to Thatcher and looked at him questioningly. He was about to turn away, as if whatever was on his mind was not worth bringing up, but Thatcher had to cave in to his curiosity.

"Is there something troubling you, Captain Drummond?" Thatcher inquired.

"I have mixed feelings about an errand I'm to attend to, but I guess it's not my place to concern myself with the potential of rekindling a smothering spark," he said, as he reached into his jacket, retrieved a note and handed it to Thatcher. He looked at Caesar and Matasaa, chuckled to himself, and bid them adieu.

Thatcher studied the note, knowing exactly who had penned it and wondering if he should further torture himself by reading her parting words, for he had come to understand that Sarah Whetstone relished cruelty and this could be her final stab to wound the lovelorn Thatcher. He sat there studying the letter, contemplating what he should do, but Caesar made the decision easier for him.

"Open it and be done with it, Thatcher. No matter what she says, there's nothing that can be done about it now."

Caesar was right, mostly. But he still had at his disposal two warships, and with the right inspiration, Thatcher would gladly utilize them for his own personal gain, including, if necessary, threatening the Royal Navy. With the last bit of hope, he tore open the letter and read the short contents of Sarah Whetstone's final missive. He began to laugh uproariously as he handed the note to Caesar. Caesar could not help but chuckle a little himself as he read her most effective parting shot.

Perhaps I shall see you in Bristol. Oh, and feel free to bring a friend. – Sarah

It may not have been a declaration of love and adoration, nor a plea to rescue her from an ungodly fate, but under the circumstances it would do, and it would give him something to look forward to should he ever return to Bristol.

The three large men climbed into that tiny boat to course their way through the devastated harbor attached to the devastated town, back to the shelter of their cove and the ships it contained. As Thatcher lay to the oars, Caesar recounted the events of the last few days while Matasaa, the ever-sober Malagasy carpenter, beamed with a pride as his chieftain related the strange and spiritual events that had transpired. While this encounter may have been nothing more than two African warrior-shamans discovering each other in the New World, these Malagasy could not help but wonder if this could indeed lead to the Maroons and these Englishmen one day charting a common course.

Chapter 8

The Emperor of New Providence
June 1704 – April 15, 1707

I

As would become a recurring theme throughout their lives, Thatcher and Caesar were victims of their own success. Their operation out of Antigua and Barbuda had been successful so much so that Spanish and French ships were giving a wide berth around the Windward Islands, making their unique hilltop outpost and signaling campaign less viable than it had been when Antigua was considered a defenseless, unimportant island. With English soldiers taking up station on the islands, their free reign was being impinged as Her Majesty's troops grew curious about the privateers' advanced messaging system that even the Royal Navy and her armies lacked. Rather than seeing this as one more safeguard for these islands, the British military began to take on a viewpoint that these privateers, though flying under the same national standard, were competition. Thus, in late spring of 1704, the *Phoenix* and *Protocol* pulled up stakes and made their way down the Windward chain to Barbados. Having struck upon a few unescorted French vessels conducting intracoastal trade between Dominica, Martinique and St. Lucia, the holds of the *Phoenix* and *Protocol* were full of freshly plundered Spanish and French goods that would find a ready market with the settlers at Bridgetown and Speightstown. As Caesar and Thatcher worked the towns, the Malagasy fanned out into the interior, questioning the slaves who appeared to be mostly of West African lineage, of any sign of slaves that looked like the Malagasy. Thatcher knew that merchants kept up on potential competitors, and he surveyed them over drinks and dinners to find out if any new Englishmen had arrived in the colonies flush with cash and short on lineage. In the weeks they languished in Barbados, their quest to catch the scent of Edward Welch's trail was unsuccessful.

Their hunt for Welch would have to go on the backburner as they sailed back to Jamaica intent on turning over the gold and silver they had netted in the Windwards to Captain Drummond for safekeeping. Making the northwest cut across the heart of the Caribbean almost assured encountering the random French merchant vessel – seeking the quicker method of profit through the direct, albeit more dangerous path between the Greater Antilles and the Netherland Antilles – or the Spanish merchant – plying the trade between New Andalusia and Hispañola or Cuba – versus the more circuitous route around the Lesser Antilles that, weather dependent, could add weeks to a cruise. If a privateer were lucky and if he did not mind running the risk of encountering a Spanish flotilla giving escort to a merchant fleet, there was always a good chance of picking off a random enemy ship for taking this bolder, more risky path. And the *Phoenix* and *Protocol* were lucky this time out, plucking Spanish and French merchanters making their way from Cartagena to Havana, and carrying their prizes to Jamaica where they discovered the loss of their corporate facilities to the Kingston inferno. Their hunt for more prizes would have to be forestalled until they could accomplish their move and build their showroom fortress on New Providence, and for a year the *Phoenix* and *Protocol* were consumed with shipping building supplies from their friends in Carolina while much of the crew was tasked with constructing Drummond Castle.

Much had changed on New Providence since the *Phoenix* set sail from her port three years earlier. Despite the cozy arrangement that had existed between the governors of La Florida, Havana and the Bahamas, war had brought a screeching halt to the lucrative protocol. As such, the successful number of privateer raids sailing out of New Providence became intolerable, inspiring Pedro Vades, the Spanish governor of Cuba, and Joseph d'Honon de Gallifet, the French governor of Saint-Domingue, to assemble a raiding party to assault Fort Nassau. Comprised of two frigates, one sailed by Blas Moreno Mondragón of Spain with 150 Spanish corsairs and the other by Claude Le Chesnaye of France who had recruited a large contingent of boucaniers, the joint flotilla set sail from Santiago de Cuba and launched a surprise attack on Nassau. With little resistance the English capital fell, its homes and shops looted and burnt, its twenty-two cannon seized and Fort Nassau's fortifications toppled. The population of Nassau was shown no mercy as over a hundred citizens met their demise. For those unable to scatter into the wilderness, 150 citizens were clapped in irons and, along with thirteen prize ships, were spirited away to Santiago de Cuba. Among the prisoners was Governor Lightfoot whose capture went unknown for months as the city was burned to ground and every ship in the harbour taken as a spoil of war. When word finally reached England of the assault on New Providence and the subsequent capture of their governor, Edward Birch was appointed the new administrator and set sail for New Providence.

Upon arriving, he found Nassau in utter ruins and depopulated except for a few miserable survivors freshly despoiled by yet another raid merely days before. He immediately returned to England to report his findings and the utter uselessness of attempting to reestablish a bastion of civilization within a far flung collection of islands inhabited by little more than pirates and ne'er-do-wells.

A once thriving town without official legal presence was an appealing prospect indeed for anyone wanting to do business far from prying eyes. Before the raid, Lightfoot had been an annoying presence to the Drummond Corporation. Because they operated under his Letter of Marque, the Governor had been entitled to excise a large portion of the proceeds from both the *Phoenix* and her prize the *Protocol*, with shares going to the Crown, to his Colony and, naturally, to himself. And so they had avoided the port of Nassau whenever possible.

But with Lightfoot now an involuntary guest of Governor Pedro Vades and these countless islands that comprised the Bahamas archipelago literally ungoverned, New Providence suddenly became the most attractive location in the Caribbean. Captain Drummond appeared within days of Birch's departure aboard his sloop *Dominion* and set his crew to work reconstructing the docks and expanding wharves of a size much larger than would be required for this small ship. In the lean-to's and mud huts passing as taverns, signs went up seeking men with construction capability for a project overlooking Governor's Hill, directing all queries to Captain Drummond aboard the *Dominion*. While most nautical types had taken to the sea to avoid such legitimate work, the likelihood of any future cash yielding prospects and a pence starved populace found a more than eager and plentiful workforce ready to sign aboard. The first project was an excavation job, where those capable of swinging a shovel and pick went about digging a very large hole that many swore was destined to reach China itself. As the unearthing was under way, others were charged with the task of locating the biggest and flattest stones they could find to cover the floor and walls of that monstrous hole. The *Phoenix* and *Protocol* at last arrived with their holds full of freshly cut lumber, felled and milled off the Albemarle Sound by Mullins & Sons, of the finest Carolina loblolly pine.

The Malagasy and their contract crew got busy framing a large structure that on the outside appeared to be a house but, for anyone who bothered to watch the thing being constructed, was a veritable underground warehouse and showroom in a style quite uncommon for the English Caribbean. The lessons learned on Jamaica and Thatcher's memories of Peter's tales of combustible Moscow went into the design of the new headquarters of the Drummond Corporation, as the Malagasy went to work mixing mud with limestone that they spread over every exposed inch of the interior and exterior of the facility, making it virtually fire-resistant. One good thing that Governor Lightfoot had done for them was to send them to St. Augustine, for the impressive and practical layout of the Castillo had inspired them in their consideration for design of their new facility. When they had received reports of Carolina's assault against St. Augustine and how impregnable the Castillo had been to both siege and fire, they knew they had to adapt key fortification elements into their model as well. For, while they never anticipated having to withstand a siege, one could never tell.

Though function and form were meticulously balanced in constructing this citadel, the Malagasy thought it entirely impractical that Thatcher insisted that enough iron be left over to fashion a latticework of iron pipe throughout the entire house. While all were happy that bathing tubs had been worked into the design, Thatcher insisted that the pipes run along the ceiling of every floor. In every room, Thatcher had installed a large, cumbersome valve, which he hoped they would never have to use. "But I can assure you, gentlemen, if anyone be tempted to set the place alight, they'll be sorely disappointed how quickly that flame is extinguished," he intoned. Once the pipe work had been completed he christened Drummond Castle and all her crew with an overhead shower as he turned a valve on the pressurized pipe and flooded the bottom floor.

One other task, barred from outsiders, involved copious amounts of iron, which the labor crews had toted up to the hill and left in a pile. The workers could observe the fire glowing ominously over the hill late into many nights and the curious disappearance of the mountain of iron could only intensify speculation from the less informed. Out of view of their prying eyes, the Malagasy were loading the iron into large stone vats, heated by a massive flame, and pouring the molten ore out of the bottom of the cauldron onto perfectly level plots of land in long flat sheets. Once it was cooled, it was man-handled by the Malagasy, under Thatcher's guidance, into that subterranean cavern where a large vault was being constructed of layers of metal sheets that no man or any amount of crew could hope to penetrate.

The crowning touches to the Drummond Corporation were again conducted exclusively by its shareholders in the dark of night, for along with that heavy cargo of timber they also carried with them eight large cannon that would crown the tower built atop their corporate headquarters. Trained in a 360 degree arc and mounted on heavy iron platforms that allowed for the cannon to be swung on an X-Y axis – left, right, up and down – these cannons were placed so that, unlike those constructed by armies with their barrels obvious and prominent, they instead slid to the center so that a casual observer peering at that curious tower atop that impressive structure would see nothing but the attractive railings, the only exposed wood visible. But these railings weren't built for form; they were built for function, for designed into them were elaborate hinges that allowed them to be swung down to provide a platform for the gun crews. To make this peaceful facade more pastoral, Thatcher and Caesar at last found a use for that oversized church bell they had liberated from the cargo of a Spanish ship en route to New Spain, bearing the cryptic word *Quiroga*. Try as he might, Drummond had not found a buyer for it, and it nearly found itself being melted down for the vault walls, gears, tracks and cannonade bases needed to construct this picturesque, covert fort. But as the tower began to take shape in their coffee-driven design plans, it struck Thatcher that such a pretty tower required a pretty bell.

"And think of the service we provide to our fellow citizens of Nassau when the next time a French or Spanish ship dare enter our harbor, or nature or man sets a structure ablaze. We, the members of the Drummond Corporation, can take the honor of sounding the alarm on our magnificent bell."

But the final touch to the tower was Thatcher's favorite, for while he loved his pretty bell, which could not help but make him think of that fireworks show in Moscow and the lovely chaotic soundtrack the cathedral bells provided, he employed one more item liberated from a Spanish ship en route to a governor with a strange fascination for astronomy. Perhaps he had intended to employ it on one of those ruined structures being discovered in the jungles of New Spain and New Andalusia that had been built by long dead ancient civilizations in a triangular shape, not unlike the pyramids of Egypt. Above the enclosed bell tower was one more platform, framed by a lovely white painted rail but open to the heavens above. Thatcher, too, loved the stars, and would look forward to those idle evenings when he could put that huge, magnificent telescope of German design to good use, exploring the heavens and, during the day, surveying the seas for any sign of enemy sail.

To an outside observer, this out-sized structure with its meticulous design and secretive aspects would appear little more than the trappings of a Caribbean robber baron, showing off his fabulous wealth in such an auspicious fashion. While the name Drummond – a successful Jamaican merchant of obvious means who had transplanted to New Providence from fear of fire and Maroons – was associated with every aspect of the enterprise, the Castle was, for all intents and purposes to its officers and shareholders, of most practical design. What the owners had learned long ago was that things should never appear as they truly are, for every exterior trifling was in truth a facade for something much more ominous. What the Drummond Corporation was erecting wasn't a temple to their success, but a fortress for the kingdom they were building.

Lumber for such a vast enterprise was not available in large quantities on these tropical islands, so Thatcher and Caesar had set out to the one place they knew they could get a good deal on sturdy loblolly pine. Upon reaching the Albemarle, they discovered that big changes were in the works for Carolina as well. While geographically this vast colony had been referred to as a "north" and "south," typically delineated by the Cape Fear River and the beginning of the barrier island chains, in 1696 the process had begun which officially divided these two vast tracts of land into separate colonies. The steady stream of settlers into the northern areas of Carolina had successfully pushed the Chowanoc and Weapem tribes off their lands, and pockets of civilized society were beginning to develop in the Albemarle, specifically the southern section reaching into Pamlico Sound, where the settlement of Bath was growing into a fairly normal, albeit primitive, town life. Settlers began to move both west and south of the Albemarle in such waves that, within the first years of the new century, the Chowan parish organized, quickly followed by Pasquotank and Perquimans, all in the northern Albemarle and critical to the development of a distinctive North Carolina society, non-dependent of either Charleston to the south or Williamsburg to the north.

In a state of war and with an ever-expanding sailing fleet, Parliament had the perfect incentive to offer to potential settlers of North Carolina with the passage of the Naval Stores Act. The British Navy had grown dependent on Holland and, during the peace, France and Spain, for those items necessary to both build and maintain a naval fleet. A few of the most critical were tar and pitch, essential elements to assure the seaworthiness and integrity of ship seams, and hemp, necessary for the thousands of miles of rope in constant demand at sea and on land. The Naval Stores Act provided a subsidy for the production of shipping essentials by providing premiums of £4 sterling per ton on tar and pitch and £6 per ton on hemp. For the Mullins family, this was manna from heaven. At last the years invested in the colony would begin to pay off tangibly, as they were on the forefront of developing one of the colony's prime industries other than tobacco. Their trees – long, straight and hard – now would become a focal point of an England at war, desperate for thick stands of wood necessary for the construction of ships, an industry now growing by leaps and bounds all along the American coast.

The primitive but picturesque clearing that had been the Mullins family settlement was now less centralized, as the brothers began to take their operations closer to the hub of activity in Chowan Parrish at Queen Anne's creek. Now with an expanding family and financial portfolio, the ladies of the Mullins clan had grown tired of the primitive, pioneer existence in their pretty settlement, far removed from town life. Patrick was the first to succumb to the demands of his wife Anne, who wanted to make sure their children grew up among people other than their kin, and he built a lovely four-room house to accommodate his three sons and two daughters. It was agreed that the boys would continue in the family trade, making their trips up the river to participate in the felling of trees that would be milled at Patrick's lumberyard. Michael, however, was experiencing a different kind of pressure from his wife Louise, who was adamant that her children have a chance at a better life than timbering. It was agreed by the family that he would move farther up the Albemarle into Pasquotank Parrish, where he, too, would open up a lumber mill and send his children to the school that had opened there. With these new opportunities in pitch and tar, there could be great opportunities to expand on the base of the family business and capitalize off this burgeoning new industry.

Seamus had always been the odd one of the family, being one of the few to express an interest in the products that went onto the lands that had been once occupied only by trees. During the harvest seasons, he had picked up extra quid by picking tobacco and taking a real interest in things that came out of the ground other than wood. With the new Act and the knowledge he had gained in tobacco, he now had a solid argument to deliver a new business opportunity to the family that would capitalize on all those thousands of acres they had cleared to take on this new product, hemp. At first, William took this all in with great reservation. He was a tree man, and he had raised his children to be tree men. But he also realized that, having lost one of his sons to a passion other than trees only to have his life snuffed out at the end of a hangman's rope, he needed to build flexibility into his thinking. The box of gold that had sat in that hole since their son's shipmates had brought it to them, minus the few coins used to book passage to New York and sustain them in that ungodly expensive city, could at last be put to good use to help his sons build their futures, still connected to the land and dependent on those trees he loved so dearly. And, as much as he hated to admit it to himself and to his wife, his daughters-in-law were correct that the children deserved better than the harsh life they had experienced for so many years. So from that chest came the money for Patrick and Michael to purchase saws and milling equipment and for seeds, plows and the family's first team of horses to help Seamus turn the soil and sow the seeds of their future.

Thatcher and Caesar were quite surprised to see how quickly the Mullins' business empire had burst to life in the few years since they had met them. Indeed, the whole region was taking on a new life, as they noted the growth of settlements on what once had been virgin stands of trees, freshly cleared courtesy of Mullins & Sons. They and the Malagasy had fully expected to come and put their backs to ax and saw, but they were pleasantly surprised when they encountered Patrick, now being rowed by laborers from his home on Queen Anne's Creek to the family settlement where William continued to hold down his shrinking fort. Patrick diverted them from their trip up the Chowan River to his rough-hewn but substantial office, where Thatcher and Caesar sat down to cups of tea on very attractive wooden chairs.

"My son William made that," Patrick beamed with obvious pride. "He and his brother David have made quite a business of it. In fact, Darby's son David – who is going now by Darby – is being lured into the business with the hope that it will keep him from following in his father's footsteps to the sea."

"We were so sorry to hear about Darby," Caesar offered. "Without him, we probably would not have survived."

Patrick's eyes grew a bit cloudy but his sadness was suddenly overcome by the anger he felt. "We couldn't talk Darby out of the sea, and my family may be pursuing other options. But we'll be damned if we see another Mullins hang for piracy, real or imagined. If we can give this boy a skill and his shot at ample gold through a real trade, well then I think that would please Darby fine."

"It was imagined, Patrick," Thatcher insisted. "Your brother was the kindest, most decent man I've known. And the sad irony is if Kidd's arrogance hadn't sent him seeking justification, if he had just waited a few more months, chances are none of this would have happened. But know, we bear much of that responsibility as well. If we had taken on caring for Darby instead of trusting him to that New York bound ship, he'd be alive today. We'll carry that with us always. So please, do what you can for young Darby, and when we see him we'll do the same."

Patrick smiled, trying to let his anger subside. "We all have to take responsibility for ourselves, gentlemen, so know that none of us hold you two accountable. In fact, in so many ways you're responsible for our success now, for without your honesty, this house, those chairs, all that equipment you saw out in my yard, never would have happened. So you tell me what we Mullins can do for you, and it's done."

For the next few days, Thatcher and Caesar enjoyed the company of the Mullins clan, who had reassembled on the old settlement once they heard their friends, these captains and their Malagasy crewmen, had returned. Since they weren't going to be charged with cutting down trees, the Malagasy took to the woods, dozens of young Mullins in tow, as they showed them the Madagascar way to bring down the deer, fox and bear that made up the sumptuous feast to be served up to the large community that had manifest overnight along the Chowan River. And it was quite the party atmosphere, as the ladies made sweets and pies while many of the cousins got together with their drums and fiddles and pipes to keep the atmosphere festive. Most of the time Thatcher and Caesar were hunkered down with sheets of paper, sketching out Drummond Tower as they calculated the thousands of board feet they would need to make this wood, stone and stucco behemoth come to life. As the jugs of Irish whiskey poured, Thatcher could not help but take his turns on the drums, dancing with all the pretty cousins who seemed to swoon at the musical, handsome sea warrior. The whiskey had its effect on everyone, as the Malagasy performed the ancient dances of their land, dragging the laughing and joyous Caesar into their circles, and from the woods the Indians watched, comparing the steps to their own. Thatcher could not help but flash back to those days at Preobrazhenskoe half a lifetime ago, where the party never stopped. Mullins and Malagasy collapsed when they could no longer tolerate another bite or drink, and off on the edge of the woods, cousins were reacquainting themselves with each other. Thatcher wasn't exactly sure when it happened or when the Irish tunes started to sound Russian to him, but all watched in amazement as that sodden Russian took to the center of the festival, dancing around in those elegant, sad steps, his arms outstretched as he danced a passionate ballet to a bottle of whiskey in front of him. When the music struck up and he attempted to do a low kicked sabre dance, his body had had enough, and he woke to find himself being lovingly attended by Mary Margaret Mullins, Sean's daughter … or was it Harry's? No matter, she was sweet and loving and giving, and he was certain the family would forgive the fact that he wasn't Catholic. Then again, neither were the Malagasy for that matter. And where they found the Indian girls would be a question they would never answer but always laugh about on those long days at sea.

It took weeks to fulfill the order and creative re-engineering of the ships to accommodate some of the lengths, but at last every board foot and a few thousand more for good measure were loaded into the *Phoenix* and *Protocol*. Their hulls had been freshly careened and decks refinished with Carolina loblolly pine and every seam and groove meticulously sealed with the tar and pitch now endlessly boiling in cauldrons at Sean's plant. The Malagasy were curious about the process and gave Sean a few tips on how to make the tar more fluid and dry less quickly to assure it seeped into the most inaccessible of seam. It was with great reluctance that the crews took to the ships to begin the return passage to New Providence. Thatcher and Caesar made a point of taking Darby aside. He was now fifteen and endlessly fascinated with all things nautical, and they felt it their duty not only to show him the ships' workings but to show him the life he had here.

"Let me tell you something about your family, Darby," Thatcher informed as he placed his arm around the shoulder of their dead friend's son. "They love you and will do anything they can to make you happy. But the sea is for people with few other marketable skills, and it's a life that you seldom grow old in. You have a trade, and I want you to make the best of it. In fact, I'm talking to your uncle, and when we send Captain Drummond in the sloop for those tables and chairs you all are making for us, I'll see if maybe they'll let you come with the Captain to New Providence to help us decide what else we need to make that place a work of art. And then when you come home, you can make it for us and bring it back to us in New Providence."

"And we'll make sure you get laid," Caesar offered, nodding his head. Thatcher shot him a look, and Caesar explained, matter-of-factly, "You offer your incentive, I'll offer mine."

Darby thought about what they had said and he turned to Thatcher with a serious look. "I think I like Uncle Caesar's offer better."

The *Phoenix* and *Protocol* at last made sail, as the Mullins family brought a large flotilla of dories, canoes and Patrick's very impressive ketch to bid good-bye to their New Providence extended family. As soon as the ships were far beyond the horizon, William and Patrick sat down and began the process of accounting the large volume of gold left behind as payment for services rendered. They recounted three times and at last came to the same conclusion: they had been severely overpaid. William took the overpayment and retrieved the old chest that had stood empty for all their investments. He placed the excess gold inside and Patrick made a note in his limited hand for future safekeeping: "Will consider this the first investment of the Drummond Corporation's North Carolina branch."

Once the Drummond Corporation headquarters had been completed and Captain Drummond set sail for Carolina, it was time for the *Phoenix* and *Protocol* to begin replenishing their vastly shrunken coffers. They took the long track around the Windwards to prey on French and Spanish ships and to pick up Edward Welch's trail where it had left off. Finding a modicum of success in the area of Trinidad, both in commandeering and unloading cargo, they eventually found themselves with a hold full of sugarcane, a perfect excuse to seek out a buyer in the Dutch port of Willemstad on the island of Curaçao.

Edward Welch had bigger plans these days than when he had been referred to as "the Little King" at St. Mary's. He had been tantalized at the notion of what Mr. Evans and Mr. Parcrick had proposed to him – the creation of a sovereign nation at the edge of the world. While Africa may one day possess limitless opportunities for ambitious men with grand designs, in this era St. Mary's was over the edge of the known world. Out there, few but the most desperate and most criminal could be gleaned into a constituency, with only he as the basis of a civil structure. Were one seeking only a minor fiefdom, it would be an ideal location, and perhaps Mr. Evans and Mr. Parcrick would one day return, find his fortress abandoned and decide to build that little kingdom they had proposed to him. When he had decided that he was going to make Curaçao his destination, he used the long journey to convince the captains that the Dutch settlement may not be the ideal location to sell their slaves. He discussed with them what he had learned about Carolina and how quickly it was growing, specifically the port of Charleston, where rice was beginning to take a foothold and slaves were gold to these plantation owners. Convinced by his sound logic of this growing market, the ships made port at Charleston and were surprised to discover how desperate these colonists were to actually receive a first-hand shipment of slaves. Since the founding of Charleston, most of their slaves had come to them by way of Barbados, who still held great sway over this colony. Despite its economic potential, the Charlestonians could not help but feel their Barbadian patrons were shipping them the worst of their slave stock. Here at last was a chance to pick from the cream of the crop rather than the bottom of the barrel, and these Malagasy, so different in appearance from the western Africans they typically received, were snatched up for prices far above what they likely would have fetched in Curaçao. While Edward Welch did not feel a sense of fear from the two young men with whom he had severed his ties, there was no reason to take unnecessary risks, and by depositing their Malagasy in Charleston it would certainly throw them off the track should they for any reason be seeking him out. Likewise, he found a ready base of customers desirous of snatching up his ample merchandise for a pretty penny. Now free of his Malagasy and cargo, he took his stocks of gold and silver to the final destination of Curaçao, where Edward Welch and all the baggage he carried ceased to exist.

Curaçao shared that common distinction with New Providence in that a man with ample gold could become anyone he wished to, including Dutch if he so chose. Thus, Edvart DeVyck was born, complete with a decent enough command of this guttural language to allow him to pass himself off as a Ceylon-born son of Eindhoven immigrants who had worked with English traders since he was a teen. Growing tired of the Red Sea, he had chosen to move to the Netherland Antilles to put his vast experience in shipping to work in the vital trade of the Caribbean. Captain Oestergaart of the *Antwerp* was happy to make the introductions and to suggest to his Curaçaon contacts that Mr. DeVyck had great insights into trade and should be consulted frequently. As a free trade port, it was critical that the masters of this black market paradise have an intimate relationship with those who had come to establish a long-term residency on the island. Jacob Beck, Governor of Curaçao, made a point of getting to know Edvart DeVyck and his insights on trade. His initial impression of DeVyck was that of a man who understood the nuances between the grey and black market and seemed not to flinch a muscle when giving consideration to the worthy applications of either as circumstances dictated. While his contacts and DeVyck's obvious accent revealed an English birth, there was no doubting that when it came to business his mind was purely Dutch. As such, Beck knew that this was one he needed to keep close.

Sailing into Willemstad, Thatcher and Caesar marveled at this mini version of Amsterdam, with its clean streets and picturesque, pastel-colored homes so unlike the rough-and-tumble life of most Caribbean towns. Like New Providence, Curaçao's governor was notorious for having his fingers in every pie and his ears in every building, and it wasn't long until word reached Jacob Beck of Englishmen inquiring about a fellow countryman of late from the island of St. Mary's. He passed a note addressed to DeVyck regarding these new arrivals and let him know, of course, that their search would be for naught. But DeVyck had to admit his curiosity and frankly how impressed he was that Evans and Parcrick had come this far to seek him out. While he felt confident in Beck's assurances, he likewise felt it was important to get them off his trail, and he communicated his concerns to the governor and his solution to this situation.

Caesar and Thatcher were returning to their ships after a long evening of drinking and carousing and desperately in need of baths. They had proposed retiring to their tubs and joining up later for a few rounds of whist while making plans for their next round of hunting. As they sauntered along the docks, they noticed a young man hovering near their boats. They looked at each other and surveyed their surroundings to see if their unexpected guest had company with him. Seeing as he was alone and the Malagasy watchman signaled no cause for alarm, they made their way to where the young man anxiously paced the length of the dock between their two ships.

"Good evening, young gentleman. We should let you know we have a full compliment and are not recruiting. However, if you would like a tour, please feel free to come back tomorrow," Thatcher offered good-naturedly, as this was a common occurrence in every port.

"Good evening, captain. I will say they are fine boats, but I am not here to sign up or tour your vessels. I am a messenger who has been asked to convey you to my employer, who may be able to answer some of the questions you've been asking."

Caesar and Thatcher looked at each other and noted the lateness of the evening. Reeking of rum and sex, it seemed that their bath time would be put off for a bit. Their Malagasy shadows would make note of their path, following at a reasonable but stealthy distance as they always did. Thatcher waved his hand to the young man, beckoning him to lead on. "Best we not keep your employer waiting, shall we?"

Their trip was not long and surprisingly ended at the front door of Governor Beck's mansion, where the young man conducted them to the study where the governor was waiting.

"Good morning, gentlemen. I hope Stefan did not tear you away from anything urgent or certainly more interesting than meeting with me in the middle of the night," Governor Beck offered graciously, as he motioned them into chairs.

"We appreciate your concern, Governor, but certainly it wasn't so pressing as to require you to meet with us so late in the evening," Thatcher replied.

"I keep very strange hours, and this is no inconvenience to me whatsoever. And if I may be helpful, I will do so." He got to the point. "I understand you are seeking out an Englishman by the name of Edward Welch, is this correct?"

"That would be correct, Governor," Caesar agreed.

"Well, I may be able to help you with that. Apparently, two ships who sailed out of my port made his acquaintance at St. Mary's and were intrigued by his offer to make their trip more successful. So apparently he arranged for a cache of slaves to be turned over in exchange for passage."

Thatcher and Caesar looked at each other in surprise that so much information was being given up so readily by the governor. "So then do you know where he ended up, Governor?" Caesar inquired.

"Oh, yes. He made his plans quite clear. In fact, he told the captains of the ships that he had every intention of continuing the relationship once he got settled in."

"So then you can tell us where we can find him?" Caesar asked.

"Oh, most certainly. I do so because so far he has not lived up to his deal, which was to keep us in ample stocks of rice, which as you know is a very solid commodity to our Spanish neighbors. In fact, I must admit, I'm a bit embarrassed as I've not yet been able to deliver on my assurances."

"Rice, you say," Thatcher probed.

"Yes, from what my captains tell me, he negotiated to keep the youngest and strongest of the males for himself by commanding a very good price for the women and children to the planters. You can find him in Carolina on a plantation he bought just outside of Charleston." The Governor stood. "I wish you luck, gentlemen. And please be kind enough to deliver a message to Mr. Welch when you see him. It is best to keep your bargains, or not to make them at all."

As he began to show them to the door, he offered one final parting word. "Oh – and I should warn you, Mr. Evans and Mr. Parcrick, there appears to be word that England is still seeking out members of Captain Kidd's crew that have not yet been brought to justice. Charleston is hell-bent to try to curry favor with England, so protect your identities well, because if the people of Charleston discover who you are, the least of your problems will be Edward Welch."

If one thing was obvious to Thatcher and Caesar, they were on a hot trail. How much the governor was to be believed, however, was an entirely different story. There were two ways to view what Beck was saying. If they were to be optimistic, they could assume he was telling them the truth, in which case it was a matter of determining exactly where near Charleston Edward Welch was holed up. This shouldn't be too difficult, as the Malagasy were quite distinctive from their fellow Africans, with their unique blend of Bantu and Polynesian features and their distinctive tongue that would make them easy to find. It was just a matter of finding one in Charleston, and from there they could find Edward Welch, no matter what name he was hiding under. Having no love lost for the people of that pretentious town, they were fairly confident they could carry out their mission against Welch, liberate a portion of the Malagasy and slip out before much could be done about it. But if Governor Beck was speaking the truth, carrying out this mission into Charleston could be very dangerous for them as well. In their first appearance aboard in the *Phoenix* they had used their real names. Apparently those names were now assumed by the powers-that-be as *noms de guerre* for Evans and Parcrick, as Welch no doubt had informed them in order to protect himself. It posed great risk to them for either the *Phoenix* or either of its captains to make port again in Charleston. They had to work out a plan with the assumption that Governor Beck was telling the truth.

And then there was the other way to view it, the most logical: that Edward Welch was here in Curaçao under Governor Beck's protection. With the two warships – aptly named the *Scylla* and *Charybidis*, for indeed anyone sailing between them would be caught between a rock and a hard place – parked in Beck's harbor, it would be very difficult to pull off an action against Welch here and expect to be able to sail out of the harbor without feeling the effects of those guns. Regardless, if Welch was here, they would find him, deal with him and work out a plan to get away with it, if at all possible. There was one way, however, that they could reach Governor Beck's ear, and that was to be of even greater value to him than sheltering Edward Welch. Governor Beck was a practical man, and if practicality dictated that these two young men, their massive ships and motivated crew could be of vital service to him, he would weigh the options and tilt in the direction where he saw the greatest long-term opportunity. This whole situation required consultation with Captain Drummond.

The fates aligned for them as a buyer for their sugar cane was quickly reached at a price not difficult to argue with. The young broker working on behalf of his client, a Mr. DeVyck, passed on a message that he was always open for business and to consult Mr. Miersma any time they reached Curaçao. Wishing to save time, they opted for the open waters that lay between the Netherland Antilles and New Providence, where hopefully Captain Drummond would have returned from the Albemarle with his lovely new office furniture.

Getting Captain Drummond into Charleston Harbor for legitimate purposes was, on the surface, simple enough. The *Phoenix* and *Protocol* escorted the good captain in his little sloop, then stood by out of sight as Drummond negotiated with the rabbinical council in the largely Jewish capital of Barbados. He unloaded a quantity of gefilte fish, lox and kosher-prepared beef and mutton they had obtained from Cartagena and sailed back to his guardians with a new trade contact for the future and a letter of introduction to key dignitaries in Charleston. Off the coast of South Carolina, Thatcher and Caesar decided to make the best of their time and sought out the Spanish and French merchant ships still brave enough to ply the coast en route to Havana and St. Augustine as the little *Dominion* made its way into Charleston Harbor.

Captain Drummond was pleased to see how readily he was received by Governor Nathaniel Johnson. While there was, at times, resentment toward their Barbadian sponsors, it was never good business to upset these wealthy merchants who had continued to pour money into that disease- and fire-plagued swamp. Governor Johnson was surprised that such a little sloop had dared cross such vast waters alone, but as Captain Drummond so eloquently pointed out it must indeed have been the hand of God himself that protected him. The Malagasy restricted their activities primarily to the docks, surveying the numerous Africans working the waterfront, for hints of their tribesmen. It didn't take long to discover that, indeed, there were Malagasy who had been brought to Charleston some years back, and Captain Drummond took note of the plantations that had taken on larger blocks of Malagasy slaves, according to the intelligence his cohorts had gleaned. Governor Johnson was delighted to arrange for introductions to the growing number of rice plantation owners, who were more than happy to welcome him for dinner and to tour their facilities. Drummond did drop hints that, as well as a strong trade in the Caribbean, he had contacts through his New Providence base with potential customers with a fondness for a product they called *arroz*. Of course, these plantation owners knew rice was called by many names and mentioned that while they may speak only one language, they would be more than happy to accommodate the captain's multi-national customer base in whatever stocks they needed. He made notes of the names and faces of the plantation owners, querying them over glasses of rum served in the beautiful Dutch crystal he had sold them, asking them what brought them to Charleston and what intrigued them about rice. And there were questions about his all-black crew, including the muscular attendant always at his elbow or near the elbow of the African servants that hovered about. After two weeks in Charleston, Captain Drummond at last bid adieu to his fine new friends, his little sloop weighed down heavily with sacks of rice. Sailing south from Charleston Harbor, he changed his course at sea to north, traveling along the Carolina coast to the mouth of the Cape Fear River where he would rendezvous with the *Phoenix* and *Protocol*. Before sailing back to New Providence, they had begun to forge a plan for a return trip to Charleston. But it was all about timing and that time was not now.

As Drummond Castle's construction neared completion, Thatcher and Caesar made a call on Patrick to return young Darby back to the settlement as he promised, with a fat order of new needs for Drummond Castle and a growing demand for these well-made Mullins chairs for desiring customers in New Providence. Darby had thrilled in that initial crossing of the tea colored waters of the broad Albemarle and Pamlico Sounds into the vast and wild deep of the dark green waters of the Atlantic and the crystal blue expanse of the Caribbean. As much as Darby lǫved the sea, he saw the real profit to be made in manufacturing quality wooden goods that could prove to be a very lucrative trade for him and his cousins. As Darby got busy turning out chairs, Patrick took Thatcher and Caesar aboard his lovely ketch and sailed around to Sean's new home, the first working model of the Mullins House, on Plum Point just outside of the town of Bath. Thatcher was intrigued to visit the frontier town, which had just last year been incorporated as the first permanent settlement of North Carolina. Sean had settled in quickly to town life, introducing him to some of the village's luminaries. He was pleased to make the acquaintance of local merchant Tobias Knight and Edward Moseley and Colonel Maurice Moore, three of the most established men in this burgeoning colonial capital. He also had the chance to meet Governor William Glover and his deputy Thomas Cary, the two men charged with governing the colony that had now fully and formally separated itself from its southern neighbor. With these men, he began to lay the groundwork for a solid trade relationship between the Drummond Corporation on New Providence and this promising colony beginning to carve itself out of the woods. He spent a few days enjoying the company of Sean Mullins, marveling at his pretty house, not far from Bath on a pretty promontory with a little creek serving this quiet cove off the Pamlico River. The peacefulness of this setting was incredibly attractive to Thatcher, and as he enjoyed the company of Mary Margaret Mullins underneath many of its trees, he could see a time in his life when such a pretty place could beckon him to build his own pretty little home.

Bidding adieu to the Mullins, they proceeded up the Carolina coast, making a rapid trip across the Chesapeake, pissing frequently in the waters they hoped would float to Jamestown and choke those arrogant Virginians, and on to Annapolis. The Maryland colony was going through tremendous growth, despite the Crown's attempts to subjugate the Catholic settlers and infuse the Church of England amongst the Papist hordes. Colonel John Seymour, the Royal Governor of Maryland, was a pleasant enough fellow despite his strident Protestant beliefs, and he was happy to hear that New Providence, despite its absence of governance, was thriving and producing such fine reputable traders as the Drummond Corporation. He welcomed the opportunity to seek trade with this company and its ample supplies of Caribbean goods.

At last they were able to push on to Philadelphia, where Thatcher was greeted at the docks by his father-in-law William Fordham and the good people of the Quaker congregation. They of course made their reunion short, knowing full well that Melanie was quite anxious to reacquaint herself with her long-absent husband. Such absences were not strange things in these days of merchant fleets and warfare. And William was pleased to hear his son-in-law Edward Thatcherev had fallen in with such a distinctive enterprise as the Drummond Corporation. They promised to sit down and discuss business after a lengthy reunion with his wife, who had taken the ensuing years to build a quite lovely home on her father's property. Mr. Fordham and the good men of Philadelphia were pleased as they sat on the back porch, sipping coffee, to hear that the reunion between Edward and Melanie was proceeding quite passionately.

"So tell me, Charles," Mr. Fordham inquired, as he turned to Caesar who sat among the assembled Quaker businessmen being regaled with the sympathy of Melanie's passionate screams. "Catch us up with all thou hast been up to since thee and Edward departed our company."

It took Caesar a moment to remember the pseudonym he had used so long ago in this port and respond. He and Thatcher had carefully worked out this timeline for the kind folk of Philadelphia, who may not be as intrigued by the more bawdy aspects of their adventures. He sipped his coffee, feeling the eyes of the Quaker gentlemen as they perched on the edges of their chairs, waiting to hear what great and exciting things had occurred beyond their great, clean port.

"Well, William, we sailed to New Providence. A war began. We discovered a good market from privateer goods, and we sailed back to Philadelphia."

"Tell us, Charles, for we feel so distant from England and the rest of her colonies. Hast thou encountered these Catholics, the French and Spanish, in thy travels?"

"Only in passing, William. They keep to their waters, and we keep to ours, for certainly we wish not to have any strange mixing going on."

The gentlemen nodded their heads in agreement, and as they sat in the silence of the evening, punctuated only by Melanie's enthusiastic demands, Thomas Peabody had to inquire, "Dost thou think they would be receptive to a visit from Friends? After all, we do not support this war and believe peaceful resolution could be obtained if we met as friends."

"Thomas, I think these French and Spanish fellows are not feeling very friendly these days. Perhaps when the war is over, you will make it a point to extend that hand of friendship when they are less likely to want to remove it with a cutlass."

Again they all sat in silence and pondered this. It had grown momentarily silent across the yard, when Thatcher burst through the rear door, plunging his head into a barrel of water, the expression of fear and exhaustion visible even in the moonlight. With scarcely time to catch a breath, the half-clad Melanie Fordham appeared and dragged him back into the house.

"Such a lovely night, friends. Would anyone care for more coffee?" William offered as he shuffled off into the house.

It was not Caesar's desire to be an asshole, but he and the crew had made it quite clear to Thatcher that, despite the long years of absence and the kindness of these Pennsylvania Quakers, this was not to be another three-month stopover. And when Day Seven finally arrived and Melanie Fordham escorted her husband to the dock, she hugged her brother-in-law, with whom she had so little time to catch up, and whispered in his ear, "Could we not have a boat follow to the end of the Delaware?"

Caesar gave her one of his firm stares and then softened into a smile. "Only as far as the mouth of the Delaware, Melanie."

"That's why I love thee, Caesar," she replied, kissing him again as she dragged Thatcher to the *Phoenix* and disappeared into the Captain's Quarters. It had been so long since she had visited Kidd's desk, and she was anxious to see how it felt on a moving sea. And at the mouth of the Delaware, she was true to her word. Taking a moment to hug each and every one of the Malagasy and thanking them for their beautiful serenades, which were as much to entertain her as to drown out the noise, she at last bid farewell to her husband.

"Promise me that it won't be six years between visits, and shouldst thou get to Bristol, tell thy mother her daughter-in-law thinks of her frequently."

"I will do all that I can, my love, and I know you understand why so long between visits. But I will do my best to come home to you soon."

She kissed her husband good-bye, knowing that in truth it could be years again. But in a few weeks, when the mornings were greeted with queasiness, she would hope that her pragmatic view would be proven incorrect. For certainly, he would wish to know his child.

II

One could never deny the industry of the Dutch. As the world's first super sea-power, their aspirations to conquer the oceans were not for such the silly reasons as the French, English or Spanish – the mere sake of planting a flag somewhere in the name of God and King – but for the purposes of commerce. And commerce was at the heart and soul of every Dutchman. Holland had worked hard to build alliances around the world that not only safeguarded their nation's shipping interests but also made it greatly difficult to really hold anything against Holland.

It was the Dutch who made the first successful inroads with the Mogul and Pashas of Mocha and locked in exclusive trade with the Moslem world for coffee. Transporting cuttings to their possessions in the South Seas, the Dutch were able to produce their first bumper crop of fine Arabica beans in 1690 on the island of Java. As the invigorating effects of coffee began to overtake the numbing effects of various alcohols among Europeans, this new global commodity fast became a highly lucrative and jealously guarded monopoly. With war once again raging between France and England, Holland had no choice but to cut off trade to its French caffeine addicts. Always pragmatic, the South Sea planters began to consider ways they might expand their crops into the Caribbean, offering ample opportunity for back door dealing with French and Spanish New World holdings. The Dutch possession Curaçao had developed a well-earned reputation of possessing the largest black market in the New World, where anything could be bought. And because of the liberal nature of the governor-general of the Dutch West India Company who made his home on the island, protected by a pair of forty-four gun frigates he owned to keep peace in his wayward post, Curaçao seemed like a natural location to consider this relocation.

Edvart DeVyck had been enjoying a dinner with Governor Jacob Beck, discussing the limitations of trade opportunities on the island by virtue of the distance that so many Dutch products had to travel. A lucrative trade in Spanish wares, smuggled from New Spain and New

Andalusia, had served to provide profitable new markets to greedy buyers in England and the colonies. But the one commodity they could not seem to hold onto was coffee. Ceylon and Batavia were half a world away, and the routes to the Western Hemisphere – either around Africa where British guns were a constant threat or through the treacherously unpredictable Straits of Magellan– made it difficult for an honest smuggler to make a decent living. Of course, neither being coffee experts, perhaps there was a reason other than Dutch territorialism that coffee production had been limited to these two distinctive regions. Out of curiosity, they decided to send survey expeditions out to the islands of the Netherland Antilles with the intention of harvesting soil samples to send to the Batavian growers for analysis. Truly, it was out of curiosity and not much more thought was given to it after the samples were sent. But even here at the edge of the world, specialists could be found in a burgeoning new science called botany, plying their trade on the island of Batavia. While England may have cornered the market on scientific theoretics, the Dutch were quietly gaining ground in scientific pragmatics, and understanding how and why things grow was critical to developing new markets. And they were happy to receive these young, bright specialists in this growing field.

In the spring of 1705, the *Spinnaker* arrived after threading that nautical chokehold of the Straits of Magellan, carrying supplies of Spanish silver and gold ware and Jamaican rum for the cash-rich planters of Batavia. As they were offloading these Caribbean specialties, they were amused by the small cargo of soil samples taken from throughout the Netherland Antilles with the thought of assessing their values for future markets. The planters were always used to some odd offer or another to expand commercial opportunities, but they were intrigued by the letter from Governor Beck of Curaçao and the solid rationale he made with respect to considering these Dutch possessions as their next expansion point. Max Weilhaus was the only person they could think of who would have the slightest amount of interest in this odd shipment. The young botanist spent his time comparing the samples from the Caribbean to the local soil where coffee had proven to proliferate, and he brought back the news of his findings. While most samples were useless and incompatible to standards of growth, two locations, specifically the heights of Saba and Curaçao, proved most promising.

"Of course, it is difficult to describe, but different soils yield different nutrient variables, and by comparing colors, compositions and fragrances, you can achieve a reasonable comparison from one to the other. And I tell you, gentlemen, these two samples are nearly identical to that of some of our soils here in Batavia. Were you ever to consider such an idea, these two locations should prove to be ideal."

Reviewing the botanist's findings fueled the imaginations of the Batavian growers. While many were against betraying their sacred oath to this exclusive possession, a small group began to advocate at least considering the possibility of this venture. For months, they debated the merits as well as the drawbacks. At last it was decided that this precious commodity would require a sizeable financial commitment and a circuitous means of shipment to assure this enterprise remained absolutely beyond scrutiny. They detailed their proposal and shipped it back to Governor Beck for his consideration. He was shocked to receive this very positive and receptive response and met with his burgeoning business partner Edvart DeVyck to arrange funding for the venture. On the next ship leaving Curaçao for Batavia, the growers were being dispatched their answer by way of the 30,000 guilder of specie.

It was decided that each planter would provide one thousand cuttings from their vast plantations to be carefully packed and shipped to Curaçao. There a portion would be planted, with the remainder taken to Saba, and word would be quietly spread that the French no longer need live without their coffee ... for the right price. It would take upwards of ten years, depending upon rain and soil, to produce the first marketable crop. But if the customers were willing, perhaps a circuitous trade of Java beans could make their way into the port of Curaçao and onto ships of any nation who dropped anchor in this free trade port. One problem with this arrangement was the fear that everyone logically voiced: what if a privateer ship or man-of-war from the French or Spanish should overtake her? Obviously, they would lose their products as a legitimate spoil of war. Or even worse: what would happen if the English got wind of a ship full of Javanese coffee plants en route to the Netherland Antilles with the intention of building a domestic market for this product? For decades, the English had been trying to coax their Dutch allies into sell them cuttings with the intention of planting coffee in the Caribbean. England's island colonies possessed some of the most startling and ideal terrain for growing these products, but the Dutch had been adamant that growth would be restricted to Ceylon and Java exclusively. Would their coffee madness put them in bad stead with their closest allies for having been cut out of the Caribbean deal?

There was only one logical answer to their shipping dilemma: Denmark. The Danish had gotten into the Caribbean colonial game in 1674 when it purchased the island of St. Thomas from the Dutch. During their seventeen years of possession, the Dutch had made no concerted effort to settle the island, which had become little more than a breeding ground for pirates. With a well-sheltered deepwater harbor, this sparsely vegetated and semi-arid island was of no real value to the Dutch as it was so far removed from the rest of their colonies in the Antilles. The King of Denmark bought the island from the Dutch and named the port town Charlotte Amalie after his wife. There was little logic for Denmark to covet this island other than to say they did and the Swedes didn't. Plus, as many of Denmark's nobles frequently whispered, it was done for no other purpose than to give Charlotte Amalie an island of her own. The Danish were for all accounts neutral with all the great powers that surrounded them. As Denmark continued its age-old struggle with Sweden, there was no capability to defend the island from hostility other than issuing Letters of Marque to those rogue bands of pirates that occupied the island on those occasions when a particular ship harassed him. For the most part, the ships of the small Danish fleet that called Charlotte Amalie their home port were traders, sailing between the rich and flourishing Caribbean neighbors for goods to carry home to Denmark. It was such a ship that made perfect sense to hire for this secretive venture, as the harmless Danish would pose no threat to anyone throughout the Caribbean.

The *Jutta Georg* set sail from Charlotte Amalie on June 1, 1706, at the start of the Caribbean storm season, to begin the long and treacherous trip to Java. There was much debate as to whether or not she should take the long way around Cape Horn and across the Indian Ocean. But her fearless captain Ole Georg would not hear of it, for such a trip, though less dangerous, would keep him away that much longer from the lovely woman for whom he'd named his ship. Captain Georg reasoned with the governor-general that, though the Straits of Magellan were a hellish course and provided more of a margin of danger, it would also cut months off the journey, a point of concern, no doubt, to their contractors. It was settled, and old Captain Georg bid his lovely ancient wife good-bye, took his white Dwarf Spitz up in his hand and set sail out of Charlotte Amalie, heading due south toward Tierra del Fuego.

Captain Georg actually preferred this passage through the Straits of Magellan. He had rounded the Horn and passed through the straits dozens of times in his career, and he always looked forward to those first signs of ice floes and the eventual towering spires of massive icebergs, as they reminded him so much of his Scandinavian travels when he was but a very young sailor. While bergs may be the curse of most captains, they made Ole Georg feel as if he were at home. And as he navigated his way through the straits, seeing his cold breath exhale before him, his little Zweigspitz Olaf tucked into his heavy coat for warmth, he took in the magnificence of the icebergs and fjords and felt the only thing missing was his beloved Jutta.

The planters in Surabaya were overjoyed to see the old Danish captain standing at the bow of his ship, pipe in his mouth and the little doggy under his arm, as he smiled a jaunty greeting to his anxious customers. To call Captain Georg flamboyant was to understate the quality of the man, for unlike most sea captains who preferred their dark jackets and tricorner hats, Captain Georg was an enigma, in his white breeches and white jacket and his odd-shaped plumed hat turned up at one corner. He had taken to carrying a cane with him, now held in one hand with the doggy resting on his arm, as he waved his pipe at the Java planters and descended the gangplank as if he were the King of Denmark himself. His long, lean and angular legs seemed not troubled by their long months at sea as he strode imperiously to his Dutch compatriots.

"And good morning to you, gentlemen," Captain Georg began, as he waved his pipe in a flourish to all of them. "It is such a glorious day today. I have always loved Surabaya and its beautiful mountains," he said, taking in a deep breath of the acrid jungle air.

"Captain George, I am Hans van Vleeck, and we are so happy to see you," one of the planters addressed him.

The captain gave him a somewhat disapproving and chiding look. "*Gyor*,'" the captain corrected him.

"Captain 'Gyor,'" Mr. van Vleeck replied, correcting himself. "Well, just know we are grateful that Denmark is assisting us in this most delicate venture. But as I'm sure you've been made aware, St. Thomas will be richly rewarded, both now and later, for your assistance."

"I am very happy to have the money, Mr. van Vleeck," the captain replied. "I do this as much for Denmark as my own love for coffee. You know, we Danes have to endure so many days without sunlight, and when we discovered coffee, it made those grey days more joyous. On behalf of my King, who needs as many bright days as possible in his struggles against the Swedes, I ask that you only do me one favor and send him a good stock of beans with my compliments."

"Well, Captain, that's perfect. You understand. Is it your intention to return the same way you came? I know most sailors prefer the safer, albeit longer, route back through the Indian and 'round the Cape."

The captain waved his hand dismissively. "No, my good Mr. van Vleeck, as quickly as you can have my ship provisioned and those delicate little plants stowed in my hold, I'll be back through the Straits before the winter can clog the passage. So," he clapped twice briskly, "post-haste! My doggie needs to take a walk. Come, Olaf," he stated as he put the little dog down and began striding to God-knows-where with those long pegs and their vast stride, forcing the little white dog to run furiously to keep up.

Over the next few days, Captain Georg supervised the load from a very comfortable rattan chair poised at the edge of the hold, Olaf in his lap barking in response like the good First Mate he was, as a Javanese servant stood beside them with a large fan to shoo away insects and the omnipresent heat. Captain Georg would gesture with his cane where he wanted every plant placed, as if sensing that every misplaced ounce would send his ship to the bottom. As provisioning and stowing was rapidly accomplished, Captain Georg at last took up an invitation from his customers for a fine lunch of monkey and breadfruit, and then as if reading a sudden change of wind, he sprang up unexpectedly, bid them all adieu and hurried down the path from the colonial mansion with little Olaf in a dead run behind him.

Captain Georg pressed all available sail on his southeast run to the Straits. He was concerned with all the extra water he carried for the plants and the clash of egos from young Mr. Weilhaus, sent by the planters to husband these little shoots to their eventual maturity. Mr. Weilhaus had a certain flare for the dramatic that Captain Georg found wholly inappropriate. But likewise, Max Weilhaus found his flamboyant captain and his Danish ways an annoyance the entire passage. Heavy winds and waves and an early chill made the journey through the Straits of Magellan much more chaotic than usual, and this odd cargo which, despite his best efforts, had been inefficiently packed, making his hold lighter than he would have hoped, making his ship feel top-heavy as those casks of fresh water quickly ran dry, lightening his load even more. Rather than pitching the empty barrels over the side, he ordered them re-filled with salt water and replaced back in the hold for ballast, much to the protest of Max, who now had to work his way around barrels of useless brine he felt posed a real threat to his fragile cargo should they accidentally bust and spill. Before proceeding north up the east coast of South America, they refilled the barrels with fresh water, which, as Captain Georg explained, they wouldn't have been able to do if they had tossed them overboard, as Max had insisted. Their journey north now, nearly a year from the day he set sail, seemed uneventful despite the week and a half trapped in the doldrums, where, at Max's demand, the plants were brought on deck to get sunlight. Those thousands of little plants were hauled up and took up every available inch of deck, making work much more precarious for the crew as Max hovered around the plants, chastising crewmen who came too close and reminding them all that he was their customer and he was not happy.

As they made their way up the coast of Brazil, Captain Georg carefully monitored a flotilla of English ships that had been raging along the coast for the last few years. Of course, he was in no danger, for his Danish flag and passports from a host of nations, including England, would result in little more than a interruption to his schedule and a tongue-lashing to whomever bothered to stop him, this Royal emissary of Denmark and a neutral flag which should receive no molestation from anyone, save pirates themselves. He had seen the fleet prowling off the southern coast of South America prior to his Magellan run. It was obvious they had noticed him as well, but as they were laying waste to a number of Spanish cities along the coast, this Danish merchant was of little concern to them, although it could be of concern to the *Jutta Georg* should Captain Georg require replenishments anywhere within Spanish-held South America. And there they were again, off the coast of Recife, where the English navy had just bombarded the harbor, causing significant damage to the port infrastructure and sending smoke plumes miles into the air from the fires set by their munitions. Their track would intersect him on their present course, and Ole Georg tacked back his sails to come across their stern, wishing in no way to appear hostile to these very aggressive English ships. In his spyglass, he took in the image of their Commodore, a young blond man, whom he could tell suffered significant wounds to his face in some prior engagement. The Commodore was duplicating Captain Georg's effort, easily spying the Danish captain, dressed head to toe in white. The young commander chuckled to his companions as they took turns on the glass, observing the sexagenarian captain in his wash of white clothing. As if to signal their obvious joy in seeing such a sight, the captain lined up his officers along the rail as they came in visual contact with the *Jutta Georg*, passing to the stern of the ships and in unison tossed him a salute. While it may have been a mockery from the young English officers, Ole Georg snapped to attention, crisply executing a salute back, his plumed hat elevated by his tilted chin as he flashed a near toothless smile that, despite its absence of teeth, revealed a cockiness young Captain Rogers and his erudite young officers could only dream to possess. Their track, Captain Georg surmised, was not carrying them to the Caribbean as they would be on a similar course with him and the *Jutta Georg*. All these months at sea with his Danish crew and the insufferable Max Weilhaus had grown stale to him, and he would have looked forward to dining with that young captain and regaling him with tales of the sea and his decades of turns around the Cape and the Horn that would send shivers down their spines. But he smiled to himself that these young officers were in the prime of their lives, and if good fortune was on their side perhaps their sailing careers could be a small reflection of his own illustrious decades in service to the Danish king.

Indeed Captain Georg was right, for Commodore Woodes Rogers, Jr., had just completed nearly two years harassing the Spanish coast. With his flotilla of five warships, he had made great sport bringing destruction up the east coast of South America, launching attacks on Rio Gallegos, Montevideo, Curitiba, Rio de Janeiro, Salvador and finally Recife. Working south from the Caribbean was Vice-Admiral Whetstone's fleet, who delivered attacks against the New Andalusia settlements of Barranquilla, Maracaibo, Puerto Cabello, Caracas, Cumana and striking blows against the French at Cayenne and the Portuguese at São Luis and Fortaleza. After launching his final attack, Admiral Whetstone sent a message to Woodes Rogers to rendezvous with him near the fifth parallel, where together the two would sail to England. Their two war fleets had gone far in delivering deadly blows against Louis' interests in the Americas and demonstrated that England's Navy was no longer in the shadow of the Spanish fleet. They had shown what England could do with its military might. As Vice-Admiral Whetstone and Captain Rogers convened at sea to begin a triumphant return to England, they would begin to put into play an event that showed that Britannia did indeed rule the waves.

Captain Georg made his noonday reading on January 1, 1707, and determined that he was at about nine degrees south, and in a few short hours his calculations were confirmed as the lookout spotted land.

"Cabo de Santo Agustinho," the captain stated to Olaf to boast his navigational prowess. From here it was just a short day's sail and he would begin his northwest swing back into the Caribbean, rounding the island of Trinidad and proceeding west past Isla de Margarita, where his Danish flag, posing threat to no one, would give him scant attention from the Guardia Costa of the Spanish fleet sailing along the coast of New Andalusia. In two days, he would make port in Willemstad, where after unloading this infernal cargo, a small provisioning and receipt of his payment he would sail northwest and in less than a week be back in the arms of Jutta.

Rounding Galera Point on the northeast coast of Trinidad, he took note of a large English fleet, sailing north along the Windwards, not realizing they were in hot pursuit of a Spanish fleet to their north. These issues were of little consequence to Ole as he prepared to make his westward swing. But off on the horizon, he saw another ship, a smaller one than the men-of-war who had just passed him. He looked at his mast to assure his Danish flag was still prominently flapping in the breeze and then gave orders for course correction. He grew a little concerned as the ship began to make an interception course with him, but again, once they saw the Danish flag they would likely move off, for as well as navy ships these waters were teeming with privateers who dared not assault a ship representing his Majesty of Denmark.

But Captain Taylor and the crew of the *Machete* cared little for flags of any nation, having spent days skulking along the New Andalusian coast, attempting to avoid both Spanish and English ships, which were crawling virtually over every square league of sea. The outsized sloop was small but fast, and with her six guns an unescorted merchant like this Dane was precisely what they had been looking for as they swooped in for the kill. There weren't many Danish ships, and Taylor had heard jokes that to pursue a Dane was always the possibility of coming up with a cargo of cookie tins. But he also knew that they often carried fair amounts of specie and possibly household goods for the pathetic little island of St. Thomas. That tiny Danish possession may have been useless and unproductive, but it seemed this king did his best to make sure his token handful of colonists was always well provisioned. And as the *Machete* sent a ball over the bow of the *Jutta Georg* and raised his *Jollé Rouge*, announcing no quarter for resistance, he was pleased to see her lower her sails and amused by the sight of the white-bedecked captain and his little dog, both yapping away at this rude intrusion.

Boarding her was no effort whatsoever, and no resistance was given, except by the little man down in the hold protecting his little flowers like they were pots of gold. The crew hauled up Max Weilhaus, laughing riotously as they tied his arms behind him, lifted him off the ground and began beating him with the backs of their swords, demanding the captain tell them where he kept the gold. Captain Georg crossed his arms in defiance, insisting there was no gold to give and that they could beat the poor botanist to death if they chose; he had nothing else to tell them. The *Machete* crew began to tear apart the *Jutta Georg*, mystified by this cargo of plants. They searched the Captain's Quarters, arrayed in all the comforts of a man accustomed to his leisure, rummaging through every drawer and tearing apart every chest and cabinet for some sign of wealth. Unfortunately, they had attacked a ship containing, to them, a virtually worthless cargo and a cash-poor captain whose meticulous ledger-sheet showed that every dime he had carried with him had been spent on provisions.

"As you can see, Mr. Pirate, you have wasted both of our time, for there is nothing of value for you here. So, if you'll be kind enough to straighten up the mess you made, apologize to me – oh, and Mr. Weilhaus – perhaps we'll just forget this incident."

Captain Taylor surveyed this strange, white-cloaked bag of bones, with his silly hat and noisy little dog, and was about to chalk it up to a bad day. But he looked at the ship, well built in the style that paid a mild tribute to the Vikings who had made their living plundering at land and sea, and realized he had something to claim for the day.

"This will do," he replied to the Captain, indicating the ship.

"Young man, I can tell you that my King will not be happy to hear that not only was one of his subjects molested but he will bring down the full wrath of Denmark on your head should you not choose to accept my offer and get along on your way."

"Cut down a boat, no oars and sails, and half a barrel of water," Captain Taylor ordered one of his men, as the rest took up the Dane, Olaf, Mr. Weilhaus and the small crew, who insisted on joining them. This close to Trinidad, Captain Georg reasoned, should find them on dry land in a day or so, and as soon as he made port he would be sending a nasty note to his king about this rude fellow, Taylor, who took his lovely *Jutta Georg*.

Captain Taylor took time to try to figure out exactly what it was this ship was carrying. The best he could surmise was they were some kind of twig sitting in dirt, wrapped in a bag, and if this wasn't a precious waste of cargo space he didn't know what was.

"Throw 'em overboard," he commanded to his crew. But, just as they had begun to descend into the hold to pitch the cuttings into the sea, a watch up in the tops of the *Machete* sounded an alert. "Ships, two sails, men-of-war comin' fast!" he shouted.

Housecleaning could wait, as the captain ordered his crew to their six guns. It was not as if he could actually face these men-of-war, but as the normal pretense of pretending they were just honest merchants would not fly with so little notice, they turned to the sails, running out maximum sheets, hoping their small size and the light cargo of the *Jutta Georg* would give them a chance to run into the shallows of Trinidad where the big ships couldn't chase. But he was disappointed to find that the two ships bearing down on him had the wind and were closing fast, and he had to make an urgent decision quickly. With his crew split, he realized that he just could not command the sail the way he wanted to, so he ordered the *Machete* alongside, set the *Jutta Georg's* sails, and his crew jumped ship back into their craft, hoping those two aggressors wouldn't split up, going one after the other. Again, Captain Taylor miscalculated as one ship gave chase to the *Jutta Georg* while the other was bearing quickly down on top of him. He ordered his guns moved to the stern as they began to fire shots uselessly at the bow of the *Protocol*, now closing in on the *Machete*. He pulled out his spyglass to see the large African man standing on her quarterdeck as she sailed beside them, coming up on his starboard to hold the wind and opening up her ports, where a row of guns ran out to prepare for a broadside. This was not what Captain Taylor had anticipated as he waved a white handkerchief in his hand, hoping this gesture would indicate no intent of malice.

But Caesar smiled, shaking his head and then pointed at the pennant that flapped from the *Machete's* mainmast. Captain Taylor's eyes moved to the top of his mast where there billowed the *Jollé Rouge*. This simple, blood-red pennant was the flag of choice for those who worked the Brotherhood of the Coast. And while Caesar was not particularly offended by it, he felt it was important to remind the captain, who had fired on him for no good reason, what that flag represented: no quarter. As none was to be given for ships that resisted, certainly none should be expected in return. Besides, if he had merely abided by the protocol, none of this would have been necessary. But Caesar felt it essential that a message be sent to this captain and anybody who survived this encounter, for breeches of protocol were bad for business. And as the captain stared at his flag, wondering why he hadn't bothered to run it down and why he opted to make the futile gesture of firing his guns from his stern, his eyes came down, met those of his opponent, and then he nodded his head in acknowledgement.

Caesar fired one solid broadside from his large ship into that tiny one. The balls of shot and shrapnel raked over the small deck of the sloop, destroying everything in their path, including sails, rigging and men. He let the smoke clear and surveyed the damage, then ordered his men to pull the *Protocol* alongside. Once they were tied together, he stepped aboard and ordered the dead tossed overboard and the dying shot. He went to her hold to survey her small, pathetic cargo of a few cases of broken dishes and Catholic iconography. Neither the cargo nor the sloop was worth his time and energy, and he ordered her sails and rigging cut down, oiled her deck and set her ablaze.

In the year and a half since the Drummond Corporation had expanded its operation to process not only its own cargo but that of any ship making its way into the port of New Providence under either a British or Dutch flag, it never ceased to amaze him how the most open secret in the Caribbean seemed not to filter down to some people. He realized there were pockets of privateers and pirates who did not realize how easy it was to do business, but even as there was an honor among thieves, that did not mean there was equal intelligence. The Caribbean had become one big blooming orchard, ripe for the picking, and easy to cart away if you knew which direction to flee. In this sea, there were three directions any enterprising young brigand could go to turn that hard-earned lucre into hard cash: St. Thomas, Willemstad or New Providence. All it took was the smallest amount of intelligence to turn any cruise, even with broken dishes, into a profitable venture. And in many ways it pained Caesar that these young upstarts had to be crushed early on in their careers for not taking a few moments to figure out who to fire on and who not to fire on.

Thatcher, in the meantime, opted to give chase to the other ship, and in his glass he could see no sign of any crew. He was aware that sometimes defenseless ships, as this small cargo ship appeared, would run their crews below decks with the hope of launching a surprise attack. But he didn't mind the risk as he brought the *Phoenix* alongside, bringing the side of his ship along her rail. Motioning for a few of his crew to follow, he jumped down on the deck of the *Jutta Georg*. He was surprised to see the Danish flag, knowing they had limited presence in the Caribbean and none of it military. So obviously this had been a prize abandoned. He had the crew slack her sail lines and took one pistol each into his hands. It was obvious someone had ransacked the ship, most likely finding little or nothing. He made his way to the Captain's Quarters, where he found it, too, in a state of disrepair. But he knew, despite the mess, he liked this captain, for though it had been well appointed with fine comforts, it also contained a good selection of books. Not being familiar with Danish was no reason to put good books to waste. He was sure that, by reducing to the Latin root and up through the Germanic, he could entertain himself on these long boring days trying to figure out this language. He began to examine the documents on the captain's desk and floor and found a set of charts indicating its passage. He noticed how it had carried him down and around the Americas and out into the South Seas, with its destination as Java. This intrigued him as he studied the manifest, billed as "fruit trees."

He departed the Captain's Quarters, following the ladder down into the hold, where there, as the manifest indicated, were indeed small saplings. He examined the thousands of carefully placed, lovingly attended plants that had survived some seven thousand miles of travel and, except for a bit of vandalism, showed themselves to be quite strong and healthy. But as he examined the cuttings and thought about their source of origin, his mind flashed back so many years ago to the tour of that São Tome plantation and his eyes brightened at the thought of what he had found. *Coffee!* he said to himself as he pondered the possibilities.

The *Jutta Georg* was tied to the rear of the *Phoenix* when Caesar and the *Protocol* at last caught up. There was no sense wasting their crew piloting this third ship, which was small enough to yield to a tow. As the two ships drew up alongside one another, lines were cast across from the *Phoenix* onto the *Protocol* as a boatswain's chair was sent across to Caesar. He hated these things and wished they'd just draw closer together so he could swing across. But he climbed aboard and the crew of the *Phoenix* slowly drew that chair across the chasm between the ships until at last he was aboard. Thatcher was waiting as he got off the chair, smiling from ear to ear.

"So tell me about your adventure," Thatcher beamed.

"They shot at us foolishly, and we blasted them to hell and sent that pathetic empty little ship to the bottom," Caesar replied in his report.

"Nothing worth taking then?" Thatcher inquired further. He loved Caesar's ability to condense every great story down into a one sentence summary.

"Broken dishes and crucifixes. No great margin for them. It wasn't worth defending."

"Well, well, sorry to hear that. But wait 'til you see what we have here."

Thatcher pulled out the manifest to show it to Caesar, who studied it and the charts accompanying. While Java was a rich and fertile island, there was scant little that grew there that was worth a seven thousand mile trip to the Caribbean. He considered for a moment and then it dawned on him why Thatcher was so excited.

"And what are we going to do with coffee trees?"

"Are you mad, brother? Do you realize the market for coffee? The Dutch have been jealously monopolizing that precious little fruit, and God knows if they've already started planting here in the Caribbean. And what a stroke of genius – they used the Danish to hide it!"

"All well and good, Thatcher, but you told me it takes a decade for this to grow. You are, of course, thinking of turning these over to a buyer or perhaps offering the Dutch a chance to buy it back, aren't you?"

"That's one option. And a good one. I'm sure Drummond could send out a few inquiries to his Dutch contacts to let them know we found their coffee trees. And the very fact we came to them versus selling them to the British interests, which would kill for these, could fetch a pretty penny. That's great short-term thinking."

"Thatcher ..."

"But, we have plenty of short-term investments. Now, let's think long-term. It's obvious the Dutch weren't announcing their new Caribbean venture, for they, too, know the value of the product. That they sent a Danish merchant to retrieve it shows they are working very hard to keep that quiet. And we should respect that silence. But likewise, we should respect the wishes of our countrymen to have an

English source for their favorite beverage. It would be very patriotic of us, don't you think?"

"What are you proposing, Thatcher?"

"She's a quick and agile ship, Caesar. The Danish like their ships quick, and I think that I can make much better time without dragging along these two behemoths and cut a hasty swath to Jamaica. Let me tell you something, Caesar. I spent many days staring at those mountains, drinking coffee and thinking how valuable those hills could be with the right crop. And it's like it just fell into our hands! We have to take advantage of this opportunity. Matasaa knows those mountains, so why doesn't he join me? You take the *Phoenix* and *Protocol* to New Providence and offload with Drummond. I'll go and begin the process of getting the ball rolling and, since they like you so much, well, you can come later to help close the deal. What do you think?"

Caesar arched his eyebrow, studying the obvious insanity of the plan and how Thatcher was not looking at the whole picture, only his role in it. "Have you not listened to anything that we have told you about the Maroons? Thatcher, they don't distinguish between Russians and Englishmen. They just know you're not an African. And if you go into those hills, they will cut you to pieces. You're letting your enthusiasm get the better of you, and you're not being sensible."

"Granted, there may be some small wrinkles. But I can iron those out with Matasaa on the way to Jamaica. And, Caesar, you know me. I'm a likeable fellow. I'll have them eating out of my hands in no time. For God's sake, man, I could sell ice cubes to Muscovites!"

Caesar and Matasaa roared with laughter as Thatcher grew huffy at the notion that all his charm and wit would still find him with his guts in his hand if he attempted to go into those mountains. The more they laughed, the more frustrated he got.

"Thatcher, you're approaching this whole thing the wrong way. Why don't Matasaa and I take the prize and sail to Jamaica and begin our conversations. You take the ships to New Providence, offload, explain to Drummond what we're thinking and then join us in the old cove. It's not as if you have any reason to set foot in Kingston anytime soon."

"But Caesar, this is coffee. These little plants need loving care the entire journey, and I don't think you're qualified, nor quite frankly attentive enough to give them the care they need despite the 'advantages' you may possess under the circumstances. We have one shot at this, because those cuttings aren't going to live forever in their little cradles."

"Then why don't we just go ahead and transfer the plants into our ships so you can keep an eye on them and give them all the water they need, talk to them if you want to for all I care. And let's just sink this boat and be done with it."

Thatcher's eyes grew like saucers. ""These are very fragile items, Caesar. I could not imagine the roughhousing they would have to endure in the process. Besides, she's a fine little ship, and perhaps Drummond can figure a way to salvage her."

Caesar usually enjoyed watching Thatcher get irrational, for in these hours aboard the *Jutta Georg* Thatcher had fallen in love again. Only this time, it was with a bunch of twigs and the pile of lumber that carried them. But what Thatcher was proposing in his long-term thinking did make sense, for a gesture of friendship to the Danes could go a long way in future enterprises. Plus, there was the salvage issue. And though it could not amount to much, it could assist in the standing of the Drummond Corporation to a whole new batch of customers in the future. He wrapped his arm around Thatcher's shoulders, understanding his infatuation with this pretty little ship and her pretty little trees. Thatcher just needed something to love. And perhaps he had a solution to it.

"I have a better idea, Thatcher" Caesar replied. "But it may require your letting go just a little bit."

Captain Georg and Max Weilhaus caught a break and were able to drift toward Port-of-Spain, where they flagged down a Spanish ship en route to the port at Trinidad. They reported their theft to the authorities, and Captain Georg arranged passage back to Charlotte Amalie. Max had no intention of setting foot on that Danish soil, and he had nothing waiting for him back in Java where he would have to explain how his cargo was stolen two days' sail from its destination. He knew the Portuguese were anxious to enter the coffee market, and perhaps he could find a way of making their pathetic efforts in São Tome profitable. So his destination would instead be the port of São Luis, a one-time French settlement in Brazil, where he would hope to find Portuguese men with designs on the trade, anxious to put to work one of those rare and unique characters who specialized in coffee plant husbandry. It may take some time, but Max Weilhaus would one day be a household name in coffee – of this he was sure.

Captain Georg was fortunate that he was able to find transport as far as Basseterre on Guadeloupe. From there, he got a local intercoastal trader to carry him into St. Johns on Antigua and then it was just a short hop back to Charlotte Amalie. He would first seek out the comfort of Jutta who would be incredibly sympathetic and understanding and grateful that Olaf did not get hurt in any way. Then he would report to the governor this depravity and hope to find someone to pay him for the loss of his ship and cargo. Unlike the English, this concept of insurance had not yet reached Copenhagen, but this incident would certainly be an impetus for it. He was making his report to the Governor von Holten when a large ship flying a Russian flag, a truly strange sight, began to make port at Charlotte Amalie. But most intriguing of all was that which trailed behind her, for tears came to his eyes as he saw his beloved *Jutta Georg*.

The typically fast-walking Ole Georg was at a dead run as his sixty-ish legs carried him like those of a boy. He ran with tears in his eyes and Olaf at his heels, watching his ship return. Thatcher stood upon the deck, studying the tear-stained face of the old man standing on the dock.

"Good morning, sir," Thatcher offered in the very limited words he had learned in Danish these past few days. "I am seeking Governor von Holten."

"And good morning to you, sir," Ole offered in Russian, appreciative of this young man's gesture at his complicated tongue. "I will be happy to direct you to him, but first I must ask, where did you find my ship?"

Thatcher, too, was pleased at the Dane's stab at Russian and the good fortune of finding the owner of the vessel here to greet him. "Ah, so, she is your ship. It was very strange. I found her adrift some three hundred miles south of here. With the Danish flag, I figured there could only be one place she belonged."

"I cannot believe my *Jutta Georg* is here again with me!" Ole gushed, tears spilling down his face. "We were attacked by pirates, and they set us adrift," Ole explained. But now, growing more hopeful with the mysterious reemergence of the *Jutta Georg*, he asked, "Tell me, was there any cargo left aboard?"

Thatcher climbed down the gangplank, withdrawing the manifest from his pocket. "I hope you do not consider me rude for intruding on your quarters, Captain, but I wished to find an explanation for such a strange mystery. I had feared I would find her captain and crew ... dispatched. But, when I saw no sign of anyone, I began to try to unravel a piece of this mystery and had only this to go by," he said, handing the manifest and charts to the captain. "Such a long journey for fruit trees, captain, don't you think?"

Captain Georg studied the documents, realizing the young man had reason to question his course and destination for seemingly insignificant cargo. But still hopeful to salvage the situation, he replied, "Yes, my customers were nostalgic for specific trees, and while I'm grateful to have my *Jutta Georg* home safe and sound, I'm still hoping I may be able to satisfy their contract and confidence in me."

Thatcher shrugged and offered a painful smile. "That unfortunately, Captain, I cannot offer you, for all I have to bring back to you is this ship. When I found her, the cargo had been stripped. God knows what those brigands did with it. If they were mere pirates, they probably saw no value and merely threw it overboard."

Captain Georg sighed and had to be satisfied with what he had been able to salvage. Already his crew, who had not strayed far from the docks, was making their way to the boat to bring her to dockside. The delightful girlish squeal Ole heard behind him made his heart leap, as he turned to see his blushing bride of forty-five years running down the dock, as spirited and sprite as the twelve-year-old girl he had met so many years ago in Nyborg. She ran up to him and embraced him, tears in her eyes.

"You've found her," she cried in her thick Danish accent, as their "child," her daughter, had come home. And of course, little Olaf and Inge, the little ball of fur Jutta held in her arms, were happy to see their sister was home, as they barked and yapped and shaked and peed with delight. As they watched the *Jutta Georg* being tied to the dock, the little family began to make their way to their object of pride and joy. And Thatcher could understand that joy, for she was a pretty little ship, and they were a pretty little family. And as much as he could see himself cruising along those Leeward Islands in this fast little boat, alas, she did not belong to him. She was betrothed to another. At least this time it made him happy and hopefully could prove to be profitable in the offing.

Captain Georg turned to the young man and said, "I will send a personal letter to your Tsar thanking him that Russia still thinks of Denmark. Who may I say did this service on behalf of his nation?"

"Thatcherev. Tell him that Yvgeny Thatcherev is happy to sail and serve in his honor and name," Thatcher replied, gallantly bowing.

Rendezvousing with Caesar off St. Kitt's, the *Phoenix* and the *Protocol* continued their eventful cruise, taking down a man-of-war off the island of Hispañola and plundering two merchant vessels. With their healthy cargo, they made their way to New Providence to meet up with Captain Drummond. Drummond swung himself onto the deck of the *Phoenix* as they related their latest adventures, Drummond laughing riotously the whole time and anxious to see if the governor of St. Thomas ever actually sent the salvage fee for the *Jutta Georg*. But the question of what to do with those thousands of trees was still a mere pipe dream and a glimmer in Thatcher's eye.

"I've given that a lot of thought, Drummond, and I can tell you that we have the perfect locale to grow these ourselves. This could make us very rich men if we can figure out how to use those vast mountains of Jamaica," said Thatcher. "I know there are issues to overcome, but when I look at those smoky heights, I see São Tome all over again. I've told you about São Tome, Drummond, and I'm telling you, I can make those Blue Mountains just bloom with coffee!"

Drummond laughed and shook his head. "That's a fine plan, Thatcher, but there's a bit of a problem there. You know as well as I that, while that island may be claimed in the name of Britain, those mountains are claimed by a totally different nation." Caesar and Matasaa nodded their heads in agreement with Captain Drummond, who saw the logic in their argument and the futility of Thatcher's plan with him at the helm. "There are many planters there who would love to gain access to those vast tracts of fertile land for a variety of crops. But I can tell you, if the British Army is afraid to go into those mountains, exactly what chance do you think you have?"

"T'atchaa has no chance," the usually silent Matasaa spoke up, then indicated Caesar. "But he does."

As the *Protocol* and the *Phoenix* set sail for Jamaica, the *Jutta Georg* set sail on a less happy mission. It was only a matter of time until word reached Curaçao that the little Danish merchant had arrived in St. Thomas before it made Willemstad, and this would create questions for her clients. Captain Georg was fortunate as he fell in with a group of Dutch merchant ships en route to Curaçao, making his journey a little less precarious but no less nerve-wracking. When the *Jutta Georg* made anchor at Willemstad Harbor, Stefan Kuyper, the governor's commercial attaché, was there with his colonial sabot to ferry the captain to the governor's landing, where Beck and his partner Mr. DeVyck were waiting for him.

"Captain Georg, at last," the governor offered, a broad smile on his face as his big hand wrapped around the thin bony one of the captain. "We had grown concerned when we heard you put into Charlotte Amalie instead of Willemstad. I hope there was no problem."

"Good morning, Governor, and let me commend you on your information network, for I was not in Charlotte Amalie twenty-four hours before I set sail for here," Captain Georg intoned as they entered the double glass doors that spilled into the library of the Governor's mansion. He took the seat indicated by the governor, trying to look as comfortable and fearless as his old bones would allow.

"Well, that's unimportant now. Most importantly, how was the trip, and how did our cargo withstand the journey? Oh, and, where is Mr. Weilhaus? I was to assume he would be joining you here today."

"My guess is that Mr. Weilhaus is somewhere in the Brazilian interior looking for new employment. What an insufferable little man he is!"

"How could Mr. Weilhaus be in the Brazilian interior by now if you've only just reached us? Did he make arrangements for magic transport in Charlotte Amalie?"

"In Port-Of-Spain, Governor. That's where we were carried to when we lost our ship to pirates."

"Pirates," Edvart DeVyck finally offered. "You were taken by pirates? So please explain how you arranged to make Charlotte Amalie in your boat?"

"That's just it, sir. I didn't make Charlotte Amalie in my boat. My boat was set adrift somewhere off the coast of Trinidad, and recovered and brought back to me in Charlotte Amalie."

"And the cargo?" questioned DeVyck.

"Stripped, sir. Every last fruit tree was removed, and it is only by the grace of God that my boat wasn't taken or scuttled in the process."

"And you can describe these pirates?" the Governor asked. "For certainly I have resources and will use them to locate them."

"Scraggly little men in a dirty little sloop, and the leader a foul man," the captain replied with a look of disgust on his face.

"Perhaps a little more description would be helpful, Captain. Did you catch a name or a ship reference?"

"We did not sit down to tea, Governor. They threw me and my crew onto my little dinghy and set us adrift. I don't know what happened after that. We drifted into Port-Of-Spain. I made a complaint to the authorities. Mr. Weilhaus said he would be appreciated in Brazil, and I and my crew made our way home. End of story."

"But what about your boat, Captain?"

The captain smiled, a dreamy expression on his face. "You do not know the sadness in my home when I returned without the *Jutta Georg*. My Jutta cried her eyes out. She is all we have. But when that Russian ship came into Charlotte Amalie, towing my little *Jutta Georg*, my wife was so happy, you should have seen her."

"Russian ship, Captain? I know of no Russian ships anywhere in the Atlantic. And praytell, do you not think that would be an object of curiosity?"

"Well, certainly. I, too, was surprised to see a Russian ship. Those vulgar Swedes and their vulgar king have done all they could to halt that great country and Denmark from honest trade. So, certainly my surprise when the Russian flag – did you know how much it looks like the Dutch flag? – but when I saw that ship with my *Jutta Georg*, and Russia had come to our rescue, I saw it as a sign, let me tell you. For I believe in signs. Russia and Denmark will be together again, and it's only a matter of time until we see Russian flags being planted in the Caribbean. That Tsar Peter, ah. Visionary."

"Captain, this is all quite wonderful, your musings of the future of Russia and Denmark, but I can tell you there are no Russian ships in the Caribbean," the Governor stated emphatically.

Captain Georg smiled and leaned back in his chair, crossing his legs, his hat in one hand, his cane in the other, as he lounged back with a look of utter pleasure. "Well, Governor, all I can tell you is that you may have a hole in your intelligence network, because that was a

Russian captain. Because I know Russian, and even if it wasn't for the language, I could tell that boy was a Russian, because he looked just like Tsar Mikhail. You know, that Peter, he's a sly one. Did you know, he toured all of Europe posing as a sailor? I would not be surprised – because I gave this a lot of thought – if that wasn't Tsar Peter himself on one of his little secret cruises. You should check with your friends in Holland to see what Peter's up to, because you may not know that he's over here exploring the Caribbean."

"You can understand, Captain Georg, my skepticism. This is quite a fanciful tale to explain the loss of an invaluable cargo, and now I'm being led to believe that the Tsar of Russia now occupies his time rescuing Danish boats in the Caribbean. Again, you understand my skepticism," Beck stated.

"This is one of the problems with you Dutch. You're too pragmatic and logical, which is why you don't understand the Slavic and Scandinavian mind. We believe in mystical things, and that was truly a mystical event. So, doubt me if you wish. But the authorities in Trinidad will verify my story, and I will give you the name of every captain who brought me back to Charlotte Amalie. And they will all tell you about how I feel about the *Jutta Georg*, and how I thought I would never see her again, and how upset I was that I had lost her. Oh, and your coffee as well."

"Well, Captain, most assuredly I will investigate this. But you can help me with a name, can't you. The ... Russian? He did give you a name, didn't he?"

Captain Georg's body movements snapped like an iguana to a fly, as his hand shoved itself into his pocket to pull out a letter, still unsealed. "I'm glad you asked, Captain. For the moment I left my lovely Jutta sleeping, I penned this letter to Tsar Peter, telling him of the great things done in his name by one of his subjects."

Captain Georg handed the letter to the Governor, who reviewed it, pushed it away from his face and looked at Captain Georg. "It's in Danish, Captain. I can't read it."

"No, Russian. It's easy to confuse the Scandinavian letters with the Cyrillic ... if you're not educated in these matters," Captain Georg replied, a condescending smile on his face.

"The name, Captain. Please tell me the name of the captain of the ship."

Áh, yes, I will never forget it. In fact, the next puppy we get, I will name him in honor of the rescuer of the *Jutta Georg* ... Yvgeny Thatcherev. And if I discover it is actually Tsar Peter?"

DeVyck sprung up and took Stefan aside. "You find the person attached to that name and the ship he sails on, if it costs every dime we pay you to do so."

"You have my word on it, Mr. DeVyck," Stefan replied as he exited the room in haste.

Until those coffee trees were found, every information resource utilized by the Governor and DeVyck would be charged with the task of finding that person. And until the coffee trees were found and until the day he died, Ole Georg would never spend another day without either of his lovely Jutta Georgs.

III

Days before he reached her, Nanani knew that Chasaa was about to return to her mountains. Word had spread the moment he set foot on the island, but even before that she had heard his voice on the waters. When they last parted, she knew she had found a kindred spirit, and though there were no plans made or any further discussion with respect to the future, she had known Chasaa was not yet done with Jamaica and the Maroons. Their time together had been one where both felt they had at last found someone with whom they could speak in real terms. As an Obeah woman, she was required to be ever mindful of her spiritual role among these people, for they needed not just another woman, not just a leader, but someone who saw beyond the British, the mountains, the island and this world. Though she had declared magic in every single person who had accompanied her from the Gold Coast to Jamaica, she had not spoken falsely, for all persons possess an element of magic no matter how dormant, insignificant or useless it may be. For the human spirit, the mind, the heart, the complex mechanics that distinguish them from all the other animals of nature was a magical aspect directly connected to this uniqueness of soul. Chasaa truly possessed a strong magic, though he did not understand it, trust it or much believe it. But his connection to his ancestors was powerful, and no matter that his tongue and his mannerisms and his clothing screamed English, his heart, his mind, his soul screamed Africa. As did Nanani's.

For the first time in his life, Caesar had found someone whom he could truly talk to about those brief years in Madagascar. For telling her wasn't really revealing something she didn't already know, it seemed, as there was nothing in his life that seemed to surprise her. In so many ways, she reminded him of Nettie, who likewise he could communicate with wordlessly. And no matter how strong his bond with Thatcher and his adoration of Abigail, Yvgeny and Beatrice, this was never anything he could explain or talk about with them because they could not fathom those experiences, nor should they be burdened with the images they seared into the mind. Thatcher had gotten a taste of it when he accompanied Caesar on his mission to seek out the Betsimsakara in Madagascar, and he had seen the ferocity and the vengeance of which Caesar was capable. He had witnessed the suffering and humiliation of the Malagasy people, but Thatcher could not see that darkness hovering all around the camp and that bright guiding light that let Caesar's eyes see beyond this realm and into the next, the one that put all pain and feeling aside and drove him in a way that was not Chasaa but purely Najas. Chasaa had been nothing but a vessel from the moment he crossed the channel at St. Mary's, for those instincts were not those of a man who had spent the previous twenty-some-odd years in a brothel in Bristol. In fact, in every moment when Caesar became a warrior, he merely stepped aside to let the spirit of Najas take over, and it was as if he were merely an observer of something more powerful, more ferocious and more ancient than he could be or wish to be.

But now, he was returning to her, and she could feel once again that he carried a burden not his own but that of someone intensely close to him. For once again, Chasaa was a vessel with a much bigger purpose, and she would have to decide if his soul was better served accepting his burden or denying it.

"You look strong, Chasaa," Nanani commented as she watched the beefy African make his way along her path of stones. There were two ways to approach Nanani's hut. There was the long way, which gave one time for reflection as it meandered through the rocks, around blind trails and at last spilled out from around a blind hairpin corner to Nanani's campfire, where she would be studying her pot of herbs and weighing your energy as you struggled along this difficult path, more concerned with the precariousness of your walk than the burden you carried on your shoulders and about which you sought her out in the first place. Or there was this way, Nanani's path of rocks in the stream, all slightly below the surface and imperceptible if you did not know where to look. Only those who truly knew Nanani knew this path, for only if she truly knew you would she show it to you. For Nanani's perch gave her a command for miles of the island from which she could remain completely invisible to you while traveling a well-coursed path that ran along the sheer cliff just a few dozen feet beneath her. And she had watched many come up this path, some English adventurers, seeking out Maroons and the bounties posted on them by the English in the settlements below. Sometimes the English themselves would travel up this path, thinking they had found the secret encampment of the Maroons and the camouflaged huts pressed against the rocks and trees. But these types never knew that these huts had been put here for their sole purpose of being found, something to search and someplace to die. For beyond the encampment stood an escarpment where those foolhardy enough to travel here uninvited and undesired would meet their final resting place a few hundred feet below amongst the twisted rotting corpses of their fellow adventurers, which the Maroons had simply dubbed "the English Graveyard." The animals of these mountains had come to know the English Graveyard well, where the carnivorous mammals, birds and insects had discovered this rich bounty of European protein and staked out these brush-covered piles of jagged rock as a place for a free meal, a gift from their brother the Maroon.

Chasaa reached Nanani's camp, where she had prepared a very fat rabbit and strong herbal tea for her guest. The rabbit's benefit was obvious, but the tea offered something else quite less overt in that it helped calm the breathing of those who had struggled up this mountain. It relaxed their muscles and freed their minds to speak honestly, not only to their hostess but to themselves as well. The pleasant hint of juniper berries created a wonderful fragrance that invited the guest to drink, relax, unwind and open up. The Maroons called it Nanani's truth serum, but Nanani understood something about human nature that few people seemed to grasp – that they were not naturally evasive and desired to speak the truth, but circumstances and ulterior motives forced them to put up barriers from honest conversation for fear that giving into the impulse for truthfulness would expose a vulnerability. And indeed it did, if one was conversing with a mere exploiter of the truth. As an Obeah woman, Nanani knew that she needed truth to help people deal with the layers of subterfuge, and the teller needed the truth so he could unburden himself from the layers of lies and deceit that barred him from honestly confronting himself. Chasaa knew the power of this tea, had felt it calm him from his long journey that first time up to these heights. He sensed that for this woman it had a magical property but noticed that she matched sip for sip with him, for she, too, was attempting to achieve a corresponding level of honesty. It had been strangely liberating to him that first trip. He understood what these Maroons were facing and their willingness and joy in retreating to these high mountains, far above the reach of English eyes and guns. And while many of the Africans who occupied these mountains had originally come from barren and flat places, they found a spiritual connection here that made them feel as if they had at last come home.

She explained to Chasaa that they had encountered each other before that first visit, or more accurately she had encountered him in that ship that carried her and her people to Jamaica. She had spent much time with his troubled spirit, reluctantly trapped between worlds, the one he'd left and the one he was going to, and while his body had followed, his spirit had resisted and remained a residue of energy in that ship. She had spent much time with that spirit, who spoke in that uncomfortable English, until she had at last convinced him that it was all right to speak in Malagasy. For while she understood its words less than that of their common tongue, she could feel its energy coalescing into a much calmer force that more clearly conveyed all he felt and all that he had experienced. It made their first face-to-face encounter that much easier and that much more natural, and she didn't need the juniper tea to hear Chasaa's truth. He needed it so he could hear himself.

When he came off that mountain many days later, he at last felt free and clear, for it had been revealed to him that pieces of his own spirit had been shedding like skin since he was a child. It was not in a spirit of defeat but in a spirit of yielding, for he had carried with him from the shores of Madagascar a piece of his father's spirit that had grown inside of him and demanded to live on. And though he was a large and powerful man, there was not room for two full-grown spirits in one body, so piece by piece, as Chasaa surrendered to Caesar on the outside, Chasaa surrendered to Najas on the inside. And now it made sense to him why he felt the things he felt and knew the things he knew and connected to the people of the Antankarana so much more naturally than he ever did to the English. Only the exterior was the Englishman who happened to be cloaked in black skin. It was the inside that was purely Malagasy and would never surrender to anything else.

"And so you come to me now, Chasaa. You come again as a vessel, not carrying your burden on the inside but on the outside, on your English side."

"This is true, Nanani. I do carry an English burden, one which I would not wish to have my brethren of these mountains shoulder were I not confident that it would be of great benefit to the Maroons as well."

"So tell me of this burden, Chasaa, and tell me how you think our taking up your burden can serve us and you."

He began explaining to Nanani about their discovery. She was amused to learn that, once again, Englishmen had developed a dependence upon a product of Africa. "And so now, these Christian English likewise partake in much tobacco and coffee as well?" Nanani mused as she smiled and shook her head. "This does not surprise me, for besides the subtle differences in the name of their earthly prophets and the color of their skin and hair, I find little difference between these Arab and these English. They seem so caught up in their idle distractions and dreaming up new ways to steal what others have spent generations to build up and sustain their families. I understand on the east coast of Africa is another group much like them called Judeans. I never had the chance to meet them, but I understand they think the same way."

"Well, the only difference is that their earthly prophet hasn't yet arrived. But beyond that, yes, they're all the same. The real difference, of course, Nanani, is that Africans have toiled for centuries, serving the passions and desires of these Arabs, Christians and Jews, not as equals but as slaves. Have you yet encountered Indians?" Caesar inquired.

She nodded her head. "Yes, here in these hills are a few remaining Arawak whom the Spanish and English were not able to kill off. We have good relations with these people. They are very African."

"This is why I wish to see the Maroons be the first African people to actually profit from English, by feeding their addictions and passions with a product we grow and control that they cannot lay their hands upon. The Maroons live in these mountains on the fickle bounty of nature and supplement their needs through simple theft of English settlements. In their minds, the Maroons will never be more than savages. What I propose will make you masters by controlling something they greatly desire."

Nanani gave this great thought as Caesar began to reach into a small bag he carried with him up this mountainside. From it he drew some pale green beans which he placed into Nanani's skillet and began to roast. When they were crackling and dark brown, swollen twice their original size, he took a stone and ground them, sifting them into two pewter cups he had brought with him, and poured boiling water from the pot dangling permanently over the fire. He passed a cup to Nanani whose nose picked up that distinctive scent she remembered from her youth on trips to see the Moslems who visited her land.

"Join me, Nanani, as we contemplate a way to own these English."

As Caesar seduced Nanani with the dark pleasures of coffee, Thatcher was forced to occupy his time with little more than his overactive imagination. It really was a shame that Sarah Whetstone could no longer distract him in these long days of waiting for Caesar. Thatcher remembered when he received news of Sarah's marriage to Woodes Rogers in the spring of 1705. He had been somewhat hopeful that, once she'd discovered how really feckless Woodes was, she would come to her senses, climb back aboard one of her father's boats – bringing the lovely Cassie with her of course – and enjoy the life she knew she much preferred. That had been obvious in her note.

Of course, it didn't mean he was completely pining away for Sarah Whetstone. As their enterprises had grown throughout the Caribbean, it became necessary to expand their reach of potential customers and to reacquaint themselves with good ones of the past who had long been neglected. Such had been his excuse to take the *Phoenix* and *Protocol* on a Colonial tour of North Carolina, Maryland and Pennsylvania. It was good that Thatcher had a chance to reacquaint and rekindle with his bride and, if pressed, Caesar would have allowed Thatcher and Melanie as much time as she demanded. But he knew Thatcher well enough to know that the longer they stayed the harder it would be to leave, and the more of him he would leave behind. And neither of them wanted that. For while they sailed the wide Atlantic, the Caribbean was teeming with ships flying a variety of standards from Royal to Rogue, hunting down any merchanter laying low in the water. Unlike the past, where ship's registry would most likely determine the port they sought to offload their booty for small stacks of gold to savor their palates and fill their ears with the tastes and sounds of the home country, these ships instead were now charting courses to New Providence. While colonists and governors may give an indication of their revulsion to piracy and the need to tolerate it, in truth they depended upon those cheap stolen goods as a source of livelihood and diversion. Legitimate cargo from homeports was terribly expensive, with both the add-ons to price from the owners and captains of ships to offset their costs and generate profit, combined with the taxes collected by the governors to satisfy the Crown and their own personal greed. For many essentials, colonists withstood the true piracy of legitimate trade and welcomed these opportunities to balance out their expenses with cheap, plundered merchandise.

As the Drummond Corporation was growing wealthier and expanding its business beyond the Caribbean, the key black markets of St. Thomas, Curaçao, Havana and Cartagena were beginning to feel the pinch, as the privateer and pirate crews that fed them such a steady stream of ill-gotten gain were beginning to dry up. Rumblings from both merchants and consumers who depended on this supplement to the steep prices of legitimate trade were causing real concern, nowhere more so than in the Port of Willemstad. It did not take long for Governor Beck to trace the source of his dwindling supplies back to the lawless and governor-less colony of the Bahamas. He sent out agents to investigate, and it came back that the Drummond Corporation, a former privateer who had set up shop as a trading clearing-house, was now doing business with anyone who entered the port flying a Dutch or English flag, that even the thin veneer of a command of either language was not a prerequisite. Beck had to begrudgingly admit how the Drummond Corporation had out-Dutched the Dutch. It was his hope that soon this war would end, and they could get back to the legitimate black-market trade that didn't require such elaborate checks and counter-checks for a simple merchant to make a decent living. But his hope had been pinned on that Danish ship that would have made him a hero to Dutch merchants worldwide.

It was on their return trip from the American colonies and their decision to make one more run down the Leewards before turning north to New Providence where that turn of events took place that would make a dramatic impact on the future of the Drummond Corporation. The taking of those French and Spanish merchant ships was all they had hoped for and had never expected to encounter that strange little Danish ship that brought them here to Jamaica. And a strange and wonderful few years it had been, Thatcher mused as he strolled the streets of Kingston, slowly coming back to life from the fire that had threatened to wipe it off the face of the map. His eyes moved to those mountains, where soon he would discover whether or not his big dream of building a coffee empire in the Caribbean would be realized or shrivel and die in the hold.

"Is that you, Edward Drummond?" he heard as he turned around to see who was calling him. He smiled when he saw one of Captain Drummond's favorite locals, conducting business with one of the new merchants that had chosen to take a chance on Jamaica. He walked to join the man with an outstretched arm.

"Why, Sir Nicholas Lawes. How very good to see you. How are your sugar canes coming along?"

"Very good indeed. Despite all we've been through, if nothing else you can count on the sugar growers to ride out anything, even those damned Maroons. So how is your uncle faring these days?"

"Very well, sir. He greatly misses Jamaica, but New Providence has proven to be quite profitable. In fact, when you're ready to ship your cane, sir, keep in mind the Drummond Corporation."

"So what brings you to Jamaica, young Mr. Drummond?" Sir Nicholas Lawes pressed.

"A bit of diversion, nothing more, sir," Thatcher smiled. "The Jamaican ladies are always a pleasure to behold and a pleasant break from the routine, so to speak."

Sir Nicholas laughed, knowing very well of the stories that had circulated about young Mr. Drummond and Miss Whetstone. It was good to see the boy was not pining away and was making productive use of his youth until some young woman made an honorable man out of him and permanently grounded his ship, so to speak.

"Well, I hope you have a chance to come up to Temple Hall and join us for dinner before you cut a wake back to New Providence," Sir Nicholas offered.

Thatcher smiled. "If my distractions here don't take up every spare moment, sir, rest assured I look forward to visiting you and your family at your beautiful plantation."

Of course, Sir Nicholas would have thought twice about that offer had he known that his pretty daughter Eleanor had been watching the exchange from the dress shop a few doors away. She remembered all the horrid and sordid stories that had circulated about young Mr. Drummond, whose eye she caught as her father returned to his never-ending business of being a merchant and Knight of the Realm.

Thatcher had every intention of making his way to that other business that never departed from fire: those bawdy, brazen women who plied their trade at the local tavern. But little Eleanor had grown up to be quite the fetching young woman, and as they both shared a love for beautiful fabric he could not help himself but to go into that dress shop and admire the fine colors and textures and, of course, was happy to help Miss Lawes in her selection. After taking her on a barrel behind the dressmaker's shop with the loveliest view of Port Royal to her stern, he was quite pleased with the offer she extended for dinner after he was done devouring his midday snack.

In the morning he rowed back out to the *Phoenix* and *Protocol*, where already the Malagasy were busy at work carefully handing up those coffee plants from the hold. Caesar had been hard at work since first light, directing the Malagasy up the trail to a point where the Maroons would take over the work of transporting those thousands of plants to a high Blue Mountains meadow.

"I take it you had success, Caesar," Thatcher smiled as he joined his brother, lifting those small saplings down into the waiting boats. "So, when do I get to meet our partners?"

"Perhaps never, Thatch," Caesar replied honestly, noting his brother's disbelief and irritation. "Certainly not on this trip, dear brother. I don't think you're ready and I know that the Maroons certainly are not."

"But who's going to make sure these plants get properly planted and cared for in the time it's going to take to bring them to fruition?"

"I am," Matasaa replied. "You are going to teach me everything I need to know to make these scrawny twigs become the magnificent trees you have spoken of. And I will teach the Maroons and we will make these plants bloom."

"This is the only way, Thatcher. Those mountains belong to the Maroons and to the African people. These trees will belong to all of us. If this plan of your works, in a few years the Maroons will have grounds to negotiate with the English that will at last bring peace to this island, to everyone, English and Maroon. But this must be a Maroon process."

"So I am just going to trust that they'll still feel this way when they have all the advantage and we have none?"

"No, Thatcher. You're going to trust me, for you know I will never fail you. What you are doing is not giving up your dream – you are expanding it. And your trust could go very far in making these Maroons trust Englishmen. Now, will you trust me?"

"Until the very last breath I breathe, Caesar."

And with a feeling of dejection and utter resignation, Thatcher filled his days supervising the careful nourishing and transfer of those thousands of delicate cuttings and his nights cutting a swatch among the lovely daughters and wives of the Jamaican planters. Over the next two months, the Maroons and Malagasy walked the dozens of miles and climbed the thousands of feet to those high meadows where the coffee plants could be assured the amount of rain and sun they would need to create the finest coffee English palates would ever drink. Despite the endless temptation, Thatcher honored the agreement, never setting foot on the path that led to the highland realm of the Maroons.

In Curaçao, Stefan Kuyper proved why he was such a valuable resource to Governor Beck and his business partners. He began with the Danish crew, pulling every man off the *Jutta Georg* and providing whatever means of coercion was necessary to get to the bottom of this highly unbelievable incident. It did not take him long to uncover that little piece of information Captain Georg either didn't share or honestly wasn't privy to – it didn't really matter. Despite his ruse, there were those in St. Thomas who knew that ship and the young man who captained her. Kuyper began to query every captain he knew that sailed in and out of Willemstad as to the dealings of the Drummond Corporation. He began to piece together this unique trade alliance they had developed with virtually every privateer and pirate ship currently plying the Caribbean. Word that Governor Beck was seeking out confirmation of a Russian ship and captain fell on the ears of one Dutch captain, who had for years been kidded for his stories of encountering Black Russians off the coast of Africa.

"It was all quite strange, Mr. Kuyper," Captain Haupt related. "We were sailing toward São Tome, prowling for French and Spanish ships, and were going to resupply when we encountered this captain who claimed to be sailing for the Empire of Russia. And I tell you, he swore that his crew was indeed Black Russians."

"São Tome, you say?" Kuyper inquired.

"Exactly. I must confess, I don't know if he was Russian or not, but he did have a command of the language, and he was aboard this large ship I swear was a galley. In fact, many believe it was the ship supposedly scuttled by Kidd off St. Mary's."

"St. Mary's?" Edvart DeVyck asked when Kuyper gave the report to him and Beck.

"That's what he said, sir," Kuyper replied.

"You know, the Portuguese have been trying very hard to husband decent crops of coffee out of São Tomé," Beck offered. "They're still years away from figuring out how to make it in bulk, but if he spent any time on that island, he learned about coffee. And perhaps enough to think he may be able to start a plantation of his own."

"What's the last reported position of the *Phoenix* and *Protocol?*" DeVyck inquired.

"About two months ago they left New Providence, making their way west toward Hispañola," Kuyper replied.

"And didn't they once have operations in Jamaica?" Governor Beck probed.

"Until the fire ravaged Kingston, sir, that was their base of operations," Kuyper confirmed.

"Ready my ships. And send word to the Spanish in Hispañola and New Andalusia that I'm calling in a favor. And I need every warship they can muster."

On April 15, 1707, the *Phoenix* and *Protocol* made sail from their cove, their crews quite exhausted from the last two months of toting some 11,000 coffee trees to the heights of Jamaica. They were all in need of much rest and relaxation after such a grueling task. It was decided that about half the Malagasy would remain with Matasaa to oversee the nurturing of the plants and to protect their interests on behalf of the Drummond Corporation. With half the complement now spread between the two ships and a short hop from Jamaica to New Providence, with only Hispañola between them, they had also made another critical decision. With so many irons in the fire, Thatcher and Caesar were going to limit the hunting to those dozens of pirates and privateers ranging these waters in a quest for their small piece of the empire pie and would at last take a break after eleven years of ranging the seven seas. It was time to go home to their mothers and to the ladies of Parker House. How they would be received would be the great question, for all these years they'd never heard a word whether there was a price on their head or a noose awaiting their necks, so it was time to take a chance and go home.

They would turn the ships over to Drummond and the Malagasy and let them outfit them with crews to do their bidding. Among the forty men remaining at sea, they would flesh out the officers' corps of these ships. Matasaa would have made the most logical Commodore, but Thatcher and Caesar knew that he had fallen in love with those mountains and the Maroon people and had found a home. For years, they had been schooling their most promising crewmen in navigation and the sailing arts. These men were brave and fearless and would maintain their loyalties and run these ships with an iron hand, but with that spirit of democracy that had turned this strange blend of English and Madagascar men into a family, for this was a family venture. And unlike Caesar and Thatcher, these waters were their home, for the Malagasy had no one waiting for them across distant waters. All they had were each other and these ships, and these lifelong native landsmen had over the years evolved into men who could think of no other place to call home but the sea.

Off the port bow, the crew in the nests gave the signal for sails ... lots of them. Thatcher and Caesar turned their glasses on an unexpectedly large flotilla of Spanish ships warping off the coast of Hispañola. Undermanned and undershipped, this was not going to be their fight, so they tacked hard to starboard, making a southwest course with the hopes of outrunning the armada. They caught the wind and began to gain the advantage until the lookouts sounded another mass of sail off their starboard bow. From what Thatcher and Caesar could tell, a total of fifteen warships were descending on them, and there was very little doubt that they were about to be overtaken. They tried to get a fix on which ships they were confronting, for even a number of Spanish ships had taken up the trade, realizing there were better prices with the Drummond Corporation than their colonial masters in Havana, Santo Domingo or Barranquilla. But what caught their attention weren't the Spanish vessels sailing in their direction but those two distinctive forty-gun brigs, the *Scylla* and the *Charybidis*, owned and operated by Governor Beck of Curaçao. Whether this was a show of force or disgruntled merchants set to right the scales was debatable, but Thatcher and Caesar were not in a mood to debate as the crews piled on every bit of sail, making every effort to lasso the wind, correcting their course due east and hoping their light ships would let them slip the noose surrounding their necks.

The intention of this flotilla became quite obvious, as each ship now opened every logical port and ran out its guns. This was to be a slaughter, and they were fish in a barrel. The crews of the *Phoenix* and *Protocol* were ordered to lock in the sail, the whipstaffs were tied off and every man went to the guns with the order to fire at will the moment it made sense. Thatcher and Caesar were the only two to remain on deck as they worked the bow guns, firing with a ferocity and desperation they never had before encountered. Being their own gun crews, they would fire, pour powder, ram the shot, aim and fire again. And though primarily fruitless, it was to show these Spaniards and their Dutch contractors that these captains were still those fearless ghosts that did not shrink from a fight. The heat of the cannons caused them to glow red-hot, and Thatcher and Caesar severely burned their hands and arms, attempting to re-load. The *Phoenix* and the *Protocol* were cloaked in billows of smoke as their gun crews delivered every round they could, while those Spanish and Dutch cannonballs slammed into every square inch of deck and hull, tearing them to slivers.

Though cloaked in the smoke of its own guns, one lucky shot from the *Charybidis* penetrated the *Protocol*, striking the powder magazine and blowing the ship apart. The flames from the *Protocol* rose, as blazing wooden shrapnel scattered across the sea and into the downed rigging and shattered deck of the *Phoenix*. Thatcher barely had time to scream, "Abandon ship!" before the *Phoenix* ignited under his feet.

Their kills accomplished, the Hispañola and New Andalusia ships peeled off, returning to their ports with their balance sheets now even with Governor Beck. Beck's crews took to the longboats, coursing through the remains of those murdered ships, looking for survivors. Periodically, they would encounter a half-dead Malagasy and put a bullet in his head as they sought out the longhaired Englishman and the bald-headed African who must be somewhere among this wreckage. Governor Beck had different plans for them if they survived, for after flaying off every inch of their skin, whether they confessed or not, he had designs for their bodies that would hearken reminders of the Spanish Inquisition. Edvart DeVyck surveyed the wreckage, looking for those two young men who should have left well enough alone but instead ended up killing every last Malagasy they knew – or so the Dutchman thought.

As night began to settle in and no signs of Caesar and Thatcher were to be found, Governor Beck ordered the barrels of oil he had carried with him cut open and cast across the debris field. Once thousands of gallons of whale oil covered the surface of the Caribbean and the longboats had been pulled back aboard, the crews of the two Dutch men-of-war loaded firepots into the bow chasers and fired, setting that half-mile-wide oil slick ablaze.

"So what do you think? Did we get them?" Beck queried as he marveled at the inferno before him.

DeVyck watched as the ocean blazed like a lake of hell and could not imagine how anyone could survive it. "Logic would dictate so, Governor. But I fear logic has nothing to do with the likes of Evans and Parcrick. I would like to believe we've seen the last of them, but I have a prickly sensation on the back of my neck that tells me those two resourceful fellows will rear their ugly heads again soon."

"What do you say, DeVyck? Should we wait?"

"Governor, those two will deal with us when they're ready. They will pick the time and place when they have control of the situation. They could be miles away from here by now, or ..." he stamped his foot on the quarterdeck, "right beneath our feet, for all we know. Waiting will do nothing more than keep us from urgent business. I suggest we attend to our business and be satisfied in the knowledge that we've put a serious dent in theirs."

Clinging to the rudder of Governor Beck's ship, Thatcher and Caesar had survived the chaos with a plan they never thought they would execute, and now they could silently congratulate themselves for having the presence of mind to imagine worst-case scenarios. As long as these ships were merely idle, they could cling to the side of the rudder blade facing the keel and escape notice from the ever-searching crew. The moment the *Scylla* and *Charybidis* bloomed those sails, Thatcher and Caesar would have to surrender their precarious hold or run the risk of being cut in half from the crushing weight of that five-ton piece of wood slicing at the water and everything in front of it. But it was much better to be at their stern than between these dangerous sea monsters and their forty guns each.

They trod water in the darkness, as the devilish flames leapt behind them, and they watched the demon that would haunt them for years to come disappearing across the deep, blue sea. Grabbing hold of a few pieces of flotsam that had escaped the waves of flame, Thatcher and

Caesar looked at the celestial light show unfolding above them, found the navigational star in the north and began kicking their way in the general direction of the Windward Passage.

Coming Spring 2013

The unauthorized biography of
Blackbeard the pirate

CHRONICLE TWO:

THE DUKE OF BRISTOL

As the world's great powers continue to contest for dominance of Europe and all its colonial possessions, opportunity brings Thatcher and Caesar Edwards back to the family brothel in their home town of Bristol, England, and its unique form of legitimate commerce. New ventures bring them into association with author Daniel DeFoe and nobleman Charles Eden, who recruit Thatcher into the shadowy realm of British espionage, as a burgeoning empire lays the groundwork to conquer its enemies – France and Spain – and ultimately rule the waves. Circumstances and old rivalries conspire against his commercial endeavors, forcing him to return to the sea and vent his rage on the enemies of his nation. When Queen Anne's War is done, Thatcher and thousands like him are cast upon the shores of the New World to fend for themselves. His associations with British intelligence provide him unique commercial opportunities in North Carolina, but the same roadblocks he encountered in England conspire against him in the Americas. Slowly but surely it dawns on him that the civilized world will never afford him the respectability and legitimate enterprise he so greatly desires. A growing discontent for England and all the monarchial powers of Europe inspire him and his fellow discontented castaway veterans to become a nation unto themselves and declare war upon the world.

Coming Fall 2013

Thatcher

The unauthorized biography of
Blackbeard the pirate

CHRONICLE THREE:
THE KING OF CAROLINA

As the United Kingdom begins the arduous task of establishing itself as the undisputed masters of the world, a new king of England finds himself having to face a growing challenge from those who helped to establish his empire. As a new form of communication known as print media begins to manifest, so, too, does the need to find sensational stories that will sell papers, and certainly there are none so riveting as those of the undisputed King of Carolina, Blackbeard the Pirate. Having evolved from privateer in service to Her Majesty Queen Anne, Thatcher now finds himself a challenger to His Majesty King George's dominance of his North American colonies. The inspiration he serves to the Brotherhood of the Coast and the fear he strikes into those who are attempting to preserve and expand empire drive him to bolder and more notorious acts. In the end, as he seeks to parlay his notoriety into power and respectability, the fear of his growing influence leads England's colonial representatives to launch a new war to eradicate this growing threat. Blackbeard's legendary last stand off the island of Ocracoke is one of the most storied battles of its kind, but it is only the tip of the iceberg to the depth and significance of this man named Thatcher Edwards. Since his death, many have searched for the notorious treasure of Blackbeard, but rather than being locked away in a water-logged grave or buried so many paces away from some long lost landmark, we find the true wealth of Blackbeard was secreted away by bureaucrats and is at last uncovered by a foreign exchange student in a dusty dead man's chest.

About the Authors

In 2006, having completed fourteen years of research, David and Penelope Carroll relocated their family to the volcanic highlands of southern Mexico to compose this work. Upon completion they returned to the United States, setting up their home on the Outer Banks, where they edited and refined this massive novel, ultimately determining to split it into three parts. They reside in Nags Head, North Carolina, with their two daughters, Abigail and Eleanor, and are busy working on their next project, also based on the magical and troubled waters of the Carolina coast.

Made in the USA
Lexington, KY
27 February 2013